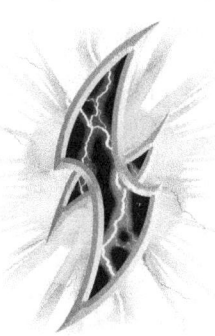

R.A.W. PRODUCTIONS PRESENTS
THE EDGE OF BEYOND:
RISE OF THE FALLEN
THE OFFICIAL NOVELIZATION

LEGEND BEARS A SYMBOL...AS
EARTH FINDS ITS TRUE PURPOSE

R.A.W. Productions LLC
"Producing a crystallized standard of quality through raw talent."

The Edge Of Beyond: Rise Of The Fallen
Print Edition ISBN-13: 978-0-692-54321-4
E-Book Edition ASIN: B07CS11PZC

First U.S. Edition: October 24th 2015

The Edge Of Beyond created by Raz Wickham.
Characters and story elements created by Raz Wickham.
Characters rendered by Joe Schlottach, Jackie Barrows, and Oudvin Cassell.
Cover scheme concept created by Raz Wickham.
Cover designs by Raz Wickham, Jackie Barrows.
Logo designs created by Raz Wickham and Damion Cronin.
Graphic design work by Jackie Barrows and Damion Cronin.
Scientific concepts created by Raz Wickham and Weston Warren.
IP taglines created by Raz Wickham.
Adapting, formatting, writing, and editing by Raz Wickham.
Production team photos taken by R.A.W. Productions LLC.

This literary series may be purchased for entertainment, educational, business, or sales promotional use. For more information, please contact us through our official email: theedgeofbeyond@gmail.com
For information regarding The Edge Of Beyond and our special engagements for nationwide interactive book signing events, find us through our social media outlets, or please visit us at our official website:
http://www.theedgeofbeyond.com

THE EDGE OF BEYOND:
RISE OF THE FALLEN
THE OFFICIAL NOVELIZATION

A NOVEL BY
RAZ A. WICKHAM

BASED ON AND ADAPTED
FROM THE SCREENPLAY BY
RAZ A. WICKHAM

THE EDGE OF BEYOND
CREATED BY
RAZ A. WICKHAM

YOU WILL BELIEVE IN ANGELS

CONTENTS

IS IT DEFEAT OR VICTORY THAT AWAITS BEYOND THE DARK?

DEDICATION

For Chelle, always

In writing to you, please know that this story is dedicated to you and your precious memory. Being fortunate enough to be a part of your life at a young age, you gave me hope even in the darkest of times. You gave me something to fight for and hold on to, knowing how precious you were, even more so being gone. Becoming a father figure, a friend, and a brother all at once, you became my burden to bear for a time and a most important one to boot. Because of that, I'm grateful that I got to see you grow during that time as you became my muse, and in a way, my personal savior.

Perhaps our time together is the stuff dreams are made of, for in a way you took care of me like a loving mother as I took care of you like a loving father, fully tolerant, and acceptant. Though we were both victims of treachery and deceit from those we had no control over, we held on and helped each other pull through the best we could at the time. As those devious forces worked tirelessly to pull us apart, I felt that I had failed you as well as myself, but I've never given up on you and never will.

In parting from you, I felt that I had truly left Heaven for Hell. Praying for your safety each day, unable to see or speak to you for so long has greatly taken its toll for the worst in many ways. Like you, I've always felt the weight of the world on my shoulders, but in caring for you, I felt light as a feather but also stronger than the world itself.

You helped me to become a better person and if not for you, the second most important character of this trilogy would not exist, which is extremely prominent. We laughed, we cried, but more importantly, we had the comfort of enjoying each other's company. The mystery that surrounds your absence torments me to this very day, for any success I may achieve through TEOB cannot be fully enjoyed without your desired blessing.

For years I've wondered; what has happened to the little girl I once knew that couldn't wait to hear my voice, and would do anything for me? Perhaps those questions have yet to be answered whether I like the truth or not. You were always the diamond in my rough, and in some ways vice versa. Even now I wonder, what you've been through, how you've been raised, and how you've endured for so long. Like me, you're a survivor, quick witted, and resilient. You are loving to the core, but also intelligent enough to see through the guise of the world and the people within it.

Sometimes life is a fairy tale and a nightmare all in one. I've tried my best to send you all the positive energy I have; perhaps that is why my journey in a literary sense has felt so negative because I gave it all to you. In truth, our strength was being compassionate for each other as a team.

It was something that no one to this day understands; pure and untarnished. A compassionate fire that sparked and burned ever so brightly, only to be faded and dimmed like a melting candle. Even now you are a true inspiration in my life and my life's work. Sadly, I don't know where you are, or where you're going, but I hope you end up in a place that brings nothing less of what you deserve; paradise perhaps, if such a place even exists.

As you probably well know by now, I've continued with my mission to keep my word to you by pushing TEOB all the way, for a promise given is a promise kept. I trust that you'll always remember me, for I will never forget you. You made life worth living, but not being able to see you flourish before my own eyes is the most unbearable thing of all. You are of strong character, perhaps even more so than I at times, but I hope that whatever character you had within you when I was around has started to truly blossom, like a beautiful Lotus flower. You're very talented and beautiful inside and out, therefore I strongly encourage you to follow your dreams, even if that means fighting for them as I always have all my life.

With all my heart, I wish I could be there as your beloved guardian angel once more, just like old times. But regardless of what's transpired, I thank you for the time we had together. And though we are now worlds apart, I wish you the absolute best in your endeavors as you grow into the person you were always meant to be. Perhaps we'll see each other again someday soon, but until then, always remember to survive, change, and adapt. I truly hope that you make the best with the precious life you've been given, so do me a favor and please make it a good one while you still can.

Forever Yours…Beyond The Dark.

PREFACE

Many live to go beyond the edge…others die trying to reach
the edge of beyond.

In 1997, a young boy introduced this phrase and a unique brand of
epic storytelling. Though sadly to his vexation, it would take him between
then and now to get to where he is, with the same profound goal, and ideal.
As far back as 1991, he began developing various world-building concepts to
support what would later become integral to his iconic story.

By 2014, he had completed the first trilogy to this epic saga in
screenplay form, with all intents and purposes of one day creating a successful
multimedia franchise, with a strong emphasis on film. I'm Raz Wickham, the
sole visionary behind The Edge Of Beyond; a Spiritual/Sci-Fi/Fantasy tale
that aims to thrill and delight audiences, around the globe.

One of the hallmarks of Science Fiction; is its ability to predict future worlds and technology. But in the realm of TEOB, as it has been so notably nicknamed, that world is ours: Earth. When it comes to Fantasy, we're taken on a journey of escapism that not only teases our minds with flights of fancy, but dares us to think big and allows us to go places most only see in dreams. But what is Spiritual/Sci-Fi/Fantasy without a great story and great characters to support it? That ladies and gentleman is where TEOB comes in…

Of all the things I can imagine artistically, it's hard to fathom that back in 1986, my 3-year-old self visited the Neuschwanstein Castle in Germany with a sense of wonder that has yet to diminish. Eighteen years have passed since I first stepped foot at Ha Ha Tonka Missouri state park, and left with the creative keys to what would become my lifelong legacy, that being TEOB. Though most would consider themselves a fan of something first and foremost, but deep down I've always been a creator first and a fan second, or perhaps a fan of creating in general.

Through various dreams of futuristic places full of utopian landscapes, angelic warriors, and advanced crystalline technology, TEOB has progressively come together as an epic spectacle that combines all the greatest aesthetic elements throughout all of entertainment history and effectively packages them together into one compact original narrative.

After many years of trial and error, I've been able to craft a story that not only intends to entertain, but educates as well. The story you have here in your hands is near and dear to my heart, one full of tragedy and triumph that has been directly inspired by many years of blood, sweat, and tears. I tried my absolute best to create the most sincere, heartfelt, and epic story possible that aims to strike various chords with people who are looking for something as thought provoking as this whilst making them laugh and cry.

In the eyes of the reader as well as myself, hopefully I succeeded. But know that there's a lot more where this first book came from, so keep your eyes out for all things TEOB related in the near future.

Prepare to enter the wondrous world of TEOB; an epic tale of tragedy and triumph that also teaches the beauty of light and darkness that resides within our souls, and in the greatest of fashion.

INTRODUCTION

In the 18 years since production began, slavery has become quite the international news story. Interestingly enough, Victor himself must rise from the darkness of his own surroundings and into the light as a result of realistic themes such as these, through pomp and circumstance. So, the question you're probably asking yourself is: What exactly is TEOB? Why should we care? In a personal sense; it is only when we are pushed to the edge and sometimes beyond that we know who we really are.

On a story front; it is a powerful manifestation of the inner and outer self, resulting in what is called ascension into the Gods' realm, or case in point, The Edge Of Beyond. From a professional perspective; it is a production standard expected from something of this quality, by pushing the boundaries of artistic criteria. You may also be wondering: What has taken so long to get TEOB up and running as a fully functional multimedia franchise? Let's just say that in the time taken to produce something tangible, not everyone shares the same work ethic or drive to succeed as I do.

For a story that is meant to entertain as well as educate, one has to wonder: What makes an audience respond to a powerful yet provocative message? Why do we enjoy Sci-Fi/Fantasy? And why do we love to escape into fantastical worlds that play into our hopes and dreams of paradise? That of course is something I hope to answer for myself with TEOB as a whole.

Another notable hallmark of TEOB has been the dedication and craftsmanship involved in keeping it alive for so long. Especially in the face of extreme adversity and shadows of an industry so heavily saturated with pop culture consumerism. With a project like this, one of the most challenging aspects has required anyone directly involved to reach a certain level of professional quality that not only matches the required visual aesthetics, but the story as well. Aesthetics involving visual, mythical, and timeless themes conjure up an epic scope necessary to tell a story of this grace and magnitude.

For TEOB specifically, I fully intend to reveal my epic creation by showing the world something it hasn't seen before. TEOB is a story with all the excitement and sense of wonder, as well as action and adventure expected in a Spiritual/Sci-Fi/Fantasy epic, plus a whole lot more. Altogether, TEOB is a culmination of 18+ years of countless hours of work ranging from story, visual, and scientific concepts, to the page you're about to read. What you are holding in your hands is the product of all my blood, sweat, and tears.

In the 18+ years that TEOB has been in development, things have changed greatly in the industry as a whole. Society has fallen victim to the idea that there isn't an audience for anything original these days. But as an original artist myself, I beg to differ. In a world full of wannabe posers and copycats, TEOB stands as an original work that dares to rise above the competition.

THE EDGE OF BEYOND: RISE OF THE FALLEN

No matter what transpires in the years to come, TEOB will continue to push the boundaries of epic storytelling. But what is a vision without the means to carry it out in a tangible form? That of course, is where you the readers and fans come in. In order to reach my audience directly, I have chosen the path of self-publication. Thus, I'm hard at work to turn years of disappointment into opportunity, tragedy into triumph.

So, witness the rise of an icon by supporting us on our journey to make this into the next big thing. Not just in the hands of Hollywood, but the world in general. There are certain things in this story that no one has ever seen before, both in concept and in a literary sense. And while I myself believe that this story is indeed great, ultimately, I understand that it's partially up to you, the fans to decide.

With your fan participation, I hope to get this entire epic trilogy into circulation, and so the world finally knows the name of TEOB, and everything this story has to offer. Deep down, I know there's an audience for a project like this, and the world needs something that shows originality is not only vital to creation, but can be popular again.

MISSION STATEMENTS:

1.) Producing a crystallized standard of quality through raw talent.

2.) Entertainment asks us to take a seat; we're asking fans to take a stand. A stand towards original work that not only entertains, but educates as well.

ACKNOWLEDGMENTS

I would like to express my deepest gratitude to those few who have helped along the way on my journey to bring TEOB to life after all these years:

Mother, for supporting my artistic endeavors and the project overall, your patience and understanding during my dark times has meant the world to me.

Father, for teaching me the real value of tough love and discipline, your hardworking efforts to provide for me growing up will never be forgotten.

Grandma Gaunt, for always being there with the friendliest and wisest care, you've always been like the Yoda of my life whenever needed, except funnier.

Uncle Arty, for always supporting my artistic endeavors with great appreciation and introducing me to Star Wars back in Christmas of 1996.

John Wickham, for being someone I could look up to during my youth whilst showing me the world of metal music and teaching me a few Megadeth songs on guitar. If not for that, I wouldn't be the musician nor artist I am today.

Yvette Hammond, for being one of the greatest blessings I could ever ask for in life. To a point, you've always loved and accepted me for who and what I am, even at my worst. You also inspired my first musical ballad, Beyond The Dark, and showed me what it means to truly love someone, for that I'm eternally grateful. Even in death, I shall remain yours and love you in return.

Weston Warren, for your loyal endorsement and aid with all science related things. Your profound moral, spiritual, and professional support is absolutely priceless in a world that continues to shun such wisdom. I shall always cherish what I've learned from you over the years, and look forward to many more.

Jackie Barrows, for your tireless work to help me with all things production related. You've more than earned your keep in my eyes, and proven yourself worthy as my assistant. Know that your loyal efforts will never go unnoticed.

Damion Cronin, for your help with graphic design work, thanks to you I have an awesome set of logos that will properly market TEOB for years to come.

Allen Childers, for your aiding with original concept art and being the only person to truly collaborate and immerse themselves in the fantastical world I've created for TEOB. If not for your help early on, my life's work would not be where it is now, as the visual origins of my characters truly shine.

Bryan K. Thomas, for pushing me to bring my creativity into a tangible form, if not for your advice I wouldn't have found the correct professional path.

Twana Turner, for being the only teacher to ever push me artistically, despite the jealousy and ridicule afflicted upon me all those years in school as a result.

Yvonne Williams, for being a fellow fighter against the evil of this world, your stand against human trafficking is truly inspiring and highly respected.

And to all those over the years who purposely held me back from achieving my goals in life, both related and non, for you only pushed me that much harder to succeed at what I do best with TEOB and my talents in general. There's a lot more where this book came from, so you better watch out.

THE EDGE OF BEYOND: RISE OF THE FALLEN

ORIGINS:
LEGENDS OF THE FALL

In the far if not near distant future, there was Earth. Ruled by man for thousands of years, humanity's so-called civil societies would soon fall victim to vanity and corruption. As the governments worldwide gathered to confront the coming storm, little would they listen to the pleas of a small team of scientists who warned them and vowed to pursue an exit strategy in order to save mankind as well as themselves.

Upon this revelation, Earth was on the verge of what has become known as the Great Cataclysm, a cataclysmic event that would take three centuries to complete. Thus, in their own selfish ignorance, mankind became the architect of their own demise through ignorance and fear. In preparation for this Earth-shattering event, the elite class of the world hid selfishly underground while the lower-class humans on the surface remained, alone and unprotected, or so was thought for the longest time.

Taking no chances upon learning that a biological homing beacon had mysteriously been sent from Earth as a distress signal into space, the team of scientists, led by two astrophysicists Atom and Evelyn prepared their own vessel with a mission they called Operation: Oblivion, a voyage that contained unknown dangers into the great beyond, with all intents and purposes to leave Earth permanently, in hopes that they would be able to sustain life elsewhere. Luckily, they were able to make their exit into the void, saying goodbye to their once beloved planet. Because the entire solar system was in the ecliptic, it was suddenly struck by a galactic super wave shortly after the team of scientists made their way into deep space. The brown dwarf planetary system, known as Planet-X, entered our inner solar system, thus leaving a trail of universal destruction behind. With various asteroids hitting the surface at random, this system left ours at a very high rate of speed, whilst shooting around the sun with great inertia and gravitational pull.

With it being so close to the Earth at the time, it became locked into a gravitational pull. In turn, our planet and moon were slung into the asteroid belt orbiting Mars and Jupiter. Due to this process, Earth's original orbit was shifted away from our natural Sun, causing it to expand four times larger in size. Because of its expansion at the same time the galactic super wave hit our solar system, the Earth's molten core was exposed to very high electro magnetic energy, which crystallized the core. Subsequently, the asteroids that existed in that orbit three astronomical units from the Sun were gravitationally pulled to Earth and absorbed by it, which in turn changed the planet's entire topography, shifting each continent to an unrecognizable state. As crystals moved to the surface from the core, countless lightning strikes from the ground up and above produced super bipolar ion clusters, which had an almost supernatural superoxide cleaning capacity that was able to heal and cleanse the Earth at rapid speed. Compared to the planet's prior orbit, which at the time was closer to Earth when the crystals were not fully developed, the core wasn't able to crystalize due to its distance away from the Sun. The galactic wave that pulsed from the center of the Milky Way galaxy effected several planetary systems, which were also in the ecliptic.

This process created four additional moons, allowing the oceans on the surface to be stronger in their high and low tides. The additional moons, now seen from the surface affected the moods and energy of all Earth's inhabitants, the gravitational pull on bodily fluids alone changed human behavior, like never before. This in turn created inner tensions and civil unrest between the two surviving factions. Due to a greater gravitational pull, the density of the crystalline structures below and above the surface as well as the electromagnetic energy that they posses created a greater gravitational pull from the molten core than what Earth used to have when it was closer to the Sun. Thus, becoming stronger biologically and metaphysically which in turn evolved all forms of life including but not limited to plants, animals, and humans as well. Ultimately, everything from the ground up evolved based on the extraordinary conditions and biology of the planet.

Since the molten core itself was under greater compression as it crystallized, it worked its way towards the surface through veins of Earth's crust, becoming thinner yet more durable. Because there were less severe radiation exposure zones near the crystals on the surface, those who were closer to these shards gathered around what seemed to be their only form of protection. Communities that developed around them were shielded in a mystical and somewhat ethereal way, which protected them from extinction. Those in close proximity to these protrusions were protected from the radiation that would have otherwise destroyed their very life source. This in turn caused genetic alterations, allowing those on the surface to develop a third strand of crystalline DNA.

After years of struggling to survive the changes caused by the cataclysm, humans who were left to die on the surface had evolved into two separate races, each with their own distinct names as well as physical and mental attributes. Those who survived in the East became known as Eudenians, and those from the West, the Enfurians. Thus, from the ashes of the once ruined planet arose two races of beings that were trapped in a perpetual state of war. They fought for control over the secrets of the ancients, which left them to fend for themselves.

The two smaller moons on the Eastside of the planet's new orbit affected the Eudenians while two larger moons on the West side affected the Enfurians. Because the Earth at this point had started to revolve slower within its new orbit, Enfurians received more days of sun exposure, four days compared to only two for the Eudenians. This counted for the Eudenians' paler skin appearance and slim but toned physique in comparison to the Enfurians' darker skin tone but larger physique.

A strange new world rises from the old; after three centuries had passed, Atom and his team of scientists had finally returned to a home they neither remembered nor had ever seen before. Upon their arrival, they were shocked to learn what had happened in the time they had been gone, realizing that the planet they so desperately left to save their own lives had become a breeding ground for humans who had evolved as well as a pure energy source. Attempting to make contact with the two evolved races on the surface, these scientists took it upon themselves to study the new crystalline formations inside and out of the planet's core.

Knowing more about the technology harnessed by its power, they were able to protect themselves through use of crystal powered Gauntlets against the Eudenians and Enfurians who seemed all too interested in fighting themselves over it. Once the team had reached a scientific breakthrough with the energy emitted from what they came to call, Chaos Crystals, they risked meeting with the leaders of both races, proposing a plan of action to help rebuild the world as they saw fit. Complying with their demands at first, the Eudenians and Enfurians worked tirelessly to bring their vision to fruition; that of a utopian society free from pollution and corruption. Realizing their position to be saviors of the world, the scientists became self-proclaimed gods in the eyes of those unwilling to challenge their scientific authority.

Though it is unknown as to what exactly the scientists went through during their long and undiscovered voyage, what is known is that upon their return to Earth, Atom came into contact with a rare biological metal which seeped into his very DNA, which mutated his entire genome. This memory based metallic alloy, which was found to be harder than diamonds, became the basis for what would later become known as Soul Gear; Earth's first bioorganic/synthetic form of technologically advanced defensive armor that adapted an electromagnetic hexagonal pattern for each bearer.

As a result, Atom became obsessed with his newfound power, which allowed him to manipulate energy naturally from direct exposure with Earth's crystals, in turn allowing him to open a gateway into an ethereal realm currently known as The Edge Of Beyond. His abilities would soon frighten his colleagues, including his wife Evelyn who sadly had been killed accidently from an incident involving his untapped power. As Atom's power grew, the others decided it was best to trap him into the ethereal realm for all eternity, not just for their own safety but for the planet's as well.

With the leaders of both races, their power waning in their attempts to overthrow each other refused to cooperate with their respective kingdoms, and instead fought for supremacy over the Gods, deciding rather that the world be divided in their favor. The Gods proposed a stable living relationship with the Eudenians and Enfurians, but their negotiations fell upon deaf ears. As tensions grew between those on the surface, the Gods began to feel overwhelmed by the sheer strength unified by the two races.

Tampering with fate, the Gods accidently created a trigger event that caused the Eudenians and Enfurians to wage war with each other. This period became known as the Chaonaissance era, which led to the beginning of what would become known as the great Chaos War. The prolonged battle between the two races engulfed the Earth, but unlike their former masters with their superior knowledge and power, one after another, humans of the past who had begun to rise to the surface after three centuries were forced to surrender their territories. Seeing no end to the bitter chaos between both races, the Gods conceived their most desperate strategy yet, a final solution to turn on the surface dwellers by leaving them behind once again.

Fearing for their own lives at this point, the Gods used human ingenuity to help create their own kingdom called Empyria, a space station that currently orbits the Earth from above. Once there, it was decided that in order to maintain control of the surface dwellers they must once again dabble in the world of science. Attempting to make warriors in their own likeness, the Gods tampered with gene splicing from Eudenian and Enfurian blood to create a supreme race, one that would defend them against any who would dare threaten their divine place of power over their new home.

Let there be light, and they were blessed by it through the creation of a new breed of Angelic warrior, which they called Archadians. Using specific genes from the most powerful of Eudenian and Enfurian warriors, they were able to create Korina, the first pureblood Angel spiritually intertwined with two other females, a Eudenian named Kitana, and an Enfurian named Kiara. After creating their own legion of Angelic warriors under a spiritual union entitled the Arch, the Gods prepared to launch a full-scale assault against everyone below in a desperate attempt to end the Chaos War once and for all. As the Chaos War reached its furious climax, the Archadians, led by the Holy Trinity Angels were sent down to Earth to end the war once and for all.

THE EDGE OF BEYOND: RISE OF THE FALLEN

What started as a never-ending battle between two powerful races; quickly became a war that was ultimately decided by the inclusion of the Archadians. Unable to match their superior power in the skies, the Eudenians and Enfurians eventually stopped fighting each other and quickly turned their sights on the Arch itself. Failing to beat the Gods' small but highly efficient Angelic army, both races reluctantly gave up in their chaotic pursuit to overthrow them. With both sides finally admitting defeat, the Gods prevailed in a victorious show of force with the aid of their Angelic creations, and thus were able to regain control over the entire Earth realm once again.

As requested by the Gods under the direct supervision of the Arch, the Eudenians and Enfurians formed a worldwide peace treaty known as the Harmony Accord, permitting both sides to coexist peacefully whilst working together once again to rebuild the kingdoms of Earth as well as their own. Knowing their Angelic army would need their own form of stability to keep the surface dwellers in check, the Gods combined their powers through use of the crystal technology and erected a self-sustaining kingdom they named Archadia. Once in the sky above the planet's surface, the Archadians would make their new home within this crystalline kingdom, in turn creating their own form of hierarchy in accordance with the Gods' will.

Seeking refuge in their own promised land in the cradle of godlike civilization, the Archadians flourished, and thus a new kingdom was born, a place they could call home, a place they could raise their descendants. Soon after, they christened their Angelic kingdom into a new age called the Archanaissance era, and it prospered under the watchful eye of the Gods. While the majority of the female Angels stayed in Archadia, the males were given the opportunity to reside in Empyria to safe guard the Gods' closely incase of another uprising. This turn of events granted them their own form of separate identity, which allowed them to be named Empyrians.

During this time, humans who sought refuge once again below the surface had risen only to become useful servants to both races in order to restore their former glory. They worked tirelessly to do their bidding and it wasn't long before the seeds of descent took root. After the Great Cataclysm, humans were always considered an inferior and subordinate class. Banished from the Gods based on their previous standing, humans were overpowered by the Eudenians and Enfurians to keep them alive only for the use of slavery in the crystal mines. Manipulated into thinking it was for their own safety, humans eventually gave in to their demands on the promise that they would be kept safe from any and all harm from others including the Archadians and the Gods. In an ironic twist of fate, those who once enslaved humanity became slaves themselves as a result of the Chaos War. Since then, things have remained peaceful between each faction…or so we think.

Welcome to a world you thought you knew; a world where freedom is history, brutality is law, and the powerful rule by fear.

MANY LIVE TO GO BEYOND THE EDGE...
OTHERS DIE TRYING TO REACH THE EDGE OF
BEYOND
R.A.W.

FROM LIGHT COMES DARKNESS, AND FROM
DARKNESS COMES LIGHT...
R.A.W.

PROLOGUE: DARK LEGACY

Beneath the ethereal edge of Earth's atmosphere, the sun begins to set, illuminating the cloud filled sky surrounding the beautiful crystalline kingdom of Archadia. For what would typically be another graceful day full of light within this floating realm of Angelic peacekeepers, this one unlike most days however, would come to a close with darkness on the horizon.

A beautiful yet mysterious Angel with long light brown hair stands inside the armory of her quarters within the interior of an Archadian Temple. With serious intent, she gears up for battle and places a small decorative piece containing a purple crystal shard atop her chest, which causes her liquid metal nanotech armor known as Soul Gear to form over her body. The Angel then grabs an Archadian Gauntlet floating inches above a small crystalline platform and places it over her arm in a graceful manner. While powering up, the Gauntlet activates the purple liquid crystalline armor to form over her bio-metallic under suit. She then presses the decorative piece bearing the Gods' symbol over her chest plate, which triggers her Angelic wings to swiftly emerge as a set of crystalline extensions materialize from her spinal armor with offset energy tails that flow graciously. A furious bolt of lightning arcs across the darkened sky with a fierce rumble of thunder, which draws the Angel's immediate attention outside, revealing the solemn concern on her face as she looks outward with intense blue eyes.

"As was foretold, the storm is coming." She determinedly whispers. Hastening for time, the Angel powers up her crystalline staff as her Archadian tiara forms a helmet securely over her head. The Gods' symbol atop her Gauntlet lights up brightly in purple as she grips it and looks on with great fortitude, knowing that fate no matter how mysterious has put her in the most unfortunate of circumstances. Moments later, the she walks down the nearest corridor heading towards the throne chamber within the temple, followed by another pair of Angels as they quickly approach her from behind.

"Everything is set, milady." One of the Archadians respectfully informs, "General Kael has arrived and is awaiting your instruction."

"Good." The Angel swiftly replies, "Tell him to ready our departure, I'll be there momentarily."

The pair nod in respect then quickly take off as ordered as the Angel reaches the end of the corridor. She pauses for a moment and sighs before entering the majestic throne chamber that's partially illuminated by the sky above to address the Supreme Arch council. Amongst them is Queen Rosalyn and King Josephus, a middle-aged couple dressed in royal attire with blondish gray hair who look upon the Angel in relief as she quickly approaches them.

"Ah, perfect timing as usual, Victoria." Josephus acknowledges from his crystalline throne, "The enemy approaches as we speak."

Victoria kneels before the council and looks upon each of them intensely. General Patrayous of the Empyrian army, a tall and stout man of imposing presence with short brown hair wearing yellow Soul Gear stands by with his wings fully spread and nods to acknowledge her presence as his Seraphine companion, Zepherus, a mid-sized dragon half cat-like creature in yellowish black fur sits beside him and howls.

"With the Holy Trinity safely at rest in the Gods' realm, it's up to us to defend the kingdom." Rosalyn explains from her throne, "General Kael is said to be Earthbound, assuming he's on his way and will be here soon."

"In the meantime, General Patrayous has just arrived from Empyria to aid us in combat against this intolerable threat." Josephus adds.

Patrayous proudly steps forward and bows in respect, signifying his allegiance to the mighty Arch as Victoria nods back in acceptance of his company.

"With his help, my sisters and I will do everything possible to keep them at bay." Victoria strongly declares, "You can be sure of that."

"Seems the war has finally arrived at your door step, wouldn't you say?" Patrayous replies sarcastically, causing Zepherus to slightly growl with his spinal shards glowing sporadically.

Victoria turns to address Patrayous directly and firmly states, "No, General; the war as you so put it has only just begun!"

Amused by her confident attitude towards the grim situation, Patrayous grins in response as she turns back to address the Arch council once again.

"If we hope to have anything left of our beloved home, then I suggest we make our stand against this legion of thunder now!" She stresses.

Patrayous confidently steps forward to address the Supreme Arch council as well. "Foolish Darchadians!" He arrogantly dismisses, "This is nothing more than a feeble attempt to honor their now fallen leader. Once we're finished, this should be the last of them to fight in his stead."

"I pray so…" Victoria suspiciously mutters as Patrayous faces her, surprised by her response as she turns to finish, "Otherwise we dishonor our people, and the Gods themselves."

Awaiting further instruction, Victoria looks upon the Arch council as Patrayous gently scratches Zepherus on the head, which causes him to purr.

"We must remain victorious against our fallen counterparts, regardless of our former ties!" Josephus announces to everyone present.

Victoria firmly nods and replies, "As an elite Angel, I harmonize that belief."

"Do what's necessary, no matter the cost!" Josephus commands.

"Don't worry your grace, I intend to." Victoria says determinedly.

"Your courage though unorthodox at times is to be greatly admired, sister." Rosalyn inspires while raising her hand out towards her in a graceful manner, "May the Gods be with you."

Victoria bows her head in respect and quickly takes her leave as instructed. Patrayous looks upon the Arch council for a moment in curiosity then takes his leave as well, with his loyal companion Zepherus at his side to do battle against the menacing Darchadians heading their direction.

While exiting the throne chamber, Victoria turns her attention towards an Archadian nursery and curiously approaches the window. She places her hand on the crystalline glass for a moment whilst looking upon the newborn Princess of Archadia who's close in age to her own. The infant with golden hair looks upward and smiles, as Victoria waves back with a comforting grin.

"I suppose the darkness has no access when the Arch's protection covers you." Victoria honorably mutters, "Farewell, Princess; it's a shame your paths may never cross, but I hope you still have a kingdom worth ruling when you're old enough to lead."

With a final compassionate glance, Victoria kisses her fingers and gently places them on the crystalline glass to bid farewell then takes her leave as the infant cries out, as though lonely without her strong presence to comfort her.

As Victoria makes her way back towards her quarters within the Arch temple, she turns a corner and finds herself nearly colliding with four other Archadians. She continues past without hesitancy as one of them moves beside her and informs, "Milady, there's an urgent matter that requires your immediate attention."

Annoyed by their disruption of her covert plan, Victoria sighs impatiently and snaps, "Can't you see I'm busy? The enemy is practically at our gates; you should be out there with the others protecting the kingdom from invasion."

"Now, *sister*!" The Archadian impatiently demands.

Victoria stops in her tracks and looks upon the four Archadians with a concern as one of them extends their arm out to lead the way through the temple. "This way please." The Archadian sternly requests.

Feeling that she has no choice but to cooperate for the time being to remain unsuspicious, Victoria reluctantly follows them as they escort her down the next corridor and abruptly turn towards her quarters in the temple. She panics at the sight upon seeing her chamber door up ahead, realizing them to be Darchadians in disguise as they unexpectedly power up their Gauntlets.

"End of the line, *Archadian!*" One of them threatens viscously with a hiss as another steps forward and callously denotes, "Seems you've become quite the troublemaker for your people lately, including ours."

Victoria suddenly comes to a halt in the corridor and prepares to defend herself as the Darchadians aim their Gauntlets. "Kill her!" The leader roars.

Composing herself righteously despite the apparent danger, Victoria sighs then closes her eyes and securely whispers, "May the Gods forgive me for what I'm about to do."

To their surprise, she unexpectedly uses her crystalline staff to emit a bright light, in turn blinding the Darchadians for a brief moment as she attempts to fight them off singlehandedly. Screeching ferociously, the Darchadians attempt to strike in unison, but are slightly incapacitated from the light emitting from her staff. Using her superior fighting prowess, Victoria strikes back furiously with her hands and staff, taking them out with ease. Pausing for a moment to catch her breath, Victoria gracefully holds her seasoned battle stance and looks onward with determination before sprinting down the corridor to her chambers before it's too late.

Upon entering her private chamber, she looks around fearfully and sees that it's a complete wreck; apparently ransacked by the Darchadians she just neutralized beforehand. Victoria quickly turns her attention towards a secret crystalline doorway as she sighs in relief, realizing that the Darchadians luckily failed to find the object of their search.

"Oh, thank heavens!" Victoria gasps as she rushes towards the secret crystalline doorway. Stopping in front of it, she clears her throat and hums an ancient melody, which causes the hidden panel to open as it reveals a male infant child with a large patch of blonde curly hair lying safely within a crystalline crib. The infant begins to cry as she cradles the child for a moment to calm him. "There, there, it's alright now, mother's here." Victoria compassionately murmurs with a smile as the infant opens his deep blue eyes. Fearful for his safety within the kingdom with the Darchadians having already infiltrated the temple, she looks away and says gently, "We'll be out of harm's way soon enough, I hope."

Hearing a sudden commotion outside, Victoria swiftly turns her attention behind her. She gently wraps the child in an Angelic cloth, which she then fastens around her neck as a sling to keep a tight grip. The noise gets louder as she approaches another Gauntlet floating inches above a crystalline pedestal within the secret doorway then grabs it and places it in her satchel.

Hoping to conceal her true intent from her fellow people, Victoria covers herself in an Angelic cloak as she approaches the balcony outside her quarters. Stepping outside onto the balcony, she sees her once beloved kingdom under attack by a fearsome fleet of Darchadians as her fellow Archadians defends Archadia alongside the Saraphine guardians flying beside them in battle with their wings fully spread.

The battle intensifies before Victoria's eyes, the clashing sight taking her aback for a moment in regret and sorrow as the Saraphine fire energy blasts from their mouths, followed by the Archadians who take aim and fire from their Gauntlets towards the Darchadians who howl and screech ferociously. The Archadians who led Victoria to the council chambers earlier approach her from the sky and float above whilst signaling her to flee.

"You're out of time!" One of them warningly shouts overhead to get her attention, "He's waiting for you!"

With a respectful nod, Victoria tightens the sling around her neck then activates her wings and suddenly takes flight, followed by the two Archadians acting as a defense around her as they fly through the kingdom now under siege. Victoria looks behind her curiously as Patrayous suddenly leaps from the balcony area of the throne chamber outside the temple and enters the fray whilst spreading his wings. As Zepherus flies beside his master with a mighty roar, the powerful pair attempt to help the Archadians and Seraphine defend the kingdom against the aggressive Darchadian fleet who have arrived as once predicted to honor their fallen leader. The battle rages on as Victoria flies through the kingdom towards an outpost with the two Archadians in tow.

General Kael; a tall man of commanding presence with a toned physique and grayish long black hair pulled back in a ponytail stands by an Arch ship with his arms crossed whilst sporting his usual green Soul Gear. While observing the powerful clash of warriors in the distance with a serious gaze, Victoria approaches him from above with the two Archadians. "About damn time!" He sarcastically greets, "I was beginning to think you weren't coming!"

Victoria lands gracefully before him and warns, "Time is of the essence, General. We need to take off now if at all possible."

"As you wish, milady." Kael replies with a respectful nod then extends his arm towards the Arch ship and says, "Get on board then. Assuming my Empyrian colleague has things under control, we shouldn't have any issues making our way safely outside the kingdom."

After nodding back, Victoria quickly turns to address the two Archadians directly, saying, "The kingdom is now under attack; please inform the council what's happening." She carefully instructs, "That should give us enough time to reach the surface and lead them off our trail." The two Archadians nod back then spread their wings and take off towards the temple as requested. Wasting no time, Victoria boards the Arch ship with the child in hand, and Kael none the wiser to what she's guarding with her life in the satchel as he rushes past her. "So, what's our heading?" He hollers back from the cockpit.

"Someplace safe, away from here!" Victoria suggests while settling into her station aboard the cargo deck in the back of the ship, "Pretoria may be a good place to start, assuming we aren't being followed."

Kael swiftly punches a few buttons on the holographic display in the ship's control deck and hollers, "You got it, setting the ship's coordinates now!"

The infant's cries catch Kael's wary attention for a moment as he looks back curiously from the cockpit, but quickly dismisses the sound to refocus his attention on the controls to fly the ship properly before the Darchadians reach their location. "Everything alright back there?" He calls back curiously.

"Yes, everything's fine, for now anyway." Victoria calmly replies.

"Good, cause here we go!" He warningly shouts.

The Arch ship hovers above the landing platform then shifts upward and takes off as the infant begins to cry. Victoria holds the child close, attempting to calm him from the violent trembling caused by various energy blasts zooming past them in the sky while observing the intense battle from the ship's cargo deck. Fearing the worst for the home that was once her sanctuary that's now being threatened by their worst enemies, Victoria looks upon Archadia one last time as it fades into the distance in the sky, then kisses her fingers and extends her arm out as if unable to let go. As they pass through the self-sustaining energy shield surrounding the entire kingdom that's powered by the Earth's core, she closes her teary eyes in distress over the extreme nature of her mysterious departure, knowing she can never go back.

Time passes, the miles slipping by in the air above the surface as Victoria carefully sets the child down onto a seat then pulls out a purple crystal shard necklace from her garb and places it into a communications control system in the cargo deck. While counting every crucial second out of sight from Kael, she records an extremely vital transmission of herself through the holographic display. After capturing the encoded data for future use, she then takes the crystal shard and places it around her neck for safekeeping. Minutes later, the Arch ship enters the southern mining continent of Pretoria and lands by the mountainside near the crystal mines. Victoria attempts to keep the infant calm by holding it closely in her arms as Kael finally steps away from the ship's control deck and approaches her from the cockpit. "Well, we're here!" He informs, "What now?"

Victoria looks around curiously and claims, "I know this area!" Trying to deduce their exact location on the planet's surface, she then turns to face Kael and asks, "This is your sector when overseeing surface ordinances, correct?"

Kael nods back and humbly answers, "It is."

"I thought so." She replies, assured of her deduction.

"Why do you ask?" He suspiciously inquires.

Hesitant to reveal the infant to him just yet, Victoria looks down into her sling and carefully says, "Don't take this the wrong way, but I need your help one last time. That is, if you're willing."

"Due to my position under the Gods, technically I'm not in a position to argue with an Archadian of your status." Kael wittingly retorts with a curious chuckle, "I'm quite aware that I owe you from our last encounter, but what is it you need from me now?"

Carefully untying the sling from around her neck, Victoria opens the satchel and finally reveals the infant as Kael looks on with surprise in his brown eyes. He then grins in response to this unexpected revelation whilst shaking his head and sternly mutters, "So, that's what this is all about. The Darchadians were after him I assume?"

"Not exactly, but knowing their savagery, they wouldn't have stopped there." She unenthusiastically replies, "It was a difficult decision, leaving Archadia the way I did, but one I felt was absolutely worth the risk." Kael looks at her with a fretful expression and mutters, "I see." He then inquires, "What is the child's name then if you don't mind me asking?"

"Victor." She graciously replies as she gently hands the child over to Kael, who carefully takes him into his arms. "Raise him well." Concerned for his well-being, Kael looks upon Victor concernedly for a moment. "Such is a heavy debt I wasn't expecting to pay in return for your previous help, for my wife is currently with child herself." He respectfully mentions, "Therefore I cannot possibly be with him at all times, even with my current rank along with Patrayous under the Gods' noble reign." Victoria nods her head in acceptance and humbly replies, "I understand."

"In order to keep him from being trafficked like so many others, someone will need to keep a careful eye on him full-time." Kael muses, "Thus, he'll need a mother, a parent of some sort."

"I'm sure there's someone out down here worthy enough and willing to take on such a responsibility." Victoria hints with a confident tone. After a moment of contemplation, Kael straightens his posture with Victor in his arms and finally assures, "Very well then, I'll take him to someone I know, he'll be safe with her. As a General of the Empyrian army, you have my word." He promises with a determined nod.

Victor begins to wail as they hear a sudden commotion outside, assuming the Pretorian Guards have surprisingly been alerted to their presence on the surface. "We haven't much time." She warns while looking out from the ship's window cautiously as Kael stands back with Victor still in his arms.

"So, what's your plan then?" He cautiously asks.

"As you can see, I'm still working on it!" Victoria impatiently replies as she swiftly presses a button in the cargo deck, which causes the landing platform to unfold behind the ship onto the rocky terrain.

"Even with your experience, don't tell me this is as far as your plan goes." Kael concernedly teases as their Gauntlets start to glow, signifying danger, "Did you come all this way just to rid yourself of another slave?"

"He's no slave!" Victoria retorts while keeping her focus outside the Arch ship from the landing platform to check for any oncoming threats as the commotion gets even louder. After composing herself, Victoria turns back towards Kael whilst keeping an attentive gaze upon Victor and calmly explains, "He's an Angel, like us, but also human."

Approaching Kael, Victoria looks upon the child and gently caresses his face, causing him to smile. "I'll create a diversion so that you can take him somewhere safe, deep within the crystal mines if you must." She suggests.

"Hold on there, we both know the mines are no place for a child!" Kael alerts with a gravely concerned voice, "Especially one so young."

"Perhaps, but as you well know by now, this is no ordinary child." She calmly infers, attempting to ease his mind on the subject.

"Why the trouble of bringing him all the way out here then?" He politely inquires, "Why not just leave him in Archadia and be done with it?"

"Isn't it obvious?" She points out as he looks on confused, "To them he'd only be an outcast and a freak, an unwanted anomaly." She clarifies, "If he were to stay, they'd eventually find out, and most likely kill him for it." Embarrassed by his harsh attitude towards her, Kael hesitates to respond and says, "I see your point. I'm sorry, milady, I didn't realize what was at stake."

"Does it really matter what he is?" Victoria strongly contests. Kael looks upon Victor in curiosity as he grips his finger tightly then smiles and mutters, "At the moment perhaps, but in general, I suppose not." Charmed by his honorable nature, Victoria smiles back and states, "It's who we are that matters, and that's exactly why we're here." Curious of his fateful future in his custody, Kael looks upon Victor once again and claims, "Due to his Angelic heritage, if he stays here for long these people may look upon him as something more one day, perhaps even a god."

"One can only hope." She comments with a proud smile, "In the end, perhaps that will be a good thing."

"I take it he's yours then?" Kael thoughtfully inquires. With a fir nod, Victoria professes, "Yes; conceived at the height of victorious bloodshed by the mighty legion of thunder. The violent storm that occurred during his birth was considered a bad omen, but now I see it as a blessing in disguise." After taking a deep breath, she reluctantly admits, "We share the same blood, and I will not see it shed like so many others I was entrusted to safeguard under my wing." She then turns back towards the landing platform and further explains, "As you can see, I can't protect him anymore, for there are many on the hunt as we speak. The crystalline structures beneath the surface should conceal his Arch aura, making it impossible for them to track him." She indicates, "Besides, they'll never think to look for him there." Surprised by her cleverness on the matter at hand, Kael nods in response and says, "Good thinking I suppose, seems you've thought this plan through very methodically, at least more so than I thought."

"Not as well as I'd hoped." Victoria says dismally, "As you and I both know, the Arch would see this as an act of extreme heresy."

"That they would." Kael apologetically concurs.

"I have to do what's best for him." She protectively vows, "And though it may be dear, it's absolutely necessary, and worth the cost."

"The price I fear could be too great as he matures." Kael forewarns.

"I know, but it's not fair for him to suffer the consequences for my actions, nor the Arch's." She says dejectedly, "Therefore, I believe it's best that he remains here for now until it's safe for him to be exposed to the surface world above."

"Regardless of my thoughts on the matter, there'll be severe consequences to pay eventually." Kael humbly cautions, "But I'm sure you already know that."

Victoria closes her eyes in despair then slowly turns and approaches Kael while removing the satchel from her waist. "I have another request for you." She informs, "It won't be easy by any means, but it must be done."

"Alright..." Kael guardedly retorts as she hands him an object from her satchel wrapped in an Angelic cloth. While holding Victor, Kael sits down to unwrap the cloth, revealing the Archadian Gauntlet with a blue crystal shard and examines them intensely.

"When the time is right, please show him how to use it." She earnestly instructs, "Train him; prepare him for the coming storm."

Confused by her bold request, Kael looks back and asks, "How will I know?"

"You are the great Alexandre Kael..." She proudly implies, "A General of the Empyrian army, are you not?" As Kael nods sheepishly, she expresses a crooked smile and finishes, "Trust me, you will know."

"I'd be foolish to see this as anything other than a noble purpose, that I'm sure of." Kael accepts as he straightens up to address her in proper fashion and declares, "I will protect this child and the Gauntlet at all costs. I swear to the Gods!"

"Not to the Gods, to me." Victoria respectfully corrects.

Kael bows his head and humbly proclaims, "I shall honor thy will, milady."

Victoria nods back in appreciation as her wings begin to flutter, signifying that danger is nearby. "I must go." She says reluctantly. As Victoria approaches Victor one last time, she looks upon him compassionately and whispers, "You will be a child of light in a world full of darkness."

She gracefully waves her hand over his face, making him smile with joy and caringly adds, "Goodbye little one; my faith in you lives on. I pray your hopes and dreams lead you to paradise someday. And if they don't, then I hope you're given the opportunity to fight for it."

Victoria holds the blue crystal shard above Victor, who looks upon it with a curious gaze. She then softly blows onto it as a glint of blue light surges through his body like a bolt of lightning.

As she turns to leave, Kael quickly extends his arm to get her attention and shouts, "Wait!" Victoria stops by the landing platform to listen as he asks, "If he's partially human, then who was his father?"

Slowly turning, Victoria sighs heavily then takes off the purple crystal shard from around her neck and hands it over to Kael, who instinctively takes it.

"You should know; he bears the mark of an old legend." She wisely implies. Kael looks on curiously as she leans over and gently kisses Victor's forehead with tears in her eyes. "Farewell my son..." She inspiringly whispers, "No matter what happens to me, know that I will always love you." Victor smiles once again in response to Victoria's comforting presence and reaches out to her. "My essence is forever bound, and will carry on through you eternally, to The Edge Of Beyond." She proudly finishes.

With a determined breath, Victoria quickly turns and finally departs the ship, fleeing into the stormy night as Kael looks on apprehensively. Distraught over her sudden departure, Victor begins to cry once again as Kael places the crystal shard necklace in his garb for safekeeping then looks upon the mysterious mark located on the infant's arm curiously and says, "It would seem that big things do in fact have small beginnings."

Pausing for a moment in her tracks outside the Arch ship, Victoria gasps with teary eyes then flees the crystal mines, attempting to make her way through undetected. In her hurry however, her cloak shifts back and the human slaves cannot help but notice her colorful Angelic wings. They suddenly kneel before her, murmuring in wonder. The crowd that forms around her draws the Pretorian Guards' notice as well, and they begin to follow her suspiciously with their Gauntlets gripped firmly. Taking advantage of the abrupt opportunity, Kael journeys deep into the crystal mines with Victor held tightly in his arms. Victoria sees him fleeing the Arch ship and begins blasting the rocks around the front gates of the mines with her Gauntlet to create a diversion, causing a pile of rubble, which stalls the Pretorian Guards as she spreads her wings and flies upwards towards a different exit. Finding his path blocked, Kael changes direction to avoid confrontation with the guards in an attempt to keep Victor safely out of sight.

Meanwhile back in Archadia, the battle against the Darchadian fleet has finally ended, with the Arch remaining victorious once more against their fallen counterparts. Within the throne chamber of the Archadian temple, several Darchadians with black trauma lines over their eyes are lined up on their knees as Patrayous walks by with Zepherus whose spinal shards glow, both anxious to destroy them at will.

"This is all that's left apparently!" Patrayous reports with a prideful stance, "At last we can be rid of them for good!"

"Let us hope you are right about that, General." Rosalyn replies, "The Arch can ill afford anymore relentless attacks such as this by their kind." Patrayous turns and kicks the Darchadian closest to him, signifying his dominance over them as Zepherus growls with delight. "Seems Kael missed out on all the action; strange, for he's usually always right there with me." He conveys inquisitively, "He must have good reason for his absence."

"One would assume, although Victoria has failed to report back as well." Josephus sternly replies with a deeply concerned tone.

Rosalyn looks around the chamber from her crystalline throne as Josephus turns to address the two Archadians who aided in Victoria's departure.

"You both last saw her earlier; where is she?" He demands.

The two Archadians glance at each other, unable to answer as another enters the chamber with two more to address the Arch council directly.

"One of our ships unexpectedly departed a few hours ago and apparently entered Pretorian air space." The Archadian informs, "The Eudenians and Enfurians are tracking its current location now."

Alarmed by this unexpected news, Rosalyn and Josephus glance at each other and shake their heads in disappointment. As Josephus frustratingly sighs, he raises his hand, signaling Patrayous to execute the Darchadians before them. The Darchadians look on with determined expressions and spitefully hiss just as Patrayous aims his Gauntlet at them. Smirking proudly, he begins to fire upon each one with great satisfaction as Zepherus roars ferociously.

Through the ghostly mist engulfing the mountainside of the Pretorian mines, Victoria flees; seemingly undetected as her Gauntlet begins to glow, signifying that danger is close. She stands ready for battle and prepares her crystalline staff as it extends before her whilst humming another musical notation, which causes it to react by shifting into defense mode. The crystal shard in her staff glows brightly in purple as she hears a familiar yet unwanted voice. "Well now, we found you after all." Raina proudly claims. Surprised, Victoria turns as the Eudenian Queen and Enfurian King stand before her, grinning with satisfaction of their ability to track her effortlessly all the way from Archadia. "Did you really think you could hide from us this long, *sister*?" Raina sneers in reference to their previous comrade.

"You were never my sister!" Victoria angrily retorts. The pair chuckle in response as Victoria looks around cautiously, trying to assess the situation as well as her immediate surroundings, then takes a calm breath and warns, "This doesn't have to get ugly you two!"

Raina and Lucian approach Victoria whilst trying to intimidate her into powering up to give her position away to the Pretorian Guards nearby.

"Don't fight it, there's no way out of this!" Lucian barks, "And don't think the Arch hasn't learned of your betrayal as we have, *Victoria Zyas!*"

Annoyed by his arrogance, Victoria scoffs and counters, "Do you really think this will help to fulfill your position as King, *Lucian Drakhan?*"

Stepping in front of Lucian, Raina spitefully insults, "You were always their favorite, that is until you turned your back on them!"

"I feel it will be too late for my people by the time they figure out what you've been doing as Queen, *Raina Demuera!*" Victoria snidely retorts.

Confident of her superiority, Raina holds out her hands with a rictus grin, and scoffs, "Come now, stand trial or face doom at the hands of yours truly." She proclaims, "Either way, you stand no chance against someone of our lineage!" Realizing that there's no way out of this deadly confrontation, Victoria sheds the rest of her cloak, revealing her Angelic wings whilst holding her crystalline staff defensively. Raina and Lucian grin with anticipation, as Victoria stands ready to fight and looks upon them intensely.

"Such fates are the wings of destiny!" Victoria states while spreading her Angelic wings as a sign of challenge, "If this is the end, then so be it!" Lucian grins in reaction to her bold claim, then aggressively leaps forward, landing in front of her as Victoria holds her ground, not even flinching as he grips his fists and shouts, "Then come on; let's get this over with! We're ready to take you on right now Archadian, but be forewarned!"

"I'm listening." Victoria steadily taunts to prove her defiance.

"Then listen well!" Lucian warns while arrogantly pointing towards her, "Your influence is great, but even you can't stop our superior power!" Knowing full well that her position will be fully compromised, Victoria gives in and finally powers up as Raina and Lucian stand ready. Looking back through the mist covering the entrance to the crystal mines, Victoria realizes that she must take the fight away from her current position in an attempt to divert their attention away from Victor and Kael. Gripping her crystalline staff tightly, she turns back and aggressively warns, "Prepare yourselves!" Without warning, she crumbles the ground beneath her feet with her energy aura as a furious bolt of lightning strikes between them, then spreads her wings and takes off into the sky. Raina and Lucian glance at each other, both sharing a devious grin then press their respective chest plate symbols, which causes their wings to emerge from their spinal armor. After powering up their energy to the fullest, they take off as well in pursuit of their worthy challenger.

High above the mountainous terrain, the two combatants find Victoria waiting for them high above in the sky. Taking the first strike, she fires an energy blast between them, which causes them both to dodge simultaneously. In retaliation, Raina fires from her Gauntlet, but also misses as Victoria gracefully maneuvers around her attack. Hoping to draw them together again, Victoria flies back, but they go to opposite sides of her in an attempt to overpower their Angelic foe. Combining their fierce strength, Raina and Lucian strike in unison, and Victoria only just evades their attack, feeling the raw power of the blasts as they quickly fly past her. Raina smirks as she watches the near hit then flies towards Victoria and strikes again.

"Our power has grown since we last met, *Archadian*!" Raina taunts with a cruel laugh whilst locking fists with Victoria. Lucian suddenly flies in and proudly claims, "That's right, we've moved beyond our previous status, making us all the better!" Victoria aggressively pushes back as Raina and Lucian attempt to strike again.

She blocks their attacks with her crystalline staff as she gracefully maneuvers through the air with her Angelic wings. "Your bloodstained crowns have blinded you!" Victoria angrily retorts as she assertively strikes back.

Lucian approaches from above as Raina attempts to distract her from below. Victoria catches a glimpse of their swift movement and turns to fly towards Lucian, firing another blast from her Gauntlet, which he blocks with his fiery aura. Preparing to strike again, Victoria powers up but is suddenly caught off guard when Raina unexpectedly comes in from behind with her energy tail, and chuckles maniacally. "Give up now, or we'll crush you when we reach the rocks below!" Raina threatens as she tightens the grip of her energy tail.

Victoria struggles for a brief moment and manages to break free of Raina's grip, forcing her back as Lucian descends from above.

"Either choice makes no difference to us really!" He exclaims.

Attempting to gain the advantage, Raina whips her energy tail towards Victoria, who easily blocks with her crystalline staff, but is blindsided by Lucian as he strikes from above, pounding with both fists locked, which forces her downward. Raina plunges towards Victoria and grips her tightly with her energy tail once again, this time forcing her down towards the mountainside with Lucian close behind. "I would've thought you to be smarter than this!" Raina arrogantly scorns, "Seems you chose unwisely; your death will mark the end of your rebellious acts!"

Looking up towards the dark sky above, Victoria realizes that she has finally been defeated. Her expression changes from one of anger to that of acceptance as she smiles confidently at Raina. "You may kill me and my memory, but my will is done regardless." She decrees to her surprise.

As Raina continues to force her downward towards the surface, Victoria's eyes begin to glow brightly in purple. Surprised by her hidden power, Raina looks upon Victoria in anger and violently breaks her wings, which causes her to scream in pain. Raina then forces her into the mountain by releasing her grip as Lucian fires a powerful energy blast out of retaliation from his Gauntlet, creating an enormous explosion below. Raina and Lucian are knocked back slightly by the energy of the blast and pause, both blinded by the light emanating from the eruption. As they blink to clear their vision, they see what appears to be Victoria's ethereal essence shoot up into the sky for a moment through a bolt of lightning and then quickly sink back into the earth.

Some distance away, the light from the explosion catches Kael's eye as he turns, looking onto the horizon from the mines and sees the bright light caused by the explosion in the distance. Sensing Victoria's inevitable demise, he looks upon the sleeping infant in his arms and sighs with a saddened tone in his breath, knowing Victor's mother just gave her own life to protect him.

As the sound of the explosion echoes violently around him, he reluctantly looks up again. "Farewell, milady; may your sacrifice not be in vain." He says determinedly, "Not as long as I can help it anyway."

He continues following the mountain path into the mines until he arrives at a door. He knocks, and it opens shortly after as a thin middle-aged woman with long black hair stands before him with a curious face. He places the joyous bundle in her arms, which causes her to look baffled. The unsuspecting woman unwraps the Angelic cloth, revealing Victor in his sleeping form. She looks upon the infant in loving shock and gently caresses his delicate face.

"The Gods be praised." She whispers with excitement while focusing her attention on Victor. She then looks up at Kael with tears of joy and politely says, "Thank you." Kael nods respectfully as they both direct their attention back to the baby, who shifts in his sleep. She grins widely with teary eyes then takes Victor inside her rustic home and sits carefully in her old chair as she begins to rock him whilst caressing the blue crystal shard around his neck. Observing from the doorway, Kael chuckles quietly to himself as Victor wakes up and begins waving his arms around excitedly. Upon taking his leave, Kael shuts the door and watches closely as Victor smiles at the woman, who touches the mysterious symbol upon his arm curiously with her fingers.

Approaching the mountaintop from above, Raina lands before several Eudenians in tow, searching for Victoria's remains. As she signals them to dig through the debris, Lucian lands a short distance away with several Enfurians waiting beside him. The Enfurians bow towards Raina and respectfully claim, "Hail Scorpius!" The Eudenians pause their search to bow in respect towards Lucian and respectfully claim, "Hail Drakhan!"
Lucian nods in response, and they all begin to search again. After a few minutes of searching, Lucian turns to face Raina, and aggressively sighs.

"Her power is gone!" He angrily bellows, "What a waste!"
Raina kneels to the ground and begins digging through the rubble frantically with her claws, getting visibly upset; as she can't find whatever it is she is looking for. After several moments of fruitless search, she looks up at the stormy sky and screams, "Damn you to hell, Archadian!"
Lucian chuckles slightly and states, "Should've known she wouldn't be foolish enough to face us head on whilst carrying a legendary Artifact. Such a pity!"
Looking both frustrated and disappointed, Raina stands as Lucian approaches her from behind whilst retracting his dragon-like helmet, revealing his bare scalp. "The hunt goes on my Queen!" He says suggestively.
With the sky rumbling with thunder overhead, Raina retracts her scorpion-like helmet as well then faces him in anger as he grins.

"I want that Gauntlet found, for we cannot allow her legacy to live on!" She spits out furiously, knowing full well that Victoria somehow succeeded in her grand yet mysterious scheme to thwart them.

END OF PROLOGUE:

ACT: 01

Deep within the crystal mines of Pretoria, resembling the bowels of Hell, thousands of human slaves are lined up by Pretorian Guards riding crystalline Scorpion diggers. Kael stands by from above, watching in repugnance as several groups of humans are scanned and placed within separate lines, each heading towards different locations to work various shifts. As if to watch over this hellish scene from beyond the grave, Victoria's voice echoes from the darkness for all who would listen:

"Faith has its reward, when there's something worth believing in. Arch Angels like myself carried out the Gods' will, to enforce balance between the two supreme races of Earth. Both were once human, but had physically evolved over time. Eudenians from the East; Enfurians to the West. As these two powerful races fought for supremacy, humans of the past became enslaved under their rule. Their endless conflict brought chaos upon the planet, until my kind were brought forth to help resolve it. In our retaliation, the war had all but ground to a halt in the flap of a wing, that is, until a new darkness arose. In the wake of this revelation, those who defied the nobles' rule were simply forced into servitude within the crystal mines. Queen Raina and King Lucian have ruled the planet through fear alongside the Titanian Emperor with a firm fist. Together, they created a utopian society built on the backs of those too weak to fight back. Since the aftermath of what has become known as the Chaos War, citizens of Earth have lived their lives; selfishly unaware of the slavish plague that inertly blankets the world in apathy. Tales of legend whisper of a power that could forever bring true balance back to the world. For years people have wondered if it was just a myth, simply told to give the captive hope. Seems that fate lies upon a legacy, one full of mystery and doubt. Tolerance is willing and acceptant, for the least among us are the most important."

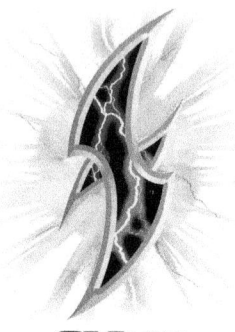

CH: 01
A FAMILY THAT STRAYS TOGETHER

During the early evening hours of Sector 12-604 within the crystal mines, several young slaves, both male and female gather to enter a primitive looking temple as the elder human priests guide them in one at a time for their weekly worship service.

"Everybody inside!" Rev. Warren shouts to get their attention, "Service is about to begin!"

As the young slaves make their way inside the temple, the second priest, Rev. Koontz looks upon them with pride and asks, "Did all of you remember to say your prayers this morning?"

"Yes sir!" The children quickly respond together.

Rev. Koontz grins in satisfaction of their cooperation as Rev. Warren chimes in, "Good; now please take your seats."

The two priests look upon the young slaves, who each find their seats in preparation for worship service, assuming everyone has been accounted for.

"That should be all of them," Rev. Koontz states with a sigh.

"Really?" Rev. Warren sarcastically retorts, "That would be a first."

With the children quickly moving past them into the temple, Koontz looks around with concern and says, "I think someone's missing actually."

"Gee, I wonder who that could be." Warren mutters sarcastically. Annoyed by the missing boy's absence, Warren quickly turns to address a couple of young slaves, the last ones in line, and sternly asks, "Alright you two, where's Victor?"

With smiles on their faces, the child slaves shrug their shoulders, acting oblivious as Warren shakes his head and sighs in annoyance over their willingness to cover up for him.

Through the midst of the fiery caverns, a young boy now with white silvery air sprints from the Pretorian Guards' camp whilst tossing several food rations to various other slaves who give thanks. Several guards search the exterior of their camp, each frustrated by the boy's theft of a food ration.

"Which way did that little brat go?" The Captain of the guard shouts. He points towards the others, attempting to outsmart the boy, then barks, "You two head that way, you three follow me!"

Attempting to lose their trail, the boy quickly climbs up a crystalline pillar protruding from overhead to hide as the Pretorian Guards continue their furious search for him. While holding on tightly to the crystalline pillar with his bare hands and feet, he listens closely to their conversation from above.

"Damn it!" The Captain grumbles, "That's the third time this week!" Feeling confident of his hiding spot overhead, the boy releases himself from the pillar, hanging down just slightly above them by the strength of his legs as he covers his mouth in amusement. After a moment, the dirt from his legs causes his ankles to slip, knocking some of the rock loose from the pillar, which falls before the feet of the guards. They quickly spot him as he drops down and lands gracefully in front of them with a big grin on his face.

"After him!" The Captain bellows as he points towards the boy. As the other guards attempt to grab him, the boy quickly turns and dashes away as they continue chasing after him once again.

"Come back here you little brat!" one of them furiously shouts. In order to avoid potential Gauntlet fire, the boy runs in a zigzag pattern, feeling confident of losing their tail. He gets some distance between himself and his pursuers as he looks back with a crooked smile, but unexpectedly runs into General Kael and falls backwards to the ground. Now with a facial scar over his right eye, Kael crosses is arms in a stern manner then looks down upon his young protégé in annoyance as the boy looks back innocently and grins. "Always be mindful of what you're running into, not just what you're running from." Kael says as he glares upon the boy sitting before him.

Feeling embarrassed for getting caught, Victor looks downward for a moment and nods in acceptance of his careless act.

"And just what were you up to this time that was more important than attending service?" Kael firmly asks.

Victor looks up at Kael, who stares back with stern displeasure. He hesitates to tell him the truth as Kael finishes; "Sonya worries herself to death whenever you pull foolish stunts like this."

As the troublesome boy stands up and quickly dusts himself off from the fall, he snaps, "Of course she does, she's my mother."

Riled by his attitude, Victor faces Kael, who raises his brow in a stern manner and says, "Who prefers that you stay out of mischief."

"You sound just like her now." Victor grumbles.

"And for good reason." Kael scolds, "How many times must I tell you that you're strictly forbidden to go anywhere near the Guards' camp?"

Hoping to justify his actions to Kael, Victor pulls out a slightly smashed food ration from his ragged clothing and replies, "I know, Master. I would've gotten away with it too if they would just mind their own business."

The group of guards finally catches up, breathing heavily from the long chase as Kael shares once last glance of displeasure with Victor.

"There you are!" The Captain angrily snarls.

Hoping to stay out of trouble in their presence, Victor attempts to hide behind Kael. Sneering down at Victor, the Captain snaps at Kael, saying "Hand the boy over for punishment!"

Putt off by their apparent lack of respect, Kael turns and faces the guards, looking the Captain up and down, then sternly stresses, "Stand down, Captain! This is my dominion!"

"Step aside, and let us do our job!" The Captain shouts back as he arrogantly steps forward to confront him.

Kael looks at the young soldier, annoyance quickly building inside him, and replies threateningly, "I'll have you all working with the slaves if you don't follow orders when given!"

"By what right?" Another guard chimes in, "He's guilty of stealing!"

"According to your mighty Emperor, that's called commerce." Kael mocks, "Besides, what could he have possibly stolen that would cause such a rise out of you?"

"The little bastard stole food from our camp!" The Captain exclaims.

With the snap of his finger, Kael signals Victor to hand over the food ration.

"Then take the ration and leave!" Kael shouts as he forcefully throws it over to the Captain.

After catching the food ration, the Captain arrogantly argues, "You're expected to help keep the peace around here, General!"

"That may be, but not here, and not in this way." Kael defends.

Realizing there's no point in arguing the matter further, the Captain signals the others to leave then turns to speak once more directly towards Victor.

"Don't you know about the order, *boy*?" He spitefully taunts, "No wonder the others mock you so much!" Offended by his words, Victor stares back intensely as the Captain leans in so that he is only a few feet away and points towards him again. "You can't hide behind the General forever! He growls, "Soon you'll have to answer to us!"

"Yeah, well I won't be here forever!" Victor confidently retorts.

"Keep telling yourself that, *slave*!" The Captain scoffs as he straightens up and leaves with the others, all of them laughing at his expense.

Kael places his hand on Victor's shoulder to comfort him as they walk back towards the slave camp. After a moment of silence, Kael determines that they are out of earshot and begins to lecture his young headstrong pupil.

"If I were you, I'd be more careful next time." Kael strongly disciplines, "I've told you time and again to keep your distance. You know I can't always be here to keep you out of trouble."

Surprised by such a reaction after going through so much woe, Victor looks at Kael with a disappointed expression as his head droops in shame and mumbles, "We just needed enough food to last the week, that's all."

As Victor's home slowly comes into view, Kael stops to face him, brow drawn in concern. "You know that if you or your mother ever need anything to just ask." He informs, "Don't go looking for trouble when you can simply avoid it altogether. Especially when it comes to stealing food for others."

"I'm not afraid of them!" Victor replies while gesturing back towards the guards' camp. "Besides, they're just foolish drones following orders!"

Trying to be non-confrontational, Kael sighs, "It's not about being afraid. Just because you don't fear them doesn't always make you the wiser." He explains, "And what of my orders? Am I foolish for following them as well?"

"Well no, but that's different!" Victor disputes, annoyed at having to justify his actions, despite feeling that he's right.

"And why is that?" Kael questions, "What makes it so?"

"Well, you don't abuse your power to hurt others for one!" Victor responds forcefully.

"And?" Kael patiently persists.

Weighing his words carefully, Victor pauses, feeling reassured of his perspective and calmly rationalizes, "You don't bully others when they don't agree with you or your beliefs."

"Well, you don't need religion to have morals." Kael interjects, "If you can't determine right from wrong then you lack empathy, not religion."

"Those in power are supposed to help people in need, but they don't." Victor finishes in a sad tone.

"Forget about them!" Kael scolds, "You can't expect to change other people for it's just a waste of time and energy."

With a disgruntled sigh, Victor mutters, "They enjoy making everyone suffer down here, especially me."

"True, but at the moment you can't do anything to change it." Kael tolerantly explains, attempting to keep him grounded. Victor grunts in response, pushing Kael to continue, "Look, I know you're angry, but you've got to let it go." Looking at him directly, Kael kneels before Victor and sternly concludes, "This better not happen again. As punishment, your training is doubled tomorrow. Also, you better hit the books or they'll be hitting you real hard. Understood?"

Though still visibly upset, Victor nods in agreement, as Sonya steps onto the porch of their home to address him. "Victor, time to eat!" She calls.

Without looking, Victor sighs disappointedly and grumbles, "Sounds like mother's calling me, I'd better go."

"You'll end up really disappointed if you think people will do for you as you do for them." Kael states, "Not everyone has the same heart as you." As Victor turns his attention behind him in annoyance of the lecture, Sonya approaches them while reaching out to shake Kael's hand, appreciative of his welcomed presence and companionship towards Victor over the years.

"It's good to see you again, Kael." She says respectfully.

"As with you, Mrs. Grace." Kael happily replies as he firmly shakes her hand in return.

"I see you've been looking out for my little trouble maker yet again!" Sonya jokingly comments with a laugh.

With a comforting grin, Kael places his hand on Victor's shoulder, slightly embarrassing him, and says, "Someone has to in a place like this."

"How are you?" Sonya asks, settling into small talk.

"I'm well, thank you for asking." He humbly replies. Sonya bows her head; acknowledging Kael's respect as he continues, "Glad to see you in higher spirits these days."

"Like most humans, we may falter from time to time, but we do our absolute best." Sonya remarks with a gentle smile, "Sometimes crystals in the hands of one person are worse than a Gauntlet in the hands of another." She expresses, "In truth, there are just some kind of people who are so busy worrying about the next world they've never learned to live in this one, and you can easily look down the cavernous streets and see the horrific results."

"I've noticed, a sad but true observation, Miss Grace." Kael responds, "By the way, how's Victor been doing as of late?"

Shaking her head with slight displeasure, Sonya smiles towards Victor and cheerfully replies, "Much better, I think." Slightly annoyed by their concern over him, Victor frowns as he steps away to extract himself from the conversation. Feeling uncomfortable with the attention, he walks a short distance away as they converse. "His birthday is coming up real soon; are you going to finally tell him?" Sonya quietly asks.

"Not yet." Kael carefully replies.

"Why not?" She probes.

Kael looks over at Victor, hoping to keep his true identity a secret for the time being, and explains, "The timing just isn't right."

"Will it ever be?" Sonya questions with a disappointed sigh.

Pleased by her intuition, Kael faces Sonya directly and states, "One day, yes, when he's old enough to understand and take responsibility for it. Though I can't speak for those around him who are even more unprepared than he is."

"Well, as you know common sense doesn't grow in everyone's garden, even in this place." Sonya sarcastically remarks.

"Unfortunately, no, it doesn't." Kael adds with a soft chuckle.

"He's a willful kid for sure." She says protectively, "Though unlike the others, he's much smarter than you give him credit for sometimes."

"I know, but he's not willing to accept certain things at this point in time." Kael discloses, "Though I admire his natural ability to look beyond his current status in life."

"Well, it is in his blood after all." Sonya jokes.

"Yes," Kael explains, "But considering his naivety to the outside world, it's as if he knows something isn't right but doesn't know how to apply what knowledge he has."

"We both know that in time he will, but we must continue to remain as we are to guide him towards the right path." Sonya advises.

"That is for certain." Kael mutters softly.

Sonya looks over at Victor, who sits on a crystal protrusion, throwing rocks one at a time into the dirt out of boredom. "He deserves better than a slave's life," she caringly expresses, "I just hope he realizes it before it's too late."

"So do I." Kael murmurs apprehensively, "I'm surprised he has yet to realize what his natural hair color is, though judging by the energy fluctuations down here, it's safe to assume that his exposure to the Earth's core has changed it permanently from its original blonde shade."

Victor walks over and stands in front of Sonya, who places her hands around his shoulders to comfort him and states, "They say it takes a village to raise a child, but sometimes I wonder if it isn't the other way around." She then gently rubs her fingers through his silvery white hair and implies, "I know he's had a few rough spots along the way, but I believe he's starting to come around thanks to you."

"I simply do what I can, when I can." Kael proudly states.

"And we're eternally grateful for that." Sonya says with a nod then looks down upon Victor to get his attention and asks. "Aren't we, Victor?"

Victor crosses his arms, trying not to get sentimental, which brings a smile to Sonya's face. A sudden whistling noise sounds off from their home as Sonya looks behind her for a moment then turns back to address Kael one last time.

"Sorry to cut this conversation short, but I have dinner to finish for this little hell-raiser." She says while rustling Victor's silvery-white hair to cheer him up as Kael nods in respect. Before heading home, she faces Victor with a firm expression. "It's almost time to eat." She informs, "Better get inside before it gets too late. And don't forget you need to wash up before you step even one foot into my kitchen."

"I'll be right there, mother!" Victor impatiently replies.

Smiling back, Sonya returns home as Victor stands beside Kael and looks on with a curious glare. "As your mother likes to say; love comes naturally for most people, whereas hate is learned, so don't let your anger get the better of you." Kael advises. Surprised by the sudden return to the earlier lecture, Victor faces Kael who finishes, "I know it's hard, but keep your head up, and take care of your mother for me will you?" As Sonya reaches the stairs leading to their small rustic home, she waves towards Kael who kindly waves back.

"Yes, Master." Victor promises, "I sure will."

"Victor, I'm not going to tell you again!" Sonya gently yells out from the front door of their home.

As a last-minute act of kindness, Kael pulls out a food ration from his garb and tosses it to Victor who carefully asks, "What's this?"

"What does it look like?" Kael retorts with a smile. Wasting no time, Victor quickly unwraps the food ration with excitement and quickly takes a small bite as Kael explains "Take it as a sign that your efforts weren't entirely wasted earlier, but also to remind you that there are other ways to get what you want and need in life."

"Thanks so much, Master Kael." Victor responds while respectfully bowing his head towards his mentor.

Kael graciously nods back in return, and says, "Take care of yourself son."

Victor smiles back in appreciation, then quickly turns to head home. Sonya waves towards Kael once more as he nods back and sighs in amusement.

"That kid is going to be stronger than all of us one day, I just know it." He amusingly mutters to himself.

Kael calmly turns away and takes his leave whilst looking upon the beautiful luminescent crystalline structures within the large cavern of the mines.

Afternoon turns to evening as Victor walks up the stairway leading up to his home with his head turned, looking behind him curiously as Sonya waits for him inside the weathered doorway.

"Something troubling you, my son?" She delicately asks.

Victor keeps his attention focused in the opposite direction for a moment as the light from the crystalline pillars highlight the worry on his young and rugged face. "Oh, it's nothing really." He calmly mutters.

Sonya scoffs in amusement as she steps out onto the porch with him and states, "I know you're struggling internally, when you're down there's no place to go but up. You may be able to fool those guards on a day-to-day basis, but you'll never fool me, no matter how hard you try."

Surprised by her intuitive response, Victor quickly turns to face her and inquires, "How did you know?"

Sonya grins, amused as always by Victor's unwillingness to accept her intuitive nature. "Lest you forget, I'm your mother; I make it my business to know." She says smiling, "The world doesn't stop because you want it to." Victor sighs in disappointment, feeling embarrassed by his actions earlier. "What have you been up to lately?" She firmly probes, "What did you do this time?"

"If you knew everything, you wouldn't ask." Victor retorts with slight condescension. Sonya raises her brow in annoyance as he smiles sheepishly then looks downward in shame and says, "Sorry, that was mean, wasn't it?"

Using a less harsh tactic, Sonya approaches Victor and drapes her arms over his shoulders once again to comfort him as they look upon the cavern lit up by the bioluminescence of various crystalline structures.

"You can't cause trouble and think that no one will notice." She patiently explains, trying to get through to him, "Sometimes the truth hurts, but in the long run, lies hurt even more."

Attempting to keep his strong composure, Victor looks on and excuses, "I was just trying to get enough food to last us the week. I didn't know I would get caught." He then finishes as he looks up to her, "I'm sorry."

Sonya lays her hand on Victor's head to comfort him as he turns to face her.

"Well, despite your valiant if not childish methods, I'm grateful." She happily acknowledges, "But don't make a habit of it, you hear me?"

"I'll try not to." Victor humbly mutters.

"I just want what's best for you and don't want to see you throw away your entire future like so many others have." Sonya softly pleas.

Victor scoffs in response and asks, "What kind of future is there to be had in this place anyway?"

"None really, but for the time being we just have to work with what we have, together." Sonya says as she places her hands on his face, hoping to get through to him. "Work as if you will live forever, and live as if you'll die tomorrow. Take time to be thankful for everything you have, you can always have more but you could also have less." Victor looks into her hazel eyes for comfort as he places his hands over hers. "I've lost so much already; we both have." Sonya continues, "I don't want to lose you too."

With a crooked smile, Victor looks into Sonya's eyes with determination and declares, "You won't, I'll make you proud eventually, I hope."

"In many ways you already have, but don't ever wish to be anything more than what you can possibly be." She advises, "One's beliefs don't make you a better person, your behavior does. And from the looks of it, I assume General Kael helped you out of this one as well?" Victor looks down, shoulders slumping in shame from her intuitive assumption. Sonya kneels, taking both his hands into her own, and explains, "You try so hard to help others that you don't stop to think about helping yourself for once. Never expect someone else will go out of their way for you, most people can't even get out of their own way to begin with." Sonya pauses for a moment, waiting for a response, which never comes. She then looks down, contemplating, then mentions; "By the way, Miss Turner gives her thanks for the food you gave her earlier today." Feeling appreciated for his efforts, Victor's head snaps up while looking into his mother's eyes once more and grins.

"There's that look again." Sonya says with a comforting laugh.

With his head cocking to the side, he asks, "What look?"

"That look you get every time you help someone in need." She tells, "Deceit is always weakness, but sincerity like yours even in error is strength."

Feeling grateful to make her smile in his presence despite his actions, Victor joyfully expresses, "I just can't help it sometimes, even when I know they can't help back, it always feels good to help others in need."

"As it always should, but charity begins at home." Sonya happily adds, "Carry out a random act of kindness with no expectation of reward, safe in the knowledge that one day someone might do the same for you. Strong people stand up for themselves, but the strongest people stand up for others as well." Victor nods, feeling he's done just that as she finishes, "Though don't forget that sometimes the best way to deal with people who stand in your way is not to deal with them at all, because when you least expect it they'll bash you with the very same mouth they begged from."

"Why doesn't everyone else stand together as a change for good?" Victor questions with a sad tone, "I can't be the only one around here, can I?" Sonya sighs disappointedly, standing slowly as she looks upon the cavern once again and replies, "Sadly, not everyone is capable of change, even when it's absolutely necessary. Some of us are just born different, and sometimes the best way to solve your own problems is to help somebody else instead." Victor listens raptly, curious to hear what she believes he was born to do.

"Some are born with the power to do great or terrible things." She elaborates, "And there are some who care nothing about the needs of others as we do. Kael once said that there's an inherit generosity in the human spirit, with one of its faces being that of a teacher and a warrior."

"Well despite not being human himself, he seems to be the embodiment of both in my opinion." Victor mutters.

"As will you someday if you're willing." Sonya comments.

"I wish I could do more myself." Victor proclaims with a determined face, sounding somewhat disheartened.

Contemplating the best approach, Sonya enlightens, "Tomorrow is but one dream away. When I was a little girl I was taught an angelic prayer, one passed down from the Arch itself." Victor listens with full attention as she reveals, "Accept the things you cannot change, have the courage to change the things you can, and have the wisdom to know the difference."

"I'm not quite sure I totally get that." Victor sheepishly admits.

"You will, but know that the world only makes sense if you force it to." Sonya strongly encourages, "Someday you will make a mark that will last forever, and when that day comes, I hope I'm there to see it."

"Me too." Victor happily adds, then with a change in tone he states, "I just wish I knew as to whether or not I'm actually worthy of a better life."

"You are, but worrying doesn't take away tomorrow's troubles, it only takes away today's peace." She tells.

"That would explain why I feel the way I do right now." He mutters.

"Whom shall I sing to sleep at night when you're grown up and gone from this place?" She questions with a smile, "I'm lonely enough as it is when you're not around."

"Assuming I ever leave, I'll always remember the melody you taught me." Victor reassures, "I can never seem to get it out of my head."

"Sometimes I wonder what I, let alone the world would do without you," she admits, "But I pray everyday to the Gods that we never find out."

"I feel as if something great awaits me out there, I just don't know what it is yet." Victor says as he looks upward into the crystalline cavern.

"You don't have to look too hard really, because you're bound to find it eventually." Sonya assures as she turns her attention upwards as well, "Don't let small minds convince you that your dreams are too big. Because without believing in yourself, your dreams no matter how big or small they may be will never come true." Feeling appreciated once more, Victor smiles as Sonya grabs his hand to lead him inside and says, "Come, let's enjoy our dinner, and forget today's troubles." As Victor follows Sonya into the rustic home, she turns, noticing the crumbs all over his shirt, then says over her shoulder, "Oh, and save the rest for later, if you don't mind."
Victor comes to a halt by the doorway, surprised that she knew about the food ration given to him by Kael then smiles as he steps inside the home.

Evening comes to a close as Sonya cleans up the kitchen area of their home from dinner, whilst feeling grateful for Victor's company. While washing the primitive dishware, she hums an ancient tune as Victor enters the kitchen and joins in, humming along with her. As they finish the final note, he approaches her and stands beside the sink area and calmly asks, "Mother?"

"Yes dear?" Sonya quickly replies.

"Why do you hum that silly tune all the time?" He carefully inquires.

"It's simple really; when life beats you down and crushes your soul, music helps to remind you that you have one." She graciously answers.

"Speaking of which, it's about that time. Can you tell me the story of the Angels when we're done for the night?" He blushingly requests.
Sonya chuckles in response to his request and retorts, "Again? But you hear that story almost every night."

"I know, but I just can't get enough of it." Victor gladly whimpers with a pleading look, "Please?"
Looking upon her adopted son with pride, Sonya laughs, "Oh, alright!" She then replies, "I guess we can take another journey to Archadia."
Sharing a warm smile, Victor attempts to leave the kitchen with excitement as Sonya looks out into the night sky from the cracked window in the ceiling.

"Even I've always wondered what Earth looks like from above." She murmurs sorrowfully, "I bet it's beautiful."
Victor stops by the kitchen entryway, concerned by Sonya's sorrowful tone as a tear rolls down her face. "Mother, are you alright?" He carefully asks.
Wiping away the tear from her cheek, Sonya takes a deep breath then nods and says, "I'm fine." With a slight turn, she looks back at him and asks, "So, are you ready to fly to Archadia yet again?"
With his eyes widened, Victor gasps as he happily retorts, "Always! Can I be the great Korina this time?"

"Of course," Sonya happily responds, "We can go through the Holy Trinity Chapter if you like." Without hesitation, Victor quickly runs into his room, feeling ecstatic. Sonya looks on and shakes her head, amused by the joy he gets out of the Archadian legends. As she walks into the living area and settles into her old but sturdy chair, Victor runs out wearing a primitive Angel costume, fists proudly planted on his hips in a heroic manner. Sonya can't help but chuckle at the sight of him in his hand-made costume with crooked seams, a broken halo, and slightly torn wings colored in blue.

"Do you ever think we'll make it there someday?" Victor inquires with an expression of wonder in his youthful blue eyes, "Archadia I mean?"
As any caring mother would do, Sonya attempts to fix Victor's tattered wings and broken halo with a smile then says, "Sweetheart, I think what you read about regarding Archadia is more like legends and fairy tales."

"I know it's real; it has to be!" Victor insists with determination.
Sonya pauses as she looks upwards through the skylight into the night sky and replies, "Oh, it's real alright, just not in the way you might imagine it. The good thing about paradise is that it's true, whether you believe in it or not. Though most choose only to see it with their eyes, not their heart."
Turning to the table beside her, Sonya grabs an old hardback book with pages made out of crystalline film and the name, *ANGELIC ARTIFACTS*, engraved on the spine. Victor notices the Gods' symbol colored in blue, pink, and silver which is also engraved on the book's cover and carefully caresses it with his fingers, saying, "This symbol, I've always wondered what it means."

"Symbols have great power for they can instill fear, hope, or in this case a deeper sense of mystery." Sonya caringly enlightens.
As he watches with great anticipation, Sonya opens the crystalline book to an old marked page with the title, *KNIGHTS OF ARCHADIA: ANGELS OF THE ARCH.* Sonya pats her hand on the seat next to her as Victor sits by, listening closely with excitement as she reads:

"Paradise; a place once believed to only be seen in your dreams. There are nights when the winds of Archadia, so inviting in their promise of flight and freedom that make one's spirit soar to great heights, but is only known to a select few. Though Archadia's beauty is like none other, it is not without a cost. Like all the kingdoms of Earth, Archadia has its fare share of dangerous encounters. Of all the threats the Arch has ever faced, the gravest was a dark entity known as, Traganus, the fallen one. Only the three legendary Angels, Kitana and Kiara led by the great Korina, were capable of defeating him, which inevitably led to his exile and imprisonment. Thus, light had triumphed over the forces of darkness, or so it seemed...."

Paying full attention, Victor listens with wondrous eyes while lying on the floor as he caresses his tattered wings in curiosity. Sonya reads on through the night as Victor closes his eyes, trying to imagine Archadia visually in his mind.

CH: 02
A LABOR OF LOVE

Through the crystalline caverns radiating with heat against the cool damp air, the human slaves work their usual shifts in various parts of the mines. Sonya works alongside other female slaves whilst preparing various crystals for transport to another sector in the mines. Earning his keep, Victor works a few hundred yards away alongside other slaves around his age, sorting through various crystals himself from a large pile before them into two smaller ones: one for those worth being polished for industrial means on the surface and the other, those which will be used within the mines. During his shift, Victor randomly finds an old aluminum soda can from Earth's previous period with a round symbol colored in red, white, and blue. Making sure no one else is looking, he carefully places the can in his pouch to add to his already large collection of old world trinkets.

After hours of sorting, Victor stands to stretch the muscles in his back as he looks around for a moment to inspect his gloomy surroundings. Half a dozen other young boys crouch beside him, hunched over their own piles of crystals as they take a break. Victor looks beyond the piles of crystals and sees two young warriors close to his age: a Eudenian with short black hair, wearing a royal purple cape with black and gray highlighting various parts of his purple Soul Gear, and a larger Enfurian with short spikey reddish-white hair whose Soul Gear is orange with black and gray highlights as well. The young warriors look around the mines curiously whilst following their escort and entourage of personal guards from their respective kingdoms. Puzzled by their unusual appearance, Victor moves forward from the other young slaves to take a closer look while observing their decorative attire inquisitively. A child slave attempting to push a cart full of crystals accidently runs into the young Enfurian warrior, who quickly turns out of annoyance and without hesitation shoves the slave back to the ground.

As the cart tips over, the crystals scatter onto the ground, the noise drawing the attention of all the slaves and Pretorian Guards in the area. With fury blazing in his eyes, Victor approaches the Enfurian as a couple of other slaves attempt to hold him back to avoid confrontation with the guards. The two warriors look upon Victor who stares at them intensely in anger. Amused by the accidental run in, the Eudenian warrior places his hand on the Enfurian's shoulder and asks, "Having trouble, Braxel?"

"I'm good, Trag." Braxel snarls as he looks around the crystalline cavern, sniffing furiously. "Let us go, this place reeks of filth."

"Boy, you said it!" Trag says in agreement with a sneering attitude.
The two young warriors look back at Victor, who's still being restrained by the other slaves and give him a condescending look. Victor meets their gazes for a moment, then slowly lowers his eyes and pulls away from the slaves holding him back. The young warriors scoff at his reluctant withdrawal as they continue following their illustrious group through the mines. Victor shakes his head in anger then returns to his stressful work with a heavy heart, feeling exhaustively worthless compared to the Eudenian and Enfurian who seem to have so much more than he feels he could ever have.

Within the temple of Archadia, Princess Elena, now also in her early teens with long golden hair sits within her chambers overlooking the beautiful kingdom as she plays a crystalline harp and hums an ancient melody. Rosalyn enters the room with Josephus and stops, both enjoying the beautiful sound.

"The energetic vibrations that come from music gives a soul to the universe, wings to the mind, flight to the imagination, and life to everything around us." Josephus explains whilst trying not to distract her.

"Have you been practicing your routine my dear?" Rosalyn asks.
Slightly annoyed, Elena pauses for a moment and sighs, "I did them earlier, but I don't see why I have to do them everyday." She replies, "Besides, it's not like I'm going to be old enough for the crown anytime soon."

"Which is why it is so important for you to learn how to use these powers while you have time as an Archling," Rosalyn stresses.

"We won't be around forever to rule this kingdom, and you'll have to start taking responsibility very soon." Josephus firmly adds, "Keeping balance across the entire planet is a serious business; thus, we can't have your frivolous ideas keep you from your true potential as an Archadian Princess."
Ignoring their advice, Elena turns her attention back to her crystalline harp then continues to play and sing along to the melody. "Elena?" Josephus calls.

"Yes!" Elena says impatiently as she stops playing her harp once again, feeling even more annoyed by their unwanted disruption.

"That is why it is so important for you to learn from us and apply the divine secrets of Archadia." Josephus warns.

"Why me?" Elena questions, unwilling to cooperate.

"Because my dear, you're the one who has to continue our work someday." Rosalyn explains, "It's your place after all."

"And what if I don't like my place?" Elena questions as she steps away from the harp, seeming bothered by the notion.

"Everyone has their place in this world, Elena." Josephus explains, "You, the soldiers, the workers. It's not all that bad being Princess, is it?"

"I suppose not," Elena murmurs as she runs her fingers through a crystalline tapestry hanging from her wall. "Would you prefer to be carting around crystals all day in the mines like the humans?" Rosalyn jokes.

"Oh mother, don't be so dramatic." Elena snaps as she steps towards the window overlooking the kingdom. "At least they seem to have some fun every now and then from what I hear." Feeling the weight of her family crown, Elena stands by the window while looking upon the crystalline kingdom and sighs as Rosalyn and Josephus glance at each other, concerned over their daughter's sudden change in behavior.

"What is it child?" Rosalyn carefully probes, "Are you concerned about being a Princess of Archadia?"

"Sometimes, I mean, what if I can't bring them peace?" Elena questions as she looks onto the beautiful sky surrounding the kingdom. She then faces them and questions, "What if I'm destined to fail by making things worse? What if I can't make them listen the way you do?"
Josephus chuckles to himself as Rosalyn shares a grin and jokes, "What if the sky turns to fire and your wings fall off?" Attempting to comfort their daughter, she continues, "I've always told you to listen with your heart; I believe now is the time to listen to it."

"But the energy around me, it's difficult to channel." Elena gripes.

"The energy of this place can help, but only the power within can truly guide you." Rosalyn states, "Trust your halo, listen to the storm within."
Taking her mother's keen advice, Elena closes her eyes and attempts to meditate. After a brief moment, she becomes utterly frustrated with herself.

"You see?" She expresses impatiently, "I just can't do it!"

"Giving up so soon?" Josephus teases, "Your progress is truly remarkable; if only we had more adult Angels of your caliber."

"Let me join the ranks and you shall." Elena states determinedly.

"I'm not quite sure the Arch is ready for an Archling like you, Josephus points out, "Besides, what would the others say if we were to allow your initiation too early?"

"That for once you let me do what I want to with my own power." Elena angrily retorts.

"With that attitude, you can see why we don't." Josephus informs, "Your defiance is reason enough to keep you at bay until you are ready."
Elena expresses a look of annoyance as they stand back to give her space.

"Now, let's give it another shot and try not lose your cool this time." Josephus caringly demands. Frustrated, Elena closes her eyes and attempts to channel the surrounding energy once again. Rosalyn and Josephus watch; impressed by her talent as she becomes even more irritated by their strict presence. "You're distracting me!" She shouts, "It just doesn't work like this!"

"It does when you want it to." Josephus states with a confident grin, "Things worthwhile don't come easy to those unwilling to try."

"The life of a Princess from her birth is well defined," Rosalyn lectures, "She must humbly serve her kingdom, play the part she's been assigned by the Gods, for she alone guards the hopes and dreams of her people. Weak and mighty, rich and poor, much like those of legend."

"All these people you speak of were victorious in some way from one generation to another." Elena denotes, "Their stories have been passed on; but why I ask unless there is any truth to them?"

"Tales of legend?" Josephus amuses, "No, only common people believe these tales as they believe most anything. As Angels, we are here precisely to educate ourselves against such foolish passions."

"But if we are superior from the surface dwellers as you say, then why do we not rule them entirely?" Elena curiously inquires to their surprise.

"How do you mean?" Rosalyn questions.

"It has always been our dream to go there." Elena mutters, "The next dimension as some people call it, our people long for such ethereal passage."

"The Edge Of Beyond has a way of swallowing men and women alike, along with their idealistic dreams of paradise." Josephus sternly warns, "Like most dreams, it promises great power but exacts a terrible price."

"But still, to think these legends can lead us forward to the greatest glory; why is it so wrong to act on them?" Elena persists to their annoyance.

"We can only teach you, not guide you." Rosalyn states, "Beware of what you dream beyond what is known or expected, for the Gods have a way of punishing such pride, even us Angels."

"An Angel must make every sacrifice for their people, for it is our sacred duty." Josephus encourages as a small fleet of Archadians fly by the window out of respect for their future Queen, "Elena, you must encourage the troops, wave to them as you would any other worthy of the Arch."

"One day when I'm Queen, I'll be able to wave to all." Elena claims.

"Don't rush the day *girl*, or you risk all!" Josephus scolds, "You needn't worry about anyone taking your crown for it is a gift from the Gods and is custom made. Thus, your crown will never fit anyone else."

Frustrated by their persistent lecture, Elena waves to her fellow Archadians for a moment then steps away from the window and enters another part of her chambers as she closes the door behind her. Rosalyn and Josephus shake their heads, knowing it won't be an easy task preparing their compassionately headstrong daughter for the crown of their beloved Angelic kingdom.

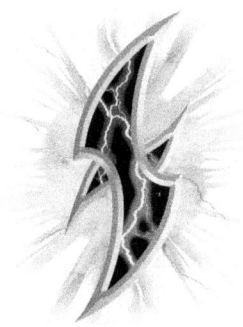

CH: 03
THE STRUGGLE TO SURVIVE

After many hours of hard labor in the unbearable heat of the mines, Victor attempts to move the last pile of crystals before the end of his shift as the other young slaves prepare to head home for the day.

"Hey Victor, you coming?" One of the boys asks.

"I'll be right there, guys!" Victor quickly replies.

The young slaves nod in response and head home, all of them tired from working for so long and hard. Victor struggles to conjure the strength to move the last few crystals when a hard shove from behind knocks him to the ground. As he wipes the dirt off of his face, he hears a condescending voice shout from behind, "Hey there, *freak*!"

Victor quickly rolls over onto his back and sees three male slaves, each a few years older in age, standing over him with his tools in hand.

"We heard about you getting into trouble with the guards the other day!" The first slave mocks.

"Yeah, what would you know about it?" Victor angrily retorts, wiping dirt from the corner of his mouth as he stands.

"We know General Kael had to bail you out, yet again!" The slave sneers in response. "Yeah, what a loser!" One of the others chimes in.

"You aren't one of us!" The leader scorns, "Half-breeds have no place among people like us here!"

With a confident smirk, Victor retorts, "Indeed you're right!"

Unwilling to fall into their trap by giving them the benefit of seeing him angry, Victor turns away to continue working, but is shoved once more.

"Don't turn your back on me; I'm talking to you runt!" The first boy yells forcefully, attempting to get a reaction out of him. Becoming angry, Victor pushes back in defense, causing the trio to laugh cruelly at his expense.

"His eyes are unlike ours." The second boy jeers, "They look awfully sad don't they, even for someone who passes as human?"

"What can you expect from eyes as blue as his?" The final boy threatens, "Do that again and we'll beat you down, punk!"

"Go ahead and try!" Victor growls, anticipating another fight.

Angered by his words, the three boys suddenly attack him. The leader punches Victor in the mouth, pushing him to the edge. Victor looks at him with disdain as the boy examines him, surprised that he has yet to bleed from their attacks. The others finally join in as Victor strikes them one at a time out of defense. Thanks to his training under Kael's protective wing, Victor fends off each of their attacks with ease.

"Is that all you got?" He taunts while laughing.

The young slaves look on in shock as a sudden spark of electricity strikes between them. Taking advantage of the distraction caused by his mysterious power, Victor finally returns the favor by striking the leader in the jaw, knocking him back towards the others as the three of them hit the ground. Standing tall and proud, Victor looks upon them intensely as the other young slaves help the leader to his feet.

"What was that for, freak!" The leader hollers.

"Don't call me that!" Victor shouts back, "I'm not a freak!"

Taken aback by his intensity, the boys crawl back away from him in fear.

"Come on you guys, let's get out of here!" The first slave grumbles nervously, hoping not to anger Victor further.

As the three boys scramble to their feet, they quickly turn to head home, and are caught off guard by Kael, as he appears standing before them. Relieved, Victor sighs, as Kael looks down upon the small group of troublesome boys in an extremely stern matter.

"Is this one such an imposing threat that you must all gang-up on him?" Kael asks as he stares directly at the leader with a stern look then states, "I think not." As the young slaves glance at each other sheepishly, he finishes, "You boys should know better than to pick on someone else's infirmity."

The leader pushes the other two away furiously then points towards Victor in anger, and snarls, "Better run home to mom! This isn't over, *half-breed!*"

Strong and silent, Victor remains unscathed as Kael stands by, waiting for him to explode at any moment. "Let's go guys!" The leader scoffs.

Victor stares back with determination as the last of the boys takes his tools and snaps the handles over his knee. "Here's your tools, *loser!*" The third slave jeers as he throws the broken tools onto the ground before Victor's feet.

"Good luck finishing your shift without them!" The second boy mocks as the others laughs. As the young slaves finally rush off, Kael shakes his head and sighs in disappointment of their harsh treatment towards Victor. Now disheartened, Victor drops to his knees and reaches to pick up the broken pieces of his tools, trying to hold back the thunderous fury inside him. He sees a glimmer out of the corner of his eye and when he turns to investigate, he finds a blue crystal shard lying in front of him on the ground.

Concerned for his mental stability, Kael looks on as Victor glances upon his cold reflection for a moment on a large crystal shard, feeling even more distressed. As his reflection stares back at him, the unwanted image reveals the cuts and bruises all over his face, the rage overwhelming him. Victor grabs the broken hammer lying next to him, gripping it tightly in his slightly trembling hand, and suddenly slams it against the crystal shard in anger, shattering it into several fragments. His reflection is multiplied from the pieces, as he looks away and closes his eyes, haunted by his own image.

"When you react, you let others control you, but when you respond, you are the one in control." Kael strongly advises, "You mustn't look for a fight, especially one you can't win, but you should never back down either."

"Either way, I still lose somehow." Victor says in a disgruntled tone.

"In some cases, you may as well get used to that, for it's the kind of resentment that your natural ability is going to invoke in others." Kael rationally states. He pauses for a moment then inquires, "Are you hurt?"
Victor opens his eyes, looks over his shoulder and sees Kael who's still standing behind him. "Should I be?" He asks quietly. After a short pause, he then mutters, "You know I'm not. Just because I'm strong enough to handle most pain doesn't mean I deserve it." Standing up, Victor brushes himself off from the fight, hoping to hide any signs of a struggle from Sonya later.

"You know that's not what I meant," Kael impatiently replies, "What I mean is, are you alright?"

"Why do they pick on me all the time?" Victor questions, his voice slightly trembling, "Why can't they just leave me alone?"

"Don't fall victim to other people's hostility or insecurities by letting them get to you." Kael says encouragingly, "No matter how badly others treat you, in the end, it's your reaction that counts." Victor listens closely as he continues, "Also, don't allow bitterness or jealousy to control your life as it does theirs. You're in control, not them. And while you're at it, don't worry about others not liking you, in this world most people are struggling to like themselves." Kael finishes while pointing at his discouraged pupil.
Victor looks into his brown eyes, and asks, "They call me a half-breed, but why?" Reluctant to answer, Kael sighs, struggling not to reveal his true origin to him. "Deep down, I know I'm a good person, aren't I?" Victor persists.

"Of course you are!" Kael firmly replies.
Hesitant to hear the answer, Victor inquires, "Then why does everyone have such a hard time believing that I am?"

"Because you challenge them." Kael aversely answers.

"How? Victor frustratingly intensifies, "I didn't do anything wrong!"

"It's not always about what we do in life that makes others resentful, though behavior itself is a mirror in which everyone shows their own image." Kael profoundly states, "In other words, it's nothing you've done so much as something you are."

Dejected, Victor motions towards the empty cavern towering over them with a furrowed brow and says, "They say I don't belong."

"Well technically, they aren't wrong." Kael respectfully chuckles, "Though keep in mind, when people attempt to undermine your dreams, predict your doom, or criticize you, they're not telling your story, but theirs."

"If that's true, then what am I exactly?" Victor continues.

"Never mind that, what they say doesn't matter!" Kael firmly replies, "Realize that not everyone around you is your friend, so don't ever let someone who has done nothing with their life tell you how to live yours."
Expressing his insecurity, Victor holds his arms out slightly before him and exclaims, "But it's true, look at me!"
Contemplating his response, Kael looks at the headstrong boy before him compassionately, and sighs strongly. "I'm always looking, Victor."
Surprised by his response, Victor looks upon Kael, feeling grateful yet sad.

"I see something that doesn't belong in this place, something they just can't see, and may never see." Kael assures.

"Because I'm different?" Victor tentatively asks while looking away.

"That, but also because you're special, and stubborn like me." Kael jokes, "But know that different doesn't mean wrong." Feeling encouraged, Victor looks at his mentor again and smiles wanly as Kael continues, "Be grateful for who you are, not what they think you are. Take pride in yourself and the life you live with honor, and integrity."

"Am I even capable of that?" Victor doubtfully mutters.

"Yes, but you must learn to pick your battles, or they'll choose you." Kael patiently explains as Victor looks downward and sighs, "You must calm the storm within if you are to ever control your anger."
Victor nods his head and determinedly replies, "I'll try to, Master."

"Someday your fate will take you far away from here, but not tonight." Kael informs. As Victor nods in response, he finishes, "Better head home before Sonya starts to worry about you." Kael smiles and gently pats his young protégé on the back as Victor turns and places his broken tools back into his worn satchel then heads home. "I know it's hard for you now, but know that someone's always watching over you." Kael calls out one last time to his retreating young friend.

"Are they?" Victor murmurs as he looks upwards to signify the Angels and the Gods, then declares, "Someday, I'll make them see."
Victor turns his head to address Kael one last time with a crooked smile, and finishes, "If I were an Angel, I'd be the best there ever was."
As Victor storms away determinedly, Kael looks on with concern in his eyes and mutters, "I believe you will be."
Saddened by Victor's inability to control his anger and by his own inability to affect his current situation, Kael sighs and takes his leave.

CH: 04
FAMILY JEOPARDY

More than a mile away in another area of the crystal mines, Sonya strives to finish her work with the other female slaves, as they converse amongst themselves.

"I don't know how you manage do to it, Sonya!" One of the women begins. Sonya stops for a moment as she turns to look at the woman, who clarifies, "Trying to work all the time while raising a troublesome bandit."

Chuckling inwardly at their apparent concern, Sonya replies, "I manage pretty well for a single mother I suppose, though sometimes I find myself losing the battle with my patience."

"We can see why!" Another woman laughs.

"Victor has yet to recover from this insane and horrific lifestyle." Sonya explains, "To be perfectly honest, it's worse for him than any of us."

The two females glance at each other for a moment, trying not to be disrespectful towards Sonya as the first one says gently, "We don't mean to pry or anything; we're just a little concerned about you lately."

Sonya looks upon her fellow workers with confusion for a moment.

"We know how strong and smart he is, but lately he's been failing all of his studies and has been picking fights with the other kids." The second slave continues the point at hand.

"Actually, they're the ones picking fights with him." Sonya calmly defends as they listen closely, "The truth of the matter is everyone makes mistakes, but that doesn't mean they have to pay for them the rest of their life. Sometimes even good people make bad choices; it doesn't mean they are inherently bad. It just means they are human like the rest of us."

"Nonetheless, he's constantly getting into some sort of trouble, and whenever we try and talk to him he's like a complete stranger to us, as well as the others." The first woman tells.

Knowing they speak the truth, Sonya shakes her head and sighs in disappointment, "I know, but in truth, he's a stranger to us all. Reality is a pretty scary thing for some people. This world is a cold and alienating place for a boy like who doesn't quite fit in."

A few Pretorian Guards notice Sonya and the other slaves conversing and decide to step in uninvited, whilst looking upon Sonya lewdly.

"Well now, what do we have here?" One of the guards teases.

"Looks like a fine working slave." The other chimes in, while looking Sonya up and down, "I bet there's more to you than that, isn't there?"

Sonya scowls upon the guards and scoffs, "More than you'll ever know!"

The guards chuckle arrogantly in response. Sonya tenses, clearly getting annoyed by their unwanted presence as she takes a deep breath and levelly asks, "What do you want? Can't you see we're busy?"

"We hear that your boy is the one who's been stealing from our camps lately!" The Captain responds with amusement evident in his voice.

"I'm sure he was just hungry," Sonya defensively replies, "That tends to happen when you're actually working like the rest of us."

The leader crouches down, leaning in face level with Sonya to intimidate her and snaps, "Last time I checked, slaves were forbidden to come near our camps at all times!"

Annoyed, the second guard turns to the leader and exclaims, "This bitch is careless, letting her bastard son get away with our food like that! It's truly unforgivable if you ask me!"

"You know, if we were all fed properly, then perhaps my son wouldn't have to!" Sonya crossly retorts. The looks on the guards' faces quickly change to that of anger as she finishes, "Maybe you should help those in need instead of indulging yourselves behind closed doors."

The leader leans in closer to Sonya, trying to bully her as the other slaves stand back in fear.

"What do you say we help your attitude a little bit by taking away your rations for the day?" He threatens spitefully, "Keep in mind, you're here to work, and nothing else! Unless you've somehow forgotten your place!"

Out of arrogance, he places his hand on Sonya's cheek, which she quickly pushes away in disgust and scowls, "If you touch me, you'll have to answer to General Kael himself!"

The second guard suddenly grabs her by her hair, trying pathetically to showcase their dominance as Sonya grunts in pain.

"You need some manners, slave!" The guard aggressively belittles.

Annoyed by her willingness to defend herself, the guards pull on Sonya's arms and drag her away from her workplace to be punished as the other slaves stand by, feeling helpless to do anything on her behalf.

"Let go of me!" Sonya cries.

"We're going to enjoy this!" The leader whispers into her ear.

A small crowd of slaves gathers around as Sonya struggles to break free, murmuring in shock and confusion. The guards tie Sonya's hands behind her back as she screams out in terror.

"Victor!" She frantically calls out, her voice echoing everywhere.
As Victor walks home from work, he hears his mother's cries in the distance. Rushing to her defense, he desperately makes his way through the crowd, trying to make sense of what caused so many people to gather. Sonya screams once again, which causes him to pause momentarily before surging forward as fast as he can. Enraged, Victor begins to shove the slaves aside in his rush to reach his mother and hollers, "Let go of her now!"
The guards turn and see Victor breaking through the crowd as he approaches them in a blind rage.

"Stand back, boy; this is for your own good!" The leader shouts.
Sonya is knocked to the ground by a strike to the back of the knees as the guards power up their Gauntlets to punish her. Victor charges towards them, but is held back by the other slaves as he panics.

"Let me go!" He yells whilst struggling against their concerned grip.
The guards blast Sonya with their Gauntlets as she tries her best to withstand the pain, crying out in agony whilst focusing her attention on Victor to keep her composure. Victor struggles even harder, trying to get to his dear mother to protect her as Sonya whimpers.

"Get out of here, Victor!" She painfully cries. "Leave now!"
The leader stops blasting Sonya and saunters over to Victor, grabbing his face aggressively, then squeezes tightly.

"Leave him alone you cowards!" Sonya screams protectively.

"You've defied us for the last time, *boy!*" The guard snarls. "We'll be sure to return the favor by sending you and your wretched mother deeper into the mines!"
Victor's pupils contract until they are nearly invisible, causing his eyes to flash brightly in blue as he unexpectedly causes the guard to lose grip. He breaks free, catching the guard by surprise as he attacks in anger and forces him to the ground. More guards quickly rush over to neutralize Victor and aggressively throw him off their subdued comrade.

"You're going to pay dearly for that, *slave!*" One of the guards snaps.
The guards stop striking Sonya to focus their attention on Victor. He is brought before everyone and forced to his knees, arms drawn back behind him and head pulled back by his silvery-white hair as he winces in pain.

"Time to pay the consequences for your actions, kid!" a guard sneers.
The guards pull Victor closer in front of Sonya, as mother and son make eye contact, each seeking the other's comfort.

"I'm sorry mother, it's my fault." Victor sobs. "I couldn't help it!"
Despite her intense pain, Sonya tries to encourage him by saying, "You wouldn't be who you are if you could. It's going to be alright."

Victor looks into Sonya's eyes for comfort then both flinch as they hear the hum of the Gauntlets charging up once again. The Pretorian Guards power up their Gauntlets as Sonya tries her best to hold back the pain to keep Victor calm. The guards begin blasting again, attempting to penetrate her backside.

"Mother!" Victor calls softly.

Sonya screams in agony, as the Pretorian Guards continue blasting her from behind. She struggles to keep her head up, eyes still focused on Victor.

"Mother, I'm scared!" He whimpers with tears welling in his eyes.

"It's alright to be scared, Victor." Sonya says weakly, "Just never forget who you are."

Concerned by the grim situation escalating further, another guard turns to address his superior officer, "That's enough, Captain!" He forcefully warns, "You're going to kill her!"

The Captain sneers with a cruel laugh and replies, "That's the point, isn't it?" As the guard looks upon his superior, unsure of what to say, the Captain continues, "A crowd has gathered, thus a lesson needs to be learned here."

The guard looks on with concern, still hesitating to speak as the Captain gives the signal and barks, "Do it!"

Following orders, the guards blast Sonya in the back once again as Victor watches in horror. "Mother, no!" He agonizingly shrieks.

As each blast hits her from behind, a wave of energy suddenly flows through Sonya's body, neutralizing her nervous system as she collapses to the ground before Victor's eyes. The crowd looks on in fear of what just transpired as the guards cease fire and power down their Gauntlets.

"Let go of me!" Victor screams, desperately struggling to reach the debilitated figure before him.

The guards restraining him violently throw Victor to the ground and walk away, laughing in amusement of their unrelenting dominance over the slaves. The concerned guard looks on as Victor scrambles over to Sonya, pushing him out of his way as he runs towards her. Victor kneels beside her near-lifeless body as he gazes upon her in sorrow and wraps his arms around her protectively. The Captain faces the frightened slaves still gathered to address them all. "Let this be a lesson to you all!" He declares, "By order of the Emperor, if you get out of line then you will be punished! Those who defy our commands as well as his will be executed without hesitation or qualm!"

Some of the slaves begin to weep from the tragedy they just witnessed as the Captain turns to address the other guards and orders, "Let's go, men!"

The Pretorian Guards march away, following their malicious Captain, while leaving behind the slaves standing around in shock that are horrified by this turn of events in their sector. As the bystanders slowly drift away, Victor tearfully clenches Sonya's dying body close to his.

"I tried to do what you told me by being strong, but it's just too hard sometimes." Victor whimpers, "At this rate, I'll never find paradise."

"You will eventually, you just have to believe in yourself." Sonya encourages with a struggling voice as she rests her head next to his, "One day you'll be at the place you always wanted to be so let your heart guide you to the light, it whispers so listen closely." While trembling from the emotional pain, Victors laments, "I wasn't strong enough mother, I couldn't save you." Sonya gently hushes him and replies, "You did what you could, and for that I'm grateful." Tears overcome Victor's face as she continues, "Don't make our mistakes, don't follow orders your whole life, think for yourself and speak the truth even if your voice shakes." Feeling her strength fade away, she holds out her hand as Victor presses his palm against hers. "You are worth so much more than you think, so never settle for anything less than what you deserve, not even second best." She encourages, "Wake up everyday to do something life changing, if you're lucky the life you change may be your own."

"If you say so, mother." Victor says softly.

With her last breath, she whispers, "I'll always be with you, even if you can't see me, and no matter where you go or what they call you, you'll always be my son. Don't ever let life pass you by, and never forget where you come from."

As the life leaves her eyes, Sonya dies in Victor's arms. Moments later, Kael arrives at the scene, looking sadly upon Victor and Sonya. Kael approaches Victor from behind and places his hand on his shoulder to comfort him, hoping to shed some of the pain for him.

"What a senseless tragedy." He sadly murmurs. "It is with a heavy heart that we must bid her farewell."

Victor closes his eyes and weeps as he grips Sonya's hand tightly in his.

"I'm sorry son." Kael tries to ease.

"It's my fault, Master." Victor mumbles sadly. Kael's eyes widen in surprise as Victor turns his head, feeling hopeless, and mutters, "If I hadn't stolen food from the camp, none of this would've happened."

Kael kneels before Victor, places his hand on his back to comfort him, and gently says, "You bare no fault in her passing; this isn't the first time someone has died by their hands."

Sobbing, Victor turns directly to look at Kael as tears threaten to flow down his cheeks, "I wasn't strong enough!"

"What did you say?" Kael asks, shocked by his response.

Victor hesitates to answer as he wipes the tears away from his sorrowful eyes.

"Had I been stronger, she'd still be alive." He finally says.

Kael envelops Victor in a hug, holding him tightly then places both hands on his shoulders to knock some sense into him.

"Now you listen to me!" He firmly states, "You didn't kill her, they did. You understand?" After a long pause, Victor releases his grip of Sonya's body and turns to fully embrace Kael, weeping into his chest. Kael holds him tightly to comfort his despair as the other slaves gather around once again to pay their respects on Sonya's behalf before dispersing back to their homes.

"I wish I could just fly away, free, like an Angel." Victor says softly. As Kael rests his chin on Victor's head, he takes a deep breath whilst preparing to speak into the silvery white hair.

"I pray someday you will." He whispers.

"Why bother?" Victor sadly mumbles, "We both know that I never get what I really want in life anyway."

"No one ever does, sometimes you just have to learn to do without." Kael reluctantly retorts, attempting to keep Victor's emotions in check as well as his own, "Fulfillment is being satisfied with yourself more than your circumstances, it's the result of developing all that you are and all you can do." Kael pauses briefly as he attempts to remain strong for Victor's sake.

"I'm not sure I can do anything because I am nothing!" Victor angrily expresses, feeling worthless.

"Nonsense!" Kael comforts, "Never give up on a dream just because of the time it will take to accomplish it; the time will pass anyway." Victor listens closely as he carefully illuminates, "You've got the makings of greatness in you, but you have to take charge of your life now, set your own course. Stick to your gut, no matter the squalls and when the time comes, you'll get your chance to really test the cut of your wings. Only then will you be able to show the world what you're truly made of."

Victor pulls back slightly and looks up at him, feeling hopeful despite the tears running down his weary face as Kael lifts his chin with his finger to encourage him. "I just hope I'm there that day to catch some of the light emanating from you." Victor looks away into the empty cavern, fearful of his future without Sonya as Kael adds, "She's gone to a better place."

"I don't understand…" Victor, retorts, "This planet, I thought this was supposed to be a better place?"

"Not yet anyway." Kael softly replies, "Sonya was a good person, inside and out. With a heart strong, and true." He states as Victor looks back at Sonya's lifeless body.

While struggling to regain his composure, Victor angrily mutters, "Had I known life was going to be this hard, I would've rather not ever been born."

"Well, under the circumstances be grateful that you were born at all." Kael caringly advises, "Don't pray for an easy life; instead pray for the strength to endure a difficult one and be the change you've always wanted to be in this world."

"Change or not, I'm truly alone now, aren't I?" Victor whimpers.

"She may not be with us anymore, but you're not alone, Victor." Kael whispers as he himself looks upon Sonya's lifeless body for a moment in sorrow and repeats, "You're not alone."

With his teary eyes full of distress, Victor looks upward into the dark crystalline cavern, hoping that one day he can be free of his slave status and fly among the Angels of Archadia in what he believes to be paradise.

CH: 05
SLAVES OF A DIFFERENT KIND

Many years later, Victor, who is now in his late twenties, kneels in front of Sonya's nearly shattered gravestone and looks upward with a more sorrowful and intense focus than before. With hair now past his shoulders, Victor looks around the all too familiar setting in the crystal mines as a large group of male slaves gather around to begin their second shift of the day. The years have not been good to them; the decades worth of hard manual labor has given them hard muscles, but has caused them to age prematurely as well. The backs of the other slaves are bent from carrying hundreds of pounds worth of crystals every day since they were children and working nonstop for their entire lives. Victor, being half Angel hasn't aged nearly as quickly due to the structure and composition of his Angelic genome.

Victor looks upon Sonya's gravestone as if to pray when a Pretorian Guard's voice booms in the distance: "Line up, you slave dogs! First shift is over!"

The slaves start forming two lines near the crystal Scorpion diggers as Victor faces Sonya's gravestone once more. He bows his head in honor of her memory and closes his eyes, long silvery white hair dropping into his intense face. He sighs, feeling disappointed of not growing up with his mother all these years as an older slave approaches him from behind to get his attention.

"Just another day in paradise, wouldn't you say?" The slave jokes.

Victor raises his head and opens his intense blue eyes, refocusing his attention towards the old slave who disturbed him. "For you maybe, but it sure as hell isn't for me." He replies, "This is no way to live, for any of us."

Unwilling to believe in anything beyond the depths of the Earth, that being the mines in which they live and work, the elder slave tilts his head back and chuckles, "You don't think that what we do is important, I mean what are you complaining about?" Victor shakes his head in annoyance as the slave extends his arms and resumes, "Incase you haven't noticed, we humans are the ones running the show; in a way, you could say that we're the lords of the Earth."

41

"Please, do us both a favor and don't talk to me about Earth, alright!" Victor snaps, "I just spent the better part of my life hauling it around under slavish conditions. There's just got to be a better place than this."
With a scoff, the elder slave retorts, "Like what, paradise?"

"You may not believe in paradise, but there's no doubt in my mind that it exists, somewhere out there, beyond this dreadful place." Victor finishes as he continues to look upward, feeling hopeful.

"A fantasy that remains forever out of reach." The elder smugly inquires, "You talk as if you've seen it first hand."

"No, I haven't unfortunately." Victor reluctantly admits.

"Well, then how do you know it's really out there?" The elder mocks. Contemplating the question, Victor humbly answers, "Some things you see only with your eyes, others you see with your heart."

"Get your head out of the clouds!" The elder slave laughs, "None of us are ever getting out of here, might as well accept that."
Annoyed by the elder's attitude, Victor turns to respond as he determinedly states, "I accept that one day I'll be strong enough to break free of this god forsaken place and make my own destiny!"

"But freedom isn't truly free at all, is it?" The elder slave contests, "It comes with the highest of costs and responsibility."

"From what I've seen, it's paid for in blood and tears." Victor firmly replies, "But that doesn't scare me away from trying."

"And what would you do with that freedom?" The slave jokes whilst gesturing towards the other slaves, signifying the many generations that have lived their entire lives in the mines. As Victor ponders the thought for a moment, the slave continues, "Even if we all could escape this horrible life, none of us would know what to do with it. Not even you."
Victor frowns at the elder slave, unwilling to accept his closed-minded viewpoint then bows in honor of the Gods and places a crystalline flower on Sonya's gravestone. The elder slave looks on curiously as Victor kisses his fingers and gently places them on the gravestone compassionately which upon closer inspection reads, *May love and fortune fill your wings with grace.*

"Rest well, mother." Victor carefully whispers.
He sighs once more in sorrow then rises to his feet whilst grabbing his gear as he looks upon an old and weathered Angel statue standing above Sonya's gravestone. Taking a closer look, he sees the name, KORINA engraved on the statue's base. "Why pray to them?" The elder slave asks spitefully, "They don't care about our kind! They only serve those on the surface, never have they come to our aid."
Victor hesitates to respond; curious about whether or not they actually exist then inquires, "Have you ever seen one?"

"Of course not!" The elder slave scoffs. "No one has, or will ever see an Angel below the surface, and neither will you."

Turning his attention elsewhere, Victor looks into the distance and mutters hopefully, "Perhaps someday, they will help free us."

"Not likely." The elder slave mutters.

"Have you ever met royalty?" Victor asks.

"Once or twice, when I was younger." The elder slave replies.

Several yards away, another elder slave suddenly falls to the ground from dehydration as the others look on in panic. Another slave waves his hand to call for help and shouts, "Water!"

A young female slave, short in size with long blonde hair looks up with her innocent hazel eyes and quickly rushes to their aid as she pulls out a small water jug from her supply pack. The old man sighs in relief as she gently lifts his head, pouring a slow and steady stream of water into his open mouth. He sputters slightly, relieved of such treatment as he quickly chugs the water.

"Thank you, child." The slave whispers in relief.

"You're welcome." The girl happily replies, feeling grateful to help another person in need.

The girl tries to slow him down to keep him from choking, then looks around for a moment and sighs from the daily fatigue. Once it's apparent that the man is taken care of, the elder slave turns back to address Victor.

"Don't rattle the cage with your childish dreams!" He sternly warns, "What makes you think they would ever help us anyway?"

Still gazing upon the old Angel statue, Victor slowly stands up and confidently states, "It's what I choose to believe, we're all in the gutter right now but some of us are still looking to the stars."

After quenching the old man's thirst, the young female slave helps him to his feet, then turns and sees Victor a short distance away as she smiles with excitement. To her surprise, a rape gang consisting of three male slaves unexpectedly approach the girl from behind as one of them moves into position and says, "Watch it, she's fairly easy on the eyes."

The young female's expression changes from that of excitement to that of intensity as her advanced goggles flip over her eyes. The three male slaves approach her cautiously as she stands her ground, preparing to defend herself.

"Not used to finding them so young these days." One of the slaves arrogantly murmurs. Victor turns his attention back towards the girl and straightens up intensely as she widens her stance. The three male slaves attempt to grab her but are caught off guard as she gracefully leaps overhead and lands safely on the ground behind them.

"Don't make this harder than it has to be!" The other slave shouts.

Concerned for the girl's safety, Victor keeps a watchful eye incase things get out of hand. As the three slaves charge towards her one last time, the girl ignites her energy whips from her primitive arm gauntlets and blows past them from in-between, forcing them all to the ground with ease. Victor sighs in relief, realizing the girl luckily has things under control.

"What the hell, *girl?*" one of the slaves angrily remarks.

"Why don't you pick on someone your own size!" The girl scorns as she pulls her energy whips away and suddenly strikes them simultaneously.
The three slaves yell from the pain then quickly jump to their feet and run off.

"That's right, you better run!" The girl proudly warns as Victor shakes his head and grins.

Confident of her ability to defend herself, the young girl retracts the energy whips back into her primitive gauntlets, straightens up her posture, and looks around as her goggles retract back over her forehead. Victor places his hand on the Angel statue one last time as the girl happily approaches him from behind and calls out excitedly, "Victor, over here!"

Victor turns and sees the young girl with golden locks running towards him as he smiles broadly in response. She quickly runs up to him then wraps her arms around his waist and cheerfully asks, "How are you today, Victor?"

"Better, now that you're here, Talia." Victor joyfully replies to his dearest friend, "I've got everything I need when you smile like that."

Talia tilts her head back, grinning up at him and says, "What can I say? My day isn't complete unless I get to see you."

"Likewise." Victor respectfully retorts. Talia smiles gleefully as he observes her new attire and says, "I see they finally upgraded your gear."

Talia observes her new gear for a moment and laughs, "You bet they did!"

Feeling restless after a long first shift, Victor wipes away the sweat from his brow and murmurs, "It's hotter than usual down here."

"Yeah, I've noticed." Talia comments.

"How is everyone today?" Victor inquires courteously.

"Only a few have fallen today." Talia replies as she turns her head in reference to the other slaves, "I've been trying to keep up so there aren't any on my shift anymore." She solemnly states. She pulls out another small jug from her supplies pack, and says, "I brought some water. Are you thirsty?"

"Yes, I'm parched!" Victor says gratefully. Talia passes the water jug to him and grins. Victor drinks deeply from the jug then pours some water over his body to drench himself for a moment to cool off, leaning his body back to enjoy the sensation of the cool liquid running down his chest. "Ah!" He relaxingly expresses, "That's ever so much better."

"Thanks," Talia beams appreciatively, "It's cleaner than usual for sure, my best yet I think."

Victor straightens his body and hands the water jug back to Talia, who places it back in her supply pack. "Thanks, Talia." He compliments, "What would I do without you?"

Feeling deeply appreciated, Talia smiles mischievously then quickly rummages through her supplies pack for something. "Oh, by the way," she laughs, "I have something to show you!"

She slowly withdraws her hand from the pack, revealing a small Seraph creature, covered in a bluish-purple pattern throughout its fur and a metallic green on its underbelly. "I found him this morning." She explains, "I think he was abandoned, poor thing. I couldn't just leave him to die, so I brought him back with me instead." Victor pets the young Seraph and laughs as it yawns from just taking a nap. "We need to find his family." She says with concern.

"What if he doesn't have one?" Victor regretfully implies.

Saddened by the thought, Talia looks upon the Seraph and happily states, "He does now." Laughter escapes from Victor's mouth, as she claims, "Everyone deserves a pet of some kind, this one just happens to be mine."

The friendly Seraph responds by licking Victor's fingers and rubs its head against his hand in approval whilst purring with its spinal shards glowing.

"He likes you, no surprise there!" Talia chuckles.

"So, I've been replaced with this little thing, have I?" Victor asks with a crooked smile.

"Victor, you know nothing could ever replace you." Talia assures.

"Nor you, Talia." Victor says respectfully.

"Looks like we have new friend," Talia jokes as she rubs her hand down the Seraph's somewhat spiny back.

"Good to know." Victor replies while scratching the top of the Seraph's head as it gracefully croons. "Does he have a name?"

"Lithia," Talia happily replies, "Like the Lithium crystals North of here, where I'm told I was born."

Victor's smile wanes slightly as he looks her in the eye with a serious gaze.

"It's too dangerous for you to be venturing out that far alone." He solemnly cautions, "Crystal denizens roam those areas, you know?"

"I know, but it's the only place I can go when you're not around that I don't feel totally alone." Talia sheepishly responds.

As the second shift chime sounds off, Victor notices the other slaves gearing up for work. Talia pulls out a set of handmade wings from her supply pack as Victor tilts his head just slightly out of curiosity and inquires, "What's that you've got there?"

"My wings!" Talia joyfully reveals, "I've been fixing them up ever since they were damaged last week."

Surprised by her craftsmanship, Victor looks upon the tattered wings colored in green and purple as he places his hand on her shoulder and encouragingly comments, "They're beautiful, just like you."

Talia looks up at him and happily asks, "Do you really think so?"

With a humble expression, Victor nods in response as Talia beams with pride. Heading toward the transport vehicles, a small group of slaves begins to pass the pair when they look at the set of battered wings in Talia's hands and scoff. Talia's head droops for a moment, feeling discouraged by their brashness.

"It's a shame they're not real though." She mumbles as she looks up into the sunny sky, longing painted on her face, then continues, "If they were, we could fly away together and find another world somewhere. One much better than this one for sure."

Sharing her vision of paradise, Victor looks upward for a moment as well, and says, "I'd be right there with you."

Talia looks back at Victor, smiling in appreciation of his shared belief then hears a condescending voice behind them. "Why do you two always look to the sky when there's nothing up there for any of us?" One of the slaves sneers, "Like most children you don't know when to stop pretending." Victor and Talia quickly turn to face the other slaves, feeling confused and somewhat hurt by the question. "Yeah!" Another slave chimes in, "Why do you both try so hard to fly when you don't have any wings to begin with?"

Hoping to cheer up his young female companion, Victor squares his shoulders in a heroic position then glances at Talia and confidently states, "We use what we've been given, and we'll run on our own legs if we have to, as long as it takes to find paradise."

Talia smiles in relief, feeding off of Victor's positive strength against their savage negativity. "Paradise?" The fist slave sneers, "Yeah right!"

"Answer me this," Victor firmly disputes, "Are we human because we dream, or do we dream because we're human?"

"How about this…" The second slave scorns with a snobbish laugh, "Keep dreaming and see where that gets you in the end."

"There's no hope in ever getting out of this place alive, trust in that." The first slave spitefully adds, "You can't just make things however you want them to be; everyone must face that reality as we've had to."

"Which is why I don't want to end up like all of you!" Victor defensively retorts, "We can't give up hope; sometimes, it's all we ever have. Besides, I'd rather have a mind opened by faithful wonder than one closed by superstitious belief."

"If you're both so divine, where's your wings?" The slave sneers.

Annoyed by their harsh treatment, Talia frowns upon them and sternly replies, "We haven't earned ours yet, but when we do, we'll be able to fly away from here."

"Either way, it's all for nothing if you don't have the freedom to do it." The second slave scorns, thinking them to be nothing but naive fools.

"Come on everyone!" The first slave laughs with the others; "We're wasting our time with these two dreamers!"

Irritated by their cruelty, Victor mutters, "If they're laughing to our faces, imagine what they're saying behind our backs. Though I suppose if our dreams weren't big enough, they wouldn't be laughing in the first place."

Feeling hurt by their harsh words, Talia slowly lowers her gaze and mutters, "You must think I'm stupid also."

"Not at all actually, it just means you have an imagination." He kindly assures, "Keep in mind, life is not always about who's real to your face, sometimes it's about who's real behind your back. Though take it from me, sometimes the hardest thing to be in this world is yourself."

"Do you truly believe that?" Talia inquires with a hopeful smile.

"I do, and I also believe that when you refuse to become a product of your environment, you can be anything." Victor humbly answers, "Unlike these people who don't seem to get the hint. Without a life mission, that being our dreams, we are subject to follow the masses to mediocrity and futility." The other slaves scoff and continue on their path towards the transports to begin their work shifts as they each give condescending looks towards them. "They may laugh at us because we're different, but I laugh at them because they're all the same." Victor defensively implies, "Kind of makes you wonder how the hell our people got like this in the first place."

"I know, but what other way would they be?" Talia queries.

Annoyed by their hateful attitude, Victor maintains stern eye contact while Talia continues to look downward, struggling to hold her tears back as she places the handmade wings back in her supplies pack. Victor turns back to Talia and delicately wipes the tears from her eyes with his rough fingers.

"Forget about them, Talia." He says encouragingly, "What the hell do they know anyway?"

"Not much it seems." Talia softly replies, sounding discouraged.

"Well I for one refuse to lower my standards to accommodate those who refuse to raise theirs, and neither should you." Victor declares, "When you lower your values to please the majority you've lost everything."

Talia's expression visibly brightens as she replies, "I suppose you're right." She pauses for a moment while digging through her supply pack once again and chimes, "Oh yeah, I almost forgot!" She quickly pulls out a blue crystal shard from another of her pack's infinite pockets, a type he's never seen before, as she explains, "I came across this where I found Lithia earlier."

Talia places the crystal shard in Victor's hands, as he examines it intensely.

"It's definitely a chaos crystal, but what kind I wonder?" He says to himself curiously.

"I'm not sure either, but I thought it would brighten your day when I'm not around." Talia comments.

As Victor slips the crystal shard into the left pocket of his trousers, he gives his young friend a half smile in appreciation of her precious gift.

"Thank you, Talia." He says cheerfully, "You just made my day."

"Don't I always?" Talia retorts with a short laugh.

Victor responds with a short bark of laughter. After a moment, he looks behind him and sighs, "I better get back to work."

He then turns back to face her and says, "I'll see you later, alright." As Victor turns away, he begins to walk up the rough path towards his crew.

Talia watches her friend moving away; her smile slightly disappearing as she joyfully shouts, "You better!"

Surprised by her sudden claim, Victor turns towards Talia, who smiles gleefully, and grins himself as he chuckles quietly for a moment then turns back to catch up with his work crew. Talia watches Victor leave with the others, as he disappears into the deep bioluminescent cavernous backdrop. Lithia climbs onto Talia's shoulder and nuzzles his head against her neck, purring as she pets him before returning to her work crew as well.

Late afternoon sets in as Victor works tirelessly to finish out his second shift. A lone drop of sweat tracks through the crystal dust coating Victor's face. Swiping the back of his right hand over his brow, he sighs and stretches his body from the daily fatigue. Suddenly, a piece of cloth stuck between the cracks in the rock catches his attention as he pulls on it, revealing an old flag of some sort covered in red, white, and blue with a section showcasing several white stars. As typical with his findings, Victor places the flag in his pouch to bring home as another trinket. Seconds later, he sees a young slave climbing down a crystalline pillar with their energy whips and watches them bring water to the other laborers, who drink in relief.

Victor waits for them to quench their thirst then waves the girl over to him. As she approaches, he looks on, amazed at the profound differences between the girl coming towards him and the one he took under his wing years ago. The young girl walks over and hands Victor a small jug of water from her supply pack, ignoring the friendly smile he gives her. Once he finishes drinking, she takes the jug and places back it into her supply pack.

"Thank you." Victor gratefully acknowledges.

The girl nods back and quickly walks away, not saying a single word to him. Victor sighs, feeling disappointed by the girl's lack of esteem then turns back to continue working. Upon thinking of Talia, he remembers the gift she gave him that morning and draws it out of his pocket. Victor examines the deep blue crystal in wonder, mesmerized by the vein of sky blue running through it like a bolt of lightning. Shaking his head, he places the crystal back into his pocket, ready to work again when he sees a spot of purple through a gap between two large rocks to his left. With curiosity overtaking his focus, Victor grabs one of his tools and wedges it into the gap and carefully forces the rocks apart, revealing a rare crystalline Lotus flower colored in green and purple. Being careful not to damage the delicate petals, Victor gently picks it from between the rocks and places it inside his garb for protection.

"You'll make a fine birthday present." He says to himself.

Last shift comes to a close as the other slaves gather their gear to head home for the day. Victor leaps down from his workstation and looks around to make sure none of the Pretorian Guards are watching then pulls out the Lotus, observing it intensely. After carefully looking around once again, he gently places it back in his supply pack with his work tools and heads home.

CH: 06
ALL THAT IS GOOD

With his last shift for the day finished, Victor trudges home, exhausted from hours of mining the coarse rock surrounding the precious crystals. His left hand drifts up and gently massages a muscle in his shoulder as he makes his way down the bioluminescent path purely by instinct. Sighing in relief of being able to go home, he drops his hand, which brushes his pocket, reminding him of his gift from earlier. He pulls out the shard, surprised by the slow pulse of the blue vein glowing deep within the heart of the crystal. Coming to a halt, Victor traces the pulse with his finger, mesmerized by it's radiance. With a tired smile, he slips it back into his pocket then looks up and sees the small shack in the distance upon the hill.

Laughter drifts across the clearing, revealing to Victor that his solitude is coming to an end by the time he enters the home. He walks up the worn steps of the porch slowly as to not miss a step, whilst enjoying the happiness in his friend's voice. Looking into the small window, he sees Talia standing in the kitchen with Lithia on her shoulder, both humming Sonya's melody while awaiting his return. Victor takes one final moment to enjoy the rare moment of solitude with a deep breath before opening the door.

As he steps through the doorway, three slaves between nine and eleven years old immediately surround him, chattering about how they are helping to make dinner. Talia turns from the large steaming pot she is stirring in the small kitchen to get their attention.

"Hey!" She scolds, "If you guys really want to help out, you should stop getting distracted!" Despite her stern words, Talia looks up to acknowledge Victor standing in the hallway and smiles, betraying her fondness for the children running around. Talia turns back to continue preparing dinner for everyone with Lithia by her side as an elderly lady takes Victor's work gear and carefully sets it down by a closet door.

Victor briefly acknowledges everyone with a nod then enters the kitchen to address Talia. "Something smells good!" He comments, "What's for dinner?"

"My specialty of course, delicious roast stew!" Talia says with excitement, which causes Lithia to chirp.

"I noticed the porch is in a poor state of repair these days." Victor mentions, "I'll need to do something about that when I get the chance."

"With my help of course." Talia happily teases.

"I wouldn't have it any other way." Victor humorously accepts.

Grateful for the meal being prepared despite their low stock of rations, Victor takes in the warm refreshing smell of the stew and places his hand on Talia's shoulder to get her attention. She quickly turns to face him as he pulls out the durable flower from his garb and laughingly touches it to her nose. "I know it's a little early yet, but happy birthday, Talia." He joyously utters.

Talia gasps at the sight while gently touching the crystalline petals with her fingers. "A Lotus flower!" She expresses with extreme awe in her voice, "Oh, thank you, it's my favorite!"

Victor chuckles in response to her excitement as he hands the flower to her and says, "I know. I'm glad I got it when I did because I wanted to wish you well and give it to you myself incase I somehow missed it this time."

Surprised by the beautiful gift, Talia examines the flower with Lithia beside her and says, "I can't believe you actually found one this time of year."

"Thought you might like that." Victor replies with a crooked smile.

As she holds the flower gently in the palm of her hand, stem cradled between her middle and ring fingers, Lithia nudges the crystalline petals with his nose, causing it to spin. Laughing, Talia tucks it into her hair above her left ear and approaches the window to look at her reflection. Lithia takes this opportunity to hop onto the counter near the stove and sip the stew from the pot, which elicits a gentle chuckle once again from Victor as Talia turns to scold him.

"Lithia!" She rebukes with her voice raised.

Lithia cowers as Talia looks at him with a humorous scowl. He launches from the counter with his wings, flying the short distance to Victor's shoulder. Victor rubs his index finger under Lithia's throat, eliciting a low purr as he jokingly warns, "Alright, you little trouble maker; better do what she says."

With a chirp, Lithia flies out of the kitchen as Talia shakes her head at Victor then steps back towards the stove to finish cooking. The meal and subsequent clean up passes through the evening with laughter and good-natured teasing as the children gather in the common area around the most comfortable chair where the old woman sits and shares stories about the Gods and Angels. Victor leans against a wall post; smiling at the rapt attention they give her as Talia along with Lithia rummage through a small closet full of old sheet music ranging from Beethoven, Vangelis, Megadeth, and Hans Zimmer. With a triumphant cry, she emerges with a couple of battered instruments resembling a blue electric guitar in the shape of a sharpened V and grey keyboard.

Excited with what little time they have every evening, Talia turns to Victor and pleads hopefully, "Come on, Victor, let's play!"

"Oh alright," he laughs, "If you insist." Victor takes the guitar and sits, warning, "I haven't played in a while, so I'll do my best to keep up."

Victor sets the V shaped guitar between his legs then takes a moment to tune it as Talia begins playing a melody on her keyboard. Victor responds by playing the same tune faster but with a more complicated rhythm, causing Lithia to hum along as he tilts his head back with his spinal shards glowing.

"Have you noticed how much better I've gotten lately?" Talia asks.

"Indeed I have." Victor proudly acknowledges, "We make such sweet music together, what say we turn up the volume?" Talia nods in agreement as the two battle each other with various musical notations.

"Every time I strike a chord I think of them as numbers in my head, which allow me to play several notes at a time." Talia happily expresses.

"As with any number, if you start learning from zero then there is no end to the amount of techniques that will emerge from within." Victor encourages while the old woman watches the children dance to the melody with Lithia still humming along.

After a much-needed evening of fun, the children scamper off to their sleeping quarters with Talia in tow, chattering happily about the special entertainment for the evening. She helps them get ready for bed, making certain the children wash their faces and brush their teeth properly, trying to prevent them from wasting any of their precious water supplies. Careful not to damage the instruments, Victor wraps them up in cloth and returns them to the closet for the night as the old woman approaches him from behind.

"Talia's become a bright student and has excelled quickly." She begins, "I trust you've helped with her studies as of late?"

As Victor closes the closet door, he turns to converse with the woman, saying, "That I have, though I must say it's a lot to take in for us both. We've currently been studying information regarding surface world governance, history, and current sovereign structure."

"Such information may seem useless to you now, but you may need it someday." The old woman says encouragingly, "Everyone needs a basic understanding of how the world works, whether they like it or not. People my age believe it's better to be aware than to remain ignorant."

Victor's left eyebrow twitches, threatening to lift in amusement as he sarcastically retorts, "Can't argue with that logic. I suppose those who don't study history are doomed to repeat it, yet those of us who do study are doomed to stand by helplessly while everyone else repeats it."

The old woman sighs, then pointedly changes the subject, "The children and I are very impressed with your talents. You two play extremely well together."

"Thanks." Victor says with a smile, "I can tell she's been practicing a lot herself lately." He then chuckles, "She's almost as good as I am now."

"You help to inspire her creativity." The old woman denotes, "She practices every chance she gets trying to impress you."

A bark of laughter escapes Victor who says, "Yeah well, it doesn't take much for her to impress me, even when she isn't trying. Truly creative people like ourselves aren't motivated by the desire to beat others, only to achieve. At the end of the day, we're just artists who listen to the beat of a different rhythm."
With her eyebrows knitted together in curiosity, the old woman grins then comments, "Your skills have definitely grown over the years. Why, who could tire of such beautiful music, or talent for that matter?"
Feeling disappointed by the possible truth, Victor heavily sighs, "Those that eventually grow out of it I suppose."

"Not everyone does, for the creative adult is just a child who has survived." The old woman encouragingly remarks, "We as humans are only limited by weakness of attention and poverty of imagination, though it is said that music is a spiritual bridge between Heaven and Earth itself."

"I pray that's a bridge I haven't yet burned." Victor jokes while heading towards the restroom as the older lady looks on and smiles once again. Inside the restroom, he cleans his teeth efficiently, using the smallest amount of water necessary and looks into the cracked mirror, examining his weary and rugged face. In the room down the hall, Talia climbs onto her bed next to Victor's and settles in as Lithia walks in and sniffs around cautiously.

"Come here, boy!" Talia happily calls.
Lithia chirps in response and climbs onto the cot, settling down next to her as she gently pets his back, careful not to snag her clothing on the crystalline shards protruding from his spine. As Lithia croons happily, Victor enters the room and climbs into his cot, ready to sleep. He positions himself, lying on the bed to settle in, when Talia chimes in softly, "Victor?"
Looking over at her hopeful face, he grins and replies, "Yes, milady?"
Talia smiles excitedly, almost forgetting what she was going to point out.

"I love it when you say that to me." She happily sighs. After a brief moment, she reaches over and grabs a crystalline music globe sitting on a nightstand and hands it over to Victor, gently chiding, "You almost forgot!"
Victor sits up from his cot, carefully takes the globe and smiles back, admiring his handy work then replies, "Of course."
The globe is roughly made, constructed by Victor himself from materials scavenged from his daily work sites: a gift given to his young friend a few weeks before for her 14th birthday. Inside the globe is a light blue Angel figure carved out of crystal, color matched to what he imagined the sky would be like in Archadia. Talia watches in anticipation as Victor winds up a small key on the front of the globe and it starts to play the melody Sonya used to hum around Victor when he was a child. The Angel inside gives a ghostly luminescence that emanates through the clear globe.

As it begins to slowly spin to the gentle melody that plays while crystalline flakes drift around it. Victor places the globe on the small table between their cots and leans over, his lips gently touching her forehead, then says, "Goodnight, Talia."

"Goodnight, Victor." Talia softly replies with a tiring yawn.

"I want you to know that when you're alone, I'll be your shadow." Victor comforts, "If you need to cry, I'll be your shoulder. If you need a hug, I'll be your embrace. If you need to be happy, I'll be your smile, and anytime you need a friend... I'll just be me."

"You know just what to say to take a girl's breath away." Talia utters to his delight, "What more could I ask for in a friend like you?"

Yawning himself, Victor lies back in his cot as Lithia hums along softly with the melody, which brings a smile to his face. Victor and Talia lie peacefully in their beds, looking up through a gap in the roof at the crystalline columns, which span the entire height of the cavern, shining brightly with the energy from the Earth's core like stars in the sky.

"Victor, look!" Talia gasps as she points upward, "They're *all* lit up tonight, just look how they shine! You know what that means, don't you?"

"Guess it's time to make a wish then." Victor chuckles softly. "You go ahead first if you like, and be sure to make it count."

A look of intense concentration covers Talia's face as she squeezes her eyes shut and moves her lips silently with excitement to make a wish. After a brief moment, her eyes open, "Got it!" She exclaims, "Your turn!"

Victor closes his eyes, sighing deeply and makes a wish, unaware of his friend's scrutiny as she smiles with excitement.

"Well," he says as he opens his deep blue eyes, "That should do it I think." He then faces her and asks, "What did you wish for?"

"Silly!" She replies with mock indignity. "You know I can't tell you; otherwise it won't come true."

"Guess that would defeat the purpose, wouldn't it?" He dryly retorts. Lithia begins to purr in his sleep as Talia smiles back and looks up, admiring her collection of hand made Angels hanging above her bed from the ceiling.

"Victor, do you believe in Angels?" Talia innocently questions.

"I believe they exist in some form or another, but sometimes they don't have wings and are simply called friends." Victor comforts, bringing a hopeful smile to her face. "Besides, who needs wings to fly anyway?"

"I believe someday we will find what we're looking for, or maybe we won't." Talia hopefully expresses, "Perhaps if we're lucky we will even find something much greater than that."

"One can hope anyway." Victor comments with another yawn.

Amused by the thought of one day meeting an Angel, Talia caresses their ragged wings, causing them to drift in lazy circles above her as Victor falls asleep to the melody playing from the music globe with a smile on his face.

CH: 07
IT'S A SMALL WORLD

The next day, dozens of slaves wake up to the call of the Pretorian Guards at the break of dawn and depart from their rustic homes in preparation for work in the mines. The slaves are lined up, waiting to leave for their first shift as the guards scan each one for roll call. The wake-up call from the guards comes too early for Victor's liking, as he starts to awake from a night of restless sleep. As he prepares for work, he buckles his belt over his tunic, causing his pouch to bounce against his pocket. He reaches into the pocket, pulling out the forgotten blue crystal, tracing the lightning like streaks on its surface once again with his fingers. Victor smiles, watching the gentle pulse of light running along the streaks. After a moment, he drops the shard back into his vest pocket, grabs his gear and opens the front door. Standing at the bottom of the steps are Talia and two other young slaves, both male, bouncing excitedly on the balls of their feet.

"Rise and shine, Victor!" The smaller of the two boys says happily.
Victor blinks rapidly in surprise and humorously inquires, "Tristan? Michael? May I ask what you guys are doing up so early?"

"It's a half day, remember?" Tristan, the smaller of the two replies with amusement apparent in his voice, "We wouldn't miss this for anything."

"We thought you could use a farewell party, so, here we are!" Michael joyously chimes in.
Amused as always by his young friends, Victor chuckles in response.

"You're our hero, Victor!" Talia explains with Lithia perched on her shoulder. "It's your last day in the West Colony, so we wanted to make it special. Soon you'll be allowed to work with the others on the surface."
Victor walks down the stairs and grips the boys' shoulders to thank the kids for their moral support, "Thanks guys, you're the best."

"Guess what you get to do when you get back today?" Michael asks in a singsong tone with a cunning smirk.

"Wait, don't tell me." Victor mutters with a suspicious smile.

"You get to show us your new moves!" Tristan joyfully expresses, "I bet you've learned some new tricks from Kael lately, haven't you?"

"Of course, how could I forget?" Victor responds with a laugh whilst placing his hand over his forehead in a joking manner.

"We want to be just like you when we grow up," Michael comments.

"Don't know why, I'm still learning myself." Victor jokingly retorts.

"Please?" Tristan and Michael both request with earnest faces.

After a moment of contemplation, Victor gives in to his would-be sidekicks and calmly replies; "I guess I could show you a few moves before I head out." Excited, Michael remarks, "He's going to teach us how to kick serious butt!"

Talia begins to laugh as Victor gently holds his arms out before them and warns, "Hold it, calm down, that's just lesson number two." Tristan and Michael straighten up as he explains; "The first and most important lesson is to be gentle, while at the same time being tough inside and out."

"That doesn't make sense. How can you be tough and gentle at the same time?" Tristan questions with a confused look on his face.

"Yeah!" Michael loudly chimes in, "I want to be tough too!"

Victor shares a glance with Talia, both amused by their extreme level of enthusiasm then he states, "I suppose it does sound a little strange at first, but the world is full of opposites, and so are you." Tristan and Michael smile in appreciation as he caringly resumes, "As Kael would say, the secret to getting ahead in life is getting started and to be a good warrior, you must first bring everything at the forefront into balance."

Confused by Victor's meaning, Tristan and Michael glance at each other while squinting their eyes.

"Let's see if this helps any." Victor suggests while motioning his arms as if to tell a story, "Think of it like this; Earth, sky, day, night, warm, cold, slow, fast, sound, silence, dark, and light."

Highly determined, Tristan and Michael nod at one another and both proclaim, "Ok, Victor, we're ready!

Victor chuckles in response to their loyal dedication and jokingly informs, "But you're still out of balance mind you."

"What do you mean?" Tristan questions.

"You're only halfway there." Victor says with a chuckle.

To their surprise, Kael approaches them from a distance as Tristan and Michael happily shout, "Hey look you guys, it's Kael!"

Victor and Talia turn their attention behind them as Kael steps forward and replies, "Why hello little warriors. And how are we doing this morning?"

"Good!" Michael quickly answers.

"Your new uniform suits you, General." Tristan compliments.

Kael observes his new green attire after years of service to the Gods and states, "Oh, the uniform, yes, now I just have to live up to it."

"Of course you will; you're very brave." Michael comments.

"Brave; in most ways, I suppose so." Kael modestly admires, "While I haven't known you guys for very long, I feel that doesn't matter when Victor's around to help look after you."

"On a side note, know that there are many in this world who are naturally born strong, while others like myself have to work hard to become strong." Victor humbly lectures to the young trio.

Kael scoffs in amusement and mutters, "Not as much as you think."

Appreciative of his comment, Victor nods towards Kael then looks upon Tristan and Michael and says, "Alright guys, time to be like an Angel and fly home. I will give you guys another lesson when I get back."

Tristan and Michael nod in response as Victor pulls out one of his tools then hands it over, and says, "Would you guys take care of this for me while I'm gone for the day?" Without hesitation, Michael grabs the tool from Victor's hand and examines it closely with Tristan. "I'll see you guys later." Victor informs, "Be safe, and prepare for a new lesson this afternoon."

"Yes sir, and we will!" Tristan and Michael reply without hesitation.

Their excitement brings a warm smile to Victor's face as they turn to leave.

"See you later, Victor!" Tristan shouts as he turns to take his leave.

"We'll be waiting for you!" Michael adds as he and Tristan take off.

Shaking his head, Kael turns to Victor and says, "You know you're never going to get that back in one piece, right?"

After sharing a chuckle with his lifelong mentor, Victor turns and walks past Kael down the path from the home, ready to join the ranks of slaves convening for their shift. "Victor!" Talia respectfully calls as her hopeful voice stops him in his tracks, "I have a favor to ask before you go."

With his usual smile, Victor turns back to face her directly and heroically retorts, "Anything for you, milady."

The joyful smile that crosses Talia's face causes Victor to chuckle lightly as she gestures towards Lithia who's still perched on her shoulder.

"Can you take Lithia with you for the day?" She asks, hopeful. "I have to work in the East Sector and don't want anything to happen to him. Please, just this once?" She finishes with a pleading tone.

Victor stifles a laugh of approval at Lithia's ruffled appearance.

"Oh, I suppose so," he replies with a long sarcastic tone, "As long as he doesn't cause any unwanted attention." He says on a more serious note.

Lithia croons softly, rubbing his head against Talia's cheek before carefully stepping onto Victor's outstretched arm.

"Thank you so much!" Talia says as Lithia climbs onto Victor's shoulder and begins to sniff his silvery white hair, purring softly in approval with his spinal shards glowing. "See!" She adds with a soft chuckle, "I told you he likes you."

"He better, cause the last thing I need right now is for him to get me into trouble with the guards." Victor jokingly murmurs.

Bidding farewell, Talia hugs Victor tightly, in which he reciprocates. After a warm embrace, Victor turns to walk away as Lithia looks on from his shoulder back at Talia. "Take care of Victor for me!" Talia says jokingly as she points towards him, "And stay out of trouble, you hear?"
Lithia chirps shortly in response as Victor looks upon him and smiles whilst heading towards his work crew to begin his first and only shift for the day.

With the hours counting down, the day passes by faster than usual for Victor, with Lithia providing company and unending amusement for him. Several times when Victor reaches for a tool, Lithia already has it ready in his mouth, playing a quick game of tug-of-war every time. When Victor hums Sonya's tune, Lithia cocks his head to the side, listening closely, then tries to croon along, eliciting a heartfelt chuckle. Before long, Victor realizes his shift is over as the other slaves prepare to head towards their transports accompanied by Pretorian Guards. Victor leaps down once again from his workstation, gathers his tools up and places them into his supply pack. He then coaxes Lithia onto his shoulders, and begins walking home.

Moments later, Victor finds the usual path home and sighs, relieved to have the rest of the day off for once in a long time. Before he can even go fifty yards, a familiar voice rings out, "Well if it isn't our old pal, Victor!"
Victor quickly turns towards the source of the voice, seeing a group of three slaves who look familiar to him. After a moment, he realizes that they are the same ones who attacked him countless times so many years ago, even on the day he lost his mother, and several times afterwards. The leader pounds his fists together, signaling the others to surround Victor, whilst trying to intimidate him as Lithia growls, feeling the need to defend his companion.

"What brings you to our sector, huh?" The leader continues, trying to look intimidating before his peers as Lithia's spinal shards glow defensively.

"Work!" Victor dryly retorts, "What else?"
The leader looks upon Victor, sizing him up and sneers, "It's been a long time since we had our fun with you! Hasn't it guys?" His remark elicits a chuckle from the other two as he motions towards them.

"I would keep to yourselves and mind your own business, if you know what's good for you." Victor sternly warns.

"What's the matter?" The second slave mocks, "Are you scared?"

"Yeah, you wish!" Victor replies, voice dripping with sarcasm.
The third slave finally chimes in, "Looks like your last beating still hasn't sunk in yet, *half-breed*!"
Victor's cheek twitches at the insult, remembering years of ridicule and torment from people just like them. Taking a deep breath, he looks upon them and calmly says, "I warn you, I'm not the same kid you fought before."

"Oh yes, we've heard about your so called 'training' with General Kael for some time now." The first one scorns.

"I bet he's the same as before!" The second one pipes up. "No way he's improved that much since then!"

Becoming more annoyed, Victor drops his bag of gear, staring upon the slaves intensely and says determinately, "Why don't you find out for yourselves then?" His words are punctuated by a deep growl from Lithia.

The leader cracks his knuckles in anticipation, rolls his shoulders, and arrogantly snarls, "Don't mind if we do!"

Victor, still surrounded by the three of them, stands his ground as they attack simultaneously. Lithia leaps into the fray from Victor's shoulder toward the leader, biting his neck and drawing his claws down the man's chest. With a roar, he throws Lithia aside as Victor fends off the other two. Ready to pounce again, the leader picks up a rock and throws it, but Lithia quickly dodges the projectile, then growls, shifting to attack position once again.

"Out of the way you beast!" The leader snarls.

The other two throw punches, which fail to hit their target, as Victor lands several blows on them. They back off slightly, when one of them trips over his supply pack. The two share a look, and one charges as the other grabs a couple of work tools. Victor easily counters the attack, but is caught off-guard when one of the tools flies through the air, hitting him solidly in his backside. He shouts, placing his hand over the already forming bruise, then turns to the man who threw the tool in order to try and block the next projectile. The other slave throws a rock, which hits him directly in the back. Becoming enraged, Victor ignores this feeble attack and focuses on the man with his tools as the other two surround him once more.

"Don't make me call down the thunder!" Victor unknowingly warns.

The slaves look on and chuckle as the leader scowls back and says, "Skies look pretty clear to us, *pal*!"

"Should've packed your bags because we're sending you home early today!" Another slave threatens as they begin to laugh more at his expense.

Sensing a sudden change in energy surrounding them due to Victor's anger, Lithia raises his head and chirps with a concerned tone as he flies behind a crystalline pillar to take cover. Unbeknownst to them is Victor's energy rising as he grips his fists then yells out with a sudden spark that eventually calls down a furious bolt of lightning from above that strikes in-between and separates them. As the slaves crash into the rock structures from the violent power surge, Victor regains his composure and rushes towards the leader, striking him in the ribs before he finally knocks the man to the ground.

Whirling to face the others, Victor takes them down with a swift punch and kick to their jaws. He then turns looking for the leader when he sees him pinned against a rock, trying to ward off the vicious attacks from Lithia whose spinal shards glow brightly in defense mode.

Breathing heavily, Victor stands proudly above the men, trying to overcome his internal rage. "Well guys, had enough yet?" He confidently asks.

"What the hell are you?" The leader angrily exclaims with a grunt.

With a disheartened sigh, Victor holds his hands out before him curiously and mutters, "I wish I knew."

Lithia turns to Victor, chirping as the leader takes the opportunity to shove him aside and jumps to his feet.

"Well whatever you are, we're going to take you down one of these days, just you wait!" He furiously grumbles.

Victor stands with pride as the gang looks upon him in complete shock of his superior yet unknown strength.

"Come on guys, we're done here!" The leader demands.

The gang pulls themselves up carefully and flees as fast as they can. Lithia flies back onto Victor's shoulder, growling at the retreating backs of the slaves. Victor scratches the scaly ridge above Lithia's eyes and murmurs, "Thanks, Lithia. I don't think they'll be coming back anytime soon."

Victor gathers up his fallen tools, noticing a few slaves roaming around in the area and continues venturing home. Eager to get home, he walks quickly along the trail when he sees a crystalline crevasse ahead, slightly off the path. He turns towards it, stepping carefully over the loose rocks, eventually reaching the welcoming shelter of the natural crystalline walls. Looking around to be sure he cannot be seen, Victor presses his shoulder into the wall for support. Doubling over in pain, a harsh groan escapes his throat, causing Lithia to nuzzle his cheek and whine, expressing concern. Victor holds his arms over his torso, trying to overcome the pain inside and out.

"Will this ever end?" Victor whispers mournfully with a cold note of fear trembling in his voice.

Regaining his composure, Victor pushes off the wall with a grunt and grabs his gear, ready to finally head home. Lithia turns his head, sniffing around curiously and chirps, gaining Victor's attention as he looks into the darkness beyond the other side of the crevasse. He hears an eerie and dreadful sound of air flowing viciously, sensing a disturbing yet unknown presence lurking about within the shadows. Lithia growls as Victor shivers, a sudden chill overtaking him, and backs away from the opening.

"Come on, Lithia." Victor persuades as he turns, tugging on the strap of his supply pack, "This place gives me the creeps."

Victor finally heads back home with Lithia who he flies next to him, trying to match his speed. As the darkness settles on the other side of the crevasse, a pair of mysterious red eyes suddenly flashes and disappears into the shadows.

CH: 08
CHILDREN OF THE DAMNED

Shortly after, Victor returns home with Lithia, only to find that Talia and the others aren't there waiting for him as expected. Victor looks around for a moment, calling each of their names, expecting some kind of response.

"That's strange, nobody's home." Victor mutters feeling puzzled.

A sudden cry draws his attention as he turns, looking upon the hill several yards away from the home. The commotion grows louder and Victor, sensing that the kids are in trouble, rushes to their aid as Lithia wraps his tail round his neck to hold on tightly. Upon cresting the hill, Victor sees a small group of Pretorian Guards crowded together nearby. Another cry reaches his sensitive ears, and he realizes the voices belong to Tristan and Michael. Panicked, he charges towards the guards, hoping to settle the matter himself.

"Time to pay the piper, *kids*!" One of the guards shouts angrily.

The guard raises his energy whip to punish the children as they cower in fear, trying to shield their heads with their arms. Talia stands by, feeling helpless, until she sees Victor rushing towards them at full speed.

"Victor!" She calls frantically.

As the guard attempts to strike, Victor thrusts himself in between the kids and the guard, shielding them at the last second from the guard's blows.

"You!" The guard shouts angrily as he points towards Victor.

Upon realizing they haven't been struck, Tristan and Michael peek out from beneath their hands and look on in relief, as Victor stands, determined to protect them like the hero he's always been to them.

"Victor?" Michael shouts, surprised to see him.

Tristan grins broadly, and exclaims with a relieved tone, "It's okay, Michael, we can always count on him!"

"Leave them alone!" Victor shouts as Talia ducks closely behind him, holding on to his leg whilst hiding from the guards' scowls.

A small crowd of children begins to form around them in Victor's defense, intrigued by the altercation.

"You dare to get in our way, *boy*?" One of the guards sneers.
Victor squares his shoulders, drawing up to his full height.

"Your quarrel is with me!" He growls back, "I suggest you leave now and let these children go if you don't want any more trouble!"
The guards surrounding the small group laugh cruelly as Lithia flies onto Talia's shoulder and growls back with his spinal shards glowing.

"Foolish slave!" Another guard spitefully jeers, "Step aside, or there'll be hell to pay!"

"Then I'm leaving with them!" Victor firmly declares, unwilling to cooperate. "Try and stop me if you can."
Talia looks up at Victor as he glances back at her to address the children.

"Come on guys, we're going home!" He sternly informs.
Tristan and Michael nod, knowing better than to disagree with their protector. Talia grips Victor's hand tightly as they all turn to leave.

"How dare you turn your back on us!" One of the guards shouts.
Seeing Victor's slight limp, they prepare to attack, believing him to be weak and defenseless. Victor sees the movement out of the corner of his blue eyes and shoves the kids out of the way, quickly turning to fight back. He counters their blows easily, which causes them to draw their Gauntlets. Victor subdues them, and the children cheer their hero on as Talia stands by with Lithia, concerned for her life long friend.
The skirmish draws the attention to the other guards as the fight escalates, with Victor unable to maintain control for long. One of the guards raises his Gauntlet to fire and Victor grabs his arm in an attempt to redirect the energy blast. The Gauntlet fires allowing Victor to subdue the guard, which severely injures him. Victor turns to continue fighting when he realizes that a child was accidently killed in the struggle. Victor stares at the child's body, completely in shock, as Talia covers her mouth in panic. When more Pretorian Guards arrive at the scene to take Victor down, he quickly turns to address Tristan and Michael once more.

"Get out of here guys, and take Lithia with you!" He orders.

"What about you?" Tristan asks with concern.
The guards power up their Gauntlets in an attempt to engage whilst preparing to take Victor down for good despite the crowd of children surrounding him.

"Don't worry about me!" Victor reassures, "I'll hold them off!"
Michael's jaw tightens, and he replies, "Alright, if you say so."

"We'll be waiting for you," Tristan adds to his comfort.
Tristan and Michael turn and flee, dodging their way through the crowd with Lithia, as Talia darts forward, gripping Victor's arm tightly.

"Come with us before it's too late!" Talia shouts with panic in her voice, trying to pull him along in their direction.

With his acute senses, Victor hears the pounding of boots approaching and turns his head slightly to look at the guards who are arriving; their uniforms are more ornate, with silver designs around the shoulders, which indicates their higher rank. One of the new arrivals looks around at the chaos and approaches the crowd as the injured guard is carried away.

"Who is responsible for this?" He shouts angrily.

The adult slaves who have gathered around selfishly point towards Victor as the fallen child is pulled into the sobbing mother's lap. Moments later, the slave master arrives and approaches Victor, glaring at him furiously.

"What have you done this time?" He asks with an irritated tone.

"I don't know; I was simply defending them and the guards killed one, just like the others." Victor mutters with shame thick in his voice, looking down at his slightly trembling hands.

The slave master steps closer, his face inches away from Victor's looking fierce, "Must have been on account of you no doubt."

"Why do you say that?" Victor frantically snaps.

"As if you didn't already know; you've brought nothing but trouble to this colony, ever since you first arrived!" He furiously scolds, "I would've expected this sort action from a child, but not from you!"

Victor stares back, feeling horrendous about the incident as the other children unknown to him back away in fear next to the guards, thinking he is now a murderer in their eyes. "Why are they moving next to them all of a sudden; do they not fear them anymore?" He naively asks.

The slave master looks upon the frightened children and denotes, "No, but it's apparent they fear something else now, don't they?" Victor struggles to keep his composure, feeling he has failed them indirectly. "I think it's time you left for good!" The slave master finishes with great disdain.

Victor scowls back at the slave master, angered, and then swiftly turns to Talia and says, "Get out of here before they see you too!"

"I'm not leaving you, Victor!" She expresses in panic.

"Don't argue with me!" Victor snaps, "Just go, now!"

Talia turns reluctantly, trying to slip through the crowd of slaves as the guards interrogate those standing around. Before she can get away unnoticed, she accidently runs into a guard, who grabs her arm roughly. When she tries to pull away, he picks her up by the neck and throws her onto the ground beside Victor. Fearful for their lives, Talia looks up at Victor with teary eyes.

"I'm sorry, Victor." She says shamefully, "I failed."

The guards finish questioning the other slaves then approach Victor and Talia. They gather around the pair as one of the higher-ranking guards shove Victor to his knees, ready for punishment, as another pulls Talia up by her hair, forcing her to watch them punish her dear friend. Panicking, she whimpers, as Victor directs his focus strictly towards her.

"Talia, hey!" He says in his most comforting tone, "Look at me."

Talia looks at Victor, trying to keep her expression as composed as possible, though unable to keep her lower lip from trembling.

"Keep your focus on me, nothing else." He calmly assures, "It's going to be alright, I promise."

As Talia looks on fearfully, the guards begin to strike Victor in front of everyone, causing her to gasp. Tears begin to form in her raging eyes, though she refuses to cry. She struggles, replacing her fear and sadness with anger, not wanting to give them the satisfaction of seeing her break. The guards continue to strike Victor one lash at a time with their energy whips, waiting for Talia to give in at any moment.

Victor takes the punishing blows, taking comfort from Talia's presence whilst gazing into her hazel eyes. The entire cavern begins to darken unexpectedly, causing the guards to look around with concern. Talia's pain and fury builds before Victor's eyes as the ground starts to tremor and crack around them, causing distress for the guards as they struggle to hold their ground from the unexpected energy force. After a moment, which seems to catch the guards by complete surprise, Talia gains the upper hand by yelling violently, her voice echoing throughout the entire cavern as the ground shakes even more. Talia attempts to fuel her inner rage until she finally breaks down, and weeps.

"Don't!" She screams loudly, "Stop it!"

As her voice continues to echo throughout the cavern with great ferocity, a sudden burst of powerful yet invisible energy forces most of the guards back onto the ground. Attempting to stop the unexplained disruption, one of the guards grabs Talia once again and viciously strikes her as another places his foot in the center of Victor's back and aggressively shoves him to the ground. Completely shocked by what just transpired before their own eyes, the guards stand back in awe for a moment as they try to assess the cause of the mysterious energy force. Seconds later, the darkness begins to clear, as Talia breaks loose from the guard's grip and moves to help her wounded friend.

"You monsters!" She snarls fiercely at the guards.

"Better take him home and attend to his wounds, *little girl!*" one of them spitefully mocks.

Another guard kicks dirt at them, causing his comrades to laugh at their expense, then they calmly walk away as Talia looks upon them in anger. A wet cough draws Talia's attention back to Victor, and when she sees the flecks of blood for the first time on his lips, she realizes that his wounds are even more severe than expected. Victor coughs up a little blood from the thrashing as she gently places her right hand on his cheek to comfort him, but he pulls it away, holding it tenderly in his left.

"Don't worry, Talia." He says comfortingly, "I'm alright."

"I'm so sorry, Victor." Talia sobs, "I should've just told them it was me to begin with."

Victor looks at his young friend, concerned by her expression and cautiously asks, "What do you mean?"

"It was I who took the food from the camp." Talia regretfully answers as she hangs her head in unbearable shame.

"What?" Victor gasps, disappointment evident in his tone and expression, "Why?"

"We all wanted to surprise you when you got back." Talia explains, "Today was supposed to be special, and I screwed it up!"

Groaning quietly, Victor forces himself off the ground and pulls Talia into a careful hug, hoping to ease her pain.

"Talia, what were you thinking?" He firmly scolds, "You could've gotten yourself and the others killed! You have to be smarter than that!"

"I just wanted to know what it was like being you for once, even if that meant getting into trouble." She attempts to justify.

Sighing impatiently, Victor stresses. "That's why I want you to be better, so that you don't have to suffer such misfortunes as I have."

"I know you do, but I was only trying to help!" Talia mumbles, her tears beginning anew.

Victor looks upon Talia, knowing that he shouldn't be too angry with her, and gently lifts her chin, forcing her to look into his eyes.

"You wouldn't be who you are if you didn't try." He says gently as he carefully wipes away her tears.

Feeling relieved, Talia replies with a wavering smile, grateful for his encouraging attitude. From several feet behind them, the pair hears an angry voice, "This is all your fault!" They turn towards the voice, facing the other slaves with confusion and see the slave master come storming back towards them. "You've always been the cause of all our sorrow in this colony, and this child is dead because of you!" He gestures towards the child's body, still cradled in his mother's arms as she weeps heavily.

Victor looks at the deceased child, and then closes his eyes in guilt at the loss indirectly caused by him.

"Everyone, please, forgive me!" He humbly pleads.

"We're not the ones you should be asking, fool!" The slave master scorns as he points upwards, signifying the Gods.

As Victor stands, he slowly turns to face the crowd that's still gathered, and states, "I know you don't believe me, but I swear it was an accident!" The slaves gathered around look upon Victor with disdain, unwilling to listen to him as he finishes, "I'm sorry, I didn't mean for any of this to happen!"

"You should be sent to the deepest depths of the mines!" The slave master snarls. "You'll be held accountable for your actions here!"

"He's not one of us!" One of the other slaves in the crowd cries out as they point towards Victor with repugnance.

"You don't belong here, and neither does she!" Another slave shouts.

Victor and Talia look at the disgruntled crowd in shock, amazed and deeply hurt by the cruel rejection from their fellow slaves.

"What was the whole point of embarrassing you in front of the entire colony like that?" Talia furiously questions, "I mean, what was that supposed to prove anyway?"

"That I have no real power here." Victor sadly retorts.

"That is so unfair though; you did nothing wrong!" Talia defends. Amused by her naivety, Victor sighs, "Yeah, well if life were to suddenly get fair for either one of us I seriously doubt it would happen in a place like this." The crowd grows silent as Kael approaches Victor to confront the matter, looking disappointed. As Victor and Talia slowly turn, they look up and see him standing behind them with intense poise.

"You just can't stay out of trouble whenever I'm gone, can you?" Kael says, clearly displeased as Victor and Talia sigh shamefully. "Talia, take Victor home now; it appears I have another mess to clean up as usual." Talia tucks herself under Victor's arm, supporting him as they begin to walk. Before they are able to go anywhere, Victor stops in his tracks and says, "I'm sorry, Kael; it's not what you think."

"What I think seems to be irrelevant when it comes to you not knowing your limits with others." Kael severely scolds.

"I know my limits, I may not always pay attention to them, but I know them." Victor sheepishly defends. Kael glances at Victor, still looking disappointed, as he remains silent.

"Don't blame him, it was my fault!" Talia defensively blurts, trying to keep Victor out of trouble in his presence. Deeply annoyed, Kael quickly turns to the pair whose spirits are now completely broken and snaps "There are no such excuses when you are in charge of others my students!" The pair is shocked by his stern and angry attitude towards them as he stresses, "You've done enough already!" Taking a deep breath, Kael eventually regains his calm composure then continues coolly, "Go home now, I'll deal with you two later." More disheartened than ever, Victor and Talia glance at each other before walking away with their shoulders slumped. Kael watches them leave and shakes his head, sighing in disappointment over his protégés' failure to stay out of trouble as expected. Upon closer inspection of the scene, Kael notices all the cracks protruding from the ground with concern as he kneels and rubs his fingers over them. Raising his brow in suspicion, he looks back towards the pair who is now several yards away from him, thinking the energy force behind the cracks to have come from Victor, though unbeknownst to him actually being Talia instead. After careful contemplation, Kael takes his leave towards the guards' camp, hoping to diffuse the situation personally if possible by finding out the truth of what transpired in his absence.

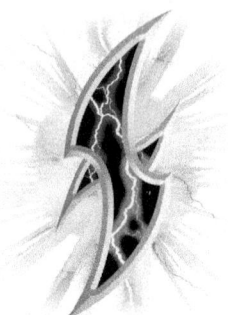

CH: 09
ALL THAT REMAINS

After walking at least mile back along the brightly lit crystalline path, Talia helps Victor into the home and sits him down in the kitchen to clean him up. She carefully helps take off his grey work vest, causing Victor to grunt slightly in pain. As Talia places his gear to the side, she pulls out the crystal shard from his vest pocket and places it in her garb for safekeeping. Victor sits by, feeling more pathetic than usual as Talia attempts to clean his wounds gently, careful not to cause him any more pain than what is apparent.

"You're the adult, and here I am patching you up as always." She displeasing mutters while shaking her head.

With a crooked smile, Victor replies, "And as always, I'm grateful."

The two share a genuine look, Talia trying hard to keep a serious face, but she soon begins to grin. "Well I should hope so." She says with a stifling laugh.

"Well, I took the hit, so I'll take the stitch." Victor shrugs, "It's better to lick your wounds and be battle scarred than to compromise your values."

"True, but you need to learn to quit picking fights with other people, especially ones that don't matter in the long run." Talia caringly scolds.

"Oh, and what makes you say that?" Victor queries.

"Because your deeds make you what you are, not your intentions." Talia expresses, "To me, true bravery is settling differences without a fight and having the wisdom to make that solution possible."

With a slight chuckle, Victor replies, "Sounds like I'm not the only one who spends time studying the ways of the Arch, though if you ever find a solution to that problem I trust you'll let me know." Lithia abruptly flies in through the window, returning home after his escape with Tristan and Michael and chirps as Victor and Talia glance at him for a moment, acknowledging his safe return. "Did you see the way they looked me?" He asks, sounding dejected.

"You mean with disgust?" Talia regretfully answers.

"Yeah, seems we have a natural talent for making enemies, don't we?" Victor jokingly mutters whilst trying to lighten the mood.

Lithia approaches Talia from the window and perches himself near the table.

"Unfortunately." Talia says disappointedly.

"And here I thought only I could draw unwanted attention with that kind of raw efficiency." Victor says sarcastically.

"Not anymore it seems." Talia mutters as she takes a moment to scratch Lithia's head, eliciting a low purr, then states, "No matter how hard we try, we can't always win every battle that comes our way. Some people lose to learn while others lose and learn. Or in other cases, they lose to win."

"Like us, right?" Victor jokes, inciting a smirk from Talia.

"Look on the bright side, things could always be worse." Talia says as she continues to patch Victor up while Lithia sits by, sniffing his dirty vest.

"How do you mean?" Victor asks politely.

"We could be them." She calmly responds, "I suppose that's the problem with having a good heart, you think everyone else has one too."

"That's why I prefer to keep it real, because I'm not afraid to make enemies." He reveals, "The truth is, I don't give anyone a reason to hate me." With a sarcastic scoff, Talia confirms, "That's because they create their own drama out of pure jealousy."

"Apparently." Victor says with a smile, "Do you think I'm ordinary?"

"You couldn't be if you tried." Talia sarcastically assures.

"Good to know, and the same can be said about you." Victor remarks, "In order to be irreplaceable, one must always be different."

"I second that motion." Talia sarcastically adds.

"It's not that I'm uncaring towards others, but they always tend to bury their heads in the dirt." Victor sighs for a moment, feeling disappointed, "I've always wanted more, more than they've wanted anyway. Just wish I had the freedom to live the life I've always imagined."

Sensing his internal struggle, Talia comforts, "People like us are extremely poor but rich by heart, besides, there's nothing wrong with dreaming, Victor."

"I know, Talia, but true artists like ourselves see what others only catch a glimpse of, which is why it's so difficult to dream in this place." He expresses, "You know, I've been thinking."

"Not your strongest suit when you're angry by the way." She teases.

"No, it's not." Victor retorts, "I've been wondering, why must we steal to survive in this place? Why can't we just earn what is rightfully ours?"

"I wish I knew, but it seems that's not the way the world below works." Talia replies, "Not sure about the one above though."

Taking in her comforting presence, Victor glances back respectfully asks, "Where would you be without me?"

"On my own, on the streets I suppose." Talia softly murmurs.

"Exactly." Victor continues, "It's a cold world out there."

"For people like us you mean." Talia cleverly denotes.

Victor nods whilst pondering the thought then curiously asks, "Do you ever feel like you don't belong? As if you're not really wanted, by anyone?"

"You already know the answer to that." Talia replies without hesitation. Victor looks at Talia, surprised by her quick response as she continues, "But unlike you, I try not to think of what I don't have, only what I do. All that truly matters right now is that we still have each other."

"That's something always worth believing in." He remarks, "But no matter what we do, the reality is, we don't belong here, and no one wants us." Slightly annoyed by Victor's discouraging attitude, Talia pauses for a moment and retorts, "You're always so negative all the time, I think that's the one thing you and I will never have in common. It's not good to think that way." Disappointed, Victor sighs and replies, "I know, I try hard not to, but I just can't help it sometimes. I guess that's the price for being me."

"You've always had a negative streak to you, which I've never really fully understood." Talia professes.

"I may not be the most optimistic person, and sometimes come off in a negative way towards others, but in actuality, I'm just realistic about everything." He clarifies.

Talia gently places her hand on Victor's shoulder and smiles as she attempts to make him see her point of view. "I hate to bring it outta ya, but you're kind of a negative person, a little grumpy, and yes you are a realistic person, but only to a degree." She informs, "You don't see any good in the world because it's not the way you want it to be."

"I suppose you're right for the most part; I'm sorry." He says dryly.

"It's alright." She comfortingly assures, "I know you mean well, so I'm not complaining."

"I hope not!" Victor laughs, causing Talia to smile. "I myself am strange and unusual to others, but I don't pretend to be something I'm not, except normal, I've pretended to be normal a few times. And I know I'm just a nobody, unimportant to the rest of the world, but at least I'm nobody who tries, whether I fail or not." He humbly declares.

"You're important to me," Talia proudly asserts, "You are who you are, and I adore you for that. But you have to admit, life would be pretty boring without me."

With a soft grin, Victor replies, "Yes, but there's only one of me and one of you, always remember that."

"Good thing too, because I think the world has a hard enough time handling the two of us as it is." Talia jokingly remarks as Victor smiles, feeling reassured by her warm affection towards him.

"Kael once told me that he believes our problem to be what is called, passive resistance." Victor explains, "In other words, we don't always do what they want us to do, hoping they won't want us around anymore."

Confused, Talia looks upon him as Lithia tilts his head in the same manner.

Feeling somewhat discouraged, Talia nods in agreement as Victor continues, "We seem to have no place in this world or the one beyond it."

"Well, it's not like we ever had a place in the world." Talia dispiritedly remarks, "At least not one we liked anyway."

"And like the world, we too must adjust, evolve to live with the drastic changes that come our way." He adds before pausing slightly in disappointment, "We alarm them for some reason, always have."

"I feel horrible for never asking you this before, but I'm curious." Talia carefully mentions, "What's it like, I mean to be surrounded by those who hate you so much on a daily basis?"

"In a way, it's like drowning, except you can see everyone around you breathing just fine. As a result, I find it hard to breathe because I'm always drowning in sorrow." Victor answers, "Some people can hate you for no reason at all, simply because your confidence and determination reminds them of their own insecurities. Over the years I've learned that growth and change are painful, but nothing is as painful as staying stuck where you don't belong." He then tilts his head back, looking upwards and grumbles, "I wonder if we'll ever be rid of this horrendous place."

"Ye have little faith." Talia says softly with a grin, "Just remember the people that are there for you on your darkest nights are the ones worth spending your brightest days with." As she finishes bandaging his wounds, Lithia brushes his head against his arm as Victor grips it tightly and looks away. Sensing his internal struggle, Talia's expression saddens as he steps away from the table to wear off the overall soreness of his battered body.

A few miles away, within the Pretorian guards' camp, Kael meets with several of the high-ranking officers regarding the previous incident, ready to defuse the situation with a firm grip if necessary.

"These slaves need to learn their place!" One of the officers shouts, "There will be unrest in the entire colony if we continue to let him live."

"There's no telling what else he'll do if he were to convince the others to revolt," another guard chimes in as Kael listens closely.

"You're absolutely right." The first guard adds, "We cannot tolerate any form of insurrection at this point in time while keep watch."

"Insurrection at this point is a relative term," Kael interrupts. "Knowing full well how your men have treated these people over the years, it makes me question just what went on exactly during my brief absence."

"We saw what Victor did!" Another guard angrily chimes in as Kael stares back, annoyed by his interjection, "He killed two people, one our own, and child slave in the process!" The guard furiously declares.

The first guard turns towards Kael to address him directly and respectfully rationalizes, "General Kael, we understand your attachment to him, but you should probably reconsider your position down here, as well as his."

Annoyed by their stance on the matter, Kael sighs, knowing there's no way to defend his young protégé to them without inciting an unnecessary argument.

"You must take action, and soon." The guard crossly finishes.

Concerned by the possible outcome, Kael crosses his left arm across his chest, resting his right elbow in his hand, and supporting his chin with his right hand. He then assures, "Understood. I'll deal with him myself if you don't mind." The officers present nod their heads in respect, as Kael finishes, "I can't have him getting into more trouble, even for my own sake. Just leave him to me, and I'll see to it personally."

The first guard gestures towards the others to signify the gravity of the situation, saying, "If we can't keep slaves like him from acting out in front of the others, then we'll have to answer to General Patrayous or even worse, Emperor Marquis himself." The guards glance at each other, concerned by the possible consequences. "You all know what has to be done, as well as I." Kael nods, knowing what he must do then walks towards the door to leave.

"Don't worry, gentlemen." He declares, "I'll take care of it."

"See that you do, General." The officer replies respectfully.

As Kael leaves to exit the camp, he sees the injured guard that Victor subdued earlier being brought to the entrance by two other guards on a stretcher.

"So, what happened to him?" He inquires.

As the guard looks up at Kael, the other two stand by to answer for him. "Damn fool, he was attacked by a slave earlier today." One of them replies.

"So, no one was actually killed as I've been told?" Kael questions.

The guards shake their heads, confused by his inquiry, "Not that we know of." The guard replies, "Just a few injuries to the one attacked by the slave."

"What really happened out there?" Kael asks with a concerned tone.

The injured guard looks at Kael once again and trembles, too cowardly to admit the truth. "I don't know!" He exclaims, "The slave just viciously attacked for no reason at all! Just to protect some stupid kids."

"Really, is that so?" Kael replies, knowing full well that he's lying. As he approaches the guard lying on the stretcher, he places his hand on the leg wound, "Tell me…" he firmly demands as he grips it tightly, causing him to yell in pain. "Does it hurt?" The guard cries out as he squeezes even tighter.

"General!" The other guard yells to stop him.

Angered by their apparent deceit, Kael turns towards the other two guards and finally loosens his grip, causing the injured guard to grunt in pain.

"If I were you, I'd be more careful about the way you treat others around here." Kael sternly warns, as the other guards look at him, confused by his sudden act of aggression. "You might not be so lucky next time." He finishes as he walks away. The two guards tend to their fallen comrade as Kael gazes upon his bioluminescent surroundings within the large cavern, knowing that the time has finally come to fulfill his promise to Victoria. Now on a mission, he heads down the crystalline path towards Victor's home.

CH: 10
A LIFE SO CHANGED

Within their small rustic home, Talia attempts to patch up Victor's wounds as Lithia keeps them company, humming Sonya's melody, which puts their minds at ease. Outside, Kael approaches the home, placing his hand on a crystalline post and sighs in disappointment. He looks behind him, closing his eyes for a moment as if to pray, then continues upward along the path leading to the front door. As Talia finishes wrapping the final bandage around Victor's chest, Lithia looks back and chirps to get their attention as they both hear the front door slam shut, followed by the thud of heavy steps approaching. "Uh oh." She mutters as she looks back at Victor with worry.

"You don't know how to pick your battles, do you?" Kael scolds as he stands inside the entryway to the kitchen and finds them waiting for him, "I thought I taught you to choose your fights a bit more carefully."

Victor glances at Kael, guilt coloring his cheeks as Talia looks at him, hoping to assuage his current guilt. "I try, Master, but I always seem to screw up regardless of what I do." He sadly expresses, "Somebody's child is dead because of me. Some leader I turned out to be." Talia places her hand on his arm, trying to make him feel better as Victor looks downward in sorrow.

"Victor, you and Talia always bear the world's problems on your shoulders." Kael encouragingly states with a sigh, "It is an admirable quality when you are protecting others no doubt, but you must realize that while at times you may not be the best at everything, it does not mean that you are the least. Mistakes are always forgivable if one has the courage to learn from them." His words bring a smile to Talia's face as Victor looks upon his mentor, his sorrow replaced by a glimmer of hope. Stepping closer, Kael resumes, "You both are strong, passionate, and loyal to a fault. These are the merits of great leaders as well, but only when tempered with compassion and humility. You must be more selective in your battles, because sometimes peace between you and others is better than being right all the time."

Victor nods, feeling reassured by his surprisingly cool attitude as Talia places her hand on his shoulder once more to comfort him.

"Now, I don't care whose fault it was, so don't bother trying to explain the minor details; all I care about and all I need to know right now is…are you two alright?" Kael peacefully soothes.

"We're fine, just a little banged up that's all." Victor replies with a short sigh of relief.

Concerned, Talia looks upon Victor and jokingly states, "I tried to get you to leave, but you wouldn't listen to me."

Amused by her gentle frankness, Victor softly chuckles and says, "Again you were right, Talia; next time wait for me to get home before you take off with the others like that."

"There won't be a next time!" Kael sternly interrupts.

Victor and Talia look back at Kael, confusion painted across their faces.

"What's that supposed to mean?" Victor cautiously asks.

"There is much to discuss," Kael states somberly, "Follow me; I have something very important to show you." Kael extends his arm to lead Victor through the living room then turns to get Talia's attention as well, adding, "You should come along too, Natalia."

Talia looks over at her Seraph companion, shrugging her shoulders then stands to walk through the living room with Lithia close behind. Victor and Talia follow Kael to their sleeping quarters where he moves a rug off of the floorboards beneath Victor's cot, revealing a trapdoor. Kael hums a musical notation, causing it to open as it reveals something wrapped in Angelic cloth. He grabs the object lying safely beneath the floor and carefully unwraps the cloth to reveal the Gauntlet that was given to him by Victoria many years ago.

"I've kept this safe for a long time." Kael explains while holding out the Gauntlet before them, "I knew when the time was right, it would be handed down to the one who could bear its true power."

Victor and Talia examine the Gauntlet with wondrous eyes as Lithia steps forward and sniffs it, which causes his spinal shards to glow and retract.

"Where did you get this?" Victor warily inquires, "It's different from yours and the others." He denotes. Kael hands the Gauntlet over to Victor, who takes it reverently. Talia caresses it with her fingers, in awe of being close to one for the first time. "It was your mother's." Kael finally reveals.

Feeling hesitant and confused, Victor calmly asks, "My mother's?"

"Yes, it was given to me personally before she was killed." Kael explains, "With her, there was always a reason behind the things she did. You see, she left it behind on purpose."

"For me?" Victor asks, touching his chest as Kael nods in response.

Fascinated, Talia points at the Gods' symbol engraved above the palm.

"Victor look!" She curiously expresses as he holds the Gauntlet upright, "There's a symbol engraved on it."

Victor inspects the Angelic design and says, "Wait a minute, I've seen this symbol before as a child. And just the other day I saw it on an old statue."

"You've seen it more times than you fail to realize." Kael points out.

"What do you mean?" Victor carefully inquires.

"It is the symbol of the Gods." Kael replies.

"The Gods, huh?" Victor says sarcastically, "I should've known."

Kael raises his arm, pointing to his Gauntlet, which bears the same symbol in green and states, "It signifies their supreme power, and ethereal realm."

Surprised by this information, Victor looks towards Talia, realizing what he means and intensely murmurs, "The Edge Of Beyond."

Kael nods as Talia takes a closer look, fascinated by this new information.

"Mother never told me about this." Victor says with concern.

"Let's just say that she couldn't." Kael woefully implies.

As Victor continues examining the Gauntlet closely before him, he inquisitively asks, "Why didn't she ever use it herself then?"

"A Gauntlet of this caliber only activates in direct correlation with the right bearer." Kael reveals.

"Other than those in high ranking positions like yourself, who would wield such a thing?" Victor anxiously probes.

"Only the fiercest among us who are willing even can." Kael informs as he hands the Gauntlet over to him. "Here, put it on."

Victor looks at Kael for a moment in hesitation and carefully reaches his right hand inside, the Gauntlet fitting snugly up to his elbow. It unexpectedly activates, taking Victor and Talia aback for a moment in wonder as the symbol above the palm begins to glow in a bright electric blue.

"Wow!" Talia whispers with excitement, "Amazing, isn't it?"

"You can say that again!" Victor comments, "I've never seen such a wondrous thing in my entire life."

"Nor would you; weapons such as these are a technical marvel yet extremely dangerous, and much more so without them in a world like this." Kael states as he smiles wanly, "Consider it a gift from the Angels above."

Victor's brow furrows with a curious expression crossing his features as he denotes, "I thought they only cared about people on the surface." He says distrustfully, "Why would they ever want me to have such a gift?"

"It was the dying wish of your mother, your *real* mother." Kael says.

"Are you telling me that my real mother, was an Angel?" Victor asks with a heavy breath as Talia looks upon him, concerned for her dear friend.

Kael nods in response, causing Victor to sit back on Talia's cot in total shock of this amazing revelation. Talia looks past Kael directly at Victor and carefully probes, "Then I guess that makes you an Angel too, right?"

"Yes, Talia." Kael answers with a soft grin, "You see, you are a warrior born, but it's up to you and you alone to live up to such a status."

Victor feels a sudden overwhelming weight on his shoulders and sighs.

"Perhaps I should've told you long ago, but your path was already chosen." Kael resumes, "The time has finally come for you to confront it."

Victor watches with a solemn glare as Talia walks out into the hallway of the home, trying to process everything that has happened, feeling ambivalent over this unexpected revelation. Victor stands up; feeling confused and hurt as a distant rumble of thunder draws his attention outside the small window in the room. Kael turns as well with a grin across his face, knowing what it is then comments, "Sounds like a storm on the horizon, much like the one that brought you here all those years ago."

After gathering her thoughts, Talia re-enters the room and walks back over to the cot next to Victor. He glances over at her for a moment then looks away while standing and sadly mutters, "All my life I thought there was something wrong with me. I've been lost for so long, I'm not quite sure how to find myself. I need some air, I need to be alone."

Deeply concerned, Talia grabs Victor's free hand, but Kael places a hand on her left shoulder, and says, "Talia, let him be." Talia loosens her grip on Victor's arm, and he slowly steps away as Kael adds, "He needs some time to think, as do we. Though in a way, the solitude he seeks can be quite dangerous." Talia listens closely as he explains, "It's truly addictive for once you see how peaceful it is sometimes you don't want to deal with people."

Realizing Kael's words to be somewhat harsh, Victor slowly turns as he reaches the doorway of the room, looks back at Talia for a moment, and says gently, "It's alright, Talia. I won't be gone long."

Talia smiles slightly, watching him walk into the hall. As she hears the front door open and close, she whispers, "You don't have to be alone, Victor." She then turns to Kael and says more clearly, "Where's he going?"

"To find his strength; sometimes being in nature allows him to be soothed and healed, and to have his senses out in order." Kael informs. Talia tears up slightly, worried about their future together as Kael says comfortingly, "Don't worry yourself, Talia. He'll be back before you know it." Now distressed, Talia mutters, "I think our lives have just become much more complicated." As Lithia climbs onto her shoulder, she wipes away her tears, "Things will never be the same will they, Master Kael?" She asks cautiously, "For him I mean?"

Surprised as always by her compassionate and intuitive nature, Kael looks at Talia with a warm expression and says encouragingly, "Nothing will ever be the same for any of us here on out, including you." Talia approaches the window with Lithia, trying to hide her tears as he caringly adds, "Your time will come soon enough; when you're ready that is. But you can't always depend on each other for your own happiness, no matter what's at stake."

"What do you mean?" Talia asks out of misperception.

"What I mean is, you've got to get out there and find out what it is you really want to do in life and then go for it." Kael patiently answers.

With a sorrowful gaze, Talia looks out the window into the stormy night with Lithia perched on her shoulder, hoping that Victor can eventually come to terms with his dark and mysterious past.

"I wish I could understand all of this, but I feel so out of place with everything, as does he." She murmurs before turning away from the darkness seen through the window then faces Kael as tears roll down her cheeks.

"That's completely understandable," Kael attempts to comfort, "But you must also have faith."

"I guess I just don't see the need to be alone all the time, to distance myself from those who truly care for me." She expresses.

"And I hope you never do," Kael remarks with a comforting tone, "For life isn't about waiting for the storm to pass, instead, it's about learning how to dance in the rain." Talia looks away towards the front door once again with an extremely saddened expression, already missing Victor's presence. "It must be both a blessing and a curse to feel everything so deeply the way you two do." Kael respectfully denotes.

"If only you knew." Talia sadly mutters.

"You and Victor are in for some hard times, so go ahead and cry if you must." Kael supports, "There's no shame in it when there's good reason. But in spite of what you're feeling inside, know that Victor needs confidence, hope, and encouragement." He states as Talia looks back at him, feeling somewhat encouraged. "What he needs now is your smile, not your tears." He then finishes, "Understand?" Kael pauses and places his hand on her shoulder, looking into her eyes as she nods, taking his advice by wiping away her tears. "Good, that's part of what growing up is all about." He praises.
Talia looks on with determination as Lithia rubs his head against her neck to comfort her. Feeling the warmth of her Seraphine companion, Talia gracefully runs her hand back and forth through his blue and purple covered fur.

"When we first took you in, I thought you might be a heavy burden." Kael professes, "After years of battle, I didn't want to see anyone else ruined by this cruel world. In many ways, darkness surrounded your birth, which is why I feared for you so. But I was wrong, so very wrong."

"About what?" Talia asks, her voice slightly rough from her tears.

"You aren't a burden at all." Kael proudly acknowledges, "In fact, you're a gift, a miraculous legacy, and a most precious one at that." Feeling better about herself, she smiles as Lithia purrs from her gentle touch. "But miracles take time to find their true purpose." Kael finishes, "Please don't ever forget how precious a gift you truly are to us, and this world."
Talia embraces Kael whilst tearing up again as she presses her face into his firm chest. Kael places his hand on the back of her head, sighing gently as he looks onward into the stormy night through the window, knowing that she'll someday learn her true place in life just like Victor.

CH: 11
SOUL SEARCHING

Searching for truth and meaning regarding his dark origin from within, Victor goes out for a long walk in the rain, taking in the cool night air whilst enjoying the bioluminescent caverns. While following the path, Victor plays with the ethereal energy fields emanating from the crystalline plant life, which causes various harmonic notes by simply touching them with his fingers. The glowing crystals illuminate the trail as he ventures down an unknown path and stops in front of a large blue crystalline pillar. Victor looks upon the reflection for a moment, wishing he knew more about his lineage and the world he wishes so desperately to be a part of. Realizing enough time has passed, he eventually turns back and reluctantly heads home after the much-needed moment of reflection in the storm.

Back at the home, Talia re-enters their room, picks up the music globe sitting next to her bed and examines it closely as she turns the key. Talia smiles for a moment as the blue Angel figure inside dances to the music that means so much to Victor. After several moments of watching it dance, she turns away from the music globe, tears welling in her eyes, wondering what will become of Victor then pulls out the crystal shard from her garb. Talia pulls a chair from across the room and sits beside her nightstand in front of the window, examining the blue shard as Lithia rubs his head against her hand with a soft pant. Suddenly, she gets an idea and opens the top drawer of the small nightstand, looking for something to write on. She pulls out a piece of parchment and a crystalline pencil then begins writing rapidly. Lithia lies next to her then begins to lick himself calmly, cleaning his colorful fur as Talia keeps an intense focus on her writing.

After wandering for over an hour outside, Victor heads home and is surprised to see Kael sitting in a chair on the porch, waiting for him. "Well, I assume you've figured out what has to be done?" He gently calls out to him.

Victor looks upon the Gauntlet still attached to his arm and nods sadly, stating, "A man should broaden his horizons sometime." He then steps closer in front of him, saying, "Nothing seems to fit, because I don't seem to fit."

"I've seen this hesitation before, but if you don't do this now then you'll never do it." Kael inspires, "Fear is temporary, but regret is forever. You can stay here, and hope for a miracle, or you can get out there and make one of your own." Apprehensive, Victor turns away, looking back along the crystalline path as Kael continues, "I know you have questions son, and someday you'll have all the answers. But first you must see through your doubts, and frustrations. See what no one else sees, what others choose not to out of fear, conformity, hell even laziness. You have the ability to see the whole world anew each day, you always did."

Victor looks out into the night, curious of the realm above whilst feeling the extreme weight of the world on his broad shoulders. "I've always wanted something more in life, something bigger." He proclaims as he turns to face Kael, and finishes, "Know that when I return someday, I'll have everything I need, and then some if I'm fortunate enough."

Standing from the weathered chair, Kael looks at Victor and inspires, "I know you're nervous, you have plenty reason to be, but remember to always look beyond your own pain. In order to take a leap of faith, it is only when we are pushed to the edge, and sometimes beyond that we know who we truly are."

Victor nods, confident for once about himself and declares, "I may not know everything in life, but I know who and what I am now."

Amused by his newfound confidence, Kael softly chuckles as he faces him and explains, "You say that now, but when the time comes, your strength in all forms will be tested, in more ways than one." Victor glances back at Kael who says, "Only then will you truly know, and it will be at that moment when you realize what you were always meant to be, and do. Who you are isn't always what you'll become, never forget that." Kael advises while firmly pointing his finger upwards towards him. Victor nods as Kael hands him a backpack full of supplies that he prepared for him while he was out. Kael wraps the backpack around Victor's arms, remembering what it was like for Sonya to do the same when he was a child.

"Will they accept me?" Victor asks with slight caution in his voice.

"The bad news is you're not going to fit in with hardly anyone, the good news is the great ones never really do." Kael answers bluntly, "In all honesty, they'll reject you, they'll fear you, but most of all, they'll envy you. Thus, it's better to meet life head on, for what makes you different also makes you dangerous. Never surrender your passion, and don't let them decide who you are to become, only you should have that right. Whatever you choose to do, make sure you do it with passion or not at all." As Kael straps the backpack tightly around Victor's shoulders, he adds, "Above all, be persistent, your dreams are worth more than you know."

With a stern gaze, Kael looks upon his protégé and finishes, "The obstacle itself is the right path, and should you be unsuccessful in what it is you set out to do, don't let your failures define you, instead let them teach you."

Victor scoffs in response to Kael's honesty and sarcastically murmurs, "The outside world doesn't sound very promising, does it?"

"Sonya and I never questioned why, but always knew that you were brought here for a reason, and that someday you would be taken far away from this place." Kael discloses, "Hardships that are greatly endured often prepare ordinary people for extraordinary destiny."

"I've never been more ready in my life." Victor jokingly replies.

"Much lies ahead of you, so be mindful of the journey." Kael warns. A dry laugh escapes Victor's throat, and he sarcastically professes, "You know, I used to think you both were just telling me stories all these years to give me guidance, but I'd be lying if I said it was all for nothing."

"The time has come." Kael informs as he places his arm around Victor's shoulders to escort him on his way. Victor looks for the crystal shard Talia gave him earlier, and suddenly realizes that he must break the news to her as he looks back towards the home, concerned for his dearest companion.

"Are you going to say goodbye to them?" Kael questions, "The children I mean?"

Sighing deeply, Victor replies, "I doubt Tristan and Michael would take the news well, so it's probably best that I don't."

"Very well then," Kael says with a respectful nod, "I'll be sure to let them down easy for you." Victor smiles sadly, then walks past his lifelong mentor and enters the home. He looks around for Talia, hoping she takes the news well. As Victor walks through the living room and into the kitchen area, he studies his familiar surroundings one last time whilst gently sliding his hand along the worn rail leading to their room. Attempting to prepare his regretful goodbye, Victor steps into the bedroom and calls out, "Talia!"

Seeing as she's nowhere to be found, he looks around a bit more then turns to leave, but stops when he notices a folded piece of parchment lying on the bed on top of his old weathered pillow. Victor grabs the parchment, and unfolds it, revealing it to be a letter personally written to him. On the front at the very top, he sees a drawing of him with angelic wings next to his name,

VICTOR ZYAS (GUARDIAN ANGEL)

Victor smiles for a moment and begins to read the letter, naturally hearing Talia's soft yet beautiful voice in his head:

> *Thank you for everything, not just for birthday gifts and dinner, all though those things are wonderful, there are more important things I had in mind. You have given me guidance, and assurance that I will succeed in life, and you have sworn me your life, and that you will always protect me, you've done a pretty good job of doing that.*

Tears well up in Victor's eyes as he woefully places his hand over his mouth.

He then takes a deep breath, hesitating to read on and reluctantly continues:

> *You've brought joy and excitement in my life, and I have greatly*
> *appreciated it. Your smile can bring happiness to me, and when*
> *you are down you can count on me to at least make you smile, and*
> *I will try my best to make you laugh, but if I don't, just know I*
> *care about you and that I am grateful for you being in my life.*

Victor notices the bottom right hand corner of the letter and smiles:

> *Love, your Little Angel*
> *-Talia Andreas*

With a saddened smile, he finishes the letter, then sighs, feeling disappointed in his decision to leave as he looks upward for a moment. He folds the letter back just the way it was and carefully places it in his pouch. Moments later, Victor steps outside the home, closing the door gently behind him and sees Kael still standing on the porch with Lithia accompanying him.

"Where's Talia?" He inquires, "I thought she turned in for the night."

"She's up there, praying to the Gods I suppose," Kael replies, gesturing towards the rocky hill in the distance beside the home. Victor looks upon the hill and swallows heavily, knowing Talia isn't going to take the news well. "Good thing too, because you'll need all the luck you can get." He adds.

"I don't need luck, I need a miracle." Victor murmurs.

"Sometimes miracles are right in front of us, even when we choose not to see them." Kael profoundly states.

Victor smiles and retorts, "Thanks for the tip, I'll keep my eyes open."

As Victor turns away, he reaches into his pockets, realizing once again that he's misplaced the crystal shard Talia gave him earlier. "I'll watch out for her while you're gone, you have my word on that." Kael encouragingly assures.

"Thank you, I feel better knowing she'll be taken care of by someone I know and trust." Victor replies, appreciatively, "Keep her safe, and whatever you do, please don't leave her alone for too long."

Knowing he must honor his pupil's final request, Kael nods in respect. Lithia hums, turning Victor's attention outward, hearing Talia's music globe playing in the distance as Kael places a hand on his upper arm.

"Words left unspoken remain a heart broken." He says gently.

"What's that? Sounds like an Angelic Proverb." Victor denotes as he rubs Lithia's belly, which causes him to purr and his spinal shards to glow.

"It is." Kael reveals, "Perhaps it's time to put all this behind you, for now at least. In the end, the whole of life becomes an act of letting go."

"I know you're right," Victor mutters, "It's just that, in letting go what always hurts the most is saying goodbye."

"Don't make promises you can't keep, for it will only lead to suffering for you both." Kael firmly concludes.

Victor nods in response, looking on with determination then takes his leave as Kael looks on whilst petting Lithia who purrs happily.

CH: 12
FOREVER YOURS

The powerful yet gentle notes of Talia's music globe bounce off the crystalline structures of the bioluminescent cavern and drift through the cool wind as Victor walks slowly up the rocky hill to find her. As he reaches the apex, he finds her standing alone on the edge of the crystalline cliff. Talia looks into the distance from afar, sadly clutching the music globe tightly as the Angel figure inside dances to the melody.

"Talia?" Victor says quietly, trying not to startle her.
Talia turns to acknowledge his presence with a half smile then looks down at the Angel figurine still spinning within the crystalline globe.

"When I was little I would look out into the sky, and could swear there were Angels flying about." She professes, "I envied them so much, but no matter what they might have been before, or what might eventually happen to them, I felt they would remain these beautiful creatures that could fly away, completely untouched, and free." Talia pauses for a moment as Victor closes his eyes, attempting to see the dreamlike world momentarily through her innocent eyes. "Do you ever wonder what's out there, beyond the rock and fire?" She continues, "What it must be like, to be an Angel?"
Victor opens his eyes with a grin and softly replies, "Everyday, same as you."

"I've always dreamed of a world beyond this one…" She explains in a hopeful manner, "A place where we can be happy, with no pain, no suffering, just paradise."

"It isn't a dream, Talia." Victor encouragingly assures, "It's real."

"Even now, I pray you're right." She mutters softly. After a moment, Talia turns to face Victor and asks, "Remember when we used to play who's the better Angel? Running around as if we were flying through a beautiful sunset sky, full of hope and wonder?"
Laughing calmly, Victor replies, "Of course. How could I ever forget?"

Talia turns back, facing the empty cavern, and continues, "I dream of that almost every night, hoping that one day we can be free, just like them." She explains, "Flying around our beautiful kingdom, with nothing but our hopes and dreams to guide us. A place where anyone can start over." She then turns to face him once again, which brings a smile to his face as she says, "That is a world I dream of, the way we were always meant to be."

Talia continues gazing upon the Angel figure dancing inside the music globe as it suddenly stops. She notices Victor's silence, waiting for a response, and slowly turns after a long pause as she looks up with a concerned expression.

"Victor?" She whispers, sudden fear overtaking her joyful bliss.

Victor kneels before her sadly, and says gently, "I have to go away."

Talia's eyes widen as she stops, completely frozen in fear whilst trying to process what just passed by her delicate ears. She takes a deep shaky breath and calmly says, "What, you're leaving?"

Feeling horrible for having to break the news to her like this, Victor nods and says quietly, "I have to; sometimes you just need an adventure to cleanse the bitter taste of life from your soul."

Trying desperately to keep her emotions under control, Talia looks away with tears in her eyes and mutters, "To run from the things you care most about is just foolish." She then faces him directly and says with a broken voice, "We're supposed to be together forever, remember?"

"I haven't forgotten that." Victor tries to diffuse, "And I know it seems foolish, but…"

"Does it really have to be this way?" Talia interrupts.

"I know this is hard, it's hard for me too, but it's the right thing to do." Victor patiently explains with tears in his eyes, becoming emotional.

"It's not fair!" Talia cries with a raised voice.

"I'm sorry," he says sadly, "But you and I both know that life isn't always fair. When you start seeing your own worth, you'll find it much harder to stay around those who don't." He encouragingly adds."

"Must it be?" She whispers, afraid she already knows the answer.

"Sadly yes, it must be." He gently replies.

Taking another deep breath, Talia says in a rush, "I know we don't belong here, but if we just stick together things will get better eventually. We just have to keep our heads up, and hope for the best."

"This is the best for us, Talia." Victor soothes, hoping to calm her emotions, "I must find my true purpose in life, as will you someday. I have to believe in a world outside of this one. I have to believe that my actions, good or bad still have meaning, even if no one remembers them."

"I'll never forget what you've done, even for me." Talia comforts.

"Please don't." Victor softly replies as he looks upward, "Someone's looking out for us from above, I'm sure of it."

"You mean the Gods?" Talia softly inquires.

"Assuming they exist, we mustn't completely trust in their plan." Victor says with a nod as he shifts his immediate focus back to her, "But, if we trust in ours, somehow we might find out who we truly are."

"Then take me with you." Talia insists with a hopeful expression. Victor sighs sadly, knowing there's no other way to handle her pain easily.

"The only way to expand our world is to go somewhere new, but I'm afraid I can't take you with me this time; where I'm going is too dangerous, maybe even for me." He explains, "I have to do this alone, so you'll have to be with me in spirit for now." Trying not to cry, Talia retains her strong composure by giving him a look of pure despair, prompting him to continue as Victor's eyes tear up as well, "Look, I know it's hard, this is difficult for me as well, but it's just too dangerous for one as young and fragile as you." He tries explaining with a broken voice. Talia looks upon him in despair, hoping to change his mind. "I may be young, but I'm not too fragile." She firmly states, "You don't want me to go cause I'm a girl, isn't it?"

"That's not it at all, Talia." Victor calmly reassures. Unwilling to let him go, Talia places her hands on his shoulder and sobs, "Don't leave me, Victor, please?" She weepily pleads, "I'll die without you here to protect me."

"You'll be fine, Talia, trust me on this." He surely encourages, "Be brave even when you are not, pretend to be if you must, for no one can truly tell the difference here. Besides, Kael will be here to look after you as always." Talia swallows roughly and weeps, "But what if you don't come back?"

"I swear to the Gods, I'll come back for you." Victor firmly declares, "We're friends and we'll always come back to each other, no matter what." Talia closes the short distance between them, wrapping her arms around him tightly, her tears dampening his grey tunic as she weeps once more in despair.

"I love you, Talia." Victor says quietly into her beautiful long blonde hair as he hugs her back, "No matter how great the distance between us, you will always be on my mind, and in my heart. A friendship like ours is worth all the crystals in the world and then some."

"I'll miss you so much." She gasps painfully into his firm chest. Victor rubs his hand delicately through her hair then gently says, "And I'll miss you, milady." Talia smiles back, grateful as always for his affection towards her while he respectfully warns. "Be strong, Talia, always believe in the person you want to become, and make sure the gates to the kingdom remain under lock and key. Life is a wild ride so please, live responsibly." With a sad nod, Talia reaches into her pouch and pulls out a necklace, saying, "I felt that you would be leaving soon, so I made this for you." She places the necklace in his hand with the shard she gave him earlier attached to it, "Now you can always see yourself through my eyes, a little rough around the edges, but clear and pure within." The crystal glows brightly in blue, signifying the harmonic energy of their unbreakable bond. "I prayed to the Gods when I made it." She happily reveals, "It'll bring you good fortune on your journey."

With an optimistic grin, she finishes, "I hope so anyway."

Victor observes the necklace in appreciation for a brief moment and places it around his neck. "I thought I'd lost it." He says in relief. Seeing her gift around his neck brings a joyful yet sad smile to Talia's face. "Thank you, I'll keep it with me always." He says kindly.

Talia holds her hand out as Victor places his against hers for a moment, a sign of true kinship between them. "No matter where you go or what you do, know that you'll always be in my heart." She says compassionately.

With a crooked smile, Victor kisses her hand, assuring, "And you'll always be in mine. You may be the only person left who believes in me, but I suppose that's enough, for it only takes one star to pierce a universe of darkness."

"Promise this isn't goodbye?" She asks, kissing his hand in return.

"I promise." Victor says with confidence, "The sun hasn't set on us yet; storms come and go but they don't last forever, not even darkness lingers eternally." Talia hugs Victor even more tightly one last time; tears streaming constantly down her face. "Always believe in yourself even when no one else does, and if someone tells you that you can't do it, prove them wrong."

Moments later, Kael walks up the rocky hill to send Victor on his way with Lithia perched proudly on his shoulder and says gently, "Victor, it's time."

Victor leans forward and mutters an old parting gesture known only between them. "Forever yours." He whispers.

Talia looks into Victor's eyes with hope, and finishes, "Beyond the dark."

They smile wanly at each other, and Victor releases her as she struggles to let him go. Lithia flies onto Talia's shoulder, rubbing his head against hers as she wraps her arms around him. Smiling, Victor stands straight up then turns to take his leave as Talia reaches out to stop him momentarily.

"Please be careful, or I'll send Lithia after you." She jokingly warns. Punctuating her remark, Lithia raises his head and chirps loudly.

"I will." Victor determinedly states, "Stay out of mischief, and always look after one another."

Victor turns to Kael, who hands him his supplies pack and respectfully guides, "Love the journey, for every destination is but a doorway to another." After sharing a brief handshake to showcase their deep respect for one another, Victor and Kael walk down the crystalline path, heading towards the cavern's exit as Talia climbs up the edge of cliff with Lithia, looking on as they leave. Talia holds her hand out as if to wave just as Victor turns around, looking up to where she stands and waves back in a confident manner. Taken aback by his kind gesture, she stands there, lonely, with tears running down her face as a cool breeze blows through her hair, pulling it around gracefully.

"Goodbye my friend." She whispers sorrowfully.

Lithia raises his head and howls with his spinal shards glowing as Talia looks onto the cavernous horizon with determination from the cliff's edge, feeling that she'll one day see Victor again, but isn't sure exactly when or where.

CH: 13
THE ESCAPE

Making their way along the crystalline path, Victor and Kael approach the East gate of the mines with caution. Kael points ahead of their direction, gesturing towards the Pretorian guards standing watch on post.

"Well I did it, and I believe that's the hardest thing I've ever done in my entire life." Victor reluctantly concedes in regards to parting from Talia.

"Trust me, I know." Kael respectfully acknowledges.

"After all this time, why help me now?" Victor hesitantly questions.

"By your mother's humble request, I knew that I needed to protect you somehow, so I kept you hidden and have waited till the time was right to bring you back to the surface as promised." Kael thoroughly answers.

"Why exactly if you don't mind me asking?" Victor inquires.

"I knew that Victoria's strength would survive with you throughout your life as a miner here." Kael explains, "I thought that if I brought you back too soon, you wouldn't be ready to face the challenges that lie ahead in the outside world. Therefore, I had to be sure. But knowing you your whole life, I now realize that you can find your way without my help, you always could."

"I suppose my life here had to end sometime." Victor sadly mutters.

"Yes, use this chance to start over." Kael encourages, "The person who follows the crowd will usually go no further, but the person who walks alone is likely to find themselves in places no one has ever been before."

"I don't even know where to begin, this is all I've ever known." Victor says to himself then asks, "What about you?"

"I've waited years for this day, and honestly I'm tired of having to watch your back all the time." Kael teases, "The best advice I can give you right now is to stay alive." He then motions his head upwards towards the ceiling of the glowing cavern as they continue walking down the path and proudly states, "Up there, you are needed more than you may ever know."

"I've failed so many times in life, I'm not sure I would ever know if I succeeded." Victor sheepishly remarks.

"Look at it this way, failure is just a key to success and each mistake we encounter teaches us something new." Kael inspires, "Regardless of the outcome, if you don't go after what you want you'll never have it."

Victor carefully ponders the thought as Kael resumes, "Take note, if you aren't willing to risk the unusual then you will have to settle for the ordinary. The right path isn't always the easiest one, but it's definitely the most important, for it's better to walk alone than with a crowd going in the wrong direction. And if for some reason you can't find a way, create one."

"All my life, I've been waiting for an opportunity like this, and here it is finally." Victor says with calm excitement, "I'm far from certain that it's devoid of danger, perhaps I should've prayed to the Gods for luck."

Kael smiles back and says, "Perhaps, but how lucky can one be if they're already dead?" Victor nods his head, pondering the thought in all seriousness as Kael continues, "The Gods are on your side; you've got all the luck you need, and then some. This is your chance to finally prove yourself."

Feeling intimidated by the spiritual path laid before him, Victor stops for a moment, gripping his Gauntlet tightly and mumbles with a concerned tone, "The mines are so vast, I'm not even sure where to arise."

"Some of the best advice you'll ever get will come from your gut instinct." Kael supports as he continues leading the way towards the exit, "Difficult roads often lead to beautiful destinations. You'll find the right path eventually, but in the most unlikely way and place."

"Good thing I've always had a good sense of direction then." Victor jokes, trying to lighten the dreary mood, "I suppose sometimes the smallest step in the right direction ends up being the biggest step of one's life."

"I'd say you're well on your way, for you see something besides the obvious." Kael patiently explains, "But don't focus on the problem at hand, otherwise you won't ever see the solution. Travel the path of integrity without focusing on the past; for there is never a wrong time to do the right thing. Also, don't waste your time looking back, you're not going that way."

"What do you see when you look at me, I mean really?" Victor cautiously inquires.

"Honestly, I see providence." Kael gently replies, "But if you don't continue to question authority, you'll quickly lose your humanity."

Kael walks down the crystalline path as Victor looks on, smiling in appreciation then continues following him. A pair of guards notice Victor walking alongside Kael with his Gauntlet and approaches them in suspicion. Kael glances back at them, strategizing the best way to confront them peacefully. "The night your mother left you in my arms, it was as if a bolt of lightning had struck you." Kael remarks, "But in truth, I think it chose you."

"For what exactly?" Victor carefully asks.

"I suppose in time you'll find out, but always stay on guard." He warns in a soft but firm manner, "What you've experienced is rarely wrong."

Victor looks ahead of them cautiously, concerned about the Pretorian guards quickly approaching them as he attempts to hide his Gauntlet behind him.

"And if it comes to pass?" He asks as Kael firmly extends his arm out before him, causing him to stop.

He turns, giving him a half-smile and replies, "Then you'll be glad that I have trained you for moments like this." Victor acknowledges his words with a nod as Kael adds, "Though be weary of all that surrounds you, for danger lurks around every corner. Everyday we have choice, fight or flight."

"How about both?" Victor sarcastically states.

Kael stands ready as the Pretorian guards approach them, and sternly adds, "Cooperation lasts only as long as the status quo is unchanged."

"Let's make sure the status works in our favor then." Victor mutters.

"Where do you think you're going with this slave, General?" one of the guards asks as they stop in the center of their path.

"Mind your own business, private!" Kael demands. "I'm taking him to the north colony towards Titania."

Victor leans forward and quietly asks, "What are you doing?"

With the turn of his head, Kael quietly replies, "Changing the status quo."

As Kael turns back, the second guard looks upon Victor and sneers openly.

"Might want to rethink that, General!" He sternly warns, "Our orders are to keep him from leaving!" Anticipating a fight, Kael quickly turns to address Victor as the Pretorian guards square their shoulders, and power up their Gauntlets to engage them. "Get out of here, I'll keep them busy!" He warns. Victor looks upon him with surprise as Kael powers up his Gauntlet in return and unexpectedly blasts the two guards back into a rock structure.

"Kael!" Victor panics, "What on Earth are you doing now?"

"Fulfilling my solemn duty to honor the oath I swore to your mother!" Kael quickly retorts, as Victor stands frozen. Two more guards move in as if to advance on the pair, so Kael turns and blasts them back into a rock structure as well and firmly shouts, "There'll be more, now go!"

Victor nods back then quickly runs up the path, attempting to escape. After a minute of running, he glances behind him and sees a couple of Scorpion diggers following close behind with Pretorian guards riding on their backs, quickly gaining ground. Victor stops for a moment then gracefully leaps onto a crystalline pillar, attempting to climb upwards. The Scorpion diggers chase Victor, causing him to grin as he runs and jumps from one crystalline structure to another. "Come and get me!" He boldly shouts from overhead.

One of the structures trembles beneath Victor as he looks down and sees the Scorpions following suit by climbing after him. Amused by their stubborn persistence to catch him, Victor shakes his head. One of them begins firing energy blasts from its tail while the other gets closer to him.

He dodges the blasts while he waits for the other to reach him, and then lunges towards it. Victor tricks one the Scorpion diggers into blasting the other by swiftly dodging in-between them, causing one to destroy the other. An explosion of smoke and debris draws the attention of all the slaves in the colony working below, who, upon realizing that the Scorpions are being neutralized, suddenly strike a nerve as they begin attacking them with their power tools. The slaves approach the one attacking Victor and begin to tear it apart, causing the Pretorian guard to fall off. As the guard looks up, he prepares to engage his Gauntlet defensively. "You all stand back!" He furiously shouts. The slaves yell in response, running towards him and begin attacking the others as well, luckily giving Victor a chance to escape. The mob of slaves looks up, amazed to see Victor holding his own against the Scorpions as the children, including Tristan and Michael look up as well; excited to see their life long hero prevailing in his long awaited escape.

"Look, up there, that's Victor!" Michael says excitedly as he points.

"Yeah, that's our hero!" Tristan proudly exclaims, "Go, Victor!"

Tristan and Michael cheer alongside the other slaves as Victor climbs the tallest crystalline pillar leading the way out. Victor briefly stops then turns and sees everyone cheering him on from below. He heroically waves back for the last time, catching Kael's attention as he looks up with a big smile on his face.

"The Gods have chosen well; may they watch over his dangerous journey." He proudly mutters. He then refocuses his attention and continues fighting the Pretorian guards by hand, blasting them away with his Gauntlet as one of them runs back towards an outpost to call for help. Several guards standing in their watchtower see the guard approaching them with concerned looks on their faces as he attempts to catch his breath. "That's a first!" One of them says, causing the others to chuckle as the arrival tries to catch his breath. "Get command on the line, now!" He shouts with his arms raised.

"What's the problem?" One of the guards questions from above.

"We're under attack and need back up now!" He says in a panic.

One of the guards signals the other who scrambles to set up a transmission through a holographic projection sitting in their watchtower. A Titanian guard suddenly appears through the image with his arms crossed and sternly demands, "What's going on down there?"

"We have a security breach in Sector 12!" The Pretorian guard exclaims in a panic himself.

"How many are there, Captain?" The Titanian guard firmly inquires.

"We're not sure, but we're taking heavy fire and need a containment unit, stat!" The Pretorian guard declares impatiently. There is a short pause as they stand by, waiting anxiously for further instructions on the issue at hand.

"We're presently inbound to your location." The Titanian guard replies, causing them to sigh in relief. "We'll inform General Patrayous that Sector 12 is currently under assault from possible rebel threat."

The Pretorians overhear the Titanian guard referring to the infamous General Patrayous and begin to panic, realizing that he's on his way to settle the matter personally as with all his business regarding the mines for Marquis himself. "In the meantime, do what you can to maintain control until we get there." The Titanian guard strictly adds.

"Copy that!" The Pretorian reluctantly responds with a nod.

The transmission ends as the guards glance at each other, concerned for their own hides. "The Titanian General, down here?" One of the guards says in a worrisome tone. "You better hope it's more than just one slave, Private!" The Captain responds annoyingly, now fearing for his own position.

The guards look out from their watchtower nervously in light of this news and power up their Gauntlets in preparation for another possible attack.

Deep within the outer portion of the crystal mines, Victor makes it through Sector 12 in the clearing and continues forward, desperately looking for a way out. His Gauntlet begins to glow brightly in blue, causing him to stop as he hears a sudden noise from behind. To his surprise, Lithia flies out from behind a crystalline structure and startles him.

"Lithia!" Victor says in utter shock, "What are you doing here?" Lithia licks his face, making him laugh. "Alright, I missed you too buddy!" He says jokingly, "How did you get out this far? You're supposed to be with Talia." A few small rocks come tumbling down, catching his attention behind him as Talia unexpectedly drops from above upside down whilst holding on to her energy whips. Knowing who it is, Victor slowly turns as he looks at her disappointingly and scolds, "And just what are you doing out here, Talia?"

"I was just hanging around." Talia jokingly replies.

"I can see that, but you were supposed to stay behind with the others." Victor rebukes. Talia loosens grip with her energy whips, landing gracefully on the ground as her goggles retract over her forehead. Slightly annoyed by his young friend's persistence, Victor places his hands on his hips and warns, "Following me could get you both killed."

"We couldn't just let you go alone!" She defensively states, "We're in this together or not at all, remember?" Victor crosses his arms in a stern manner as Lithia flies onto Talia's shoulder. "Lithia got scared and followed you here…" She adds as Lithia peeps, "He's somehow able to track you."

Amused by her undying loyalty to him, Victor shakes his head and jokingly mutters, "I'll never be rid of you, will I?"

"Never!" Talia replies with a big smile on her face, "As always, we must take adventures together in order to know where we truly belong."

Trying to figure out what to do with his extra companions, Victor looks away and sighs. Disheartened by his recent departure, Talia tears up slightly and says, "Tristan and Michael looked up to you, as I always have. You were their hero, as well as mine." Feeling that he let them down, Victor turns back to face Talia who fearfully probes, "Victor, why would you leave them behind?"

With a slightly dispirited sigh, Victor looks upon his young female sidekick and reluctantly says, "They were better off staying, for now anyway."
Gesturing upward, he patiently clarifies, "There's a whole new world out there, full of wonder and danger."
Talia suddenly grabs his arm, holding it up to signify his Gauntlet, and points out, "Don't you see? This is it, the answer to all our problems."
Annoyed by the suggestion, Victor quickly pulls his arm back and declares, "Forget it, there's absolutely no way you're coming with me!"
As he steps away, Talia follows closely behind, grabbing his arm again and inquires, "What about all those stories? Surely you remember them!"
Victor stops, trying not to offend her and calmly retorts, "Of course I do, but I'm afraid that's all they'll ever be, just stories, nothing more."
Talia looks up at him, worried about his negative attitude towards her and asks, "Are you saying this because it's true, or because you really don't want me to go with you?" Victor sighs impatiently as he ponders his response for a moment then says encouragingly, "Truth is, I want you to go with me, and I honestly can't say for sure if those stories are true or false."

"Maybe it won't work out, but if it does it will be the best adventure of our lives." Talia comments, "Don't you want to experience that together?"
Talia sighs, feeling somewhat disappointed as Victor places his hand on her shoulder and claims, "Well, we're too far to turn back now, so I guess I'm stuck with you all the way." Talia's eyes widen with excitement as Lithia raises his head and chirps back. "Really, you don't mind?" She asks politely, trying to hold back her excitement. Victor nods, causing her to smile gleefully as Lithia flies onto his shoulder once again, rubbing his head against his cheek in appreciation. "Well, come on then!" Victor says as he waves them forward.
The three continue down the crystalline path of the bioluminescent cavern as a shadowy figure with glowing red eyes observes them from a distance above. The mysterious entity's eyes flash then swiftly disappears into the darkness.

Back in Sector 12, Kael keeps up his strong defense but is eventually outnumbered by a dozen Pretorian guards riding upon their Scorpion diggers. Kael stands ready, realizing he's surrounded and finally gives up the fight, hoping he gave Victor enough time to escape. "Cease your attack, General, or we'll be forced to take you down for good!" One of the guards announces atop a Scorpion. The Scorpions take aim with their spiked tails; ready to fire as Kael chuckles loudly then powers down his Gauntlet and calmly submits, "You win, boys! Better take me in before I change my mind!"
The Pretorian Captain departs from his crystal Scorpion then approaches Kael to confront him face to face and begrudgingly mocks, "You can't reason your way out of this one, General."

"Yeah, we'll see about that." Kael scoffs in response as the Captain signals his men to escort him into custody for interrogation, confiscating his Empyrian Gauntlet in the process as they finally cease control of the incident.

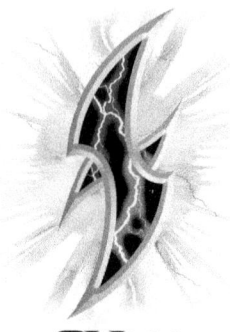

CH: 14
DENIZENS OF THE DEEP

Venturing deeper into the mines together like an adventurous duo, Victor and Talia continue moving upwards, using Lithia as a guide.

"Do you even know where you're going?" Talia inquires curiously.

"Not really, but Lithia seems to know the way." Victor jokingly replies, causing Lithia to turn his head back and chirp. "Is it any wonder that we've lost our sense of direction all of a sudden?"

"Nope!" Talia teasingly retorts.

A few moments later, Lithia stops and begins to growl with his spinal shards glowing. "What's wrong boy, cat got your tongue?" Victor jokes.

Talia sees Victor's Gauntlet begin to glow, causing them both to stop as they look around cautiously. Lithia growls more ferociously as Talia stands back to back with Victor. She presses a button on her primitive arm gauntlet, which causes her goggles to shift over her eyes, ready to use her energy whips at any moment in defense.

"Victor, I'm a little scared." She whispers in slight fear.

"Don't be, it's probably nothing." Victor quietly assures.

"What do you think it is?" Talia softly asks.

"I can't be sure." He replies, focused and alert.

Lithia attempts to fire an energy blast from his throat for the first time, which lights up part of the cavern, revealing a large creature of the unknown.

"Victor, what is that?" Talia panics at the sight.

"I don't know!" Victor unnervingly retorts.

As Lithia growls at the creature, the Gargoyle returns the favor by growling back even more ferociously, the sound echoing throughout the entire cavern.

"Whatever it is, it doesn't seem to like us!" Victor sarcastically states while powering up his Gauntlet.

The denizen Gargoyle suddenly attacks the trio, catching them off guard as Victor extends his arm to shield Talia with his Gauntlet.

"Talia, stay back!" He shouts.

Victor readies his Gauntlet and attempts to battle the creature singlehandedly. The Gargoyle strikes, causing Victor to block then forces him back with its wing. As he looks up, he notices the Gargoyle turning its attention towards Talia and immediately goes after her.

"Talia, run!" Victor yells.

Talia attempts to run away and uses her energy whips to maneuver around the crystalline structures, trying to confuse the creature. Lithia bites the Gargoyle's wing as Talia leaps out from one of the pillars and trips it with her energy whips. Victor takes this brief moment to blast the Gargoyle back into a pile of falling rocks crashing down from above. As the dust finally settles, Victor powers down his Gauntlet and turns towards Talia, sighing in relief as Lithia lands back on her shoulder with a confident chirp.

"Phew!" Victor sighs as he faces her, "You alright?"

"Yeah, more or less." Talia sarcastically replies as her goggles retract from her face back over her head, "You see; you can't leave without me."

"Good to know," Victor acknowledges, "Let's get out of here then."

"Yeah, without anymore surprises if possible." Talia mutters.

The three continue moving upward within the mines, hoping to avoid another confrontation that may harm them along the way.

Outside of the Pretorian mines; a Titanian ship lands before the entrance as several Pretorian guards look on with concern covering their faces. General Patrayous, now with a facial scar covering his left eye with a crystalline pattern departs the ship with his companion Zepherus in tow and heads towards the mining entrance. The Pretorians bow one by one as Patrayous' grey cape flows past them. Patrayous walks by with Zepherus close behind as he growls with his spinal shards glowing. The guards look on, feeling intimidated as Zepherus' razor sharp claws retract with each step while following his master.

Furthering deeper into the unknown, Victor and Talia reach the top of a cliff, only to find that their route has been cut off by heavy debris.

"Damn it, that figures!" Victor says disappointedly. Lithia sniffs around, trying to pick up another scent as Victor turns back to face Talia. "We need to find another way out." He looks upward, realizing that there's only one way out from their current position then says, "Well, I guess if we want to make good time, we better start climbing."

'Sometimes when you hit rock bottom, the only way out is up." Talia confidently states as her goggles shift back over her face. She then uses her energy whips to pull herself onto the next platform with ease.

Victor looks up with surprise as her goggles quickly retract back over her forehead and with an assertive smile, she informs, "This way!"

Amused by her confidence, Victor shakes his head and mutters, "Show off!"

Talia leads the way, using the night vision feature within her goggles as Victor and Lithia follow close behind. The three companions climb up the large rock pile and upon reaching the very top, they take a brief moment to look around and catch their breath.

"That was easier than I thought it would be." Victor says in relief as Lithia growls once again with his spinal shards glowing, causing him to power up his Gauntlet in preparation for the worst, "Oh, great! What now?"

The same Gargoyle from earlier ambushes them once again as Victor attempts to fire upon it with his Gauntlet. Talia tries to maneuver around the creature, but is knocked back into the rocks.

"Talia!" Victor cries out.

Talia hides behind the pile as the creature tries desperately to grab her. Victor aims his Gauntlet and attacks the Gargoyle from behind, trying to divert its attention away from her.

"Come on you ugly beast!" He shouts, "I'm over here!"

The Gargoyle turns, staring back at Victor as Lithia pulls at its tail with his small but sharp teeth. Victor fires once again, trying to bring the creature down for good, using Lithia as a distraction. Talia suddenly jumps out from behind the rock pile and strikes the Gargoyle's face with one of her energy whips, using the other to wrap around its feet and knock it onto its back. She lands gracefully in front of the creature on her hands and knees then stands to brush herself off, as Victor looks on, impressed by her swift agility.

"I have to say, that was a little too close for comfort." Victor warns with a chuckle. Feeling somewhat inferior to what she just did, he compliments, "You did well back there."

"Thanks!" Talia replies with a smile as her goggles retract from her face back over her head once again. She then turns and says, "You know, you're not the only one who's learned a thing or two from Kael over the years." Victor grins in response as she continues, "Looks like I'm winning at my own game of who's the better Angel," she finishes whilst holding out two fingers, "That's twice you owe me now."

"I suppose you're right." Victor jokingly retorts.

"What would you do without me?" Talia asks with a confident smile.

Victor smiles back for a moment then suddenly his expression changes to one of panic as the cliff behind her begins to crumble and cave in.

"Talia, look out!" He frantically shouts.

Talia looks down in shock as the ground beneath her feet starts to crumble. The Gargoyle begins to fall with the edge of the cliff as it quickly reaches for her. Victor attempts to blast the creature away with his Gauntlet, but is suddenly pulled to the edge by it.

He hangs on to the edge of the cliff with both hands, struggling to move as Talia and Lithia attempt to pull him up.

"Get out of here Talia!" Victor shouts to keep them at bay, "There's nothing more you can do!"

"Nonsense! Don't say such things!" Talia caringly disputes, "We're going to get you out of this together!"

With a determined chirp, Lithia flies down to distract the creature so that Talia can pull Victor up. The Gargoyle uses its tail to knock Lithia away and suddenly grabs Talia instead, attempting to pull her off the edge as Victor reaches out with his other hand, grabbing her in midair. Victor is now hanging onto the edge of the cliff with one arm, whilst trying to hold onto Talia with the other, and being weighed down by the Gargoyle itself.

"Don't let go, Talia, I've got you!" He sorely assures her. Talia grunts, using all her strength to hold on for dear life as Victor grunts himself and carefully instructs, "Try to climb up my back if you can!"

Talia grunts once again from the struggle and nods with determination, saying, "I'll try, just don't let go, alright?"

"I swear I won't let go!" Victor replies with a painful expression.

Talia tries to climb up Victor's back whilst holding onto his other hand. The Gargoyle sees Talia climbing upward then detaches itself from Victor's leg, and fully grabs her instead. Struggling to use what strength he has left, Victor is now holding on to Talia with one arm as the Gargoyle holds on to Talia's feet. Lithia latches onto Talia's back, trying to pull her by flying upwards, but to no avail. As Victor watches her dangle above the bottomless well of gloom, he begins to lose grip with his Gauntlet and panics, knowing that there's no possible way for him to save Talia much less himself with the creature still holding on to her.

"Hang on!" He painfully shouts.

"You can't hold us both!" Talia exclaims in a fearful tone.

"I can, and I will!" Victor retorts determinedly.

Talia looks down unto the darkness below in fear and closes her eyes for a moment then looks back up at Victor, realizing there's only one way out of this debacle.

"Don't quit on me, Talia!" Victor says, attempting to put her mind at ease. "We're going to make it through this! Just hold on a little longer!"

With tears running down her cheek, Talia smiles momentarily as Victor looks upon her, terrified, knowing she's up to something. Lithia struggles to pull Talia up as she calmly gestures, "Lithia, take care of Victor for me."

"Don't say that!" Victor agonizingly cries out, his voice breaking, "I'm going to get you out of here!"

Talia gazes into Victor's eyes with a compassionate expression and calmly says, "It's going to be alright, Victor, I believe in you." Victor yells out painfully, doing his best to pull her up as he grips her hand tightly within his. "If you ever find it, I'll be waiting for you in paradise." She calmly adds.

"Talia, don't!" Victor yells, the tragic seconds counting down.

"I wish we had met under better circumstances, but I'm grateful to have known you as well as I have my whole life." She says serenely. Tears roll down Victor's face, doing his best to keep a strong composure as Talia finishes with her last words, "I'm sorry I can't be with you, Victor." She utters peacefully, "Say hello to an Angel for me, will you?"

Almost without warning, she closes her eyes and unexpectedly lets loose as Victor loses grip of her hand. Hanging off the edge of the cliff, he watches Talia being pulled down below by the Gargoyle, feeling absolutely helpless. Lithia stays latched onto Talia's back whilst flapping his wings as they both fall into the darkness of the crystalline cavern below.

"No!" Victor excruciatingly cries out. He pulls himself up just in time before the rest of the cliff begins to crumble down as well and falls to his knees, yelling in agony. "Talia!" He cries out once more. His voice echoes throughout the lonely cavern as he struggles to keep his composure, looking downward in despair with tears welling up in his deep blue eyes.

"If paradise lies beyond this place, I'll find it for you, Talia." He says gently before raising his arm and his voice, "I swear to the Gods I will!"

Victor observes his Gauntlet with determination then closes his teary eyes for a moment in sorrow. Gripping his fists tightly, he finally loses control then falls completely onto the ground and begins to weep into the cavern's emptiness. After a few moments, Victor regains control over his emotions and slowly pulls himself up. He stands there for a moment, shaky, and takes a deep breath, holding his hands out as he grips them intensely once more, then moves on as planned in her honor, attempting to make his way out of the mines for good.

Being escorted to the north gate of the mines by Pretorian guards, Kael is shoved to the ground. Annoyed by their harsh treatment, he grunts then looks up and sees Patrayous standing before him with Zepherus. With his spinal shards glowing, Zepherus growls as Patrayous looks down upon Kael, oddly surprised and annoyed by his presence.

"Alexandre!" He says with slight condescension.

"Kraven!" Kael irritatingly responds.

"Fancy meeting you here like this." Patrayous mocks.

"Likewise." Kael harshly replies.

Patrayous grins then turns to address the Pretorian guards as he points towards Kael, "So, is this the man responsible?" He commandingly inquires.

One of the guards approaches Patrayous and hands over Kael's Gauntlet.

"Yes Sir!" The guard quickly replies, "It appears he was helping the slaves to escape as well."

Annoyed as usual by the Pretorians, Patrayous shakes his head and states, "How many times must I be called down here to restore order, Captain?"

"There was some sort of riot, our defense post was under attack!" The guard answers defensively, triggering Zepherus to growl.

Patrayous glances at Zepherus, silently giving him the signal as he unexpectedly strikes the guard with his long-spiked tail, knocking him back several feet into a wall. Zepherus roars ferociously as Patrayous grabs the other guard by the neck and holds him up forcefully before the others, who stand by fearfully in his presence.

"It's no wonder why you and your men lost control down here!" Patrayous intolerantly snarls, "If I had to guess it's because you Pretorians are further down the evolutionary ladder just above humans."

"It wasn't our fault, Sir!" The guard painfully pleads, "We tried to…"

"You panicked, and your weakness has cost the lives of several others!" Patrayous impatiently interrupts.

"We didn't know the slave was armed!" The guard once again pleads as Patrayous pulls him close.

"No excuses, Captain! I've heard enough of them already!" Out of anger, Patrayous aggressively throws the Captain to the ground then turns his attention back towards Kael, who stands by with is usual calm composure.

"Alright, Alex, start talking!" He strictly demands. "What have you been doing down here?"

"Come on, Kraven!" Kael replies to his old comrade defensively, "Let's not pretend to ignore the real travesty of this place!"

"For someone in my position I am deeply respectful of the laws that have kept our people safe, but when it comes to humans I couldn't care less about them." Patrayous vainly states.

"I thought you were better than that; the man I once knew showed a little more compassion towards others." Kael mutters.

"You say that as if we were still friends." Patrayous responds, apparent condescension in his voice as Kael scowls. "Like me, you've been a fine officer." Patrayous haughtily states, "You have discipline, courage, and ability, but you seem to have a certain weakness for the lower classes, that which I've always found quite disturbing."

"Not as disturbing as your arrogant pride!" Kael angrily retorts.

"You may still be a high-ranking General through human eyes, or perhaps even the Arch, but you're nothing but a nuisance to me!" Patrayous snaps.

"Then you'll release me, if you know what's good for you." Kael warns, still confident of his position under the Gods as an Empyrian General, "Despite our previous falling out, you and I no longer have quarrel, and most importantly we have peace."

"For now." Patrayous scoffs impatiently. He then turns to face his men and with the wave of his hand, he frustratingly orders, "Let him go!"

The Titanian guards glance at each other for a moment then look towards Patrayous, confused by his command. "Sir?" One of them questions.

Holding his arm up in a non-threatening manner, Patrayous calmly replies, "It's all right, Commander; Kael and I go way back." He then turns to face Kael directly and confidently says, "Don't we?" Patrayous suddenly tosses Kael's Gauntlet to him as he glances back in annoyance.

"Unfortunately!" Kael sternly retorts, triggering a devious chuckle out of his old Empyrian comrade, "I decided to put as much effort into contacting you as you have with me over the years."

"That's only part of why we don't consult with each other anymore." Patrayous states with a selfish grin then points his finger towards Kael and firmly warns, "Consider this a favor, old friend. But I better not see you anywhere near the mines again, if you know what's good for you."

Irritated by his former friend, Kael scoffs in response as Zepherus growls. A couple of Titanian guards approach Kael to escort him away.

"Come along, Kael!" One of the guards claims, "No sense in you being down here anymore!"

"That's General Kael to you!" Patrayous warns with a serious glare.

The Titanian guards stop in their tracks as Kael looks upon Patrayous, surprised by the small shred of respect still left in his old partner in crime.

"Like me, he's earned the right to carry the rank, more than you'll ever know." Patrayous informs, "So handle him carefully, and show a little respect while you're at it!"

"Right, as you wish Sir!" The guards awkwardly respond as they turn back towards Kael, cautiously taking their hands off of him and respectfully order, "This way, General."

The Titanian guards walk off with Kael as he looks back at Patrayous, staring off once more. Kael leaves the area with the guards as Patrayous shakes his head and scoffs before turning to address another of his troops.

"How many slaves actually escaped?" He sternly inquires.

"It appears only one made it past the Scorpions, Sir." One of guards states as he steps forward to speak directly.

"Hmm, just one?" Patrayous mutters as he looks away suspiciously.

"With your permission, General, we'd like to begin our search for this slave immediately." The guard requests as Patrayous ponders the thought, he then carefully inquires, "Shall I send a couple of squads to begin searching the East and West sectors?"

"No, that won't be necessary." Patrayous replies as he turns back.
One of the guards places their hand on the side of their helmet over their scouter, and states, "Our scouters have picked up an energy signal East of here, but we're unable to pinpoint the exact source."
Patrayous glances over at Zepherus who growls in anticipation with his spinal shards glowing once again, then curiously replies, "How strong is the signal?"

"It's faint, but it's possible the slave took one of their Gauntlets and accidently fired it up!" The guard replies.
With a slight chuckle, Patrayous announces, "The slave is probably well on their way towards the surface then."

"He'll likely continue in that direction." The guard suggests.
Zepherus looks towards a certain direction, lifting his head up and growls. Trusting his senses more than anyone else's, Patrayous looks up as well; realizing his prey, that being Victor will most likely head north instead in an attempt to escape.

"You won't find him East." Patrayous says with total confidence.
Zepherus growls in a sinister manner as Kael continues following the Titanian guards. As they make their way towards the exit, he looks upward in hopes that Victor is triumphant in his escape.

As a man on a dangerous mission, Victor continues venturing outside of the mines and sees light shining at the end of the crystalline path. He hesitantly follows the path leading out of the mountain and steps out as it suddenly stops raining from the overnight storm. As the sun rises, Victor looks upon the Harvester fields and sees various ships flying in the distance. He closes his eyes for a moment and sighs heavily in relief.

"I made it, finally." He says softly.
He then slowly opens his eyes, amazed at the sight before him as a tear drops down the left side of his weary face.

"May the Gods find me worthy." He whispers.
Victor looks upon the sun filled horizon spreading over the beautiful yet unknown landscape for the first time in his life, curious as to what sort of wonders and dangers lie beyond Earth's surface.

END OF ACT: 01

ACT: 02

CH: 15
VALE OF PLENTY

Through the darkness of the chasm below, Talia lies unconscious from the fall. Lithia climbs onto her back, trying to wake her and she suddenly awakens, breathing heavily as she coughs. Looking upward in despair, she realizes that Victor is gone and has never felt so alone in her life.

"Victor!" She calls out hysterically.

Frightened, Talia hears nothing but her fragile voice echoing throughout the dark cavern then sighs. Lithia climbs onto Talia's lap and licks her face, trying to comfort her. "He's gone." She mutters with disappointment in her voice, "I sure hope he made it out safely."

She looks around and sees the music globe lying on the ground next to her, shattered in pieces. Lithia pushes the globe towards her with his head as she reaches out and grabs the crystalline Angel figure, luckily still intact but cracked slightly all over. Talia looks upon the Angel figure in sorrow, then grips it tightly with determination and says, "I'll never forget you, Victor."

With his spinal shards glowing, Lithia chirps to get Talia's attention as she hears voices in the distance drawing near. A few Pretorian guards commence their search for Victor, causing Talia to panic as she whispers, "Oh no!"

Realizing she's too weak to escape in time, Talia places the Angel figure in her garb then turns to address Lithia and says, "Lithia, find Victor!"

Her words cause Lithia to pant with concern as the Pretorian guards scan the area, coming closer with each step. She tears up for a moment then grabs a rock and throws it towards Lithia to scare him away.

"Get out of here before it's too late!" She cries, voice trembling in despair, "It's for your own good. I don't need you anymore!"

Disappointed by her sudden harsh attitude, Lithia pants sadly in response then flies away. Talia watches her small furry sidekick fly upwards, weeping from the guilt of shunning him away for his own safety.

"I'm so sorry, Lithia." She whispers in despair.

Refocusing her attention elsewhere, Talia pulls her leg loose from beneath the creature, groaning slightly from the pain and sees the Pretorian guards approaching from behind. The guards shine beams of light from their Gauntlets and find her lying restless next to the Gargoyle.

"Captain, we've found something!" The first guard announces.

The Captain turns to face them and eagerly approaches them, "What is it?" He asks, "What have you found?"

"One of the slaves, and it looks as if there was some sort of cave in." The guard replies whilst pointing the light from his Gauntlet towards Talia who looks back with a painful scowl on her face.

"Good! The Captain responds, "Inform General Patrayous of our findings, that should brighten his day." He finishes with a chuckle.

"What of the girl?" one of the guards asks.

The Captain looks upon Talia for a second with a confident grin then orders, "Take her into custody, she'll be interrogated with the others when Lord Tannis arrives."

The other guards look at their superior officer for a moment in apprehension.

"The Emperor, he's coming here?" One of them asks hesitantly.

"Of course he is!" The Captain explains, "You know how the Emperor likes to deal with these matters personally."

The Pretorian guards glance at each other with concern before taking Talia into custody. Attempting to break free with what little strength she has left, Talia shouts, "Let me go!"

The Gargoyle suddenly opens its intense red eyes, breathing heavily as the guards look around with caution.

"What is that?" One of the guards queries.

"Just a breeze!" another guard replies, "Wind of rather chaotic nature flows constantly throughout this sector."

To their surprise, the Gargoyle rises to its feet and roars ferociously, the sound echoing throughout the cavern, which causes the guards to quickly take aim with their Gauntlets in retaliation.

"Look out men!" One of them yells, "Take aim!"

Before getting a shot off, the Gargoyle glances at Talia for a moment with its glowing red eyes as she stares back, alarmed by the creature's mystifying acknowledgment of her.

"Fire at will!" The Captain commands.

The Pretorian guards begin firing upon the creature as it roars once again and swiftly strikes them all back with its wings then takes the opportunity to fly away, heading upwards.

"That could've been worse!" The Captain states as him and the others pull themselves up off the ground. "You men should be more cautious next time you venture this far out." He sternly finishes.

One of the guards still holding onto Talia pulls her aggressively in his direction and says, "Come on, let's go!"

The guards take their leave with Talia in custody as she looks back for a moment, hoping Lithia finds Victor before it's too late.

"Farewell, Victor." She whispers sadly.

Hanging onto a crystalline pillar high above the dark cavern, the Gargoyle watches the search party as they leave with Talia in their grasp then grunts before taking off into the shadows.

Outside the entrance to the Pretorian mines, another Titanian ship arrives as Patrayous and Zepherus stand by. A Titanian guard approaches Patrayous and inquires, "So, is this our urgent errand, Sir?"

"I don't take your meaning, Captain." Patrayous responds.

"Why does a disloyal human from the mines command such careful attention from the Emperor's General? The guard inquires, "So much so that he himself would come to retrieve him personally?"

"Because the Emperor has a special interest in this human, whoever he is." Patrayous answers.

"We know nothing of this interest." The guard points out.

With a devious grin, Patrayous informs, "Neither does he, not yet anyway."

Emperor Marquis, a tall man of slimmer build and short blonde hair wearing decorative iridescent attire departs his ship; surrounded by several elite Titanian guards while tapping his decorated fingers along the landing platform's railing. As Patrayous bows in honor of his mighty superior, Tannis approaches him and Zepherus with a rictus grin on his face.

"Welcome, my Lord." Patrayous greets in a respectful tone.

Holding his right hand upward elegantly, Tannis signals Patrayous to stand up and replies, "At ease, General." Patrayous stands as Tannis looks past him towards the dreary mountainous backdrop, and inquires, "What's the status on this slave who supposedly escaped Sector 12?"

Patrayous turns his attention behind him also, and replies, "He's been difficult to track, but our scouters have picked up an energy signal heading north of here." He then turns back and says, "It won't be long till we find him."

With his arms crossed, Tannis places his left hand over his chin as if to ponder for a moment then inquires, "How did a slave escape such a heavily secured area, and with a Gauntlet in hand?"

"That we aren't sure of yet," Patrayous murmurs, "To my knowledge, humans aren't even able to activate such equipment naturally."

"No, but somehow this one did." Tannis denotes as he looks upon the Pretorian guards standing by the entrance to the mines, "Seems the guards can't keep our pets under control here."

"Apparently not." Patrayous cynically adds.

"Well, if that's the case, then we'll just have to do it for them, won't we?" Tannis insinuates whilst looking upon the mountain before them.

"The mines are vast, and can be extremely difficult to navigate through." Patrayous cautions.

"For someone inferior to you I suppose." Tannis pompously comments, sounding assured.

"Indeed, but Raina and Lucian have dominion over the East and West sectors, so we've begun sweeping the outer rim in the Neutral Zone near the Everwylde." Patrayous clarifies.

"Excellent!" Tannis says as he turns to face his ship, signaling the Titanian guards to stand watch, "I trust you'll do what is necessary when you find him then."

Zepherus growls as Patrayous scratches his head and asks, "What is thy will?" With his back turned, Tannis gazes upon the horizon once more, curious of the human fugitive's whereabouts.

"Continue scouting the outer rim." He calmly orders, "We need the slave to change course, so we can bring him into our custody."

"Won't that be an issue with Raina and Lucian if the slave is captured in one of their territories?" Patrayous asks with a smirk on his face.

"That's not too much for concern if they don't even know about it." Tannis replies with a confident chuckle then faces him and orders, "Force the slave north through the Neutral Zone, and he'll surely be ours for the taking."

"That shouldn't take long with Zepherus by my side." Patrayous declares as Zepherus chirps lowly in appreciation with his spinal shards glowing and retracting. "Being a Seraph, his senses are far more attuned than that of my own."

"I'm sure they are," Tannis mutters as he walks past Patrayous towards the mining entrance then says, "Report back when you have him."

"Will do." Patrayous determinately declares.

"Oh, and one more thing, General." Tannis adds as he turns back to face him directly, "I want that Gauntlet fully intact."

"Of course." Patrayous replies, "And what of the slave?"

"Alive!" Tannis retorts with a condescending laugh, "That is if the Everwylde doesn't kill him first."

"Understood my Lord." Patrayous says while bowing his head in respect for his Emperor.

With a quick turn, Patrayous takes his leave with Zepherus as they board their ship to begin hunting Victor on the surface. Prideful of his mighty General, Tannis looks on and grins as a Titanian guard approaches him from the ship.

"Orders, Sire?" The guard inquires.

Hesitating to answer, Tannis places his decorated hand over his chin once again, pondering his next move as the guard waits patiently for a response.

"Send a squad out to the borderlands, but don't get too close." He cunningly orders, "We can't allow the Eudenians, or Enfurians to get their hands on him first."

"We'll see to it he doesn't get close enough to gain their attention." The guard confidently proclaims.

"Make sure the squad doesn't do anything reckless, or they'll have to answer to me." Tannis firmly warns.

"Understood, Sire!" The guard reverently retorts.

The Titanian guard signals several others to board their ship as a few more approach Tannis, ready for action.

"Where are we headed, Sir?" one of them inquires.

"Into the mines!" Tannis quickly informs. "I have some questions that need answering immediately. And the only way to get them is to go directly to the source."

Followed closely by a several Titanian guards with their Gauntlets at the ready, Tannis approaches the entrance to the mines and wastes no time entering to investigate the urgent matter personally.

CH: 16
A WHOLE NEW WORLD

Venturing through the Harvester fields undetected, Victor gazes upon the beautiful crystalline landscape for the first time with wondrous eyes. He smiles in relief whilst taking in the cool spring breeze and continues moving forward. Flying out of the Pretorian mines, the Gargoyle follows close behind from a distance; paying close attention to Victor's movements then suddenly disappears into the shadows as its red eyes flash mysteriously.

Victor stops by a crystalline waterfall creek near the forests of Eldria to drink some fresh water and drenches himself as he closes his eyes in reprieve. After a moment of relaxation, Victor slowly opens his eyes and sees several exotic horse-like creatures roaming around the creek bed. The creatures communicate to one another through various grunting sounds as Victor sneaks around through the foliage to get a better look. Stepping out carefully, he gets close enough to one and extends his arm out gently. The creature hesitates for a second, sniffing cautiously then rubs its head against him, allowing Victor to pet it. Victor carefully places his hands around the creature's head and chuckles, causing it to calmly snort back in response. The surrounding creatures snort in response then quickly turn their attention behind them as Victor looks on with concern.

"Hey now!" He says with a smirk, "What's the matter?"
A loud screeching hiss abruptly echoes throughout the creek bed, scaring the creatures away as Victor looks around cautiously and powers up his Gauntlet in preparation. A pair of female Darchadians with black trauma lines over their eyes, one with long black hair named Raiven and the other, Celeste with faintly short spiky red hair appear behind Victor, floating above him silently with their Angelic wings fully spread. "Long way from home, aren't we?" Raiven sneers. Sensing their unexpected and unwanted presence, Victor swiftly turns and raises his Gauntlet in defense with a look of annoyance. Raiven smirks and deviously inquires, "What's your destination stranger?"

"No place in particular, I'm just passing through." He firmly replies.

"Don't be shy!" Celeste chuckles in response, "We don't bite, much."
With a curious expression, Victor sternly inquires, "What the hell are you?"
Amused by the inquiry, Celeste shares a devious grin with Raiven and replies, "Let's just say we're made of sugar, spice, and everything not so nice."
Realizing his position to be compromised, Victor looks around cautiously with a sigh, "Damn!" He grumbles, "I'd hoped to put enough distance between me and any pursuers."

"Others pursue, we find." Raiven sarcastically comments.
Trying to size up his female foes floating before him, Victor scowls upon them and asks, "What do you want?"

"Something we don't mind killing for!" Celeste confidently answers.
Victor takes a look at his arm, realizing that they're referring to his Gauntlet then firmly declares, "If you're looking for trouble, then I suggest you look elsewhere, whoever you are!"
The two Darchadians float towards Victor, trying to intimidate him.

"Now, that's no way to treat a lady!" Celeste viciously scorns.
Keeping a calm composure, Victor firmly holds his position, unwilling to budge and warns, "Take a hint, ladies!"

"We don't take hints, we give them!" Raiven viciously mocks.
Raiven and Celeste power up their Gauntlets, ready to fight and hiss whilst trying to trigger a defensive response from him.

"Would you prefer the hard way?" Celeste warns harshly.

"Makes no difference to us if we kill you in the process!" Raiven threatens venomously as she and Celeste laugh at his expense.
Still holding his ground, Victor steps into attack position just as Kael once taught him and announces intensely, "You can try!"

"So be it!" Raiven gladly squelches.
Realizing there's no way to take them head on; Victor quickly takes off and attempts to flee into the Eldrian forest. Raiven and Celeste howl with high-pitched screeches as they begin their furious chase to retrieve his Gauntlet. They fiercely fire energy blasts from their Gauntlets, trying to take him down as he leaps in and out of the trees in defense by firing back with his.

"Come back here you white headed freak!" Celeste angrily shouts.
Victor maneuvers in-between them and fires, catching them off guard as they accidently fly into separate tree branches. After smiling confidently for his ability to hold his own against them, Victor continues fleeing as Raina and Celeste force themselves through the branches in anger, toppling one tree after another as they fire several energy blasts from above. Running for his life, Victor heads towards the edge of a crystalline waterfall cliff and stops.

"Nowhere to go!" Raiven shrieks from a short distance overhead.
Victor turns his head slightly in reaction, sudden death from above then looks around, frantically trying to strategize his next move.

"Wait till we get our hands on you! Celeste yells furiously.

Before Victor can attempt to fire upon them coming towards him, Raiven and Celeste fire a couple of energy blasts simultaneously, which suddenly forces him off the edge, causing him to fall into the river below the crystalline waterfall. Raiven and Celeste land on the edge of the cliff, hissing as they attempt to track Victor through the watery mist surrounding the cascade.

"You can run, but you can't hide!" Celeste screeches wrathfully.

After crashing into the river below, Victor attempts to swim away undetected.

"Well sis, I guess there's no need to report this one, if you know what I mean." Raiven cynically suggests.

"I know exactly what you mean, sis." Celeste retorts with a nod while raising her Gauntlet, and then fires an energy blast towards the water below.

A chaotic ball of untamed energy sits below the cusp of the water, which brings panic to Victor's eyes, widened by the sight as he tries to swim away to safety before it detonates. Celeste holds her hand out and jokes, "How would you like this one cooked sis, medium or well done?"

"Well done thank you!" Raiven cynically replies.

After sharing a cackle with Raiven, Celeste grips her fist tightly, causing the energy ball to suddenly detonate, followed by an explosion, which creates a huge wave that shoots up towards the cliff where the two Darchadians stand. Victor attempts to swim away but if pushed back by the heavy wave and crashes into a large tree branch, breaking it in two with his head as he struggles to keep himself conscious.

"Nice shot, sis." Raiven compliments, "I think you fried that one."

"A little overcooked I suppose." Celeste sarcastically responds.

The pair laugh once again as the water eventually settles below. Shadowy wings spread then disappear like ethereal smoke as a mysterious male Darchadian known as the mighty Traganus suddenly appears behind them overlooking the river from above with the infamous black trauma lines over his eyes like all those who serve him. Darkly intense in presence with long black hair and dark grey Soul Gear with hints of silvery blue, Traganus steps out of the shadows, his face mostly hidden beneath his Archadian like helmet.

"This one is strong." He curiously remarks, "Find him!"

The trouble-making duo quickly turns towards their master to respond.

"In this?" Raiven asks with a confused look.

"He probably won't survive with that kind of current." Celeste states while laughing.

"He'll live." Traganus firmly states, "This one's different."

"What makes you so sure?" Raiven suspiciously queries.

As Traganus steps forward near the edge of the cliff, he looks upon his two female officers and says, "I can tell." He then orders, "Bring him in so we can direct his path towards that of our own choosing."

Raiven and Celeste glance at each other, slightly concerned by the request.

"As you wish." Raiven murmurs.

The deadly pair flies towards the bottom of the river to hunt Victor down, taking different paths to cover more ground as Traganus vanishes back into the shadows. Unbeknownst to them, Lithia witnesses the whole thing whilst sitting on a tree limb several yards away and continues to track Victor's whereabouts as well. With a short howl of relief, Lithia spreads his wings and quickly takes off to find his second companion as requested by Talia.

Battered and bruised, Talia is taken into custody by Pretorian guards back in Sector 12 and lined up with the other slaves, waiting to be interrogated. Moments later, Tannis enters the crystalline cavern whilst being escorted by several Titanian guards and approaches the Pretorian Captain who reverently bows before him.

"Welcome back, Lord Tannis." He greets, "It has been too long."

"Not long enough it seems." Tannis replies with a sigh of annoyance.

"Our apologies for bringing you out here on such short notice." The Captain apologizes. Unmoved by his gesture, Tannis scowls back as he continues, "We've verified the trace, but have most unfortunate news."

"Cut to the chase, Captain!" Tannis impatiently scoffs, "I have not traveled across the vastness of the Everwylde for your meager pleasantries! Time is fleeting, so I ask that you not waste mine!"

"Of course, forgive me." The Captain replies while bowing his head.

"Now, how many actually escaped?" Tannis inquiries.

The Captain gestures towards Talia standing beside the other slaves and explains, "We've captured a child in the East sector of the mines, and it seems one got away."

"Really? Tannis responds with his eyebrows raised, "Only one?"

"Yes Sire!" The Captain carefully replies.

Amused by this revelation, Tannis steps towards the slaves and says, "Let me get this straight. One slave got the best of your men, correct?" The Captain nods his head sheepishly in response as Tannis looks upon the guards and states, "Seems impossible considering the tight security down here."

Leaning her body out of line in curiosity, Talia listens closely to their conversation, hoping to be unnoticed as Tannis approaches the slaves.

"He wasn't alone!" Another guard chimes in to get Tannis' attention then clarifies, "The slave was armed, and somehow attacked our defense posts singlehandedly." Talia sighs, assuming she has been overlooked but is startled when Tannis unexpectedly approaches her with a confident grin.

"Well now, you're just a child." He remarks out of amusement as she looks up at him, too scared to say anything. "How could a child slave make it that far out alone I wonder?" He calmly mutters.

Tannis kneels before Talia to confront her face to face as she slowly backs away in fear. "I assume you were with the one that escaped then?" He probes. Talia scowls towards Tannis in anger, refusing to answer, which causes him to chuckle. "I'm not here to hurt you, but I do need answers." He calmly clarifies, "If you tell me where he is, then I'll have you released immediately." Looking surprised, Talia gives her true feelings away as Tannis grins, knowing she was in fact with Victor. She quickly turns her head back, still refusing to speak as Tannis waves his hand over her and chuckles.

"You have spirit girl, I'll give you that." He comments, "But I can't guarantee the safety of you or your friend if you don't cooperate." Talia turns back curiously, pondering his words as he implies with a confident smile, "As you probably already know, it's a dangerous world out there." After carefully thinking things over, Talia gives in against her better judgment, hoping she can help Victor by cooperating with him.

"Yes, I was with him." She regretfully admits.

"See, that wasn't so difficult, now was it? Tannis replies, amused by her concern, "I assume he helped you to escape then?"

Talia looks away for a moment then turns back, hesitating to answer.

"Actually, I helped him." She calmly answers.

Surprised by her response, Tannis examines her attire, realizing what her slave status is. "I see now. You're a life support slave, aren't you?" He politely asks. She hesitates to speak once again and nods in response. "Impressive to say the least considering your age." Tannis compliments. Attempting to get answers, he leans towards Talia, caressing his hand over her firm shoulder pad then asks, "It's clear that you have a few toys of your own," he gestures while placing her hand in his as she looks into his eyes, "But tell me child, what toys does your friend play with?" Talia stares back, unsure of what to say at this point without giving too much away as Tannis grins deviously.

"There are rumors regarding the incident." One of the Titanian guards chimes in, "The Pretorians claim that the slave used an unfamiliar Gauntlet to make his way through their defense."

Surprised by this bit of information, Tannis turns back to face the guards and says, "Really, is that so?"

"We can't substantiate the claim just yet, for we don't know how or where he got it." The guard informs.

With a grin on his face, Tannis stands up and claims, "I think I have an idea."

"Also, it apparently didn't give off an energy signal like that of our own." The guard finishes concernedly.

Tannis looks upon the guard, surprised by this sudden revelation and quickly deduces, "Interesting, so that's how he escaped."

Another Titanian guard places his hand over his scouter covering his ear and announces, "My Lord, I've been informed that Queen Raina and King Lucian have been asking questions regarding the incident."

Shaking his head in annoyance, Tannis looks away, sighing impatiently then says, "Of course, as if the situation couldn't get any worse than it already is."

"Sire?" The guard carefully asks with a confused look.

Tannis steps away from Talia, looking upwards towards the top of the cavern and states, "If they're already asking questions, then their Champions are likely preparing to hunt as we speak."

"Trag and Braxel you mean?" The guard asks to clarify.

"Yes." Tannis asserts, "It's safe to assume that they've been waiting for an opportunity like this for a long time."

A Pretorian guard steps in to address Tannis directly in defense and claims; "General Patrayous was the closest to our aid when the incident occurred. We've tried our best to keep them out of it."

"No matter," Tannis proclaims, "I've already sent someone else to intercept the slave, and this Gauntlet you spoke of."

Thinking the worst about Tannis having Victor hunted down, Talia tries to intervene by pleading, "Please, whatever you do, don't hurt him!"

Amused by Talia's persistence, Tannis turns back to face her and deceitfully claims, "I'm not going to hurt him, yet." Talia frowns upon him, annoyed by his arrogance as he clarifies, "I need him alive long enough to find out more about this Gauntlet he's supposedly carrying."

Talia sighs, feeling relieved over Victor's safety for the time being as Tannis turns his attention back towards the gathered slaves in curiosity and asks, "Remind me Captain why you've brought these people before me?"

"These are the ones who witnessed the incident." The Pretorian guard replies whilst pointing towards the slaves who look back in distress then finishes with a laugh, "They're a robust stock to say the least."

To her surprise, Talia notices Tristan and Michael amongst the group of gathered slaves and waves to them as they cautiously wave back, hoping for the best possible outcome. She then turns her attention back towards Tannis, fearing the worst for her and her friends.

"Ah yes, a perfect example of excessive individualism; it doesn't seem too long ago when fear allowed them to give up their civil liberties entirely, and like children they need to be reminded of the order of things." Tannis confidently states, "Such people will fight to protect their enslavers to escape any form of responsibility, but if you want to keep their feet on the ground you must put some on their shoulders." Thinking upon the subject, he places his hand over his chin and mutters, "For the most part they indulge me really, though eventually they become real tiresome, for they are a paradoxical people. And in spite of their vitality, they are fundamentally stupid and primitive beings that cannot survive without our divine nobility to rule them."

As he looks upon the fearful slaves lined up for interrogation with selfish delight, he steps onto a crystalline platform surrounded by fire and brimstone to address them directly as Talia listens closely with the others.

"The situation's very simple!" He proudly announces, "You wanted protection, and we've done so, by keeping you safe! But there's always a price for such security! Your food, shelter and supplies; it all adds up eventually!"
The slaves stare back, feeling he is untrustworthy for someone in his position as he continues, "By now, each of you has accumulated a debt worth a fortune! That means until you finish paying off your said debt, I own you!"
Concerned by his cruel statement, the slaves glance at each other as Tannis holds his arms up, trying to ease their harsh view of him and proclaims, "Please understand, for it is not my intention to cause any of you misery!" He eases whilst holding up a crystal shard in his hand, "You see, we're all in this together really, so technically that makes us business partners!" Tannis drops the crystal shard as it lands before the slaves who look at it dreadfully.

"Everyone present knows that the life of an individual doesn't matter in the grand scheme of things on this planet!" He explains harshly, "What matters is the colony you're willing to live, fight, and die for! There's more to be had in the lives you share down here, but be very certain, that if anyone tries to escape, someone dear to you will pay the ultimate price!" Tannis bitterly warns, "So if you get the urge to do something that might threaten our arrangement, and you will likely get that urge, and learn to control it! Or inevitably, someone close to you will be hurt, and may even die as a result!"
The slaves glance at each other once again and tremble, fearful for their lives.

"Your course is reciprocal to our demands!" Tannis further explains, "And since you all seem so fit to take it upon yourselves to infringe onto my domain, I must ask for some sort of payment in return!"
He then raises his Gauntlet and fires upon the crystal shard lying on the ground. The energy blast causes a bright light, shattering it into several pieces as the slaves gasp, feeling powerless before their oppressors.

"Follow the order set before you, and you'll one day be free!" Tannis convincingly declares, "Rebel, and you will all perish at my feet!"
Feeling they have no choice but to continue following orders in their hellish domain, the slaves shake their heads in despair.

"Do yourselves a favor while you're at it; don't evolve, for it only leads to chaos!" Tannis strongly finishes with a confident grin, "The choice my fellow Earthlings, I leave to you!"
The slaves continue looking on in fear and finally head back to their quarters to rest as Tannis steps down from the crystalline platform. "Excellent speech your Majesty!" The Pretorian guard praises.

"I thought so, for he who wishes to be obeyed must first know how to rule." Tannis asserts with a firm grip, "As history dictates, there are two ways to conquer and enslave people; one is by force, and the other by debt." While gazing upon the cavern curiously, he concludes, "My business is done here, Captain. I'm feeling rather generous at the moment, so take the slaves back to their quarters, and put them back to work first thing tomorrow."

"Yes, my Lord!" The guard humbly responds.

Tannis signals the Titanian guards to take the slaves who witnessed the incident away and informs, "I want this place up and running at full capacity as usual!" As he turns back to face the Pretorian guard, he calmly states, "I can't afford any delay whatsoever with tomorrow's shipment if the traffickers are to receive what they've already paid for in advance."

"Understood!" The guard replies then points towards Talia and asks, "What of the girl?"

Tannis looks upon Talia once again and grins, as she looks back, confused by his cheerful yet unnerving mood. "She's coming with me!" He says whilst signaling her to step forward.

"My Lord!" The guard interjects with serious concern, "Shouldn't she be punished and put back to work with the rest of them?"

With a stern glare, Tannis faces the guard and states, "Do not question my authority Captain! My will is the will of the Gods, and it will always be so!"

"Yes sire, as you command." The guard says politely, and bows before taking his leave with the others.

As Talia approaches Tannis, he extends his arm out in an unthreatening manner and claims, "These won't be necessary."

With the flick of his decorated fingers, Tannis breaks the energy shackles from her wrists as she rubs them together in respite then looks up at him and says, "You're freeing me, just like that?

"Just like that." Tannis replies with a soft chuckle.

Confused by his sudden change of heart, she carefully asks, "Even after what I just told you?"

"If you really want to know the truth, you're mine now, and you'll do what I ask." Tannis crudely states. Talia sighs impatiently, hoping to have been officially freed of her slave status, "Or I'll just put your shackles back on, and let the guards have their way with you." He scornfully gestures.

Realizing this to be the best alternative, Talia shakes her head and with a dejected voice, says, "No! I'll do anything, just don't hurt him."

Her touching reaction causes Tannis to chuckle slightly again in response.

"Cooperate, and I'll see about getting your friend back in one piece." He implies, "Assuming the Eudenians or Enfurians don't find him first."

Talia looks away in a fearful manner, curious to Victor's whereabouts.

"Come child," Tannis kindly invites while extending his arm out to escort his young acquaintance outside the mines, "Let us leave this god forsaken place for good."

With Talia at his side, Tannis leaves the mines and heads towards his ship outside, followed closely by several Titanian guards who continue to guard him closely as well as his new guest.

CH: 17
FATEFUL RENDEZVOUS

At the end of the stream, Victor is carried down the river current through Eldria and is seen by Pretorian slave pirates as he passes out completely from the head injury. One of them kneels to check Victor's pulse by placing their fingers beside his neck.

"Well, is he alive?" The leader asks impatiently.

The slave pirate feels Victor's strong pulse pounding and grins as he turns back, saying, "And well it seems."

"Good, bring him aboard!" The leader says whilst signaling two others to carry Victor away, "Our first catch of the day."

Victor is taken aboard their Harvester ship as the leader takes his Gauntlet away and observes it in curiosity before boarding himself.

A few hours later, high above the surface aboard the Harvester ship, several slave pirates observe the mark on Victor's left arm in curiosity as their leader enters the room, causing them to back away reverently. The leader slowly approaches Victor and strikes his face with his bare hand to wake him up. In quick reaction, Victor awakens in energy shackles and painfully grunts.

"Man, talk about a rude awakening." He grumbles. After gathering his full attention, he sees the slave pirates standing before him with his Gauntlet in hand and sternly asks, "Where am I?"

The leader turns to acknowledge his crew as they begin to laugh in response.

"Consider this your lucky day!" The leader says condescendingly.

"Oh yeah, and why is that?" Victor scoffs.

Victor is suddenly cut loose and shoved to the ground before the crew.

"Cause you work for us now!" The leader starkly retorts.

Angered by their harsh treatment, Victor sighs intensely as the leader holds out his Gauntlet to taunt him.

"This will surely fetch a pretty price." The leader remarks while carefully examining the Gauntlet, "What a remarkable piece of equipment." The leader then hands the Gauntlet to one of the elite crewmembers and signals him to lock it away for safekeeping.

"Glad you approve." Victor scoffs with an intense scowl.

"You know for a human, you don't look so normal." The leader cynically teases on Victor's behalf.

Victor stands up to address the leader face-to-face; staring back intensely and says, "Perhaps I should take that as a compliment. What is normal anyway?"

"That wasn't a compliment." The leader ridicules, "You see, normal is what everyone else is, and you are not."

As Victor slowly approaches him in anger, the leader suddenly kicks him in the abdomen and signals two others to grab him. Victor coughs once again from lack of air as the leader turns to take his leave aboard the ship's deck and orders, "See that he doesn't escape!"

"No problem!" The slave pirates respond with great satisfaction.

Unable to break free, Victor is escorted to the lower deck to work as the two pirates shove him onto the floor and laugh. As Victor looks up to catch his breath, he turns and sees an old Angel statue with the name, *KITANA* engraved on it and bows in respect as if to pray.

"Please watch over Talia, and take good care of the others for me." He whispers in a hopeful tone, "Tristan and Michael will need some sort of guidance while I'm gone."

Victor is unexpectedly struck from behind by one of the pirates, as he turns to face them, grunting angrily in pain.

"Get to work, *slave*!" The pirate furiously shouts.

The slave pirates take their leave towards the next deck as Victor looks away for a moment, feeling at this rate that he'll never be rid of his slave status.

Hunting for any remains of Victor through the watery mist as ordered by their master, Raiven and Celeste reach the river's edge in Eldria and shake their heads at one another in annoyance.

"Where do you suppose that human went?" Celeste irately asks.

"I don't know; but his tracks stop just a few feet from the river with these others." Raiven replies while pointing towards the footprints left by Victor and the slave Pirates.

A sudden low-pitched screech catches their attention as they quickly turn and look above them. Overhead, Traganus flies with his red wings fully spread then suddenly stops mid-air while signaling them to move forward.

"Well sis, better do what he says." Raiven advises.

"That stupid human better hope he survives long enough for us to find him." Celeste sneers.

Traganus continues flying overhead as Raiven and Celeste press the symbols on their chest plates to activate their wings and quickly take to the sky as well to resume the hunt for Victor.

Having also lost Victor's trail just outside of Eldria near the desert border of Sahria, Patrayous and his men come to a stopping point at the end of the river shortly after Raiven and Celeste. The Titanian guards scan the area as one of them quickly approaches Patrayous and informs, "The slave's tracks seem to have stopped here, General."

Curious of this new Intel, Patrayous kneels to examine the tracks left by the slave pirates, trying to deduce Victor's exact whereabouts.

"It's highly unlikely that he would venture back through Eldria's forestry area, or the Celestial pass." The guard suggests.

"Perhaps you're right." Patrayous responds, "A Harvester ship must have picked him up."

The Titanian guard nods in agreement as Patrayous looks upon the sky and sees Zepherus approaching from above. The mighty Seraph lands before him, growling with his spinal shards glowing as he gestures upward with his head.

"Good work, Zepherus." Patrayous says whilst scratching Zepherus' head, which causes him to purr in a low tone.

"Orders, Sir?" The Titanian guard inquires.

Knowing Victor has left the surface area, Patrayous turns his attention upwards and announces, "Gentlemen, we're taking to the skies!"

The Titanian guards scramble together as Patrayous and Zepherus board their vessel to hunt down the closest Harvester ship traveling north side.

High above the surface area of Sahria within Pretoria, the slave Pirates decide to change course in hopes of avoiding confrontation along the borderlands. Avoiding the Pirates' attention as much as possible within the Harvester ship, Victor looks around for his Gauntlet and is suddenly struck down from behind by a crewmember's energy whip.

"Slaves like you should learn to mind their own business!" The first Pirate savagely barks.

After pulling himself off the floor, Victor turns to face the three slave Pirates standing before him with scheming grins on their faces.

"Why is that, because you have something to hide like everyone else?" Victor retorts, "Or perhaps you have something that belongs to me!"

"Enough with the attitude!" The second Pirate yells out irritably, "Your senses don't work so well here!"

"Then perhaps we should knock some into you!" The third Pirate arrogantly chimes in.

"That's too bad, cause my senses seem to be working just fine!" Victor claims with a confident smirk as he stands his ground in defense.
The slave Pirates extend their energy whips in an attempt to punish him, then all of a sudden, a loud rumble is heard, causing the entire ship to shake. Victor feels the disturbance and hears the ship's crew panic from above.

"The ship is under attack!" one of the Pirates announces frantically through the ship's intercom, "We're taking heavy fire!"
The three pirates look upon Victor in annoyance then begin to act as ordered, shouting, "All hands on deck! To battle stations people!"
The crewmembers scramble to their defense posts as two of them stay behind to guard Victor, who sighs disappointingly, failing to escape once again.

Rising to the surface outside the Harvester ship, the crew struggles to defend their vessel as a small fleet of Archadians unexpectedly swarms towards them at high speed from above, firing energy blasts all over the deck with their Gauntlets. Several slave Pirates are taken out in the process as the Archadians quickly board the deck to seize control of the ship. A couple of slave Pirates stand together defensively then look up as a large black male Empyrian with a bald scalp named Marcus flies in overhead.

"Look out below!" He shouts humorously as he knocks them down simultaneously upon landing on the deck.
The Empyrian fights, taking out one crewmember at a time, followed by a second Empyrian named Yuri who lands on the ship near the first.

"Anyone care to dance?" He also shouts humorously in response.
Having an oriental ethnicity, this Angelic warrior with short spikey black hair is smaller in size but faster in his movements as he fights against the pirate crew beside his fellow comedic Empyrian comrade, Marcus.

Below the Harvester ship's deck, the crew begins to panic from the commotion above. Chattering amongst themselves, one of them points towards Victor, regarding his presence and infers, "They must be after him!"
The slave pirates quickly turn to face Victor and grin, as he looks back, concerned for his life.

"Give me my Gauntlet!" He forcefully demands as he tries to break his energy shackles, "Let me fight for my life!"
Chuckling in response, the Pirates slowly approach him with their energy whips protracted, as one of them says, "Better rid ourselves of the extra cargo then, huh boys?"

"Yeah, no need for dead weight!" The second one selfishly adds.

Victor braces himself with his feet firmly planted on the floor as the Pirates step forward and attempt to kill him, but are suddenly taken out by an energy blast ripping through the ship's hull. As the dust settles, Victor looks around and jokingly mutters, "Couldn't agree with you more on that one."

After finally breaking free of his energy shackles, Victor attempts to look for his Gauntlet aboard the ship's lower decks to aid in his escape.

Outside, the Arch ship itself fires an energy blast towards the Harvester ship's engine compartment, causing it to lose momentum high in the sky. The attack on deck continues as the two Empyrians fight side by side against the bloodthirsty slave Pirates.

"I'm already three up on you today, Yuri!" Marcus proudly declares, "Looks like you're buying tonight!"

"Don't count on it, Marcus!" Yuri confidently retorts.

Marcus looks on with surprise as Yuri quickly jumps in front of him, taking out three crewmembers simultaneously with his energy sword, then turns back with a grin on his face and sarcastically says, "Who's buying now?"

Yuri's show of force brings a smile to Marcus' face as they continue to fight the persistent group of slave Pirates along with several Archadian comrades.

After a few minutes of searching below deck of the Harvester ship, Victor finally locates his Gauntlet sitting atop a pile of unused crystals.

"There you are!" He murmurs in relief.

Not wasting any time, he quickly grabs the Gauntlet and places it back over his arm. The Gods' symbol lights up brightly in blue once again as he begins to power it up, regaining confidence over the situation. With his Gauntlet in hand, Victor stands ready to take on anything in his path and heads towards the upper deck, hoping to flee the Harvester ship for good.

Attacking specific parts on deck outside, the Archadians eventually neutralize the Harvester ship's floatation device, causing it to finally stop in midair. One of the Archadians with pink and light grey Soul Gear flies in from above and lands gracefully on the ship's deck, ready and alert as her helmet shifts back from her tiara, revealing her face, who turns out to be Princess Elena now older. Beautiful but deadly, the blondish brown-haired Angel looks up with serious intent emanating from her intense blue eyes. With her crystalline staff in hand, she stands ready as several slave Pirates rush towards her and quickly takes them out with deadly grace. Elena draws Marcus' attention, who turns and quickly taps Yuri's shoulder.

"Uh oh!" He says, "Better hold off the bet, Yuri!"

"Come on, Marcus, don't tell me you've lost count already!" Yuri laughs whilst retracting his energy blade back into his Gauntlet.

Marcus fires an energy blast towards one of the slave Pirates without flinching and continues, "Of course not, but I see someone else couldn't wait to get a piece of the action as well!"

Yuri looks over and sees the Elena fighting then turns back towards Marcus and says, "Ten shards say she takes out more then both of us."

"You're on!" Marcus confidently replies as he and Yuri pound their fists together in accord.

Finally making his way to the upper deck of the Harvester ship, Victor is shocked at the sight of Archadians taking on the pirate crew. Without hesitation, he joins the fight; helping to take out the slave Pirates single handedly. Yuri notices Victor fighting alone and gestures towards Marcus as he inquires, "Who's that over there?"

Marcus looks towards Victor with confusion and replies, "Looks like a human to me! But since when do humans carry Gauntlets these days?"

"Beats me!" Yuri responds, shrugging his shoulders, "Guess we'll find out soon enough though."

Marcus and Yuri continue their bout, as does Victor who takes on one slave Pirate at a time. Elena fends off a group of slave Pirates single handedly, but is suddenly blind-sided by an explosion erupting from the Harvester ship's core, which knocks her off deck. Seeing this all unfold, Victor quickly runs then leaps down to save Elena from falling off the ship, grabbing her just in time as he hangs on to the edge of the lower deck.

"I've got you!" He shouts while hanging a few yards below the top deck with his legs wrapped tightly around a broken beam, "You're strong."

Elena looks up at Victor with surprise then grins, saying, "I know, so are you. She presses the Gods' symbol in pink bearing over her chest plate, which causes her Angelic wings to appear. Victor looks back, amazed by the sight of her wings as she gracefully pulls him back up to the top deck. Extending his left arm in a protective manner, Victor holds his Gauntlet before him then turns his head and alerts, "It's too hot, milady! Stay low, I'll hold them off!"

Several slave Pirates rush towards them as Victor stands ready to protect the unknown Angel but she unexpectedly intervenes by taking them out herself with her crystalline staff. Victor looks on in shock as she holds her graceful stance then turns with a friendly expression on her face. Seconds later, Elena confidently approaches Victor who stands silent.

"Tell you what, you cover me, and I'll hold them off." She jests as she grabs a torn piece of clothing from Victor's attire. As she wipes the sweat off her beautiful face, she faces Victor with a comforting smile and teases, "Let me know when it gets hot, alright?"

Smiling back, Victor nods and sarcastically mutters, "Yes mam!"

With the battle raging on and the ship's crew dwindling, Victor fights side by side with Elena as they take turns striking down each slave Pirate with great finesse. Victor sees what appears to be the last slave Pirate then raises his Gauntlet and yells, "Come on!"

The slave Pirate rushes towards Victor and is easily subdued, though unbeknownst to him, another one tries to attack from behind, but is suddenly taken out by Elena who fires an energy blast from her Gauntlet. Victor quickly turns and sees Elena floating in the air with her Gauntlet aimed, surprised by her instinctive attack.

"Hot enough for you?" Elena says jokingly as she pulls her arm back. Grateful, Victor smiles upon her as he sighs in relief then sarcastically replies, "You could say that!"

Elena smiles in return as Marcus and Yuri power down their Gauntlets.

"You lost, pay up!" Yuri teasingly demands.

Marcus sighs, slightly annoyed by the losing bet and responds, "You got lucky this time bro!"

Two other Archadians, Valorie who is also oriental with short black hair, and Vennessa a taller black female with long dread locks, step up to address everyone after the battle ceases.

"The crew has surrendered, and their ship has been crippled!" Valorie proudly announces.

Vennessa raises her Gauntlet and also declares, "Victory is ours!"

A couple of slave Pirates are brought to their knees and begin to attack each other in anger, as Elena swiftly turns away from Victor in annoyance.

"You know the rules!" She strictly informs with her crystalline staff pointed towards them, "There'll be no brawling on this ship!"

Valorie and Vennessa separate the two slave Pirates, forcing them to the ground with their crystalline staffs as they look up at Elena indignantly.

"Unless of course you wish to join the others who are now unable to speak." Elena taunts as the two Pirates quickly shake their heads in response. Elena looks upon the other slave Pirates and sternly announces, "Any further offenders will be confined to the brig for the remainder of the voyage." She then turns back to address the two Pirates kneeling before her and firmly says, "Am I clear?" The two slave Pirates nod sheepishly in response, bringing a smile to Victor's face. "Good!" Elena finishes graciously with a grin.

The Archadians take the remaining slave Pirates into custody aboard their ship as Elena shakes her head, annoyed by their very existence. Valorie and Vennessa stand by Elena to keep patrol as Marcus and Yuri approaches them, awaiting orders. Unsure of who or what he is, a couple of other Archadians circle around Victor, puzzled by his strange presence as they inspect his Gauntlet, causing him to guard it closely to his chest.

"Look well Angels!" Elena calmly intervenes with her hand raised, "It seems we have a guest onboard this floating death trap."

Victor looks upon Elena in curiosity then slowly approaches her and politely asks, "Who are you?"

Insulted by his apparent lack in manners, Vennessa strikes Victor in the abdomen with her crystalline staff, causing him to grunt in pain as she clearly states, "You do not speak unless spoken to, peasant!"

"My mistake!" Victor replies with a slight chuckle as he looks upon Vennessa and sarcastically says, "Does that apply to you as well?"

Angered by his lack of respect, Vennessa strikes Victor again, this time knocking him to his knees as Elena extends her hand out and firmly shouts, "That's enough sister!"

Vennessa looks back at Elena, annoyed by her sudden request.

"Leave him be!" Elena calmly finishes whilst lowering her hand back to her side, "There will be no such punishment while I'm around."

Taking one last glance at Victor, Vennessa scoffs impatiently and slowly backs away. Valorie approaches Victor and takes his Gauntlet away as he looks upon her, shaking his head in annoyance.

"Seems I'm treated no differently here." He sarcastically mutters.

Elena signals the others aboard the ship's deck to stand down and commands, "Steady sisters, he's not a threat!" Taking a moment to look upon Victor in curiosity, she respectfully asks, "Have you a name?"

Looking around, Victor hesitates to respond then faces Elena and calmly says, "Victor, Victor Zyas."

"Victor, huh?" Elena replies, "It is a strong name, one I haven't heard in my lifetime." Victor smiles in appreciation as she points her crystalline staff towards him in a non-threatening manner, and states, "Judging by your attire, I'd say you've had a rough journey."

Laughing softly in response, Victor replies, "You could say that."

"You're from Pretoria I presume." Elena curiously implies.

"Not exactly," Victor calmly explains, "I come from a place of pain, and suffering. Where people are forced to work in fire and brimstone."

"I see." Elena respectfully acknowledges, "Can't say I've ever met a strong person such as yourself with an easy past."

Valorie approaches Elena with Victor's Gauntlet and hands it to her, then informs, "We found this on him. It's old, but appears to be one of ours."

Vennessa steps forward as well, staring back at Victor with a scowl and murmurs, "Is it possible to think he killed one of our own and took it?"

Victor looks back, concerned by their position on the matter as Vennessa unexpectedly aims her Gauntlet at him and says strongly, "If so, then he must suffer the consequences like the rest of them!"

Elena places her hand on Vennessa's Gauntlet to diffuse her anger by easing her mind, "Don't be absurd, sister!" She assures, "He may not be a noble, but he didn't use it to harm any of us mind you."

Concerned by Elena's attitude, Vennessa reluctantly lowers her Gauntlet. Angered by Vennessa's harsh stance, Victor sighs as Elena looks to him and gently points out, "As a matter of fact, he saved me."

Victor nods back in respect with Elena following suit whilst grinning.

"He is now a guest of the Arch, and is to be treated as such." Elena announces as she looks directly towards Valorie and Vennessa then finishes, "Understood, sisters?"

Valorie and Vennessa nod in response while keeping a suspicious and somewhat detestable gaze upon Victor.

"Looks like you're getting rusty my friend." Yuri says humorously, poking Marcus' side.

Marcus looks upon his short pal and says, "Oh yeah, why do you say that?"

"That human took out at least ten pirates himself." Yuri replies whilst motioning towards Victor, "Guess I should be thanking him for the much-needed win today."

"Yeah, and I'll be the victor next time." Marcus scoffs, "Assuming we don't have any further interruptions from uninvited guests."

"Fair enough." Yuri says with a grin.

Still kneeling out of respect, Elena signals Victor with a graceful hand gesture and says, "Rise, Victor. Do not fear us for no harm will befall you, at least not while I'm around."

As Victor rises to his feet, he looks around for a moment then calmly says, "I'll ask again, if I may this time." He finishes with a stern glance towards Vennessa who scowls back. Elena responds with a smile and nods in return as Victor politely asks, "Who are you?"

"I am Elena Saltora, Princess of Archadia." She replies to his surprise, "I shall grant you one request in exchange for your gallantry."

"I simply wish to continue my journey north." Victor humbly asserts, "Without any trouble of course."

After a moment of considering his bold request, Elena responds once again with a smile and says, "Very well. We will take you to Titania, where you shall receive food and shelter for your services to the Arch."

Victor sighs in relief, hoping to be that much closer to his ultimate goal.

"Where you go from there is entirely up to you." Elena clarifies, "But we can at least offer you a ride as a 'personal thanks' from me."

"Why would you do that for someone you don't even know?" Victor carefully inquires, trying not to sound offensive towards her.

"Perhaps he's smarter than he looks." Valorie mockingly comments directly to Vennessa, who grins.

"Because, like it or not you are a guest, and I am honor bound to protect you." Elena clarifies, "For honor is the backbone of our civilization"

"Thanks so much, you are most generous, milady." Victor says whilst bowing his head in respect.

Glancing at him curiously, Elena denotes, "If I had to take a wild guess based on your primitive attire, I'd say that you're pretty upfront about yourself."

Victor cracks a smile and sarcastically retorts, "For the most part anyway. In truth, I'm a simple person with a complicated mind, but given the circumstances I have no reason not to be."

Amused by his honest approach, Elena admits, "Yeah, I suppose it always catches up to you if you're not."

Looking upon her curiously to determine her exact demeanor, Victor tilts his head and asks, "Correct me if I'm wrong, but you're one of those crusading heroine types, aren't you?"

"You could say that, but no more than you apparently." Elena teasingly replies as he smiles back in amusement. She then raises her hand in signal formation to conclude their brief conversation and respectfully calls, "Sisters! Please take our new guest on board if you don't mind."

Valorie and Vennessa grudgingly approach Victor and peacefully escort him onto the Arch ship floating next to the damaged Harvester ship. Elena then turns to address Marcus and Yuri as she hands them Victor's Gauntlet.

"Marcus, Yuri!" She also calls as they step forward, then firmly requests, "Clean up this Gauntlet, and see if you can find out its true origin if you would please."

"Yes, your Highness." Yuri responds with a nod as he takes the Gauntlet in hand, "It shouldn't take long for me to calibrate its crystalline core." Examining the Gauntlet closely, he finishes, "Though from what I can already tell, it's a very impressive design."

Marcus steps closer to Elena from behind with a look of concern and says, "Do you want us to keep an eye on this guy? He somehow took on these pirates single-handedly."

"I take it you're volunteering then?" Elena suggests with a grin as she turns to face Marcus who looks back, confused. "He may be a stranger to us, but he risked his life to save mine." She expresses, "It would be wrong of me not to return the favor, don't you think?"

"If you say so, Princess." Marcus replies apprehensively.

"Anything on the signal we were tracking earlier?" Elena queries.

"Nothing yet, but we'll definitely keep you posted." Yuri replies.

Elena nods, looking disappointed as Marcus and Yuri take their leave aboard the Arch ship, followed by her moments after observing the damaged Harvester ship one last time. As the Arch ship floats several yards away, Elena turns firmly with her crystalline staff raised towards the Harvester.

"Prepare to disengage; destroy it!" She sternly orders.

The Archadians blast the ship's hull with a powerful energy beam, causing the Harvester to fall and crash onto the surface below as the Arch ship takes off at full speed, heading north towards Titania.

CH: 18
PATH TO HEAVEN

Entering the highly advanced continent north of Pretoria, Tannis' ship arrives in Titania air space, landing on the port of Edge City. As Tannis and his crew depart the ship, two Titanian guards take Talia into custody.

"Take her to my quarters!" Tannis orders with the wave of his decorated hand. "See that she's fed and cleaned up before I return."

The Titanian guards bow their heads in respect and reply in unison, "Yes my Lord!" The guards shove Talia forward and rudely say, "This way, *slave!*"

Talia follows the guards, amazed by the sight and size of the dominant looking metropolis towering over her.

"My gosh." She whispers while looking around in curiosity and wonder, "Where am I?" She follows the guards as Tannis trails his personal escort to his tower shaped like a giant *T* in the center of the large city.

Aboard the Arch ship also heading towards Titania from Pretoria, Elena finds Victor sitting alone in the cargo deck and cautiously approaches him. Victor looks up and is surprised to see her standing before him.

"I wanted to thank you for helping me earlier today." She happily acknowledges, "Whether you meant to or not, it was very brave."

"You seem like an honorable person yourself, I'm sure you would've done the same for me." Victor comments with a soft grin.

"I suppose the first to help you up are the ones who know how it feels to fall down." Elena kindly denotes on his behalf.

"Something I know all too well." Victor concedes, "I'm sorry if I speak out of place, it's just that, well, I'm not very good with people."

"It's quite alright, I myself don't have lots of friends, I just happen to know a lot of people." Elena caringly shrugs, "Honesty has a power that very few people can handle; luckily I'm not one of them."

Feeling hesitant at first, she respectfully probes, "Forgive my intrusion, but I'm curious. Why did you help me, not knowing who I am?"
After a short pause, Victor slightly chuckles and says, "Guess you could say I was just following my instincts, which told me to act without question."

"They must be really good then, in a virtuous type of way." Elena teasingly suggests. "Really?" Victor calmly asks, "How so?"
Gesturing towards his armor-less body, Elena remarks, "You held your own quite well for not having any Soul Gear. I wonder what someone like you could do with that kind of power, should you ever attain it."

"Well, I sure as hell wouldn't use it to hurt others if that's what you're implying." Victor firmly retorts.
Trying not to offend him, Elena shakes her head and clarifies, "Not at all, but the more powerful you become the more the world expects of you."
Taking her view into consideration, Victor looks at her and respectfully asks, "As an Angel I assume you're expected to look after the people of Earth?"
Elena sits next to him and replies, "Yes, to some degree." Thinking of what to say next, she looks away then faces him, chuckling, "You know, it's funny, in some ways technology has connected the world and disconnected everyone all at once." She professes, "I used to observe people living their lives upon the surface, and for some strange reason, I envied them greatly. But if there's one thing I've learned through all my years watching from above…"

"It's that people aren't always what they seem." Victor interjects.
Elena nods in agreement to his thoughtful interruption, "Yes, I think it's a good thing to try and inspire goodness within people of the world." She says softly, "But I've come to learn over the years that it only goes so far, for they too must also take action if they ever want anything in their life to improve."
With a sigh, Victor nods and says, "A sad yet horrible truth to be sure."

"People of the world need us but they don't always like us, for we must be light in a too often dim world." Elena reveals in a disappointed tone, "They depend on us to be strong when they are vulnerable." Victor ponders the thought as she continues, "And when there's a conflict, they tend to blame us for it now. Can you believe that?"

"I guess most people will believe whatever they want to nowadays, whether its true or not." Victor carefully comments.

"Naturally." She affirms, "And though my people and I don't always agree, it's still my sacred duty to watch over everyone, even people like you."

"Amazing how many have lost faith in such things as guardian Angels." Victor remarks, "Even I have from time to time."

"A lot of people do, that is until they need one." Elena states with a smile, "But without help from above, who will survive on the surface?"
Surprised by her courageous statement, Victor looks upon her intensely and infers, "Seems a lot is expected of your kind above the clouds."
Elena nods back, "In more ways than one actually.

And what is expected of you? Is there something you honor as well?" Disheartened, Victor pulls out the crystal necklace from around his neck, examining it intensely and answers, "A promise."

"To someone very important I'm sure." She inspires while placing a hand on his shoulder, "Was there someone special where you come from?" Nodding in a sorrowful manner, Victor tucks the necklace back under his tunic and answers sadly, "Sort of, but for all I know they're dead now." Saddened by his answer, Elena looks away and says, "I'm sorry to hear that."

"Don't be, it's my burden to bear." Victor calmly says in respect. Elena tries to cheer him up with a positive thought by stating, "Perhaps one day you will fulfill that promise with honor, and dignity."

"If I was given the opportunity, there's no telling what I could accomplish." He says determinately. While trying to read his thoughts, Elena stares into his deep blue eyes and says, "I don't presume to know your past, but I can tell you've been through a lot, a great deal of pain and suffering." Victor stares back, feeling the warmth of her comfort unlike any before. "You have a spirit that fights to survive, like mine." She denotes, "Though, I sense a lot of hate within you as well."

"Very perceptive of you." Victor utters with a laugh, "Though I'm probably not as complicated as one might think. I simply do what is necessary to keep moving forward, even if I'm the one who must suffer in the end." Elena waves her hand gracefully over his face, sensing a mysterious aura as he looks back curiously. "If you haven't noticed already, I'm sort of an empath, meaning I can sense other people's presence." She claims, "I'm not sure why exactly, but I sense something very different about you, something good, but also dark and mysterious." Victor grins, confident of his difference to others of the world. "Do you believe in Heaven, Victor?" She curiously inquires. Looking upward, Victor sighs heavily and says, "I've been living in Hell for so long, I'm not sure what I believe in anymore." He then looks upon her once again and compassionately insinuates, "But if you represent what Heaven is, will you please take me there?" His impulse brings a smile to Elena's face as she places her hand on his shoulder once again and teases, "We'll see."

"Figured it was worth a shot." He jokingly mutters. Elena laughs then says, "One of the most elusive things to find in life is balance, though contrary to popular belief it's not typically our position to interfere with the domestic affairs of other cultures on the surface."

"But you can interact, right?" Victor queries.

"Of course, how can we learn otherwise?" Elena replies, "Our role in this world is not to judge or figure out if someone deserves something, our job is to lift the fallen, to restore the broken, and to heal the hurting." Victor grins while motioning towards her, and asks, "What about you then?" Surprised, Elena places her hand on her chest plate and says, "Me?" Nodding back, Victor persists, "It's obvious you are resilient as well."

He then motions towards everyone aboard the ship and says, "Unlike the others, you seem to have a strong sense of compassion."

Curious to his keen observation, Elena looks upon the other Archadians and replies, "I'm sure you have many questions about us Angels." Feeling somewhat disappointed, she looks away and explains, "I'll admit that I myself am very different than my fellow brothers and sisters, for unlike the rest of my people I have a social and political obligation to the less fortunate."

"You have such a big heart for someone in your position." Victor says out of respect as she nods in appreciation.

"Well despite what you may have heard, being a Princess isn't all it's cracked up to be." She reveals, "I'm more of a free spirit; most don't like that but that's just the way I am. You know one of the biggest tragedies in our society is that so many people eagerly offer up hatred, yet willingly withhold their love, empathy, and kindness from others including themselves."

"And you?" He curiously probes.

"Not at all." She admits, "Though perhaps that will be the end of me someday, but I'd be living a lie if I didn't stay true to who and what I am."

"What you are is apparent, but who are you, really?" Victor asks.

"A survivor, like you." Elena answers softly with a confident smile.

"You speak my language very well it seems." He proudly denotes.

"And you mine." She happily replies, "How fortunate we must be."

"Incase you were wondering, I'm hard to get to know and near impossible to forget." Victor humorously challenges, "Though I'm humble enough to know I'm not better than anybody in this world, and wise enough to know that I'm different from the rest."

"I don't doubt that one bit." She accepts, "I can relate myself."

The friendly pair laughs over their likeness, feeling a close if not strange connection between them as the Arch ship continues flying towards Titania.

High above Edge City within Tannis' imperious tower, Talia wanders around the throne room, scared and alone as she observes various crystalline trinkets on display in curiosity. Upon closer inspection, the wall closest to her reveals to have numerous weapons on display as well, spanning hundreds of years worth of artistry from Earth's people such as various firearms and blades, generations before the Great Cataclysm. She picks up a metallic looking plate sitting on a table and observes it intensely. Her eyes widen with surprise upon seeing her reflection engulfed in shadow. Frightened by the image, she accidently drops the plate onto the table and mutters, "Whoa, that was scary." She then sees a random document lying on the table and hesitates to pick it up as she views the cover that reads: *TRISHARD INDUSTRIES: OPERATION X-NINETY SEVEN: LOCATION UNKOWN!* After flipping through the pages, she places it back onto the table and continues to look around curiously. In memory of her former setting in the mines, she pulls out the crystalline Angel figure from her garb and caresses it sorrowfully.

"Did you get enough to eat child?" Tannis says in welcoming fashion as he unexpectedly enters the throne room.

Startled by his intimidating presence, Talia tries to place the Angel figure back in her garb unnoticed and turns to face him, replying, "Yes, thank you."

Tannis shares a confident grin then approaches her, holding out his hand as she backs away in fear. "What's that you've got there?" He calmly asks.

Talia looks downward at the Angel figure sitting in her pocket as she tries to act ignorant by saying, "Oh this? It's nothing, really!"

"It must mean more to you than that if you guard it so carefully." Tannis denotes as he circles around her, extending his hand out once again. "Don't be shy, let me see it." Hesitating to comply, she pulls the Angel figure out of her pocket once more as Tannis slowly takes it from her hand and studies it intensely. "A primitive piece for sure, but a beautiful sculpture nonetheless." He respectfully regards. Talia glances at him worrisomely, in hopes that he doesn't take it away or destroy it. "Your friend must have given this to you." Tannis deduces as she nods, "Better you keep it then." He says as he tosses the Angel figure back to Talia who instinctively grabs it, holding it tightly against her chest protectively. "As you can see, I have plenty of my own trinkets on display that I've collected over the years." Tannis states as he motions towards the various knickknacks displayed on the walls of his throne room. "Besides, I have no need for such useless decorations anyway." He rudely asserts. After a sigh of relief, Talia quickly places the Angel figure back in her pocket for safekeeping. "Have no fear, child." Tannis declares while looking out from his window overlooking the busy city, "No one in this kingdom will harm you, but know that there are plenty who definitely would." Tannis extends his arm towards her as she steps cautiously towards the window to look out onto the city a few feet from him.

"You're very fortunate that I'm the one who brought you here; otherwise you'd become just another sex slave in the hands of others." Tannis explains as she places her hands on the crystalline glass; "Luckily for you though, I'm above that sort of harsh treatment." He clarifies, as Talia looks towards him, concerned by his meaning. "Your emotions give you away, so you must learn to control them." He confidently informs with his attention still focused outside the window overlooking the large city. "And while you're here in my custody, you will do what I ask. Understood?" He says facing her.

Talia looks away and nods, distraught over her current position in his hands.

"When we find your so-called friend, and believe me we will, he better cooperate as you have for his own sake as well as yours." Tannis warns, giving her food for thought as he steps away from the window, approaching his crystalline throne while tapping his decorated fingers across it. Talia turns her attention behind her, following his movements as he finally sits down. She then looks back onto the city through the window with a depressing sigh, hoping that Victor is unharmed as promised by her prestigious captor.

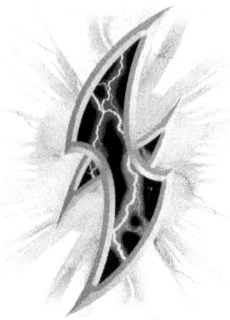

CH: 19
GRAVITY OF THE SITUATION

Continuing his search for Victor in the skies above Pretoria aboard his ship, Patrayous stands by with Zepherus, anxiously awaiting Intel as they look out the cockpit window. A Titanian guard approaches from behind to address him as Zepherus growls to get his attention.

"What is it, Commander?" Patrayous asks in stern tone.

"We're picking up energy fluctuations around a crash site near the border lands, right outside the Neutral Zone in Sahria." The guard replies as he punches a few buttons on a holographic display projecting from his Gauntlet then informs, "I've already debriefed the trackers."

"And what's the report thus far?" Patrayous inquires.

"Well, this slave is one shadowy character." The guard remarks.

"Get to the point already!" Patrayous impatiently demands.

"They lost his trail at the edge of the river in Eldria." The guard informs as Patrayous carefully contemplates their next move, "Shall I send a squad to investigate?"
Patrayous glances at Zepherus for a moment as if to run the idea by him first then states, "No! That's completely out of our jurisdiction."

"Are we to cease our search for the slave then?" The guard queries with concern and respect.

"It's likely the ship we're looking for is the one that crashed." Patrayous denotes as he glances out the window once again in annoyance, "Looks like the two Champions we'll get this one after all unfortunately."
Zepherus snarls in disappointment until Patrayous hands him a piece of raw meat from behind a cabinet to chew on viciously.

"What do you think could've possibly caused it to crash all of a sudden outside the Neutral Zone?" The guard reverently inquires.
With his strong and stern posture, Patrayous turns back to face the guard and admits, "I don't know, I can't say for sure at this time."

"General!" Another guard abruptly shouts, "They've just confirmed that it was in fact a Harvester ship."

"Tell your men to fall back!" Patrayous immediately shouts.

"Fall back, Sir?" The guard asks cautiously.

As the other guard looks upon his mighty superior in question, Patrayous explains, "If the ship crash landed near the borderlands, then it will be up to Raina and Lucian to investigate the matter further. Consequently, we are not permitted to get in their way."

"With the Champions, you mean?" The other guard inquires.

Zepherus raises his head with his spinal shards glowing, gaining Patrayous' attention as he announces, "The slave may still be headed north on foot! We'll continue tracking him there, assuming he hasn't changed course yet."

"Right away, Sir!" one of the guards replies before facing the others and orders, "You men, tell the squad to fall back immediately!"

The Titanian guards set up a transmission to contact the squads still searching on the surface below for the wanted fugitive. Patrayous looks upon his Gauntlet and groans in annoyance of having to change course to avoid confrontation with Raina and Lucian. Sensing his frustration, Zepherus chirps towards him as the ship changes course from Pretoria, now heading back towards Titania instead.

Within the Eastern continent of the kingdom Eudenia, the Eudenian Champion Damian Trag, tall with short black hair sits alone inside his private quarters. Sitting in a meditative state, eyes closed, he focuses his mind in the form of his national martial art known as Eudetsu before a crystalline Scorpion statue with his arms calmly at his side. Moments later, a Eudenian guard unexpectedly enters the chamber to address him.

"My apologies, LT!" The guard politely announces.

Quickly opening his intense brown eyes in annoyance, Damian turns his head and firmly asks, "What is it?"

The guard steps forward to respond directly, saying, "Queen Demuera has summoned you, she's awaiting your presence."

Damian turns back; closing his eyes once again and says, "Very well then, inform her of my leave, I'll be there momentarily."

"Will do, LT." The guard replies before taking his leave quietly.

With an intense sigh, Damian refocuses his attention, curious as to why his nation's ruler as summoned him in the first place.

Moments after the Eudenian guard leaves, Damian opens his eyes once again, stands up and approaches a crystalline display case several feet away. Damian grabs his Eudenian Gauntlet and places it over his arm, which powers up his Soul Gear lined with hints of purple. He then grabs his royal purple cape and wraps it around his neck as it locks into place onto his shoulders. Gripping his fist tightly, he looks onto the kingdom from his window above the kingdom in anticipation of the Queen's formal request.

Within the Western continent of the kingdom Enfuria, the Enfurian Champion Adrian Braxel, large in mass while tall with short reddish white spiky hair and tribal tattoos covering various parts of his body, sits alone inside his private quarters. Sitting in a meditative state, eyes closed, Adrian focuses his mind in the form of his national martial art known as Furikan before a crystalline Dragon statue with his arms crossed. Moments later, an Enfurian guard unexpectedly enters the chamber to address him.

"I'm sorry to disturb you, LT!" The guard politely announces.

Opening his hazel eyes quickly in annoyance, Adrian turns his head and rudely responds, "You should be!"

The guard steps forward to respond directly to him, saying, "King Drakhan has summoned you, he's awaiting your presence."

Adrian turns back with a grunting sigh; closing his eyes once again and says, "Alright then, tell him I'm on my way."

"Right away, LT." The guard replies before taking his leave.

Moments after the Enfurian guard leaves, Adrian opens his eyes once again, stands up with a groan and approaches a crystalline display case several feet away. Adrian grabs his Enfurian Gauntlet and places it over his arm, which powers up his Soul Gear lined with hints of orange. He then grabs his tribal effects and locks them into place on his stocky shoulders. Pounding his fists tightly, he looks onto the surrounding kingdom from his window in anticipation of the King's formal request.

Within the hour, Damian enters the throne chamber of the Eudenian palace and approaches Raina, who's sitting in her crystalline throne shaped like a large Scorpion. She looks upon Damian with pride as he kneels before her and says, "You summoned me, my Queen."

"Yes, Trag." Raina replies as she taps her decorated fingers together, "There is an issue at hand that requires your immediate expertise."

"What is thy will?" Damian willfully asks.

Raina sits back in her crystalline throne and explains, "A Harvester ship has crash landed near the borderlands in Pretoria. I want you to investigate the matter personally, and report anything you may find there."

Slightly confused by the request, Damian raises his head and cautiously inquires, "That's typically a job for General Patrayous, is it not?"

"Typically, yes, but there may have been someone on board carrying something quite valuable." She clarifies, "So valuable in fact that I want you to retrieve it first before anyone else does."

Damian stands to address Raina directly and with a concerned tone, he questions, "What if we should run into the Enfurians while we're there?"

Chuckling to herself in response, Raina places her hands on the armrests of her throne and states, "If you're wondering about Braxel, he's likely aware of the situation as well." She reveals, "It is of no consequence though, for they will not be a threat thanks to our peaceful alliance with Drakhan."

"I shall leave immediately then, Lord Riana." Damian declares as he bows his head in respect then turns to take his leave, flipping his purple cape past his left shoulder in a pompous manner.

Curious of the situation at hand, Raina turns in her throne and mutters, "What an interesting turn of events this has become."

Contemplating the outcome of his search, Raina stands from her crystalline throne and looks upon the Eudenian kingdom from above, shining brightly under the cool Eastern moonlight that illuminates the city structures below.

Within the same hour, Adrian enters the throne chamber of the Enfurian palace and approaches Lucian, who's sitting in his crystalline throne shaped like a large Dragon. He looks upon Adrian with pride as he kneels before him and says, "You summoned me, my King."

"Of course." Lucian replies as he pounds his fists together tightly, "I'm need of your services once again."

"How do I honor thee?" Adrian willfully asks.

Lucian sits back in his crystalline throne and explains, "A Harvester ship was somehow taken down near the borderlands in Pretoria. You will go and investigate the matter first hand and inform me of anything unusual."

Adrian raises his head, slightly confused by the request and cautiously retorts, "We're doing Patrayous' dirty work now, are we?"

"Not exactly." Lucian clarifies, "The ship just happened to crash beyond his jurisdiction, giving us the right of passage."

Adrian stands to address Lucian directly and inquires, "I assume the Eudenians have been alerted as well then?"

With a deep chuckle, Lucian places his hands on the armrests of his throne and reveals, "Trag and his men will surely be on the hunt also, so proceed with extreme caution." He warns.

"Understood." Adrian sternly acknowledges.

"Report back when you've found the ship and whatever remains you may come across in the process." Lucian orders.

"As you wish, Lord Lucian." Adrian declares as he bows his head in respect then turns to take his leave.

Suspicious of the situation laid out before them, Lucian turns in his crystalline throne and mutters, "So, the hunt the continues."

Unsure of the necessity regarding his involvement, Lucian stands from his crystalline throne and looks upon the Enfurian kingdom from above, gleaming under the hot Western sun, which magnifies the light beaming off of the city structures below.

CH: 20
USEFUL SERVANTS

Arriving at the Northern continent Titania in the early evening hours, Elena's Arch ship lands at the port of Edge City. As the landing platform opens, Marcus and Yuri prepare to depart the ship along with the others.

"Time to eat!" Marcus announces, "I'm famished!"

Shaking his head in amusement, Yuri glances at Marcus and jokily comebacks, "You're always hungry!"

"Guess I worked up quite an appetite today." Marcus adds.

Yuri smacks his hand on Marcus' shoulder and leads the way outside the ship, saying, "Come on, you're buying."

"Yeah right!" Marcus sarcastically mutters.

Marcus and Yuri take off towards the city to find food as Victor and Elena depart the ship shortly after with Valorie and Vennessa who stand guard. Before moving forward, Elena turns to face Valorie and Vennessa, requesting, "Make sure the ship is ready for take off when we get back."

"Yes, your Highness!" Valorie and Vennessa jointly reply.

"I don't plan on being here long enough to relax if I can help it." Elena mentions with a stern tone.

Valorie and Vennessa nod in response, and keep guard over the Arch ship as requested. Victor looks around in wonder of the cityscape towering over him and inquires, "What is this place?"

"Titania…" Elena replies as she leads Victor closer into the city, "Also known as the land of trade, where the Emperor reigns."

Victor stops for a moment to Elena's surprise and cautiously asks, "His keep is somewhere inside there, huh? Within this huge city?"

Sensing Victor's apprehension, Elena grins slightly as she clarifies, "It's a remote stronghold left from a golden age, which is currently being ruled by rich and powerful industrialists."

With an accepting nod, Victor continues following Elena into the large city, saying, "I'm beginning to think its appearance is aimed at first time visitors like myself to create strong feelings of smallness and inadequacy, though I'd be lying if I said it wasn't working."

"In regards to the imperial prerogatives running rampant, you're probably right." She fully explains, "The nobles call it the lost city; a kingdom that is a treasure trove of various types of culture. At its center is the globalist empire and Tannis Marquis controls it all. Like its surrounding continents Eudenia and Enfuria, Titania is a highly structured if not feudalistic society, for they're an enemy combatant political system with an economic globalist regime. And for the most part they're exceedingly proud of their worldwide occupation that I myself am not too fond of even in the slightest."

"What is it the nobles trade here exactly?" Victor inquires as thousands of people roam the market place within the city, trading for various goods and supplies as well as human slaves between the nobles of Earth.

"Most barter for food and supplies," Elena continues to explain, "While others for power and wealth, using human slaves as currency."

Angered by this revelation, Victor stops once again and says, "You mean to tell me that humans are traded like cattle here as well?"

Sensing his frustration on the subject, Elena tries to clarify her stance, "It's revolting I know, but the Emperor controls the trade market here, and currently he's hated by many yet confronted by none due to his diplomatic immunity." Stepping past her, Victor looks upon the scandalous metropolis, sighing in anger over the peoples' selfish power over his kind. "His influence on the Senate, as well as the mob allows him to control slaves for the nobles of Earth." She continues, "People are trafficked without a glimpse or care of compassion in this place as well as the rest of the world I gather."

"Sounds more like equal results for the less fortunate than equal opportunity to me." Victor says, dispirited by his journey to the surface, "Just like home I guess, though I expected better things from a place like this."

"I know, it's horrific to say the least." Elena attempts to ease, "Sadly, this is the world we currently live in."

Victor turns to face Elena and says with a stern voice, "It's easy to turn a blind eye towards people you don't even know or care about, especially when they're the ones suffering." Elena looks upon Victor, feeling his pain as she nods in agreement. "I suppose people on the surface are no better than the ones below it." Victor gripes as he looks back onto the busy city in anger.

"They're not all bad." Elena assures as she motions him to continue following her into the city, "They simply obey the Emperor out of fear, or they believe he's right and have simply lost perspective on most things in the world." She reveals, "People critical of him have been known to simply disappear; government officials, activists, journalists, even average civilians aren't immune from such precarious judgment."

"Why does no put an end to it?" Victor questions, his brow lowered. Elena turns to face him and replies, "There are some in the Senate who have dedicated their lives to the people of Earth and the Gods themselves."

"Any candidates I should be aware of while I'm here?" Victor sarcastically queries, jaded by the possibility of any good people in the area. In response to Victor's persistent nature, Elena grins and patiently explains, "Nikolas Hammond for example, one man above all has shown such dedication to the cause, along with his loyal colleague, Julius Griffin."

"Who are they?" Victor respectfully asks. Senators Hammond and Griffin wave to Elena from a distance as she smiles and waves back then further explains, "Two of the only nobles that can be relied on these days. You could say they're from the insider class and system for they make great diplomats, and you will meet them soon enough." Victor sees Hammond and Griffin approaching them from several yards away, unsure of who they are exactly at first glance. "Hammond and Griffin have allied themselves with the Arch to bring change within the world Senate," Elena proclaims, "But sadly, humans are still seen only as slaves here."

"That's unfortunate." Victor scoffs, trying to hide the anger apparent in his voice, "Sounds like the Emperor must be heavily connected then."

"Very." She responds with a disappointing nod, "Because of his monopolistic practices, the Emperor has dominion over the entire Earth realm, first only to the Eudenian Queen and Enfurian King. The Senate itself is full of his sycophantic followers who help push his selfish ideologies."

"More like educated fools if you ask me." Victor comments.

"For the most part, you're right." She acknowledges, "But as long as he controls them, he controls everyone. Until the people begin to wake up from their pathetic dream state, no one will ever lift a finger to stop it." Stopping once more, Victor looks upon Elena, expressing that of concern.

"But you're an Angel." He asks, "Can't your people put a stop to it?" Elena stops also, sensing his elevated frustration and replies with a troubled tone, "They would, but it's a lot more complicated than that I'm afraid."

"Why does it have to be?" Victor asks impatiently.

"Because we can only intervene to uphold balance, as is stated in the Arch code set by the Gods centuries ago." She explains, "As long as the Eudenians and Enfurians aren't fighting with each other under our watch, then slavery will only continue to grow and fester."

"I hope to one day have a hand in ending it once and for all." Victor declares as he places his right fist within his left hand tightly. Elena places her hand on his shoulder to comfort him, and supportively concedes, "As do I, Victor, as do I." Victor smiles back, feeling comforted by her graceful tone, "Come, you must be hungry." She concludes. A low grumbling noise is heard as Victor places his hand over his stomach.

"As a matter of fact, I'm starving!" He says with a painful laugh.

A small group of people approach Elena as Hammond, a middle-aged white male somewhat tall in stance with short brownish grey hair, and Griffin, a slightly taller black male around the same age with no hair, bow their heads in respect to greet her properly. "Greetings, your Highness." Griffin welcomes, "I trust your journey was pleasant if not tolerable enough on your way here."

"Not quite." Elena says with a grin, shaking her head, "I must speak to the Senate at once, assuming you can arrange a meeting while I'm here."

"You sound troubled, milady." Hammond points out.

"That I am." She says directly to Hammond before lowering her voice with caution, "We recently came across a Harvester ship near the Neutral Zone in Pretoria."

Griffin chuckles and remarks, "It's not unusual for Harvesters to trade near the borderlands as you well know."

"Obviously." Elena replies, slightly annoyed by his remark, "But these were slave Pirates, the illegal kind."

Hammond and Griffin glance at each other for a moment with concern then turn their attention towards Victor to lighten the mood.

"I see, and who is this young lad you have yet to introduce us to?" Hammond humbly inquires as Victor steps forward to be properly greeted.

"This is Victor Zyas." Elena answers as she motions towards him while gently placing her hand on his shoulder to make him feel at home.

Hammond extends his arm out to shake Victor's hand in respect and says, "Greetings, Victor. You've been in good hands I see."

Bowing his head in respect, Victor responds, "Thank you sir, she's been very hospitable and generous enough to me as it is."

Elena looks away for a moment, gently raising her hand to her mouth in amusement while slightly flushed by his kind acknowledgement.

"I must admit, it's very unusual for the Princess to bring about a guest here in this fashion." Hammond says with slight suspicion.

Regaining her serious composure, Elena looks upon Hammond and states; "He was wrongfully held captive on the Harvester ship we encountered earlier. Please see to it that he receives your upmost respect and hospitality."

Griffin glances at Hammond, who slightly chuckles in response to her appeal and says, "A large request for someone we've just met, but granted."

"Our people will give him secure accommodation, you have our word on that, Princess." Griffin respectfully adds.

"Thank you, Senators." Elena responds with a peaceful nod.

Hammond raises his hand and signals his people to take Victor into his hospitable custody as Griffin walks with them towards the city. Victor turns to face Elena and nods respectfully, whispering, "Thank you."

"Don't mention it." She softly replies, her hand sliding off Victor's shoulder as he moves forward with Hammond and Griffin. To her surprise, he unexpectedly turns back to face her and asks, "Will I ever see you again?"

Amused by his compassionate attitude, Elena smiles and retorts, "When the time is right, I'm sure." She then motions towards her friendly Senators and gladly informs, "Hammond and Griffin will take care of you from here."

"What about my Gauntlet?" Victor inquires with grave concern in his voice, "What do you intend to do with it?"

Hesitating to answer, Elena looks back towards Valorie and Vennessa whom stand by the Arch ship then turns back to face him. "My people will want to study its origin." She clarifies, "For your protection, it's best that you don't carry it here anyway. It will be safe with us for the time being, I give you my word." She kindly assures.

"Right now, your word seems to be the only one that means anything to me." Victor commends, which brings a smile to her face, "Until next time then, milady." He finishes while bowing his head in respect as he pulls her hand towards him and gently kisses it.

After a brief and somewhat flirtatious sendoff, Victor walks away with Hammond and Griffin, escorted by their servants into the city. Elena looks on, shaking her head with a big smile across her usually intense face from his kind gesture, hoping the best for him. After a moment of curious observation, she then moves towards the city with business of her own.

As the sun sets upon the ever-growing Edge City, the busy streets continue to fill with Titanian citizens whose activities range from various forms of entertainment and trading. High above the urban area within Tannis' tower, Elena approaches the throne chamber and sees two Titanian guards by the entrance. "Halt!" One of them commands, "What's your business?"

"Surely his majesty would not refuse an audience with a visiting Princess of Archadia, would he?" Elena sarcastically questions as she stops before them. As she stands by the entrance awaiting security clearance, one of the guards raises his Gauntlet and without hesitation sets up a transmission to inform Tannis of her arrival. "My Lord, the Princess has arrived."

"Excellent." Tannis replies through the intercom, "Show her in."

The Titanian guard extends his arm to grant Elena entry and respectfully says, "This way, Princess." Elena bows her head then walks past the two guards through the large doorway and enters the throne room. Sitting in his crystalline throne, Tannis turns to face her as she comes to a stopping point to converse. "Greetings, Princess, this is a pleasure most rare." Tannis starts as he looks upon her curiously, "What brings you here on this fine evening?"

Stepping closer to be heard properly, Elena replies, "To bid farewell. My crew and I are heading back to Archadia tonight."

Tannis stands from his throne then approaches Elena to address her directly, saying, "I see, and what of this mysterious visitor you brought here?"

"I wasn't aware you knew." Elena answers, annoyed by his knowing.

"Someone in my position has to know everything regarding his own kingdom, even if it's something small." Tannis condescendingly proclaims, as Elena nods in slight agreement. "It's highly irregular for random guests to be given such hospitality before getting security clearance from me or the Senate. Don't you agree?" He finishes as he pompously walks past her.

"Consider him a friend if it makes you feel any better." She defends.

"A friend, how unlikely." Tannis jeers cynically.

"He's in Senator Hammond's care now, that's all you need to know." Elena says without flinching, "I'm sure with your proper upbringing you realize that it is rude to refuse a request of a guest no matter who they are."

"I suppose you got me there." Tannis says before snapping his fingers towards a guard securing the entrance, signaling him to move towards a separate doorway. "Would you like a drink before take off?" He asks civilly.

"No thank you, I'm good." Elena politely refuses.

The Titanian guard opens the other door in the opposite direction of the entrance as Talia unexpectedly enters the room with a platter holding a crystalline bottle of wine and two highly decorated glasses. As Elena watches in repulsion, Talia approaches the table sitting several feet in front of the crystalline throne. She carefully places the tray on the table, trying not to break anything as Tannis grabs a glass and pours himself a drink.

"Why thank you, dear." He calmly acknowledges.

Talia bows her head in respect and steps aside, glancing at Elena in curiosity of her Angelic attire. Elena looks back also, concerned for the young girl's position. "You know something, there is almost no discipline nor real knowledge with today's youth." Tannis arrogantly comments, "I try to set an example, but it is extremely difficult as you can imagine. Personally, I blame the current state of our media, but that's a whole other story."

"Definitely one I don't have time for." Elena sternly mutters.

"Tell me, Princess, have you ever seen a harvest before?" Tannis inquires before taking a sip from his wine glass.

With a stern look, Elena faces him and replies, "Can't say I have, but I hear there's plenty of pain to go around in the process."

Tannis chuckles by her response and confidently states, "It's quite humane really. Those that don't survive would merely thank us for our mercy to end their pathetic lives." He then raises his glass and conceitedly remarks, "Let us be thankful that we live in more enlightened times."

Looking back at Talia once again, Elena sighs with annoyance evident in her deep breath, "There's nothing of the sort when you consider an entire race of people under the lash of your beck and call."

"They are nothing more than livestock, a disease for which there is no cure for the human condition." Tannis haughtily claims, "We prey upon them as you would any other beast."

"You can't attack people for things they can't control." Elena refutes.

With his attention turned outside, Tannis finishes, "And I shouldn't have to put up with them for things they can't control either. Though by now you'd think they would have evolved with a better sense of being overall."

Elena looks away, disgusted by his attitude towards humans and retorts, "Maybe they choose not to given the way you treat them. If it weren't for them, you wouldn't have a crystalline pedestal to place yourself on."

"I've earned my position as Emperor, thank you very much!" Tannis snaps after taking another sip from his drink.

"But as workers, they control the means of production, not you." Elena disputes as she turns back then comments, "You know as well as I do that people aren't objects to be possessed."

After finishing his wine, Tannis sets the glass back on the table and responds, "Perhaps not, but in this case a necessary evil."

"What's necessary is their independence." Elena claims on a serious note, "It's a miracle they haven't fought back yet."

Stepping towards the window overlooking the city, Tannis argues, "There are those who have profited from such miracles." Standing next to his crystalline throne with his back turned, he lectures, "This is the rule of nature." Tapping his decorated fingers on his throne, he then turns and hypothetically asks, "Would you dare to take that away from them?"

"You know I would in a heart beat." Elena proudly declares, "For it's not Mother Nature's rule, it's yours and yours alone."

"And as a rule of nature, they will continue to behave like animals." Tannis states with a rictus grin, trying to justify his point.

"They won't if you introduce them to the general population." Elena argumentatively suggests.

"And why would I want to do that?" Tannis questions with a smirk.

"People trapped in cages will behave like animals." Elena explains, "Give them they're freedom, and they'll soon remember their humanity."

"Gestures suffice for slaves as indeed for any other beast of burden." Tannis states with a soft chuckle then mocks, "So that's your plan, is it? To create an enlightened society?"

"Well, yes." Elena retorts, "Is that really so difficult to fathom?"

"Do I sense skepticism in your gesture?" He contests.

"I'm just curious to know if you really believe an entire race of people whose crimes are so heinous that they justify imprisonment." Elena denotes, "Sadists who find gratification in the debasement of others and those cowards who send people to their deaths in scenarios they themselves would avoid altogether. Except for humans, I believe most if not all of them can be rehabilitated often by the simple act of having their dignity restored."

"Those people on the surface and below are free to choose their own destiny, but they are not free from the consequences thereafter." He mocks.

"Sounds like a double-edged sword if you ask me." She scoffs.

Amused by Elena's unbending character, Tannis laughs, as Talia looks back with a dispirited expression covering her features. "Struggle breeds greatness for those who survive the pecking order, as it were." Tannis proclaims while scratching his fingers over the armrest of his throne. "Besides, humans are known for their idiosyncratic attitude towards protocol." He condescendingly expresses as he finally steps away from his throne with hands behind his back. "Weakness is behind all the problems of the world, including our own." He resumes, "Yet, regardless of their weaknesses, they're strategically important, for they're innovative in a minimalist sort of way. Though one would get the feeling they don't exactly trust us." He finishes with a cynical tease.

"I wonder why!" Elena harshly replies, "Can't say I blame them." As Tannis faces her with a scowl, she adds, "It takes a very special kind of people to live in such desolation, perhaps visionaries who see the planet not as it is, but what it once was and could possibly be again."

Puzzled by Elena's position on the subject, Talia listens closely to their conversation whilst trying not to attract any unwanted attention to herself.

"Nonsense!" Tannis hollers, turning Talia's attention away from Elena, "Humans simply provide us with the necessities of life, and we provide them with the necessities of living. It is a fair exchange when you stop and think about it, for they are a stubborn people to say the least."

"No more than you or I." Elena assertively states, "That too can be a positive trait, even in the eyes of the Gods."

"From what I've seen, there's not much to redeem them." He mocks, "Kind of makes you wonder just how their tragic species ever survived the Great Cataclysm in the first place."

"Decades of perseverance and suffrage I'm sure." Elena impatiently murmurs whilst looking at Talia, who smiles back.

"Regardless of how they've survived this long, our societies are intertwined in a symbiotic relationship." Tannis affirms regarding the notion.

"With one society profiting at the expense of the other!" Elena firmly debates while motioning towards Talia.

"Most would consider it a mutual understanding." Tannis remarks.

"But there's absolutely nothing mutual about it; it's exploitation pure and simple." Elena contests, "You've caused all of this suffering and hardship only to make your pitiful lives easier, and all of it based on a lie."

"That's how you see it." Tannis says with a devious smirk as he signals Talia to leave. Without hesitation, she bows her head and takes her leave with the tray in hand. "Someone has to mine the crystals of this world, for they play a vital part in our military industrial complex alone." He excuses, "A lifetime of slavery sounds pretty dull if you ask me."

"Of course it is!" Elena argues, "Any form of slavery is a dull if not pointless existence. This refining process of which you are so proud is only to increase productivity of the crystals and tighten your grip."

"Then who do you prefer serves it, us, or them?" Tannis contests. Shaking her head in frustration, Elena looks on in disgust of Talia's treatment as she glances back and suddenly trips, falling to the ground. As Tannis turns his attention towards the noise, Elena rushes to help her. Holding her head down out of embarrassment, Talia quickly tries to clean up the mess as Elena places her hand on her shoulder to comfort her and gently asks, "Are you alright, child?" Talia ignores Elena, trying not to offend Tannis with her usual outspoken personality as she focuses on cleaning up the mess.

"Here, let me help you with that." Elena kindly gestures as she kneels to help her with the mess now covering the floor. Irritated by Elena's act of kindness, Tannis places his hand over his forehead, rolling his eyes in disdain.

"Don't concern yourself with me," Talia says discouragingly while trying desperately to wipe away the wine, "I'm fine."
Helping her to clean the floor, Elena looks upon Talia and encourages with a smile, "It's alright, everyone needs help from time to time."
Surprised by her comforting presence, Talia grins in appreciation as Elena pauses for a moment in shock, sensing something mysteriously special about her and cautiously asks, "Who are you?"

"I'm nobody, really!" Talia replies, trying not to draw too much attention to herself once again in front of Tannis.

"Nonsense!" Elena caringly persists, "What is your name?"
Talia looks upon Elena curiously, finding the strength to answer from her encouraging presence and says, "Natalia Andreas."
Elena takes this small opportunity to gracefully wave her hand in front of Talia's face, and to her surprise realizes her to be of Angel descent. She then smiles to comfort Talia who smiles back, unsure of her sudden excitement.

"Where did this girl come from?" Elena inquires as she turns her head directly towards Tannis.

"That's none of your concern!" Tannis infuriatingly replies as he approaches them, "Though if you really want to know, this is my way of giving people who've made mistakes in their lives an opportunity to rise above themselves, to move beyond the bars of containment as it were."

"Like those on the surface?" Elena scoffs, "Last I checked any and all humans were still considered slaves under your fiendish rule."

"She's my slave, and I will do what I want with her thank you very much!" Tannis firmly proclaims.

"Not anymore!" Elena declares as she faces Talia and stands before her with her hand extended, "Get up, you're coming with me."

"What?" Talia responds, hesitating to move against Tannis' wishes as Elena motions towards her. Talia finally takes her hand as she helps her up.

"What do you think you're doing, Princess?" Tannis asks furiously.
As Elena turns to address Tannis, she stands behind Talia with her hands placed on her shoulders and reveals, "I sense an Arch aura in this child."

"Impossible!" Tannis exclaims, "She's merely a human slave!"

"More than that I'd say!" Elena contests with a grin as she looks down at Talia who smiles back, feeling hopeful.

"You have no right to such a claim in my kingdom of all places!" Tannis argues, "The Senate itself would not approve of this defiant act!"

Moving towards the entrance, Elena prepares to leave with Talia by her side and says; "I must present her before the supreme council in Archadia for evaluation." She then turns to face Tannis one last time and finishes, "If you and your people have any regard for me or the Arch, then you will respect my sacred duty as an Angel of this Earth."

Tannis scowls upon her in anger, as Elena turns to exit the chamber for good.

"Come with me, Natalia!" Elena calls to get her attention as she quickly follows suit. The Titanian guard opens the large crystalline door as Elena stands by, waiting for Talia to catch up. As Talia takes her leave in Elena's safe custody, she glances back at Tannis, sighing in relief as he scowls.

"Well played, Princess." Tannis says angrily to himself as he kneels to pick up one the wine glasses that's still intact, "And now for my turn."

As the guards shut the door, Tannis looks on with a devious grin and breaks the glass with his bare hand then turns to approach his window once again.

Outside the city under the night sky, Elena and her crew prepare to board the Arch ship with Talia in tow. "Take her onboard, and make sure that she's comfortable." Elena requests as Valorie and Vennessa nod in response.

Elena looks onto the city one last time as Marcus approaches her from behind and jokingly comments, "Another pet I presume?"

"I must take her before the council for evaluation immediately." Elena firmly responds before turning to face him.

"I'm not sure it would be wise to bring a human slave with us to Archadia." Yuri cautions as he approaches the Arch ship, "Your parents will likely disapprove of this act no matter how noble it may be."

Slightly annoyed, Elena sighs and states, "I truly appreciate your concern in the matter, but it's my burden to bear." Talia stands by, awaiting instructions as Elena motions her hand towards the Arch ship and orders, "Take her onboard and fire up the ship."

"As you wish." Yuri responds as he and Marcus glance at each other, slightly concerned by her strange request. Yuri finally boards the Arch ship with Valorie and Vennessa as Marcus looks upon Elena for a moment, expressing his concern with a glaring eye. After shaking his head, he then follows suit and boards the Arch ship with the others as Elena turns to Talia and informs, "Time to go, Natalia."

Hesitant to move, Talia looks onto the city one last time, hoping her friend is somewhere safe, and whispers, "Where are you, Victor?" Turning back, she finally boards the ship with Elena. Moments later, it hovers above the landing platform and swiftly takes off into the lustrous evening sky towards Archadia.

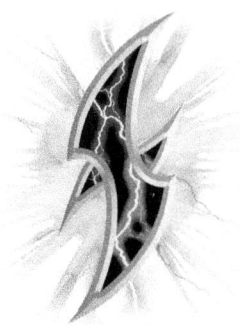

CH: 21
FUTILE RESISTANCE

Enjoying some of the perks Edge City has to offer, Victor is cleaned up and fed as requested by Elena within a fancy penthouse building. Attempting to prevent any damage, Victor slides Talia's letter under a pile of towels as he undresses himself to enter a hot bath. Embarrassed by their attention to detail, Victor laughs as the female servants struggle to bath his entire body. One of the servants tries to take the crystal necklace off of Victor's neck as he instinctively grabs it, holding it close to his chest protectively. The servant exhales impatiently as Victor shakes his head, warning her to back off. As the servants finish up their cleaning, Victor holds the shard before him, examining it closely as he sighs, feeling disheartened without Talia's comforting presence. Shortly after, Hammond and Griffin enter the room and chuckle at Victor's expense as they approach him.

"I see my servants have already taken good care of you." Hammond denotes with a grin. As Victor looks up, he sees the two Senators standing before him then responds with a laugh, "Yes they have, perhaps too good."

"We hope the food is to your liking." Griffin implies.

"The best I've ever had actually." Victor compliments.

The female servants finish with Victor and take their leave, each bowing their heads to Hammond and Griffin in respect. Victor looks on, amused by the attention given to him by the servants and says, "Thanks again for your hospitality, it's much appreciated."

"You're very welcome; it's the least we can do for an acquaintance of Archadia" Hammond respectfully replies, "If ever you should need anything, please don't hesitate to ask, for any friend of Elena is a sure friend of ours."

"Good to know." Victor murmurs as he steps out of the bathing pool to dry himself off with a blue towel given to him by the servants, "Forgive me, but I didn't expect such kindness from people like yourselves." Hammond and Griffin glance at each other and chuckle once again.

"Can't blame you for that honest observation considering the fact that public service is mostly elected by greed these days." Hammond jokes.

"Though unlike most in the Senate, we strive to work towards the good of all people, not just our own." Griffin confidently states. As Victor steps behind an enclosure to dress himself with a set of Titanian attire, the two Senators continue conversing. "Unlike everyone else in office, we haven't been swayed by the Emperor's rule." Griffin resumes.

"Indeed, many have fallen victim to the aristocratic lifestyle, along with a small cadre of former rogues whose loyalty have either been bought or coerced." Hammond divulges, "The current system in which we reluctantly live in was designed with the sole purpose to subdue the masses."

Victor steps out from behind the closure whilst buttoning his new blue dress shirt and says, "From what I've seen the system only works for those who own it and it appears your government manufactures chains, nothing else. Though you both seem to manage well for not being slave owners yourselves. You're lucky to still have your own free will in a place like this."

"That we are." Hammond responds, smiling, "As far as the trade market is concerned, they travel the world in search of mercantile and territorial opportunities, mostly within a negative form of means."

Sitting down in a chair to place the new pair of shoes over his feet, Victor listens as Griffin interjects, saying, "That's putting it lightly. To be perfectly honest, they are the worst quality of capitalists, for they conduct their affairs of commerce on the ancient principle."

"And what principle is that?" Victor cautiously asks.

"Let the buyer beware." Hammond warningly answers. "While we're all for a company's right to profit, it's a real shame it had to be at the sacrifice of quality and humanity. Such is life in these times."

"Too bad we can't go back." Griffin sarcastically comments.

With a scoff, Hammond replies, "At this point, why would anyone want to?"

Victor nods in agreement and sarcastically says with a smirk, "I'm sure glad that you're not like them; otherwise I'd be in deep trouble."

"Quite so." Hammond says with a nod as he steps towards the window overlooking the city from above. "As requested by the Princess herself, you're welcome to stay here as long as you need."

"Hopefully not too long." Victor implies as he looks upward.

Hammond steps away from the window and stops in front of Victor to address him directly and suggestively warns, "I'm sure we can find something for you to do as a form of compensation for both of us, but if you look for trouble, you'll find more than you can possibly handle in this place."

Victor scoffs and mutters, "In my case, trouble always seems to find me."

Griffin signals two servants who enter the chamber and bow their heads, "These men will show you to your private quarters when you're ready." He informs, "They'll see to it that you're fed properly since you look famished."

"I'd say I've had my full for now, but thanks anyway." Victor states.
A pound on the entrance doors grabs Victor's attention as Hammond and Griffin quickly turn to look behind them with confusion.

"Well now, I wonder who that could possibly be at this hour." Hammond says curiously.

"You got me." Griffin remarks while shaking his head.
Concerned for his own safety, Victor quickly places the letter back in his new garb then looks on with fretful eyes as Patrayous and Zepherus break through the doors and enter the room unannounced, followed by a group of Titanian guards who aim their Gauntlets at him. "Perhaps you spoke too soon." Griffin says in annoyance while glancing back at Hammond.

"Can I help you, gentleman?" Hammond carefully asks, "If there is any trouble here then perhaps you can tell me what it is first."
Hammond and Griffin both scowl, annoyed by the forced intrusion as Patrayous approaches the group with Zepherus and stops to address them.

"By order of Lord Tannis himself," Patrayous declares as he points towards Victor, "This slave is to be taken back into custody, immediately!"
In preparation for a fight, Victor rises to his feet as Zepherus growls with his spinal shards glowing. Patrayous expresses a confident smirk as Victor stares back with a scowl also. "What is the meaning of this, General?" Hammond demands, "You have no right to barge in here without probable cause!"
With a poised chuckle, Patrayous glances at Hammond and Griffin, and then snidely informs, "Oh, I have cause alright."
Raising his right hand, Patrayous signals the Titanian guards who approach Victor and place energy shackles on his hands and feet. Victor struggles to break free as the guards grab him aggressively to subdue him.

"Let go of me!" Victor angrily shouts.

"Silence, *human*!" Patrayous furiously shouts back.
Feeling powerless to do anything, Hammond and Griffin stand by and watch as Zepherus steps forward between them and Victor. As Zepherus shoves him back with his spiked tail, Victor runs into Patrayous who stands firmly and says, "Lights out, *slave*!" Victor swings his arms back in an attempt to strike but is suddenly struck by Patrayous, knocking him out cold. Hammond and Griffin shake their heads, angered by the situation as Patrayous signals the guards to take Victor into custody. Zepherus takes this moment to raise his head towards Hammond and Griffin, growling as they stand perfectly still, trying not to provoke him.
As Zepherus turns to follow the Titanian guards, Patrayous stands before them and calmly says, "Excuse my forceful entrance, Senators, but if you'll kindly step back I'll be out of your way. I've got to report back to someone who has a very big interest in him." Sighing out of annoyance, Hammond and Griffin nod in respect as Patrayous nods back then takes his leave with Victor in his grasp, followed by Zepherus who turns back and growls once more.

"The Princess isn't going to be happy about this, Nikolas." Griffin warns with a concerned tone.

"I know, Julius." Hammond responds disappointedly, "But until we fully understand the nature of these extreme circumstances, for now it's probably best that we keep it to ourselves."

"Knowing her temper, I definitely agree." Griffin wittedly murmurs.
Unable to help their new guest, Hammond and Griffin stand by, looking on with concern evident on their faces as Patrayous exits their chamber with his captive held firmly in his grasp.

At the crack of dawn, the sun rises upon Edge City, another day full of mischievous trade and entertainment. Somewhere beneath the city underground inside the human slave pit, Victor slowly wakes up in energy shackles from the foul stench left behind by those who have died. Taking a moment to remember what happened to him the night before, he places his hand over his head in pain, and shouts, "Damn that hurt!"
Edging his way through the energy bars within the slave pit, Lithia suddenly appears and chirps to get Victor's attention from above.

"Lithia?" Victor calls, as he looks up, surprised. Chirping once again in response, Lithia rushes to Victor's aid, landing in his lap as he smiles in relief. "Boy, am I glad to see you!" Victor says excitedly as he wraps Lithia in his arms, causing him to lick his face. "I'm surprised to see you alive!" Lithia responds with a purring noise. "Well, seeing as how you made it this far, I trust Talia made it out too?" He says, looking hopeful.
Panting sadly in response, Lithia lies down as Victor sits back, closes his eyes for a moment and sighs disappointingly, unaware of what has become of his dear friend since his escape from the mines. As Victor holds Lithia in his lap, he gently pets him as Tannis and Patrayous watch from above on a higher crystalline platform with Zepherus standing beside them with his spinal shards glowing. "Who is he?" Tannis sternly inquires.

"The one we were warned about." Patrayous reveals, "I believe this is the slave we've been looking for this whole time."

"So it would seem." Tannis mutters with an annoyed breath, "Does the slave have a name?"

"I overheard Hammond and his servants refer to him as, Victor." Patrayous respectfully answers, "An unusual if not archaic name to be sure."
Victor hears them conversing and looks upwards as does Lithia who tilts his head curiously with his spinal shards glowing. "Oh well, it doesn't really matter because he's mine now." Tannis proclaims whilst gripping his right fist tightly before him. Patrayous expresses a look of guilt while facing him and professes, "Forgive me for not bringing this to your attention earlier, but General Kael is the one who's believed to have aided in his escape."

"I already know that you questioned him back in the mines," Tannis implies with an unsympathetic voice, "Yet you failed to mention it until now. Why is that I wonder?" Slightly embarrassed, Patrayous attempts to clarify, "Guess you could say I was distracted by the thrill of the hunt. Besides, he's no real threat to us now that we've finally captured him in our own territory." Annoyed, Tannis scolds, "You still have a bad habit of ignoring the fine details when in combat, General. Apology accepted for now, but see that it doesn't happen again."

"My Lord?" Patrayous asks, confused by his remark.

Hoping to escape, Victor looks around for a possible exit as Tannis faces Patrayous and denotes, "We both know this isn't the first time Alexandre has interfered with my affairs, don't we?" Patrayous nods sheepishly as Tannis begrudgingly infers, "As I recall you were with him the last time something like that happened."

"Yes, but as a result my allegiance was faithfully sworn to you." Patrayous assures, "Mind you that I haven't considered him a comrade in a very long time because of that particular incident."

"And because of that instance, you are forever indebted to me." Tannis sternly informs, "On that we are agreed?"

"We are, my Lord." Patrayous respectfully replies.

Bringing a grin to his face, Tannis insists, "Water under the bridge as far as I'm concerned. He's most likely returned to Archadia by now, so be sure to keep a closer eye on his activities from hear on out." He finishes.

"Of course." Patrayous replies before motioning towards Victor below, "Should I dispose of this slave once and for all then?"

Contemplating the idea, Tannis answers back, "No! Leave him be."

"You're keeping him alive?" Patrayous asks, concern in his tone.

"Does my General in his superior wisdom object?" Tannis firmly questions as he turns to face him. Patrayous shakes his head as Tannis turns back with a grin and pompously murmurs, "I didn't think so."

Zepherus growls viciously at Lithia as Victor rubs his backside, trying to calm him by saying, "It's alright, Lithia." Standing guard on his shoulder with his spinal shards glowing, Lithia attempts to roar as Zepherus roars back himself.

"That'll be all, General." Tannis calmly says, waving of his hand.

While bowing his head in respect, Patrayous stares Victor down for a moment, and then takes his leave with Zepherus close behind.

Victor looks up frustratingly as Tannis turns, locking eyes with him for the first time. "My apologies for the zealous nature of my security." He proclaims, "Perhaps if you had just turned yourself in to begin with, all this misfortune might have been avoided."

Lithia reacts by chirping as Victor scoffs, saying, "I highly doubt that."

"You've had quite the journey, haven't you?" Tannis indicates as he circles around from above, "I'm still unsure on just how you escaped."

"My instincts, guess I qualify." Victor sarcastically retorts.

Nodding in amusement, Tannis acknowledges, "I'm surprised you even made it through the Everwylde, or past the borderlands in one piece."

Victor's looks back with a smirk and claims, "I had a little help along the way." Lithia complements with a purring noise to signify their friendship.

"So I've heard." Tannis says with a devious grin, "They should've killed you before then." His remark causes Lithia to growl as Victor looks up with determination and asserts, "Believe me, they tried."

"And just how did you make it through Pretoria unharmed?" Tannis inquires in suspicion, "Let me guess, just like the old human tales would suggest; a guardian Angel came swooping in to your rescue?"

"Something like that." Victor firmly replies. Amused by his response, Tannis chuckles as he steps closer from above. "Who are you?" Victor cautiously inquiries, unsure of his true intentions.

As Tannis walks down the steps heading towards the slave pit, he cryptically answers, "Oh, you could say that I'm an ancient soul in a modern body with a futuristic state of mind. Truthfully, I'm nothing more than a journeyman, a partisan of progress if you will. Though some would say I'm a trafficker of information, and power." He finishes as he stops several feet above him.

"You mean people?" Victor infers with a lowered brow.

"Naturally, amongst other things." Tannis claims as he places his hand over his chin, "I simply give them shelter in a cold and dreary world."

"Actually, you give them a painful death." Victor crossly retorts.

"Don't be caged by your own perception." Tannis cautions, "I will tell you something to take with you; people must be broken to remain whole again. Many of them are far sweeter forced than many are willing. In truth put to it, I think not all of them truly object to their current lifestyle."

"If you knew what it's like to live such a horrid life, you would know otherwise." Victor sternly replies, "I myself prefer the hardships of a free man over the comforts of the most well treated slave."

With a rictus grin, Tannis enlightens, "Since you appear to be unaware of whom I am, allow me to introduce myself." Victor rolls his eyes, irritated as he glances at Lithia. "I am Tannis Marquis, Emperor of Titania." Tannis proudly announces as he pulls out a pink crystal shard from his garb and tosses to Victor who instinctively catches it. He then probes, "I assume you know what this is?"

Examining the crystal closely with Lithia still perched on his shoulder, Victor coolly answers, "A painful reminder."

"Crystals such as these are for pleasure, not pain." Tannis remarks.

"You seek to profit from our pain." Victor scorns as he examines the pink crystal once more, "Looks like a typical crystal to me."

"Obviously, much like the one around your neck." Tannis amusingly indicates to his surprise.

Victor places his hand on the crystal necklace, realizing that it's surprisingly still around his neck and sighs in relief. "Like any other bio-organic mineral, it's just a piece of rock that handled stress exceptionally well, but in actuality, it's also a token of fortune and power." Tannis decrees, "You see, crystals such as these are a common currency here on Earth, also referred to as Chaos Crystals since chaos is what they generally finance."

"If crystals are so common, why not share the wealth with everyone on this planet?" Victor suspiciously inquires.

"That would be a short lived corporate venture, for we are not in the habit of giving away that which has not been paid for." Tannis enlightens, "The crystals which yield the most power grow only in remote areas of Pretoria like the colony you escaped from. It is there where they must be painstakingly cultivated and harvested to purify, a complex and expensive process as you can imagine. A single shipment of crystals represents an enormous investment for myself as well as my trusted shareholders, thus the wealth you speak of comes at a price, we can't just give it freely to everyone." After inspecting the crystal shard, Victor throws it against the wall and shouts, "Spare me your hypocrisy! You'd rather see them die than share?"
Tannis chuckles in response, "For the moment anyway; you see your life is but a small part in an ever-growing industry." He spitefully affirms.

"An industry made up of slaves who have no idea how little their lives are to be valued by the likes of you!" Victor despises.

"They're not as oblivious to their purpose in this world as you may think." Tannis explains, "In truth, we map out in detail how they contribute to our society overall. That way we can assess who's valuable and who's expendable, it's just business really."
Victor scoffs and mutters, "An extremely evil business if you ask me."

"Welcome to the real world." Tannis scornfully counters.

"Your world, where my people work like drones and have no idea of what freedom actually is." Victor angrily retorts.

"They have freedom to be themselves." Tannis reassures.

"No they don't!" Victor disputes, "They don't even have the luxury of courts in this world."

"We have our own judicial system full of courts, and you'll be in ours soon enough." Tannis warns with an alienating gaze.

"Why are you doing this?" Victor inquires, becoming impatient.

"Why? Because I can." Tannis pompously states, "It's simple really, you create a political problem, which has become my problem, as of late."

"I haven't done anything!" Victor shouts as he swings his arms back, anger rising within him.
Smirking deviously, Tannis responds, "No, you and your kind never do."

"Elena asked your people to shelter me, not enslave me!" Victor exclaims to the point at hand while gripping his fists tightly.

"Ah yes, that she did, didn't she?" Tannis selfishly clarifies, "But as you can see, she doesn't make the rules around here."

"Then who does?" Victor sarcastically asks, "You?" Tannis chuckles once again, angering Victor even more as he looks upon him with a hardened scowl then snaps, "Why would you blatantly betray the trust of an Angel?"

"Please!" Tannis condescendingly snaps back, "The Angels only exist to keep balance amongst the people of Earth, nothing more."

"Wouldn't this count as disrupting the balance?" Victor firmly questions, raising his arms up from the energy shackles in a defiant manner.

"Perhaps, then again the balance was disrupted when you escaped the mines." Tannis rudely alludes. Staggered that Tannis knows where he came from, Victor looks away furiously. "You look surprised." Tannis mocks, "What do you think that symbol on your arm means, a good luck charm?" Victor glances at the mysterious symbol marked on his arm curiously, then sighs, feeling discouraged by its unknown significance. "It means that you're my property, and I will do what I want with you, when I want with you whether you like or not." Tannis confidently threatens. Regaining his stern composure, Victor raises his fist towards Tannis and exclaims, "You can't rule something that's meant to be free!" He then swings his arm back furiously.

"Freedom is an illusion, a construct created between those with power, and those without." Tannis pompously argues, "Much like love." Victor scowls in response to his pretentious captor who looks back, confident of his status in life. "Unlike you, I answer to no one." Tannis states, "There's a natural order to this world, and it must be protected at all costs."

"There are man made laws and there is spiritual law, I choose the latter myself." Victor proclaims against his arrogant stance, "There's something very wrong with your character if opportunity controls your loyalty to the people of this Earth." He then raises his brow, tilting his head back and asks, "How do you justify balance to the Gods if you've enslaved an entire race of people on this planet?"

"I don't!" Tannis vainly answers, puzzling Victor as Lithia growls. "Consider yourself fortunate that you don't understand the true ugliness of this world, and the next." He mysteriously indicates. Stepping forward to address him closely, Victor grunts and aggressively retorts, "I've seen my fair share of hostility over the years!"

"I'm sure you have, but you'll never know what it's like to be free before your end." Tannis assuredly teases.

"What are you talking about?" Victor snaps as Tannis turns his back towards him from above, "What is it you expect me to do?"

"Stay alive!" Tannis answers while coming to a stop, "That is of course, if you can. You're going to fight in the arena with the other slaves." He reveals as he continues to circle around Victor overhead.

"Oh yeah?" Victor cautiously probes as he turns to follow his captor's movements, "For what purpose?"

Tannis faces Victor once more and proudly informs, "For the sake of entertainment of course! I'm preparing a special event for the world's finest." He says while approaching Victor from ground level just behind the energy bars, "They're going to have fun with you."

Victor steps forward and stops in front of the energy bars to address Tannis face-to-face and warns, "You think you can keep me in here forever?"

"I have no reason to think otherwise at the moment." Tannis taunts.

"I got out once, and I'll surely do it again!" Victor lashes out with a confident grin, "When Elena finds out, we'll see who's smiling then."

"What makes you think she'll even remember someone as tragic and unimportant as you?" Tannis inquires with a curious smirk.

"She'll remember me." Victor firmly contests.

Amused by his fortitude, Tannis laughs, "You still don't get it, do you?" You're my property, and you'll do as I command, or perish with the other slave fodder." He threatens, "I can't have you dead before the big event."

Shaking his head, Victor grins and reiterates, "You're still forgetting about the Angels! Elena will surely intervene, and set me free eventually."

Tannis looks away and sighs impatiently, annoyed by her name being mentioned then murmurs, "Indeed, the Princess has over stepped her bounds many times before. Though idealism and compassion aren't technically incompatible, I can assure you that there's nothing she can do for you now."

"So you think!" Victor scoffs, assured of himself.

Confident of his grip over him, Tannis tilts his head to the side and denotes, "You won't make it past the first round anyway, so why worry about it?"

"What makes you think I'll fight for you?" Victor barks irritably, "I'm not here to entertain you, or any crowd for that matter!"

"You will fight in my arena, or die in the mines!" Tannis states with a firm tone, "And if you choose the latter, I will make sure there is no way you can possibly ever escape again."

Knowing that the dangerous odds are stacked against him, Victor looks away, contemplating his grim chances as he glances at Lithia, who chirps. He then queries, "So if I fight, and I win, what will you do with me then?"

"Tell you what..." Tannis calmly explains as he walks back up the stairs above him, "If you can survive the event in one piece, then you will be freed, no fuss, no questions asked."

"Sounds easy enough, but why don't you put your money where your mouth is?" Victor cautiously implies, "What's the catch?"

"No catch." Tannis clarifies, "As a free man, you'll be able to simply do as you please, but you will not be allowed to leave this kingdom, ever."

Glancing back at Lithia, Victor considers the crude but potential offer and responds, "If all I have to do is survive, then we have an accord."

"Foolish human!" Tannis laughs in response; "No human slave has ever survived in my arena, not since the days of the great Chaos War."

"And what if I do?" Victor questions with a crooked smile.

Grinning facetiously, Tannis replies, "Then we won't be having this conversation afterwards, will we? Keep in mind, there's no place in this big world for little people like you." Victor frowns back as Tannis turns to face the Titanian guard standing by and says, "Captain!"

"Yes sire?" The guard replies as he quickly steps forward.

Pointing towards Victor rudely, Tannis orders, "Take this slave to be prepped for the games, and keep an eye on him this time. That'll be the least of it!"

"Do you want him with the lower-class slaves?" The guard inquires.

"No!" Tannis quickly answers, "Put him with the elite class, and begin his initiation with the others as soon as possible."

The Titanian guard chuckles in response and mutters, "Like all slaves, some for killing, and some for dying, right my Lord?"

"Indeed." Tannis responds with a grin, "Though he'll be lucky enough to make it to the games if they have their way with him."

Staring back, Victor proudly declares, "You underestimate me! I'll fight in your arena, Marquis, and I will win!" Lithia supports with a deep growl.

Turning away from the guard, Tannis warns, "You forget, the Gods favor only the strong, never the weak. Only the mighty ever prevail on this planet."

Victor smiles in response and boldly states, "Well then it's a good thing they've smiled upon me thus far."

"Unfortunately." Tannis mutters in annoyance then continues, "Assuming you behave yourself under my watch, I'll be sure give you your own quarters, and as a show of good faith, I'll increase your rations and send down more fresh water as a noble addition to your stay."

"Why would you go out of your way to do that?" Victor questions out of suspicion for his tyrant imprisoner.

"Because unlike the Gods, I'm not cruel." Tannis affirms, "I'll check in on your progress, and should they extend your life, we shall see just how long they continue to do so. Won't we?" He finishes with total self-assurance.

"Yes, we shall." Victor confidently replies.

Tannis shakes his head in response and leaves with the Titanian guard. Victor looks on as Lithia tries to comfort him by licking his face, "I should've just told Elena what I was to begin with, but if I survive, then I can seek out her help in Archadia." Victor quietly proposes, "A fine plan if I do say so myself." Concerned for his safety, Lithia pants in sorrow. "Don't look at me like that, Lithia." He says directly towards him on his shoulder before looking upwards and sadly closes, "It's what Talia would've wanted."

Lithia purrs in response to honoring Talia as Victor sits back down, caressing his fingers over the mark on his arm and sighs, hoping he made the right decision to fight for his freedom in the deadly arena.

CH: 22
HOMECOMING

In the late morning hours, high above the Earth's surface, the Arch ship arrives in the skies of Archadia. Looking out the window with excitement, Talia sees the crystalline kingdom floating ahead in the distance for the first time and whispers, "Oh my gosh there it is."
Elena senses Talia's enthusiasm and grins, envious of her joy from seeing the home she's so used to being a part of on a daily basis. As Talia extends her arms out in a birdlike manner, she feels like she's floating through heaven as the clouds pass by, glistening with beauty from the sun's rays.

"Is that Archadia?" Talia excitingly inquires as she points out the window from the cargo deck.
Elena approaches her from behind, gently placing her hands on her shoulders and calmly replies, "Indeed it is, the kingdom of Angels."

"It's so beautiful." Talia utters softly as she looks up at Elena who smiles back, trying to share her delight.

"We're preparing to land, Princess!" Valorie respectfully calls out from the ship's cockpit.

"Very good!" Elena acknowledges.
Vennessa turns back as well and calls out, "Shall we inform them that we have a guest onboard?"
Elena turns to face the cockpit and replies, "That won't be necessary, I'll take her before the council myself!" She states as Talia smiles back.

"As you wish!" Valorie responds.

"Prepare for landing, sisters! Vennessa announces.

"And brothers!" Marcus jokingly calls out to get their attention.
Yuri glances at Marcus and they begin to laugh, as Elena shakes her head, amused by her two comical Empyrian bodyguards.

"Princess!" Valorie calls back once again to get Elena's attention, "It seems we have a message from Titania!"
Elena approaches the cockpit and inquires, "What's the word, sisters?"

Valorie quickly turns from her seat to address Elena and reveals, "Senators Hammond and Griffin just informed us that the Senate has agreed to meet regarding the matter in Pretoria."

Pleased and annoyed by this news, Elena murmurs, "Wish they would've come to that conclusion before we headed back home so soon."

"We can head back now if you like." Valorie respectfully suggests.

Looking back towards Talia, Elena points out, "Well, considering we have a young one on board," she then turns back to finish, "I think it's best if we drop her off first."

"Probably not a bad idea, for we don't even need to be there technically." Vennessa suggests.

"I'll head back with Marcus and Yuri myself then." Elena explains, "Since we're not heading into a combat situation, we should be fine."

"Very well, Princess." Vennessa responds with a dutiful nod.

Elena steps away from the cockpit, approaching Marcus and Yuri as they look back and chuckle.

"So, they finally responded huh?" Marcus says sarcastically.

"Yeah, finally." Elena jokes, "Wouldn't you know they'd wait right until we got home to tell us."

Yuri chimes in and puns, "Well what do you expect from a realm full of self important politicians?"

Shaking her head once again in amusement, Elena grins as Marcus and Yuri jokingly pound their fists together. Still looking out the window in excitement, Talia stares into the cloud filled sky with wondrous eyes. Elena approaches Talia from behind and kneels, attempting to prep her for their arrival, she encourages, "Things are going to be much different now that you're here."

Slight hesitation strikes Talia's expression, as she turns and says with a soft voice, "I know, but what if they don't want me?"

"Why do you think that?" Elena asks lightly with a curious grin.

Looking out the window once again, Talia mutters, "Guess I've never quite felt so welcome before in the arms of strangers." She then faces Elena with a fearful look and asks, "What if they send me back?"

"They won't, you have my word as an Archadian Princess." Elena promises as she gently places her hand on Talia's face, "I'll do everything in my power to make sure that never happens. Believe it or not, everyone needs a home, you included."

Feeling a motherly connection, Talia hugs Elena tightly with tears of joy in her eyes, and whispers, "Thank you."

Sensing Talia's sorrow, Elena looks out the window in hopes that her people will accept her young friend without qualm. After a few hours flight, the Arch ship passes through the surrounding energy shield then enters the crystalline kingdom and lands on the port of Archadia.

As the crew departs the ship, Talia looks on from her position and hesitates to move, uncertain about of her new surroundings floating peacefully in the sky above the surface. Amused by her timid demeanor in light of their safe travels, Elena stands by on the landing platform with her hand extended and says, "Welcome to Archadia, Natalia. My home as well as yours."
Talia steps onto the landing platform and takes Elena's hand, departing the ship as she looks around in wonder of the miraculous kingdom before her.

"I wish you could see this for yourself, Victor." Talia whispers to herself, unbeknownst to Elena.
Several Archadians approach the crew as Elena raises her left hand and proudly announces, "Sisters, we have a guest!"
The Archadians begin cheering in a tribal manner, welcoming Talia to their home whilst raising their fists in the air, which causes her to blush in reaction. As Valorie and Vennessa depart the ship they approach Elena, who motions towards the kingdom and says, "Take her to my quarters, and see that she's comfortable."

"Yes, your Highness." Valorie and Vennessa respectfully respond.

"Take this Gauntlet as well," she informs as she carefully hands Victor's Gauntlet over, unseen by Talia, "I will speak with the council upon my return." She finishes with a confident nod.
Valorie and Vennessa nod back as they wrap the Gauntlet up in Angelic cloth and approach Talia, who looks upon Elena with her glossy hazel eyes and asks, "You're leaving already?"
Elena glances at Valorie and Vennessa for a moment, realizing that she forgot to warn Talia ahead of time during their flight then kneels before her and calmly explains, "I'm sorry I didn't' tell you about this sooner, Natalia, but I'm afraid I have to abroad again on a diplomatic mission for the Arch."

"Why so sudden?" Talia softly inquires.

"I'm not at liberty to say at the moment, but hope is very scarce upon the surface, so I need you to pray for the both of us." She simplifies, "Can you do that for me?"
Talia nods in agreement and asks, "Can I come with you?"

"Conventions of this nature in Titania are very complex, therefore I must go alone." Elena clarifies, "I won't be gone long."

"I hope not." Talia mutters.

"From now on your life is here, for this is your birth rite." Elena assures, "My people will take good care of you till I get back."
Longing to stay at Elena's side for her own safety, Talia tears up slightly and softly gestures, "Will I ever see you again?"
Taking this moment to comfort her new young friend, Elena embraces Talia once more and says, "Of course you will, but I'm needed elsewhere at the moment." She reassures, "I'll return as soon as I can."

"You promise?" Talia whispers, looking hopeful with joyous eyes.

"I promise, from one Angel to another." Elena reassures with a comforting nod, "Get some food and rest while you're at it, you'll be safe here." She concludes, "Trust me."

Talia nods back as Valorie and Vennessa escort her into the kingdom. Before enough distance comes between them, Talia turns and waves, with Elena returning the sentiment. As Talia follows the two Archadians, Elena turns to board the Arch ship with Marcus and Yuri at her side.

"Looks like you have two pets now." Yuri jokes, triggering a sarcastic smile from Elena.

"Yeah, except this time you picked the runt of the litter." Marcus interjects with a playful laugh, "She's not like the others we've encountered, that's for sure."

"Do you think the council will accept her?" Yuri carefully inquires.

Elena stops for a moment, turning back to look upon the kingdom once more, "I don't know," she replies as she watches Talia being safely escorted into the kingdom by Valorie and Vennessa, then finishes, "But I have to try."

"For duty's sake?" Yuri humorously implies.

"More importantly, a promise." Elena resolutely answers.

Marcus and Yuri glance at each other with concern over Elena's sudden change in behavior as she steps onto the Arch ship's landing platform and firmly states, "The Senate will be gathering soon, we better get going."

Shrugging their shoulders with slight apprehension, Marcus and Yuri board the ship as well and prepare for take off once again. As the ship fires up, Elena looks out the window from the cockpit, hopeful that Talia will be welcomed with open arms amongst her people. Moments later, the Arch ship hovers above the landing platform then suddenly flies off into the cloud filled sky, heading back towards Titania.

CH: 23
RETURN TO NOWHERE

In preparation for the arena event during midday in Titania, Victor and the other slaves are gathered in the slave pit before Tannis, who enters the chamber, followed closely by Patrayous and Zepherus. Lithia watches closely from above as to not draw unwanted attention to himself or Victor. As Tannis walks by slowly to examine each would-be gladiator, one of the slaves turns to Victor and jokingly inquires, "So, what's your story pal?"

"Guess you could say I somehow ended up where I don't belong." Victor sarcastically implies.

"How does that sort of thing happen?" The slave jokes in response.

"You give up a few things along the way I suppose." Victor states while looking upward towards the sky above, "Chasing your dream for one."

"Was it worth it?" The slave asks as Victor faces him, "Your dream?"

"Honestly, I don't know." Victor murmurs, shrugging his shoulders with a depressing sigh, "I hope so."

"Sounds to me like you've given up already." The slave remarks as he turns his attention towards Tannis, who continues to walk past each fighter with him arms behind his back while Patrayous and Zepherus trail him.

"Perhaps, just a life long obsession." Victor calmly mentions as he reluctantly turns his attention back towards Tannis as well, "But I'll get over it eventually, or maybe I won't. Either way doesn't appeal to my heart."
Tannis finally stops in front of Victor and looks upon him with disdain as he denotes, "I trust the other fighters will whip you into shape in no time."

"I don't need their help for that, I have my own skillset." Victor scoffs in annoyance of his unwanted presence.

"I take it you think of yourself as unique?" Tannis annoyingly probes. Victor scowls back and says, "Why shouldn't I?"

"Well, just because you're unique doesn't mean you're useful by any means." Tannis says confidently.
Confused by his meaning, Victor inquires, "Useful, to what?"

"The society in which we live in, generally speaking." Tannis cunningly replies, "Seems to me that you overrate your gift."

Laughing in response, Victor states, "Underrated is more like it."

"You humans are puny and weak!" Patrayous harshly interjects.

"Perhaps, but our spirit is indomitable." Victor proudly counters.

"And still you are powerless to break free." Tannis cynically mocks.

Victor attempts to strike, but is held back by the energy shackles as Tannis grins, unmoved by his uncontrollable anger.

"You don't like me very much, do you?" Tannis mockingly asks.

Realizing there's no way to escape at this point, Victor attempts to keep his cool and replies, "Is that a requirement in this place?"

Patrayous chuckles in response to Victor's tenacity as Tannis quickly joins in and denotes, "You sure have a problem with authority, for unlike the rest of your pathetic species, you rebel even when the odds are stacked against you."

"Consider it my highest quality, for I will not be coerced by anyone I see as a potential threat to my wellbeing." Victor states with a smirk.

"It appears you don't have a choice." Tannis taunts, "Still, there's a sense of beauty to your pitiful resistance, isn't there?" He then insultingly infers, "At this point you should consider the others here your greatest allies."

"This may come as a shock to you, but I don't play well with others." Victor grumbles with a confident glare.

"Perhaps not, so be careful which friends you do play with." Tannis scornfully advises, "If you do what I want, I'll consider making all your recent criminal transgressions go away, and let you get back to that pathetic excuse of a life in the mines."

"You think I should be like you?" Victor snaps, "Be all selfish with crystals? I bet their deaths are a real comfort every time you look at yourself in the mirror."

With a harsh glare, Tannis stands face to face with him and retorts, "A small price I paid for my people, and my planet."

Changing his expression from that of confidence to annoyance, Victor responds, "Powerful men like you don't have to be so cruel about it."

"Sure I do, so believe me when I say, it comes with the territory." Tannis defensively states with a firm grip.

Scowling upon him, Victor informs, "Don't let it slip your mind that I'm only fighting for my freedom, not you or anyone else for that matter."

"Fool!" Tannis barks, "Keep this up and you'll have no future whatsoever, you'll be exiled from everything and everyone you've ever loved."

"Too late for that." Victor sarcastically grumbles.

"To know one's place in the order of things is truly a blessing." Tannis states, "You think the rules do not apply to you, and that you are in someway special. But the truth of the matter is, you're wrong about both."

"Am I?" Victor proudly contests, "Judging by my ability to make it this far, it would seem the Gods themselves would think otherwise."

"Some pearls of wisdom; what one man calls a god, another calls the laws of physics." Tannis cryptically mentions with a confident smirk.

Amused by Victor's persistence, Patrayous scoffs, "A man in your position should never trust too much in the Gods anyway, for they do not smile upon weak men who cannot accomplish things through strength of will."

"Well then I guess it's a good thing that my real strength comes from my will to survive against such odds." Victor confidently proclaims, "Tell me I can't do something then watch me work twice as hard to prove you wrong."

"You know, for one so feisty you have yet to prove your worth against your own slave kin." Patrayous pompously counters.

Scowling back, Victor replies, "Yeah well, we'll see about that."

"Yes, I'm sure we will." Tannis finishes with great poise as he turns to address the other slaves. Zepherus looks upon Victor and growls as Patrayous places his hand on his head to calm him. "In the coming days, each of you will fight!" Tannis announces as he paces in before the slaves gathered, "Some by their own volition, others, by chance!" Attempting to get a rise out of Victor, Tannis glances back, signifying his current situation and resumes, "Some of you will refuse to fight, while some of you probably can't!"

Victor sighs impatiently from his current predicament as Patrayous looks over whilst crossing his arms and grins.

"Rest assured that either truth will come to light, when you all go toe to toe with a Eudenian and an Enfurian!" Tannis continues, "Ultimately, you're all dead anyway, and will be inevitably forgotten in the days to come!"

Patrayous looks upon the slaves, grinning with confidence of his position over them as Zepherus raises his head and growls.

"At the moment, what matters is what you do with the time you have left on this Earth!" Tannis explains as he steps closer to the slaves, "Sadly though, you don't get to choose how you meet that end, but know one thing!" Tannis turns back towards Victor with a grin and finishes, "I will be there when you fall!" Victor scowls back at Tannis, who chuckles then concludes, "I'll be in touch. Oh, and try to stay out of trouble, if you can."

The slaves glance at Victor as Tannis takes his leave with Patrayous and Zepherus. Sighing once again in despair, Victor looks upon the sky with hope, then closes his eyes and is suddenly attacked by the surrounding slaves, knocking him face first into the ground. "What the hell was that for?" He angrily shouts as he rubs his hand over his cheek.

"Always be prepared!" One of the slaves forewarns.

As Victor rises to his feet in anger, the slaves attack once again, putting him on the defense. Holding back his true power for their sake, Victor tries to subdue them one at a time, and yells, "Come on you guys, I don't want to hurt any of you, but I most certainly will if you force me to!"

"You won't have a choice in the arena!" Another slave yells back as they quickly surround him from all sides. After a short pointless brawl, Victor lowers his guard and is struck down once again. Disappointed by their harsh treatment, Victor scowls as one of them steps forward and condescendingly states, "Better get used to this, *pal*, because there's no going back now!"

Victor rubs his neck to rid of the pain inflicted upon him as the slaves quickly disperse. "Watch your back, and always be prepared." The slave insists.

"For what exactly?" Victor inquires with a hateful scoff.

Inciting a small grin on his face, the slave slowly turns and warningly states, "You'll know soon enough."

As the slaves walk away to their rustic quarters within the pit below the arena floating in the sky above Edge City, Lithia flies to Victor's side and pants.

"I'm alright, Lithia." Victor claims with grave disappointment in his voice as he brushes off the dirt from his arms and shoulders.

Victor stands as Lithia perches himself on his shoulder once again and chirps, causing him to grin slightly. Keeping his focus on the other slaves, he looks upon them in anger, realizing that he must play along for the time being in order to accomplish his ultimate goal of reaching Archadia. Upon entering his primitive quarters near the other slaves who have retired, Victor randomly thinks of a precious moment from his past.

Several years before, Victor has a flashback of a time when enduring Kael's intense training in the mines as a troublesome child.

"Get up!" Kael shouts as he engages Victor, "Move faster!" Victor is knocked to the ground as he looks back in anger. "Again!" Kael firmly shouts with his back turned. "Protect what's inside you by making it stronger, because there is no greater defense than a mind filled with absolute certainty. Though on any given day you can be beaten."

Infuriated, Victor slams the ground with his fists, then pulls himself up and rushes towards Kael in a blind rage, attempting to land a hit.

"You'll have to control your anger better than that if you expect to win!" Kael warns as he counters the angry young boy's every move, "As with everything in life, if you continue to pull your punches you're the one who's going to get hit." Kael is taken aback by Victor's natural strength considering his young age and strongly advises, "Always assume that your opponent is going to be bigger, stronger, and faster than you."

"Why?" Victor shouts angrily as he punches through a pile of rocks, barely missing Kael who dodges.

"So that you can learn to rely on technique, timing, and leverage rather than brute strength alone." Kael sternly replies.

Taking advantage of an opening, Kael suddenly trips Victor, knocking him onto the ground once again which causes him slight pain.

"Choose your battles wisely, because if you attempt to fight them all you'll be too tired to win the really important ones." Kael forcefully adds.

Feeling discouraged and angry, Victor looks up at Kael, who grins.

"Don't be so human, Victor, either give up or grow up!" He sternly encourages, "If you truly want to separate yourself from the rest, know that the coward never starts, the weak never finish, but the warrior never quits. Life comes with pain so don't ever let anyone tell you otherwise. What matters is not trying to dodge every obstacle but using them to forge in you an impenetrable character of crystal from which you'll face every future adversity." He then turns to take his leave and says, "We're done for the day!" Breathing heavily, Victor pounds the ground once again in frustration, unable to channel his aggressive side properly without losing control from within.

Seconds later, another flashback strikes Victor's memory, this one of Sonya tending to his wounds within the kitchen area after the intense training with Kael earlier that day. "Lucky for you, these wounds will heal quickly." Sonya murmurs with a comforting tone, "Like always it seems."

"Then why waste your time?" Victor asks impatiently with a grunt.
Sonya chuckles as she prepares a crystalline cream ointment for his wounds.

"Even still, you're not completely immune to pain." She enlightens, "Regardless, I need to clean these up to prevent any infection while you're out there working." Struggling to sit still, Victor moves around as Sonya places her hands on his shoulders and informs, "Hold still please!"

"I'm fine, mother!" Victor angrily retorts, refusing to be patched up properly and in a timely fashion.
Attempting to calm him down, Sonya pulls Victor close, causing him to match his heavy panting with her calm breathing. "This may come as a surprise to you, Victor, but we all feel pain." Sonya calmly explains, "Regardless of how much we or the outside world try to prevent it."

"I know!" He replies irritably.
Pulling away, Sonya looks upon Victor and states, "After all, no matter what we do, in the end, we're only human."
Victor's breath begins to calm, as he looks into her brown eyes and with a disheartened tone, he mutters, "Unfortunately."
Sonya places her hands on Victor's face, hoping to comfort him as he places his hands over hers. "Don't expect too much of yourself, take time to have fun and when you get tired, learn to rest not quit." She advises whilst continuing to patch his wounds up, which causes him to gasp slightly.

"I'll try." He says softly.

"That's all I ever ask, otherwise what's the point of living?" Sonya says gently with a smile, "Stand for what's right even if you stand alone."
Shortly after, Sonya stands up from the chair and gathers her medical supplies. As she leaves the kitchen area, Victor extends his arm, surprised by the fact that he feels better from her attempt to treat him and smiles in appreciation as he looks upward through the sky light in the ceiling, his deep blue eyes full of curiosity and wonder to world still unknown to him.

CH: 24
FINDERS KEEPERS

Upon the rocky surface within Pretoria under the moonlit sky, Damian and his crew arrive at the crash site near the borderlands to investigate. Moments after departing their ship, Damian raises his arm and announces, "Check the perimeter, and cover any possible escape routes!"

As requested, the Eudenian guards check the perimeter for any possible threats related to the crash. Damian and his team approach the crashed Harvester ship with caution, unsure of the cause behind its destruction. Stepping closer to investigate, he and the other Eudenians are startled as Adrian and his men appear unexpectedly on the other side of the crashed ship with their Gauntlets aimed.

"What are you doing here, Trag?" Adrian inquires in annoyance.

"I might ask you the same thing, Braxel, but I already know the answer." Damian firmly responds with his Gauntlet still aimed.

"If you're hunting, then you've come too late as we have." Adrian informs, sounding disappointed, "Once we realized the level of destruction we knew it could not have been any of us."

"Who do you suppose is responsible then?" Damian queries.

"We haven't got a clue yet." Adrian replies, "We were kind of hoping you would know."

Damian and Adrian stare at each other intensely for a moment as the Eudenians and Enfurians troops stand by, awaiting orders from their would-be Champions. Moments later, Damian raises his fist, signaling his crew to back off as Adrian respectfully follows suit. "Stand down!" Damian orders.

"Sir?" one of the Eudenian guards asks, looking confused.

Continuing his serious gaze upon Adrian, Damian then turns to respond, saying, "Fall back, there's nothing out here."

Adrian turns his head suspiciously, smelling something unfamiliar as he snorts, "Are you sure about that?"

Damian looks at him curiously as their high-tech scouters pick up an enemy signal near by. "There's definitely something out there." Adrian asserts.

"Other than the spontaneous energy readings, how do you know for sure?" Damian cautiously inquires as Adrian glances at him with concern. Adrian faces Damian and claims; "I can smell them, whatever they are." The pair signal their men to power up their Gauntlets whilst surrounding the crashed Harvester ship, preparing to engage any possible threat.

"Stand together everyone!" Damian commands as the Eudenians and Enfurians hold their positions in front of the wreckage, "Create a barrier!"

"Whatever they are, they'd be foolish to attack us all at once." Adrian denotes with an intense breath. As both teams prepare to engage, Raiven and Celeste suddenly appear out of nowhere from both sides.

"What the hell are these things?" Damian sternly inquires.

"At the moment I'm not quite sure, but assuming they're rebels of sorts I've seen firsthand that they can be destroyed." Adrian confirms as he and Damian stand their ground with their troops while Raiven and Celeste float above them and hiss. "Can we play too?" Celeste cynically teases. Adrian scoffs in annoyance, as Damian shouts, "We have no time for games!"

"That's too bad, cause we certainly do!" Celeste cynically jeers.

"So you're what all the fuss is about." Raiven deviously implies.

"The same could be said about you!" Adrian barks in return. The two Darchadians circle around both teams from above, whilst hissing in an attempt to trigger a defensive response.

"What do you suppose these things are?" Damian respectfully asks. Adrian smirks in response, and replies, "No clue, but they look like Angels of some kind, though extremely dark ones."

"Looks like they've taken dark to a whole new level." Damian states, "I've never seen Angels like this before."

"Neither have I." Adrian murmurs with a short-tempered voice. The two mischievous Darchadians float closer overhead, continuing to circle around both teams in unison as a pair of red eyes flashes in observation from a short distance above them.

"Well, if we're going to do something about this little charade, I suggest we get started." Damian firmly proposes.

"Your call, assuming you're willing to take responsibility for anything that goes wrong." Adrian deferentially cautions. Before Raiven and Celeste can cause any real mischief, a sudden screeching howl is heard in the distance, causing both teams to look around cautiously. Raiven and Celeste glance at each other, knowing what it is and grins.

"That's our exit cue!" Raiven announces with a confident smirk, "Your presence in this area is not wanted, you may tell your superiors that we are back to reclaim what's ours!"

As the two Darchadians prepare to take their leave, Celeste turns and hollers back, "See you around, *boys!*"
Screeching with high-pitched howls, they quickly take off into the night sky. Confused by their sudden departure, Damian and Adrian glance at each other and power down their Gauntlets with their troops following suit.

"Not sure what that was all about, but I'm sure glad it's over." Damian says in relief.

"Same here." Adrian retorts, "Not much on pleasantries, are they?" Damian shakes his head in agreement and utters, "Apparently not."
Both teams stand down and continue investigating the crash site together.

"By the way," Adrian confidently informs whilst facing Damian, "I look forward to seeing you in the arena, assuming you'll be there this time."

"Keep dreaming!" Damian scoffs, "We've made some progress here, let's not ruin it with unnecessary posturing if you don't mind." He then turns his attention towards the ship, "I don't believe the crash and the proximity to be a coincidence."

"Nor do I." Adrian agrees as he looks towards the ship as well, "Assuming we were sent here for reasons unknown, we should probably keep tracking while we're here before heading back to our respective kingdoms."

"I greatly concur with that." Damian finishes with a stern nod.
As both teams continue to scout the perimeter around the Harvester ship with caution, the same pair of red eyes glows within the shadows several yards away, as Traganus stands by, observing them curiously from above.

"Impressive," Traganus says intensely, "And so it begins."
After a moment of watching the Eudenians and Enfurians survey the area, Traganus suddenly disappears into the night to avoid confrontation.

Sitting by himself in the slave pit below the arena the next morning, Victor gathers his thoughts as Lithia appears with a food ration in his mouth.

"Lithia, over here boy!" He calls, waving him over in his direction.
Lithia flies towards him and drops the food ration from his talons. After wasting no time to open it, Victor quickly scarfs down the food and affirms, "Don't be shy, Lithia, there's plenty for us both so dig in." Victor places part of the ration on the floor next to him as Lithia begins to happily chow down. Appreciative of not having to break his energy shackles, Victor pets Lithia's head and calmly says, "Thanks for being there for me." Lithia raises his head and chirps in response, "I know she would greatly appreciate it too."
Lithia purrs, acknowledging Talia and continues to eat as Victor turns and sees an old Angel statue with the name, *KLARA* engraved on it.
Taking a moment to savor the food, Victor approaches the statue then bows in honor and humbly prays, "Please watch over Talia and Elena, I trust the will of the Gods is divine, and just."

One of the slaves approaches Victor from behind, causing Lithia to growl slightly in protection of the food ration left for him.

"To whom do you pray?" The slave respectfully asks.

Refocusing his attention behind him, Victor slowly turns to respond, and says, "Who do you think?"

"Perhaps you should pray for the strength to engage then." The slave retorts with a condescending laugh.

"That's never been a problem for me." Victor firmly states as he stands to walk back over to Lithia to finish eating.

"Then why are you holding back?" The slave inquires as Victor stops for a moment, hesitating to answer, "Whether we like it or not, we all must fight to survive." He prudently advises.

Victor glances at the mysterious symbol on his arm, feeling disheartened and retorts, "What's the point of living if it means throwing away your pride, your dignity?" He then turns to face the slave directly and declares, "I'm not afraid to fight, never have been and never will."

"Perhaps you should be." The slave warningly argues, "Fighting for the Emperor is how we maintain our pride. In fact, it's the only way really."

"Why do you fight for him anyway?" Victor queries in annoyance.

Laughing once again, the slave sits down on the ground, points to Victor and says, "So that we don't end up where you are." Unamused by his reference, Victor scowls in response as the slave explains; "The nobles despise us, so if we fight for them they pretty much leave us alone, for the most part anyway."

Victor approaches the slave whilst motioning towards the others listening in and furiously scorns; "You're lying to yourselves, just so you all can live a miserable life and die a miserable death in this place?"

"You've gotta do what you can to survive!" Another slave interjects defensively, "Keep acting like that and you'll surely be killed in no time!"

"Like what?" Victor disputes, "A man who's supposed to roam freely amongst his peers?"

The first slave shakes his head and states, "You know what your problem is? You draw too much attention to yourself."

Looking around the entire slave pit with his arms extended, Victor raises his voice to make sure everyone hears him loud and clear as he angrily shouts, "Have you all given up your pride as well then?"

"Pride doesn't count for much when you're dead!" The second slave retorts with his arms raised as well, "We honor the Gods by fighting in the most prestigious of all battlegrounds, the arena!"

Everyone cheers in response, angering Victor further as Lithia flies onto his shoulder in his defense and growls with his spinal shards glowing.

"You should consider yourself lucky!" The first slave points out.

"Why?" Victor asks impatiently.

"Because, the Emperor gave you the chance to fight and die with dignity before the people of Earth." The slave proudly proclaims.

Looking around the chamber, Victor locks eyes with everyone watching and refutes, "I shouldn't have to, and neither should any of you!" Shaking his head disappointedly, he finishes, "Not like this!"

"Fool!" The other slave ridicules as Victor and Lithia look back with stern faces, "Let's see how that attitude holds up in the arena. Here you will face death itself, and when there's no one left to fight, only then will you be free." He firmly clarifies then finishes, "Your enemies must be slain if you are to live, for it is the way of life, the way we have trained our entire lives for."

Unwilling to accept their point of view, Victor shakes his head once again and exclaims, "I can't do that, and I won't!" Lithia adds to his stance with a growl. The second slave scoffs before taking his leave then turns back to address Victor once more, saying, "If not, then what will you do?"

Angered by his attitude, Victor grunts impatiently as the slave leaves the chamber. He glances at the symbol on his arm once again and sighs in sorrow as Lithia rubs his head against his to cheer him up. As the slaves disperse, Victor sits back down with Lithia to finally finish eating the food ration.

"Why do you do that?" The first slave sensibly inquires as he and another approaches him.

"Do what?" Victor snaps.

"Why push yourself away from those trying to help you?" He questions, trying to make peace with him.

"If you only knew." Victor mutters as he rests his head back to relax, "I've got to find a way out of this prison."

"Your ambition is the only thing that makes it a prison." The second slave humbly informs.

"Without my ambition, I'd be just like everyone else." Victor states.

"Is that a sign of the Gods?" The first slave respectfully asks while pointing at his arm.

"I'm not sure," Victor replies as he gently caresses the symbol with his fingers, "I used to think so."

"Perhaps it signifies freedom then." The slave kindly suggests.

Sighing impatiently, Victor examines the symbol once more and responds, "Maybe, but freedom from what exactly?"

"I guess that's our job in life to figure out, isn't it?" The other slave jokingly implies with a chuckle.

Victor looks upon the two slaves as they all laugh together in response.

"Guess I should stop telling myself that I'm lost because I'm not." He humbly concedes, "I'm simply on a road with no destination; flying with hope that I'll find a place to my liking that I fit in, and I'll stay there forever."

Now bored, Lithia shakes his head and rolls his eyes as Victor looks upward, hoping to one day fulfill his destiny from above as he's always dreamed.

CH: 25
COURT OF DECEPTION

During mid-day in Titania, Elena and her crew arrive back in Edge City to attend the Senate meeting. The Senate chime sounds off, echoing throughout the entire city as hundreds of politicians approach the Senate Hall to conduct a world's summit. Shortly after, the Senators take their seats within the hall to begin the meeting as Tannis enters the chamber, followed by Patrayous and Zepherus. Senator Malik, a thin white male with short dark hair and a mechanical eyepiece takes his seat behind Hammond and Griffin as Elena enters the chamber with Marcus and Yuri, who guard her closely.

"Such a glorious thing, the dance of politics." Malik comments as he leans over from behind. Annoyed, Hammond and Griffin turn to face their competitive politician. "Am I right?" Malik cynically implies.

"Guess that depends on the purpose of the dance," Hammond calmly replies as he and Griffin share a glance, "Wouldn't you agree?"

"Dance outside the lines and you'll know soon enough who your true allies are." Malik snaps as he motions towards the stadium full of politicians.

"Perhaps we should tread carefully near those who might betray us then, for the easily offended are in turn easily manipulated." Griffin jeers as he and Hammond turn back in their seats.

Malik scoffs in response as Hammond and Griffin grin in amusement of his pretentious behavior. Moments later, the Chancellor enters the Senate Hall, escorted by two elite Titanian guards. Entertained by the large attendance, Tannis looks around the Hall and grins. "This meeting will come to order!" The Chancellor announces whilst taking his seat amongst the Supreme Earth Council members. The Senators hush down; ready to hear the issue at hand as Patrayous stands by with Zepherus to guard the proceeding. Marcus and Yuri stand a few feet behind Elena as they look upon the gathered crowd in awe.

"Princess Elena, you have the floor now!" The Chancellor calls.

"Thank you, Chancellor." Elena responds with a respectful nod

As she approaches her podium to speak, she takes a moment to look around the Senate Hall then calmly addresses everyone, "For those of you unaware, a new and mysterious threat has emerged; lurking in the shadows of our great societies." Each Senator glances at each other; unsure of her meaning, "Though their numbers are unknown at this time, it's possible they could soon threaten all the kingdoms of Earth." She decisively informs.

"Though as you said," Tannis smugly intervenes, "Their numbers are unknown, and for all we know they may not even be a threat to us at all." The Senators nod in agreement, pushing Elena to change her diplomatic tactic, by declaring, "Point taken, but if they do become a threat then it will be the duty of my people to handle the matter before it gets much worse." Chuckling softly with Patrayous, Tannis turns back and arrogantly proclaims, "There hasn't been an enemy presence like that in decades. Whoever they are, their numbers are surely too small and weak to threaten us now." Retaining her composure, Elena retorts, "True, there hasn't been an enemy presence for sometime, but just because there isn't a war doesn't mean there's peace either. I would expect everyone to know this by now regardless of..."

"And our forces are stronger than ever before," Tannis interrupts as he steps before the eager crowd, "Surely any enemies lingering about our beloved planet would know better than to challenge us at this point in time."

"Here, here!" Patrayous shouts with a raised fist, which causes the crowd to applaud in response. Elena looks back at Marcus and Yuri, shaking her head in annoyance as they nod back to encourage her. Nodding towards her Empyrian guards, she turns back to face the crowd and calmly informs, "A few days ago, my crew and I conducted a sensor sweep of the Neutral Zone in Pretoria and came across a Harvester ship near the borderlands." She pauses for a moment then finishes, "We took control, and destroyed it."

"What was its point of departure?" Tannis curiously questions.

"We're not sure exactly." Elena answers without hesitation.

"So, the cause of its destruction has been ascertained by the Arch then?" Tannis inquires out of suspicion as he paces before the large crowd.

"Of course." Elena clarifies with a grin, "Collapsed implosion due to the extreme negligence of their own crew."

"Pretoria in general is mainly a foreign Neutral Zone these days." Tannis enlightens, still pacing back and forth, "I'm sure it just strayed off course doing its duty." Stopping with his back turned against the crowd, Tannis faces Elena and continues, "That tends to happen when you have dangerous animals in those areas of the world you know? Unlike us, nature knows nothing of mercy, such are the many dangers of the Everwylde I'm afraid." He finishes with a shared chuckle amongst the mob of Senators. Shaking her head impatiently, Elena argues, "I get your point, but please keep in mind that this wasn't a typical Harvester ship."

"Really?" Tannis carefully probes, "How so?"

"The crew had a malicious intent, and were carrying a lone human slave onboard." Elena discloses as the Senators whisper amongst themselves, giving her an edge over Tannis in the debate as she civilly inquires, "I thought it was forbidden for humans to be brought North through the Neutral Zone after processing, especially by slave Pirates?"

"It is, Princess." The Chancellor respectfully assures, "Any ships traveling that far North from the mines would need clearance to do so, which as we all know has been prohibited for some time now since the peace treaty known as the Harmony Accord between all kingdoms forbids it."

"From my own observation, I've noticed that there's a growing number of people in this world that regard those underground as not only geographically beneath them, but socially and spiritually as well." Elena firmly states, "Last I checked, no wealth is ever truly decreased by giving charity."

"You're overlooking something, *Princess*." Tannis alerts.

"Am I now?" Elena proudly contests with a smirk.

"You ignore the fact that slavery is so interwoven into the very fabric of this great society that to destroy it would be to destroy us as a people." Tannis harshly informs with a confident posture, "Modern slaves aren't necessarily in chains, for they are in debt more than anything else."

"Goes to show how tolerant you are when your views are being challenged." Elena mocks, which causes everyone to argue, "If you only build amenities that certain groups can enjoy then you make no progress at all."
Annoyed by this debate, Malik quickly stands to address everyone and hollers, "What are we talking about here? Who cares about the slaves?" He callously states with his arms extended, "Look at the political polls, we have urgent problems of our own! Only our lives matter anyway, so why not let the lower races fend for themselves?" He finishes after swinging his arm back.

"The fact that humanity has to clarify that any lives matter should be concern enough regarding our way of life, for extremism in defense of others is no such vice." Elena states with a stern expression, "Though technically, all the people of Earth were human once. That is until we let race disconnect us, politics divide us, religion separate us, and wealth classify us."

"Aye, and let us not forget about natural selection through means of evolution." Malik snaps, "Next you'll be telling us these fiends have a soul."
Arguing amongst themselves, the Senators begin to chatter as Hammond and Griffin look around the hall, concerned for their stance on human rights.

"Compose yourself, Malik, for you do not have the floor!" The Chancellor warns as he rises from his chair, "There'll be no suppressing any opinions here today on either side!" With a scoff, Malik sits back down behind Hammond and Griffin. Sitting down also, the Chancellor extends his hand towards Tannis and permits, "My Lord, you may continue please."

"So you destroyed a Harvester ship without investigating its true origin or objective?" Tannis disputes as he approaches Elena's podium.

"We had good reason." She responds with a serious tone.

"Oh, and what reason might that have been?" Tannis cynically infers as he motions towards the crowd with his arms extended, "Perhaps you would be so kind as to share such confidential information with all of us here today, enlighten us if you will."

"Very well…" Elena utters with an impatient groan, grinning with confidence on the matter, then exposes, "We honed in on what appeared to be a Darchadian signal aboard the ship." Surprised by this revelation, the Senators whisper amongst themselves once again with grave concern in their scheming voices. "Is that certainty, or speculation?" Tannis contends.
Staring back at him, Elena proclaims, "Certainty."
Irritated by the idea, Tannis shakes his head along with Patrayous as the Senators continue to argue amongst themselves. "There will be order here!" The Chancellor yells to silence the crowd. Marcus and Yuri glance at each other, slightly amused by the sudden change of mood amongst everyone present. "That will get them talking." Marcus surely derides.

"Yeah, about how they can all avoid doing anything as usual." Yuri jokingly adds with a scoff himself.
Seeing their fellow Senators argue like children, Hammond and Griffin smile with satisfaction of Elena holding her own against Tannis and the Senate. Glancing back at Patrayous who frowns, Tannis paces once again and disregards, "No matter how mysterious they may be, the Darchadians are nothing but a myth at this point. A horror story told only to scare the likes of children. There's no empirical proof of their current existence on this planet."

"You know as well as I do that from what we've found there's much evidence to support it." Elena confidently disputes.

"Theories, that's it." Tannis firmly contests, "In case you forgot, facts in this case matter, though you seem to be unacquainted with them."

"I've forgotten nothing of the sort." Elena confidently retorts, "Just because something has yet to be discovered, doesn't mean it does not exist."

"You'll forgive the Senate if they're all too easy to dismiss this extreme if not bizarre conjecture." Tannis skeptically informs.

"Of course anyone could, but truth is the pill that everyone wants yet can't seem to swallow." She upholds, "You should look at the facts at hand."

"Find some, and we will." Tannis suggests as he approaches her once again and resumes his argument, "To muse and blabber about such things in front of this particular crowd, demonstrates a level of ineptitude that edges faintly on the imbecilic. And I mean that in the most respectful way, Princess." He finishes with a civil nod.

"I seriously doubt that." Elena dismisses before turning her attention back towards the crowd, "My words may not be for the faint of heart, but that doesn't change the fact that I know what I saw. Whether you like it or not, the Darchadians have indeed returned in some form or another."

"Such is a fallacy!" Patrayous forcefully declares, "The factors do not lead to that conclusion, and there's no such evidence to support your claim!"

"He's right, Princess, the case you're making is not only divisive but wrong." Tannis adds, evoking a scowl from Elena, "Trag and Braxel were sent to Sahria recently to investigate the matter first hand, and found nothing more than a small resistance. Human radicals no doubt, for such deviants and defectives are in their own classification." He implies with an assertive grin.

The Senators whisper in agreement with Tannis as Elena sighs impatiently and states, "I may not be able to prove where the signal came from exactly, but regardless, a Harvester ship carrying any human slaves, especially one piloted by Pirates shouldn't be allowed anywhere within the Neutral Zone."

"The mysterious nature of this encounter is enough for grave concern amongst everyone here." The Chancellor humbly adds to her case.

"Exactly!" Elena quickly defends and illuminates, "For a mystery is only a mystery as long as it's uninvestigated." She then looks upon the entire crowd to address them all directly, "Passivity in terms of powerlessness is one of the most dangerous epidemics in our world today. And the only way to counter such spates is to take action against what we know for sure with the evidence we currently have at our disposal."

The Chancellor glances at the others on the Supreme Council and states, "This is a considerable deliberation, and does raise the question of our patrols out there, General!" He finishes with a stern glare towards Patrayous.

Patrayous steps forward to address the Chancellor directly, saying, "If you're suggesting our people need fear a Darchadian threat, then what does your grace offer for a solution?" He questions as he motions towards Elena.

Seeing this as an opportunity for everyone involved, Hammond nods at Griffin then quickly stands to join in on the conversation as Malik shakes his head in annoyance.

"Well isn't it obvious, General?" Hammond interjects, gaining Tannis and Elena's attention as they look upon him with surprised expressions.

Yuri gently jabs his elbow into Marcus and states, "This just got interesting."

"And who says politics is boring?" Marcus jokingly infers.

"Senator Hammond..." The Chancellor calls, rising from his chair once again, "The council has not recognized you to speak at this time!"

"For reasons obvious to all of us present!" Malik cynically hollers.

The Senators all laugh in response as Zepherus raises his head and growls with his spinal shards glowing and retracting.

"My apologies fellow Senators, but it seems the Princess is simply requesting a little help in the matter." Hammond states as he steps away from his seat and approaches the Supreme Council in an unorthodox manner.

Curious to hear Hammond speak, the Chancellor sits back in his chair as Tannis looks on with a scowl and firmly cautions, "This doesn't concern you or your colleague, *Hammond!*"

Hammond approaches Tannis with a confident grin and assertively retorts, "Oh, I think it concerns all of us actually!" Listening closely, Elena watches from her podium as Hammond walks past Tannis and continues to address the entire Senate. "If we are indeed on the brink of a Darchadian uprising, then it seems only fair that our Champions help in resolving the matter personally." Hammond surely proposes.

Angered at Hammond for interfering, Tannis glances back at Patrayous, who shakes his head in displeasure. "Are you suggesting that we send a team to investigate, Senator Hammond?" The Chancellor intriguingly inquires.

"Precisely, if we don't act now, then our way of life might be at stake." Hammond proclaims as he stands before the crowd facing the council, "We wouldn't want a repeat of the great Chaos War now would we?"

Getting louder in their arguments, the Senators quietly discuss the debate as Tannis and Malik glance at each other in annoyance. "If there isn't a threat, then no harm gained." Hammond strongly suggests, "But if there is, then who better than Trag and Braxel to take up the task?"

"And just who would be leading this team, might I ask?" Patrayous irritatingly questions.

Raising his left hand in response, Hammond turns to signify Elena, and willingly pronounces, "Why none other than the Princess herself, with the Senate's permission of course."

Patrayous is angered even further as Tannis looks upon the crowd getting louder with each argument. Marcus and Yuri look around the Hall, observing the hostile atmosphere caused by the Senate as Elena glances at Hammond with surprise and gratitude.

"Order please!" The Chancellor calls out once again, struggling to maintain stability within the crowd, "There will be order here!"

As Hammond approaches Elena to address her directly, he expresses a large smile and murmurs, "You're welcome, milady."

Shaking her head in amusement, Elena replies, "I appreciate your help, Senator, but I can handle myself here as well as any other place."

"I know; it looked like you needed a little help though." Hammond peacefully rationalizes, "Someone has to speak for my people, even if they don't always see eye to eye."

"Good to know there's someone in this corrupt political web that still cares about justice the way I do." Elena lightheartedly infers.

"More than you know." Hammond says as Elena smiles back.

After a few moments of harsh argumentation, the Senate quiets down as the Chancellor converses with his colleagues, preparing to speak once again.

"Princess Elena, though the Senate supports your concern on the issue, they however do not agree that you should be the one leading the team." He respectfully informs.

"Really, and why is that?" She asks apprehensively.

"If the threat is indeed real, then it's only fitting that we allow our own Champions to lead." He sternly clarifies.

"We don't need any interference from your people anyway," Tannis rudely adds as he faces Elena, "The Arch does not dictate policy on Earth."

"However!" The Chancellor interrupts, causing Tannis to glance back angrily, then clarifies once more, "The Senate does support Hammond's suggestion of your involvement."

"What sort of involvement?" Elena cautiously inquires.

The council members nod towards the Chancellor as he turns back and announces, "The Senate has agreed upon you aiding the team through the investigation, but you must allow Trag and Braxel to lead." He explains whilst pointing directly towards Elena.

"What exactly are you requesting of me, Chancellor?" She queries.

Leaning back in his chair, the Chancellor calmly instructs, "To watch over them, and aid in combat if absolutely necessary." Elena looks away, slightly annoyed by the request as he continues, "We can't afford for our Champions to be in harms way. Therefore, you will help to make sure that any and all Darchadians are destroyed on sight."

As Elena nods reluctantly in agreement, Tannis approaches the Chancellor and mentions, "The council mustn't forget about the games coming up."

"Indeed, well put, Marquis." The Chancellor acknowledges with a nod as he addresses the entire Senate, "The investigation will not begin until after the upcoming arena event. Thus, our people mustn't be alarmed by the chance of any possible threat whatsoever."

Shaking her head in disagreement, Elena defends; "Chancellor, I don't think it would be wise to postpone the investigation any further." The council looks upon her with serious doubt as she pleas, "We must proceed quickly if we are to uncover the truth behind this facade."

"The games will proceed without delay!" The Chancellor sternly declares, "We cannot give our people a reason to fear coming, for it is a worldwide tradition." Elena sighs impatiently as the Chancellor motions towards Tannis and says, "Lord Tannis will be hosting the games as usual, and we will not do anything at this time to interfere with his plans."

"Thank you, Chancellor." Tannis says while bowing his head in respect, "I promise it will be most spectacular for everyone involved."

"I'm sure it will be." The Chancellor retorts as he stands up from his chair to address the Senate directly, "We shall reconvene at a later time regarding this dark matter. In the mean time, I suggest everyone remain calm, meeting adjourned!" He finishes with a pound of his crystalline gavel.

The crowd disperses as the Chancellor and his colleagues take their leave from their crystalline podium.

"Looks like we're getting our hands dirty after all." Yuri comments.

"Finally," Marcus says in relief, "I'm tired of hunting slave Pirates."

"You and me both." Yuri jokingly adds as he and Marcus approach Elena to securely escort her out of the Senate Hall.

Feeling she failed to get through to them, Elena rushes out of the Senate Hall as Tannis attempts to follow her. Zepherus growls as Patrayous scratches his head and motions towards the exit. "Come, Zepherus." He calmly orders as they follow Tannis towards the exit.

Hammond stands by Elena's podium overlooking the Senate Hall as Griffin approaches him from behind and says, "Good going, Nikolas, you even had me convinced."

Smiling in response, Hammond turns and says, "Let's hope everyone else was convinced as well."

"Rightfully so." Griffin murmurs as he and Hammond take their leave within the crowd while Malik watches from above, suspicious of his fellow Senators. Shortly after outside the Senate Hall, Tannis approaches Elena to converse, followed closely by Patrayous and Zepherus.

"Forgive me, Princess, for the ill temper of my colleague here." Tannis kindly expresses as Elena turns to face him in irritation, "We are but your humble servants." He finishes while bowing his head in respect.

The stern expression on Elena's face goes unchanged as she stares back and says, "Such flattery will get you nowhere in my eyes." She then waves her hand, signaling Marcus and Yuri to head back to the Arch ship without her. Marcus and Yuri bow their heads then head back to their ship as Elena turns to face them. Patrayous gives a snarky look, trying to play it cool as Elena shakes her head impatiently, unmoved by Tannis' fake gesture.

"My apologies, for I too may have come across a bit rash." Tannis conveys as he extends his arms in a hospitable manner with a slight bow, "You're always welcome to my assistance should you ever need it." Tannis motions towards Patrayous and finishes, "Isn't she, General?"

"The Titanian army is ready at your command, my Lord." Patrayous declares as he steps forward in a prideful manner, "There's no force on this Earth we can't handle. If the Senate decides that it is so, then we'll gladly take over if need be."

Zepherus howls in response to his master's claim, as Elena rolls her eyes and says distrustfully, "Such are the words of a closed mind too accustomed to military privileges."

Patrayous scoffs as Zepherus motions towards her and growls with his spinal shards glowing. Elena scowls back, hinting at her extreme power as she hones in her Arch aura for a split second, which causes him to snarl and back away.

"You know for someone in your high-ranking position, you have such hostility." Elena sternly denotes.

"As if being driven to succeed in life is a character flaw." Tannis condescendingly contests, "It has always been my philosophy that in order to be successful, one must project an image of success at all times."

"If this event is so important that you would delay a time sensitive investigation, then why don't you challenge those combatants in the arena yourself?" She mockingly proposes.

"Not I." Tannis says with a pompous grin while placing his hand delicately on his chest, "For I am merely a spectator, as well as a man of great wealth, and importance."

"With all your divisive rhetoric, you sure have a big mouth for someone so frail." Elena insults.

"You know everybody says that about me," Tannis states with extreme condescension, "But what can I do? I am Emperor after all."

"Incase you haven't figured this out by now, I don't much like you, or your colleague." Elena scorns, attempting to retain some class over him.

"Well, not many do." Tannis replies with a confident grin.

"Your confidence is most overbearing." Elena scoffs, "If I'm ever in such desperate need of help, you're the last person I would ever depend on."

"Don't be so sure, Princess." Tannis belittles, "When the time comes, you may find that you'll need all the help you can possibly get."

"We shall see about that when the time comes, won't we?" Elena counters as she glances at Patrayous with a firm glare.

As Elena quickly turns and walks away in a cold manner, Tannis smirks and conceitedly mutters, "Yes, we shall."

Zepherus growls once again as Tannis and Patrayous glance at each other, amused by her insolent attitude towards them. Moments later, Elena catches up with Marcus and Yuri near the city's port and prepares to board their ship.

"So, what's the plan?" Marcus inquires.

"Guess we'll have to hold off on the hunt till further notice." Elena answers while stopping in front of the ship overlooking the city, "Though hopefully, the delay will be minimal."

Standing on the landing platform, Yuri leans over and informs, "We can't cause tension between the two Champions if they are to lead your team."

"Agreed." Marcus chimes in.

"The signal is enough concern for us at the moment." Yuri adds.

"I must speak with the Arch council, they'll know what to do." Elena notifies as she steps onto the ship's landing platform, "Let us return home so we can strategize our next move."

"Better hope Trag and Braxel are up to the challenge then." Marcus implies as Elena stops for a moment to listen, "What if the threat is more than they can handle, or we even?"

Elena turns, looking back at the city once more and calmly states, "Then just as Tannis said; we'll need all the help we can possibly get."

Confused by her statement, Marcus and Yuri glance at each other as Elena finally boards the ship. They soon follow and fire up it up; moments later the ship takes off from the landing platform, heading back towards Archadia.

CH: 26
EPHEMERAL DREAMS

After days of training beneath the arena, Victor earns the respect of the other slaves and is given the nickname, *ARCHELUS*. As the slaves continue to prepare themselves, Victor stands by with Lithia perched on his shoulder and notices the mistakes made during their training. Victor glances at Lithia who shakes his head while chirping in disapproval of their efforts and decides to step in. Lithia watches from the sidelines as Victor approaches the group and shouts, "Hey!"

Confused by his sudden call, the slaves look upon Victor and shrug their shoulders, saying, "What?"

"You're not doing that right!" Victor informs with a serious face.

The slaves glance at each other, feeling insulted by his remark as the head slave steps forward and says, "Alright, Archelus. If you're so well versed in our combative ways, then why don't you show them how it's done?"

"Sure, why not?" Victor replies with a smirk, "Don't mind if I do."

The head slave steps back from the others, sitting on the ground with a curious grin then states, "I'll just sit back and watch for a change."

Amused by Victor's concern for their training, the head slave decides to sit back and watch him take a crack at it. Trying not to offend them, Victor approaches the slaves and begins to show them some tactics he learned from Kael growing up. The head slave looks on and nods, impressed by his skills as Victor attempts to instruct them in the form of Chaota, which was taught to him by Kael during his youth. As the gladiatorial training commences, Lithia watches for a brief moment then lies down out of boredom to bath by licking himself with his paws. While Victor puts his skills to the test against the other would-be gladiators, he digs deep into his memory and has a sudden flashback of undergoing Kael's intense training as an adult.

Feeling discouraged in the heat of the moment during training, Kael continues to push him to his limits one strike after another.

"Keep it up!" Kael firmly shouts, "Don't stop when you're tired, stop when you're done!" Victor defends against Kael's attacks and surprises him with a few hits, eventually subduing him on the ground.

Thinking he has finally subdued his mentor, Victor smiles, assured of himself and demands, "Yield!"

"You really think you've beaten me?" Kael jestingly mutters.

"I wouldn't be so sure if I hadn't!" Victor retorts with a grin.

Kael responds with a grin and retaliates by pushing Victor back, forcing him to use all of his strength as they lock fists together. Victor comes close to overpowering Kael, but his strength begins to drain as Kael takes the opportunity and knocks him back into a rock wall. Falling to his knees, Victor looks up; breathing heavily as Kael slowly approaches him and advises, "Know your limits. Mastering others is strength, but mastering yourself is true power." Angered, Victor grunts as he takes a moment to catch his breath.

"You're angry, that's good, that is if you know how to channel it properly. But those who anger you, conquer you." Kael enlightens, "Though you must project strength in order to avoid conflict no matter how much you may want to enter one." He then extends his hand out as Victor looks upon him and scowls for a moment. "One of the best lessons you can learn in life is to master how to remain calm when facing adversity." Seconds later after calming himself, Victor finally takes his hand as Kael finishes, "Always remember to use it wisely, and every time you train, train with the motivation and purpose that you will be the hardest person someone ever tries to kill." Victor nods in response to his stern lecturing as Kael pats him on the shoulder and turns to take his leave, saying, "We must all suffer from two different types of pain, the pain of discipline or the pain of regret."

"What's the difference?" Victor humbly questions.

Kael faces him once more and explains, "The difference is that the first weighs ounces while the latter weighs tons, choose wisely. Discipline itself is the bridge between goals and accomplishment, but should ever that bridge burn then one must learn to fly." As Kael walks away, Victor crouches and slams his fists back into the wall behind him, feeling disappointed by his failure to overpower his mentor.

While continuing to train with the other slaves, Victor also thinks back to a time when Talia tends to his wounds by routine in their small rustic home after his intense training with Kael. Sitting in the chair next to the table in the kitchen area, Victor plays the role of patient just like before when Sonya was still alive. "It's a good thing you heal quickly." Talia lightly says in relief as she attempts to treat his wounds.

"Yeah, I suppose that is a good thing in a place like this." Victor sarcastically retorts with his head tilted back.

Talia grabs the last few bandages and attempts to wrap them around Victor's arm and into a sling, "If Master Kael doesn't let up soon, I'm going to run out of places to patch you up." She cautions, causing Victor to laugh in response. As Talia finishes patching his wounds, she gladly says, "There, all done!"

Victor lets out a calming sigh; appreciative of her helpful nature as Talia gathers what medical supplies they have left to put them away for future use in her handy supply pack. "Thanks, Talia." He inspires, "You're a life saver."

Talia places her hand on his shoulder, shaking her head in amusement and with a warming smile then says, "You're welcome."

Smiling back, Victor stands up from the chair to wear off the soreness then looks on, grateful for her hospitality as she exits the kitchen area and places the medical supplies back where they came from.

Finished with his reminiscent thoughts, Victor and the other slaves continue their intense training as a team of gladiators for the upcoming arena event in the days to come.

Returning from Titania of an early evening, Elena and her crew arrive back in Archadia as the ship lands on the port. As soon as Elena departs the ship with Marcus and Yuri in tow, Valorie and Vennessa approach them.

"What's this, a welcoming party?" Marcus jokes.

"Well, we did survive yet another political farce in Titania." Yuri sarcastically replies.

"Good call, bro." Marcus responds as he and Yuri pound theirs fists together, showcasing their comedic bond.

Elena shakes her head and grins in response to their usual wisecracks as Valorie gracefully lands before them with Vennessa and informs, "Your presence has been requested by the council your Highness."

"They're becoming impatient." Vennessa adds as a warning.

"Very well then, let's get this over with." Elena sighs with a slightly concerned attitude as she swiftly waves her hand over her shoulder to signal Marcus and Yuri, "Don't worry about me guys, I've got this!"

As Elena prepares to take off with Valorie and Vennessa, Yuri looks over and shouts, "Good luck!"

"And try not to stir up too much trouble while you're at it!" Marcus jokingly chimes in.

Facing them with a poised smile, Elena assures, "I'll try not to."

"We'll be around if you need us." Yuri informs.

Elena nods back then activates her wings and takes her leave with Valorie and Vennessa into the kingdom to confront the Arch council as requested.

Inside the throne chamber of the Arch Temple, Elena confronts her parents Rosalyn and Josephus alongside the Arch council members who are still alive and present.

"If the people of Earth are willing to let their Champions aid you in the investigation, then so be it." Josephus firmly states.

"We find it strange that they've chosen to delay, but it's their way and we shall honor their decision regardless." Rosalyn chimes in as Elena nods unwillingly in agreement.

"Now that you're here, we can finally ask." Josephus says while signaling two Archadians standing by the side entrance to open the doors.

"To what are you implying exactly?" Elena cautiously inquires.

The Arch council waves for Talia to enter the chamber while Elena looks upon her and smiles with confidence as she smiles back.

"Why have you brought a human girl to our kingdom?" Rosalyn questions as Talia stands before the Arch council, feeling awkward.

"I don't think she's human, not entirely anyway." Elena proclaims.

"Introduce your protégé." Rosalyn respectfully demands.

"It is an honor to present this young girl to the Arch." Elena proudly announces as Talia stands in front of her, "I've seen first hand that she has greatness within her, a grand destiny so to speak."

"Perhaps that is so, but we must be certain of her loyalty." Rosalyn suspiciously comments.

Elena glances at Talia and assures, "You have my word."

With a slight chuckle, Josephus retorts, "We are the Arch, and as such we require much more than words, even from you."

"I understand that, but there's more to her than what she seems." Elena informs as Talia smiles, looking hopeful. "She has a powerful Arch aura, I can sense it."

"Indeed she does, but whatever she truly is, her aura is somehow familiar in a dark sense." Rosalyn reveals, "One thing's for certain, it's neither Eudenian or Enfurian."

"I've gathered that as well." Elena surely denotes as she glances at Talia, who looks back with concern.

"Is it possible that she's been mistaken for a human in captivity this whole time?" Josephus queries.

"I don't know honestly," Elena replies, "It would appear that way."

"Then what exactly makes you think she is even worthy of the Arch in the first place?" Josephus contests wit a stern voice.

Elena looks upon Talia once again, attempting to comfort her worry and states, "I believe that with our help, she could become a powerful ally."

Rosalyn and Josephus glance at Talia briefly, curious of her true origin.

"You presume to think that she will become an Angel like you then?" Rosalyn suspiciously probes.

"I do." Elena answers with an assertive nod.

"Why?" Josephus says eagerly.

"It's what I believe," Elena firmly retorts as she looks upon the Arch council directly, "Finding her was the Gods' will no doubt, I'm sure of it."

"But you have virtually nothing on her." Josephus points out, "No real background, no history. As a Princess of this kingdom, you should know everything about her before expecting us to add her into our collective."

Keeping a stern gaze, Rosalyn adds, "The last we checked there are certain procedures that must be followed, I believe it's called vetting."

With a sigh, Elena defends, "I'm fully aware, and I know what I'm doing."

"Knowledge is power and yet you know nothing substantial about her." Rosalyn sternly disputes.

"A person is a person no matter how small." Elena strongly contests, "Besides, how much do you have to know when people are in need? I don't think there's a gray area when it comes to helping others. And while we obviously don't know the full extent of her power just yet, what matters most is that she needs our help."

"You do realize there are more important matters at hand?" Rosalyn firmly points out as she motions towards the edge of the crystalline podium. Everyone slowly turns their attention towards Victor's Gauntlet, which is floating above a small crystalline platform.

Shaking her head in annoyance of the Gauntlet being in their grasp without her approval, Elena declares, "If the council will not grant my wish, then I respectfully request to train her myself."

Talia looks up with surprise as Elena waves her over and places her hands on her shoulders from behind, signifying her stance on the young girl's behalf.

"Alright, Elena, it's apparent that your will to safeguard her well-being is undeniably righteous." Josephus recognizes as Elena nods in respect, "But the girl must first pass a test if she is to ever become one of us."

"What sort of test?" Elena probes as she holds Talia close.

"As your Archling apprentice, we require that she be by your side at all times." Josephus informs.

Concerned for Talia's safety, Elena carefully inquires, "For what purpose would that possibly serve?"

"A great one, for the girl must prove her loyalty to you before she can be granted sisterhood into the Arch." Rosalyn reveals, "Defend her in times of trouble and she'll be safe for a day or two, but teach her to defend herself when the time comes and she'll be safe for a lifetime."

Elena runs her hand through Talia's hair in a calming fashion, and states, "Don't you think it's unsafe to bring her along if I'm hunting Darchadians?"

Josephus stands from his chair, leans with his hands over the crystalline podium and exclaims, "It is the will of the Gods!"

Annoyed by her father's stern attitude, Elena frowns as Rosalyn steps in and humbly diffuses, "We will seriously consider you proposal, Elena."

"Thank you." Elena calmly responds as Talia smiles with excitement.

"If she proves her loyalty by the time this investigation is over, then she'll be allowed to face the Arch trials, assuming she can." Rosalyn finishes.

Pleased by this invitation, Elena replies, "Understood." She then bows her head in respect and takes her leave with Talia by her side.

The Arch council glances at Rosalyn and Josephus who look on, concerned over the mysterious situation. Feeling somewhat discouraged, Talia follows Elena outside the Arch Temple, confused by the Arch council's decision. "What will happen to me now?" Talia cautiously asks as she stops a few yards outside the temple's entrance.

Sensing her discomfort, Elena faces Talia and kneels, "The council has requested that you stay by my side for now." She explains, "So I want you to stay close and learn from me as we venture out into the unknown together."

"I will try, but I'm not sure I understand any of this." Talia mutters with extreme doubt in her voice.

Placing her hands on Talia's arms, Elena encourages, "Believe me, with sufficient time and training, you soon will." Talia looks up in curiosity as Elena stands back up and professes, "The council may not see it, but I sense there is great power in you."

"Really?" Talia anxiously inquires, "What sort of power?"

"Guess we'll find out soon enough." Elena comforts with her hand extended, "Come along, Natalia." Talia takes Elena's hand and walks beside her down the Temple stairs, but before they can reach the bottom, Valorie and Vennessa approach them whilst floating from above.

"Your Highness, we should probably make our way back to Titania if we are to make good time." Valorie informs.

"What's the rush?" Elena says with a grin, "We just got here."

Vennessa floats closer to address Elena directly and says, "It's time for the games, unless you've forgotten already?"

Elena places her hand over her head and murmurs, "Not that such a thing truly matters, but thank you for reminding me, sisters."

"That's what we do." Valorie puns.

Smiling, Elena inquires, "I assume our things have been packed already?"

"Yes," Vennessa answers, "Just waiting on you."

Disappointed in having to leave so soon, Elena nods and respectfully states, "We'll be right there."

Valorie and Vennessa nod back in esteem then take off towards their ship.

"Change of plans, Natalia." Elena reluctantly warns.

"Where are we going now?" Talia asks in curiosity.

Sighing in response to her concern, Elena says, "For now it's probably best that you don't know, but don't worry you'll be safe in my hands, I promise."

Elena presses the pink Gods' symbol bearing over her chest plate, which causes her wings to emerge from her spinal armor. Talia looks on with surprise as Elena wraps her arms around her and suddenly takes off.

As they fly through the air towards their ship, Talia looks upon the beautiful kingdom from above and gasps at the sight while spreading her arms, pretending to fly. "Oh, wow!" She happily expresses, "It's so far."

"It's the world dear; did you expect it to be small?" Elena teases.

"No, just smaller in general." Talia mutters as Elena smiles in reaction to her excitement. Moments later they approach the Arch ship on the landing platform. Marcus and Yuri fire up the ship as Elena lands gracefully behind them with Talia in her arms. "Was that fun or what?" She jokes.

"Yeah!" Talia replies joyously, "Can we do that again?"
Her excitement causes Elena to laugh as she places her hand on Talia's head and states, "Sure thing, as soon as we get back."
Talia smiles then looks back at the kingdom once more, yearning to stay, as Elena places her hand on her back and ushers her onboard the ship.

"Everybody ready to say goodbye to Archadia once again?" Marcus satirically announces from the Arch ship's cockpit.

"Ready!" Talia happily shouts as she and Elena share a laugh.

"We should arrive just in time for the games." Yuri announces.

"Let's make this trip as short as possible!" Elena calls back, "I'm not looking to stay in Titania any longer than I have to."
Talia looks upon her, worrisome of running into Tannis again. Elena smiles to comfort her new companion, which causes Talia to smile back, assured that she'll be unharmed by her side. Valorie and Vennessa take their seats behind Marcus and Yuri as the Arch ship hovers above the landing platform then quickly takes off towards Titania. Talia looks out the window once again and sighs, placing her hand on the crystalline glass as she looks towards the crystalline kingdom quickly fading into the cloudy distance.

Finished with their gladiatorial training, Victor along with the other slaves receives a new mark on his arm, signifying "*ELITE.*"

Deep within the Enfurian palace inside Lucian's throne room during a hot day summer day, Adrian is given his ceremonial invitation to the arena event from Lord Tannis himself. He gratefully accepts the honor and prepares to board his ship as Lucian looks on with pride.

Attempting to push himself even further, Victor continues his intense training, becoming stronger and more confident with each day in preparation for the arena event.

Deep within the Eudenian palace inside Raina's throne room on a cool summer night, Damian is given his ceremonial invitation to the arena event from Lord Tannis himself. He reluctantly accepts the honor and prepares to board his ship as Raina looks on with pride.

CH: 27
TENDER MEMORIES

After many long days of intense preparation, Victor along with the other slaves is finally ready to fight. As night falls onto the floating arena in Titania, Lithia lies next to Victor whilst humming Sonya's melody. Remembering the letter Talia wrote to him earlier, Victor pulls it out then unfolds it as he examines it closely for a moment and sighs sorrowfully.

"What's that you've got there?" One of the slaves inquires.
Confused for a second, Victor then realizes that he's referring to the letter in his hands, and replies, "Oh this?" He says while holding it up, "Perhaps nothing to others, but it's the only proof I have that I ever meant anything to anyone in this world."

"Must mean more to you than that if you've been able to hold onto it for so long." The slave respectfully denotes.

"You could say that." Victor calmly mutters.

"You know, you're an unexpectedly sentimental guy for someone in your position." The slave concedes with a chuckle.

"Yeah well, everyone has their weaknesses I suppose." Victor retorts as he glances at the letter once more.
Sighing once again in disappointment, he then folds the letter up and places it back in his garb as Lithia purrs peacefully in his lap.

"It seems the Gods favor you, Archelus." The slave mentions.

"Why do you say that?" Victor asks with a curious grin.

"That creature hasn't left your side since you got here." The slave points out while motioning towards Lithia, "It's rare for a creature of Earth to bond with a human these days."
Victor sighs peacefully in response, "He's not really mine, though I do enjoy his company." He explains while petting Lithia from head to tail, "I'm not so lonely with him around."

Raising his head, Lithia happily chirps in response, which brings a smile to Victor's face. Lithia makes a loud purring noise, acknowledging that he enjoys being with Victor as well.

"Might as well enjoy an evening of peace and tranquility, for it may very well be our last." The slave reluctantly informs.

"I don't feel the same as you about that, but I'll take your advice and enjoy it anyway." Victor mutters.

Turning to fall asleep on the cold floor, the slave advises, "Either way, better get some rest for tomorrow, you're going to need it."

After petting Lithia for a minute, Victor looks up into the night sky for a moment, then pulls out the crystal shard necklace from under his tunic and carefully caresses it in wonder.

As Victor caresses the crystal shard, he thinks back to a precious time a few years before when playing with Talia in the mines as they both pretend to fly around with custom self-made wings attached to their backs. Victor rushes past Talia and leaps onto a crystalline pillar, causing her to stop for a moment in her tracks, realizing she's lost sight of him all of a sudden.

"Victor!" She frantically calls, "Where are you?"

"Close your eyes." Victor whispers from the shadows as she listens closely trying to track him in a playful manner, "Sense my presence, follow my energy, and you'll find me."

Talia closes her eyes and walks around with her hands extended to feel around. She stops for a moment, thinking she knows where he is, then quickly turns and opens her eyes. Unable to see him, Talia suddenly loses her balance then falls backwards as Victor quickly jumps down from the crystalline pillar and catches her just in time right off the edge.

"If you can't find me, know that I'll always find you, even in the dark." He inspires confidently.

Talia sighs in relief as Victor stares back with a confident grin.

"You'll always be there to catch me, won't you?" She happily states with total belief in him.

"Am I a guardian?" Victor asks with a curious expression.

"You're more than that," Talia proudly assures, "You're my most trusted and loyal friend."

"That will do." Victor calmly retorts with a crooked smile as he gently pulls her up over the edge to safety.

"You're always looking out for me, aren't you?" Talia whispers as she embraces him for a moment in appreciation.

"Just doing the best I can really." He says softly.

"I just don't know what I'd do without you," Talia professes, "You're the best person I've ever known, and the best friend I've ever had."

Taking in her comfort, Victor feels reassured of his guardian like position while looking out into the bioluminescent cavern and happily sighs.

"This may not be any of my business, but you're bound to find a significant other someday." Talia encouragingly expresses, "Perhaps one day, someone will fly into your life and make you see why it never worked out with anyone else."

"I'm not taken, not technically anyway." Victor professes, "I'm simply on reserve for the one who truly deserves my heart. I haven't had opportunities like everyone else, and that's partly because no one wants me."

"Sounds to me like you need someone who's tough enough to know what she wants yet soft enough to know how to get it." Talia kindly denotes. Nodding in agreement, Victor admits, "Perhaps, I'm really tough on the outside myself, but deep down I'm probably no less sensitive than others."

"I figured as much, but never allow yourself to be so desperate that you end up settling for far less than what you deserve." Talia informs, "You should only trust someone who can see these three things in you."

"Three things, huh?" Victor sarcastically responds, "Is that all?"

"Pretty much." Talia says with a confident voice.

"I see, and just what are these three things you speak of?" Victor jokingly questions, curious to hear the answer.

With a precious smirk, Talia states, "The sorrow behind your smile, the love behind your anger, and the reason behind your silence."

Victor ponders the thought for a moment, realizing her words to be more profound than he expected, "I suppose those are but a few things worth remembering in life." He jokingly comments.

"You bet they are!" Talia excitingly retorts, "Everything comes to us in the right moment, so be patient and grateful when it finally comes."

"That goes for you as well." Victor jokingly inspires, "Although I feel that one day I'll wake up and there won't be any more time to do the things I've always wanted."

With a curious expression, Talia asks, "What makes you say that?"

"Because contrary to popular belief, dreams do in fact have time limits." Victor reluctantly answers.

"Then I suggest we better get a move on then." Talia happily teases. Feeling even more appreciative of his female companion, Victor embraces Talia once again, their indestructible bond growing that much more.

After a moment of reminiscing what few good memories he has, Victor rests his back on the cold floor of the slave pit and reaches his hand upward towards the starry sky as if to make a wish. Lithia climbs onto his torso and lies on his stomach, purring softly as he quickly falls asleep.

"Good night, Lithia." Victor says calmly as he scratches his furry friend's head once more before turning in for the night himself.

Lithia responds with a loud purring noise as Victor takes a deep breath and falls asleep soon after as well.

CH: 28
SURVIVAL OF THE FITTEST

High above the kingdom of Titania over the cusp of Edge City, thousands of Earth's most influential citizens gather inside the floating arena to attend the event hosted by Tannis. As everyone takes their seats within the gladiatorial venue, Tannis greets select individuals one at a time with Patrayous and Zepherus standing by. Hammond and Griffin take their seats overlooking the arena in front of Malik, who leans over and infers with a condescending tone, "Well, I must say I'm surprised to see you both here enjoying the pleasures of the vulgar crowd."

Annoyed by his presence, Griffin sighs, "As a matter of fact we detest violence," he then faces Malik, "And we're even less fond of people like you."

Malik chuckles and waves over a few female human sex slaves, who surround him in a sensual manner. "Incase you haven't noticed, I'm above your petty remarks, as well as most of the people here." He pompously declares.

Shaking his head in disgust, Hammond strongly remarks, "Well unlike you, Senator, we don't pretend to be above the people, for we'd much rather be one with the people. And incase you've forgotten, we are an enlightened order of people who believe that a tournament of this nature is preferable to total warfare as a means of solving differences, not exploiting them. "

"Speaking of which," Griffin sarcastically chimes in, "What are we to wager on this outcome your grace, humans again?"

"Why not?" Malik retorts, "Other than crystals, there's nothing else more valuable to those of us in need of indentured servants. Besides, they're an expendable commodity." Hammond and Griffin turn back in their seats, repulsed by his behavior as Malik toys with the human sex slaves and states, "Relax, Senators, a little pleasure will do you good, and take years off your lives, as well as your faces. Thanks to the Emperor himself, whatever your pleasure, I can authorize. And with whatever company you so choose."

"Another time perhaps, for a speaker of truth has no such friends, or company for that matter." Hammond grumbles impatiently.

"Your self-restraint and foolishness astounds if not puzzles me sometimes." Malik scoffs, "You both continue to deny yourselves every benefit your noble positions have to offer." Hammond and Griffin glance at each other, rolling their eyes as Malik infers, "Quite suspicious if you ask me."

"Not really, in fact we prefer to share such benefits with all the people of Earth." Hammond cleverly disputes as he turns to face Malik once more, "Surround yourself with wise people and you'll become wiser; surround yourself with fools then you're the biggest one of them all."

Malik scoffs once again and proclaims, "Consider me a fool then because in this world, to get along you've got to go along. What's most bewildering to her majesty, Princess Saltora, is this arrogant belief towards independence from the Senate. After all, if you cannot rule the Senate, then you simply cannot rule whatsoever."

"As anyone in the courts will tell you, *Malik*, it's the independence from our Senate that keeps us free from the tyranny of others, the Emperor included." Griffin begrudgingly argues.

"For now, anyway." Malik deviously mutters.

Annoyed by his gluttonous nature, Hammond and Griffin turn their attention back towards the arena. Raina and Lucian arrive shortly after and approach Tannis to be properly greeted as he bows his head and says, "Greetings my King and Queen; I trust your distant travels were most luxurious."

"It's been a long time since we've attended an event of this magnitude." Lucian responds as he looks upon the heavy crowd.

"You've prepared quite the spectacle this year, Marquis." Raina compliments, "We've been looking forward to it for some time now."

"Indeed I have your majesty." Tannis responds with a grin.

"This event celebrates the acknowledgement of our new Champions' place in this world." Lucian mentions, "Our people expect a good show, be sure they get it." He finishes while firmly pointing at Tannis.

"As your humble host, I assure you both that you won't be disappointed." Tannis says while bowing his head once again, "I shouldn't like to impede your view so I've reserved the best seats in the house." He then extends his arm to show them to their seats, saying, "This way please."

Raina and Lucian approach their seats and raise their hands in honorable fashion to acknowledge the crowd as everyone solutes them out of respect before sitting down. Damian and Adrian arrive moments later, both eagerly waiting to be seated. "Greetings, Champions." Tannis welcomes while motioning behind him, "I trust you'll find your seats most accommodating."

Confident of his Enfurian prowess, Adrian looks upon Damian and mocks, "Beware, Trag, for I will be victorious this time, whatever the cost."

"It's just a game, Braxel, a friendly little competition." Damian scoffs, "You simply work up a sweat to entertain the crowd, you have a few laughs, and possibly make new allies while you're at it."

Adrian scoffs in response and says, "If winning is not important even to the likes of you, then why bother keeping score in the first place?"

After staring each other down intensely for a brief moment, Damian and Adrian continue towards their seats in front of Raina and Lucian as Elena and her crew arrive seconds later to be greeted as well.

"Princess, how nice of you join the festivities on this fine day." Tannis remarks with a grin as he turns to face Elena.

"Spare me, if we could dispense with the formalities please." Elena comebacks firmly, "I could care less about your festivities this day or any other, Marquis." She clarifies as Tannis casually nods, "I'm here strictly as an emissary on behalf of my people, and nothing else."

"Very well." Tannis says with a chuckle, "You may be considered a personal guest, but that doesn't change the fact that this event helps to keep the peace between us, as well as our Eastern and Western neighbors."

Elena turns her head and scoffs as Tannis extends his hand behind him and finishes, "This way please."

As Elena and her crew walk past him towards their seats, Tannis looks on in annoyance, seeing Talia by her side in semi-formal Archadian attire as she glances back with a scowl. After the crowd fully gathers in anticipation, the Titanian guards open a large crystalline doorway and signal the human slaves to enter the arena.

Victor sees the Titanian guards standing by the entrance to the slave pit, then glances at Lithia standing next to him and says, "Well boy, I guess that's us!"

Lithia growls in anticipation with his spinal shards glowing as the head slave stands up and shouts, "Everyone, it's time!" The slaves nod back determinedly as they all rise, "Prepare yourselves!" He cautions as they walk past him and get in line before the entrance into the arena. Victor shakes his head and stands up as well then turns to address the other slaves.

"Well guys, we didn't come all this way for nothing!" He comments.

"You know, sometimes your spirit annoys us!" One of the slaves mocks while getting in line.

As the other slaves approach the entrance, Victor glances at Lithia who perches himself on his shoulder and mutters, "Well, Lithia, no time like the present." Lithia replies by growling in anticipation, ready for some action.

Victor follows the other slaves and walks past the Titanian guards who hand them each a primitive Gauntlet to fight with. The slaves are brought into the arena as they look upon the large crowd for the first time in awe.

"By the Gods!" One of the slaves murmurs, "Look at that crowd!"

Victor looks upon the arena in shock, overwhelmed by its sheer size as Lithia chirps to comfort his sudden anxiety.

"Many worthy foes have gathered here today!" The head slave informs everyone as they follow him into the center of the arena, "Whatever the Emperor has in store for us isn't going to be pleasant!"

"We'll be lucky enough to make it through this alive!" A second slave states discouragingly.

"Yeah, I suppose none of us will be able to prove anything to the world today!" another one chimes in disappointedly.

As Victor walks with his group, he calmly mutters, "Something tells me I'll get my chance soon enough."

The other slaves chuckle at Victor's expense, incapable of understanding what he's truly capable of, "What chance could any of us have by the time the Champions arrive?" One of the slaves questions.

"I hear Trag and Braxel are honorary guests for this particular event," another slave mentions in a fearful tone.

"Good reason not to hold back on anyone then." Victor remarks.

"A lot of good it will do in the end anyway!" Another slave grumbles.

Without feeling distracted, Victor states, "You'd be surprised how much one can do when they try!"

"Well put, Archelus!" The head slave chimes in with his head turned.

As Victor and the others reach the middle podium in the center of the arena, each slave is lined up and put on display to be showcased and rated for all the zealous slave traders to bid on. High above the main audience, Traganus, unbeknownst to anyone else, enters a secret booth overlooking the arena with Raiven and Celeste as his escort, completely unnoticed by the crowd. Traganus looks upon the arena while focusing his attention specifically on Victor as Raiven and Celeste stand watch, disguised as Titanian guards. Victor steps forward in line in the arena's center as a Titanian guard motions towards him and demands, "Come on, you're next!"

Stepping onto the higher platform to be showcased and rated, Victor looks upon the bloodthirsty crowd, feeling determined to survive the event. Elena looks on from the arena balcony in curiosity as the Titanian guards order Victor to face each direction for the slave traders to examine.

"Yuri, who is that human down there?" Elena inquires while pointing directly towards the arena floor.

"The one they just introduced?" Yuri replies.

Elena nods in response as Talia looks over, unsure as to whom they are referring to. "I'm not sure," Yuri explains, "But from what I just overheard, they refer to him as Archelus, whatever that means."

"He who falls and rises, I believe." Elena curiously deduces.

Knowing who it is after taking a closer view; Marcus looks on with surprise and says enthusiastically, "I don't believe it!"

"What?" Elena quickly probes with concern.

"Take a look!" Marcus excitedly informs while pointing back towards the arena floor.

Talia turns her attention as well then stands to take a closer look and to her surprise, she notices her friend Victor among the other slaves being rated.

"Oh my gosh!" She says in panic and excitement, "It's Victor!"

Startled by Talia's sudden reaction, Elena quickly turns to her with a curious expression and asks, "Wait a minute, you know him?"

"Of course I do!" Talia expresses, thrilled to see Victor once again, "We grew up together, I've known him my whole life!"

Surprised by this revelation, Elena turns her attention back towards the arena floor, "I see now," she mutters in disappointment, "You must've been the one he was referring to earlier."

"You've met him before?" Talia questions.

Feeling slightly embarrassed, Elena patiently explains, "Yes, but I never expected to see him again like this."

"How did he end up in a place like this anyway?" Talia asks with a deeply concerned tone.

"I don't know," Elena clarifies, "I was promised he would be taken care of, not made to fight in the arena of all things."

As Victor steps down from the portable stage after being rated lowly, Talia looks on from the balcony and sighs, feeling disheartened.

"It seems you've been deceived, Elena." Marcus respectfully points out; "Though Hammond and Griffin failed to warn you ahead of time."

Elena sits back in her chair and places her hand over her head in frustration over this turn of events, saying, "How could I be so foolish to think for one second that Tannis of all people would ever keep his word?"

"No disrespect, milady, but he is the Emperor after all." Yuri informs, "Point being he has full ownership to any and all slaves here."

"What can you do?" Talia asks with glossy eyes.

After a moment of thinking the situation over, Elena determinedly claims, "I'm going to bargain for his life, that's what I'm going to do!"

Talia looks upon Elena, surprised by her strong commitment to him as she places her hands on her shoulder.

"He would never part with one of his own without a price, even from you, Elena." Yuri carefully warns.

Looking back at the arena floor, Elena sternly professes, "You guys may not understand, but I have to help him."

"We understand, but there's nothing that can be done about it right now." Marcus humbly informs.

With hope gleaming from her eyes once again, Talia looks on as Elena places her arm around her shoulders to comfort her.

After mingling with specific attendees, Tannis finally takes his seat and gives the signal to the Titanian Announcer, who stands from his seat and approaches the crystalline podium above the arena floor. With the crowd sitting in both silence and anticipation, Victor looks up just as the Announcer extends his arms to address everyone.

"Each of you are witness to the greatest tradition to ever grace this planet!" He entertainingly exclaims as Elena rolls her eyes in repulsion, "Today, we honor our Eudenian and Enfurian Champions by giving you the best show you will ever see on Earth!" Damian and Adrian glance at each other and nod in respect as the Announcer resumes, "The decisions of this event are final, and binding!" Victor glances back at the other slaves, as Lithia remains perched on his shoulder and growls, "In the name of any and all survivors, we hope that you honor us with your willingness to fight for your lives! By the Gods' blessing, may the peace between us, and our people be forever kept!"

Tannis looks upon Raina and Lucian as they nod back in respect. The crowd continues to remain silent as the Announcer takes a moment to look upon the arena then gives the signal and enthusiastically shouts, "Let us begin!"

Victor and the other slaves look around with grave concern as they hear several loud roars. Lithia growls back as Victor places his hand on his wing and gently says, "Easy boy, we don't know what's out there."

Several Titanian guards open three large crystalline doorways as several animalistic denizens enter the arena.

"We do now!" The head slave chimes in as Victor sighs impatiently.

The denizens approach the small group of slaves and begin their attack as Victor helps them to fight. Cheering with bloodthirsty excitement, the crowd watches the slaves battle the creatures to the death. Proving too fast for the creatures, Victor quickly maneuvers around them and takes out a couple of denizens single-handedly as Lithia chirps to help keep watch over his surroundings. Elena turns away in disgust as she tries to cover Talia's eyes, and says, "Come on, Natalia, you don't need to see this."

"Yes I do!" Talia responds as she pushes Elena's hand out of the way, fearful for her dear friend.

Slightly bothered by her persistence, Elena sits back as her and Talia continue to watch Victor and the others fight for their lives. With the last denizen attempting to kill the slaves, Victor leaps in-between them and leads the creature elsewhere as it begins to chase after him. Outsmarting the denizen with ease, Victor runs as fast as he can towards one of the walls then leaps onto it and back over the creature as it charges head first into the barrier. The impact kills the creature instantly as Victor lands gracefully on its back and raises his fist, signifying his ability to overcome the first round, which causes the crowd to cheer and applaud.

After a short but gruesome battle, the first round ends with a majority of the slaves taken out. Several Titanian guards force the remaining denizens back into their chambers behind the arena walls while riding their crystal Scorpion warrior drones, as Lithia flies back onto Victor's shoulder. Victor stands surprisingly unscathed as the surviving slaves quickly approach him with their wounded as if to seek his protection.

"So, that was our fight?" Victor sneers with total confidence, "What we've been training for this whole time?"

"You forget, that was just round one!" The head slave points out while helping another slave walk back to their rustic quarters underground.

"Still not near as bad as I thought it would be though." Victor claims.

"Just wait, it gets much worse, trust me." The head slave warns as he helps the others back into the slave pit.

Victor looks at Lithia, shrugging his shoulders then follows the other slaves back into the depths of the arena. As the slaves make it back into their quarters behind the arena walls, the Announcer stands up once again to the crystalline podium, extending his arms out in a theatrical fashion.

"That concludes round one!" He proudly announces as the crowd cheers in response to the carnage of the battle, "Enjoy the rest of the festivities during the break! Combat will commence for round two shortly after our intermission!" He finishes as the crowd disperses towards the lobbies to enjoy various hospitable refreshments and convenience facilities.

Standing within the secret booth above the arena floor, Traganus keeps a close eye on Victor and chuckles softly, sensing his mysterious Angelic power as Raiven and Celeste glance at each other curiously through their Titanian helmets. As the Titanian guards begin to shut the large crystalline doors behind them, Victor looks back for a moment, sighing with determination and helps the remaining fighters back into the slave pit to prepare for the next round. The doors suddenly close with a big bang, as the chamber greatly darkens by being cut off from the external light.

Outside the arena in the main lobby during the break, Tannis and Malik approach a few Pretorian trade servants, followed closely behind by Patrayous and Zepherus. The trade servants bow their heads in respect as they hold out a crystal shard file. "We trust that you will be most pleased with the current productivity of our new weaponry that's sure to accommodate your extremely high standards, Emperor." One of them respectfully surmises.

"If you're trying to get on my good graces after your last attempt, I'd say it's working." Tannis compliments as he briefly examines the holographic shard file and grins, "Well gentlemen, you've certainly peaked my interest." The servants glance each other, pleased to hear his positive reaction as they grin deviously in response. "The quality is admirable to say the least." Tannis explicates as he hands the shard file over to Patrayous who instinctively takes it to inspect himself, "Very exceptional work if I do say so myself."

After viewing the information carefully, Patrayous hands the shard file over to Malik who examines it closely as well before handing it back to the servants.

"No doubt you have applied your technology from other industries to the refinement of this new product line under our banner." Malik denotes.

"We have no other industry, but one would be foolish not to take advantage, for it's mutually beneficial." One of the servants responds with a devious chuckle as the others quickly join in.

Looking confident, Tannis states, "Like my father used to say, if what you offer is unappreciated then you simply reduce supply to increase demand."

Another servant places his hands together and says, "Speaking of demand; thanks to your wonderful contribution of human slaves, our Harvester shipments now run faster than ever through the trade routes in Pretoria."

"I should hope so for all that I've done for you over the years." Tannis smugly claims before motioning towards Malik, "But you have Senator Malik here to thank for your current ease of transportation."

The servants bow their heads in respect towards Malik as he nods in return.

"Since we are fortunately ahead of schedule, the traffickers await your approval on the next set of cargo drops." The servant informs.

"Excellent." Tannis quickly retorts with great pleasure over this news, "Luckily they won't have to wait too long given their obedient slave labor."

"Shall we prepare an order for you as soon as possible then, Sire?" another servant carefully inquires.

Tannis glances at Malik, who nods in approval of their new production line then places his hand over his chin and says, "You may tell your fellow colleagues that I am very interested in their high-quality merchandise."

"How would you like them allocated?" One of the servants inquires.

"Evenly across their shared accounts if it's not too much trouble." Tannis respectfully requests.

"Why, none whatsoever." The servant humbly replies.

"With Trishard now leading the industry, we are on a tight schedule, so see to it that things move quickly if you will." Malik also requests.

"Of course, as you command my Lords." The trade servants reply while bowing their heads in respect.

Infuriated by Victor's current predicament, Elena finds Tannis during the break and quickly approaches him as Zepherus turns his head and growls. Patrayous taps Tannis' shoulder to get his attention as he turns and smiles.

"Tannis!" She calls impatiently, "I need to speak with you at once!"

Tannis grudgingly faces Elena and extends his hand out beside him, saying, "Later I suppose, first I have some unfinished business to attend to, a deal that needs closing." Elena sighs impatiently, annoying him as he clarifies, "Can't you see that I'm in the middle of something important, Princess?"

"Unfortunately for you, my business takes precedence over theirs." Elena sternly proclaims.

Tannis signals Malik to escort the trade servants back to their ship before the intermission's end then faces Elena once again as they take their leave.

"I take it you aren't impressed with my livestock this year?" Tannis rudely infers, already knowing what she has to say.

"If you're referring to this so-called victimization through violent entertainment, then absolutely not!" Elena states with an aggravated voice, "I was promised that Victor would be protected under Hammond's care!"

To their amusement, Tannis and Patrayous glance at each other and deviously grin as Zepherus groans.

"Ah yes, the *human.*" Tannis cynically responds, "Well as you know, politicians shouldn't make promises they don't intend to keep."

"Release him at once!" Elena angrily demands, "I didn't bring him here to become another of your bargaining chips!"

"You have no control over my property!" Tannis firmly argues, looking extremely annoyed, "Just like all the other slaves on this planet, he's already mine, as payment for my allegiance to our people, and the Gods."

"We'd been looking for him since he escaped the mines in Pretoria," Patrayous selfishly chimes in, "And now he's back where he belongs."

"Perhaps you should swap places with a human for once and see how well you like it!" Elena impatiently retorts.

Zepherus growls in response with his spinal shards glowing as Patrayous approaches Elena, staring her down intensely. Raising his right hand, Tannis signals Patrayous to stand down as he scoffs in annoyance.

"For a moment, I thought I heard a threat implied, but that would be foolishness." Tannis condescends as he looks back at Patrayous and grins.

"Something to be carefully avoided for sure." Patrayous warns.

Elena steps forward to address Tannis face-to-face and threatens, "If you don't release him then I'll have to take matters into my own hands. And don't you dare think for one second that I won't!"

Patrayous chuckles as Tannis looks away and scoffs, "How noble, yet utterly pointless." He arrogantly states, "You're overestimating your authority as it is." Tannis explains, angering her even further, "And as far as the Arch is concerned, you have none."

"I don't know about that," Elena contests, "As with everything else on this planet the rules of the game must be balanced accordingly."

"Come now, Princess, we both know there's nothing you can do for him at this point." Patrayous intervenes as he steps behind her, "Wouldn't want to disrupt your precious balance now, would we?"

Shaking her head in frustration, Elena scornfully retorts, "Your followers hold you in such high esteem, Marquis, yet they fail to realize their true purpose as they fight and die for your own selfish amusement." Tannis nods in agreement as she continues, "And worst of all, my people as well as your own participate in this archaic absurdity!"

"Indeed they do." Tannis comments with a condescending smirk, "It's an interesting thing for sure."

"Not interesting enough." She bitterly insults, "You're nothing but a facilitator for violence and corruption!"

"Low if not harsh words from someone of your elevated status, Princess." Tannis snaps while attempting to keep his cool, "In actuality, I facilitate that which brings profit to those in need of such services, and like any other business person will tell you, you can't truly exist without one."

"I'm done arguing!" Elena aggressively asserts as she swings her arm back impatiently, "How much?"

Patrayous chuckles once again as Tannis looks back and grins.

"Astute as always." He denotes as he walks past her, looking upward towards the top of the arena, "Don't tell me you forgot your purse at home."

"Not at all, let's do business." Elena confidently affirms.

"You obviously have the means to make such an expensive purchase, but I'm afraid you'll have to wait till after the games." Tannis finishes with his attention still focused upon the arena and his back turned.

Elena steps forward irately and stops beside him, saying, "You know as well as I do that he may not even survive the games!"

"That's not my problem now, is it?" Tannis remarks as he turns back to face her, "The people have come to see a spectacle. They cheer for blood, and they shall have it." He explains, "I can't disappoint them, and therefore his freedom will have to wait."

"If he even survives!" Patrayous says with a laugh as he and Tannis begin to rudely walk away.

"Damn you, Tannis!" Elena hollers, "You won't get away with this cruel business of yours for long!"

Tannis turns once again to face Elena and proclaims, "On the contrary, Princess, my business has just begun!" Elena scowls back as he approaches her and assures, "Once the games are over, you have my word as Emperor that the human is yours, assuming you want him in one piece that is."

Taking a brief moment to regain her cool composure, Elena calmly inquires, "Name your terms."

"Alright then," Tannis politely wagers, "Should he die, I will give you the souls of all those who fall in combat today. A very reasonable offer, wouldn't you agree?"

With a disgusted grin, Elena shakes her head and scoffs, "I get it. You stand to lose nothing either way the challenge goes. You are so cavalier with the lives of others, it sickens me to the core."

"Not just others," Tannis selfishly defends, "I'd offer my life as well, but you see I'm more important than everyone else in this world, and plan on living a very long time."

"If you think that's the way to win favor amongst your peers, you're doing a horrible job so far." Elena insults.

"Kingdoms are won with armies, but empires are made by alliances." Tannis confidently disputes, "As for the slaves you seem to care so much about, I've taken nothing from them they've not been long without."

"You couldn't possibly understand the proper value of life, even if it struck you in the face." She ridicules as she looks away impatiently.

"Oh, we understand that it is a highly pleasant thing, but after all unimportant to the likes of humans." Patrayous arrogantly counters.

"Will you not take my odds?" Tannis inquires with a devious smirk.

"I wager you, but if he survives or even possibly wins, you will acquit him of all you think he owes you." Elena informs.

"And if he loses?" Tannis curiously counters, "Even I would lose money if I were to wager that one."

"Then I will gladly pay his debt in full." Elena assures, "My factor will call upon your grace's factor. If he's permitted a fair fight in the arena and wins, what will you make then?"

"I suppose that would recoup his loss from his last wager," Tannis carefully ponders to her displeasure.

"He must have a fair fight if he is to have one at all." Elena stresses.

"Of course, I would have it no other way." Tannis respectfully teases, "I'll see to it that he gets one."

"Good, as long as we understand each other then." Elena adds.

"All this just to save the life of one human?" Tannis questions. Turning her back against her stubborn naysayers, Elena sighs impatiently with her head turned, and claims, "I don't care what it takes, just see to it that he's properly taken care of."

"That will depend greatly on whether or not he endures," Tannis teases once more, "I highly doubt it."
Facing them again, Elena angrily retorts, "Slaves against gladiators is never a fair contest. This is not how it's supposed to be!"
Feeling impatient, Tannis comebacks, "If you're serious about purchasing his freedom, then validate your claim now while you still can." Elena nods in agreement as he continues, "But if he dies, your payment is still mine in full."
Once again angered by his pompous attitude, Elena looks away and exhales aggressively, "I will hold you to our bargain, *Marquis*."

"And I you, *Saltora*." Tannis rudely concludes; "Senator Malik as well as my General here are more than capable of handling things when I'm away, so if you have any further concerns you can bring them to their attention."
Elena shares a scowl with Patrayous as Tannis finishes; "Now if you'll kindly excuse me I have others to attend to, for I have very important clients in need of service more specifically local dignitaries."
Tannis walks away followed by Patrayous and Zepherus as Elena looks back, shaking her head and frustratingly warns, "I will expect the terms to be met!"

"You have my word as Emperor of Earth, *Princess!*" Tannis starkly replies with a quick turn of his head. Realizing she hasn't the luxury of time nor clearance to free Victor herself, Elena heads towards the holding cells within the slave pit, hoping to speak with him before the second round starts.

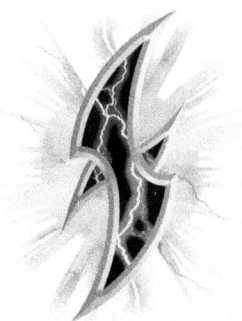

CH: 29
SIZE DOESN'T MATTER

Rushing through the crowd during the tail end of the intermission, Elena enters the holding cells beneath the arena in an attempt to meet Victor. She sees a pile of greyish cloth lying near the entrance and quickly wraps it over herself like a cloak to hide her Angelic appearance from the Titanian guards. Flying above the crowd in the arena, Lithia suddenly dives in and grabs a piece of food from what appears to be a large turkey leg with his talons from an unsuspecting audience member just as they sit down in their seat. Sitting alone in his cell, Victor looks around, confident of his ability to take on the next round as Lithia flies through the window with more food.

"Thanks, Lithia." Victor regards as Lithia stands next to him and happily shares some of the food.

Elena enters the holding cells and approaches the guards, as one of them turns and rudely informs, "If you're here to collect, you'll have to wait!"

"I'm here to speak with the one they call, Archelus." She says delicately, "I've purchased him from Lord Tannis himself just moments ago and would like to inspect my claim personally if you don't mind."

The Titanian guards glance at each other, unsure of her intentions then motions towards the slave pit behind them.

"He's in cell number ninety-seven!" One of them says as he raises his hand with his thumb pointed behind him, "You better hurry though, cause the second round is about to begin." The second guard warns.

"I'll be sure to inform the Emperor of your good work." Elena politely responds as she nods in respect then cautiously walks down the corridor, disgusted by the site of humans being treated like animals as the wounded scream in agony from the first round. After a minute of searching, she locates Victor's cell in the slave pit and quickly approaches him as he prepares for the next round, this time with a full stomach.

"Would one be so kind as to point me in the direction of the one they call, Archelus?" Elena says gently as to not give herself away just yet.

Victor quickly looks up with surprise; not realizing who it is and sternly replies, "I am he."

Lithia sniffs around with his spinal shards glowing, sensing Elena to be an Archadian then chirps. Elena's eyes widen at the sight of Lithia, surprised to see a young Seraph like him in a place other than her home back in Archadia.

"I see you have a furry companion." She curiously denotes, "To my knowledge creatures like that are native only to Archadia."

Victor glances back at Lithia for a moment and replies, "I don't know where he came from exactly, but he's been a big help ever since I first met him."

"I should hope so," Elena softly implies as Lithia brushes up against her decorated hands, "I hear you're the best warrior in the arena."

Bringing a slight grin to his face, Victor humbly informs, "Perhaps, but you see I wouldn't be here if not for my comrades."

"Perhaps." Elena says in return as she steps closer to the energy bars surrounding the cell, "Do you plan on winning today, Victor?"

Confused by her unexpected query, Victor slowly looks upon her and asks, "How do you know my name?"

"How could I forget the name of the one who once saved my life?" She softly replies with a slight chuckle.

"And you are?" Victor inquires, feeling somewhat annoyed.

Elena finally sheds the grey cloak to reveal herself to him as Victor looks on in shock and quickly bows in her honor, saying, "Forgive me, Princess, I didn't realize it was you."

Amused by his chivalry, she looks upon Victor compassionately and says, "No, I'm the one who is sorry, for bringing you here." She then asks, "It's been pretty rough down here, hasn't it?"

"Actually, I've seen rougher." Victor lightheartedly retorts.

"How are they treating you here?" Elena caringly inquires.

"No worse than the people back home really." He calmly answers.

"That's good to know." Elena says with a calming sigh. Relieved by her response, Victor grins as she looks back to watch for any oncoming guards, then says, "I can't be seen consorting with a slave so I must be quick."

"This is no place for you, milady, you shouldn't even be here." Victor cautions, as he stands to converse face-to-face.

"Nor should you, and yet, here we are." Elena responds before turning back. Sensing his concern for her, Elena looks upon Victor and says gently, "Are you sending me away?" Victor pauses momentarily and shakes his head, "I thought not." She confirms with a grin.

Feeling embarrassed, Victor looks down for a second then locks eyes with her and says, "I wondered if I would ever see your face again."

"I'm sorry for what Tannis has done, I truly am." She apologizes.

"Don't blame yourself for his selfish actions, Elena." He calmly reassures, "It's not your fault."

"But it is!" She shamefully admits, "I had no idea he would treat you like this after we parted. I should've seen to this before, but I didn't know."

"Hey, don't worry yourself about it." Victor says smiling, "Believe it or not I'm actually quite familiar with this setting, though I've seen better days." He says while grunting from the pain all over his body, realizing that he took more physical punishment than previously thought during the fight.

Hesitant, Elena tilts her head and gently asks, "You're the one who escaped the Pretorian mines, aren't you?" Looking into her eyes compassionately, Victor nods sheepishly in response, "You have no idea what has happened since we met." She says with excitement in her voice.

"It was a difficult decision at first, but I felt it was worth the risk." Victor professes, "I'm sorry if our encounter has caused you any grief."

"None whatsoever," Elena assures, shaking her head with a smile, "Your escape has brought hope to those who have none, and those of us who wish to see an end to slavery once and for all on this planet."

Chuckling slightly, Victor replies, "They weren't exactly singing praises when I left, but I'm hoping to change all that someday."

"Really, how so?" Elena curiously probes.

Victor looks around the slave pit for a moment then moves in closer and undertones, "I've got plans to make others see me and my people a little differently." Elena grins as he extends his arms, signifying his current position and states, "Though as you can see, my plans seem to have gone astray."

"Not this time," Elena happily encourages whilst shaking her head, "Unfortunately for you, I am bound by the rules of the Arch code which order me not to interfere with other cultures. If I were to tell them any of this, even me being here I would technically be violating that prime directive." She carefully explains, "And if I had it my way you would already be free, but you must survive the arena before I can do anything to help you."

Curious to her kind offer, Victor stares back intensely and carefully asks, "How can you possibly help me now?"

"You forget, I'm an Archadian Princess, I have my own power." Elena answers with a smile of confidence, "Besides, you'd be dead already if the Gods hadn't spared you."

Feeling disheartened, Victor grips the energy bars and states, "Yet I am still at their mercy, and the only power I have is at the expense of the Emperor."

"Then use that power to fight against him." She inspires, bringing a grin to his face, "Stay focused, and concentrate on what you must do."

"I'm trying." Victor retorts with disappointment in his voice.

"I truly hope so." She graciously inspires, "You have no idea just how important you've become to us, and to me."

Elena gently places her hands on top of Victor's through the energy bars to comfort him as he looks down for a moment and says softly, "I didn't realize I was still important to anyone, especially you of all people."

"Well you are, more than you may ever know." Elena proudly comforts with a smile.

Whilst looking deeply into her light blue eyes in sorrow, Victor sadly concedes, "I don't know how much fight I have left in me."

"I guess we'll see in a moment's time, won't we?" Elena implies. Victor nods in agreement as she attempts to sense his inner thoughts then gently asks, "Would you fight for an Angel?"

Taking a moment to think, Victor shakes his head and softly replies, "No." Surprised by his answer, Elena's expression hardens slightly as Victor clarifies, "But I'll willingly fight for you."

Flattered by his kind response, Elena looks upon him, smiling once again and says, "Then fight for me you shall, and win your freedom."

Now beaming with determination, Victor nods with a crooked smile as she queries, "What's your current condition, if you don't mind me asking?"

"At the moment, could be better, could be worse." He replies as he looks over his entire body, covered in bruises. Elena suddenly kisses Victor's forehead, which causes a glint of light to appear when her lips gently touch his skin. "What was that for, if you don't mind me asking?" He says jokingly.

"For your protection, you may need it." She humbly informs.

"I've been in continuous practice, I'll win by the odds." Victor says with a confident smirk as he and Elena grip their hands through the energy bars and look into each other's blue eyes compassionately for a brief moment.

"Times up, *lady*!" a Titanian guard rudely shouts, "Have to get the slaves ready for the second round!"

Disappointed by their ruined moment, Elena turns back to address the guard and exclaims, "I understand!" She then turns back to face Victor as she gracefully waves her hand in front of his face.

"I promise this isn't goodbye," she says warmly in a confident manner, "May the Gods watch over you."

"And you, milady." Victor respectfully adds.

Elena smiles once more then covers herself with the grey cloak and walks away from Victor's cell towards the exit. As Elena passes by the Titanian guards, she holds her out hand and places money in their armored pouches then utters, "For your trouble."

"Sure, whatever lady." One of the guards rudely dismisses as he and the other beside him drools over the amount she gave them.

Feeling more confident than ever before, Victor sits back in his cell as Lithia chirps in anticipation of the next round.

Shortly after the intermission, the crowd returns to their seats to continue watching the arena event. The remaining fighters are lined up once again in the center to face the second round as the crowd yells in excitement. Victor looks around, feeling more determined than ever to take on the next challenge as Lithia sits perched upon his shoulder and growls in anticipation. Elena rejoins her crew and sits back in her seat, as Talia looks upon her, worrisome for Victor. "Where have you been this whole time?" Yuri inquires.

"Just visiting a friend." Elena calmly replies.

"You missed out on the half-time show," Marcus informs, "It was surprisingly better than last year's."

Elena looks over and replies, "Sorry guys, I had more important business to take care of during the break."

"Don't tell us, you went to see Victor, didn't you?" Marcus teases.

Elena's expression gives her intentions away, concerning Talia even more as she looks upon her and questions, "Is he alright?"

"He's fine, Natalia, don't worry." Elena assures while placing her hand around Talia to comfort her.

"I hope he makes it through." Talia mutters, fearing the worst.

Sensing her deep concern for him, Elena rubs her hand over Talia's head and says, "So do I, Natalia." She then turns her attention back towards the arena floor and finishes, "So do I."

Taking the opportunity to gamble, Marcus jabs at Yuri's side and jokingly bets, "Ten to one odds he makes it to round three."

"And the odds of him being the last human standing?" Yuri jokingly replies as he jabs back.

"Deal!" Marcus settles as he and Yuri pound their fists together once again to honor their bet.

Annoyed by their constant dealing, Elena shakes her head whilst trying not to be distracted. Talia sits close to Elena, concerned for Victor's safety as she counts the minutes passing by in her head.

"Your precious human has done well!" Tannis arrogantly teases from his seat, getting Elena's attention as she turns to face him, "Shall we see if he can survive round two?" He mocks with a confident expression.

Staring back at him intensely, Elena grins with confidence herself and states, "You underestimate the power of will, don't be surprised if he's victorious."

"No human will survive today's event, you can be sure of that!" Tannis claims with a crude laugh; completely assured of himself.

Elena scowls for a second then turns back to focus on the arena floor with Talia. As Tannis leans back in his chair, he signals the Announcer to speak. The Announcer acknowledges the signal with a nod then steps up to the crystalline podium once again to address the entire crowd.

"Citizens of Earth, let us begin our second half of today's special event!" He proudly announces, "The second round will now commence!"

The crowd cheers in excitement as Victor and other slaves enter the arena and take their positions once again. Tannis leans forward in his chair with his hands held together while placing his elbows on his knees and excitedly mutters, "And now for my favorite part of the game."

The large crystalline doors on the arena walls unlock in unison, which causes a loud noise that gains everyone's attention. Lithia growls as Victor powers up his Gauntlet in preparation and grips it tightly with caution.

"Survival of the fittest." Tannis finishes with a selfish grin.

"No quarter will be asked or given!" The Announcer proclaims, "Attend to your Gauntlets, and commence upon my mark!" As the other combatants power up their Gauntlets, the Announcer extends his arms dramatically and shouts, "Let the second round begin!"

The large doors open and the second round begins as several Eudenian and Enfurian warriors unexpectedly enter the arena, quickly approaching the human slaves to engage them. With the help of his furry companion, Victor is able to target several foes at a time thanks to Lithia's ability to warn him with a loud chirping noise every time someone approaches them. The slaves stand their ground and put up a good fight, but are easily outmatched. Victor's Gauntlet begins to malfunction all of a sudden as a Eudenian and Enfurian trap him in a corner. Lithia chirps from overhead, giving Victor an idea as he discharges the drained shard from the primitive Gauntlet then pulls out the shard necklace from around his neck and places it inside to power it up. The Eudenian and Enfurian warriors stand back for a moment with caution, as Victor successfully powers up the primitive Gauntlet to its full capacity.

"Alright now, who's next?" Victor calls as he looks back intensely.

The Eudenian and Enfurian warriors glance at each other, surprised by Victor's confidence then quickly rush towards him. With a grin crossing his angular face, Victor swiftly leaps out of the way and blasts them from above, catching them off guard as he lands safely behind them while gracefully holding a battle stance. Lithia flies back towards his shoulder as he looks upon the defeated warriors and scoffs.

Surprised by Victor's persistence, Tannis turns to address Patrayous directly behind him and says, "Impressive for a human slave, no wonder you and the others had trouble finding him."

Patrayous grips his fist tightly, annoyed by his failure to capture Victor as Zepherus growls in response. As the battle on the arena floor resumes, Lithia continues to aid Victor in combat; helping to target oncoming combatants by chirping each time they attempt to strike. Tannis looks over at Elena with disgust as her and Talia smile back with confidence.

"You've known him longer than I have." Elena denotes.

Looking back at her, Talia replies, "Yeah?"

"Is he always this good in battle?" Elena jokingly inquires.

Talia laughs in response, and happily informs, "Of course, but you should see him when he's angry!"
Curious to Victor's true power, Elena mutters, "Not sure if I ever want to."

"You would if he was trying to protect you." Talia proudly states, which brings a smile to Elena's face as she continues watching the deadly battle before them.
Victor forces several Eudenians back then takes out a couple of Enfurians behind him. As the fight ensues, he grips his hands tightly; feeling more powerful with the new shard in his Gauntlet then steps forward with his arms raised to address Tannis directly before the crowd in a confident manner.

"Call forth a worthy Champion, if you can!" Victor proudly exclaims. Elena and Talia smile at one another, feeling there is still hope for their dear friend. Damian chuckles in response, as Adrian scoffs angrily, annoyed by Victor's pretentious claim. As Victor continues to hold his own against the Eudenian and Enfurian warriors, Adrian loses patience then approaches Tannis from his seat to address him. Surprised by his competitive Enfurian counterpart, Damian watches as Adrian unexpectedly kneels before Tannis.

"What is it, Braxel?" Tannis respectfully asks.

"Wondering if I should make a quick end of them?" Adrian infers.
Slightly amused, Tannis says, "I always though you were one for tradition."

"I am; forgive my intrusion, Lord Tannis, but I request permission to take out the human slaves once and for all!" Adrian firmly requests as he points towards the arena floor and says, "Especially that one!"
Tannis looks upon the arena floor, realizing that he's referring to Victor and chuckles, "Always the pride with you Enfurians. What's the matter, LT., don't enjoy seeing your own kind taken down by one of my absolute best?" Adrian grunts in response as he mocks, "Your turn will come soon enough."
Angered by his crude insult, Adrian sternly retorts, "With all do respect, Emperor, he's dishonoring my people! Allow me to take him out before this whole thing gets out of hand!"

"And what do I gain from granting such a bold request?" Tannis inquires as he looks upon Adrian intensely.

"Our loyalty and service, as always." Adrian replies while bowing his head in respect towards him.
As Tannis considers the bold request, Raina and Lucian look on in curiosity as Adrian turns towards them and nods, signifying his honorable request.

"Oh, very well, Braxel, he's yours." Tannis carelessly states, "I'm beginning to find this whole thing rather tiresome anyway." Adrian grins, as he looks towards Damian who frowns back, unsure of his intentions. "I realize the stakes are a bit hemmed, but I do hope this slave will challenge you enough to make the match interesting for everyone present. Do as you please at my expense, but don't kill him." Tannis clarifies, "Crush him into the dust and enjoy, but if he fares against you well enough then I want him alive."

"I wouldn't worry about that," Adrian scoffs pretentiously, "He won't make it past me."

"I have no doubt about that." Tannis sarcastically infers with a devious grin as he signals Adrian, allowing him to do as requested.

Confident of his powerful Enfurian stature, Adrian walks past Damian who stares back curiously of the situation. As Adrian approaches the end of the balcony, he watches the battle below, disgusted by the sight of Victor faring well against his own. Victor helps the remaining slaves fend off the Eudenian and Enfurian warriors, pushing them back into a corner. Adrian looks towards Lucian as he nods in approval then yells out a war cry and proceeds to jump into the arena unexpectedly, causing the ground to shake as the crowd cheers loudly. Elena stands up from her chair, looking panicked then turns towards Tannis and scowls as he grins in return.

"What's going on?" Talia asks with grave concern.

Angered by Tannis for manipulating the event, Elena sighs then sits back down and replies, "More than what I expected unfortunately."

"What do you mean?" Talia asks with a fearful expression.

Elena looks upon her and gently says, "Things are about to get rough for Victor, so do us both a favor and pray for his safety, alright?

"Alright, if you say so." Talia retorts as her and Elena turn their attention back towards the arena floor.

As Victor and the slaves prepare for their final attack, Adrian points towards the other warriors in an arrogant fashion.

"Leave the rest to me boys!" He exclaims, "It's my turn now!"

The Eudenian and Enfurian warriors look towards Adrian behind the group of slaves as Damian leans his chin on his right fist and shakes his head, annoyed by his comrade's prideful act. Adrian cracks his knuckles as the warriors back away from Victor and the slaves. Surprised by their sudden change to disengage, Victor and the slaves turn their attention behind them as Adrian slowly approaches them. Breathing heavily with concern, Talia fears the worst for Victor as Elena wraps her arms around her to comfort her.

"You lose, Marcus!" Yuri jokingly states, "Care to concede that bet?"

"Hell no!" Marcus sarcastically snaps.

"Well there's no way he's going to make it now!" Yuri comments.

"Maybe not, but I probably could!" Marcus scoffs.

"You and what army?" Yuri teasingly snickers, "The both of us perhaps, but not by yourself!"

"I could if I had the chance." Marcus claims as he glances back at Damian, "Trag on the other hand hasn't fought in the arena in years." Unsure of his intended look, Damian looks back as Marcus turns back and quietly adds, "He probably thinks it's beneath him to fight against humans anyway."

"Or perhaps he knows better than to get in the arena with someone like Braxel!" Yuri sarcastically implies.

"Don't be too sure of that." Marcus tries to dispute; "I bet you he's been holding back all these years, purposely letting Braxel have all the fun."

Yuri suddenly gets an idea from the notion then holds out his fist and bets, "Ten to one odds he's holding back?"

"You're on!" Marcus settles as he and Yuri pound their fists together once again in agreement.

Annoyed by their gambling banter, Elena shakes her head once again in annoyance. Assessing the situation, Victor looks upon Adrian and realizes he must face him alone for the sake of the others who are too weak to fight.

"Get out of here guys!" Victor warningly shouts to the other slaves standing by, "He's mine!"

"What?" The head slave replies, "You can't take him all by yourself! Do you even know who that is?"

"No, but I'm sure I'm about to find out." Victor calmly retorts.

Adrian stares down Victor from a distance with disdain, and snarls.

"He's the Champion of Enfuria!" The head slave mentions with a scolding voice, "You don't stand a chance against him!"

"Don't worry about me, I'll be fine!" Victor eagerly exclaims, "Leave now before he decides to come after all of us!"

"Are you sure about this?" The head slave inquires.

"Not at all." Victor sarcastically mutters.

"I didn't expect you to be so foolish, Archelus!" The head slave irritably expresses as he helps the others to their feet.

"Don't worry about me!" Victor hollers, "Focus on yourselves!"

The head slave shakes his head, concerned by Victor's stubbornness, then shouts, "Come on everyone, do as he says!"

The slaves head back towards their quarters behind the arena wall, as Victor slowly turns with Lithia still perched on his shoulder to face his new adversary with dignity. As Adrian approaches him, he raises his hands, exciting the crowd as they cheer and applaud. Victor looks upon the crowd in curiosity of their reaction as Adrian lowers his arms and faces him with a disgusted look. Still sitting in his chair, Tannis leans over to get Elena's attention and says, "Looks like the tables have finally turned, wouldn't you say, Princess?"

Hoping to lighten the dreary mood for Talia's sake, Elena glances at her and says, "Ready, Talia?"

"Ready!" Talia quickly replies, looking excited.

Thinking his words have fallen on deaf ears, Tannis is taken aback as Elena and Talia quickly face him and stick their tongues out in a childish manner. Tannis pounds the armrest of his chair in anger, feeling insulted, as Elena and Talia turn back and giggle together like a typical pair of sisters. Patrayous scowls in response to Elena's childish act as they turn their attention back onto the arena floor, hoping Victor can hold his own against Adrian.

"You fight well, for a *human*!" Adrian arrogantly exclaims with each step, "But this is my showground!"

Victor glances at Lithia and asks, "So what do you say, Lithia, yay or nay?"

Lithia shakes his head and snorts, signifying a negative response.

"My thinking exactly." Victor puns confidently.

Adrian approaches Victor and shouts, "Welcome to my arena!"

Trying to intimidate him with each step, Victor stares back, trying to size him up. The crowd continues to cheer as Victor nods towards Lithia, who nods back and flies away towards a perching point to stay out of harms way. Victor powers up his Gauntlet and stands in battle stance, preparing for the worst possible outcome. "On Earth, there is only one law, survival of the fittest and glory for the greatest." Adrian declares as he steps even closer, "Therefore it is customary to pay tribute to the Gods in such a warrior like manner. And as you can see, the crowd wants one thing to happen right now!"

"Oh yeah, and what is that?" Victor scoffs.

"Your defeat at the hands of yours truly!" Adrian proudly states as he points towards himself with his thumb sticking out of his fist.

"You know, you remind me of the crystal denizens that flock the East sector of the mines!" Victor sarcastically mocks in an attempt to break his spirit, "Except you're much uglier for sure!"

Angered by Victor's remark, Adrian scoffs as he pounds his fists together to showcase his significant stature and states, "You're going to eat those words!"

"Not today!" Victor retorts with confidence, "My mother used to say that the giant in front of you is never bigger than the god inside you."

"Enough of this!" Adrian swings his hand back furiously then points towards him, "It's just you and me, *freak show*!"

Victor frowns upon his insult, reminding him of the bullies back in the mines. Adrian looks back towards the balcony with anticipation, awaiting the signal to begin as Tannis stands before the crowd and grins.

"Finally, something we haven't seen before." Raina says in relief.

"Indeed, this should be good." Lucian responds with slight excitement in his voice.

Elena and Talia share a frown in response to their remarks while trying to focus on the fight at hand.

"Come on, Victor." Talia whispers as she holds her hands together tightly as if to pray, "I believe in you."

The Announcer respectfully steps aside as Tannis approaches the crystalline podium overlooking the arena. The crowd waits in anticipation as Victor and Adrian stare off intensely. As Tannis raises his right arm, he gives the signal by swinging it downwards and the fight begins. To Victor's surprise, Adrian powers up and quickly charges towards him without hesitation, trying to smash him into the ground as he quickly dodges.

"Come here, *you*!" Adrian angrily shouts.

Adrian chases after Victor, trying to pummel him to the ground, but Victor proves too quick for the large Enfurian. The crowd cheers, getting louder with each attack while Adrian charges towards him once again and misses as Victor quickly moves out of the way.

"You're quick, but even lightning can be stopped!" Adrian bellows, looking up as Victor leaps overhead and lands gracefully behind him.

Smiling with confidence, Adrian quickly changes his tactic by pounding the ground with his fists, which causes several crystalline pillars to shoot up from beneath the arena floor as Victor tries his best to dodge them one at a time. Adrian charges through the debris caused by the protruding pillars, striking Victor a few times as Tannis laughs in amusement with Patrayous.

"Better watch out, I'm coming for you!" Adrian furiously proclaims as he continues his attack against him.

Victor stops for a moment to catch his breath and notices that the crystalline pillars remind him of climbing and leaping in the mines growing up as a child. With his acute sense, he can hear Adrian, but can barely see him through the debris so he changes his tactic as well. Hoping to outsmart his opponent, Victor jumps onto one of the pillars, holding on with his hands tightly gripped then closes his eyes for a moment, waiting for Adrian to come closer.

"I have you now!" Adrian pompously shouts as he finally locates Victor through the debris.

Adrian charges towards Victor at full speed and attempts to strike, but is caught off guard when Victor opens his intense eyes and quickly leaps out of the way, jumping onto another crystalline pillar.

"Is that all you've got you big brute?" He mocks with a confident smile while firmly holding his position.

Becoming angrier, Adrian crushes the pillar with his bare hands and tries to follow Victor's movements from one pillar to the next. Victor is able to land several good hits on him using this cunning tactic, taking advantage of his Angelic agility. Becoming more confident in his abilities, Victor strikes Adrian face first then again as their fists pound together, causing a slight energy wake. Watching from the balcony overhead, Elena glances at Talia, who cheers Victor on with excitement. Elena continues to watch the fight in astonishment of Victor's ability to hold his own against Adrian, considering the possibility of him having Archadian blood like that of Talia. With their fists locked together, each trying to overpower the other, Victor smiles in confidence of this feat as Adrian attempts to strike with his other fist and misses yet again. Adrian yells in anger as Victor rolls to dodge and swiftly leaps onto another pillar. While retaining his usual crooked smile, Victor confidently shouts, "Take your best shot tough guy!"

"How dare you mock me!" Adrian furiously shouts.

Victor raises his Gauntlet, signifying his edge over him as Adrian changes his tactic again and fires energy blasts at each pillar, causing them to crumble.

Confused by this approach, Victor is struck by an energy blast and falls off the pillar, hitting the ground hard as he looks up and sees Adrian jump, approaching him from above. "Now you're mine!" Adrian roars, "While I enjoy a good game, playtime's over and I always win."

Adrian thrusts towards him from overhead with his fist as Victor attempts to block but is knocked back several yards, hitting the dirt. As Adrian turns with a grin, he proclaims, "I believe the odds are back in my favor, *human!*"

Angered by his arrogant remark, Victor suddenly blasts Adrian back with his Gauntlet as the crowd continues to cheer. Tannis is surprised by Victor's endurance as Damian looks over at Elena with concern himself. Watching from above in his secret booth, Traganus watches the fight closely, carefully studying Victor's every move as if to size him up.

Victor holds his hands out, surprised by the power harnessed from his Gauntlet as Adrian runs towards him and fires energy blasts around his feet. Using his speed once again, Victor dodges each blast but suddenly loses balance. Seeing an opening in his defense, Adrian grabs him by the neck and slams him hard against the ground then kicks him back several yards into the dirt. Losing control over the battle, Victor struggles to hold back his inner rage as Adrian fires an energy wave towards him. With anger burning in his intense blue eyes, Victor rises to his feet, attempting to block the attack.

Concerned for the crowd's safety, Damian looks on whilst quickly devising a plan to neutralize the escalating battle. As Victor regains control of his power, he aims his Gauntlet and fires back at Adrian as the two energy waves clash, hitting head on before the crowds' eyes. Adrian steps towards Victor, attempting to push him through the arena wall with his energy wave. Growing angrier by the second, Victor's eyes suddenly begin to glow brightly in blue as he pushes Adrian back with his energy wave as well.

"Time's up, *human!*" Adrian shouts, feeling confident of his victory over him as he pushes even harder with his energy wave from his Gauntlet.

Talia rushes towards the edge of the balcony, concerned for Victor's life as Elena quickly approaches her from behind to hold her back. Yelling furiously, Victor retaliates with a more powerful energy blast as Adrian struggles to push him back whilst holding his ground. Realizing that the fight is getting out of control, Damian takes it upon himself to intervene as he unexpectedly leaps out of his seat and into the arena. As the energy waves become drastically unstable, Damian lands between them and the beams with his Gauntlet, hitting the ground hard, which cause both energy waves to bounce back towards Victor and Adrian. Reacting instantly to Damian's attempts, Elena quickly activates her wings from her chest piece and flies down just in the nick of time, pulling Victor

out of harms way as the energy wave knocks Adrian back and crashes him through the arena wall. Both waves violently hit opposite sides of the arena, knocking holes into the walls as the crowd stands in awe at the sight.

Elena pulls Victor away towards Damian as the crowd settles in silence for a moment. Angered by Damian and Elena's interference, Tannis and Patrayous scowl as Raina and Lucian look on, surprised by this exciting outcome. "Well done, Marquis, bravo." Lucian compliments with a smirk, "You didn't disappoint us after all."

"You've truly outdone yourself this time, and here we thought you would fail to deliver." Raina facetiously adds with an amused tone, unbeknownst to Tannis' anger. Annoyed by their amusement, Tannis stands up, completely speechless. As the dust settles, the crowd remains silent as Elena shields Victor with her Angelic wings. After a long moment of silence, the crowd begins to cheer and applaud even louder than before as Damian approaches Adrian to help him out of the rubble from the arena walls.

"I think you bit off more than you can chew this time, Braxel." Damian teases as Adrian suddenly bursts through the debris with extreme anger, "Looks like he got the best of you."

"I would've taken him out had you not interfered, Trag!" Adrian scoffs as he wipes off the rubble from his body.

"You left me no choice," Damian explains, "That blast could've hurt a lot of people, and you alone would've been held responsible."
Adrian holds his hand over his chest in slight pain and angrily retorts, "Don't insult me just because you're too afraid of getting in the arena yourself!"

"Sorry to ruin your pride and all, but if it makes you feel any better, you would've won anyway." Damian states, "Even without going full power."

"Don't patronize me!" Adrian furiously snaps.

"You sure do have a lot to learn about proper sportsmanship, don't you?" Damian jokes at his expense.

"Mind your own business next time, or it'll be you who's on the receiving end!" Adrian grumbles.
Amused by his comrade's stubbornness, Damian rolls his eyes and extends his hand out to help him up, saying, "Come on, better show the people what a good sport you really are."

"Yeah right!" Adrian snarls back in annoyance.
Damian helps Adrian up from the rubble then approaches Victor and Elena standing in the center of the arena floor. The crowd continues to cheer and applaud as Tannis looks around for a moment, taking in their reaction with surprise, which causes him to grin. Uncertain of what just happened, Victor looks his body over and says, "You healed me, didn't you?"
Elena retracts her wings back into her spinal armor and with her back turned, she states, "Consider it a parting gift, the kind you can never give back."

"But why?" Victor inquires.

"Let's just say we're even now," Elena gladly divulges as Victor expresses a surprised look, "And you're welcome." She finishes while facing him with a confident smile.

Appreciative of her help at the last minute, Victor nods back in respect and murmurs, "I suppose a 'thanks' is in order?"

"I hope it was enough." Elena jokes as she lightly slaps her hand on his arm, "What would you do without me?"

"As of now, I hope I never have to know." He says with a smirk as he discharges the crystal shard from his Gauntlet then carefully places it back around his neck and caresses it.

"Now that I was not expecting!" Damian states as he and Adrian approach them from the other side of the arena. "That sure was a close call." Elena quickly turns and with a nod says, "Indeed it was, but it looks like I wasn't the only one who intervened!"

"I don't know about you, but I was merely preventing a disaster." Damian explains as he motions towards Victor, "You saved this human's life in the process. Why I wonder?"

Victor smiles once again in appreciation as Elena places her hand on his shoulder and replies, "The same reason you saved them I suppose."

"Next time you won't have someone swooping in to your rescue!" Adrian proclaims irritably.

"He has a name you guys!" Elena impatiently retorts.

"Ha!" Adrian scoffs, "And what might that be?"

Victor steps forward and proudly declares, "The name's Victor, *friend*!"

"Victor, huh?" Damian responds, "I won't forget it anytime soon." He then chuckles while jabbing Adrian's side, "Who could forget the name of the person who took on Braxel singlehandedly?"

"I'd like to see you do better, *Trag*!" Adrian scoffs in annoyance.

The group refocuses their attention elsewhere and notices that the crowd is still cheering and applauding as they rise from their seats, yelling Victor's gladiatorial name repeatedly with excitement.

"Archelus! Archelus! Archelus!" The crowd chants loudly in unison.

Amazed by their positive response, Victor looks around the arena and observes the crowd as they continue to cheer his name with excitement.

"Hear that, Victor?" Elena whispers encouragingly in his left ear as she places her hands on his shoulders from behind, "That's the sound of freedom, and worldwide acceptance." Victor slowly turns, looking upon Elena compassionately as her smile causes him to smile back. "Come on," she says gently as she takes his hand to walk him before the entire crowd on the arena floor, "Your freedom awaits."

Damian and Adrian follow suit as the four of them walk towards the front of the balcony to await Tannis' reaction. Excited, Lithia takes off overhead as Victor waves to get his attention, and he responds with a chirp. Patrayous glances over at Tannis, unsure of what his reaction will be as Zepherus snarls. Talia looks on, relieved to see Victor alive and well as she covers her mouth with her hands, gripping them together in a fist.

As Lithia flies to her, Talia gasps, more excited than ever by the sight of her furry companion. "Lithia!" She calls as he lands gracefully before her on the balcony's edge, "How did you end up this far?" Excited to see her as well, Lithia chirps then begins licking her face as she holds him close in her arms and delightfully mutters, "I'm so glad you're safe!"

As the group below stops before the balcony, Tannis approaches the crystalline podium overlooking the arena to address the crowd.

"People of Titania!" He proudly announces with his arms extended away from him dramatically, "It seems we have a draw on our hands, and a most unusual one at that!"

The crowd cheers and applauds in response as Elena playfully bumps into Victor with her hip, inciting a lighthearted grin.

"Behold your Champions, Adrian Braxel of Enfuria!" Tannis announces with his left open hand motioned towards him.

Adrian raises his fists to acknowledge the crowd as they happily cheer him on.

"Damian Trag of Eudenia!" Tannis announces secondly with his right open hand motioned towards Damian.

Damian moves his royal purple cape behind him in a graceful manner and takes a bow as the crowd continues to cheer and applaud. Taking in the moment of their uncontrollable reaction, Tannis pauses for a moment then extends his left open hand towards Victor.

"And behold, the first human to ever challenge a Champion of Earth, and survive!" Tannis reluctantly points out.

Victor raises his Gauntlet in approval, gripping his fist tightly as the crowd cheers and applauds louder than ever.

"Archelus! Archelus! Archelus!" The crowd continues to chant.

"As always, thank you all for attending this year's event!" Tannis concludes, "May your travels and business affairs be safe and luxurious!"

Shortly after, the crowd begins to disperse as Tannis looks towards Victor directly, and mutters, "I'll be keeping a close eye on you."

Tannis glances back at Patrayous while grinning then turns to leave the balcony. Patrayous observes the arena for a moment; surprised by Victor's power then he and Zepherus follow close behind Tannis. Raina and Lucian continue observing the arena from their seats on the balcony, alarmed by Victor's surprising strength.

"Seems the human race isn't as weak as we once thought." Raina unwillingly admits.

"It would appear that way, but how I wonder?" Lucian responds apprehensively to the notion. After a few minutes of looking upon the arena in curiosity, Raina and Lucian take their leave with the other nobles.

Watching from above in his secret booth, Traganus shares a confident grin with Raiven and Celeste then turns away and mutters, "Well done, a man with spirit triumphs over all. Finally, someone among us is actually worthy."

As Traganus turns to take his leave, Raiven and Celeste glance at each other, concerned over their inability to capture Victor themselves. Traganus exits the booth; disappearing into the shadows as the two Darchadians glance back at the arena for a moment then quickly turn to follow him out.

With the evening hours settling in, Tannis stands in front of the window overlooking the arena from above in his private chamber with Patrayous and Zepherus standing by. Moments later, Elena enters the chamber to confront him, which causes Zepherus to growl with his spinal shards glowing as Patrayous frowns upon her. Confident of her gambling claim, Elena smiles back as she stops several feet in front of them.

"Well Princess, I suppose you're here on a matter of honor." Tannis says edgily with his back turned.

"I am here to assure you settle it honorably." She firmly replies.

"You expect me to uphold our agreement then?" Tannis questions.

"Of course, if it's not too much trouble." Elena boldly responds, "Considering our previous wager, I am entitled to substantial compensation."

"Very well, a deal's a deal." Tannis sighs as he turns to face her and waves his hand, "As always you are my guest and since he is your property now, as long as he doesn't the betray the trust of your people or mine, he lives. Therefore, you may take your prize anytime you like."

"My men are already on their way to retrieve him now." Elena informs as she steps forward to address him directly, "He's none of your concern anymore, therefore our business is concluded, indefinitely I hope."

As Elena turns to take her leave, Tannis glances at Patrayous for a second and says, "Just one more thing before you leave, Princess!" Annoyed by his persistent arrogance, Elena sighs then turns back to listen. "You do realize that if he slips up just once, he'll be taken back into my custody." Tannis proclaims as he steps away from the window towards her.

"This time for good!" Patrayous proudly declares while gripping his fist as Zepherus growls in accordance.

"Not a fair bargain considering he rightfully earned his freedom from the clutches of your own hands." Elena scoffs as she steps closer.

"Fairness, such a human conceit." Tannis calmly mocks with a grin, "You must think more imaginatively."

"I can imagine what will happen should you choose to dishonor our agreement." Elena firmly retorts, "I pray the Gods show more compassion than you, Marquis." As she turns to take her leave, she stops for a moment, then turns back and finishes, "You may need it someday."

Elena leaves the chamber impatiently as Patrayous scoffs at her remark. Tannis grins; amused by her never ending tenacity then continues gazing out the window overlooking the arena, sighing calmly as if to scheme once more.

CH: 30
REUNITED

Outside the floating arena shortly after the event has come to a close, Victor exits the slave pit while being escorted by Marcus and Yuri.

"Not exactly sure who won back there," Marcus jokes, "How about we call the bet off for now?"

"Sounds good to me," Yuri acknowledges, "Guess we'll be the only ones leaving this place empty handed."

Stopping for a moment to enjoy his freedom from Tannis, Victor closes his eyes, extends his arms out and takes a deep breath, exhaling in relief before hearing a familiar voice that suddenly cries, "Victor!"

Shocked by the familiarity of the voice, Victor opens his eyes then quickly turns and sees Talia running towards him with Lithia.

"Talia?" Victor calls back in relief.

Tears well up in his eyes as Talia rushes towards Victor and jumps onto him, hugging him tightly with excitement as Lithia licks his face. "Praise the Gods, you're alive!" Victor says while gently placing his hands over her delicate face.

Placing her hands over his face in return, Talia tears up with a joyous smile and says softly, "I found you."

"Yes you did." Victor calmly responds with a joyful expression as he kisses her forehead, "But how did you escape? I thought you were...."

Talia motions behind them as Victor looks up and sees Elena approaching them with a smile. Victor smiles back, surprised and relieved that Elena was able to help her as well.

"I'm so glad to see you, Victor." Talia comforts as she holds him tightly, closing her eyes in reprieve.

Holding her close, Victor brushes his hand gently through her blonde hair, "As am I, Talia." He whispers, "As am I."

Wiping away his joyful tears, Victor looks upon Elena again in appreciation and says, "I am truly in your graces now, I can't thank you enough."

"No need," Elena assures, "She was held captive here as well."

"Let me guess, Tannis." Victor deduces as he looks over Talia's shoulder at the arena towering over them while Elena nods in response, "You saved our lives, I believe I now have a debt of honor to you."

"Against your wish?" Elena jokes.

"No man, woman or child should ever beg for their life, not ever." Victor states.

"You didn't," Elena reveals, "I did on your behalf and meant nothing offensive by it of course."

"How can I ever repay you?" Victor respectfully inquires.

"Think nothing of it." Elena says with a confident smile.

Victor nods in respect as Talia loosens her grip around him and looks upon Elena curiously.

"Are we going back now?" She asks, holding back her excitement.

"Yes we are." Elena answers with a comforting smile.

Victor looks into Talia's hazel eyes, feeling hopeful and mutters, "Archadia?" Talia nods with excitement, triggering a sigh of relief from him as she looks upwards and says, "You're going to love it!"

"I'm sure I will!" Victor says with a chuckle as he looks upward as well, "Let's just hope it's not too good to be true."

Talia smiles as everyone approaches the Arch ship on the landing platform.

Standing above their quarters on a platform overlooking the arena's exterior, Raina and Lucian watches the group board their ship in curiosity.

"The Princess is keen on defying the Emperor, isn't she?" Lucian sternly denotes, "The Arch must have great interest in him, whoever and whatever he is."

"This human is quite impressive indeed, for a mere mortal anyway." Raina curiously acknowledges, "He isn't a threat now, but he could soon become one in their hands."

Lucian turns to face Raina and warns, "There's no telling what he'll become; therefore, we must be cautious."

Turning their attention back in displeasure, they watch as the Arch ship hovers above the landing platform then quickly takes off towards Archadia.

High above the planet's surface, Victor happily sits beside Talia in anticipation aboard the Arch ship as it flies towards Archadia.

"Victor, look!" Talia excitedly informs while pointing towards the window in the cargo deck, "There it is!"

Excited and slightly nervous, Victor raises his head and approaches the window next to Talia, "Well I'll be damned!" He states with excitement in his voice, "Paradise does exist after all."

Tickled by their enthusiasm, Elena looks over at them and grins.

"Yep, just like you said!" Talia expresses with delight.

As a tear runs down Victor's cheek, he sighs in relief of finally seeing Archadia with his own eyes for the first time as Lithia stands beside them near the window and chirps. Moments later after passing through the energy shield surrounding the entire floating kingdom, the Arch ship lands on the port of Archadia. Hesitating to move, Victor sits still with a prolonged gaze out the window as Talia grabs his hand and says, "Ready, Victor?"

"Are you kidding?" Victor happily retorts as he takes her hand and stands up, "I've been ready my whole life!" As everyone departs the Arch ship, Victor looks upon the kingdom for the first time in wonder and mutters, "Well mother, looks like I finally made it after all." He then clears his throat and states, "Wow, Archadia is so much bigger than I expected."

"Isn't it beautiful?" Talia cheerfully implies as she motions towards the crystalline kingdom floating before them.

Victor turns his head towards Elena as she departs the ship then softly mutters, "Yes, beautiful indeed."

Elena approaches Victor from behind, gently placing her hands over his arms and says, "I'd like to show you around, but first I need you to follow me."

"As you wish, milady." Victor calmly murmurs.

Victor walks beside Elena and Talia as Marcus and Yuri follow close behind with Valorie and Vennessa in tow.

"There must be something special about this guy as well if she brought him all the way up here." Marcus skeptically implies.

"I'm not one to question Elena's judgment most of the time, but I can't say that I see whatever it is she sees myself." Yuri adds.

"That makes two of us." Marcus finishes with a lowered brow.

Lithia flies next to Victor and Talia, the reluctant trio, back together at last as the group enters the Angelic kingdom, admiring the breath-taking sights.

CH: 31
THE HEALING PROCESS

Shortly after making their way into the crystalline kingdom, Victor follows Elena within the Archadian Temple and into a mysterious chamber as Talia and Lithia look around in curiosity.

"What is this place?" Victor inquires.

Standing a few feet before him, Elena extends her arm out gracefully and replies, "The Angelus Chamber."

Slightly hesitant at first, Victor looks around for a moment and carefully asks, "Why did you bring me here?"

"You'll see." Elena answers as she walks past him and approaches a cryogenic chamber covered in Archadian scribe. She then extends her hand towards Victor as he and Talia glance at each other curiously. Victor takes the crystal shard necklace from around his neck and hands it to Talia, saying, "Hold onto this for me, will you?"

"Of course." Talia nods in response as Victor slowly enters the Angelus Chamber with caution.

As Victor settles comfortably inside the Angelus Chamber, Elena begins to punch a few buttons on the holographic screen and informs, "You may be free of the Emperor's grasp, but we have to be sure."

"About what?" Victor questions while raising his head.

"That any and all darkness within you is properly cleansed; technically we don't judge, we simply reveal and heal." She explains while continuing to press a few buttons, "We call this the Angelus Process, and it will surely fix you up in no time, though keep in mind that physical as well as spiritual detox in and of itself is quite a process. When it's complete it should give you great spiritual insight and perspective, the kind you haven't before."

"Do all your guests have to go through this sort of initiation?" Victor jokes, trying to lighten the mood.

Stopping for a moment, Elena steps away from the control screen to clarify, "For someone of your age, yes, but before you can be allowed to roam our kingdom freely, you must first earn our trust by demonstrating yours."

"And how do I do that?" Victor carefully asks.

"By showing that you won't become a danger to us, or yourself." Elena finishes as she steps back before the holographic control screen.

"Last time I checked, I'm not like anyone else." Victor attests.

"That you'll have to prove." Elena firmly retorts.

"All right, if you say so." He mutters before nodding at Talia who nods back with a smile.

Elena presses a button on the holographic screen to activate the Angelus Process, which causes the chamber to enclose and move upward as Victor studies his surroundings. "This may hurt just a bit." She cautiously warns.

"I've heard that before." Victor says with a slight chuckle.

As the chamber moves into position, Talia steps onto a higher platform with Lithia to observe the procedure. Victor looks up through the chamber and smiles while Talia stands above with Lithia, smiling back as she kisses her hand and presses it against the crystalline glass to comfort him. Returning the sentiment, Victor kisses his hand and places it against the crystalline glass in front of hers. "Don't worry about a thing, your body's natural ability to heal is far greater than anyone has ever permitted you to believe." Elena assures while standing before the chamber, "Just try to relax and you'll be fine."

"Who says I'm worried." Victor retorts with a smirk.

"Come, Natalia." Elena calls while holding her arm out to her, "This will take a while." Talia jumps down from the higher platform with Lithia and walks past her to exit the chamber. Stepping closer, Elena places her hand on the crystalline glass and says, "I'll see you when you've awakened."

Victor responds by placing his hand in front of hers on the glass as well and says, "I'm looking forward to it."

Elena smiles as she places her hand over his briefly, then steps back as he passes out from the chemicals released into the Angelus Chamber. "I don't know who you are or where you come from, but I hope me bringing you here was worth it." She whispers with a concerned look. Laying there peacefully and unconscious, Victor undergoes the healing process as Elena exits the chamber with Talia and Lithia by her side. Moments later, Victor yells and screams as the cellular reproduction from the Angelus Process finally begins.

A few hours later, Victor floats above a crystalline platform in the Angelus Chamber, still unconscious. Elena stands by, observing him and the holographic screen intensely with Rosalyn and Josephus present.

"His energy reading is unlike anything we've ever seen before." Elena calmly informs with a puzzled expression.

"How is that even possible for a human?" Rosalyn inquires.

"He's much more than that." Elena says with an annoyed tone.

Sharing a serious glance with Rosalyn, Josephus asks, "What is he then?" Standing by in the next room with Lithia, Talia listens closely to their discussion as she looks into the Angelus Chamber. Keeping her focus on Victor for a moment in curiosity, Elena's eyes widen as she carefully answers, "He appears to be a hybrid."

"Impossible!" Josephus argues, "How could a hybrid of this caliber stay undetected all these years?"

"I'm not entirely sure, but I have a theory." Elena implies while looking over at Victoria's Gauntlet floating above a small crystalline platform. Surprised by this revelation, Rosalyn and Josephus glance at each other with concern. "Makes you wonder just how long his power can last," Elena infers while facing her parents, "Think of it, all that energy coursing through him. He's the first and only one of his kind."

"That we know of." Josephus sternly adds.

"Even so…" Elena continues as she slowly turns back towards Victor, "Who's to say how powerful he might become eventually?"

"There's no telling what he's truly capable of, that's what makes him dangerous." Josephus sternly implies.

"Yes, and if his body could sustain this much power as a half breed, then what would it take to kill him?" Rosalyn cautiously questions, "The gaze in his eyes alone, they're almost haunting."

"Or perhaps they suggest a level of passion." Elena assuredly implies. Josephus points towards different areas of Victor's body and mentions, "Look at all these lightning marks, like that of the Darchadians, the Gods mark them all with similar scars. His inner wounds are beyond our means to fully heal." He finishes with a concerned expression, "No matter what we do, he will be forever scarred, inside and out."

"There is great power within him that still lies dormant, for whatever blood flows through his veins, it resembles that of a Darchadian." Rosalyn carefully denotes, "Imagine the mass hysteria if the public knew about this." Shocked by this stunning revelation, Elena steps away while placing her hand over her mouth, deeply worried for Victor's future within their kingdom.

"Do we have any idea what this one Angel could do?" Josephus points out, "His power alone, if used improperly it could completely shatter the people's faith in the Arch." He then sighs and adds, "There will be unrest within the Senate if they were to learn of this, especially the Gods."

"Then for now, it's probably best that they don't." Elena retorts as she faces them, "He could be a powerful asset, should he pass for one of us."

"Perhaps." Josephus says with uncertainty as he faces Elena directly then states, "Your heart has softened, Elena." Concerned by his meaning, Elena looks upon him as he points towards Victor and mentions, "There is much mystery that surrounds his aura. Did you bring him here to justify your own assumptions about the Arch's history in conjunction with humans?"

"It's not about the past, it's about the future, and now." Elena firmly says in defense, "Sharing the history of other marginalized groups with our own is crucial to the unification of Earth's people."

"Our history is already greatly solidified and acknowledged widely," Josephus scolds with displeasure in his voice, "Years ago you would've slain someone like him on sight."

"Years ago, our people had better things to do than to hunt down our own kind at the edge of the world!" Elena defensively retorts while approaching them.

"The Darchadians are not our kind!" Rosalyn sternly chimes in, "Besides, the people are content, and have complete faith in the Arch's ability to keep them forever safe."

"Are they?" Elena carefully mutters, "I'm not so sure these days."

"Elena, it is not our place, nor our people to question the Gods!" Josephus states with a firm tone.

"Because they don't know any better!" Elena disputes impatiently, "I dream of a world where truth is what shapes people's politics rather than politics shaping what people think is true. We ourselves are a great people, and now our kingdom is threatened to lie in ruins should we continue to remain apathetic." Surprised by her sudden intensity, Rosalyn and Josephus look at their daughter in trepidation. "He could be the answer to all our prayers," Elena calmly justifies while placing her hand over the crystalline glass, "The one who could bring true balance back to the world."

"Don't be ridiculous!" Josephus scoffs, "Only a prophet or a fool could make such a claim!"

"Anything that fits out of the ordinary scares you." Elena insults.

"No..." Rosalyn remarks, "Only things that threaten the very balance we try so hard to sustain."

Frustrated by her parent's attitude towards her, Elena sighs then caresses her fingers over the crystalline glass and justifies, "To be prepared for any contingency is the greatest of virtues, which is why a single feather can tip the scale. One person alone may be the difference between victory, and defeat."

Sighing impatiently, Josephus warns, "I don't care how much potential he may have, you risk too much letting him stay, Elena!"

"That may be, but the truth of the matter is, Victor is a mysterious if not sacred asset." She peacefully rationalizes, "And as Angels, we must continue to uphold the Arch's most important law." She finishes while turning to face them directly.

"Oh, and which law is that?" Josephus sneers.

"That all life is sacred; our job is to love others without stopping to inquire whether or not they are worthy." Elena protectively states, "You keep praying for help, and when someone like him finally comes along who might actually be able to save us, you simply reject him."

Stepping towards Victor, Rosalyn argues, "But he is not one of us, nor is he Angel born, technically."

"Neither are we." Elena scoffs in frustration, "And does it really matter what he is? We can't keep protecting what is only familiar and pushing away what is new just because it scares us."

Annoyed by their daughter's stubbornness, Rosalyn and Josephus glance at each other once again in a stern manner then share a calming sigh.

"Forgive us, daughter, you're right." Rosalyn articulates, "Perhaps your parents care too much for your wellbeing. I wish we could spend more time together like we used to when you were the sweetest little girl."

"There's never been time, *mother*." Elena strongly emphasizes, "Since I was a child I was groomed to ever be the best." She then looks upward and states, "The Gods would weep if they could see how far we've fallen."

"You must never confuse your feelings with your sacred duty, for a Princess of your status must make public gestures for the common people and nobles alike." Josephus sternly stresses.

"I know, but our people haven't known true honorable warfare since ritual combat began." Elena mutters with a depressing breathe.

"Which is why our people have always had a role in it, Elena!" Josephus snaps, "Those tournaments in the arena exist for a reason, and have such for centuries and will likely continue to do so."

"These events are rare, but we have a commitment to making ourselves capable of them." Rosalyn adds, "It is a time-honored tradition."

"I know, but it's your tradition, not mine!" Elena debates as she approaches Victor once again and states, "If someone like him could unlock the secrets to our past, then perhaps we can save our future."

"No! Our way of life is preserved," Josephus contests, "It is the way things are, and it will always be."

Rosalyn approaches Elena, hoping to diffuse the argument and calmly says, "Elena, when you take the throne one day you will understand."

"Please!" Elena edgily replies while following her movement, "I can only hope to one day be as uncompromising as you two."

As Rosalyn stands next to Josephus, she explains, "Sometimes there is no such luxury as compromise, even between the people of Earth. A notion you must learn to accept if you are to ever rule this kingdom."

Sighing impatiently, Elena faces Victor once more, feeling hopeful of his presence and says, "Imagine what people could accomplish if we all loved and respected each other the way we were always meant to. In our world, he could change everything we know."

"For better, or worse though?" Josephus seriously questions.

Elena presses a button on the holographic display, which causes the scanners to attack any remaining dark energy lying within Victor whilst continuing to heal his entire body inside and out.

"Soon it will be time for you to take your place among our people with a significant other of our choosing." Josephus informs, "Many look to us for divine strength, and someday they will look to you as well."

"You should be greatly honored by that." Rosalyn finishes.

Turning to face her parents once more in annoyance, Elena softens her expression and replies, "I am, more than you'll ever understand, though in the practice of tolerance, one's enemy is the best teacher." As Victor's body continues to undergo the Angelus Process, he yells in agony, making it difficult for Elena to endure. "This may take longer than expected," she says with small doubt in her voice, "I'll check back on him later when the process is finally complete." Elena leaves the chamber with Rosalyn and Josephus as the Angelus Process begins to fully regenerate Victor. A set of mechanical arms places a decorative piece on Victor's chest and presses the Gods' symbol crested on top, which causes the Archadian Soul Gear to form over his body. Hearing the process near its final stage, Elena stops by the entrance then looks back once more and whispers, "I pray I'm right about you."

She then leaves the chamber while the Soul Gear forms completely over Victor's body as the Gods' symbol bearing over his chest lights up brightly in blue, signifying a perfect neurological connection.

After hours of hearing Victor in agony, Talia enters the chamber and sees him lying peacefully on a crystalline bed. Careful not to wake him, Talia approaches the bed and caresses her hand over his new Archadian Soul Gear in curiosity. She then lies on the bed and carefully cuddles next to him, taking in his every breath for comfort.

Time passes, and Victor finally awakens while rubbing his hand over his head. After a long sigh of relief, he sees Talia lying next to him dead asleep with the crystal shard still in her hand. Trying not to wake her, he carefully takes the shard out of her hand and places it back around his neck. Victor notices his body covered in the dark greyish Soul Gear and that the slave mark on his right arm is completely gone but the other mark on his left arm remains. Taking a moment to relax, Victor hums the melody taught to him by Sonya whilst caressing Talia's beautiful face as she lies there peacefully.

After a moment of calm relaxation, Elena quietly enters the room to address Victor and says, "So this is who you've been spending all your time with in Pretoria, huh?" Raising his head, Victor looks up with a smile and sees Elena standing at the doorway then mutters, "What can I say, she gets me. They say blood makes you related, but in my eyes, loyalty makes you family."

"Indeed," Elena mentions, "I'd say she's had a long day."

"I know, we both have." Victor replies, "Much like everyone else in the mines, we were raised hand to mouth so she's pretty used to it by now."

"That's probably good and bad." Elena denotes with a soothing grin, "I can tell she's a little taken with you, and doesn't want to leave your side."

"I'll never forget the look on her face when she realized I wasn't able to save her." Victor carefully professes, "I hope never to relive a moment like that ever again as long as I live." Refocusing his attention on Talia, he looks upon her compassionately whilst continuing to gently caress her young face, saying, "I thought she was dead, I'm sure she thought the same about me." He pauses for a moment then continues, "I've never seen her so peaceful, she seems to be resting better than ever."

"That's because she is loved." Elena implies as she approaches him.

"To my knowledge, she always has been." Victor claims, "This whole time, I never knew she was of Angel descent." He then looks upon Elena and inquires, "You're going to make her into a warrior someday, aren't you?"

Stepping closer, Elena looks upon Talia and says, "In a way she already is, she was just never encouraged properly. The tools we give her will allow her to utilize what power she has, and bring out her vision eventually."

Slightly concerned for Talia's future, Victor retorts, "It could take years to learn how to do that, I for one would know."

"It will happen more quickly than you think, she just needs devoted care and attention to flourish properly." Elena explains as she sits on the edge of the bed and caresses Talia's face as well, "Behind every beautiful face is some kind of pain, seems her origin is just as mysterious as yours." She then looks directly upon Victor and inquires, "Did she have any foster parents?"

"No, just me really." Victor responds while shaking his head, "Somehow, I always knew she was special, now I know why."

Elena gently runs her fingers through Talia's hair, causing her to moan in her sleep and states, "An Angel's love makes anything possible, and perhaps that's why she survived as long as you have." Feeling appreciative of their likeness, Victor shares a grin as she enlightens, "Thanks to the Angelus Process, you've reached optimum physical condition."

"How is that?" Victor quietly asks.

"Archadian technology," Elena quietly explains, "A water based nanotech which increases the tensile strength of bone and muscle tissue by several thousand percent." Victor looks upon his Soul Gear once again as she continues, "Thus, your recovery has been greatly accelerated."

"I'm sure that will come in handy someday." Victor remarks.

Elena smiles back with a nod and finishes, "Cellular regeneration is vital to keeping ourselves intact, inside and out. It took longer than expected, but you seem to be doing well."

Feeling stronger than ever before, Victor examines his body and states, "I feel as if a tremendous weight has been lifted from my shoulders, and my heart."

"Good, that means it's working." Elena informs, "You should feel a tremendous difference in your physicality overall."

"I've never felt better actually," Victor calmly describes, "I'm a little dazed, but good nonetheless."

Elena leans over from the edge of the bed and examines his profile with her hands, saying, "I can tell the extraction took its toll on you, any disorientation should wear off soon." She then leans back and finishes, "Though there might be some residual effects."

Victor looks directly into her eyes and calmly says, "Thank you."

"For what?" She asks with a curious smile.

Looking around the chamber, Victor motions towards his body and Talia, stating, "For this, and, for her."

"You're welcome." Elena happily replies before turning her attention back towards Talia compassionately, "She's unique and strong, isn't she?"

"That she is," Victor jokes, "Even stronger than me I'm afraid."

"She doesn't really belong anywhere, does she?" Elena probes.

"No, I think she belongs here." Victor surely claims, "They say home is where the heart is, but to me home is wherever you are in the moment."

"I believe you're right, for blood is much thicker than water but loyalty is far greater than both." Elena proudly informs, "Even the children in this place have already grown to love her from what I hear."

"And why not?" Victor remarks, "She's strong, brave, and beautiful. But like me, when she's mad even the demons run for cover."

"She's a chip off the old block then, huh?" Elena teases.

Amused by her comment, Victor smiles and replies, "You could say that. Though in some ways she's just as strong as any boy, only smarter."

"I take it you haven't many friends?" She carefully inquires.

Hesitant to answer, Victor raises his brow and replies, "I've never had the luxury of friends, just her."

"You feel very compassionate about her, in a devoted kind of way, I can tell." Elena respectfully denotes.

"I can tell it will be very hard to keep secrets from you in this place." Victor sarcastically replies.

Elena chuckles softly in response, and says, "We'll let her rest for a bit." She stands up from the edge of the bed and urges, "Follow me, there's something I want to show you."

Victor nods in respect then softly kisses Talia's forehead before leaving, and whispers, "Sleep well, milady."

Standing before him, Elena extends her hand in a welcoming manner. With a crooked smile, Victor takes her hand and leaves the room. Moments later, Lithia enters the room then climbs up on the bed and lies next to Talia, joining her in a nap. Opening her eyes, Talia sees Victor and Elena holding hands as they quietly leave the chamber. She pulls out the Angel figure from her garb and holds it closely to her chest with a sigh of relief. She smiles at the sight as she carefully caresses Lithia's back, which causes him to purr loudly. Unbeknownst to her, some of the cracks in the Angel figure begin to heal, a sign of compassionate energy flowing from Talia to the crystal itself.

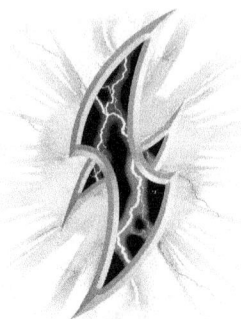

CH: 32
DYING TO BE AN ANGEL

As the afternoon turns to early evening, Victor and Elena walk along the crystalline path outside the Archadian Temple, admiring the view.

"Welcome to my kingdom," Elena says while motioning her hand towards the crystalline structures before them, "Archadia is a place where the sun warms the skin and the moon eases the mind."

Stopping abruptly to take in the stunning scenery for a moment, Victor states, "I'm speechless. It's more beautiful than I ever imagined."

"You haven't seen beautiful until you've seen a sunset up close and personal." Elena comments as she turns her attention towards the sky.

"I don't know about that," Victor flirtingly compliments as he turns directly towards Elena, "Besides, I thought Angels were beautiful no matter what time of day?" Feeling bashful by his remark, Elena smiles then moves on as he follows. "Do you remember much from your past?" She inquires.

Continuing his gaze upon the kingdom, Victor reluctantly professes, "I try to forget most things, leaving bad memories behind in the dark, hoping they never see the light of day. Other than Talia, I have no family so nothing to miss really; you see I've never been the fit in and play nice type anyway."

"What of your parents?" Elena probes, "Do you remember them?"

"Sadly, I knew never knew them." Victor unhappily reveals.

"Well whoever they were, they must've been very strong." She says.

"Someone took care of me during my youth, a surrogate of sorts, but she wasn't my real mother apparently." Victor says disappointedly.

Elena stops, feeling she struck a nerve and politely says, "I'm sorry."

"I'm not," Victor calmly murmurs as he turns to face her, "She did what she could while she was alive. Can't ask for more than that I suppose."

Stepping towards him, Elena continues to probe, "Don't you ever long for them, wonder who and what they were; your real parents I mean?"

"I'm sure when the time is right, I will." Victor sighs as he turns his attention back towards the kingdom.

A tear rolls down his face as he stops to look at the bright sun for the first time up close. Sensing the struggle within him, Elena comforts, "I'm sorry if your arrival or perhaps this place isn't exactly what you hoped for."

Embarrassed, Victor shakes his head, saying, "Please don't mistake my childish fantasy for disappointment." Feeling reassured; Elena nods in respect, "From what little I've already seen, this place truly is amazing." He clarifies while facing her, "I feel deeply honored to be here."

"I truly hope so." Elena says with a smile while walking past him.

"Being poor all my life, I've had only my dreams to carry me." Victor sensitively concedes, "I wasn't supposed to see any of this."

Elena turns back and concernedly questions, "Why do you say that?"

"I lack the memory of positive experiences." He explains, "For one, I've never seen a sunrise or sunset. Well, not the way you see them anyway."

Sympathetic towards his perspective, Elena eases, "I knew it, you are sensitive, an uncommon quality in a man of your stature. I can see why you would long for something beyond the norm of your previous surroundings."

"Have you ever been in a place from which hope is completely gone, where all that's left is faith and patience?" Victor queries in a soft tone.

"In a way, though I'm sure not near as devastating as what you're referring to." Elena regards, "Our training grounds underneath the kingdom can bring much solace to those who actually survive the Arch trials."

"My world is dark and lonely, while yours is bright and comforting." Victor expresses with slight discomfort.

"You've lived a whole life of severe oppression, that's not living." She sympathizes with concern in her voice.

"No, it's not, but it's all I know." Victor sighs in a disheartened manner, "Misery has a way of clarifying one's convictions, for it was in the mines that I realized what my life's work would be. Not to labor amongst the wretched and friendless, but to give those poor souls some small measure of hope and kindness in a world that knows all too little."

"That's truly a shame, I never knew it was like that where you come from." Elena empathizes, "I mean in Archadia, well, I guess we just let the Gods make all the decisions for us." Hoping to ease his mind, she motions towards the kingdom and offers; "You're more than welcome to stay here with my people among the clouds, if you like."

Grateful for her hospitable nature, Victor quickly responds, "I appreciate the generous offer, but I don't want to intrude."

Elena places her hand on his shoulder and says, "Trust me, you wouldn't be." Bringing a warm smile to his face, Victor comments, "Your people seem to be doing well enough here without someone like me getting in the way. I'll stay, but only if I'm wanted."

"My people will gladly give you shelter, you needn't worry about that." Elena happily reassures.

Looking away, Victor says, "Actually, it's not their approval I seek." Surprised by his meaning, she tilts her head as he finishes, "It's yours, and yours alone." Elena looks upon him and smiles compassionately, unsure of what to say then continues walking forward along the crystalline path.

"I'm sure by now you know that we aren't so different, you and I." She jokingly implies, "In fact, I think you're different, just like me."

"I've known for a while actually." Victor teasingly informs.

Stopping once again, Elena looks upon him and asks, "Really, how?"

"When we first met." Victor softly admits, "By the way, what were you doing in Pretoria that day?"

"I guess you could say I was looking for a little trouble of my own." Elena says with a slight chuckle.

"Well, I too attract trouble." Victor sarcastically replies.

"You know, I've got a rebellious streak myself." Elena jokes, "Many have found me to be a royal pain sometimes."

"I can only imagine," Victor adds, "And I a reluctant disaster."

"Have you always been this strange?" Elena teases as they make their way towards the end of the crystalline path.

"Why?" He questions, "Do you think I'm strange?"

"Well you are, sort of." She teases, "You do know that, don't you?"

"Maybe, but that's not the word I would use." Victor murmurs as he tilts his head back to take in the purified air flowing throughout the kingdom.

"Well, I like it." She admits, "You're not like anyone else I've met."

"Now that you mention it, there is a certain strangeness to me that's kind of a bizarre quality to others." Victor professes, "Some have said freak, but I think it's complimentary in a world full of posers and copycats." He then looks directly at her and comments, "I'm glad to know I'm not the only one in this world with such qualities."

Feeling flattered, Elena smiles while blushing and whispers, "Victor, I..."

"Victor!" Talia abruptly calls from a short distance away.

Surprised by the sudden interruption, Victor and Elena turn and see Talia waving as she rushes towards them with Lithia down the crystalline path.

"Looks like you have a fan." Elena amusingly remarks.

"I guess so." Victor jokingly mutters before refocusing his attention back towards her, "You were saying?"

Caught off guard, Elena slowly opens her mouth to speak, but is quickly interrupted by Talia who comes to a halt after running towards them.

"There you are!" Talia says while trying to catch her breath, "I've been looking all over for you!"

"Have you now?" Victor jokes as Elena and Talia join him in a laugh.

"You're easy to find when Lithia's around." She happily informs.

Perched on Talia's shoulder, Lithia then flies up and licks Victor's face, which causes him to laugh again. Amused by their playfulness, Elena giggles as Victor falls onto the ground, trying to calm their furry friend down.

"Alright, Lithia, that's enough!" Victor jokes as he pushes him away. Lithia stands back and chirps as Victor looks up at Elena and amusingly shrugs his shoulders. "We can talk about this later." Elena says with a smile. Excited for their new home in the sky, Talia grabs Victor's hand and excitedly shouts, "Come on, Victor, follow me!" Talia pulls him along the pathway towards the bottom of the crystalline waterfall as Elena follows closely behind with a smile on her face. Victor and Talia stop by a small pond with various crystalline creatures lurking about as Elena slowly catches up. Thrilled to see other Seraphs like himself, Lithia jumps in the water, trying to scare them off in a playful manner. "Lithia!" Talia calls with a stern tone. Lithia turns and chirps in response as a few Seraphine fly away in annoyance.

"Well what are you waiting for, an invitation?" Victor says directly to Talia, "That water looks awfully pure to me!"

"Huh?" Talia replies, looking confused. To her surprise, Victor suddenly picks her up in his arms and jokingly says, "Come on, it's your turn now!"

"Victor, don't!" She playfully cries, "You wouldn't!"

"Oh yes I would!" Victor claims as he throws her into the air. Smiling with confidence, Talia wraps her arms around her legs and splashes into the water unharmed. Elena laughs as Victor glances as her humorously, anticipating Talia's reaction. Lithia flies above the water, concerned for Talia as she unexpectedly pops her head out and tags him with her fingers while spitting water in his face. "You're it, Lithia!" She spiritedly teases. Smiling back, Lithia jumps in the water as well and begins to splash around playfully with her. Pleased by their joy, Victor laughs as Talia swims gracefully through the pond below the crystalline waterfall. She is surprised as a few Seraphine creatures suddenly surround her with their spinal shards glowing.

"This place certainly makes for an interesting habitat." Victor says on Lithia's behalf, "There's so many; I didn't know there were others like him." Elena smiles in response to Victor's naivety and says, "He's a Seraph alright."

"A Seraph?" Victor inquires, "Like the ones told in legend?" Curious, the Seraphine approach Talia who smiles, knowing now that there are in fact others just like Lithia and that he has an extended animalistic family after all. "The Seraphine are extremely sentient and have helped to protect our kingdom from invaders for generations." Elena explains, "Their acute senses have been helpful to us in many ways over the years." Talia plays with the Seraphine creatures and laughs as Lithia joins in. Trying to show off, Lithia hums Sonya's tune as the others look back confused. As he continues to hum the melody, the other Saraphine catch on and imitate the notes through harmonic chirping, which brings a smile to Talia's face.

"I don't mean this in a literal sense," Victor probes, "But do you think it's possible for two people such as Talia and myself to go back in time, undo the hardships we've endured?"

"In this place, anything's possible." Elena answers as she watches them play in the water, "You and Talia are now members of this society, and that will not change unless you make it so."

"I see." Victor mutters, "I hope not to disappoint anyone."

"All in all, it is up to you to make the transition as easy as possible for her and yourself." She respectfully clarifies.

Victor nods determinedly and declares, "I'll do what I can to help her, cause at this point, there's nothing we can or should do to change it."

Kneeling before the edge of the pond, Victor feels the dirt and water with his bare hands as Elena approaches him from behind, overlooking the crystalline waterfall, rushing with a constant flow.

"I know our worlds are different, but you'll soon grow accustomed to us." She encourages, "In time, you'll come to love it here. I'm sure of it."

Closing his eyes, Victor hums along with Lithia and takes a deep breath, taking in the watery mist then says, "There's a certain tranquility to this place. I never thought I'd live long enough to see paradise with my own eyes."

Victor picks up a small rock and skips it across the water, which splashes into Talia and accidently scares off the Seraphine creatures surrounding her.

"Victor!" Talia jokingly hollers.

Laughing at her expense, Victor smirks as she playfully frowns in response.

"To a point, we humans maintain a great perspective on life below the surface because we're always looking up, though I have to admit, the smarter we get the more dangerous we become." He says with a wary expression, "Still, I wish the others could see this place for themselves."

"Perhaps someday they will." Elena inspires.

Rising to his feet, Victor wipes off the dirt from his hands with the pond water then turns to face her, "I hope so, cause I'm going back for them someday." He declares, "One way or another."

"You never know what will happen." Elena encourages with a smile.

Victor conclusively steps away from the pond and stands beside her, saying, "No, I guess you never do."

"From my perspective over the years as an Archadian Princess, the greatest problem in the world today is tolerance." Elena strongly denotes.

Curious to her meaning, Victor question, "How so?"

"Because it seems everyone is so intolerant of each other nowadays." Elena respectfully implies, "Though to us, equality is about giving everyone an equal chance, not about giving everyone an equal result. Popularity for example is something I assume you lacked growing up."

Sighing disappointedly, Victor admits, "The only thing the Pretorians hated more than the others was me."

"That's unfortunate." She regards with a saddened tone.

"Most people despised me, but I didn't always hate them in return." He humbly explains, "In fact, I pitied them." He then looks directly at her, saying, "And do you know why?"

"Because most people will never know anything beyond what they see with their own eyes." Elena replies without hesitation.

Surprised by her intuition, Victor looks upon her compassionately as they both smile, acknowledging each other's likeness. He then turns his attention overhead as Valorie and Vennessa suddenly approach Elena from the sky. As they float above them, Elena looks upon her fellow sisters in curiosity.

"Princess, you've both been summoned." Vennessa announces.

"They're waiting for you." Valorie respectfully adds.

Elena nods her head in respect and says, "We'll be right there."

Valorie and Vennessa nod back then quickly take off as Victor looks upon Elena and inquires, "What's going on?"

"Follow me, there is much to discuss." Elena informs as she quickly turns to take her leave. Victor follows Elena then slowly turns back to address Talia before leaving and warns, "You two stay here, and stay out of trouble!"

"When have I ever done otherwise?" Talia replies with a cute smile.

Amused by her playful attitude, Victor shakes his head and follows Elena back towards the Archadian Temple. Talia turns her attention back towards her furry friend and says, "Alright, you heard him, Lithia."

As Talia and Lithia continue splashing around the pond, Victor turns his head once more and smiles while following Elena along the crystalline path.

Deep within the Archadian Temple, Victor and Elena walk down the corridor leading towards the throne chamber as he looks around, admiring the Angelic architecture. "You ready?" Elena asks.

"Guess we'll see soon enough." Victor retorts with a nervous grin.

Elena smiles back then opens the crystalline doorway leading into the throne chamber. As they enter, Rosalyn turns to face them with a pleasing look.

"Welcome, Victor." She calls, "We've been expecting you."

"Oh, have I been the subject of conversation lately?" Victor sarcastically comments, attempting to lighten the mood upon his first impression as Rosalyn and Josephus chuckle in response.

"Indirectly." Josephus states, "Come, join us if you will."

Hesitant, Victor glances at Elena who holds his hand to comfort him and says gently, "It's alright, don't be afraid. You can speak freely here."

Feeling somewhat reassured, Victor sarcastically mutters, "Speaking my mind is easy, doing it tactfully, not so much." After sharing a brief smile with Elena, the pair calmly approaches her parents to converse within the chamber.

"Our daughter's become quite the missionary as of late." Josephus denotes, "Though her prescient nature is impeccable at times."

Looking back at her, Victor jokingly puns, "Thanks for the warning."

Elena smacks her hand over his arm in a playful manner and grins as Victor calmly chuckles to himself. "We see you've survived the arena safely in one piece," Rosalyn compliments, "Impressive for a human of your stature."
Feeling somewhat insulted, Victor glances back at Elena once again with a lowered brow, unsure of their meaning.

"That was meant as a joke by the way." Elena carefully teases.

"Sorry, I was not amused." Victor jokingly scoffs in return.

"You guys should've seen it," Elena describes to her parents ecstatically, "Tannis had the nerve to put him up against Braxel of all people."

"Really?" Josephus inquires, "And just how did you manage to handle that by yourself I wonder?"

"Things were getting out of hand, so Trag and I intervened." Elena clarifies with a childish smile.
Rosalyn and Josephus look upon her with concern as she and Victor grin.

"Is that so?" Josephus queries, "Your timing is fortuitous, and since we all seem to be standing on ceremony, allow us to introduce ourselves." He finishes while bowing his head, "I am Josephus Saltora, King of Archadia."

"And I am Rosalyn Saltora, Queen of Archadia." Rosalyn adds in the same respectful manner.
Victor also bows his head and says, "It's an honor to finally meet you."

"I must say, your presence couldn't have come at a better time." Rosalyn informs with a soft sigh of relief.

"I'm not sure why," Victor curiously retorts, "But is anyone going to tell me why I'm here?"
Trying not to give themselves away, Rosalyn and Josephus nod at Elena as she faces Victor directly and informs, "We need your help, Victor."

"My help?" He cautiously inquires, "For what exactly?"
Slowly circling around Victor to examine him carefully, Josephus points out, "You survived the arena, did you not?"
Confused by his intentions, Victor keeps his focus on Josephus and responds, "Yeah, but what makes you think I have what it takes to be an Angel?"
As Josephus stops, Rosalyn respectfully interjects, "You have very low esteem for someone capable of such courage."

"A human trait no doubt." Josephus seriously adds.
Victor glances at Elena then extends his arms out, "Look, this is all very flattering, but you don't want me." He clarifies, "I'm only human."

"And an Angel!" Elena chimes in protectively.

"I think you misunderstand what it is that we do here," Josephus enlightens, "A common misconception that has yet to be remedied among the surface dwellers of Earth."
Rosalyn extends her arm out and invites, "Please, walk with us, Victor."
Elena places her hand over Victor's back, encouraging him to go along.

"Relax, we have much to discuss." Josephus eases.

Victor nods out of respect and follows Rosalyn and Josephus outside onto the balcony of the temple as Elena follows close behind.

Everyone stands on the balcony of the Archadian Temple overlooking the kingdom under the beautiful sunset as Victor looks on in amazement of the view from their current height. "Since time immemorial, the Arch has served as the keepers of peace, order, and justice throughout the world." Josephus proclaims with his attention focused on the kingdom, "To be chosen, to join its ranks is the highest of honors, and the greatest of responsibilities."

Rosalyn steps forward and continues, "Whenever a child of Earth is chosen, or in other words blessed with an Arch aura, they are given asylum into our kingdom for eternity." She then adds, "Should they choose the virtuous path of an Angel that is."

"Though the people of Earth govern themselves, we watch over them, and act whenever necessary." Josephus finishes.

Curious of their actual purpose, Victor looks upon them and respectfully inquires, "What of the Gods?"

Rosalyn glances at Josephus then looks upward, signifying the orbiting space station, and explains, "As you can see, they rule from their kingdom Empyria, and give us strength as we safeguard the world you know. Their intelligence is much more advanced and for us that means efficiency functioning on multiple levels and sometimes multiple dimensions in a spiritual sense."

"If your power is so great, then what keeps anyone from just leaving this planet altogether?" Victor queries.

"An interesting notion, but all the energy derived even from the most powerful of chaos crystals is useless when trying to breach the Earth's atmosphere." Josephus enlightens.

"I take it you've tried?" Victor carefully inquires.

Josephus shares a glance with Rosalyn for a moment, impressed by Victor's intuitive nature then answers, "No, but there are many who have."

"Though all of them failed in their feeble attempts to go beyond, and simply died." Rosalyn adds.

Nodding, Victor looks onto the horizon and mutters, "I see."

"To fully answer your question, it would take more power than we ourselves currently possess to do so without the proper key into their realm." Rosalyn clarifies as Elena stands next to Victor by the balcony's edge.

"The Gods made sure no one could ever use the crystals' power beyond our world for their safety, as well as our own." Josephus informs.

Victor scoffs in light of this information and says, "Probably so that no one could ever use it against them." He then sneers, "Sounds no different than the mines in Pretoria if you ask me."

"A thought-provoking analogy to be sure, but make no mistake about the real difference." Josephus defends, "For it is an honor to serve them in return for our way of life."

"Way of life?" Victor asks as he glances over at them.

"A life that grants purpose, but when the people of Earth are threatened it becomes a threat for us all." Rosalyn explains, "People never do evil so completely and cheerfully as when they do it for religious conviction." Victor looks back at Elena with a concerned expression and sighs, "Sounds like a double-edged sword to me. There's a lot more to this, isn't there?" Rosalyn looks upon Victor curiously and asks, "What do you mean?"

"I've seen another of your kind before," Victor reveals as he leans back against the railing with his arms crossed, "They attacked me in Pretoria after I escaped the mines. I'm not sure why exactly, but it seems they were after my Gauntlet, which I assume is still here." Elena nods to reassure him, as they glance at each other with grave concern.

"Are you sure about that?" Rosalyn questions.

"Absolutely." Victor continues, "Never thought I'd ever see one in person, not that close anyway." Concerned by this news, Josephus attempts to simplify, "They killed our own kind when they were supposed to be our allies. They simply believe other races to be a waste of purpose and skin."

"That couldn't have been more obvious to me." Victor murmurs.

"The last time we encountered them ourselves was centuries ago, which cost thousands of lives." Josephus sternly adds.

"I can believe that." Victor states in a respectful manner.

"We are an ancient power, but we've greatly suffered for it." Rosalyn continues, "Our history is littered with the deaths of those who wanted more." She explains, "Nothing was ever enough for them, so we evolved a simpler way of living. For whatever is taken, something must always be given in return."

"That seems an equitable code." Victor commends. Josephus leads the way down a crystalline path from the balcony and continues, "It's brought us peace anyway, though unfortunately there are those that wish to destroy what's left of it." He explains, "Heaven and Hell can be earthly, for we each carry them both inside us."

"What you speak of are none other than what we refer to as, the fallen." Rosalyn discloses. Victor stops next to Elena, concerned by the name and asks, "The fallen?" Rosalyn turns and responds, "Angels that have fallen from their divine place among us. We call them Darchadians, for in contrast they've become damned by the darkness within them."

"I've heard of them before, but only in stories." Victor references.

"The Darchadians lack a sense of morality, and have always been our most dangerous adversaries." Josephus assuredly claims, "They intended to upset the balance of war and peace, but their presence has been nonexistent for some time now."

"They sure looked like Darchadians to me," Victor reveals as Elena looks upon him with concern, "Both were extremely dark and twisted."

Unsure of his exact description, Josephus states, "You could be confused with those on Earth who foolishly attempt to imitate our kind. But if that's not the case, then Archadia needs all the best Angels it can get to defend itself from such possible threats."

Shaking his head in disbelief, Victor scoffs, "All the more reason to choose someone more qualified then."

Elena steps in front of him and calmly informs, "We didn't choose you."

Confused by her meaning, Victor's expression changes to that of concern as Rosalyn clarifies, "As a matter of fact, the Gods chose you, as they have chosen all of us here."

"You're a child of both worlds, but in truth we were curious and merely took a chance on a fate." Josephus acknowledges.

"Where I come from, chance is nothing more than a fool's paradise." Victor replies irksomely.

"Consider us fools if you must, but the Angelus process has never been attempted on a human before," Josephus retorts, "As you are the first to ever be chosen."

Feeling uneasy about his position, Victor firmly inquires, "If I was chosen, then what of my people? They're still a part of me, and always will be."

Sensing his disappointment, Elena looks into Victor's eyes, hoping to ease his mind of any dark thoughts still lingering within.

"But none of them accept you, do they?" Rosalyn implies.

Disheartened by their words, Victor says, "No, they don't." He then looks into the sunset, taking in the last bit of warmth from the sun's rays.

Taking this opportunity to sway Victor away from his past, Rosalyn deduces, "To fit in, they demanded you change the one thing that sets you apart from them. Instead, you resisted their sinful ways, that too is the mark of an Angel most worthy of recognition." Out of reminder, Victor glances at the mark on his arm curiously as he caresses his fingers over it then lowers his head discouragingly. "It's safe to assume that those around you did not understand, for you apparently frightened them." Rosalyn explains, "They shunned you, cursed you, even called you vile names, and you knew not why."

Victor raises his head, knowing Rosalyn speaks the truth.

"Even now, you don't fully understand why you are so driven, why you can't relent, repent, confess, or perhaps even obtain." She resumes as Victor nods unwillingly, "But how could you possibly know, assuming there have been no others to lead you to that knowledge?" She finishes.

Discouraged, Victor glances at Elena who smiles and places her hand on his shoulder to comfort him. "We know that you've been shunned by those below, lost, and alone." Josephus regards, "But the truth is, you're nothing to them and likely never will be."

"That's enough, father!" Elena firmly scolds, annoyed by their persistent badgering towards him. Josephus scoffs as she tries to comfort Victor, saying, "I apologize for my parents' behavior." She explains while motioning towards them, "Seems they're totally out of practice when it comes to ancient methods of decorum." Victor looks back at her parents for a moment and politely articulates, "At least they're honest; I can respect that." Rosalyn and Josephus nod in respect as Elena counters, "Yes, but sometimes they never let up. Our style of complete honesty frightens most people."

"I'll admit their honesty is a bit tenacious, but absolutely necessary in this case." Victor says with a nod.

"I've never heard it described in such a way, but it is an Archadian attribute." Elena says jokingly, "I promise I'll try to be only half as annoying."

"Only half, huh?" Victor jokes with a crooked smile.

Elena smiles in response as Victor sighs to regain his confident composure.

"You must excuse our unruly daughter, for she's always been an independent woman of her own mind." Josephus apologizes.

"And my parents have always been experts at making my excuses time and again." Elena jokingly retorts.

As Victor walks past Elena, he approaches the edge of the crystalline path, and observes the beautiful kingdom, trying to evaluate the responsibility that comes with such a proposed status of being an Angelic warrior in their midst.

"There is nothing left for you back in the mines," Rosalyn persuades, "Everything, is in Archadia now."

"Not everything." Victor contests, "There's a part of me that's still searching from the storm within."

"You will be welcome here until we learn of the Darchadians' true intentions, if they are indeed to be revealed as such." Rosalyn assures, "In the mean time, we ask that you stay with us safe within this kingdom, above any hardships you may encounter on the surface below."

Too prideful to accept their generous offer, Victor turns his head and declares, "Thanks, but I go my own way, always have." Looking back towards the sky, he takes a deep breath and finishes, "I'm just not sure I can reconcile all this with the world I know below."

Josephus approaches him and explains, "It's your choice. You can go back, sure, and pray that they'll one day accept you. Or you can stay, have a life of freedom here if you want it; earn your place among us and the Gods."

"Like my mother?" Victor mocks intensely, regarding Victoria.

Elena glances at Rosalyn, both looking concerned as Josephus profoundly regards, "There is an ethereal energy more powerful than any of us that rules over Earth; it defines right from wrong and governs all our destinies. Point being, what happened to her was indeed tragic, but make no mistake, for it was the Gods' will." He finishes while stepping away, "You should be eternally grateful that they chose to spare you, for you at least survived."

Victor quickly turns and firmly retorts, "Did I?"

"Of course!" Josephus says with a chuckle, "The Gods are never wrong, though occasionally they do tend to disagree from time to time."

"And though your presence raises many questions, let us hope we understand your true purpose before it's too late." Rosalyn cautions.

Elena gazes upon Victor compassionately, hoping he can quickly come to terms with all of this. "We have to believe that an intelligence that advanced knows what they're doing." She strongly encourages, "All that's required on our part is faith." Turning back, Victor looks upon Elena whilst hesitating to speak, then calmly queries, "A sense of adventure you mean?"

"You can reclaim your birth rite, renew your halo so to speak." Josephus coaxes, "We're offering you the chance to be one of us, an Angel."

"No!" Victor strongly retorts, "You're offering me a chance to pretend to be an Angel, nothing more." Elena is surprised by his response as Josephus sighs impatiently to his stubbornness like that of hers.

"No doubt your oppressed childhood made you into the man you are today, but know that each of us has a higher purpose regardless of our setting, though yours simply has yet to reveal itself." Rosalyn calmly informs.

Crossing his arms, Victor refutably says, "I just got here, and already you expect me to risk my neck for those I don't even know or have never met?"

Josephus frowns, feeling slightly insulted as Victor clarifies, "I respect your position, I really do, but until you give me a better reason I won't do it."

Calming himself to Victor's rebelliousness, Josephus states, "Your pride demonstrates your noble character, regardless of your breeding."

"I appreciate the sentiment, but you can't sell dreams to someone who has walked through nightmares." Victor scorns, "If you're going to expect someone to save the world, you should probably make sure they like it the way it already is first."

"There's no doubt that your deprived childhood made you into the man you are today," Rosalyn kindly suggests, "Perhaps you'll reconsider our offer after you've had a chance to think things over."

Concerned for his current state of mind, Elena frowns upon her parents.

Sighing disappointedly, Victor looks away and mutters, "I need to be alone."

As he turns to walk away, Rosalyn settles, "Victor, if ever you should change your mind; know that you will always find refuge here."

Victor walks away to clear his head as Elena steps forward then stops as she watches him leave, sensing the pain buried deep within him.

"He's afraid, even after all this time it seems he's still questioning his place in the world." Rosalyn cautiously denotes.

"That's because he has nothing to fight for." Josephus infers, "If there's one thing he's hiding, it's his questionable disposition, for he's headstrong and in some ways dangerously idealistic."

Elena impatiently turns her head for a moment, annoyed by their claims.

"Don't blame him, Elena, it's in his nature to survive." Rosalyn explains, "That's why there's so many of him and so few of us."

"Even still, we must be cautious, for what lies within him resembles that of a shadow heart." Josephus forewarns.

Elena quickly turns to face them, upset by their pretentious assumptions.

"It's apparent that he is driven by passion," Rosalyn continues, "But his power derives from emotions he was never taught to control."

Josephus steps towards the edge of the crystalline path, while watching Victor make his way down towards the waterfall bottom and says, "He may be more Angel than he realizes, though his rage has unbalanced him." He then turns back to address Elena directly, "If he is to stay, then he must learn to control his fear. Otherwise he will not be given sanctuary by us, or the Gods."

Stepping forward past her parents, Elena looks away and sighs, hoping her instincts aren't wrong about Victor. "You may find him to be unusual, and maybe he his, but I've sensed remarkable depth in him." She justifies.

"He may be half Angel but that doesn't make him one of us, for he'll always remain human as well." Josephus firmly retorts.

Irritated by her parents' remarks, Elena rushes off to find Victor as Rosalyn and Josephus glance at each other with concern.

Standing alone at the end of the crystalline path below the waterfall, Victor looks up into the evening sky as the sun finally sets upon the kingdom.

"Who are you, Victor?" Elena calls out as she walks down the path.

Victor quickly turns and sees her approaching him with an intense look.

"I'm nobody, for whatever that's worth." He pathetically mutters.

"Don't give me that!" She demands as she suddenly stops before him, "What is your purpose?"

"My purpose?" He asks, confused by her sudden change in attitude.

"Yes!" She forcefully pursues, stepping closer as if to examine him closely, "You do have one, don't you?"

"What do you take me for, Princess?" He scoffs in annoyance.

Put off by his wary tone, she states, "A man who's lost in the scramble for his own identity. Though despite all that, you're someone in need of a mission, something to accomplish, and the Gods could use a person like you."

"Really?" Victor guardedly inquires, "And why is that?"

"Because your heart is open." Elena says with a softer tone.

"Right now, my heart hunts for a place to be free." Victor asserts.

Hoping to sway his view, she places her hand over his chest and says, "You hold nothing back, and give all of yourself to those in need." As Victor takes in the comfort of her delicate touch, she resumes; "Such heroism inspires courage and sacrifice, by asking others to be better than what they are."

"So, that's why the Gods spared me is it?" Victor sarcastically questions, "To be a symbol?"

Pulling her hand away, Elena looks upon Victor intensely and informs, "Yes, and it's why the nobles hate you. I saw the shame in their eyes when the crowd praised you back at the arena." Victor turns away irritably as she persists, "Don't you understand? Yesterday the world saw a slave become more powerful than the Emperor himself."

"I highly doubt that." Victor scoffs in amusement, "You give me more credit than I possibly deserve."

Elena steps beside Victor, hoping to help him see her perspective.

"Listen to me!" She insists, "The Emperor has enemies, most of all in the Senate. But while most of the people follow him, no one would dare stand against him, not until you came along."

"If they oppose him, then why don't they do something about it?" Victor questions with anger evident in his voice.

Stepping towards the pathway's edge overlooking the kingdom, Elena clarifies, "Suffice it to say because they play the rules of the system and are too afraid to act. And while he rules them, he rules everything below on the surface." She finishes with her head turned.

Joining her on the pathway's edge, Victor profoundly denotes, "So let me get this straight, they justify criminal behavior and glorify violence; as a result, they've based everything on a fraudulent narrative." Elena nods in response as he scoffs, "What makes you think anything's ever going to change that?"

"There's nothing people in power hate more than to be made irrelevant in the eyes of those with less. Don't you see?" She pleas, "You're the only one who can bridge the gap between two worlds, each distinct from one another. And the world below needs a hero now more than ever."

Victor places his hands on the railing and sighs, "I'm not saying you're wrong, but what good is a hero if no one remembers who they are or is changed by what they did?"

"Even small deeds don't go unnoticed by those who truly matter." She strongly pursues, "Do you not see the virtue of our cause?"

"Everyone thinks their cause is virtuous in nature, Princess." Victor rudely claims as he turns to walk away.

"Even so…" Elena responds as she rushes towards him, hoping to change his mind then says, "Is there nothing about my kingdom that appeals to your heart in some way?" Stopping in his tracks, Victor faces her, whilst pondering the thought and questions, "Aren't you afraid of anything?"

"Unlike most others you may have encountered upon the surface, I can't afford to be afraid, even when I have a reason to." She proudly answers, "Don't you have any fear?"

"Fear is all I really know." Victor mutters with a depressed groan.

"Just think of it, if your hate could be turned into electricity it would light up the whole world." She encourages.

"It would do much more than that I'm afraid." Victor retorts.

"You're the missing link that can make a difference for all the people of Earth." Elena enlightens as she approaches him and places her hand back on his chest, "The Archadian within is the missing piece to your heart. If you embrace it, and except it, you can do anything."

Trying not to give his true feelings away, Victor responds, "You make it sound so poetic, but no good will come out of me fighting your war."

Elena pulls her hand away and denotes, "You must have something to fight for if you've made it this far in life."

Gazing upon her compassionately with sorrowful eyes, Victor admits, "I do fight for something, I'm just not sure if I'm strong enough to protect it."

Pausing briefly, Elena nods, realizing that he's not only referring to Talia, but herself as well. "If you had the means to save others, would you not take any action possible to make it so?" She asks softly, expecting a specific answer.

"Of course I would, I just don't know if I can." Victor expresses, "In the long run, it's probably best that I don't get involved."

"Why?" Elena questions, "So that your ego can rest assured of your own uniqueness?"

"Is that a problem?" Victor firmly contests with a stern gaze.

"Unique or not, you belong here as much as anyone, and maybe more." She rationalizes, "You wouldn't be here if there wasn't something special inside you. I see it. Why can't you?"

Staring into her eyes intensely, Victor professes, "I see you."

Flustered by his attempt to woo her, Elena turns away, looking up at the moon, and states, "If that is true, then you see my purpose, my duty. I would lay down my life for Archadia as it is my sacred duty." She then turns back and finishes, "What is yours?"

Looking away, Victor searches deep inside himself and claims, "I'm just a fool of a man who can only maintain his pride through suffering, by fighting."

As she looks upon him with concern, he extends his arms and reluctantly states, "Deep down, I've always known I was meant for something greater, but I have so many questions." Lowering his arms, he looks directly at her and says, "Where do I come from? Why am I even here?"

"Our present defines us, not our past." She encourages while placing his hand in hers, "Forget what you were and embrace who you are. Like me, you were chosen by the Gods to be their instrument of salvation."

Raising his hand while slowly turning it back and forth, Victor simplifies, "I want to show the world that humans aren't slaves, we're more than that whether anyone believes it or not." He finishes with a closed fist.

Elena steps away as she continues her gaze upon the scenic kingdom before them, stating, "Earth dwellers think of us as mere decorations for the Gods, but they do not know nor can they even conceive the brutal unseen war that has been brewing around them for years now. A war that may one day determine the very fate of this planet."

Victor listens with full attention as she faces him and informs, "Indirectly, whether you like it or not, you have been drawn into this spiritual war. Understand; there comes a time in everyone's life when we are called upon to make a difference, for you and I in particular, I believe now is that time."
Hesitating to make a decision, Victor sighs, "It seems I have no choice then, for slavery is an eternity I hope none of you ever have to face."

"I'm sorry you had to endure such a horrible life, but you do have a choice." She reassures, "Never be defined by your past for it was just a lesson, not a life sentence. Highly evolved people such as ourselves have their own conscience of pure law which allows us to move past our daily hardships."
After a moment of contemplation, Victor finally comes to his senses and says, "If there's one thing my mother taught me as a child, it's that if you don't have much then you simply work with what you've got. And when you don't have anything, you take what you can get." Elena nods in agreement as Victor straightens up and declares, "All right, I'll join your ranks, but if I do this, I do it as a human, nothing more and nothing less."
Elena closes her eyes for a moment in relief then says, "But you're not just human," opening her eyes, she finishes, "Are you?"

"Perhaps not, but I know I can't do it alone." He states determinedly while stepping closer to her.

"You won't." She inspires with her hand extended before him in a warrior like manner, "When you are born into a world you don't quite fit in, perhaps it's because you were meant to help create a new one instead."
Accepting his decision, Victor nods with a grin and says, "Oh, what the hell." He grips her hand in covenant as she nods back, smiling with confidence of his choice. In response to his noble decision, she pulls out a basic Archadian Gauntlet from her garb and hands it to Victor who instinctively takes it. He places the Gauntlet over his arm with feet firmly planted as it powers up his Soul Gear. Elena observes the energy reaction and chuckles quietly; Victor is taken aback by the sudden power surge and grunts as the crystalline armor forms over his body. Stepping towards the pathway's edge, she informs, "Now that that's settled, if you're feeling up to it we're going to fly now."
Surprised by her gesture, Victor questions, "What do you mean, fly?"
Elena approaches him and presses the blue symbol bearing over his chest, which causes his wings to activate for the first time as they emerge from his spinal armor. "You're half Angel, remember?" She spiritedly prompts, "Your wings already exist; all you have to do is utilize them properly."
Shocked by the sight of his blue Angelic wings, Victor takes in a heavy breath to keep his composure and expresses, "I can't believe what I'm seeing!"
He exhales and moves his wings up and down effortlessly to get a feel for them, saying, "They're really mine, aren't they?"
Elena nods with a smile then presses the pink Gods' symbol on her chest as well, which causes her wings to activate and emerge from her spinal armor.

Victor's eyes widen as she steps towards the edge of a crystalline rock structure, and states, "Come on, I'll lead the way." She then steps off of the structure and gracefully floats in the air before him.

Observing her pink Angelic wings curiously as they flow up and down gracefully, Victor approaches the cliff and whispers, "Incredible."

"Now you try." Elena convinces while motioning towards him.

Concerned about the gravity of the situation, Victor looks over the edge of the cliff and mutters, "Guess there's a first time for everything, isn't there?"

"Better late than never I suppose." Elena encouragingly jokes, "When it feels scary to jump, that's exactly when you do it, otherwise you end up staying in the same place your whole life."

"And that I cannot do." Victor sternly admits.

"But if you truly want to fly, you have to give up the things that weigh you down by taking a leap of faith." Elena graciously inspires.

"I suppose you're right, how hard can it be anyway?" Victor states as he closes his eyes, and carefully steps off the edge. He falls for a second but stays afloat as his wings react neurologically to his natural instinct to fly.

"It's a lot harder than it looks sometimes." Elena teases with a laugh.

"Good thing I'm a fast learner then." He claims, "We're flying now!"

Laughing excitingly, Elena looks upon Victor who attempts to maneuver himself in midair. "You see, it's not so bad." She assures, "In every flight with nature one receives far more than they seek."

Excited, Victor looks left and right to examine his wings then grips his fists tightly and shouts, "Wow, this is great!" He laughs while quickly moving up and down in the air with ease.

"Care for an evening stroll?" Elena requests.

"Oh yeah!" Victor exclaims enthusiastically, "I was born for this!"

"Good!" She cheerfully responds, "Follow me then."

Elena suddenly flies off as Victor grins with determination mutters, "With pleasure." Trying to stay afloat, he follows her closely as she leads him through the kingdom to showcase its true beauty. She then flies in closer and reaches out to grip his hand to help him sustain his balance. "No offense, but your race seems to be more primitive than I expected." He jokingly nitpicks.

Amused by his instigating comment, Elena replies, "We may seem primitive at first glance, but our technological abilities aren't always apparent because we have chosen not to employ them in our daily lives."

"We too believe that when you allow technology to work in place of the people, you take away something extremely vital from them." Victor remarks as he looks around curiously, "Speaking of which, what do your people do for fun around here anyway?"

"We're not as dull as you surface dwellers may think." She replies with a soft chuckle then points towards a specific section of the kingdom and says, "See that?"

Turning his attention elsewhere, he sees the professed spot where several Archadians challenge each other though various night sports as she explains, "Nothing reveals a person so well as the games they play."

"Seems more accurate that people reveal themselves in how they play." Victor comments, "I gather there's no hard feelings between anyone?"

"Here we don't begrudge one another due to lack of skill or power." She proudly proclaims, "Life is much more simple up here in terms of class." Looking around from above, Victor asks, "What's the real challenge then?"

Triggering a smile, Elena looks over at him and amusingly responds, "The challenge as you so eloquently put it is to improve and enrich ourselves, to enjoy everything life has to offer though nothing in excess." She enlightens, "With a certain level of discipline and obedience of course."

"A life like that does present a certain fascination to one looking for a change in pace." Victor states with a childish smirk.

"We Angels may not always be the smartest or the strongest people on the planet, but we are without a doubt the most righteous." Elena informs whilst continuing to lead the way through the crystalline kingdom, "A lot has changed over the centuries, at least for my people that is."

"How do you mean?" Victor curiously probes.

"Material needs for the most part no longer exist for us." She explains, "We don't obsess over the accumulation of things, for we've eliminated hunger, want, and the need for worthless possessions." Victor glances at the crystal shard necklace still wrapped around his neck, feeling it to be anything but worthless as she continues, "Unlike those below, hate has no place in our society for we've grown out of our primal infancy."

"Some people on the surface would say you've got it all wrong." Victor respectfully challenges, "Not all belongings are completely worthless just as not all people are hateful. Though it has never truly been about possessions or even hate, for me anyway, it's about power really."

Curious to his bold statement, Elena glances back at him and carefully inquires, "Power to do what exactly?"

"To control one's life, one's destiny." He confirms while feeling the cut of his wings for the first time through the cool sky as Kael once cited.

"Some would say that kind of control is an illusion." She contends.

"Probably, but I'm here, aren't I?" Victor points out to her surprise, "I should be dead, but I'm not, not yet anyway."

Elena leans her head back as she closes her eyes in relief of the cool evening breeze, and says, "We Angels enjoy such things as music and flying, not to escape life but for life not to escape us. When I'm up here I don't even feel the troubles of the world below, purely, I just feel…."

"Free." Victor thoughtfully interjects.

Surprised by their intuitive nature to finish each other's sentences, Elena opens her eyes then glances at Victor, sharing a compassionate smile.

Victor turns his attention below him, observing the Angels training together with great finesse as Elena motions towards them and states, "As you can see, we help each other to grow, so that we can act as one."

"Wish my people would learn to do the same." Victor sadly mutters.

"All people are capable of working together…" She encourages while directly facing him as he looks back curiously, "They just have to believe." Victor firmly nods in agreement to her bold sentiment as she smiles back determinedly and teases, "Try and keep up, if you can!"

Feeling that he's ready to utilize his Angelic wings without help after finally letting go of his hand, Elena spread hers and suddenly flies off at high speed, taking Victor aback as he stops for a moment, trying to maintain his balance in the air. "You want it, you got it!" He announces with a determined grin.

Victor fully spreads his wings in return and swiftly takes off, trying to keep up with her as they fly throughout the kingdom at high speed. Learning to balance himself properly whilst flying, Victor speeds up trying to catch her and accidently runs into a crystalline structure being handcrafted by a fellow Archadian. "Sorry!" He apologetically exclaims with his head turned as the Artisan raises his fist and shakes his head in annoyance.

"You're going to have to do better than that if you want to catch me!" Elena jokingly warns, as she looks behind her with a grin then suddenly takes off at full speed. "As you wish, milady!" Victor says determinedly.

Attempting to catch her once again, Victor flies at full speed, as Elena looks behind her and sees him suddenly changing course between buildings. Elena flies through several crystalline waterfalls, trying to lose him as he follows closely behind. Flying through another waterfall, Elena stops to see if Victor is capable of tracking her instinctively. Surprised, Elena looks on as Victor slowly appears through the crystalline waterfall and graciously wraps his upper wings around her. A moment of true connection is made as they look into each other's eyes passionately and lock their hands together for a moment whilst floating above the rocks behind the peaceful waterfall.

Shortly after their bonding experience, Victor and Elena come to a stopping point and land gracefully above the waterfall. "I see you're getting the hang of it." She says with a smile. Victor grins in response as Elena extends her arm towards a small crystalline tree and says, "As you've probably noticed by now, love of nature is a common language that can transcend political and social boundaries."

Curious, Victor approaches the small tree then kneels before it and humbly concedes, "I've never seen a tree quite like this one before."

"I suppose when you're born into privilege, you don't notice such things as much because it seems all too natural." Elena reluctantly admits.

"The same can be said about being born into suffering." Victor adds as he carefully caresses the crystalline branches, "What is it?"

"We call this the Tree of Life." Elena reveals as she approaches him from behind, "It is said to have been the first form of organic life that sprouted when the Gods blessed us with this floating kingdom."

The tree sparkles with beauty, illuminated by the moonlight beaming from the sky above as Victor looks upon it in wonder. "In truth, it symbolizes that of wondrous power and growth, the evolution of Earth's people, as well as the balance between what you surface dwellers call Heaven and Hell." She resumes, "It represents the divine root that contains our life essence, and memories passed down from those before us."

Cogitating her profound meaning, Victor stands up and deduces, "In other words, paradise." Elena nods, amused by his intuition. Gazing into the night sky, he mutters, "Seems there's so much I have yet to learn in this world."

Standing close beside him, Elena looks into the night sky as well, and states, "In our society, we devote ourselves to the obligation of making life work, for everyone, not just ourselves."

"In mine, we share the responsibilities, and the pain equally." Victor says softly while closing his eyes, taking in a deep breath.

"As do we, which is why I'm here with you now." She happily assures, "Preserving life, all life is very important to us."

Slowly opening his eyes while exhaling calmly, Victor faces her with a curious expression and respectfully asks, "Why exactly?"

"It's simple really." She clarifies, "We believe everything in the world has a right to exist, despite its origins."

"An interesting belief which most do not share unfortunately," Victor states as they watch the sun finally disappear into twilight on the other ends of the Earth, "Everything seems so perfect up here, especially with you."

Flattered by his remark, Elena blushes for a moment then turns to take her leave, saying, "Tomorrow your training begins." She stops while pointing towards a tall crystalline shrine in the distance and instructs, "At dawn, see to it you reach the top of that tower." Victor looks upon the towering shrine in curiosity as she continues, "There will be a surprise waiting for you up there."

Willing to honor her request, Victor nods with determination as she activates her wings and calmly informs, "I must go."

As Elena prepares to take off, Victor quickly takes her hand in his, and says, "Elena, wait!" Turning back slowly, Elena's looks into his eyes passionately. "Where are you going?" He kindly persists, "The night is young."

"Rest well tonight, Victor. You'll need your strength," Elena says softly then turns and firmly states, "I'll see you tomorrow bright and early."

Disappointed by her sudden departure, Victor looks on as Elena swiftly takes off to her quarters within the Archadian Temple in the distance.

As the stars glisten with beauty, Victor takes in the moonlit sky once more then sighs as he activates his wings also and quickly takes off back to his quarters to rest for the night as requested.

CH: 33
ANGELIC INITIATION

Early the next morning in Archadia, Victor climbs up the tower as requested by Elena, stopping for a moment to gaze upon the cloudy domain. He makes it to the top then looks over the edge, amazed at the height while admiring the view from above as the sun rises, illuminating the entire kingdom. Suddenly, to his surprise a familiar voice calls, "I'm surprised to see you've traveled this far, and on foot no less!" Victor slowly turns and sees Kael standing behind him. "You have wings now, so why not use them?"

Hesitant to speak, Victor's eyes widen as he looks upon Kael for a moment in shock and says, "Master Kael."

Kael slowly approaches his lifelong student with a grin, saying, "Welcome to Archadia, Victor. I knew you'd find your way eventually, despite the difficult obstacles you faced along the way."

Looking over the edge upon the kingdom with his old mentor, Victor mutters, "I suppose your faith in my abilities helped guide me this way."

"Indeed," Kael says with a pat on his shoulder. He then steps away from the edge and says, "As an authority figure, I inspired you, it's what I'm supposed to do. That's why I've been sent here to greet you in person."

"I felt the worst had befallen you." Victor sadly professes as he faces Kael then carefully asks, "What happened?"

"Let's just say you're not the only one with friends in high places." Kael replies with a soft chuckle, "Archadia is an advanced culture, centuries old, self-contained with incredible technical sophistication, whilst providing the daily needs of all its citizens." He explains, "So they can turn themselves completely over to art, culture, and certain paths of enlightenment." Victor is slightly emotional, thinking Kael had been killed during his daring escape from the mines. Being the only father figure he's ever known, Victor does his best to keep his strong composure in his presence. "I'm glad to know Talia made it out safely as well." Kael adds on a more personal note.

"So am I." Victor says with a solemn nod.

"The two of you have always had an unbreakable bond," Kael illuminates, "The kind that others have fought and died for. Many have found it disturbing in some ways cause you both were so close for so long." He then chuckles quietly to himself, "At first even I didn't understand it, but I soon learned to see it for what it always was."

Stepping away from the edge overlooking the kingdom, Victor approaches Kael and inquires, "Which is?"

"Beautiful, beyond compare." He softly proclaims.

Nodding in agreement, Victor grins as Kael senses his inner sorrow and asks, "How is she by the way?"

"She's safe." Victor responds with a rough voice, "I know she'd be excited to see you too."

"All in good time I'm sure." Kael states decisively as he steps closer and surprisingly holds out Victoria's Gauntlet, "Here, put it on."

Stunned, Victor looks upon the basic Archadian Gauntlet given to him the night before by Elena then slowly removes it from his arm and hands it over to Kael. Victor hesitates to grab Victoria's Gauntlet from him then reluctantly places it over his arm once again, remembering how much better it feels.

"From the looks of it, you'll need a new shard to power it up properly." Kael informs, "The original seems useless at this point."

With a sudden thought, Victor grabs the crystal necklace given to him by Talia from around his neck and places it into the Gauntlet. To his surprise, the Gods' symbol lights up brightly in blue and activates his Soul Gear, becoming even more powerful with his body connection. To Kael's delight, Victor holds his hands out as the Soul Gear forms a specific crystalline uniformed armor design around his body, courtesy of Victoria's Gauntlet.

"What kind of power is this?" Victor curiously inquires.

"The kind that's lied dormant within you all these years," Kael states, "It is the energy harnessed from the chaos crystal in your Gauntlet." He points towards his Gauntlet and continues, "Its power is derived from the planet's crystalline core." Feeling a sense of wonder, Victor observes his Archadian Soul Gear as Kael explains, "It in turn charges the crystals, which in turn charges your Gauntlet. Even your Soul Gear is powered entirely by its energy, acting as a body sealant, or in other words, appendage armor."

After a moment of examining his Soul Gear, Victor asks, "Why crystals?"

"I figured that would be clear enough to you by now, for design should always be second to function." Kael retorts, catching him off guard, "The Gods harnessed the core's power because it was the strongest source of energy after the Great Cataclysm. During the metaphysical state of the Chaos War, people the world over united with infinitely greater purpose in pursuit of war than they ever did in pursuit of peace."

"Is that why humans were enslaved?" Victor apprehensively denotes.

"A society intermixed with crystal technology has no doubt had tremendous advantages and a few disadvantages." Kael clarifies, "To keep up with demand, they were forced to work in the mines, a horrific result of the Chaos War as you well know by now."

"Such is complete subjugation!" Victor angrily expresses, "Do people not realize this? Excess in all things of this fashion is the undoing of men."

"That is why as Angels we are far superior, for we practice control of our senses and through moderation." Kael points out.

"Such fortune though, Archadia itself will soon corrupt if it hasn't already." He argues, "Wealth in great quantities brings all kingdoms below."

"Not for those who fight to keep it alive." Kael proudly states.

"Perhaps, but by weaponizing something that was meant to be pure, the world has already fell victim to their own demise. They've fallen in love with all the things in life that threatens to destroy it!" He then raises his arm, signifying his Gauntlet and exclaims, "We work ourselves to death for this?"

"The Gods are in the business of sustaining life overall, not looking out specifically after humans below the surface." Kael patiently divulges.

"Then they should make it their business to change that!" Victor angrily retorts as he examines the blue crystal within his Gauntlet, "Maybe the crystals are too powerful, maybe they should remain buried with the dead."

"But your people," Kael contests, "They've regained so much from them as well. Could you put them through darkness all over again?"

"In case you forgot, they're already in darkness." Victor contests.

"I would've thought you learned this through your studies as a child," Kael implies, "But apparently not."

"Learned what?" Victor inquires with an impatient breath.

"Humans once enslaved their own kind centuries before the Great Cataclysm ever took place." Kael informs, "There has never existed a civilized society in which one segment did not thrive upon the labor of another, as far back as one chooses to look, to ancient even biblical times, slavery has always been with us in some form." He then finishes, "And according to the people of Earth, neither is sinful or immoral, but rather as war and antagonism are the natural states of man, so too is slavery as natural as it is inevitable."

"My viewpoint greatly differs than that of Earth's." Victor states. Sensing his anger, Kael attempts to clarify, "You must understand, the crystals' power helped Earth's races rebuild their societies as they saw fit. In doing so, the Gods consolidated their power, thus, creating a one Earth form of government." Victor moves his hand back and forth then sighs depressingly as Kael continues, "Democratic institutions were swept away to enforce a world congress. Separate sovereignty between continents just happens to keep peace between everyone for the time being."

"But they enslaved my people in the process!" Victor argues while swinging his arm back furiously.

"An unfortunate turn of events for sure, nevertheless it is the way things are." Kael states as he walks past Victor then stops, turning his head and says, "Who are you to change it?"

Feeling frustrated, Victor looks back and declares, "Someone who's willing to use their power for the greater good of all people, not just my own!"

"Really?" Kael mocks with a confident grin, testing his protégé. Victor frowns in response, feeling discouraged. "You may not understand the Gods' will, but their teachings influenced all cultures of the world, a touch of Archadia goes a long way." Kael explains, "The Arch code is not just a set of rules, it is a philosophy and a very correct one. History has proved time and again that when mankind interferes with a less developed civilization no matter how well intentioned that interference may be the results are invariably disastrous. The Arch itself follows many codes, but one stands above all others." Kael states as he looks onto the kingdom once again from above.

"Oh yeah? Victor impatiently asks, "And what code is that?"

Facing him, Kael patiently answers, "That the needs of the many outweigh the needs of the few."

"Is that so?" Victor scoffs, unaccepting of the ancient code.

"I don't technically agree with it myself, but when the time comes you will understand what it truly means." Kael resumes as he paces around Victor, "Some of the darkest chapters in the history of the world involve oppression of a small group of people to satisfy the demands of a large one. I hoped that we as a people would eventually learn from our mistakes, but it seems that most of us haven't."

Carefully pondering the thought, Victor insinuates, "You're saying that one person can't make a difference no matter how small?"

"Ah, but the one." Kael confidently responds, "One is a warrior, but many are an army." He explains while pointing towards the Gods' symbol on Victor's chest, "Though if one stands for something that others can follow, a symbol of sorts, then he or she can bring the others back with them as well, even from the depths of oblivion."

"What if I can't?" Victor questions, sounding disheartened, "What if I'm not strong enough to?"

"Then it will be at that moment when you realize what it is you were always meant for." Kael replies as he walks towards the center area of the tower, "As always, the dream is free, but the hustle is sold separately."

Victor sighs with determination and follows as Kael stops in the center of the decorated floor and says, "The courage of an Angel is tempered, for they neither fear death nor do they foolishly rush to meet it." He suddenly powers up his Gauntlet and proclaims, "To be an Archadian, you must have cunning and balance, as well as speed and strength in your arsenal at all times."

Victor looks on curiously as Kael raises his Gauntlet and motions it towards him, saying, "To master your power, you must first master your will to use it. Your Gauntlet is only limited to what you can harness from within." Kael quickly aims his Gauntlet and fires a powerful blast of energy, destroying an old statue with ease. "Your turn!" He calls, just like the training days of old.

Hesitant at first, Victor looks over his Gauntlet intensely for a moment then powers it up determinedly. "Concentrate, initiate your armor, ignite your energy, and calm the storm within." Kael encourages.

Attempting to harness the energy from within as instructed, Victor closes his eyes and powers up as energetic lightning surrounds his entire body for the first time. Moments later, he opens his intense blue eyes and fires a blast of energy, destroying a barrier as well. Kael chuckles and says, "Not bad, though be sure to keep your harmonal balance in check, otherwise your power and armor will act accordingly by being more chaotic in nature as well."

"It's hard to believe I'm capable of doing this." Victor admits while holding his hands out, then turns and asks, "This power, where did I get it?"

"The power has always been within you, as well as your talent." Kael informs, "The Gauntlet is just a tool to help you develop it. It's what you were always meant for, even Sonya knew that before her passing."

"I get that!" Victor retorts while gripping his fists tightly, "But where does the source of this power connection come from exactly?"

"The Angelus Process of course." Kael describes, "The cerebral upload of your Soul Gear activates the Gauntlet's higher functions, including a working knowledge base of any and all Archadian energy tactics."

Amazed, Victor observes his hands once again and mutters, "Fascinating!"

"Your Soul Gear is made from self-regulating metallic molecules that's wired neurologically in a biological state, allowing instant active and reactive movements, giving you various offensive and defensive capabilities." He further explains, "It acts as a defensive bio-organic crystalline structure, a second skin that adapts to your body's individual needs which continues to arm itself naturally the more you sense or afflict any sort of bodily damage."

Holding up his hands in shock, Victor exclaims, "This feels incredible!"

Confident of this new power, Victor continues to fire his Gauntlet, destroying several target barriers, which brings a prideful smile to Kael's face.

"Your Angelic aura, like that of the other Angels is infused with the power to become strong and righteous, whilst creating a protective barrier against most attacks." Kael wisely informs, "Also, the things you think about and feel on a daily basis determine the overall quality of your power when armored. Even your Soul Gear takes on the spiritual color of your thoughts."

"Is that why it changes color depending on the bearer?" Victor asks.

As Kael nods in response, Victor stops firing for a moment and excitedly retorts, "Outstanding!" He then continues to test his Gauntlet's powerful capabilities with each energy blast.

"Try to separate yourself from the technique when fighting; separate yourself from yourself if possible." Kael advises as Victor follows suit with each move, "Know that true power comes in response to a need, not a desire. And if you have no need, then it simply becomes a matter of survival."

Quickly turning to acknowledge Kael's advice, Victor nods in response and respectfully replies, "I see, mind over matter."

"Precisely, but it's also a matter of survival." Kael motivates, "You have within you the ability to magnify the power of your attacks." Victor grins with confidence as he continues to test his own power. "Though while you're busy playing offense, you mustn't forget about your defense." Kael warns while stepping back, "Like your wings, the Gauntlet will warn you when there is an imminent threat through different spectrums of illumination."

The Gauntlet begins to glow, catching Victor's attention right before he is struck from behind by an energy blast, knocking him to the ground as Kael chuckles humorously. Marcus and Yuri arrive unexpectedly, floating above Victor as Kael motions towards them and informs, "These particular threat's names are Yuri Kuran and Marcus Durrante."

Victor looks back in annoyance as the two Empyrians land before him and say, "Hey there, how's it going?"

"They'll be your combat training officers during your stay, so it's time to make friends who'll force you to level up your power." Kael infers as Victor sizes them up and scoffs, "Your whole life I've trained you in the old ways of Chaota, but from now on you'll be learning a new fighting style in which the Angels call, Archeron."

Acknowledging their position with a nod, Victor stands up and is suddenly knocked back down as Marcus lands in front of him. "Let your guard down at your own peril, *human*, but never surrender your defense!" Marcus exclaims.

Victor scowls in response as Yuri steps forward and announces, "Welcome to Angel boot camp; a power placement also known as Angelic initiation!"

Marcus approaches Victor, who stares back intensely, trying to intimidate him, and adds, "Or as I like to call it, the worst day of an Archling's life!"

Irritated by his attitude, Victor rises to his feet and powers up his Gauntlet defensively, which causes Marcus to laugh. Trying to size each other up, Marcus observes Victor for a brief moment in curiosity, then faces Yuri and calls, "Hey Yuri, ever seen a human like this before?"

"No, Marcus can't say I have!" Yuri replies while approaching their would-be comrade in arms.

"If you've come to fight me, here I am!" Victor proudly exclaims.

"Not here." Yuri sternly informs.

Facing Victor, Marcus proclaims, "Earthlings; like all surface dwellers, you think you're the center of the planet." He mocks, "But first and foremost, if you want to become an elite Angel like us, then you've gotta train with Angels and fully commit yourself to the Arch!"

Marcus raises his arm and fires a blast of energy from his Gauntlet, signifying a new addition to the kingdom of Angels then quickly activates his wings and takes off with Yuri in tow. Confused by their sudden exit, Victor glances back at Kael who nods, then activates his wings and instinctively follows them outside the tower. A long distance away from the tower at the other end of the kingdom, Marcus and Yuri prepare to train their new comrade. Moments later, Victor arrives and lands before them intensely. Marcus glances at Yuri and motions towards Victor before approaching him arrogantly. Kael arrives seconds later on top of an adult Seraph and lands a few yards behind Victor. Prepared to fight, Victor stands ready as Kael stands by the Seraph to watch.

"Alright, *human*!" Marcus warns, "Time to teach you some humility!"

"More like humanility, as if I don't know enough already!" Victor sarcastically retorts.

Marcus comes to a halt, motioning his hands in a challenging manner and states, "Now then, show us what you've got!"

"All right, but don't hold me accountable is you get hurt!" Victor warns with a confident smirk.

Marcus chuckles while looking back at Yuri who approaches him as well.

"So confident," Yuri mocks, "Let's see you try!"

Victor stands in a battle stance and is put to the test as Yuri begins blasting away, attempting to test his speed as he quickly dodges back and forth.

"Your power is only going to be as strong as your will, and from what I can tell, your will is absolutely pathetic!" Marcus sneers.

As Victor swiftly dodges and deflects each energy blast, Yuri informs, "Our job is to rigorously and ruthlessly train the humanity out of you, by making you into something far better!"

"Oh really, and what is that?" Victor confidently asks while deflecting an energy blast between them with his arm.

Surprised by this daring move, Marcus raises his brow humorously as Yuri proclaims, "We're going to make an Angel out of you!"

Yuri continues to fire upon Victor, who dodges back and forth once again, trying to get close enough to strike. Changing his tactic, Victor activates his wings and leaps into the air whilst trying to stay firmly afloat.

"We're going to work you, and hit you until you're strong enough to be worthy of those wings!" Marcus decrees as he aims his Gauntlet towards him and fires. Victor is suddenly blasted out of the air, and falls to the ground. Determined, he quickly jumps back into the air with his wings as Marcus and Yuri chuckle.

"Next lesson!" Yuri announces as Marcus begins firing energy blasts all around Victor, trying to make him dodge whilst flying around effortlessly through the air. "Feel that?" Yuri tests as Victor tries his best to stay balanced in the air with his wings fully spread, attempting to stay afloat from the intense force of each energy blast.

"Makes flying through the air very dangerous," Marcus forewarns, "And like ego, the bigger you are the harder you fall!" He then fires a more powerful energy blast towards Victor, the explosion knocking him back to the ground as he chuckles, "Gravity's a bitch, isn't it?" As Victor attempts to catch his breath after hitting the ground, Marcus approaches him with his hand extended and says, "Need a hand, bro?"

Assuming his gesture to be sincere, Victor takes his hand as Marcus unexpectedly punches him in the gut with Yuri striking from behind. Dazed from the hit, Victor places his hand over his head and stomach as they laugh.

"So much for a fair fight!" Victor angrily mutters.

"There's no such thing as a fair fight if you truly know what you're doing." Yuri states as Victor pulls himself up, "Like all combat, the odds should always be in your favor when in battle because your enemies aren't going to fight fair under any circumstances."

"If you're feeling a little slow, know that your strength and speed can and will be developed throughout your training." Marcus informs. Angered by their attitude, Victor looks upon them as they circle around him in unison. "Remember, you don't have to be good all the time, just when it truly matters." Marcus cautiously warns.

"That's good advice." Victor replies with a confident smirk.

Marcus approaches Victor once again to continue their initiation and attempts to strike but is caught off guard as he quickly maneuvers around then strikes him in the face, ending with a kick to the gut. Grunting in pain, Marcus drops to his knees as Yuri laughs at his colleague's expense. As Marcus looks up in annoyance, Victor approaches him and mocks, "Thanks for the lesson, *bro!*"

"Interesting move!" Marcus painfully regards with a grunt while fixing his posture, "What technique was that anyway?"

"You could say that of a desperate man." Victor sternly tells.

Marcus finally stands up and retorts, "I'll be sure to keep that in mind."

"I sure would." Victor nods with a poised grin as he glances at Kael who encouragingly nods back.

"Well, Marcus, it looks like he got the drop on you." Yuri jokes.

"That's not all he dropped." Marcus grumbles, "Lucky shot, *human!*"

"Gotta think fast to be fast, right?" Victor taunts while shrugging his shoulders in a prideful manner.

Marcus scoffs while shaking his head as Yuri jabs his side to get his attention. Victor turns as well and sees Damian and Adrian approaching them.

"So, this is the defiant human who slipped through General Patrayous' fingers in Pretoria." Damian scornfully implies as Adrian scowls towards Victor who stares back, annoyed by their unwanted presence. With a cold stare, Damian circles around Victor while carefully sizing him up and evaluates, "When we learned that the Gods had chosen a hybrid of all things, we felt there had to be a mistake of some sort."

As Victor follows his movements intensely, Damian stops beside Adrian, who looks back and mocks, "Care to prove us wrong?"

Trying to intimidate him, Damian and Adrian stare Victor down intensely as Elena flies in from above with Valorie and Vennessa behind Marcus and Yuri.

"What are they doing here?" Marcus intolerantly asks.

Walking between them, Elena informs, "The more we know about each other on a combative level, the greater chance we'll survive. And if we're going to work as a team, then we must train as one."

Kael steps away from the Seraph and approaches the group, nodding in respect as Elena nods back to acknowledge his welcomed presence.

"She has a point, Marcus." Yuri respectfully points out.

As Elena approaches Victor, Damian looks back towards Marcus and Yuri then informs, "We'll take it from here guys if you don't mind!"

"You might as well let us handle it!" Adrian mockingly adds.

Annoyed by their arrogance, Marcus scoffs, "Don't have too much fun with him, he's got a few tricks up his sleeve!"

"Make sure to save some for the enemy!" Yuri advises as he and Marcus prepare to take their leave to let them deal with Victor.

The two Empyrians quickly take off to let Damian and Adrian continue the training as Elena stands before Victor and looks upon him compassionately.

"Good luck, Victor." She calmly inspires, "You'll need it."

Victor smiles as Elena steps back and suddenly flies away with Valorie and Vennessa in tow. Victor sighs, then turns to face Damian and Adrian.

"You seem somewhat familiar with that silvery white hair of yours," Adrian rudely points out, "We've met before the arena, have we not?"

"Not that I know of." Victor cautiously replies, "Then again who knows, but I'd surely remember the likes of you."

"Time will tell." Adrian states whilst staring Victor down, amused as he sniffs his unwanted presence from several feet away. "Hey Trag!" He calls, "Don't know about you, but I do believe I smell fear."

Looking upon Victor penetratingly, Damian responds, "Good call, Braxel."

Curious to his hybrid presence, Damian approaches Victor whilst trying to intimidate him, saying, "Are you afraid, *human*?" Victor stands his ground as Damian steps closer, now face-to-face. "Well, are you?" He harasses with an aggressive shove. Displeased by their bullying, Victor stares back intensely, anger swelling in his eyes as he warns, "I wouldn't do that if I were you."

Adrian steps forward and mocks, "Ha! Give us a reason not to! We are Champions of Earth, we fear nothing!" He declares with his arms out, "We're the best of the best, and just like the Archadians, we strive to become better!"

Victor grunts as Damian retains his usual calm composure, stating, "The team is only as strong as its weakest link, and we will tolerate no weak links." He then rudely points towards Victor and stresses, "Understood?"

"Sure thing, but don't think of me as a pushover." Victor defends.

"Strong talk, but we know otherwise." Adrian arrogantly snarls.

"We're only here to realize your full potential, for you must overcome fear if you are to become a Champion of Earth." Damian sternly explains while stepping back, "But in order to do that, you must not care as to whether you live or die."

Looking at the two imposing Champions standing before him, Victor disputes, "There's no point in living if you have nothing to care for."

As Adrian scoffs, Victor reacts by standing in a battle stance, bringing a grin to Damian's face. Damian nods while taking a few more steps back. As the next lesson begins, Adrian suddenly strikes towards Victor who quickly dodges while gracefully holding his battle stance. "Fear is the enemy of will, because will is what makes you take action, whilst fear stops you, and makes you weak!" Adrian proudly advises as he fires an energy wave towards Victor who blocks while trying to deflect the beam, "Renders your attacks feeble!"

"And contrary to popular belief, warriors like ourselves are not made of art and science; we are forged in battle." Damian firmly adds.

Pushing the energy wave towards Victor, Adrian finally knocks him to the ground. Looking back with determination, Victor quickly jumps to his feet and flies into the air with a grin as Damian swings his purple cape back and leaps in from above to attack. Catching him off guard, Damian strikes Victor down and attempts to strike him as he keeps rushing back to attack each time.

"Impatient, how human!" Damian mocks while countering every move, "Too easy, your tactics are one dimensional, just like you!"

Out of anger, Victor strikes Damian back whilst trying to subdue him, as Adrian stands by, amused by his attempts. Surprised by his willingness to show him up, Damian stands ready and extends his arm out towards Victor to taunt him. Assured of his position, Victor rushes towards Damian in anger as he tries once again to subdue him, matching him almost blow for blow.

"When you're afraid you can't act, and when you can't act you can't defend, thus, when you can't defend…." Damian teases as he subdues Victor to the ground intensely and finishes, "You simply die like everyone else."

Pushing back in anger, Victor grunts as Damian turns away with confidence.

"Try not to enjoy this too much guys!" Victor furiously warns.

Damian quickly turns and informs, "We're trying to help you live."

"I gathered that much!" Victor mockingly exclaims.

"Incase you haven't noticed by now; the world doesn't play by your rules." Damian seriously warns, "Therefore you must learn to become more adaptive as we have."

"In other words, get with the program or get the hell out!" Adrian arrogantly chimes in, "Fight well, or die badly my people always say."

Approaching Victor, Damian respectfully extends his hand out towards him. Victor hesitates for a moment then takes his hand then stands up as Damian denounces, "I'm sorry to say, but you reek of fear, Victor Zyas."

"Amongst other things." Adrian scornfully adds while waving his hand past his nose then turns his head in disgust of Victor's human scent.

"The Angels are great warriors, and you insult the Gods by wearing their symbol." Damian informs as he points towards Victor's chest.

Victor observes the Gods' symbol over his chest, feeling partially inadequate.

"That's enough!" Kael demands as he steps away from the Seraph. As Victor places his hand over the Gods' symbol on his chest, Damian and Adrian turn their attention towards Kael, who approaches them and firmly scolds, "We have no time for petty insults! You will restrain yourselves here!" Annoyed by his interruption, Damian scoffs, "General Kael, former leader of the Empyrian army, how good of you to grace us with your presence here."

"At ease LT., he's much stronger than you think!" Kael states as he loyally steps beside Victor, who looks upon him and grins in appreciation. Adrian scoffs at his remark and stares Victor down intensely as Damian looks towards him, and amusingly retorts, "So we've heard, even so, I still don't see why we need another person on this team, especially one that's going to be nothing more than a liability."

Acknowledging his rightful place among them, Kael nods towards Victor who lowers his Gauntlet and closes his eyes for a moment in despair, "I can see we're getting off on the wrong foot here but this is a team effort, therefore we must be willing to accommodate others who are willing to fight beside us."

"Your power is nothing unless you know how to use it!" Adrian contemptuously advises. Victor quickly opens his eyes and faces Adrian, irritated by his constant negative remarks. "It doesn't matter where you go or what you do, for you will never be one of us!" He insultingly finishes.

"It's an unlikely chance that we'll be working together for long, *human*." Damian rudely states as he and Adrian turn to take their leave.

"Might want to rethink that, gentlemen!" Kael sternly interjects as Damian and Adrian turn back in annoyance, "If your cover's blown, then you'll need someone like him shadowing you."

Displeased by Kael's insistence, Damian glances back and condescendingly responds, "I'm not asking permission, *General*!"

"Maybe not, but you will follow my lead while you're here!" Kael strongly informs as he steps face-to-face in front of Damian.

Surprised by his interference, Victor looks on as Damian sighs impatiently, "Come on, Braxel, we have better things to do with our time."

"For once we agree on something, Trag." Adrian sarcastically replies.

Victor and Kael look on as Damian and Adrian calmly take their leave.

"This harsh initiation…" Victor mentions.

"What about it?" Kael curiously interrupts.

"Somehow I get the feeling this is all at my expense." Victor jokes.

With a slight chuckle, Kael responds, "You're absolutely right about that."

"Are they always this charming?" Victor sarcastically inquires.

"Relax, you're in better hands than you should be." Kael assures.

"Thanks for the reassurance," Victor says with a condescending grin, "I was beginning to think otherwise."

"Don't let them get to you, for they too have much to learn." Kael encourages, "Your rage is one hell of a defense mechanism, but you mustn't rely on it fully if you are to overcome your adversaries."
Victor looks upon his lifelong mentor for a moment then jokes, "And to think all those years I thought your training was unbearable."

"You're welcome!" Kael sarcastically replies, unamused as Victor stretches to wear off the soreness, "You've been given reserves and strength unlike ordinary men. It's time to put that experience to good use."
While observing the crystalline kingdom floating before them, Victor shakes his head and remarks, "Everyone here must have a lot of faith in my abilities considering they treat me as if I know nothing."
Kael nods with a grin and inspires, "You'll learn, but know that the world isn't in need of a perfect Angel, just a different kind."
Victor lowers his head then smiles as he faces Kael and states, "One thing's for certain, they got something different when they chose me."

"There's no room for doubt in this picture, which as you know kills more dreams than failure ever will." Kael informs, "True strength comes from mastering yourself as well as your enemies, therefore you must surround yourself with those on the same mission as you during your heroic journey."

"This I already know." Victor proudly retorts.

"Any fool can know; the point is to understand." Kael states as he walks past him, "And to know one's abilities, one must first know their limits, but your training has just begun, for nothing worth having comes easy."

"They won't make me give up, no matter how hard they try!" Victor heroically declares.

"Keep that attitude with you always." Kael strongly encourages whilst facing him, "You must disguise your weaknesses as strengths in the eyes of your opponents. The truth of the matter is that like the Princess herself, you are powerful beyond measure." Feeling more determined, Victor attempts to power up as his energy aura glows furiously with energetic lightning. Kael looks on with surprise, sensing his hidden power, and kindly mentions, "You may have celestial blood, but your heart is mostly human. Like Talia, you have the potential to serve greatness, should you choose to do so. But when it comes to being an Angel, you have to earn it, just like everyone else."

"Alright then, let's do this!" Victor proudly decrees as he positions himself in a battle stance to take on his lifelong mentor for the first time on equal terms. Ready to further his training, Kael looks on with pride and powers up himself, saying, "Begin when you're ready!"
Smiling back confidently, Victor swings his arms behind him and charges towards Kael, who in turn does the same to test his lifelong protégé's power.

CH: 34
SPIRIT OF LIGHT

Well on his way to becoming an Archadian warrior, Victor, now with slightly shorter hair trains night and day to keep up with his future colleagues. Deep within the Archadian Temple, Elena shows Victor the Arch reactor within the center chamber whilst sharing the Arch's history as Kael looks on from above, sensing that their bond is becoming much stronger each day.

"The Arch is a perpetual grace, a respected religious order with missions all across the world." Elena informs, "This kingdom itself was built in the middle of Earth so that everyone could be equally close to the Gods."

"I like that, the symmetry." Victor comments with a nod, "The geometry of belief; makes one feel more secure and righteous at times."

Elena nods in response, contemplating the thought process behind his profound comment. "In a way, the two realms are geometric echoes of each other." She adds, attempting to stay on point.

"Much like us it seems." Victor mutters, causing her to blush slightly, "I never realized Archadia was so technologically advanced, though I can't say I'm surprised." He remarks while looking around curiously, "It's much more so than what I've seen on the surface."

"Their technology is estimated in someway to be generally equal to that of our own, but that doesn't mean identical." Elena explains, "We are no doubt advanced in some areas, and they in others."

Victor faces her and asks, "I assume it's the same with your power as well?"

Elena nods and replies, "I suppose so, but when it comes to Archadian technology, our engineers always base their designs on real world things."

"Like the Arch reactor?" Victor inquires as he motions towards it.

"Yes." She answers, "It may not be dangerous in nature, but it could still be an Archadian war machine if it were to fall into the wrong hands."

"Let's hope it doesn't." Victor mutters in a serous tone.

"Growing up, I've learned that certain weapons of Archadia contain untold power." She carefully reveals.

"If you're right, that's an understatement." Victor sarcastically retorts whilst raising his Gauntlet before him then places his hand on a crystalline structure, admiring its unique design and says, "The craftsmanship of this place is extraordinary. I feel that there's a certain kind of poetry to it."

"It's the work of our ancestors, you see art is how we decorate space whereas music is how we embellish time." Elena explains as she places her hand on the crystalline structure also, "Even now we have students that are ready to become apprentices." Several Archlings roam around the chamber playfully as Victor watches and smiles, "In the years to come, some of them will take their rightful place among the Angelic Artisans." She finishes.

"Technically, I've felt like an apprentice my whole life." Victor jokes.

"As have I." Elena drolly retorts, "As you can see with the ancestral pattern throughout, the ancient history of our people rests within this place."

"I've come to dislike certain parts of history myself," Victor remarks, "When I look back, I see nothing good from the past."

"In general, nobody truly hates history, only their own." Elena adds. Victor sees an Angelic statue then points to it and asks, "Who's that?" Elena turns her attention behind her and replies, "I believe this was your mother, Victoria, if I remember right."

While observing the highly decorated Soul Gear present on the statue, Victor mutters, "Well now you know where I get my dramatic flare from."

"To worship before such icons, to kneel before the statues of the Holy Trinity is to remember all those who were robbed of their power and who were once oppressed." Elena passionately explains.

Coming to a stopping point, Elena points towards the Arch reactor several feet in front of them and informs, "Each color represents a certain type of personality." She then motions towards a beam of light colored in pink and admits, "Due to my spiritual being, I've always preferred this one myself."

"You can probably guess which one I'm partial to." Victor puns, referring to the blue beam of light as Elena smiles in response. He carefully approaches it in curiosity and respectfully nods towards two Archadian elders who guard it closely, "Amazing." He gasps, "What does it do exactly?"

"It frees us from all unnecessary burden, takes care of all our needs by regulating the energy of our daily lives." Elena informs.

Victor places his hand upon the Arch reactor, and inquires, "Who built it?"

"The Gods of course, many centuries ago." She asserts.

Gently running his fingers across the Arch reactor's front, Victor probes, "What is its power source?" Eager to answer, one of the Archadian elders kindly interjects, "The Earth's core. Is that truly important though?"

Victor glances back at Elena for a moment and quickly replies, "To a curious mind like mine, yes, I'd say it most definitely is."

"It does what we expect it to, always has." The second elder explains, "What difference does it make how it works so long as it works?"

"If you don't know how it works, then how can you ever repair it?" Victor questions in disbelief. Elena chuckles in response to Victor's curious nature as the two Archadians hesitate to answer, "Why would we need to?" The first one amusingly retorts, "To our knowledge it's never needed repair since it's initial construction, for it is energy efficient."

Looking back at the Arch reactor, Victor comments, "Everything requires maintenance from time to time, even one's belief in something."

With a grin, Elena motions Victor to follow her as the two elders glance at each other, confused by his persistent viewpoint. "Our ancient technology, the Arch reactor, shares its energy with that of the Earth's core." Elena specifies as they tour other parts of the crystalline temple, "In effect, acing as an operational nexus for a pure self-sustaining energy source that permeates throughout our kingdom. You can feel it can't you, flowing around us?"

Stopping to study his Angelic surroundings, he deduces, "Somewhat, almost like an Angelic tomb, right?"

"In a way, but know that Angels aren't born to live normal lives." She clarifies, "They are the stuff of legend, of future memory passed down for many generations to come." Victor nods in acknowledgement as he continues looking around in curiosity. "The metaphysic energy emanates from the planet's crystalline core, which continually regenerates our genetic structure," Elena adds, "Surely you've felt the effects by now."

"I've just begun to." He realizes before facing her and asks, "I assume the regenerative state doesn't take full effect till maturity?"

Nodding, Elena infers, "Theoretically, though as the Arch code states, death cannot separate us, for one life is born from the other. Energy is passed down from one another, sustaining power for all."

"Makes sense, but as you know, there's always a price for power." Victor remarks as he turns his attention elsewhere and sees an old mural of Eudenians and Enfurians fighting each other over crystal technology during the legendary Chaos War he heard so much about as a child growing up.

"As you've probably heard countless times by now, light and darkness are in constant fluctuation back and forth." She enlightens, "Though every so often, these forces are perfectly balanced. Thus, if the balance shifts in any way shape or form, then evil will inevitably rise."

"You seem to know a lot about light and shadow." Victor denotes.

"Yes, I suppose I do." Elena points out, "Except I think we only understand a fraction of what the crystals can teach us at this point."

"Well, I know that none of it would be possible without people like you." Victor compliments, "You weren't kidding when you said you and I weren't so different."

"How do you mean?" Elena questions with a curious grin.

"Your people touch the corners of the globe, teaching and healing, doing great good in the process." He happily clarifies.

"But they also did great harm, almost destroying the world and themselves." Elena says, "I've read the old scriptures. Even my parents feared the temptation to abuse our power would be too great, so they hid it away."

"The secrets you carry is neither good nor bad, but a strong leader must also have the wisdom to know when to share that knowledge." He adds.

"It would be wonderful if my people did not try to remain hidden up here in the clouds," Elena expresses, "To have them walk the surface of the world again beside the people of Earth, such would be a wonderful thing."

"I suppose it's the Gods' choice in the end." Victor murmurs.

Moments later, several young Archadians approach Elena with excitement as she kneels to greet them all. Amused by their presence, Victor smiles as they look upon him out of suspicion. "Princess Elena, who's that?" One of them curiously inquires as they point towards Victor. Elena looks back at him and smiles as the Archlings continue to study him. "Why, he's one of us." She calmly explains. "One of us?" Another chimes in, "Are you sure?"

Chuckling in response to their curiosity, Elena clarifies, "Yes I'm sure."

Taking her word, the Archlings cautiously approach Victor as he kneels before them and grins. As the Archlings examine his unusual features, one of them comments, "He doesn't look like one of us." Victor laughs as the Archlings warm up to him and play with his silvery white hair.

"If it hasn't struck you as obvious at this point, the search for knowledge is always our primary position." Elena mentions, "Our entire biological system, the brain and the Earth itself work on the exact same frequencies. Though sadly most people have no idea how to tune in."

"I noticed you spend a lot of time in the children's hospice." He denotes, "It's very kind of you to take time for all the kids in need."

"Many have been killed during battle over the years, so out of necessity I taught myself the art of healing." She reveals, "I believe that it's important to always smile back towards those who are young; to ignore them is destroy their belief that there is some good left in the world."

"I wholeheartedly agree with that mentality," Victor supports as he looks upon the Archlings with a certain sense of pride, "If I could be like you, I would protect all of Earth, and no one would ever get hurt." Enjoying their company, Victor shows his playful side while interacting with the Archlings.

Shortly after, Elena begins to delve into the Arch's history with the young Archadian students, as they focus their attention specifically on her. Standing by the entrance with Lithia, Talia listens in, feeling somewhat left out, as she is too shy to interact with the other kids whilst trying not to interfere with Victor's time currently tied up with Elena.

The next morning inside the Angelic cathedral, Victor sits beside Talia as the Archadians conduct a church like ritual in honor of the Gods. Victor and Talia observe the ritual in curiosity as the Archadians perform music and give sermons.

As the ritual ends, several Archadians stand in line, each taking their turn to honor the Gods' statues as Rosalyn and Josephus stand by with Elena. Elena nods to each Archadian walking by in respect as Victor looks over at her, feeling too shy to talk to her while she looks back for a moment and smiles. As Talia and Lithia interact with the other young Archlings, Victor watches Rosalyn and Josephus take their leave from the cathedral and conjures the courage to approach Elena. Finishing up with the last Archadians in line, Elena notices Victor approaching her and smiles.

"I thought it would take longer, but it's apparent that we can read each other quite well." She teasingly remarks, "Souls like ours recognize each other by vibes not appearances."

"Really?" Victor jokes, "Can I take that as a compliment?"

"Absolutely." Elena humorously retorts as she and Victor laugh together. Calmed by his presence, she looks into his eyes and says; "I don't know why exactly, but I've only ever felt this way with you."

"I'm flattered." Victor says with a smirk, "Do I have competition?"

"Not at all!" She jokes, "Though I have a lot of practice to endure."

"I'm still in practice myself." He jokingly admits.

Taking a moment to wave towards the Archlings who are excited by her graceful presence, Elena concedes, "Eventually, I believe we can work in concert, assuming we're going to be together a long time."

"I'd like nothing more." Victor responds with a confident grin.

Feeling bashful, Elena smiles as Talia looks over, sensing the bond between them becoming stronger. Victor looks up towards the top of the cathedral as the light from the morning sun shines down through the crystalline glass.

"The energy from the light up here is truly amazing." He comments.

"What's amazing about it is when you see something like that it's like the Gods are looking right at you." Elena remarks, "And if you're careful, you can almost look right back."

"You could say I've been looking my whole life." Victor jokes.

"And what do you see?" Elena inquires.

"Paradise." Victor softly replies, "What is it that you search for?"

"Purity, energy, things others generally dismiss." Elena replies, "I'd be lying if I said there wasn't a definite energy between us."

"I feel it also." Victor admits, "It tends to surge through both of us."

Talia smiles briefly then looks away, concerned about whether or not their bond could ever pull her and Victor apart. Sensing her sorrow, Lithia looks at Talia, who is disheartened, then chirps in an attempt to cheer her up. Unable to keep a serious face, she cracks a smile and pets Lithia's neck as he purrs loudly. Turning her attention back, Talia sees Victor and Elena leave the cathedral together then sighs, hoping things work out for the best.

CH: 35
THE DAMNED AND DIVINE

Somewhere near the outskirts of Pretoria inside a fortress, a small fleet of Darchadians gathers around in the main chamber as Traganus makes his mysterious entrance and looks upon them intensely. Raiven and Celeste stand by as Traganus steps forward to take on any would-be challengers.

"Proceed!" He commands with a deadly serious tone.

Sitting on his knees, Traganus closes his eyes as Raiven and Celeste give the signal. Several Darchadians attempt to subdue him as Traganus deflects each attack with ease. Raiven and Celeste glance at each other; concerned as the Darchadians try their best to land a single hit on him. Unable to defeat him after several attempts, Traganus stands and extends his red Angelic wings, pushing them back towards the chamber walls with great force. Traganus looks around for a moment and scoffs in annoyance of their defeat.

"Hesitation is a weakness the enemy will not share!" He exclaims.

Raiven and Celeste stand by and grin as Traganus looks upon the fallen Darchadians in disappointment. The small group Darchadians stand up and back away from Traganus, feeling intimidated by his overly dark presence.

"As Darchadians, you must be stealthier than the night, and deadlier than the dawn!" Traganus proudly proclaims while glancing at Raiven and Celeste for a brief moment, "When it comes to your comrades in arms, if they stand behind you, give them protection. If they stand beside you, give them respect, but if they should stand against you, show no mercy!" As Traganus turns his attention back towards the other Darchadians, he firmly concludes, "When you inspire others to do the same, that's what makes us a tribe. Dismissed!" Discouraged by their failure to impress him, the Darchadians look on as Traganus takes his leave and enters his throne room.

Raiven and Celeste glance at each other, ashamed of displeasing their master then continue to train the Darchadians for the coming battle.

As the weeks pass by, Marcus and Yuri continue to train with Victor in Archadia as Elena and Kael observe. Damian and Adrian stand by also and are surprised by Victor's progress as Talia watches from above with Lithia.

"Seems you've been at it nonstop." Yuri teases, "Perhaps it's time for others to have their turn."

"When I'm finished." Victor sarcastically replies.

"I have to hand it to you, Zyas, you never stop practicing." Marcus compliments while he and Yuri try to land a hit on him.

"What can I say, I'm a quick study." Victor confidently retorts.

"Perhaps that will make you the best someday." Yuri adds.

As Marcus and Yuri attempt to strike, Victor easily blocks their attack and confidently retorts, "No, maybe just better in general."

Marcus and Yuri chuckle in response as they and Victor back off from one another and bow their heads in mutual respect.

"Preparedness is a perquisite for victory in all circumstances, the Darchadians are likely preparing for battle as well." Yuri, informs, "To help you survive against them, the Arch has requested that you be provided with Archadian weaponry the same as us. The Gods gave their Angels such weapons because even they knew that evil cannot technically be defeated only with tolerance and understanding."

Victor looks upon his Gauntlet and Soul Gear in appreciation then smirks.

"We use our spiritual tech to equalize the battlefield, for Darchadians can only descend upon defeat." Marcus chimes in, "Angelic Gauntlets are sacramental by bearing the mark," he raises his Gauntlet and points towards the top of the palm, "A symbol of the Archadian order, as well as the Gods'." Acknowledging their guidance, Victor raises his Gauntlet as well and examines it closely in a prideful manner.

"The best defense against those who do evil is good people who are skilled at tactical violence like us." Yuri states, "It is said that when a Darchadian is killed, their energy descends unto the Earth's core. Though unlike ours, it remains trapped there for eternity."

"So, what happens when an Archadian descends?" Victor carefully inquires as Elena approaches them from above whilst hovering in the air with her pink Angelic wings.

"We are sacramental beings of light, we ascend." Elena enlightens as she lands gracefully before him, "Unlike them, we rise to the occasion, we do not fall into darkness as they do. Thus, our energy is given back to the planet's soul." Victor listens carefully as she continues, "But in order to defeat a shadow, you need simply shine a little light." Victor nods in respect, gripping his fists tightly as a sign of confidence. "Victor, you have incredible mental discipline and clarity of perception," Elena concedes, "And judging by how far and how quickly you've progressed I'd say you've made elite status faster than anyone in Archadian history, present company included."

While sizing him up curiously with a grin, she then asks, "But the real question is, are you really that good?"

"Yes I am, the Arch's finest." Victor proudly proclaims.

"One of, most definitely." Elena teases.

Confident of his current status as an Archadian warrior, Victor smiles upon her, and says; "Care to put that to the test?"

Elena glances at Marcus and Yuri for a moment then faces Victor and grins with confidence herself, "Sure, why not? I thought you'd never ask."

Grinning with excitement, Victor signals Marcus and Yuri to step back as he and Elena prepare to spar for the first time. Talia looks on curiously as Lithia chirps with excitement. Moving back several yards, Marcus and Yuri glance at each other and grin. "Now this I gotta see." Yuri utters while rubbing his hands together excitingly in anticipation.

"My bet's on Elena." Marcus undoubtedly claims.

"Same here." Yuri quickly replies, "And if Victor lands a single hit?"

"Right on!" Marcus settles as he and Yuri pound their fists together humorously in agreement.

Everyone looks on in curiosity as Victor and Elena power up their Soul Gear and position themselves in Archadian battle stances.

"I hear you're fast, but I wonder just how fast you are in comparison to someone such as myself." Elena taunts.

"Guess there's only one way to find out." Victor sarcastically states.

"You ready?" Elena calls.

"Whenever you are!" Victor calls back with a grin, "Ladies first!"

"Good!" Elena says then without warning, flies towards Victor at full speed and strikes him back several yards, unexpectedly knocking him to the ground as everyone watching chuckles at his expense.

Talia expresses concern for a moment then begins to chuckle as well, covering her mouth with her hands so as to not be heard. Surprised by her intensity, Victor looks upon Elena as she gracefully lands in front of him.

"Guess I should've warned you beforehand; don't hold back just because I'm female." Elena mocks with a confident grin, "Let it out!"

Amused by her powerful presence, Victor repositions himself and boldly retorts, "Alright then, you asked for it!"

Elena grins in preparation as Victor suddenly charges towards her at full speed and attempts to strike, "Pardon me!" He teases.

"Oh, very stylish." Elena wittily replies.

"What can I say?" Victor jokes, "I learned from the best."

Reacting instinctively, Elena blocks his fist as they lock eyes intensely for a moment. Marcus and Yuri cheer in excitement as Damian and Adrian nod their heads towards each other in respect of their colleagues' power.

"Don't tell me that's all you've got?" Elena taunts with a smile.

Smiling back, Victor proudly claims, "Far from it actually."

As the sparring match continues, the two Angelic warriors counter each other's movements in a graceful yet intense manner.

"Your strength, speed, and stamina are far beyond that of most Angels." Elena encourages while attempting to land a hit on him.

"But not yours, huh?" Victor puns, trying to find her weak spot.

Elena grins in response as Victor suddenly takes the offensive.

"Use those gifts to your advantage, take sides in a war that you are inherently a part of." She inspires while deflecting each attack.

Victor powerfully strikes as Elena swiftly blocks, he then asks her curiously, "And what exactly are you a part of?"

Slightly confused by his query, Elena's expression changes as Victor uses this opportunity to catch her off guard and quickly maneuvers around her. Attempting to follow his movements while striking each time, Elena is taken aback as he gracefully subdues her in a dance like bow. Breathing heavily with excitement, Elena looks upon him, and laughs, "That works too I suppose, though it lacks a certain finesse."

Sharing a confident grin, Victor jokingly retorts, "For now anyway."

Not expecting this surprising outcome, Marcus quickly turns to Yuri and says, "Well damn! I guess it's a draw."

"For once we both lost on a bet!" Yuri jokingly retorts.

Marcus holds his hands close to his cheeks and shouts, "You guys finished, or are you just going to stand there looking like fools all day?"

Embarrassed by the remark, Victor helps Elena stand up properly as she looks deeply into his intense blue eyes. Keeping her focus on him, she says softly, "Remember my words."

"I always do." Victor assures with a crooked smile.

After sharing a grin, Elena approaches Kael as Damian and Adrian glance at each other curiously. Victor waves upward at Talia who waves back with excitement as Lithia chirps, then turns to address Damian and Adrian directly.

"You guys want a taste?" Victor provokes with his arms extended.

Damian and Adrian shake their heads in annoyance as Victor grins, confident of his Angelic stature. Trying to catch her breath, Elena sits next to Kael as he looks upon her and jokingly states, "I'm beginning to think you two are an equal match in more ways than one."

"I was merely toying with him as I'm sure he was with me." She humorously responds, "He's come a long way it seems."

"That he has." Kael states in a prideful manner.

Elena and Kael watch as Marcus and Yuri continue to spar with their new comrade, "Again!" Victor teasingly challenges.

"I suppose he has you to thank for his strong moral fiber." Elena respectfully implies.

Kael chuckles, and retorts, "I did what I could, when I could, never knowing if it was enough at times."

"I've noticed that he's still avoiding everything regarding his past." Elena stresses with a deeply concerned tone.

"That's because he's tried to erase his childhood." Kael informs, "Honestly I don't know which is worse for him; trying to remember certain things, or unable to forget them. Difficult childhoods I believe make for the most interesting adults sometimes."

"I thought he'd be more open by now, but there's a mysterious side to him that I can't seem to penetrate just yet." She reluctantly admits.

"All I can say is to keep trying," Kael encourages, "I'm sure you'll get through to him eventually."

Continuing to watch Victor and her two Empyrian bodyguards spar, Elena probes, "Why doesn't he ever talk about it openly?"

Hesitant, Kael sighs and responds, "It's not that he can't, he just won't. You see he keeps his emotions locked away, deep inside."

"Why is that?" She questions, wanting to know more about him.

"So no one can hurt him again." Kael patiently reveals, "What happened to him in his youth was tragic to say the least. But in time, he'll learn to open up more and free himself from such heavy burdens."

Elena nods while keeping her focus on Victor, who looks back and teasingly salutes in her honor. "There is much strength within him, I've felt it." She regards, "His aura is extremely powerful, rising, like a fallen Angel."

"In a way, he's naturally stronger than all of us, but his true strength comes from his bravery to fight for those he cares about." Kael adds, "Everything that he does comes out of him being hurt."

Victor pushes Marcus and Yuri back with his energetic lightning as they look upon him with surprise then nod back in respect of his superior power.

"Though I can sense that he fights with anger in his heart as well." Elena denotes, sounding deeply concerned for him.

Getting bored, Talia climbs down from above with Lithia to get a closer look.

"That he does, but hopefully our work will bear fruit." Kael divulges, "Like the rest of his human counterparts, he has an extreme quality of growth, which most possibly fear, hate, or even admire at times."

As Marcus and Yuri finish with their sparring, Talia approaches Victor with Lithia by her side and embraces him. Elena watches closely, sensing their unbreakable bond as they converse out of earshot. Rosalyn and Josephus approach Elena from behind while observing Victor's interaction with Talia.

"We've heard good things regarding Victor's progression through his training." Josephus indicates as Elena quickly turns to face them.

"May we suggest he attend our courting ritual to let him experience having seen the royal might and majesty of Archadian society?" Rosalyn kindly suggests on Victor's behalf.

"He doesn't know our customs." Elena cautions.

"It's time he learned then." Josephus firmly states.

"To subject him to that kind of scrutiny would be kind of unethical, don't you think?" Elena carefully points out.

"I don't understand," Rosalyn infers, "If he's an Angel, then why shouldn't he fit right in?"

"Excellent notion my dear." Josephus chimes in, "You will bring him to the ball, prove to us that he's as civilized as you claim, and we shall possibly grant him a higher rank to prove our appreciation in return."

Once Talia steps away, Victor looks towards Elena and nods as she smiles back. Talia waves Victor over in her direction as Elena turns to take her leave, contemplating Victor's true allegiance between Talia and the Arch.

Back in Titania during the late evening hours of the always extremely hectic Edge City, Raina and Lucian meet with Tannis in his throne chamber as Patrayous stands by with Zepherus.

"We've just received confirmation that our Champions have been preparing for combat against this so-called threat, and will soon be ready for deployment." Raina informs.

With his back turned, Tannis looks onto the city from the window and replies, "Excellent, that's the best news I've heard in a while."

"Our sources have also informed us that the human will be fighting alongside them as well," Raina adds, sounding annoyed," They indicate that his powers are growing rapidly through his training with the Archadians."

Sighing out of annoyance, Tannis mutters, "So I've been told," he then turns to face Raina and Lucian, saying, "I have only myself to blame for not realizing first hand that he is in fact part Angel."

Feeling slightly embarrassed by not realizing beforehand himself, Patrayous assures, "Don't blame yourself, my Lord. None of us were able to pick up on his Arch aura because his human self was able to disguise it so well."

"The Arch must have initiated him into their collective then, and granted him sanctuary if he's to do battle with Trag and Braxel." Tannis deduces with a curious tone.

"Unfortunately!" Lucian chimes in as he and Raina glance at each other with concern, "Though he appears to be a gifted warrior, despite his bloodstained lineage."

Unwilling to accept Victor for anything other than a slave, Tannis states, "Yes, but he threatens everything we've built, as well as what we stand for."

Raina and Lucian look upon Tannis curiously as Patrayous listens. "Seems you have a valid point to make, Marquis." Raina curiously prompts, "Do tell."

Tannis steps in front of his crystalline throne and explains, "Before us, Earth was nothing. We brought all the kingdoms together. We ourselves created a world of prosperity from crystals and slaves." He pauses for a moment then finishes, "We build the future, not them, nor his pathetic kind!"

As Tannis retraces his steps, Lucian scoffs and proudly discounts, "Well put, Marquis, but I believe you overestimate this fool and his abilities."
Stopping in his tracks beside his crystalline throne, Tannis slowly turns, and sternly replies, "Do I now?"

"Only time will tell who and what he truly fights for, cause at the moment he seems to be loyal to no one, including the Arch." Raina notifies.

"General Kael and Princess Elena are believed to be the only ones he currently listens to," Lucian implies, "Though extreme circumstances could easily change that, in our favor of course."

"This is ridiculous, we run the show, not him!" Tannis grumbles, "It is we who decides who to unify on this planet, for not even the Gods have such superiority. This man is nothing but trouble, nothing!"

"Will you shut up and just let the team do their thing!" Raina impatiently chimes in, "You might be surprised to see what this hybrid is truly capable of in the heat of battle."
Zepherus growls with his spinal shards glowing as Patrayous shakes his head in annoyance and mutters, "What a shame really."
Puzzled by his expression, Raina and Lucian quickly turn towards Patrayous and curiously inquire, "What is?"
Patrayous faces them and insolently explains, "That your Champions are going to be fighting alongside a *slave* of all people. The highest of nobility, given to a human immigrant, and protected by the Arch."

"What's your point?" Lucian irritably asks, becoming heated.
Curious of his General's attitude, Tannis looks on intriguingly as Patrayous approaches Raina and Lucian, declaring, "I alone have the military proficiency to direct this entire operation and I sure as hell wouldn't need the help of a human slave to wage war against my enemies."

"And what do you know of such matters?" Lucian snaps.
"Quite a bit actually." Patrayous arrogantly states.
Lucian heavily grunts in anger as Raina places her hand on his shoulder to calm him and warns, "Do not presume to speak above your station, General." Retaining his intense composure, Lucian furiously mocks, "That's right, Kraven, as if you could do any better than us?"
Patrayous chuckles slightly as Zepherus stretches and scratches himself.

"Oh, as a matter of fact, I know I could." Patrayous proudly states.
Angered, Lucian approaches Patrayous and looks down upon him, as they stand face-to-face intensely. "Is that a challenge, Empyrian?" Lucian growls.

"Heavens no, I wouldn't dream of challenging the King of Enfuria, much less the Queen of Eudenia in a chauvinistic free for all without the Emperor's consent of course." Patrayous calmly retorts as Raina and Lucian furiously scoff. Somewhat amused by his colleague's arrogance, Tannis grins as Patrayous instigates, "That would be a dangerous play, though if you're both up to it I'm sure we can find a way to make it happen. Your call really."

"It's not wise to annoy us, *Kraven!*" Raina angrily warns.

Taking a moment to retain control of the social exchange, Patrayous calmly states, "Forgive my combative nature, for I mean no offense whatsoever."

"Too late for that!" Raina snaps.

"Call it an old Earth tradition, habit of the beast if you will." Patrayous clarifies with a confident smile.

"Do not forget your place, for you aren't an Empyrian General anymore!" Lucian exclaims as he points his finger towards Patrayous and jabs it firmly into his chest as a severe warning, "You lost that privilege when you foolishly decided to turn your back against the Gods along with your former associate, General Kael."

"Need you remind me?" Patrayous scoffs as he pushes Lucian's hand away, "Don't forget that I too have had my fair share of combat in the face of death and disaster, just as you both have."

Raina and Lucian scoff, anger evident in their mannerisms, as Tannis steps forward to neutralize their current displeasure.

"Whatever happens, just keep us informed of their progress." Lucian demands as he turns his head towards Tannis.

"Will do my Lords." Tannis replies with a respectful bow.

Raina steps towards Tannis and articulates, "We'd prefer that our Champions make it through this alive, with or without the Arch's involvement."

As Raina and Lucian impatiently take their leave, Tannis and Patrayous glance at each other in amusement. With the doors to the chamber closing behind them, Tannis approaches his throne once again as Patrayous follows.

"Let me take my own squad to Pretoria to investigate," Patrayous forcefully pleads; "I can finish this quicker and much more adequately then they possibly can!" He finishes by pounding his fists onto the table.

Annoyed by his arrogant ambition, Tannis looks upon Patrayous and sternly replies, "No!" Patrayous grunts, dissatisfied with his order as Zepherus stands up and growls. "You shall remain here and let the Champions take care of it for now." He commands.

"My Lord?" Patrayous firmly questions, concerned by the request.

"The scenario is bad enough as it is," Tannis clarifies, "I don't need you getting involved just yet. Are we clear?"

"Crystal, Sir" Patrayous replies with a stern yet respectful tone.

"You would do well to learn some patience my friend." Tannis advises as he approaches the window overlooking the city once again.

Frustrated, Patrayous scoffs as Zepherus steps beside him and groans.

"Don't worry, General, you'll get your chance soon enough." Tannis assures while looking out the window, then turns back once more, "Events of this nature can be dangerous, for accidents do tend to happen."

Patrayous grins, followed by a growl from Zepherus in anticipation as Tannis continues his gaze upon the large city and smirks with absolute certainty.

CH: 36
HARMONIOUS RITUAL

During the evening hours, many Archadians gather for a courting ritual banquet within the Archadian Temple in honor of the teams' training. Victor approaches the temple with Kael from the bottom of the stairs outside and stops for a moment whilst examining his custom made black and blue dress attire with a touch of grey. "Do I really have to wear this stuff?" He gripes while trying to get comfortable in his fancy new suit, "I mean, it's nice and all, but kind of unnecessary don't you think?"

"Everything is unnecessary in your eyes if it doesn't make sense to you at first glance." Kael mocks then firmly states, "I don't expect that you would want to offend the Princess by choosing to lower yourself."
Contemplating the thought, Victor attempts to justify, "No, but…."

"Their craftspeople made this for you," Kael interrupts in a scolding manner, "The least you could do is honor their efforts for one night, so you're going to wear it with pride whether you like it or not."

"Look at me though, I feel absolutely ridiculous!" Victor pathetically mopes, "Like a silly butterfly!"

"Listen to me!" Kael hollers to get his attention. Victor sighs edgily as Kael attempts to fix his dress garb, and calmly explains, "Tonight you are to enjoy some mandatory fun, and make some friends if possible. Timing is everything, for this is an opportunity for you and your people to become more familiar with each other."

"How much more familiar can we get?" Victor scoffs.

"A lot; this is just an event to showcase their appreciation for those willing to fight for the Arch." Kael patiently explains, "All you have to do is show up, don't look too conspicuous and mingle while you're here. I trust that isn't too much to ask for considering the fact that you've been graciously welcomed into their kingdom with arms wide open." Victor reluctantly shakes his head in acceptance, realizing that he must respect their graces.

"They say if you're civilized, you can fit right in, but it's the elite of Archadian society." Kael informs, "Etiquette is the most important thing to remember while you're here and first impression can often be the right one."

"Shouldn't be too difficult then." Victor jokes, feeling assured.

"There are a million ways you can insult someone, believe me I know." Kael informs, "And if you slip up just once, Tannis will make sure everyone on the surface knows about it."

"Well then, I better not slip up." Victor declares, "I can't learn their ways alone, but you can help me. What must I do?"

"One must dare to be himself however frightening or strange that self may prove to be unto others." Kael inspires, "In other words, just be yourself, and show what personality you have."

"Exactly what part of my persona can I possibly show that they don't already know about?" Victor questions with a slight chuckle.

Kael chuckles quietly and answers, "Charm." Feeling encouraged, Victor faces the temple stairs and slowly approaches them as Kael smiles on behalf of his protégé and follows closely behind. As Victor makes his way up the stairs, he sees a row of familiar flowers growing outside the temple and carefully picks one. "That sort of flair should suffice." Kael teases.

Slightly embarrassed, Victor shakes his head and jokingly scowls as he places the crystalline flower in his garb and continues walking up the stairs, followed by Kael who smiles at his expense. After reaching the top of the stairs, Victor takes a deep breath and enters the cathedral, looking around nervously while enjoying the view. Elena converses with several Archadian guests then sees Victor and Kael from a distance and approaches them.

"Milady." Kael says while bowing his head in respect.

Returning the sentiment, Elena bows her head as Kael pats Victor's shoulder and walks off to mingle with the crowd. Observing his dress attire closely, she happily expresses, "Well look at you, glowing like a shooting star."

Victor laughs and politely responds, "Still not as bright as you though."

"Maybe not, but you're going to rock the stars eventually." Elena encourages, "I just know it." Feeling less awkward with his noble attire, Victor grins in appreciation as Valorie and Vennessa approach Elena from behind. "You look so sharp and handsome." She praises, "If I didn't know any better, I'd say you're starting to look more like a noble."

"Thanks, you look great as well." Victor compliments, taken aback by her graceful beauty. Elena blushes in response, trying to hide her expression from Valorie and Vennessa to avoid any possible awkwardness.

"Look but don't touch!" Valorie sternly warns.

"Can't you see she's out of your league?" Vennessa rudely chimes in.

Annoyed by their remarks, Elena sighs as Victor pulls out the crystalline flower from his garb and respectfully hands it to her.

Elena instinctively takes it and inquires, "What's this?"

"A gift." Victor softly replies, hoping not to have offended her. Holding the flower close, Elena closes her eyes in appreciation, then opens them and says softly, "How elegant."

"You make it so." He flatters with a crooked smile. The flower suddenly changes back and forth between pink and blue as Elena watches with a surprised expression. "It's a chameleon rose," Victor reveals, "It changes color with the feelings of its owner."

"It's very thoughtful," Elena kindly accepts, "Thank you."

"You're very welcome, milady." Victor responds while bowing his head in respect. Elena bows her head in return as Victor walks away towards a table to find a seat. Observing the crystalline flower closely, Elena caresses the pedals with her fingers as Valorie and Vennessa glance at it in curiosity.

"What a nice token of gratitude." Valorie acknowledges.

"Yes, even I wonder what such a present symbolizes." Vennessa suspiciously adds. Highly amused by their stern naivety, Elena smiles and happily mutters, "Maybe where he comes from it means love."

"Only a true romantic can tell." Valorie cynically murmurs.

"He may be somewhat coarse on the outside, but unlike you two, I can see past my nose whenever I so choose." Elena retorts as she frowns upon them, "Deep down, there's something more."

Acting as his typical loner self, Victor sits down to observe the festivities, watching Talia enjoy herself with Lithia perched on her shoulder. Shortly after, Elena approaches Victor and sits next to him while observing the crystalline flower inquisitively. "No one's ever given me a gift like this before." She compliments.

"Don't see why they wouldn't," Victor praises, "Every good woman deserves a flower to compliment their beauty, inside and out." Elena smiles in appreciation as he looks upon her passionately and states, "You know, you remind me of the old tales my mother used to tell me when I was a child."

"How do you mean?" Elena jokingly inquires.

"I used to think most Angels had no names, just beautiful faces." Victor professes before turning back to face her, "But now I know for sure with my own eyes that they're beautiful no matter what they're called."

Listening penetratingly, Elena beams as Victor resumes, "If I could have just one thing in life, it would be to stay up here with you and Talia, forever." Elena looks on passionately, trying not to give her true feelings away as Victor looks upon the joyous crowd within the temple in curiosity and self-consciously mutters; "I feel so out of place in this setting."

"Why is that?" Elena calmly asks.

"I'm not quite at home around others sometimes." Victor jokes while watching the others before them, "These people, they're more your crowd than mine. Though come to think of it, I've never really had my own crowd."

"You do now!" Elena chuckles softly in retort as they laugh together.

Talia approaches them with Lithia perched on her shoulder and excitedly demands, "Come on, Victor, ready for a little fancy footwork?" She then grabs his hand and pulls, "Let's dance!"

"Come on, Talia!" He playfully excuses, hoping not to embarrass himself, "You know I don't know how!"

Talia teasingly scowls at him, placing her hands on her hips as Lithia chirps. Knowing there's no way out of it, Victor glances at Elena who smiles back and cons, "I think you better do what she says."

"Yeah, *Victor!*" Talia teases, followed by a chirp from Lithia.

Victor looks back at Talia for a moment then smiles while shaking his head, then finally gives in, "Oh all right, if you insist!"

Frowning once again in a teasing manner, Talia pulls Victor from his seat and leads him to the dance floor. Valorie and Vennessa stand beside Elena as she watches Victor trying to keep up with Talia, laughing at his lack of rhythm. Making his presence known throughout the crowd, Kael approaches Elena and nods towards Damian and Adrian in respect as they slowly nod back.

"Never thought I'd see him come this far," Kael jokingly mentions, "A noble, who'd have thought?"

"Guess you had a hand in that." Elena compliments, "You've been a great mentor to him over the years, I can tell."

Taking a seat next to her, Kael reveals, "I simply taught him to take the good with the bad, but it wasn't all me. Sonya was a great benefit while she was alive, and you've helped as well it seems."

Flattered by his comment, Elena says, "I know, but it's good to see he had someone to look up to growing up, despite his past surroundings."

Kael chuckles in response, and states, "I don't know if I'm a good example, but I'll gladly take what I can get at this point."

Amused by his comment, Elena grins as Rosalyn and Josephus sit in their crystalline thrones and signal the Archadians to begin the courting ritual. Surrounded by several Archadians who begin to dance, Victor and Talia join in, both trying to blend in with the others as Lithia flies around them and hums to the music. Damian and Adrian stand by whilst observing the festivities and respectfully nod towards Marcus and Yuri who stand by doing the same. Soon after as the dance ends, everyone in the cathedral claps while the Archadians take a bow. Trying to catch his breath, Victor sighs in relief and says, "I think I'm going to sit the next one out if you don't mind."

"Alright, guess I'll just dance with Lithia then." Talia jokes as her furry companion lands back on her shoulder.

"He's probably better at it than I am anyway," Victor teases as he looks directly towards Lithia, "Hope you can keep up with her, boy." Lithia chirps loudly with his spinal shards glowing, causing Talia to laugh as Victor bows his head then walks back towards the table and sits beside Elena.

Clapping humorously, Elena teases, "Well done, Archelus, well done."

"At least I tried anyway." Victor chuckles along with her, "I came, I saw, I made it awkward for everyone, myself included."

As the Archadians prepare for the next dance, Kael approaches Talia dancing alone with Lithia then extends his arm out, and says politely, "Milady."

"Why thank you, Sir." She kindly responds then turns to address Lithia still perched on her shoulder and says, "Sorry, Lithia. Time to beat it."

Grunting in slight disappointment, Lithia flies away towards the crystalline chandelier-hanging overhead as Talia looks on, shaking her head and smiles by his reaction. Talia takes Kael's hand as they prepare to dance with the others. Victor and Elena look on in delight, watching Talia having a good time with Kael as they begin to dance. "I trust you've been treated fairly during your time here?" Elena curiously infers.

"Naturally, your people have treated me as can be expected." Victor respectfully retorts.

"But is that all you expect?" She curiously probes.

Hesitant, Victor looks away and replies, "Honestly, it's all I've ever known."

"It doesn't have to be." Elena encourages.

"Your people seem normal enough, on the surface anyway." Victor teases as he and Elena smile at one another, their bond becoming stronger with each passing moment. "For years I've lived mostly with the same faces." He professes, "It's strange to meet new people every single day. Each person I come in contact with has new thoughts, new ideas to share. Your world has so much to offer; I hope one day that my people and the world they live in can offer as much."

"There's no reason they can't." Elena comforts, "Your people can make a difference in the world just like we do on a day to day basis."

"But with me gone, it's up to the people to raise their little ones in peace." Victor jokes in reference to taking in Talia, Tristan, and Michael under his wing for so many years. As the second dance ends, Elena stands up from the table and politely says, "Please excuse me for a moment."

"Of course." Victor respectfully murmurs.

Elena gives a teasing smirk then turns and approaches Kael on the dance floor. Talia sees Elena walking towards them and bows her head in respect.

"Has she worn you out yet?" Elena teases while placing her hand on Talia's shoulder to acknowledge her welcomed presence.

"Only a little, not too much." Kael sarcastically retorts.

One of the Archadian band members quickly approaches Elena from the staging area and informs, "Milady, we're ready for you now."

"Excellent," Elena happily replies, "I haven't practiced my whole life for nothing." Talia glances at Kael for a moment in curiosity as he shrugs his shoulders, both unsure of what Elena is about to do. As Elena quickly approaches the stage, the Archadian band positions themselves and their crystalline instruments in preparation for the next musical number.

With a beautiful yet passionate voice, she begins the ancient number with her childhood melody and gracefully sins;

"He who…dares fall from the light, through all darkness…an Angel shall rise."

"He holds…a place in my heart, forever yours…beyond the dark."

Struck by Elena's beautiful voice, Victor turns his attention behind him and suddenly gets the urge to walk towards the Archadian band playing on stage. As he approaches one of the guitar players, he politely asks, "May I?"

The Archadian guitar player gives a respectful nod and gently hands over the guitar while moving to the side of the stage. Victor straps the crystalline guitar over his shoulder and begins to pluck away with Elena's melody. Surprised by this action, Elena glances over at Victor who smiles back. Shaking her head in amusement, Elena continues playing her crystalline harp and sings once again:

"He who…dares fall from the light, through all darkness…an Angel shall rise."

"He holds…a place in my heart, forever yours…beyond the dark."

The dance floor lights up as Victor and Elena play their hearts out to everyone's enjoyment. As the musical number ends, everyone in the cathedral cheers. Elena steps away from her instrument, blowing kisses at everyone then turns and waves Victor over. Hesitant, Victor sets the guitar down and steps beside her to take in the moment as well. As the band prepares for the next number, Kael walks up to the stage and asks, "Care to dance?"

"Sure, why not?" Elena says with a bow as she steps off the stage.

After being complimented by a few other Archadians' regarding his playing, Victor steps back towards the table and sits down to enjoy the next number. Smiling with joy, Talia bows her head once again to Elena then heads back towards Victor at the table. Enjoying the festivities, Victor looks around then turns as Talia stands before him unexpectedly with a silly looking face.

"Hi!" She says with a cute expression. The friendly pair laughs together as Lithia sits perched on the crystalline chandelier overhead and chirps. As the Archadians move onto the dance floor, Kael bows in respect and extends his arm as he and Elena begin to dance. She looks over his shoulder and sees Talia having a good time conversing with Victor as usual.

"So, what's the story with those two?" Elena inquires, "You would think they were brother and sister or something."

Looking over her shoulder, Kael glances at Victor and Talia with a grin and replies, "He's definitely left an imprint on her for sure, they seem to bring out the best in one another despite what they've been through."

"That couldn't be anymore obvious." Elena says with slight sarcasm, "Sometimes people with the worst paths end up creating the best futures."

"Truth is, they looked out for one another back in the mines." Kael illuminates, "If not for him, she would've been a prime target for abuse, every man's punching bag. During years of mistreatment, they found comfort in themselves, thus their bravery and care for each other is quite innocent, and completely boundless."

"I suppose those reasons are plentiful and mysterious, though it seems like you were training them to be some kind of warriors without them even knowing." She respectfully denotes.

"I suppose it takes someone strong to make others strong." Kael specifies, "I simply helped them to find the power within, so they wouldn't remain victims of their surroundings. They were both taught at an early age that all life no matter how big or small has value."

While keeping her focus towards Victor and Talia, Elena infers, "Can't say I've ever seen anything quite like it before. Though, I suppose they had no one else to depend on but each other when you weren't around."

"Most are simply afraid of what they don't see or understand." Kael enlightens, "Their bond seems strange at first, but it's one of those happy stories that also makes you kind of sad too." Elena ponders the notion as he continues, "The love they have for each other transcends beyond anything anyone could ever fathom, but in a platonic kind of way."

"I know what you mean." She inquisitively discloses as she glances at Victor who smiles back, "Sometimes you can feel a kinship with others even when they're not related. Like my mother used to say to me when I was little, Angels of a feather flock together until their wings become broken."

"Quite so, milady." Kael augments, "His care for her drives his compassion. She's been the only one worthy in his eyes for sometime now."

"I've noticed." Elena lightheartedly confesses, "There's something about those eyes of his. So mysterious, yet so intense."

Continuing to lead the dance, Kael informs, "He finds you worthy too."

"Apparently, he thinks I'm beautiful." She embarrassingly mutters.

"And so you are, though souls such as yours recognize each other by vibes more so than appearance." He compliments. Surprised, she looks upon Kael, who adds, "I'm sure he acknowledges your inner beauty as well."

"Really?" Elena inquires, "Does he acknowledge love as well?"

"I believe so, but to tell you the truth, I think he could use some work on that." Kael says with a grin, "He's a man that certainly knows what he wants in life, but nobody's ever wanted him in return."

Curious of Victor's true intentions, Elena pulls out the crystalline flower from her garb and examines it curiously as it continues to change colors.

"I suppose a flower that blooms in adversity can be the most rare and beautiful of them all." She says softly, "Though most would probably argue that true beauty is often found where it is least expected."

Kael nods in agreement as they resume their dance. Watching from the table with Talia, Victor taps his fingers to the rhythm of the music being played and says, "Well, Talia, this is a big night for you."

"What do you mean?" Talia questions, looking confused.

"Dressed up all lady like in the midst of high society." He willingly compliments, "Tristan and Michael would be so proud."

"Well I've already got Elena's approval." She sarcastically retorts. Thinking quietly to himself, he inquires, "You like her, don't you?"

"I like her just fine, and I can tell you like her too." Talia professes. Examining the thought for a moment, Victor caringly retorts, "I certainly do, but all I want is for you to be happy, Talia."

"I just want you to be happy, Victor." Talia assures with a smile.

"I appreciate that." Victor commends as he turns his attention back towards the dance floor, watching Kael and Elena dance.

Hoping to ease his mind, she taps Victor's shoulder and teases, "What are you waiting for, Mr.?" Confused, Victor turns directly towards Talia, who teases once more, "It's not everyday you get to dance with a Princess you know?" Acknowledging her sentiment, Victor smiles then stands from the table, looking determined and says, "Well, I guess there's no time like the present."

As the dance ends, Talia looks on from the table, smiling excitedly as Victor approaches Elena and Kael. "Mind if I cut in?" He asks with a crooked smile. Elena turns and sees Victor standing before them and smiles back.

"I suppose not." Kael says jokingly then bows his head in respect and steps away from the dance floor as Victor steps in.

Victor and Elena look at each other compassionately as the Archadian band prepares for the last dance. "I'm sure you're probably tired of hearing this by now, but you look beautiful." Victor compliments.

"From others, yes, but from you, I could never tire of hearing such words." Elena says with a smile, "I suppose you've come to ask me to dance."

"Believe me, nothing would please me more right now." Victor admits while extending his arm in proper fashion, then bows his head in respect, feeling hopeful and asks, "May I have this dance, milady?"

Looking upon him with firm excitement, Elena takes a deep breath and calmly says, "Why yes, you may sir." Elena wraps her arm around Victor's as several others take their places on the dance floor. Smiling excitedly, Talia watches from the table as Victor and Elena get into position with the others for the last dance of the night. "I'm no good at this so forgive me if I fumble, I've never truly danced before." Victor informs, trying to lighten the mood.

"You'll be fine; all you have to do is hold on." Elena humorously comforts, "Just lead the way, and I'll take care of the rest."

Encouraged, Victor looks upon Elena as she smiles back with confidence in him. As the Archadian band starts to play the last musical number, Victor and Elena dance for the first time together, standing out from the entire crowd.

Marcus gently jabs his elbow into Yuri's side to get his attention, and gags, "Looks like Victor's got some smooth moves, if you know what I mean."

"I know what you mean, but sometimes I question whether or not you do." Yuri sarcastically retorts as he and Marcus share a sarcastic laugh. Looking bored as usual, the two Champions watch the festivities as Damian teases, "Well, we've seen your moves in the arena, how about here?"

"Get real!" Adrian snaps, "Making a fool out of one's self isn't my style. But if it's yours, then by all means, be my guest." He mocks while motioning his hand towards the dance floor.

Shaking his head, Damian scoffs and says, "Is it just me, or are you Enfurians always this stubborn?"

"Yeah right!" Adrian grunts impatiently, "No more than you Eudenians." Standing beside the dance floor, Talia claps her hands to the musical beat, as Adrian sternly concludes, "I'll stick to what suits me, and you stick to yours, got it."

Damian chuckles in response to Adrian's smug attitude, then turns his attention back towards the dance floor and mutters, "Fine by me."

Adrian scoffs in annoyance as Damian shakes his head once again and grins. Victor and Elena continue to dance, looking into each other's eyes passionately as if to search for something deeper within themselves.

Meanwhile, as Victor and Elena dance together in Archadia, a small group of Archadians looks out onto the horizon from their post outside of an Arch Temple above the surface in Pretoria. Unbeknownst to them, Raiven and Celeste stand by as Traganus suddenly appears out of the shadows and signals them to approach the Arch Temple undetected.

As Victor and Elena continue to dance the night away, Talia laughs, having the best time of her life as Lithia remains perched overhead on the crystalline chandelier and hums along whilst moving his tail back and forth.

"You don't seem to be having as much difficulty adjusting to your current surroundings as Talia." Elena humbly denotes.

Hoping that Talia is having a good time as well, Victor looks over Elena's shoulder at her and says, "Like me, her life has been extremely difficult over the years. She probably doesn't want to get too attached too quickly if you take my meaning."

"That's completely understandable." Elena kindly regards with a nod as she looks into Victor's eyes for a moment, trying to sense his true feelings then says softly, "I belong to this kingdom. Where do you belong?"

"Here with you, forever." Victor softly replies with an intense gaze projecting from his deep blue eyes.

"Better hope forever is long enough." Elena calmly teases as she and Victor stare into each other's eyes deeply and passionately.

Rosalyn and Josephus watch them with grave concern over their obvious bond, which emanates with extreme passion.

"Your eyes, they never leave me, do they?" Elena curiously implies while continuing to look into his intense eyes.

Self-conscious, Victor takes a moment to gather his thoughts and answers, "Of all the wonders I've ever seen, I've never looked upon anything or anyone as stunning as you."

Smiling, Elena teases, "Perhaps you ache for what you've never known."

"Perhaps you ache for what you cannot have." Victor sarcastically counters with a crooked smile. Realizing that Victor is much more than he appears to be inside and out in an extremely profound way, Elena gazes into his eyes intensely as they continue to dance within the crowd.

Catching the Archadians off guard in Pretoria, Raiven and Celeste begin their attack upon everyone in the Arch Temple as Traganus watches from the shadows. The Eudenian and Enfurian monks attempt to flee out of fear as the Archadians violently succumb to the dark and deadly sister duo.

Back in the Arch Temple in Archadia, several young Archlings play with Lithia, trying to get his attention as they throw pieces of food at him from below. Distracted, Lithia flies down from the crystalline chandelier and accepts the food in their hands as they pet his backside, causing him to purr. Concerned for her lifelong friend, Talia watches Victor and Elena closely, hoping neither one of them ends up getting hurt by their fast-growing bond.

"I assume your power developed here like all the others?" Victor inquires whilst getting the hang of their dancing.

"As with any other Angel I suppose." Elena sarcastically replies.

"Does it come from the Gods as well?" He curiously probes.

Elena chuckles in response, saying, "Always the skeptical one, if you stay long enough that will surely change."

"Would it?" Victor sarcastically retorts as Elena nods, then states, "I suppose if the world stopped worrying about what happened yesterday, stop planning like there's no tomorrow, then perhaps we could all enjoy the simple things in life without fear of losing everything we already have."

"There's beauty in such simplicity." Elena adds with a nod as she pauses for a moment, getting lost in his eyes then says softly, "Have you ever experienced a perfect moment in time?"

Taking a few seconds to ponder the profound thought, he calmly responds, "A perfect moment, like this one I presume."

"Sometimes you will never know the true value of a moment until it becomes a memory." She enlightens, "But when time seems to stop completely, then you can almost live in that moment forever."

"Like seeing the outside world for the first time." Victor suggests.

"Exactly, there's nothing more complicated than perception because thought is the basis of all reality." Elena claims, "Though the best and most beautiful things in the world cannot be seen or even touched, for they must be felt in the heart instead."

Looking around to acknowledge his beautiful and peaceful surroundings, Victor states, "All life, all consciousness is indisputably bound together in some way or another. Spiritual knowledge itself is unseen knowledge."

"Indeed, it's all part of the same thing." She articulates, "You explore what the world has to offer; we've discovered that a single moment in time can be a universe in and of itself. Full of powerful forces most people aren't aware enough of the present to even notice."

Chuckling quietly to himself, Victor mutters, "I suppose the best way to predict your own future is to daringly create it. Time stands still for no one, though, I wish I could spare a few centuries to learn."

"I know how you feel," Elena inspires, "It took my people centuries to learn it doesn't take that long to do so at all."

Talia looks on, resting her head over her hand whilst leaning against the table and sighs joyfully. She looks over and smiles as several young Archlings try to grab Lithia's tail in a playful manner. Watching Victor and Elena dance, Rosalyn turns from her crystalline throne to address Josephus.

"They seem to be getting along well." She happily regards.

"Yes, perhaps too well." Josephus gripes, "I trust our daughter knows better than to involve herself with a low-level half-breed."

"Do you suppose she has feelings for him?" Rosalyn probes.

"I don't know, but I can tell he has feelings for her." Josephus states. Annoyed by his attitude, Rosalyn shakes her head and defends, "My dear, there's no harm in them dancing. Why, I remember when you used to dance."

"That was long ago, before it bored my interest." Josephus scoffs while keeping his focus closely on Victor and Elena.

Put off by his selfish remark, Rosalyn turns her attention back towards the dance floor and mutters, "Like everything else it seems."

Josephus scoffs once more as Rosalyn watches their daughter dance and smiles from the joy of seeing her happy for the first time in ages.

Meanwhile, back at the Arch Temple in the outskirts of Pretoria, Raiven and Celeste combine various energy attacks with their Gauntlets and take down the remaining Archadians, who struggle to hold their defense against them. Laughing maniacally at their expense, the deadly pair roams throughout the temple halls in search for something extremely valuable and powerful in nature.

Within the Arch Temple of Archadia, Victor and Elena dance together to the peaceful music being played by the band as Rosalyn and Josephus converse. "I think it's wonderful to see her finally getting along with someone so well after all these years, don't you?" Rosalyn cheerfully infers.

"As long as they both know their place." Josephus sternly claims after taking a sip from his crystalline wine glass, "You know as well as I do that a union between them is strictly forbidden, regardless of their bond."
Confident of her stance on the matter, Rosalyn calmly dismisses, "Through the Gods' eyes maybe, but I think you worry too much my dear."

"Perhaps you don't worry enough!" Josephus scorns.
Turning her attention back towards Victor and Elena, Rosalyn proclaims, "Friendship can be a bond not so easily broken, just like love."

"We'll see." Josephus sneers, "I keep forgetting where our daughter gets her overly compassionate side from." Rosalyn chuckles in response as Josephus joins in. Standing by himself away from the dance floor, Kael notices that everyone is watching closely as Victor and Elena dance perfectly in harmony together. "Tell me something, how is it possible that someone like you has never been taken?" Victor asks as she looks at him confused, "Why haven't you married?" Surprised by his inquiry, her eyes widen as he adds, "Surely there are plenty of worthy people between here and Empyria."
Contemplating the best way to answer, Elena humbly replies, "What's the rush? Despite my current rank, I just haven't got around to it yet."

"How come?" Victor persists.

"We've always known that to survive we must sometimes remain apart as to not distract ourselves from our sacred duty." She explains.
Nodding seriously, Victor responds, "Guess that makes sense."

"You seem intelligent and creative enough yourself; why are you still single?" Elena awkwardly probes, which causes him to chuckle softly.
Victor wittily retorts, "Apparently I'm overqualified to most standards."

"As am I for the most part." Elena drolly retorts, "As you probably already know, it hasn't been easy, for many of our people want to know more about the world below." She clarifies, "They're attracted to stories of a faster paced lifestyle."
Confident of his ability to finally lead her in the dance, Victor looks around and states, "Most people who live that faster lifestyle would likely sell their own souls to slow it down just a bit."

"But not you, huh?" Elena humorously inquires.
Victor turns his attention back with a serious face then expresses a crooked smile and says, "There are days, more than I like to admit anyway."

"I'm glad to know you don't live up to your previous reputation." Elena respectfully comments.

"Well, in defense of humans, I'm sure there are others like me, at least more than the world wants to see or believe." Victor wittily indicates.

"I wonder if you're even aware of the trust you engender?" Elena intriguingly probes, which brings a look of curiosity to Victor's face. "In my experience, it's unusual for an Angel, especially for one so alone."

"I'm not alone with you beside me." He says softly.

Feeling flattered and somewhat distressed, Elena abruptly stops in her tracks for a moment as Victor looks upon her with concern, sensing that he accidently struck a nerve with her. Seconds later, the dance ends as Victor and Elena refocus their attention as to not reveal that anything's wrong, smiling as they clap softly. Kael begins to clap as well, inciting everyone else to join in as they applaud in their honor. Sharing the spotlight, Victor and Elena bow before everyone as Talia joins in as well, joyous to see her two closest friends being acknowledged. Moments later, a sudden look of panic strikes Elena's face, sensing trouble of unknown proportion upon the planet's surface.

"Something wrong?" Victor inquires, concerned by her dreaded look.

Experiencing a mental overload, Elena places her hand on Victor's shoulder to retain spiritual balance, and says, "I could use a breather, how about you?"

"I suppose a break is in order." Victor politely obliges.

Elena smiles for a brief moment then turns to approach Rosalyn and Josephus as the Archadian band plays the closing number. As Elena approaches her parents, Rosalyn curiously inquires, "Having fun?"

Elena smiles back and says, "Why yes, more than I've had in years actually."

"For your sake, we hope you don't get too comfortable then." Josephus firmly warns. Confused by the stern warning, Elena looks upon her parents curiously and asks, "With what are you referring to?"

"We sense that Victor has grown very fond of you, Elena, and quickly I might add." Rosalyn cautiously informs.

"We're just having a good time." Elena jokingly shrugs, then motions towards the crowd, "That is kind of the point of this whole thing, is it not?"

"Yes, but unlike your previous suitors, we can tell he's much more persistent." Rosalyn carefully reveals to her, "We respect the admiration you apparently have for each other, but don't let your emotions cloud your judgment. Especially at this time."

Annoyed, Elena frowns and says, "It's a shame you can't find enjoyment without always finding fault somewhere. You should be happy really."

"Why?" Josephus probes as he leans back in his crystalline throne.

Motioning towards Victor, she answers, "Because he's nothing like them."

"We hope not." Rosalyn cautions, "You may see a hero in him, and maybe there is, but that's not all that lies within him."

"You sound as if he doesn't quite measure up in your eyes or is unworthy of my attention." Elena says with a disgruntled tone, "Are you implying that I'm incapable of telling who he is, inside and out?"

Rosalyn looks over and sees Victor conversing with Talia as he glances back, then implies, "Eyes like his seek out danger, not love."

"He seems to be having good time to me." Elena defends.

"But that's not a smile," Josephus informs, "That is nothing more than a mask hiding years of pain and suffering."

"He likes you, it's quite obvious." Rosalyn suspiciously implies.

Elena looks back at Victor once again and mutters, "It would seem so."

"And you like him we assume?" Josephus firmly inquires.

Turning back to face her parents, Elena hardens her expression and admits, "I trust him, that means a lot, and I appreciate that he's a good warrior."

"Let us hope that is all you dare to perceive." Rosalyn warns.

"Why do you always do that?" Elena questions, becoming annoyed.

"I'm sorry?" Josephus states, oblivious to her true feelings.

"Whenever I dare to get close to anyone, you always find a way to alienate me." She assertively defends, "How can you look at someone and not realize that you share a special connection, despite what others may think?"

"Because we know where our duty lies, first and foremost." Josephus firmly states to her displeasure.

"Do you?" Rosalyn chimes in, putting her on the spot.

"I'm sorry, I don't follow." Elena says while shaking her head.

Sighing impatiently, Josephus explains, "Those eyes, they belong to a man who's torn by extreme conflict, and the desperation that comes with fighting for his own life against others."

"Well at least he knows what it's like to be independent and fight for something noble!" Elena defends, "That's something we both seem to share."

"That may be, but you must ask yourself if a man like that even knows how to love." Josephus contests.

Elena glances back at Victor and concedes, "From what I can already tell, he has more compassion than anyone I've ever known. I for one appreciate such diversity because there's always so much to learn from others like him."

"Regardless, do not give him hope where there is none, for it can and will be used against both of you." Josephus sternly warns, "For only a fool wants what he cannot have."

"And only fools can't appreciate something beautiful sitting right in front of them." She quickly turns back and retorts, "Like a bond between two people, kindred spirits." She justifies, "If that sort of thing scares you, then it's no wonder why I've been so alone my whole life."

"There will be none of that!" Josephus sternly expresses, "Remember daughter, you are to be married soon and you have your solemn oath."

"As always, I keep forgetting." Elena murmurs disappointedly as she looks away, "You're right, unfortunately."

Attempting to calm her defiant attitude, Rosalyn explains, "This man is different somehow though. You don't want to let your guard down, for he is possibly dangerous and could very well lead to the destruction of our entire order if we aren't careful."

Chuckling in response, Josephus confidently states, "No my dear, I assure you that the Arch won't be weakened by the inclusion of a commoner like him in the family. Of that I am certain." He says arrogantly, "Like the Gods, we will also protect our sacred beliefs from outsiders, for those who would plunder our kingdom to betray our secrets will answer to them."

"There are ancient powers that will make certain our secrets are kept, and you more than anyone should understand this." Rosalyn stresses.
Frustrated by her parents' harsh attitude towards Victor, Elena shakes her head and scoffs as she takes her leave impatiently. Rosalyn and Josephus look on with concern, hoping their daughter doesn't do anything cavalier.

After a grueling slaughter, Raiven and Celeste step over several dead Archadians through the burning Arch Temple in Pretoria while approaching a secret chamber. As they force themselves inside, they observe an Archadian Artifact, an Angelic tiara sitting inside the hands of the Holy Trinity statue, specifically the legendary Enfurian Angel, Kiara.

"Why don't you do the honor, sis?" Raiven suggests with her hand motioned towards the Angelic statue.

"Why thank you, sis, you're so kind." Celeste jokes as she steps forward and aggressively pulls out the Artifact from the statue's hand. With the first of three sacred Angelic Artifacts in their grasp, Celeste proudly states, "One down, two to go."

"So much for resistance, huh?" Raiven mentions while admiring their destructive handiwork throughout the now ruined temple.
A dying Archadian from several feet away looks up at Raiven and Celeste and attempts to blast them with their Gauntlet, but misses as they both turn in anger. "Why you!" Celeste screeches furiously. As they aim their Gauntlets, Traganus appears out of the shadows through the flames and strikes the Archadian with deadly intensity. Intimidated by his dark prowess, Raiven and Celeste glance each other as Traganus retains his intense yet graceful battle stance then straightens up and proclaims, "That will get their attention!"

"If this doesn't, nothing will." Raiven pompously states.

"We've got what we came for." Celeste states, "What now, Master?"
Retracting his wings into his spinal armor, Traganus faces his deadly female duo, and informs, "Their move, we'll let them come to us." Raiven and Celeste glance at each other and grin in anticipation as he steps closer and fiercely adds, "In time, we'll bring the fight to them."
Nodding in agreement, the pair chuckle quietly as Traganus raises his fist intensely and declares, "It's been so very long, and it will be our time again, for soon they will be draped with failure, and us with triumph." Raiven and Celeste share a devious grin as they follow him out of the burning temple with the Holy Artifact in hand.

CH: 37
A SACRED OATH

The next day in Archadia, Victor is finally ready to receive his official initiation alongside Earth's Champions. At the start of the ceremony, he walks between a fleet of Angels as they raise their Gauntlets upward in honor with their wings fully spread. Victor bows before the Arch council to speak the sacred oath as Kael approaches him in his own decorative attire.

"Those who are gathered here today are the elite, the best and bravest the Arch has to offer." He announces as he glances at Damian and Adrian who nod back in respect, then turns his attention back towards Victor and decrees, "Yours, Victor, is a heroic mission, one that requires you to transcend your humanity, by protecting others. Embody the highest of the Arch's principles, that being obedience, order, and control." Victor nods in respect as he glances at Elena and grins as she smiles back. With a stern expression, Kael finally questions, "What is your mission?"

Taking a moment to refocus his intense composure, Victor proudly declares, "I pledge myself, now and forever, to the Gods, and in their service, declare an oath to the people of Earth. And with that oath, I solemnly swear by the ordinances of the Arch with irrevocable intent, to defend against those who would do harm upon them, and my kingdom." He finishes while humbly bowing his head before the Arch council in their honor.

"You're very lucky to have made it this far in such a short amount of time," Kael strongly advises, "Don't squander your good fortune." Victor nods respectfully, hoping to make good use of his abilities in service to the Arch and the Gods. "As an Angelic warrior, you're going to see things you may want to stop with every fiber of your being, but if you're the one making the call, just be sure it's the right one." Kael cautions, "Loyalty is everything in this world, so look out for those who look out for you."

"I'll be sure of that." Victor confidently replies.

"Very good." Kael admires, "I'm proud to have taught you all the necessary skills in life." He then smiles and says, "Be sure to use them well."

"Believe me, I will." Victor proclaims with a crooked smile.

Kael bows his head then steps aside as Elena approaches Victor before the Arch council and smiles. Victor smiles back as Kael nods towards Elena in respect. "I'm so proud of you, Victor." She says softly, "You are ready."

Nodding with determination, Victor glances over at Talia who waves back with Lithia perched on her shoulder as always.

"Like most warriors, Angels are those who choose to stand between their enemy and all that they love or hold sacred." Rosalyn respectfully states, "We see within you the potential of what you are, and what you can be."

"I hope to one day be recognized as such, an Angel worthy of my wings." Victor proudly claims.

"But you will be, and a great one." Rosalyn proudly assures with a grin, "To be an Angel is to have the courage to look within and learn from yourself. You must leave the known by entering the unknown, in turn you must develop the strength to survive defeat inside and out, for this is the true essence of the Arch."

Victor smiles in response as Josephus takes his turn to address him and seriously infers, "There are some among us who are suspicious, yet the majority feels we have no choice but to trust you."

"Can't say I truly understand the source of your misgivings, but I appreciate what faith you have in me at this time." Victor humbly responds.

"Make certain that faith is not misplaced, for loyalty given is loyalty earned." Josephus carefully advises, "It is great solace to know that you along with our other Angels will be fighting for the sanctity of the Arch itself."

Victor firmly nods, anxious to attain his new status in life, "With full humility and upmost gratitude, I accept this great honor." He declares, "I promise I will do my absolute best to represent my people, this planet, and the Gods on this historic journey. I thank you all from the bottom of my heart."

"It is said that a new breed of enemy requires a new breed of hero, therefore a new breed of Darchadian requires a new breed of Angel in general." Josephus resumes. "Rise, Victor Zyas." He proudly declares with his hand raised, "Rise an Angel!" As Victor rises to his feet, Talia looks on with tears of joy running down her cheeks as Lithia attempts to lick them away.

"May the Gods give you strength, now and forever!" Rosalyn proudly declares with her hand raised as well. Glancing back at Talia, Victor smiles, hoping to comfort her joyful sorrow as she wipes her tears away.

"The Gods bless those who fight and die for honor and truth," Josephus announces, "The Arch embraces you; hence forth you will be forever known as Archelus, an Angel of Archadia." He then graciously adds, "We are what we do, and what we do in life echoes in eternity."

Elena places her hands below her chin, excited to witness Victor's ascension.

"Be without fear in the face of your enemies, bring hope to the hopeless and safeguard the defenseless when called into action." Rosalyn adds, "Never give up, and never surrender, even if it leads to your demise." Victor nods once more, as Josephus concludes, "We are who we protect, what we stand for, and should you ever face death on the battlefield in service to the Arch, know that it will be the greatest glory anyone could ever achieve in their lifetime." Rosalyn and Josephus bow their heads in approval as Victor faces Damian and Adrian who approach him in respect. Marcus and Yuri also glance at each other in approval, as do Valorie and Vennessa. Damian and Arian place their arms on Victor's shoulders, standing together in a stance that forms a trinity as they each speak the oath together in unison:

"Brothers in arms, together we fight, through life and death, from night till dawn, with honor and grace, through dark of light, to the edge of beyond."

Elena and Talia look on with excitement over Victor's Angelic final initiation as Lithia proudly chirps. "Remember these words, and you will taste victory." Kael informs with a poised stance, "Vanquish your fears, or they'll vanquish you. You all know your jobs, you've been trained, tested, thus you've earned the right to bear those Gauntlets, and wings." He finishes with a stern grin towards Victor, "Sacrifice, the price you pay to be all you can be. Keep the team unified, and you shall always succeed."

Successfully swearing the oath as a team, Damian and Adrian nod in respect towards their new comrade, who nods back in an honorable fashion.

"Ready for battle?" Damian motivates.

Determined, Victor chuckles quietly to himself with a crooked smile and gladly replies, "As ready as I'll ever be I suppose."

"Good, with an attitude like that you just might make it after all." Damian encourages, "We'll need your strength for sure. If we know you have our backs then rest assured we will always have yours."

As Victor nods in agreement, Adrian chimes in, pointing towards the blue Gods' symbol bearing over his chest, and states, "In the end, an Angel's true strength comes from the warrior within. Give respect and honor to your comrades, and it will be returned in full."

"In other words, be sure to fight with your head." Damian jokes while tapping the side of his brow.

"I fight with my heart." Victor proudly asserts while looking at Elena.

"Better hope it's enough." Adrian cautions, "You may be a half-breed, but there's an Angel in you as well. Be sure to bring it with you."

"Don't worry, I intend to." Victor affirms.

"Welcome to the team, provisionally of course." Damian warns, "We'll be proud to have you fight by our side, so that we may also keep an eye on you. You bust your wings for us, and we'll bust our backs for you."

"As brothers in arms, we either fight for you or with you." Adrian respectfully concludes as the three of them nod towards one another.

As Damian and Adrian take their leave, Victor turns his attention towards Talia, who stands by, feeling too shy to approach him. Lithia chirps as Victor approaches her, looking upon her old friend with a new sense of joy and somewhat distraught curiosity, "Well, Talia, none of this would be the same without you." Victor gratefully regards with his arms extended in a friendly manner, "So, what do you think about all this?"

Hesitant, Talia looks upon her lifelong friend curiously, then places her hand over his arm, and says softly, "It's wonderful, I'm so happy for you, Victor." Hoping to comfort her, Victor places his hands on her shoulders as she looks into his eyes in a hopeful manner, tears still running down her face.

"You know I'm not the only one worthy of this recognition." He encourages, "Someday, you'll be right where I am."

"I hope you're right about that." She says modestly with a hopeful voice, "Do you really believe so?"

Victor chuckles in response and assures, "As a matter of fact, I know so."

Trying to gather her thoughts, Talia looks away for a moment, struggling with her emotions, and mutters, "This is all so sudden."

"I know, but it's for the best I'm sure." He comforts.

"You're the only good thing that's ever happened in my life." She sadly professes, "I'm scared to lose you simply because all the good things keep going away."

"I'm not going anywhere." Victor calmly reassures.

"I hope not, just promise you won't forget about me." Talia says, looking into his eyes with extreme hope.

"How could I?" Victor laughs, "You're a part of my life the same as yours. We're stuck together, best friends, and we always will be."

"I hope so, cause there's only one of you." Talia utters.

"Only one of anybody really." Victor jokes with a crooked smile.

Deeply heartened by his words, Talia embraces Victor, feeling a new sense of hope for him and his new status in life. "I know you pride yourself on being the outsider sometimes, but aren't you tired of being something you're not?" She asks, "I know I am."

"All this responsibility though, it's not me." Victor professes while pulling away from her embrace. He then the motions towards Elena and says, "It's more her thing really." Talia looks back towards Elena, who smiles back at them. "I've always been good at certain things, maybe it's time I tried something I'm not." He finishes.

"I think you're missing the point, Victor." Talia explains as she slowly turns back, "I mean; you're officially an Angel now, what an honor that must be. I'd be pretty excited myself."

Amused by her keen perception, Victor smiles and says, "I am, but you see, I've never been like you in that sense."

"What do you mean?" Talia softly questions with a curious smile.

"You know exactly who you are, you always have." Victor clarifies, "But a part of me is still looking unfortunately."

Without hesitation, Talia states, "If you look too hard you may just miss whatever it is you're looking for."

Victor smiles in response to her honesty, and admits, "I know that I'm not as worthy of this status compared to someone like Elena, and I've never met my mother, or father for that matter."

"So?" Talia retorts, attempting to keep his mind on a positive track.

"So, what does that make me?" He cautiously inquires, expecting his young friend to comfort him in some way.

Talia places her hand over the Gods' symbol on his chest to comfort him, saying, "I think what you're searching for isn't out there, it's in here." She encourages, "Maybe you just don't see it yet, but know that it's always there whenever you need it."

"Maybe, but you know there has to be something else out there, something even beyond this place." Victor suggests while looking upward.

"I think for now you should just be happy with what you have, which is a lot if you ask me." Talia caringly advises.

Smiling at one another, Victor and Talia chuckle quietly as Lithia flies onto his shoulder and chirps in acceptance of his new Angelic status.

"I know it's probably none of my business, but I have to ask." She mentions apprehensively. "Ask away." Victor humorously responds.

Choosing her words carefully, Talia inquires, "So what do you get out of all this when you're finished? The day you get to hang up your wings for good?"

Thinking it over carefully, Victor replies, "I don't know, it's too early to tell."

"I bet by then you'll get something out of it." Talia inspires.

With a curious expression, Victor asks, "Like what?"

"Maybe, you get to be the hero this time, and perhaps even more." Talia happily encourages with a smile, "Whose name are people going to yell when you leave for battle?"

"No one I guess." Victor sadly mutters.

"Then who's going to scream your name when you return?" She asks.

"Honestly, I don't think anyone ever will." Victor says sheepishly.

"Why not?" Talia persists.

"The truth is, it takes more than looking to really see one's worth in this world." Victor replies.

Hoping to encourage him, Talia asserts, "Someday you'll be ready, and when you are you'll find her and she'll find you."

With a cunning smile, Victor says, "Nah, what could possibly ever change?"

"Everything." Talia enlightens, "Things are changing for us; so be sure this is what you really want in life. Years from now make sure you can look back and say you chose this path and didn't settle for it."

"Yes mam." He replies with a devious grin.

"Your job is to live the fantasy other people only dream about." Talia informs, "The job of an Angel must be quite an undertaking."

"It's one thing to dream about such things, and quite another to actually do them." Victor jokes.

"Exactly." Talia explains, "Don't go in halfway, dream big or go home. Live the life you have to the fullest."

"That goes for you as well." Victor points out, bringing a smile to Talia's face. "No regrets?"

"None whatsoever." Talia happily retorts with a slight chuckle then infers, "By the way, I've seen the way she looks at you."

"Who, Elena?" Victor inquires. Talia responds with a joyful nod as he hesitantly looks over at Elena and says, "I'm quite fond of her myself, but unfortunately for her, there's not much to see."

"Then just like everyone else, encourage her to look again." She informs, hoping not to lead him astray, "If she's as smart as I think she is, she'll have no problem seeing you for who you really are inside and out."

"Like you." Victor teases which makes her blush.

Nodding with a grin, Talia admits, "It's still strange seeing you with them."

"What, you don't think they need me?" Victor queries.

"Actually, I think they do." Talia informs, "But you need to be sure that this team is really a team, and that they truly have your back because they're not your friends unless they have defended you in your absence. They're the closest anyone can get to being a god, but they need someone like you to keep them grounded, down to Earth if you know what I mean."

"I do," Victor comments as they share a comforting smile, "But you know the best part about being an Angel..." She looks upon him with a curious expression, "You get to fly." Talia smiles with excitement as he continues; "You've got to try it sometime, assuming you earn your own set of wings in the near future. Nothing makes you feel more powerful," Victor glances at Elena with a crooked smile and finishes, "Well, almost nothing."

Elena smiles back as she turns her attention towards Valorie and Vennessa who receive a sudden transmission then quickly approach her. Victor looks on curiously of their movement towards Elena as Talia wipes her tears away. As Valorie and Vennessa approach Elena, Marcus and Yuri step beside her as well to listen in. "Your Highness, we have a situation." Valorie informs.

Concerned, Marcus and Yuri glance at each other, unsure of what to expect.

"It's urgent." Vennessa adds.

Elena's expression becomes intense, knowing that there's danger lurking about then turns towards Victor and Talia as Lithia chirps to get their attention. Finishing his conversation with Talia, Victor wraps his arms around her comfortingly as Elena motions her head elsewhere, signifying there's an issue. Sighing concernedly, Victor stares back and nods as Elena takes her leave with her crew to confront the Arch council.

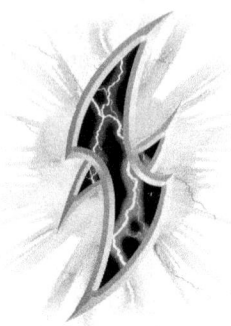

CH: 38
HOSTILE IMMINENT

Shortly after the initiation ceremony, Elena enters the throne chamber to confront the Arch council as Kael stands in the back of the room listening in with Talia and Lithia beside him. Lithia makes a purring noise, which causes Talia to shush him as to not offend the council.

"Your presence is unexpected, Elena." Rosalyn suspiciously calls, "Have you been summoned?"
Elena steps forward, and replies, "No, and for that I apologize."

"We've just inducted another into our harmonious collective." Josephus states, "What matter of business do you have then?"

"I would not disturb you all if this matter were not of the upmost importance, but I felt you should know what's happened as of late." Elena explains with a concerned tone.
Josephus waves his hand and grants, "Very well then, you may proceed."
Glancing upon each council member, she informs, "One of our temples has recently been attacked, and several of our fellow Angels have been killed." The Arch council glances at each other with concern as she continues, "Annihilated by an unknown threat that possesses a dark and mysterious power. An enemy against whom we seem to have no real defense, one, which discounting rumor, we know very little about."
Whispering amongst themselves, Rosalyn and Josephus glance each other as if to know more about the situation than previously thought.

"We know it originated from somewhere within Pretoria, near Eldria." Elena further explains, "We know it grows more powerful with each deadly encounter. Many were apparently killed in the struggle, and according to their last transmission, they seemed to know who and what it was."
Keeping them in suspense, the council members remain silent until Elena finally reveals, "They claim that it's Traganus, the fallen Darchadian leader."
The Arch council gasps, concerned for their kingdom once again as Elena shares a nod with Kael in support.

After quieting down, Josephus states, "We are aware of the threat, and are presently assessing the situation!"

"While you assess, innocent lives will be endangered, maybe even lost." Elena exclaims as she steps closer to address her parents directly, "Our survival depends on knowing any and all adversaries beforehand."

"Elena, there is much of which you are not yet aware." Rosalyn implies while shaking her head.

Concerned by her parents' tone, Elena looks upon them intensely, and cautiously inquires, "What are you saying?"

"If the threat is as great as we suspect, then we must act carefully." Josephus informs, "Given what has happened, and assuming Traganus has indeed returned, his power could be vastly superior to ours by now."

"That is a natural if not obvious assumption; either way it's a certainty we cannot sustain." Elena sarcastically replies with an annoyed tone. Contemplating her peoples' safety, she then asks, "Considering the dark history of our past, do you think this enemy can defeat us?"

The Arch council members glance at each other for a moment with concern, unable to answer until Josephus reluctantly admits, "Possibly."

"Then let me take my team to face this new adversary at once!" Elena requests with great determination, "We must formulate a strategy and act immediately while we still can. We have to hit them hard, and fast."

"That is impractical and provocative!" Josephus argues, "You're assuming that your team has the power to sustain such a daring tactic?"

"Victor included?" Rosalyn curiously chimes in.

Confident, Elena decrees, "With his help, I believe we stand a good chance."

"Fight fire with fire you mean?" Rosalyn implies.

"Yes, though more like lightning against thunder!" Elena retorts, "They've already acted against us. Isn't that alone considered an act of war?"

Rosalyn and Josephus glance at each other for a moment, nodding in agreement as Kael places his hand on Talia's shoulder to comfort her.

"We appreciate your advice and concern, dear daughter, but this is not the time for rash actions, for we must proceed in a calm and orderly manner." Rosalyn sternly informs, "Assuming we run out of options here, how do you suggest we clarify their intentions?"

"We go in; if we prepare for the worst and nothing happens, we've lost nothing." Elena proclaims, "May I at least take my team to investigate?"

"That would be prudent." Rosalyn calmly states, "Your team may be slightly unprepared and outmatched, but we believe in their abilities to overcome what challenges may lie ahead of them."

"Though it would be best if Victor completed the Arch trials first, at this point I'm afraid we have no choice." Josephus cautions.

Confused by her father's claim, Elena queries, "Afraid, of what exactly?"

"You know the danger should he fight before purging his fear." Rosalyn sternly forewarns. Elena sighs impatiently, unwilling to accept him as anything less at this point. "The last thing we need right now is for him to fall." Josephus cautions, "Remember what happened to your former comrades, Raiven and Celeste when they eloped?"

Feeling reassured, Elena nods with a stern expression, knowing they are right then says, "Of course, how could I ever forget. Regardless, the enemy is likely on the move, therefore I urge you to engage them with all haste."

"Very well then, it has carefully been decided." Rosalyn orders, "Prepare your team, and seek out this enemy."

"Do whatever is necessary!" Josephus firmly adds.

Elena bows in respect then takes her leave with Talia, followed by Kael and Lithia as the Arch council glances at each other once again with concern.

"You two go ahead." Elena insists, "I'll catch up later."

Sensing she has other business, Kael responds, "As you wish, milady." He then turns to Talia and says, "Come along, Natalia."

Talia follows Kael with Lithia perched on her shoulder and glances back as Elena examines her Gauntlet for a moment, having a sudden thought. Determined to waste no time, Elena quickly takes her leave to find answers.

Afternoon turns into evening; Elena enters the Archives within the Archadian Temple to investigate the true origin of Victor's Gauntlet. As she finds a quiet place to do her research, several Archadians tend to their usual duties, preparing to close up shop for the day.

"Alright, let's see what we can find here." Elena mutters as she attempts to look through the holographic archives but is unable to find any current information regarding the Darchadians or Victor's Gauntlet. Moments later, two Archadian Elders approach her from behind. "Good evening your Highness," one of them greets, "We're told that you specifically requested the best Archivists currently present in the kingdom."

"That's right." Elena sternly replies.

"Anything we can possibly help you with before we close up tonight?" The other elder adds.

Turning to face them directly, Elena looks upon the two elders curiously and replies; "Yes, actually. I need some information regarding the Gauntlet I brought back with me several weeks ago."

"You mean the second-generation model?" One of them specifies.

Elena nods in response, saying, "You would think that our technology would afford us to go back in time to find the truth about such things."

One of them nods back and explains; "True, but we don't know a whole lot about it ourselves, other than it was customized by someone long ago."

"How long?" Elena carefully inquires.

"Oh, as far back as we can remember." The second elder responds, "Long before you were born anyway."

Curious to their actual knowledge regarding Victor's powerful Gauntlet, Elena probes, "You can tell that much about it already?"

The elders glance at each other with concern; unsure as to how much information they're allowed to give. Finally, one of them says, "It's unclear how old it is exactly, but we have an idea of who it may previously been in contact with during its use."

"Who exactly?" Elena persists. Hesitant to respond, the elders look upon her with deep concern, "Tell me, please?" She pleas, "I need to know."

Sighing in response, one of the elders professes, "Your parents probably wouldn't approve of us giving you this information at this time, but if you're that concerned then we'll tell you." Elena respectfully nods as the other explains, "From what we've gathered, the last Archadian to come in contact with it before it arrived here was definitely one of our own."

"You mean an elite like me, right?" Elena suspiciously asks.

"Yes, but one who's actions became somewhat questionable in the aftermath of the Chaos War." The other elder informs. Trying not to offend her, the elder finally reveals, "Her name was Zyas, Victoria Zyas."

Shocked by this revelation, Elena looks away for a moment in distress as the elders express concern over sharing this information.

"This explains everything." Elena murmurs as she faces them then sternly asks, "Why was I never told about this before now?"

Realizing they've already said too much, the elders glance at each other, then one of them states, "It's not particularly important."

"Well it must be if it's been kept a secret this whole time!" Elena impatiently retorts, "As an Angel, these are intelligences unknown to me."

"They are known to you now." The elder firmly states.

"I'm uncertain of your exact meaning?" Elena challenges.

"Your parents have expressed dire claim that it is not to be discussed with fellow Angels, unless deemed absolutely necessary." The first retorts.

"They thought it best to keep it from you." The second one adds.

"Why?" Elena questions with a concerned voice.

Trying not to anger her further, the first elder calmly explains, "For fear that it would cause problems between you and Victor during his training."

"So, you knew about his connection with it already?" Elena deduces.

"Yes, and that's the only reason why he was ever allowed into our kingdom in the first place." The first elder justifies.

Attempting to rationalize, the second elder cautiously informs, "His current involvement with the Arch is also not to be on record."

Elena scoffs while continuing to flip through files on the holographic screen, and mutters, "Makes me wonder what else isn't on record in this place."

"Any information regarding his involvement and or any assignments has intentionally been kept off the grid." The first elder continues, "As requested by your parents as well."

"Why, because they're embarrassed by his bloodstained lineage?" Elena angrily retorts as she swipes the holographic screen aggressively.

Sensing her immediate frustration, the second elder clarifies, "So they could see to it personally that he doesn't become a Darchadian, like the others. For whoever fights monsters should see to it that in the process they do not become monsters themselves." Irritated by this info, Elena stands back from the holographic screen, and states, "Speaking of which, I've sifted through all the past antidotal data and can't seem to find anything regarding their current status. Since we've had no contact with them for some time now, we must consider that the information they have about us is also out of date."

"The lack of information between us seems to be what this is all about." The first elder implies, "We take this to mean the enemy is completely unfocused in their actions and have no apparent goals."

Looking around the Archives at the other Archadians, Elena firmly surmises, "Their goals are quite clear for I believe the Darchadians want confrontation; not just specifically with us, but everyone who dares to stand in their way." Concerned by her claim, the elders glance at each other as she explains, "They know the Arch will send their absolute best, that alone will give them a perfect chance to see first hand just how far we've advanced both in technology and technique."

"Your reasoning is perfectly sound." The second elder supports.

Realizing that matters are possibly worse than she expected, Elena faces the two elders and respectfully concludes, "Thank you both for your time."

"Of course, your Highness." The first elder replies as they both bow their heads in respect. Elena bows in return then quickly takes her leave, as the two elders look on, concerned for her tenacious efforts to seek the truth.

Shortly after leaving the Archives and making her way through the Arch Temple, Elena enters the Armory as Talia and Kael look upon her curiously. Talia grins as Elena places her hand on her shoulder, hoping to keep her out of harms way and smiles back as Lithia chirps.

"Everything alright, milady?" Kael respectfully inquires.

Facing him with deep concern, Elena calmly sighs then says reluctantly, "Something extremely nefarious awaits us. Is everyone ready for tomorrow?"

"More or less, as can be expected anyway." Kael answers.

"I fear the same about our enemy," Elena states as she looks onto the kingdom from above under the late evening sky, "I've heard nothing but wicked things about their kind growing up."

"It's true that they are known for their barbarity and their slavish devotion to their senses, but I wouldn't worry too much, Princess." He encourages, "Heck, they may know as little about us as we do about them at this point in time."

Turning back to face him, Elena stresses, "Except they already know that they've got us right where they want us."

"Where exactly?" Talia chimes in unexpectedly.

Amused by her intuition, Elena smiles upon Talia and says, "In deep trouble."

"If so, then the real question becomes what do they intend to do with that knowledge?" Kael indicates.

Talia looks upon Kael, fearing the worst as Lithia pants in a sorrowful tone.

"To my knowledge, there's been no contact with them since their leader fell years ago." She explains, "Everything we know about them beyond that point is based on rumor or conjecture. So the question I have is, what's the connection? Why now, what's their true objective after all this time?"

As he prepares several Archadian Gauntlets for battle, Kael informs, "As I understand it, the Arch's strategic decision is to send one team, but you could get out there and find yourselves greatly outnumbered, and overmatched."

Nodding in agreement, Elena sighs, "True enough." She then jokes, "As Marcus and Yuri would say; it's a gamble." Elena caresses Talia's hair to comfort her as she smiles back, then resumes, "This first encounter coming so suddenly after all this time, we have to assume it's a setup."

"I concur." Kael firmly states.

"If force is absolutely necessary, we will use it, but that would mean we have failed in our prime directive." Elena says discouragingly.

Kael places a few Gauntlets on the table, ready for combat and states, "The ultimate goal here is to establish some kind of communication with them, assuming they even want to communicate." Talia carefully rubs her fingers over one of the Gauntlets as he explains, "If we don't succeed to convince them of our resolve, the general feeling in Archadia is that they are seeking confrontation of the upmost extremity."

"That's what worries me." Elena fearfully mutters, "If what you say about them is true, then they will likely read our intent, which could force them into taking a similar posture. Meaning they'll want to engage in battle."

"There is sufficient evidence to support that theory." Kael adds, "The temple in Pretoria is expected to be nearly destroyed and countless lives have already been lost." Talia accidently activates one of the Gauntlets, causing the Gods' symbol to light up brightly in red as Kael quickly moves her hand away. "Careful dear, they're dangerous." He gently warns.

Expressing a silly frown, Talia moves back towards Lithia, as Elena shakes her head in amusement. "They may want to test themselves in battle against us to see how far we've advanced." Kael continues as he presses the Gods' symbol on the Gauntlet to power it down, "That alone would explain why they're so animalistic in nature, for they seek the darkness over the light."

"Well, if that is truly the case, then we should prepare for the worst." Elena says determinedly, "What do you recommend, General?"

"Not sure I have a specific notion at this time." Kael admits as he places more Gauntlets on the table. He then faces her directly and suggests, "Perhaps we should take the initiative ourselves and see what happens."

"My thinking exactly." Elena confirms, "This may be our only opportunity to make sure the situation doesn't escalate, we should seize it."

Placing the prepared Gauntlets into a storage container, Kael explains, "The strategy is built on a single premise, the hostile intent of the Darchadians. If the premise is sound, then so is the proposal, theoretically that is."

"But if their intention isn't truly hostile, then what is it?" Elena questions while looking upwards towards the starry sky, she then sighs as Talia pets Lithia's backside, which makes him purr loudly.

"Don't stress out, Princess." Kael reassures, "They've been training for weeks now and already seem to work well together."

As Elena approaches the wall covered in Archadian weaponry, she cautions, "We'll be facing a fierce enemy, one that is highly skilled, and whose cruelty is known to be ever reaching." After taking a moment to add to her supplies, she then turns to address Kael directly, and says, "Are you sure you want to join us on the hunt?"

"The team still has much to learn, for they have not spent enough time working together as a single unit yet." He professes, "They're strong no doubt, but they'll need guidance against such malevolence."

"I know there is much pressure on Victor's shoulders right now, but the world needs something they can believe in, a hero." She professes.

"You don't need to be an Angel or a God to be a hero, you just need to believe in your own abilities to do heroic things." Kael attests, "It's what worked for him, but what the hell do I know? I should've been dead by now."

As Elena walks past Talia, she informs, "We head out at first light." Talia follows her movements as Elena stops by the entrance and requests, "Tell Victor I need to speak with him tonight if you don't mind. It's important."

"Why not now?" Kael respectfully inquires.

"I'm not quite ready to receive his company at the moment." Elena discloses, "You see I'm having something special prepared as a gift and wish to give it to him personally when it's ready."

"As you wish, milady." Kael replies with a respectful nod.

"Thank you." Elena utters softly, then turns towards Talia and says; "Rest well tonight, Natalia. I'll see you in the morning."

"You too, Elena." Talia politely responds.

Elena activates her wings then swiftly takes off into the night as Kael looks on and grins. Looking out into the evening sky with concern, Talia hopes the best for her friends as Kael stops what he's doing to comfort her.

"Don't' worry yourself, Natalia," Kael eases, "They'll be fine."

Gazing up at the stars, Lithia purrs as Talia mutters, "I truly hope so."

Kael takes his leave as Talia glances at Lithia, who rubs his head against hers and chirps. Trying to be optimistic about the situation, Talia smiles and hugs Lithia for comfort, wishing she were old enough to join them in battle.

CH: 39
SOULS OF ENCHANTMENT

As the night settles in, Victor sits by himself atop the crystalline waterfall, observing the Tree of Life, which is illuminated by the bright moonlight. Kael finds Victor sitting alone and approaches him to converse.

"You should probably turn in for the night," Kael advises as Victor faces him, "You have a long day ahead of you tomorrow."

"I know." Victor calmly retorts with a depressing sigh as he turns his attention back towards the Tree of Life.

"You've always stayed up till all hours of the night." Kael says as he steps towards the waterfall's edge, "Even longer than you probably should." Chuckling, Victor humorously replies, "You know me, I've always been more energetic at night. Besides, I've got too much on my mind right now, I couldn't sleep anyway."

"Understandable, nor could I." Kael admits with a grin as he steps back several feet from the waterfall's edge. Curious of his mentor's presence, Victor asks, "Is that why you're out strolling the kingdom so late yourself?"

"Not exactly." Kael calmly mentions on her behalf, "The Princess has requested your presence, she's expecting you now."
Surprised, Victor inquires, "She is, really?" Kael nods in response as he looks away and mutters, "I'm almost too afraid to ask why." Careful not to reveal his true feelings, he then says, "One thing's for certain, she has a mysterious yet exotic vibe to her, and seems to have a genuine belief in one's duty."

"How beautiful it is to find someone who asks for nothing but your company." Kael sarcastically implies, "Still, nothing is what it seems."

"No, except her." Victor murmurs, "To me she embodies everything that a strong woman has become in this day and age."
Sensing his young protégé's reluctance, Kael implies, "You admire her."
Looking at him directly, Victor humbly professes, "Yes, but not because of her status. It's more than that really."

"Because like you, she stands for something." Kael kindly regards, "Something that can't be bought or broken."

With a firm nod, Victor remarks, "Amazing how many are so flawed by those two things." He then grins and jokes, "Sure glad I don't have to worry about that myself anymore."

As Victor sits in silence, Kael sighs, looking for the right thing to say then finally encourages, "Victor, sometimes to fear nothing is to love nothing. But if there's nothing to love, then what joy is there in this life, or the next?"

Gazing into the night sky on the waterfall's edge, specifically at the kingdom Empyria floating above Earth's atmosphere as the stars shine brightly, Victor states, "I'm not so sure I know what true love is, but I have an idea."

Attempting to teach him another valuable lesson in life, Kael steps beside Victor on the edge, and specifies, "There are many forms of affection, but to you, love is just a vestigial word for a feeling you've never truly felt before."

"I'm starting to feel it now." Victor confirms with a crooked smile.

"Even if you hadn't grown up a slave, you'd still be lost." Kael explains, "For there are no trails through a pure woman's heart." He then turns his attention upwards towards the night sky and finishes, "Besides, an Angel of her beauty doesn't just fall out of the sky and flutter into oblivion."

"This one did." Victor says apprehensively, "You see, in a way, she's perfect in an amoral world."

Kael chuckles quietly, and retorts, "True, but at the moment you seem all too interested in exterminating our enemy." Victor laughs in response as he continues, "Perhaps that is your destiny; you envy your human emotions and yearn to share the warmth of another's heart."

"Always have." Victor calmly responds, "Beauty is entertaining no doubt, but that along with great depth is much more impressive to me."

"Certain things will catch your eye, but pursue only those who capture your heart." Kael infers, "The truth is you think it's impossible for someone like you to fall in love, especially with someone of her caliber. Looks and talent don't always go together, but in this case fairly exceptional."

Faintly annoyed, Victor looks directly at Kael and warns, "You're out of line!" Realizing he insulted him, Kael calmly clarifies, "Forgive me, I know it's difficult. You've always felt alone because you've been searching for one thing your whole life." Disheartened, Victor looks away and sighs as Kael explains, "You've survived so long without it, the fact that you may have finally found it, simply terrifies you. Perhaps even more so than dying on the battlefield."

"Yes, it does." Victor admits with apprehension in his voice.

"But not as much as the fact that you're afraid to get close to anyone again for fear that you will lose them as well." Kael counsels, "Like Talia, always looking for hope but still feeling helpless and unsure about all things."

"Can you really blame me?" Victor scoffs irksomely, "Considering where I grew up, I haven't quite developed a defense for that yet."

Kael pauses briefly then firmly states, "Even so, it is beyond your control. Just accept the fact that somebody can love you for who and what you are."
Turning his attention elsewhere, Victor looks towards Elena's quarters in the temple several yards away and sighs, "What do you suggest I do?"

"She's an honorable woman, just tell her how you feel." Kael insists.

"How can I?" Victor questions, "What would she say in return?"

"Sorry, I can't help you with this one, it's something you'll just have to find out for yourself." Kael explains, "You're a strong and worthy soul, the kind she will stand and fight with, thus, I believe you're finally ready."
Victor continues his gaze upon Elena's quarters high above them and sighs once more with a depressing breath.

"Your heart is speaking to you, always has." Kael inspires, "The question is, do you have the guts to listen to it?" Victor grins while pondering the thought for a moment as Kael resumes, "Whenever her name is even mentioned you react with such intense emotion. I don't want to interfere with your personal life, but unresolved strong emotion of that magnitude can greatly affect your judgment, especially in combat." He carefully explains, "Confronting deep personal issues has never been easy for you because you tend to suppress them. Perhaps you should use this time to analyze your true feelings and put them into perspective with someone who truly understands."
As Kael motions towards Elena's quarters in the temple, he finishes, "I think someone's waiting for you." Pleased by his stance on the matter, Victor faces Kael, who jokingly instructs, "Well, get going!"
Smiling in response, Victor nods in respect then heads towards Elena's tower, making his way upwards by climbing the old-fashioned way. Kael looks on, fully aware of their bond and walks away while shaking his head, amused at him for not using his wings once again. Savoring each step he makes, Victor climbs up the tower attached to the temple and finally reaches her balcony. Feeling nervous in her divine presence, he looks around for a moment whilst hesitating to enter. "You summoned me, milady?" He calmly addresses.
Elena quickly turns, facing him in relief with a surprised look, then calmly says, "Yes, please, come in." Victor bows his head then enters the room with caution. "I was hoping to catch you before you turned in for the night, sometimes on the eve of battle it's harder to be alone." Elena mentions as she approaches her nightstand, "I have something for you."
Curious, Victor stands silent and looks on as she opens a crystalline chest, revealing a new suit. To his surprise, Elena holds out a custom-made Soul Gear attire, lying dormant within a new decorative piece bearing the Gods' symbol in blue with lightning marks. "I had this customized, for when the time is right." She informs. Victor observes the Soul Gear in appreciation, whilst caressing the V design covering most of the torso below the Gods' symbol. "I may just make a nobleman out of you yet." Elena happily teases. Grateful for the gift, Victor looks upon her, and says softly, "Thank you."

"You're welcome, but it's me who should be thanking you really." She inspires with a soft grin.

"For what?" Victor queries with a confused expression.

As Elena gently takes the Soul Gear from him and places it back on her nightstand, she replies, "For everything you've done, and are about to do."

"Don't thank me yet, we still have a battle to fight." He says lightly.

"I know, but you have to measure your successes and your failures within." Elena enlightens as she faces him directly, "Not by anything that I or anyone else might think. When this is all over, in one night, you will have done more for the world than a million diplomats ever could." Victor looks upon her passionately, as she stares back, unsure of what to say in his presence then asks, "By any chance, are you tempted by immortality?"

"Everlasting life?" Victor considerably muses, "What a random concept; sounds like a fantasy only one could dream of."

Smiling, Elena comments, "For most I'm sure, but the things we're most passionate about in life are not random, for they are our calling."

"Even with such a calling, I imagine it would be very lonely." Victor expresses, "Though, who wouldn't be tempted by perpetual youth?"

"I believe your temptation comes from wanting to make the most of what life you've been given." Elena indicates while leaning against her nightstand, "Very admirable, but perhaps if you had someone to share it with, someone to love, then it might not be so lonely."

Charmed by her sentiment, Victor retorts, "You couldn't be more right. I'm still not sure why I was chosen to do this, but you make it worth while."

Sighing impatiently, Elena clarifies, "Victor, the Gods didn't choose you because of your fearlessness."

"Then why did they choose me?" Victor quickly probes.

"Because of your ability to overcome it." She calmly answers as Victor looks upon her with a surprised expression. She then simplifies, "They see your strength, and courage, much like that of a legend."

"Every legend bears a symbol of some sort." Victor proclaims while gazing upon the Gods' symbol over his chest as he caresses it with his fingers.

"Think of your gifts as a blessing, not a curse." She advises, "Because right now they're much needed here."

Refocusing his attention towards her, Victor respectfully comments, "It's a good thing I plan on surviving then. For me, it's an honor to protect my people, and my family while having the freedom to do it."

"You would die for honor then?" Elena carefully inquires.

"I would simply die doing what's right, yes." He proudly decrees, "I prefer peace, but if trouble must come, let it come in my time so that my people may one day live in harmony with everyone else in this world."

Elena looks away, trying to not to give her true feelings away, saying, "I see." She then faces him and asks, "So if you come back, what will you do then?"

Entertained by the thought, Victor responds, "There are many things of importance I want to do in this life, some more than others. But if I can help it, I prefer not to do them alone."

"Was there no love in your life before you came here?" Elena carefully probes, curious to his answer.

Shaking his head dejectedly, he replies, "No, not really. What little I know about it is that it's something money can't buy." He then looks directly at her and states, "Not if it's true anyway."

"It's also unconditional, to a point." She implies.

Sensing the time passing by quickly, Victor informs, "I can't stay too long."

"Then you'll leave without knowing my biggest secret." Elena teases.

"Wait, there's more?" Victor carefully inquires with a smirk.

"Actually, just one." She retorts with a cunning smile.

Dying to know what she's referring to, Victor questions, "And that is?"

"How I feel." Elena reluctantly professes.

As Victor stares back intensely, he asks, "And just how do you feel?"

"From what I can tell, the same as you." Elena answers, hoping not to offend him in the slightest.

"Which is?" Victor carefully persists.

"Deeply." She sadly reveals to his surprise as she looks upon him passionately then encourages, "You don't have to be alone, Victor, I'm sure you'll find someone special eventually. After all, this place is full of wonders where true paradise can be found, inside and out."

"Seems my search has finally come to an end, for I've already found someone special." Victor firmly claims with a serious face.

Wary to his claim, Elena asks gently, "I see, and does this person know?"

"I hope so, because when the fighting is over, I'll come back for her." Victor softly hints as he steps closer to Elena who faces him and stares into his intense blue eyes, looking hopeful as he finishes, "For you."

"But deep down something scares you, and dares to keep your heart at bay." Elena cautiously implies, sensing his hesitation.

"This is my life, and I'm not sure it can be shared." Victor sadly professes, "Especially with anyone who cares for me as deeply as you."

"You're afraid of me." Elena denotes.

"No, I'm not afraid of you, I'm afraid for you." He reluctantly states.

"Why?" Elena probes with a concerned voice.

"Because I've finally found something that I never thought possible in this world full of death and misery." Victor reveals, placing more distance between them, "You mustn't care for me the way that you do."

"That's for me to decide, don't you think?" She infers, "Besides, how do you know it wasn't me that drew you to this place from the very start?"

"I don't," Victor admits, "But I do know that your essence is pure enough to sustain whatever darkness lies in my heart."

Looking into each other's eyes passionately, Elena tears up slightly, as Victor expresses, "That is if you would have me, but I dare not kiss someone so lovely, for I have but one heart to break."

"May our hearts become one then." She softly gestures.

Victor and Elena come in close and suddenly kiss, showing their true affection for each other with extreme passion. As their lips separate, she places her hands on his face and smiles as he holds them tightly within his, and whispers; "Now that's what I want to come home to." Elena smiles in response, feeling grateful as tears of joy run down her face. "That's what I want to think and dream about while I'm gone." He happily confesses.

"Me too." Elena whispers with a heartfelt expression.

Gesturing towards the world below, Victor states, "Even your kiss is a promise of paradise, therefore I want to know that the worst is behind me, and that the best part of my life still lies ahead, always there waiting for me."

"So do I." Elena happily affirms.

"All those years in the mines, I dreamed of getting out and being with a real family, a perfect one." He confesses.

"Trust me, it's never perfect really." She comforts.

Feeling each other's comfort, the Angelic pair kiss once again as they look into each other's blue eyes intensely. Elena looks out into the starry sky and says, "Look outside, it's beautiful."

"Yes, you most definitely are." He respectfully compliments with a comforting whisper, "You're even more beautiful on the inside."

Elena tears up, deeply touched by his comfort as they hold each other in their arms then says, "Do you really think there's more to me than what you see, that I have something else to give beyond my royal crown?"

"I do." Victor soothingly assures.

"I've never met anyone like you." She sadly professes, "I mean, you understand the world better than anyone I've ever known."

"Do you really think so?" Victor inquires.

"I do." Elena replies with a soft nod, "Deep down, I know that more than anything you want to be an Angel among us." She whispers in his ear.

"That may be true, but that's not all I want in life." He says softly.

"I can feel that." Elena acknowledges, "I know you truly care within those limits, but I'm not exactly sure what you feel outside of them." Unsure of what to say, Victor looks away as she gently asks, "Are you listening to me, do you hear what I'm saying?"

"Every word," Victor softly replies, "I'm just...."

"What?" Elena kindly asks.

Facing her, Victor replies, "I'm just worried that I won't live up to your expectations. Not just as an Angel, but a man who genuinely cares for you."

"As far as I know, you're nothing like the enemy." Elena reassures, "For they are cold, and vicious in nature."

"How do you know I'm not like that?" Victor cautiously asks.

"It's your eyes that give you away." She articulates out of concern for her loving companion as she looks into his eyes once again, unsure of what he's truly feeling inside.

"I'm not the person you think I am, but I want to be, more than anything." Victor professes, unsure about his bond with her.

"You're afraid the truth will scare me away." Elena insists.

"From what I've seen of you, no." He replies, "All this, it's not who I truly am inside." Victor calmly explains while gesturing towards the kingdom, "Deep down, there is more, a lot more."

"I've always known that." Elena states confidently, "You take risks, I like that, or maybe I'm the one taking a risk on you."

Victor shakes his head, trying to come to terms with his current life, and specifies, "This whole thing, me being here, is still bizarre to me."

"I understand completely." She comforts while placing her hands gently on his sorrowful looking face, "Just be honest with yourself, the world may be undeserving of your presence, but you need not hide your true feelings from me. Not now, not ever."

"I'm trying, but I'm kind of new to this." Victor responds, feeling confused and disheartened.

Elena smiles as he holds her close in his arms, then says, "Others treat me like I'm some precious thing to be bartered, or put on display and possessed."

"It's not like that with me, I assure you." Victor calmly soothes.

"No?" Elena asks with concern in her voice, "How is it different?"

"Because it's you who possesses me." He softly inspires.

Hearing the midnight chime from inside the temple, Elena expresses a look of worry, unable to let him go as he turns his attention behind him towards the balcony, saying, "It's getting late, I should probably go now." Placing her hands on his chest, she nods disappointingly with tears in her eyes. Sensing her inner turmoil, he says softly, "Sleep well, Princess."

Victor kisses Elena's forehead then turns to leave as she clings to his hand, slowly letting go and calls softly, "Victor?" Bound by his passion for her, he immediately stops at the edge of the balcony, turning his head slightly as she stresses, "Look at me and tell me you don't love me."

Disappointed in his inability to truly express himself, Victor sighs while refusing to face her fully then calmly mutters, "I do love you, always will." Elena smiles in relief as he finally turns to face her, saying, "But you have your place, and I have mine." He finishes while bowing his head in respect.

As Victor turns back, he activates his Angelic wings and takes off as Elena looks on from the balcony's edge. After watching him disappear into the moonlit sky, she walks back into the room and stands behind a crystalline pillar with tears in her eyes after slightly weeping, realizing that she and Victor have truly fallen for each other after all, despite their forbidden bond.

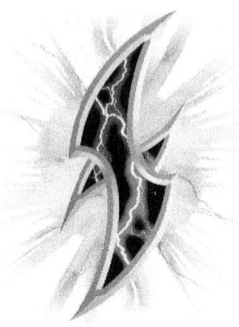

CH: 40
A STORM ON THE HORIZON

Meanwhile, deep within the Darchadian lair in Pretoria, a small fleet of Darchadians prepare themselves for the oncoming battle. Raiven and Celeste walk through the crowd of anxious warriors, and enter Traganus' throne room as they approach him with his back turned.

"Master!" Raiven informs, "We're ready."

"Good, there's been a slight change in the game." Traganus replies. The two sisters with deadly finesse glance at each other; then Celeste cautiously inquires, "Should we be concerned?"

Traganus stands from his crystalline throne and turns to face them directly, stating, "Consider it a sensible precaution."

Confused by his statement, Raiven carefully asks, "Is it practical though?"

After a slight pause, Traganus proclaims, "Yes, one I believe will work to our advantage, and may very well lead us to our prime objective."

"What is thy bidding?" Celeste asks with a bloodthirsty voice.

Stepping away from his crystalline throne, Traganus approaches them and says, "I need you to be my eyes and ears." Raiven and Celeste grin in response as he walks past them and observes the Darchadian fleet preparing for battle below. "Find them, and punish them!" He demands.

"And just how will we know of this advantage you speak of?" Raiven carefully inquires, trying not to annoy him.

"We should know what to expect ahead of time." Celeste chimes in.

Traganus chuckles as he turns slightly, and confirms, "You will, for there's a wildcard at play." He then turns back, facing the Darchadian fleet and says, "They'll be impossible to miss." Raiven and Celeste smile at one another, anxious to spill some blood. "Something is happening," he enlightens, "I can feel the darkness stirring, and it's nearing its perpetual flux."

"The enemy will never know what hit them till it's too late!" Raiven proudly proclaims while swinging her hand back.

"Not even in the afterlife!" Celeste cynically adds.

Amused by their enthusiasm, Traganus turns to face them and sternly warns, "Prepare yourselves, sisters, they'll be here soon."

"Not soon enough!" Celeste sneers with a devious grin.

Acknowledging their crude sentiment, Traganus nods then turns his back once more, still overlooking the Darchadian fleet below and firmly concludes, "Greet them warmly."

Bowing their heads in respect, Raiven and Celeste reply, "Yes, Master!"

As the pair takes their leave, Traganus approaches the wall behind his crystalline throne and places the retrieved Artifact beside two other empty slots. After a moment of admiring his Angelic trophy on the wall, Traganus turns his attention behind him and grins as a secret door in the side of the room suddenly opens, revealing a mysterious cloaked male figure.

As the sun rises the next morning in Archadia, Elena enters the armory inside the Arch Temple and approaches Kael as Talia stands by with Lithia perched on her shoulder.

"Good morning, milady." Kael says politely.

"Good morning, General." Elena replies with a smirk.

"According to our latest Intel, the Darchadians' sole purpose has been to instigate a response." Kael informs.

"And they'll soon have one." Elena says with utter confidence then asks, "Have any of you seen Victor yet?"

Kael glances at Talia, who shrugs her shoulders, then says, "No, not yet."

"Do you know where he is?" Elena quickly inquires, "I need to talk to him about something."

"He left early this morning," Kael informs, "Probably couldn't wait to get away for a while before take off."

"I see." Elena calmly mutters.

"He usually prays to the Gods on some mornings." Talia informs.

Contemplating his exacts whereabouts in the kingdom, Elena looks away and utters, "I bet I know where he is."

Elena turns to leave as Valorie and Vennessa enter the armory to address her.

"Everyone's ready, Princess." Valorie informs, "We must depart for Pretoria as soon as possible."

"Yes I know." Elena firmly retorts.

"We should probably leave now if we are to make good use of our time." Vennessa strongly advises.

Turning her head impatiently, Elena affirms, "Haste my sisters, we cast off within the hour."

She then takes her leave as Valorie and Vennessa glance at each other curiously. Anxious, Talia looks on and sighs, still unsure of whether or not to fully trust Victor and Elena's apparent bond.

As the morning sun brightens the entire kingdom, Victor enters the cathedral inside the temple and looks around in wonder as beams of light shine through the crystalline windows, illuminating his path in the center of the chamber. Taking in the sun's warmth, Victor extends his arms out while approaching the Holy Trinity statues bearing the legendary names, *KORINA, KITANA,* and *KIARA,* then humbly kneels before them.

"I don't know if you can hear me, or if you're even there." He prays, "But if you are, I hope that you simply listen to my thoughts, and prayers."
Moments later, Elena enters the temple in search for Victor and stops by the cathedral entrance behind an Angelic statue to carefully listen in.

"I know I'm just an outcast, and probably shouldn't speak to you." He continues, "But still I pray and wonder if you were once an outcast too." After a short pause, he takes a heavy breath and resumes, "Divine spirit of the Arch, protect my brothers and sisters and give me the strength to face the dark force I fear is coming. With upmost sincerity, I pray that you watch over everyone on our journey, and that they all return home safely."
Elena grins, intuiting his deep sincerity as he resumes, "Lords of light, I also ask that you help my people, who look to you still. Help them to be better than what they are, for they will someday see the light ahead to guide them through the darkness."
Sensing his sorrow, Elena leans against the statue and looks downward whilst caressing its crystalline wings.

"I ask for nothing of myself, other than the strength to endure." Victor decrees, "So that I may protect those I love from harm. Let me not bring misfortune to my people. Help me to lead my comrades well, do not let me dishonor them and please help me to regain my family's' honor."
Elena closes her eyes as a tear runs down her cheek from the shared connection. Pausing for a moment, Victor looks upon the ceiling of the cathedral and sees a mural of the five Gods creating the Arch with a sixth unknown entity colored in blue in the middle surrounded by the Holy Trinity.

"I know I ask for things I can't possess myself, but I'm lucky to be where I am, alive and well." He resumes after clearing his throat; "Your Angels have blessed me and surely lead me to this point. Especially one in particular." He acknowledges as Elena opens her eyes and smiles, knowing that he's referring to her.

"Please let them continue to do so." Victor calmly pleads as he looks upon the faces of each Angel statue standing silently before him.
After finishing his prayer, he rises to his feet as Elena leans her head out from behind the statue curiously whilst trying to remain out of sight. As Victor turns to take his leave, he suddenly stops, feeling he left something out.

"Oh, and another thing." He says turning back then concludes, "Give Talia the strength to endure as well. She needs it more than I do."

Smiling once again in appreciation, Elena takes this moment and quietly leaves the cathedral. Victor gazes upon the Holy Trinity statues one last time in curiosity, sighing calmly.

"Rest well, mother." He whispers, hoping her soul is at peace.
Expecting no response from the blank stares carved into the Angelic statues, Victor turns to take his leave, taking his time to meet with the others for departure whilst regaining his strong composure.

Shortly after exiting the temple unnoticed, Elena approaches Kael and Talia on the landing platform by their ship on the port as Lithia chirps to acknowledge her presence.

"Did you find him?" Kael inquires.
Elena nods and replies, "Yep, sure did."

"He's coming with us, isn't he?" Talia carefully asks.
Bringing a smile to her face, Elena looks upon Talia and reassures, "He'll be here any minute now, you'll see."
Marcus and Yuri, along with Valorie and Vennessa approach Elena on their way towards the Arch ship.

"We're ready when you are, Princess." Yuri informs.

"Good," Elena replies, "Prepare the ship for our departure then."

"You go it!" Marcus responds as he and Yuri head towards the ship.
To her surprise, Valorie and Vennessa firmly stay put, both with concerned expressions over their faces.

"Yes, sisters?" Elena asks, slightly annoyed by their lack of space.
Valorie shares a glance with Vennessa then states, "I hope you know what you're doing, with him I mean."

"So do I, sisters." Elena calmly retorts, "So do I."

"Assuming he can hold his own with the others, we shall still be weary of the outcome." Vennessa infers as she and Valorie step away towards the Arch ship with Marcus and Yuri.
Lithia chirps to get everyone's attention as they turn and see Victor finally approaching them from the temple. Relieved to see him once again, Elena grins as Victor moves his arms around, trying to get comfortable with his standard issue Soul Gear. He and the team prepare to board their ship as Kael looks upon them with pride.

"Ready to take on the might of our new enemy?" Kael motivates.

"Of course we are!" Adrian scoffs as he approaches the ship.

"Be cautious, for these foes are unlike anything or anyone you've ever faced before." Kael sternly warns.
Stopping to address him directly with a confident smirk, Damian proudly states, "We can handle ourselves out there, General."

"You got that right!" Adrian sarcastically retorts with a sure grin.

"For your sake, let's hope so." Kael cautions while nodding towards them in respect. Damian and Adrian nod back in return then board their own ship as Victor approaches Kael seconds later.

"Remember your teachings." Kael advises while shaking his hand in respect, "For your true power to be realized, you must not let emotion over power you in any way shape or form."

Victor grins determinedly, and asserts, "I won't."

Prideful of his young protégé, Kael nods as Victor turns to address Talia and Elena who approach him.

"I wanted to thank you before we depart." Victor mentions.

"For what?" Elena queries.

"For helping me get this far, and for caring enough to see me through." Victor humbly expresses, "Apparently that isn't the easiest thing for anyone to do."

"Well maybe that's because you opened up to me and no one else, other than Talia of course." Elena regards as she motions towards Talia.

"Please be safe." Talia calmly pleads.

Greatly appreciative of her usual concern, Victor grins and attempts to comfort, "Not to worry, we're in good hands now."

"I know, but sometimes you act before you think." Talia cautions.

"Oh, and you don't?" Victor teases with a crooked smile.

Talia grins, trying to retain a serious composure as Victor chuckles quietly.

"Elena has you well looked after, so be sure to stay close to her at all times." He affirms while motioning towards Elena.

"I will." Talia proclaims. She then motions towards Lithia perched on her shoulder and requests, "Do you mind taking Lithia with you?"

Victor nods in agreement as he pets Lithia's head and says, "I don't see why not. I could use his senses anyway."

Lithia chirps in approval as Victor turns to face Elena.

"The council has requested that she stay by my side until this conflict is over," Elena informs, "I'll guard her with my life."

"I know you will." Victor responds with a grin, "Good thing too, because I'd be devastated if anything were to happen to her."

Talia smiles, appreciative as always of his friendly concern over her.

"We won't be far behind." Elena ensures.

"I'm counting on it." He says while nodding in respect. Knowing Victor truly has something to fight for, Elena smiles. "You ladies be safe, alright?" Victor cautions as he motions towards them.

"The Gods will be watching over us." Elena guarantees.

"I've seen too much reality to trust them completely, and I'm not alone, for nobody has much faith anymore." Victor sadly professes, "Not where I come from anyway." Still trying to get used to the new Soul Gear, Victor rotates his neck to get comfortable and states, "I sure hope this new gear does what it's supposed to do when the time comes."

"Your suit represents a state of the art in dynamic adaptive design." Elena reveals, "In other words, it learns from each encounter and improves itself whenever necessary in combat. Though the real question is, can you?"

"Well, I guess I'm about to find out soon enough whether the world likes it or not." Victor jokes, trying to lighten the mood for Talia's sake.

"The people need a hero, they need someone to look up to." Elena comforts as she places her hand over the Gods' symbol on Victor's chest, "Talia believes in you; bring us peace, and I'll believe in you too."

Victor nods confidently then turns to board the other Arch ship. Lithia chirps then flies off of Talia's shoulder and onto Victor's. Damian and Adrian step onto the landing platform as Elena approaches them, and respectfully requests, "Look after him you guys. I know he's not exactly one of you, but bring him back alive if you would please."

"As long as he doesn't get in our way, he'll be fine." Adrian remarks.

"We don't have all the answers yet, so all I ask is that you keep your eyes open at all times." Elena stresses.

"That's sound advice at anytime." Adrian mutters before heading onto the ship to find a place to secure himself properly.

Putt off by his comrade's prideful attitude, Damian faces Elena, and stresses, "Our presence in the area will be a vital show of force. We're going to be in sorry shape if things turn ugly."

"I'll be sure to keep the odds in your favor then." Elena pledges.

"We'll signal you if we run into any trouble." Damian replies with a respectful nod, "Assuming we will."

Elena nods in return as Damian turns back and boards the Arch ship. Standing close by, Talia looks upon Elena, tugging on her hand, and asks, "We're going too, right?"

With a small grin on her face, places her hand on Talia's shoulder to comfort her, saying, "Patience, Natalia. We'll be there to help them if they need it, won't we?" She encourages.

Talia nods with determination as Elena turns her attention back towards the Arch ship getting ready for take off.

"May the Gods be merciful." She says softly with a graceful gesture.

The Arch ship hovers above the landing platform as Elena, Talia, and Kael stand beside each other looking on. As the ship prepares to take off, Victor looks out the window for a moment and waves towards Talia and Elena, who wave back, hoping to inspire him even more.

He then refocuses his attention aboard the ship, unsure of what to expect as it swiftly takes off towards the southern continent, Pretoria. Elena looks away, expressing concern as Marcus and Yuri approach Valorie and Vennessa to board their ship as well.

"That's strange, for a moment I swear I could suddenly feel his fear escalating." Elena mutters.

Catching his attention at earshot, Kael glances at Elena and asks, "What do you suppose would cause that all of a sudden?"

Alarmed, Elena turns to face him and says, "I sense deliberate concealment."

"Of what?" He inquires.

Elena steps forward, concerning Talia and Kael as she continues her gaze into the distance past the floating kingdom, and carefully denotes, "I don't know for sure, but whatever it is, it's extremely intense."

"Guess it's a good thing you're going along with them," Kael jokingly points out, "Someone that intense can be extremely unpredictable. If other members become disoriented for any reason, it could create additional problems, perhaps increase the danger also."

Feeling uneasy about Victor's involvement, Elena nods in agreement while facing Talia then looks upon her with hope and states, "At this rate, the level of danger is expected to increase."

"I'll be at the Archadian outpost above Pretoria should you need me." Kael respectfully informs.

"No offense, but I hope we don't." Elena jokes with a serious tone.

Kael bows his head in respect and approaches another Arch ship, followed by several Archadians. Marcus and Yuri stand by their ship with Valorie and Vennessa, waiting for Elena and Talia as they wave to get her attention. Acknowledging their signal, Elena nods in response then turns to address Talia, inquiring, "You ready?"

"Of course." Talia replies determinedly then asks, "Aren't you?"

Expressing a strong sense of dread, Elena looks away and carefully mutters, "Not as much as I'd hoped."

Elena refocuses her attention on the mission at hand then motions towards the others as Talia follows her. After boarding the ship with Talia, Elena straps her in and prepares for departure. Feeling nervous about joining them on such a dangerous mission, Talia pulls out the Angel figure from her garb, examining it closely in hopes that everyone returns home safe and sound. Moment later, the Arch ship hovers above the landing platform then swiftly takes off towards Pretoria to aid the team against the mysterious threat.

END OF ACT: 02

ACT: 03

CH: 41
ENTER THE DARK

A few hours later, the team head towards their destination, followed by Elena and her crew aboard their ship to investigate the distress call in Pretoria as they each prepare for battle.

"Alright everyone!" Adrian calls, "Listen up!" Several Eudenian and Enfurian soldiers sit in their buckled seats as Damian and Adrian approach them from the cargo deck. "We've arrived at the edge of the Neutral Zone where we'll have an opportunity to learn first hand what happened to the Arch's distant outpost." Adrian pauses for a moment to study the troops' reaction then informs, "This should be a quick in and out mission, but our enemy is unknown for the most part!"

Victor looks upon the Eudenian and Enfurian soldiers as he listens closely.

"Keep formation, and stay alert at all times!" Damian chimes in as the soldiers shout in response, "Let's keep this smooth, and by the numbers!" Adrian walks in front of everyone to motivate them, warning, "They can sense our power, so don't ever let your guard down!"

"Elena and the other Angels will halo over our position should there be any strife!" Damian firmly adds.

"Prepare yourselves!" Adrian concludes while glancing at Victor to get his undivided attention as Lithia chirps with his spinal shards glowing.

Victor looks towards Damian and asks, "What exactly is this Neutral Zone I keep hearing so much about?"

Damian faces Victor and replies, "This particular zone acts as a political buffer between the Titanian Empire, our kingdoms, as well as the Arch."

"Why does that make me even more nervous?" Victor mutters.

"I don't know, but you're not the only one." Damian comments.

"We won't be inviting them to our party, will we?" Victor asks.

"No, that would not be appropriate at this time." Damian answers.

Victor holds onto his Gauntlet tightly in anticipation as Damian walks towards the ship's landing platform with Adrian and says, "Communications between the Arch and the temple have been lost for some time now."

"As can be expected, failure to communicate is inherently a sign of hostility." Adrian cautiously denotes.

Damian nods in response, and says, "Let us hope it doesn't become a defense matter, or else we may be in serious trouble."

"Especially if our new comrade fails to pull his own weight." Adrian mordantly retorts in spite of Victor.

Glancing back at Victor and the troops for a moment, Damian quietly advises, "Stay sharp, and no surprises this time." Adrian nods in agreement as he finishes, "I would rather out think them than fight them if at all possible."

"Agreed." Adrian asserts as he prepares his Gauntlet for battle.

"LT!" one of the Eudenian pilots calls from the ship's cockpit.

"What is it?" Damian inquires.

"The source of interference is destroyed, but luckily we still have a clear signal." The Eudenian pilot replies.

"Lock it in!" Damian orders, "We'll have to track it from the air."

"Yes Sir!" The pilot responds with a nod.

Damian and Adrian look onto the horizon from the ship's window in preparation for the worst as Victor looks back and sighs, feeling edgy.

Minutes later, the Arch ship lands on the rocky surface in Pretoria as the troops prepare for battle. Victor glances at Lithia perched on his shoulder with slight hesitation then stands to fall in line with the others.

"Alright everyone, saddle up!" Damian orders while waving his hand.

"Prepare to move out!" Adrian adds, doing the same.

Everyone including Victor departs the ship to locate the distress signal with caution. As the team checks the perimeter for the signal's origin, Victor looks around with Lithia floating next to him with his wings whilst observing the Pretorian landscape through a thick fog. Victor steps out of line as Damian approaches him from behind, placing his hand on his shoulder to get his attention, and calmly advises, "Stay close, Victor."

Victor quickly steps back into formation with Lithia as the team moves on through the eerie fog. Attempting to track, Adrian kneels to feel and smell the Earth while observing a holographic image projecting a faint bio-signature trail from his Gauntlet. Damian abruptly stops beside him, cautious and alert, then carefully asks, "Find anything yet?"

Adrian looks around for a moment, trying to sniff out a scent, and replies, "Hard to say with all the pheromone signatures left around in the area. They don't give off an energy reading like us, but I've come across this stench before." He informs while motioning towards Victor.

Damian looks back at Victor, unsure of his connection to the energy reading.

"Even despite all the scent molecules, I smell death in the air." Adrian says while standing up and motioning ahead through the thick mist, "There's a strange bloody fog hovering the area, as if Hell itself lies beyond." Concerned, Damian looks around, having trouble with his Gauntlet readings, and says, "I would've hoped the Gods had sent us this haze for protection, but our instruments seem to be malfunctioning at the moment."

"Yeah, even my senses seem to be a little distracted ever since we got here." Adrian states with slight frustration.

"We need to find a vantage point, and quick." Damian strongly suggests, having difficulty finding a correct path himself. Adrian extends his arm as he punches a few buttons on his Gauntlet, and states, "Search pattern initiated!" Damian watches as Adrian's Gauntlet fails to map out directions towards the distress signal's origin. Adrian shakes his head in annoyance of the disruption, "I got nothing!" He informs, "The heavy magnetism of this place appears to be disrupting our instruments."

"How is that even possible?" Damian suspiciously queries, "The coordinates said the temple should be located somewhere in this vicinity."

"Well, if you want my honest opinion, I suggest we find an alternate route." Adrian proposes. Sighing in disappointment, Damian requests, "Alright then, keep tracking and let me know when you find something."

"No problem." Adrian utters before moving forward determinedly. Victor walks cautiously with his Gauntlet aimed as Lithia turns his head and suddenly chirps with his spinal shards glowing to get his attention.

"What is it, boy?" He curiously inquires. As Lithia motions his head towards a certain direction, Victor grins with confidence, and says, "Good going, Lithia, I knew you'd be of some use." Lithia chirps in response as Victor turns to address Damian and Adrian, waving them over, and calls, "Hey guys, over here!" Damian and Adrian glance at each other, expressing concern then quickly approach him in curiosity.

"Find something, Victor?" Damian asks. Victor nods as Adrian chimes in, "Please tell me you found some trace of the enemy presence in this hell hole."

"Actually, I found something better." Victor states with a smirk.

"Like what?" Damian cautiously inquires. Taking a moment to assess the situation, Victor then asks, "The Darchadians supposedly attacked one of our temples, right?"

"That's the word anyway." Adrian sarcastically states. Hearing Lithia chirp within the mysterious fog, Victor points towards a specific direction and says, "The temple is that way, and the signal must be coming from that direction as well. I'm sure of it." Damian and Adrian glance at each other once again, unsure of his assessment.

"I don't see any path." Damian irritably denotes.

"That's because there is none." Victor proclaims.

"Then how the hell do we know where we're going?" Adrian asks.

"By trusting my instincts, that's how." Victor assures.

Adrian scoffs and informs, "There's more than brush and trees here in Eldria. You don't just cut through it when you please without some kind of preparation. And you sure as hell don't want to be stuck here at night."

"We don't have to worry about running into any real danger out here, believe me." Victor asserts.

"Are you sure?" Damian asks with disbelief.

"Yeah!" Adrian chimes in, "How do you know?"

"I don't know how I know, but I know." Victor seriously claims as he faces them directly, "Trust me on this, I've got a nose for these things."

"I'm sure." Adrian cynically remarks with a sigh.

Damian steps forward and says, "Well how are we going to get there exactly? We're having enough trouble mapping out the environment."

"Leave that to me." Victor reassures as he steps in front of them.

"We don't even know where we're going!" Adrian grumbles.

Slowly walking forward without stopping, Victor calmly retorts, "I do."

"How is that?" Adrian inquires, "None of us can see in the dark much less this ghastly fog."

Victor turns slightly towards them, looking intense and says, "No, but I can." He then motions towards the others and announces, "Everybody stay close!"

"You better be right about this." Damian cautions.

"We'll be all right as long as we don't separate." Victor affirms.

Realizing that there's no other solution, Damian extends his hand out and says, "Fine, you lead the way since you're so eager."

Victor nods then turns back, heading into the fog with Lithia, as Damian and Adrian glance at each other, concerned by their limited options. Adrian extends his arm out and jokingly invites, "After you, friend."

"I guess cowardice substitutes for bravery when necessary, doesn't it?" Damian jokingly counters.

"Ha!" Adrian scoffs, "Very funny."

Damian follows Victor into the fog as Adrian signals the Eudenian and Enfurian soldiers to follow suit then orders, "Should anything come out of this mist men, remember to hold the line!"

Moving through the fog with ease, Victor uses his heightened acute senses as Lithia chirps once again to get his attention. Victor suddenly stops and looks towards a certain direction, realizing them to be closer than they thought as Damian and Adrian catch up to him with their Gauntlets aimed cautiously.

"The temple has to be around here somewhere." Damian states.

Lithia chirps once more as Victor looks up and sees the top of the temple through the fog, calmly saying, "Well guys, we're here."

Damian and Adrian quickly look up as the fog mysteriously clears around the entrance to the temple a few yards in front of them.

"Well I'll be!" Adrian professes, "Guess your senses work better than mine in this fog. I can't see a damn thing right now."

Keeping a serious composure, Victor informs, "It's easy to move in the dark when you aren't blinded by the light."

Adrian chuckles as Damian faces the troops and orders, "Let's move people!"

Victor looks upon the temple with determination beaming from his eyes as the team approaches the entrance with extreme caution.

"Since when do Archadian temples look so dark and dreary?" Adrian implies with sarcasm evident in his voice.

"You got me," Damian steadily retorts, "I was beginning to think the same thing myself."

Damian steps onto the stairs before the temple entrance as Adrian looks up and warns, "It could be a bad omen."

Stopping cautiously, Damian frowns upon the dreary looking temple, and mutters, "Yeah, maybe. Whatever it is, it doesn't look or feel natural."

"Agreed, there is a certain darkness surrounding the temple, and the shadows have reaped all that was once pure here." Victor informs, "Things will not change until its power is broken."

"Thanks for the heads up." Adrian sarcastically responds.

As the team reaches the top of the stairs in front of the entrance to the temple, Lithia floats before them and chirps with a concerned tone. Victor looks around for a moment behind him, trying to sense any oncoming threats then turns around with Lithia and steps back in formation to follow the team.

Anxiously standing by, Elena and her crew land several yards away from the team's ship.

"Everyone stand ready, and wait on my mark to proceed should they need us!" Elena announces.

"Got it!" Marcus and Yuri answer as they prepare themselves for possible battle alongside Valorie and Vennessa.

Elena nods her head, signaling Yuri to open the landing platform. She then glances at Talia who looks out from the ship with a sense of dread. Marcus and Yuri prepare their Gauntlets and approach the back of the ship, followed closely by Valorie and Vennessa. Elena steps onto the landing platform, cautious and alert as Marcus and Yuri stand by to guard the ship with Valorie and Vennessa in tow. Sensing the worst, Talia fearfully peeks her head out, as Elena looks around with a stern expression, ready to take on anything in their path as her tiara forms a crystalline helmet over her head in preparation.

Inside the entrance to the temple, Victor closes up the team's tail as they infiltrate the structure with intense caution.

"Well, we finally made it inside." Adrian jokes, "What now?

Facing the troops, Damian raises his hand and orders, "Use your scouters!"

Following orders, the Eudenian and Enfurian soldiers activate their scouters, which appear over their right eyes from their helmets. "We don't know how many of them may still be in the area if at all!" Damian cautions.

"Just because you don't read anything yet doesn't mean they're not lurking around somewhere!" Adrian adds with a stern tone.

The team moves through the base of the temple as Victor looks around cautiously, feeling a sensual overload from the mysterious structure.

"Elena was under the assumption that these things might be waiting for us." Damian infers.

The entrance doors suddenly slam shut behind Victor, as everyone looks back with their Gauntlets aimed, cautious and alert. Victor glances at the entrance doors then scoffs and slowly turns back towards Damian and Adrian as they shake their heads in annoyance, thinking it was him.

"I'm beginning to think she's probably right." Adrian murmurs.

"Anticipation of this deadly nature denotes some form of combative intelligence." Damian states apprehensively.

Looking upward, Adrian mutters, "Yeah, they're probably watching us right now. Only a fool would willingly come to this damn place unarmed."

"Unless they were already damned." Victor mutters to their surprise.

Damian and Adrian lead the team forward as Victor looks back at the door once more in curiosity then continues following them up the stairs.

"It's strange, there's almost nothing left of the temple's interior, whereas the exterior remains fully intact." Damian denotes.

"Must have been one hell of a fight." Adrian comments.

"You can say that again," Damian suspiciously remarks, "Sensors indicate no evidence of conventional attack either."

"Can you determine what happened?" Adrian curiously asks.

"The temple wasn't just destroyed from the inside, it's as if some great and powerful force just wiped it off the face of the planet." Damian indicates with a surprised expression.

"Could it be a natural phenomenon?" Adrian inquires.

"Insufficient information at this point." Damian informs.

Lithia flies around cautiously and chirps as Victor suddenly stops in his tracks behind the troops. Sensing something dark lurking about, Victor sets his attention towards a shadowy pathway below the main floor. Contemplating his next move, he glances at the team for a moment as they take the stairs leading upwards. Determined, Victor sighs intensely and reluctantly follows the shadowy pathway with Lithia, splitting him from the team.

CH: 42
SHADOW HEART

Minutes later, Victor follows the shadowy pathway below the temple and hears several young voices in the distance. Lithia pants fearfully as Victor enters a mysterious cold and damp chamber with dozens of slave cages hanging from the ceiling. There are dozens of human slaves held captive as Victor approaches one of the cages and looks upon two kids struggling to breath. As he steps closer to investigate, his eyes widen, realizing the two kids to be Tristan and Michael. The two boys turn their attention outside the cage, seeing their childhood hero and whisper, "Victor, is that you?"

The boys reach out to Victor who kneels before them as he places his hand through the cage, gripping their hands in despair to comfort them.

"What have they done to all of you?" Victor says in panics.

"You're going to get us out of here, aren't you?" Michael asks.

Unsure of his ability to free everyone, including his two young friends, Victor replies, "I'll do what I can." He then turns his attention beyond the cage, and says, "But first I need to find out who's responsible for this."

"We believe in you, Victor." Tristan says softly with pain in his voice. Victor turns his attention back to them as Tristan suddenly passes out in Michael's arms from a fever. As Michael attempts to keep his friend's body temperature cool, Victor rattles the cage in anger then closes his eyes in despair, feeling somewhat responsible for their current predicament. With his spinal shards glowing, Lithia growls at something drawing near as an eerie and dreadful sound of air flows viciously. Victor slowly opens his eyes, full of rage then stands and looks around for a moment with concern; unsure of the dangerous mess he feels he and the team have stepped into. Sensing that he's being watched, Victor powers up his Gauntlet in preparation as a mysterious figure suddenly appears from behind, revealing himself to be Traganus.

"Looking for something?" Traganus curiously denotes.

Without hesitation, Victor quickly turns and attempts to fire several energy blasts, but misses every time as Traganus dodges in and out of the shadows.

Traganus chuckles and taunts, "Aren't you're the zealous type, I like that."

"What have you done with my friends?" Victor furiously demands.

"If you're worried about the little ones, don't be, for I've done everything in my power to help them survive in a sad cruel world." Traganus replies, "As for the others, they've been cast into the dark abyss below."

"No!" Victor exclaims with a panicky voice.

"Your feelings for them are strong." Traganus infers, "Their pain rests on your shoulders, but it could not be helped." Victor looks around, cautious and alert as Traganus, now unseen attempts to toy with him, saying, "You can't fight what you can't see."

"Luckily for me, I've spent enough time in the dark." Victor retorts.

"Have you now?" Traganus questions, sounding amused.

"Finding you is only a matter of time." Victor proclaims.

"Like you." Traganus professes, "You're a hard man to find."
Still cautious and alert, Victor takes each step carefully within the chamber and mutters, "Perhaps it's because I don't want to be found."

"Or in this case, understood." Traganus states, "For those who deal in violence, typically attract violence. Therefore, I welcome your presence."

"Not exactly a warm welcome." Victor scoffs.
With his voice echoing through the shadows, Traganus firmly states, "Perhaps not, but if I wanted you dead you wouldn't be here now."

"Whatever, if you say so." Victor mockingly retorts then cautiously inquires, "Who are you?"

"That's a much bigger question than you think." Traganus says, "For I'm the one who understands you, and like you, I'm one of the damned."

"Assuming you're the Darchadian leader, I would say that to most people in this world you are merely a legend at this point." Victor deduces.

"A legend I am, but one rooted in scientific fact." Traganus declares.
Determined, Victor attempts to fire again with his Gauntlet, and misses, confused by Traganus' exact location as he continues, "Assaulting me is useless, I wouldn't recommend it!" As Michael looks on from his cage with Tristan, Victor grips his Gauntlet tightly, annoyed by his failure to successfully track his dark foe. "Taking me head on is a mission for morons and fools?" Traganus proclaims, "Which are you I wonder?"
Lithia perches himself on Victor's shoulder, gripping it tightly with his claws and growls ferociously in his defense. "Actually, I'm neither." Victor says with confidence, "You see I'm a force for good, and a nightmare to you!"
Traganus, still unseen chuckles quietly and states, "Brave words, I've heard them before." His voice echoes all around him, "From thousands of people across thousands of miles, since long before you were created." His voice now centers before him, "But they all fell in time, just as everyone else does."

Looking around cautiously, Victor tries to track his movements as Lithia sniffs around to help him out, he then retorts, "Unlucky for them, for I am unlike anyone you've ever encountered before."

"Is that so?" Traganus mocks, "You look like a mere warrior trying desperately to become a triumphant hero."
Confident, Victor expresses a crooked smile and calmly retorts, "I'm no hero, nor warrior; in fact, I'm something else entirely."

"Yes, and like most people in this world, you are an imperfect being; honoring an imperfect ideal, created by imperfect beings." Traganus asserts.
Lithia expresses concern with a deep growl, as Victor sarcastically states, "Yeah well, nobody's perfect." Victor's expression changes to that of concern as he looks upon his Gauntlet, which suddenly lights up brightly in blue, signaling that danger is close. "Strange that your energy reading didn't register before now." He curiously mutters.

"Perhaps your instruments are useless." Traganus suggests.

"Maybe." Victor coolly retorts, then looks around, finally realizing to whom he's talking to, "You must be the one they call, Traganus." He cautiously inquires, "Am I right?"

"That I am!" Traganus proudly asserts as he slightly reveals himself through the shadows, "The beginning, the end; the one who is eternal. Do not be afraid, for I'm not your enemy, yet." He states, as his voice suddenly appears to be on the other end of the chamber.
Victor continues along the shadowy corridor with Lithia, and says, "Afraid? You don't seem so threatening!" He makes his way into the next chamber and asks, "What makes you think I'm afraid?"
Surprised, Victor finally sees Traganus walking along on a crystalline bridge across the large cavern and heads after him with Lithia.

"You may not be afraid of me, but you are afraid of something, aren't you?" Traganus boldly implies.
Victor steadily approaches his mysterious new adversary while gripping his Gauntlet, then says, "You think so huh?"

"I know so!" Traganus proclaims with a confident tone, "It's only a matter of time before your weakness is found, and it will soon be exploited."
As Victor enters the next chamber, he sees Traganus standing upon the edge of a tall crystalline pillar with his back turned.

"Your pain runs deep, very deep." He denotes, "I can sense it."

"Oh yeah!" Victor scoffs, "What would you know of my pain?"

"Plenty." Traganus reveals, "Each person hides a secret pain within. It must be exposed and reckoned with in order to overcome it. It must be dragged from the darkness and into the light."
Victor slowly approaches the crystalline pillar with caution as Lithia growls with his spinal shards glowing and retracting defensively.

Traganus turns his head towards them and states, "People's greatest fears, yours is that you'll never belong, to anything, or anyone for that matter." His words cause Victor to scowl, "I bring order to chaos, and right now you are in chaos, Victor Zyas."

Shocked by hearing his name, Victor looks upon him as he stands ready and alert, unsure of his intentions. "How do you know me?" He cautiously asks.

"At this point, who doesn't?" Traganus teases as Victor sighs impatiently, "Do not mistake my intensity as a threat…" He then finally turns to face Victor as his helmet shifts back, revealing his full face for the first time, "For appearances can be deceiving."

Sudden panic flashes in Victor's eyes, as he slowly backs away, feeling the dark energy emanating from him. Lithia chirps to get his attention as the chamber suddenly fills with shadows, causing Victor to be spun around. He becomes disoriented as he aims his Gauntlet in all directions and fires whilst struggling to keep his composure. "Who are you, really?" Victor irately asks.

"Does it matter?" Traganus taunts to his surprise as he explains, "Like you, I feed on conflict. Until recently I'd been starving. I sensed the return of aggression, sought its cause, and its source led me directly to you."

"It's done more than that I'd say!" Victor exclaims, "It's brought us all here, and for what purpose?"

Traganus' red wings suddenly emerge from his spinal armor and he floats above Victor, stating, "The Arch's reign has nearly eliminated conflict on this planet, which had left me virtually powerless, till now." As Victor grips his Gauntlet once again, Traganus swiftly spins with his wings, causing the crystalline pillar to be engulfed in complete shadow. "I'm curious about you, Zyas." Traganus taunts, "I sense danger in you, but I can't read you as well as I thought I would. I can read all men, like reading scrolls of flesh but you, you I can't see past your scowl. Why is that?"

"And just what exactly are you hoping to find behind it?" Victor questions whilst preparing to fire his Gauntlet in defense.

"Perhaps some riddles aren't worth solving." Traganus evaluates.

Traganus unseen yet again chuckles, as Victor studies his surroundings, unsure of his exact location then looks back towards the cavern's entrance.

"Though I can show you what you truly fear." Traganus claims.

Surprised, Victor realizes he's right back where he started as Lithia growls.

"You were born into bondage and have been found wanting, yet worst of all, you do not know why." Traganus continuously taunts, "Why were you chosen, to be like this? A shadow heart."

Looking for an exit, Victor discovers that some time type of mysterious force field has suddenly blocked the cavern's entrance as Traganus' shadow encroaches upon him. To his surprise, Traganus mysteriously appears out of the shadows directly in front of him.

"Well fear not…" Traganus states as he holds out a blue crystalline Angel figure floating above the palm of his hand just like the one Victor made for Talia. The figurine suddenly turns dark, shifting into a typical shard shape as Traganus finishes, "For the answer to that, is right here." Lithia growls fiercely as Victor's eyes widen at the sight of the dark blue shard, one he's never seen before. "The thing you fear the most contains the very thing you need." Traganus finishes as Victor focuses on the shard intensely.

Meanwhile in the temple above, Damian and Adrian continue tracking the signal with the team and notice debris all around the interior structure. As they finally come to a stopping point, everyone looks around with concern, trying to track any possible threats.

"What happened here?" Adrian cautiously inquires.

"I don't know, but it looks like we were too late." Damian replies disappointedly, "There's no telling if our presence would've even helped."

"This place is an absolute wreck." Adrian mentions while glancing at the holographic schematic projecting from his Gauntlet, "There are no life signs at all, meaning this place is already dead."

"We shouldn't be surprised considering the historical nature of these things." Damian indicates.

Taking a moment to study their surroundings, Adrian sees various blast marks on the walls and curiously denotes, "I know one thing, there's been some intense fighting going on here."

"These things must be in a different league altogether." Damian says while looking around cautiously then asks, "Suppose they're still around?"

"Not likely, but we can't be too sure." Adrian cautions as he swipes the schematic away from his Gauntlet.

"We should probably stay together, assuming our new comrade will draw attention." Damian suggests as he signals the troops to move upward.

"Yeah, and not all of it welcome either." Adrian sarcastically utters.

Noticing Victor's sudden absence, Damian looks behind him and inquires, "Where is Zyas by the way?"

"Probably got scared and fell behind." Adrian says while motioning below the stairs, "Should we go after him before he gets into trouble?"

"No," Damian utters while looking down the stairwell, "If he falls behind then it's up to him to catch up. We can't be expected to hold his hand every step of the way. That's his responsibility, not ours."

"Knowing him, I'm sure he'll catch up with us sooner or later." Adrian suggests then turns back to face the others, saying, "We shouldn't waste anymore time here."

Damian nods in agreement and replies, "Right, let's keep moving then."

"Gladly." Adrian mutters while gripping his Gauntlet tightly.

The two brave Champions continue moving upwards cautiously within the distressed temple, followed closely by the Eudenian and Enfurian soldiers.

Waiting outside the Arch ship several yards away, Marcus and Yuri stand guard with Valorie and Vennessa as Elena stands watch on the landing platform. Talia sits inside the cargo deck and pulls out the Angel figure; examining it curiously in hopes that Victor makes it back safely and sighs, extremely anxious for his return.

Deep below the temple, Victor observes the dark crystal before him intensely as Traganus continues to taunt him. "Do you want it, Victor?" He probes, "True power?" Still perched upon his shoulder, Lithia growls as Victor hesitates to respond. "Everything you wanted to know, is in this shard?" Traganus states while holding the shard closer to him, "The crystal draws you into its brilliance, and to your end." Victor fights the impulse to grab it then closes his eyes whilst struggling to make a decision. "Join me on my quest, brother." He persuasively requests.

With his eyes still closed, Victor calmly asks, "What is it that you truly seek?"

"What all have sought since time began, ultimate power, or as you earthlings like to call it, The Edge Of Beyond." Traganus forcefully states while gripping the shard tightly in his fist, "Just like the Arch, the true message behind it was written from crystal in the language of science. Though had it been strictly religious in nature, it would contradict its own power. But if you truly wish to find the secrets of the world, you must first think in terms of energy." Struggling to clear his mind, Victor listens closely as Traganus resumes, "Like all living things on this planet, crystals are at the very beginning of creation, with each having a specific frequency and vibration. And when it comes to such ethereal frequencies, even music itself acts like a magic key to which the most tightly closed heart opens."

Victor opens his eyes and carefully asks, "Why are you telling me all this?"

To his surprise, Traganus has disappeared once again. Lithia motions his head elsewhere as Victor follows his shadow down another corridor and sees him standing before them once again. Every time Victor turns, Traganus moves in and out of the shadows within the chamber.

"Why did you end up like this, an Angel without a halo, a shadow heart, like me?" Traganus teases in all seriousness, "Both unable to reach out to anyone." Annoyed by his pestering, Victor grips his fists tightly in anger whilst struggling to keep his composure. "You want answers so badly, it's burning you up inside." Traganus continues, "You want to grab them and fly off with them, but you're afraid of what they, your comrades will think." Victor's breath quickens as Traganus pushes him into a corner, saying, "You're afraid of disappointing them. Well, let me ease your mind about one thing. They'll never accept you, not really."

The darkness slowly overcomes Victor who closes his eyes and crosses his arms close to his chest as Lithia chirps with a concerned tone. "Stop it!" Victor cries furiously while holding his hands over his head, "I know what you're trying to do!"

Traganus chuckles and retorts in a confident tone, "Do you now?" Opening his eyes, Victor struggles to hold back the rage burning within him. "We're both struck from the same mold, built to seek and destroy." Traganus states.

Lithia pants as Victor places his hand over his head once again, trying desperately not to let his anger get the better of him in front of his adversary.

"Look past the hero you wish to be, and you'll surely find a monster lurking within." Traganus confidently implies, feeding off of Victor's inner rage, "After all, you're not one of them, and never will be."

The shadows back away reluctantly as Traganus appears before him once again. Victor instinctively aims his Gauntlet in anger, his arm shaking as he exclaims, "You don't know what I am!"

Traganus back away a few feet and claims, "Of course I do, darkness follows you wherever you go. Why, it's here with you now." He suddenly tosses the dark crystal shard to Victor who instinctively catches it, then proudly informs, "People like us, we are blessed and cursed by our times."

Lithia growls ferociously with his spinal shards glowing and retracting once more as a warning for Traganus to back off as Victor looks up with terror in his eyes, and says softly, "What is this?"

"More to the point, Victor, what are you?" Traganus contests.

As Victor looks upon his opposition with confusion, he explains, "You may not even be aware, but from what I can tell, you are a living contradiction. A human who wishes to be an Angel, and vice versa."

Regaining his composure, Victor looks upon Traganus with determination, and says, "If you know so much about me, then you're aware that I am an Angel! And as an Angel, I aspire to evolve, to better myself."

As Traganus circles around him, he claims, "We too are on a quest to better ourselves, evolving towards a powerful state of perfection."

Amused by his claim, Victor mocks, "Forgive me and my ignorance, but Darchadians such as yourself do not evolve, you simply conquer."

"We conquer our fear, chase our dreams, not our reality." Traganus enlightens as he stops before him, "Your reality is that you're still a prisoner of this world, shackled by society. Your dreams however, lead you to believe that there's something greater. You may still be enslaved by your reality, but you can free yourself, as I once did."

"What you fail to realize is that I carry no such burden anymore!" Victor proudly exclaims, "I'm already free!"

"So you think, but if you shy away from expressing your very nature, you will never reach the highest peak of your true potential." Traganus scoffs as he turns his back towards him and begins to walk away, "Therefore you must fly through the light to find your shadow like the rest of us."

Curious to his true intentions, Victor carefully inquires, "What sort of power do you hold over others?"

Traganus stops in his tracks and turns his head slightly to respond, "Contrary to what you've been told, I don't control people, I simply free them." Victor looks upon him intensely; listening closely as Traganus slowly turns, and states, "Yet, beneath the surface of any would-be hero, lies a monster lurking inside. A diamond in the rough if you will."

Lithia growls once again and suddenly flies towards Traganus as he backs away into the shadows, becoming one with the darkness.

"Lithia, no!" Victor frantically calls.

Eager to attack, Lithia flies towards the shadow and suddenly disappears into the darkness as Traganus laughs maniacally. Angered, Victor powers up and charges forward, striking at nothing as Traganus quickly dodges.

"The things you fear to face hold the answers you seek." Traganus cruelly torments, "Confront the beast that haunts you, only then will you find peace. I know from experience, no matter how far you run no matter how fast you go, the darkness will always follow, for Angels such as yourself cannot escape their own fate."

Victor charges towards the shadows again in anger and suddenly flies out of the darkness, ready to strike. Looking around, he suddenly realizes he's forgotten something. "Lithia!" He frantically calls again.

Victor turns to re-enter the chamber, only to find himself face-to-face against an Angelic statue with broken wings, some distance away from the temple outside. As he looks on curiously, he sees the name, *VICTORIA* engraved on the statue's base. Gripping his Gauntlet tightly, Victor's eyes widen in fear.

"Wings help one to soar beyond the dark and into the light, when they're not broken." Traganus taunts out of sight, "When an Angel falls from grace, they are forever separated from their previous bonds, and once the darkness settles in, it never goes away."

Trembling in fear at the sight of the statue, Victor falls to his knees in despair, realizing the name on the statue to be that of his own real mother.

Back in the temple, Damian and Adrian make their way towards the top floor with the others as they look around cautiously from the stairwell.

"Where are we?" Adrian inquires with a grunt, sounding impatient from all the walking.

"Some place we don't want to be." Damian sarcastically answers.

Each soldier attempts to tread quietly behind them, trying not to give their position away too soon. "It's likely to become more dangerous the further we venture." Adrian firmly cautions.

"Probably." Damian mutters in agreement.

Sniffing around in disgust, Adrian turns his head and says, "I smell danger in the air, and my blood is on fire."

"So is mine." Damian quietly professes.

Facing his Eudenian comrade directly, Adrian asks, "Have you ever fought an Angel like this before?"

Damian shakes his head as he looks around, ready to strike and responds, "Technically, no. Have you?"

"No, but I guess we'll find out." Adrian fearfully surmises.

Damian and Adrian continue looking around the top floor alongside the team with their Gauntlets drawn, mindful of anything harmful that draws near.

Still standing by the Arch ship outside the temple, Elena positions herself beside Talia, sensing danger then approaches the landing platform as she looks onto the misty horizon with concern.

"What is it?" Talia carefully asks.

Elena continues looking around as Valorie and Vennessa take their positions beside her to stand guard while Marcus and Yuri nod at one another and quickly follow suit.

"Something isn't right, there's a great energy here." She sternly warns.

Talia approaches the landing platform as she looks onto the horizon as well, then asks, "How do you know?"

"I can feel it." Elena confidently states.

Marcus and Yuri search around the back of the ship with their Gauntlets drawn, catching on to her intuitive vibe.

"You're right about that, Princess!" Yuri informs, "We sense it too!"

With his Gauntlet drawn carefully, Marcus curiously inquires, "What kind of energy are you sensing?"

As Elena readies her crystalline staff by powering it up, she looks upon Marcus intensely and firmly replies, "Dark!"

Talia looks on from inside the Arch ship, slightly frightened as Elena and her crew stand guard by the landing platform, ready for anything that may bring them or the team harm.

As Damian and Adrian continue investigating the top floor of the temple, they approach the main corridor with the team close behind.

"Guess nobody's home." Adrian jokes.

"If only we were that lucky." Damian sarcastically retorts.

While observing their mysterious surroundings, Adrian reluctantly professes, "You know I've been to all kinds of places before, but...."

"But what?" Damian asks impatiently.

"I've never felt such a great sense of danger as I do here." Adrian explains, "Every hair on my body is on end."

"What are you so nervous about?" Damian scornfully teases with a stern look, "We haven't found anything yet."

"My point exactly." Adrian affirms, "This stupid place is freaking me out a little, and I don't like it, not one bit."

Damian chuckles quietly and jokes, "Well there's something new."

"How do you figure that?" Adrian sternly questions.

"I figured Victor would've been the one complaining," Damian mocks, "Though I never expected to hear someone like you wine so much."
Unamused by his snide remark, Adrian grunts, saying, "It's a normal reaction under the circumstances. We've never faced an enemy like this before, therefore we have no idea what we're really up against."
As Damian signals the others to close up their back end, he jeeringly suggests, "Well why don't you just go back then, leave the rest to us while you're at it?"
Adrian scoffs in defense of his position then humorously retorts, "And leave all the excitement to you? Not a chance pal!"
Damian grins in response as they continue moving forward. As the team enters a large chamber at the top of the temple, Damian turns and accidently stumbles upon a dead Archadian with broken wings. As he looks upon his Gauntlet, Damian sees that the distress signal has suddenly disappeared. He then signals everyone to come to a halt as Adrian approaches him from behind. "What do you got?" He carefully inquires, "Talk to me!"
Damian looks upon the energy reading from his Gauntlet once again as it suddenly reappears, then says, "It's strange, the energy readings went blank for a minute, and now they're getting stronger all of a sudden."

"That can't be good," Adrian forewarns with a deeply concerned tone, "Must be quantum interference from the temple's crystalline structure."

"Let's hope that's all it is." Damian mutters as he examines the dead Archadian lying before him.

"Why do I get the feeling we've been following a trail of bread crumbs this whole time?" Adrian sarcastically implies.
The two Champions suddenly hear a low screeching noise as the team looks around with their Gauntlets defensively drawn.

"What was that?" Damian cautiously asks.

"Maybe somebody's home after all." Adrian humorously states.
As Damian and Adrian prepare their Gauntlets, they hear multiple screeching noises this time as they glance at each other with concern.

"There it is again," Damian quietly warns, "It's getting louder this time." He then asks impatiently, "Thoughts please?"

"I'm thinking shoot first, ask questions later!" Adrian declares.

"Likewise!" Damian firmly replies in agreement.
Damian and Adrian power up their Gauntlets as the troops get into attack position. Confused by their current situation, Damian looks around for a moment then turns his attention back towards the dead Archadian with broken wings. Panic flashes in his eyes upon realizing that the Archadian's body to have been the signal's origin the whole time.

"It's a trap!" Damian warningly shouts.

The team is suddenly surrounded by a small group of Darchadians who hiss ferociously, trying to intimidate them.

"Why do I get the feeling these things don't like us very much already?" Damian sarcastically questions.

"That's because they know we're here to kill them!" Adrian confirms. The Eudenian and Enfurian soldiers quickly aim their Gauntlets, awaiting orders as they prepare for attack.

"We have visual range!" a Eudenian soldier exclaims.
An Enfurian soldier stands next to the Eudenian and adds, "Lock on target!"
As the Darchadians fully surround the team, Damian and Adrian stand back to back defensively with their Gauntlets pressed firmly against their chests.

"Looks like we've got company!" Damian exclaims.

"Yeah, and lots of it!" Adrian jokingly adds.
The pair firmly holds their positions to show their defensive prowess.

"Now we know who placed the bread crumbs," Damian denotes, "We're not here by accident!"

"So much for a vantage point!" Adrian sarcastically mutters while shaking his head, "Looks like we'll have to fire line of sight."
Wasting no time, Damian quickly presses a button on his Gauntlet to activate a holographic schematic, saying, "Tactical analysis!"
The Darchadians fly around the team, waiting to strike in anticipation, as Damian expresses a look of shock from the schematic.

"So what do you think, friend or foe?" Adrian sarcastically inquires.

"Most definitely foe!" Damian retorts as he swings his purple cape behind him in preparation to fight.
Hissing intensely, the Darchadians slowly approach the team as Damian and Adrian give each other a respectful nod then power up in unison.

"Prepare to engage!" Adrian orders as the troops follow suit.
The Darchadians begin their vicious attack, putting the team on the defense.

"Careful men, they're ruthless!" Damian warns. The team attempts to force the Darchadians back as they attack in groups. "Stand your ground, and kill and anything that moves!" Damian orders.
Confident of his power, Adrian pounds his fists together tightly and shouts, "Come on you punk ass fairies!"
Damian and Adrian fight side by side whilst attempting to hold their own against the deadly Darchadians. Moments later, Raiven and Celeste enter the chamber and see the team fighting against their own.

"Not bad!" Raiven comments, surprised by the teams' prowess.

"Let's make it bad!" Celeste sneers as she smiles towards Raiven then raises her arm to signal the Darchadians, and orders, "Bring us their heads!"
Several Darchadians nod in response then quickly take off towards the team. Raiven and Celeste glance at each other for a moment and grin as the team endures the most intense battle of their lives.

Sensing the conflict from afar, Elena suddenly powers up as everyone looks upon her with concern. Turning back from the landing platform, she orders, "Talia, stay here!"

"I'm not going anywhere!" Talia affirms whilst shaking her head. Concerned by her sudden intent, Marcus approaches Elena and inquires, "Elena, what are you doing?"

"We don't have time to just stand around!" She exclaims defensively as she presses the Gods' symbol over her chest, which activates her wings. Concerned for Talia's safety, Elena quickly turns to address the Archadians still aboard the Arch ship, and orders, "Keep the ship steady, sisters!"

As the few Archadians nod determinedly, Elena points towards Marcus and Yuri as Valorie and Vennessa prepare for battle as well.

"You guys with me!" Elena commands. Marcus glances at Yuri as they pound their fists together with excitement.

"Finally, some action!" Marcus exclaims with excitement.

"You said it!" Yuri jokingly retorts. Elena looks back towards Talia intensely, signaling her to stay put as her pink wings prepare to take flight. "Angels, fly!" She commandingly orders.

While causing a slight energy wake from her aura, Elena quickly takes off at full speed with Valorie and Vennessa towards the temple to aid the team, followed closely by Marcus and Yuri. Observing from a short distance, a Darchadian suddenly steps out of the shadows while turning their attention towards the Arch ship, watching it closely with deadly intent.

With their numbers dwindling, the team continues their fight against the Darchadians as Raiven and Celeste move in closer to corner them.

"This doesn't look good!" Adrian warns.

"No it doesn't!" Damian impatiently retorts, "It's safe to assume they don't believe in diplomatic solutions!"

"Of course not, they've already drawn first blood!" Adrian states angrily, "This is more like aggressive negotiation!" Attempting to lighten the already grim mood, Damian jokes, "Isn't that the universal greeting when negotiations fail?"

"I believe it's the universal greeting for when you don't like someone!" Adrian jokingly retorts as he suddenly pounds the temple floor with his fist, knocking back several Darchadians with the energy wave, which gives the team a brief moment to get back into formation. Raiven and Celeste look on in annoyance as the team regroups, hopelessly trying to gather what troops they have left in the deadly skirmish.

"We're greatly outnumbered here!" Damian concernedly warns, "There are too many of them!"

Unsure of their next tactical move, Adrian quickly looks around and conveys, "Well I'm all out of ideas, how about you?"

"Nothing at the moment!" Damian replies.
Adrian scoffs then inquires, "What do you want to do?"
Realizing there's no hope for themselves or the team, Damian quickly orders, "Signal the general abort directive, we must request retrieval now!"

"Way ahead of you there!" Adrian responds with a smirk after pressing a distress button on his Gauntlet.
Raiven and Celeste signal the remaining Darchadians to approach the team once again as Damian and Adrian stare back with concern over their faces.

"I don't see anyway out of here from this height, do you?" Damian asks, hoping for a quick answer.

"Not that I've noticed!" Adrian sarcastically shouts after pushing back a Darchadian, "Looks like they're blocking our escape route!"

"I can see that, thank you!" Damian annoyingly snaps after striking a Darchadian with a swift kick, "We have to hold out as long as we can!"
Taking this slight opportunity before the Darchadians attack again, Damian and Adrian discharge the crystal shards from their Gauntlets and reload with new ones from their armored belts. Amused by the teams' unwillingness to give up, Raiven and Celeste glance at each other in amusement then suddenly aim their Gauntlets towards the ceiling.

"Time to send these fools to another dimension, don't you agree, sis?" Raiven cynically implies.

"Indeed I do!" Celeste retorts, "Let's see how well they play with fire!" Raiven and Celeste suddenly fire energy blasts upon the ceiling with their Gauntlets, causing the temple to catch fire. The rabble-rousing pair laughs maniacally as Damian and Adrian look towards them intensely, concerned for their own lives as well as the teams'.

"Like lambs to the slaughter!" Celeste states with a confident grin.

"Or in this case, a feast!" Raiven cynically adds.
Confident of their demise, Raiven and Celeste screech loudly, as Damian and Adrian continue fighting through the flames, one Darchadian at a time.

Outside, the two Archadians stand aboard the Arch ship to guard Talia and sense an imminent threat approaching. Afraid, Talia looks on from inside the ship as the two Archadians prepare their crystalline staffs. As they look out from the ship, they are suddenly taken out by energy blasts from two other Darchadians. Watching in panic, Talia attempts to hide aboard the ship, hoping not to be found. The two Darchadians quickly board the ship and look around, sensing Talia's innocent presence.

"Raiven said there would be more." One of the Darchadians informs.

"She also said for us to retrieve some random Archling, but we have yet to find her." The second one indicates.

The other points towards the front of the Arch ship, and orders, "Check over there! That Archling has to be around here somewhere!"

As the two Darchadians begin their search aboard the ship, Talia does her best to keep calm with tears running down her face. One of the Darchadians walks right past her as she looks up and sees their dark looking wings.

"Oh god!" Talia frighteningly whispers.

The Darchadian aggressively shoves a container onto the floor as Talia accidently squeals then quickly covers her mouth and closes her eyes in panic.

"Come out come out wherever you are!" one of them playfully calls.

Realizing where she is, the Darchadian at the back of the ship nods at the other as she quietly points towards Talia's hiding spot. The Darchadian closest to her leans overhead and says, "Well now, what have we here?"

Terrified, Talia slowly opens her eyes and hesitates to look up as the Darchadian stands above her with a grin. Talia looks on in fear as the Darchadian aggressively reaches for her, which causes her to scream in terror.

Some distance away, Victor finally makes his way outside of the Darchadian lair beneath the temple as his eyes fill with dread, realizing where he is. Victor sees the temple burning through the fog and panics at the sight.

"Oh no!" He says frantically, "What have I done?"

While watching this all unfold, Victor is completely heartbroken, feeling solely responsible for this unexpected yet tragic outcome. Victor activates his wings by pressing the Gods' symbol over his chest, which causes them to emerge from his spinal armor, and without hesitation he quickly takes off towards the temple, hoping to help the team before it's too late.

The fight continues within the temple between the team and the Darchadians, as the situation looks even grimmer. Damian and Adrian attempt to hold their own but are quickly drained of power from lack of energy in their Gauntlets.

"I think we underestimated their fighting prowess!" Damian exclaims with a disappointing tone.

"Gee, what made you come to that conclusion?" Adrian sarcastically retorts while shaking his head.

"Because we seem to have lost this fight already!" Damian replies.

"Considerably!" Adrian mutters.

Raiven and Celeste signal the remaining Darchadians to move forward as Damian and Adrian quickly strategize their next move.

"They have us right where they want us!" Damian warns.

"Yeah, in their sights!" Adrian jokes, which causes Damian to grin.

With each intimidating step, the Darchadians hiss ferociously towards their Eudenian and Enfurian prey.

"What do we do now, Trag?" Adrian irritably inquires.

"Your guess is as good as mine, Braxel!" Damian sternly answers, "The chances of us making it out alive aren't going to be easy."

"That couldn't be more obvious." Adrian sarcastically mutters.

Feeling combatively overwhelmed for the first time in their lives, Damian and Adrian position themselves to make their final stand against their deadly foes. Suddenly, like an answered prayer from the Gods, Elena flies in unexpectedly through the temple ceiling and lands gracefully between them and the Darchadians. Surprised by her sudden entrance, the Darchadians hiss as Valorie and Vennessa, followed closely by Marcus and Yuri land next to Elena defensively as well. Sighing in relief, Damian and Adrian glance at each other as Elena turns her head towards them intensely.

"You guys alright?" She firmly asks.

Scoffing in response, Adrian humorously replies, "We are now!"

"Looks like you could use some help." Elena sternly denotes.

"More than a little." Damian reluctantly admits, "Can't say we're not glad to see you."

Elena nods in respect then quickly turns back to face the Darchadians as Raiven and Celeste look upon her in anger.

"What's she doing here?" Celeste furiously questions.

"Beats me!" Raiven irritably answers.

Marcus and Yuri stand guard alongside Valorie and Vennessa with Elena as she looks upon the Darchadians with serious determination.

"Get them!" Raiven orders as she waves her arm furiously.

The Darchadians quickly approach Elena and hiss ferociously as she suddenly kneels, causing a bright light to emanate from her crystalline staff, which illuminates the entire chamber. Slightly blinded, the Darchadians quickly cover their eyes and screech angrily. Elena uses this brief moment to rush towards Damian and Adrian's side as Marcus and Yuri fend off the remaining Darchadians alongside Valorie and Vennessa. As Elena flies beside the two Champions, she exclaims, "Come on! We have to get out of here now!"

"About time we got reinforced!" Adrian sarcastically comments as he watches the battle ensue before them.

"Didn't think we'd need you so soon!" Damian admits as he swings his cape behind him and powers down with Adrian to conserve energy.

"Neither did I!" Elena says with a stern gaze as she quickly looks around for a moment with concern, realizing that Victor is nowhere to be found. "Where's Victor?" She inquires.

Damian and Adrian glance at each other for a moment in disappointment.

"Where do you think?" Adrian angrily retorts.

Elena frowns upon Adrian in annoyance as she turns towards Damian and asks, "What happened to him?"

As Damian tries to help a Eudenian soldier stand, he looks back with a disappointed expression and calmly says, "He fell behind."

Devastated, Elena looks upon the two Champions, shaking her head and mutters, "No!"

The whole temple is suddenly engulfed in flames as it begins to crumble down piece by piece. Realizing what kind of temple they're in, Elena looks around with alarm, and states, "I know this temple's design!"

"What?" Damian impatiently asks with a quick turn to face her.

"This place, it's a temple housing one of the Holy Artifacts!" She informs while keeping a close eye on the enemy.

As her crew attempts to hold back the Darchadians, Elena turns her attention behind her, wide-eyed with concern, realizing that the Darchadians likely stole it beforehand in order to incite a reaction from the Arch.

"You do have a plan for getting us out of this mess, right?" Damian inquires while laying one his comrades down on the floor that just died.

As Marcus and Yuri take out several Darchadians alongside Valorie and Vennessa, Elena faces the two Champions and holds her hands out before her. Determined to end the bloodshed, Elena powers up intensely and creates an exit route by blasting a big hole through the roof of the temple. Surprised by her sudden intensity, Damian and Adrian take cover as the debris hits the floor from above.

"Go now!" Elena firmly orders.

"Right!" Damian replies with a respectful nod.

Adrian nods also as he and Damian turn to make a break for it. Marcus and Yuri quickly approach them to lead the way, followed closely by Valorie and Vennessa as they stand guard to cover their escape route.

"This way guys!" Yuri informs.

Elena stands behind them, focusing her attention on the Darchadians as Marcus approaches her and says, "Come on, Elena!"

With the help of her crew, the Champions makes a break for it through the roof as the temple continues to crumble down. Elena prepares to take off then suddenly hears a couple of high-pitched screeching hisses from behind. Annoyed, Elena turns to look through the fire and sees her two former comrades standing there with devious grins on their faces. Raiven and Celeste stare off against Elena for a moment, completely separated by the fire before it causes them to flee. Elena activates her wings then quickly takes off through the roof, as Raiven and Celeste quickly turn to address the remaining Darchadians, and shout together, "Let's vanish!"

Raiven and Celeste screech loudly and quickly fly off, followed closely by the other surviving Darchadians as the temple finally comes crashing down from the intense battle.

CH: 43
FAMILY FEUD

Shortly after the battle, Victor approaches the burning temple at the base, ready to fight and suddenly hears coughing with a rustle behind him.

"Victor!" Damian calls. Victor quickly turns with his Gauntlet drawn then sighs in relief as Damian and Adrian appear out of the fog, having just come from the intense battle. They're exhausted, wild-eyed and distraught from their unbearable defeat at the hands of the fearsome Darchadians.

"Where were you?" Adrian angrily inquires.

"I got a little sidetracked." Victor sheepishly replies while powering down. Seeing his Eudenian and Enfurian comrades in rough shape, he then carefully asks, "What happened?"

Annoyed by his obliviousness to the situation, Damian looks back and heatedly retorts, "The Darchadians ambushed us, leaving none wounded!"

"What do you mean none wounded?" Victor questions.

Damian and Adrian glance at each other then shake their heads in anger.

"It means no one else made it out alive, incase you didn't know!" Adrian exclaims impatiently. Shocked by this news, Victor looks upon Damian and Adrian, realizing his absence cost them and the team more deeply than he expected. "They are without honor, and don't take prisoners apparently." Adrian sternly explains as he brushes past Victor, purposely leaning into his shoulder to push him aside in disrespect.

"Or stress diplomacy for that matter." Damian firmly adds as he stands beside Adrian, both looking upon Victor intensely. "Well?" He asks impatiently with a disgruntled tone.

"Well what?" Victor retorts in annoyance.

"Are you going to tell us why you didn't have our backs up there?" Adrian mockingly instigates.

Knowing there's no easy way to explain his case, Victor sighs in dismay.

"Victor!" Elena calls, grabbing everyone's attention over head.

Victor, along with Damian and Adrian turn their attention above them as Elena arrives with Marcus and Yuri as they all land to rejoin the group. Victor and Elena glance at each other in relief, but hesitate to say anything due to feeling awkward about the situation. "They destroyed our ship!" Yuri annoyingly states as he angrily kicks the dirt and kneels to calm himself.

"That's unfortunate." Damian calmly responds.

Hesitant, Marcus motions towards Damian and Adrian, saying, "Guess we'll have to ride back with you guys if you don't mind."

"No problem." Adrian says in respect.

Elena approaches Victor then places her hand on his shoulder in relief, and gently asks, "Are you alright?"

Sighing in disappointment, Victor glances at his broken teammates and mutters, "I'm fine, for the most part I guess."

"You seem shaken." Elena implies with her intuitive sense. Victor looks upon Elena, feeling discouraged as she turns her attention towards his trembling fist lying by his side. "What is that?" She carefully asks. Mortified, Victor holds his hand out as he opens his fist, revealing the dark crystal shard given to him by Traganus as Elena examines it intensely and cautiously asks, "Where did you get this?"

Victor looks upon the dark crystal shard for a moment, hesitant to speak the truth and says, "I was, it's…"

Elena looks around, suddenly realizing that Talia is nowhere to be found, then questions, "Where's Natalia?"

Panicked by the sudden thought of his friend, Victor looks upon her and fearfully expresses, "I don't know, I thought she was with you!"

"She was, but we were split up during the attack!" Elena fearfully expresses in return.

Confused by her statement, Victor inquires, "Wait, she didn't come back?"

"Not that I know of, I figured she went to find you!" She explains.

Victor turns away in distress, unsure of what to do about Talia's absence.

"I'm sorry, but we told you there would be risks." Elena justifies.

"You also told me that she'd be under complete protection the entire time!" Victor rightfully disputes.

"The operation didn't go as smoothly as we anticipated!" She argues.

"I'd say that's an understatement." Victor spitefully comments as Damian and Adrian look upon their hybrid comrade in contempt. Concerned, Elena looks upon him with a frightened expression, and says, "Victor?"

Turning back to face her, Victor hesitates to respond as Valorie and Vennessa fly in from above and land gracefully with a Darchadian in hand. Elena turns away from him, as Valorie and Vennessa drag the unconscious Darchadian.

"We've searched the perimeter, but she's nowhere to be found!" Vennessa informs.

Everyone looks on with surprise as Vennessa aggressively shoves the Darchadian to the ground before them intensely and says, "She was taken by people wearing the same attire as these idiots!" Concerned for Talia, Elena glances back at Victor, who steps forward, breathing heavily as the rage within him builds even more so than before.

"It's as if they did everything in their power to separates us." Valorie reveals, "Seems they got their hands on that girl in the process."
Feeling him to be responsible for her capture, Elena shakes her head disappointedly with a tear running down her face as she glances at Victor.

"Oh Victor, what have you done?" She says dejectedly, "What's happened to her?"
Upset by Talia's assumed capture, Victor looks upon Elena with glossy eyes, feeling disheartened. Adrian approaches him while gripping his fists tightly in anger, and interrogates, "That is why you weren't there?" Victor looks upon him with teary eyes, "You were with them?" He questions furiously.

"Calm down, Adrian!" Elena firmly orders with her crystalline staff extended towards him.
Angered even further, Adrian turns to address Elena directly and exclaims, "Don't tell me to calm down!"
Losing control of the teams' moral, Elena sighs impatiently as Adrian looks back towards Victor in anger.

"No, listen guys, I'm sorry!" Victor tries to explain, "I didn't mean for any of this to happen, I swear!"
Adrian attempts to calm himself down and steps away as Victor looks on frustratingly at his Enfurian teammate.

"Who are you, and why the hell would you lead them to us like that?" Damian sternly inquires.

"Look, it wasn't intentional!" Victor defends as he turns to face him.

"Our problem with you is that you're reckless!" Damian scolds, "We trusted you to help lead the others as a team, and for whatever reason, you were no where to be found."

"I knew some of them better than you did!" Victor snaps.

"Oh I see, so that makes it all right then?" Damian disputes.

"No!" Victor impatiently barks, "It doesn't make it all right, but somehow they knew beforehand."

"Knew what?" Damian questions.

"It doesn't matter, I found him, didn't I?" Victor argues.

"Found who? Damian questions in disbelief, "Their leader?"
As Victor nods, Elena steps forward on his behalf and states, "Yes you did, that's what you do and that's why we need you." She praises, "You have an insight, you know darkness. You can feel it, you can sense it."

"Yeah, what's your point?" Victor harshly replies.

"You said they knew, what did you mean by that?" She inquires.

"They knew I was coming." Victor replies sounding disappointed.

"What are you then?" She asks, unsure whether or not to trust him.

"I'm trapped between two worlds, that's what I am." Victor states.

"Is that all?" Elena questions with a concerned expression.

"What are you trying to say?" Victor queries, disgruntled by her tone.

"What she's trying to say is this whole thing is a farce because in the end, after you've killed, after you've captured every Darchadian out there, there's still one left, you." Adrian claims as he points towards Victor, jabbing his finger firmly into his chest.

"I wish I could be more gracious," Victor exclaims defensively as he pushes Adrian's hand away, "But I'm not one of them!"

"Really?" Adrian mocks as he slowly turns to face him then angrily questions, "Then what the hell are you?"

Hesitating to answer, Victor looks away in despair, as Elena furiously chimes in, "He's an Angel, incase you forgot!"

"Ha!" Adrian scoffs, "A coward is more like it!"

Elena sighs impatiently as Victor scowls towards Adrian and furiously exclaims, "Who are you calling a coward?"

Adrian grunts ferociously as Victor powers up suddenly in anger and uses his energy to push him back several feet. Surprised by his intense reaction, everyone looks directly at Victor, realizing him to be an apparent threat to them. Elena closes her eyes in disappointment and slowly shakes her head, knowing Victor's inner rage has yet to be tamed.

"Enough with the charade!" Adrian shouts as he approaches Victor.

"Who says this was a game?" Victor sternly retorts.

Adrian yells in anger over Victor's arrogance towards him and finally exclaims, "That's it! He has to go, now!"

Victor looks upon Adrian intensely and stands face to face with him in anger, showcasing his powerful stance as everyone excluding Elena powers up their Gauntlets in defense, hoping to keep the situation from escalating. As the two warriors stare off, Adrian suddenly strikes Victor back to the ground, and laughs. As Victor's eyes begin to glow from the rage within, Elena suddenly strikes Adrian back several feet, knocking him to the ground as well.

"Get a grip, guys, we didn't come all this way just to lose our nerve at the first glitch!" She informs while stepping in-between them, "We're all on the same side here!"

"Step back, Elena!" Damian warns in a threatening manner with his Gauntlet aimed towards Victor, "This runt needs to be taught a lesson!"

Confused by which side to take, Marcus and Yuri stand beside Valorie and Vennessa with their Gauntlets aimed as well.

"He's not the enemy!" Elena justifies, "You've been fired upon by the enemy!" She then motions towards Victor and says, "That's not him!"

"Did he not just strike one of our own?" Damian sternly implies.

"He has a point, Princess." Valorie interjects, "If this is the real him we don't like what we're seeing already."

"What did you expect?" Elena irately defends as she faces Damian, "You provoked him!"

Rising to his feet, Adrian approaches the group and furiously states, "I don't care who or what he is, he doesn't belong on this team!"

Feeling his comrades have officially turned their backs on him, Victor scoffs, and murmurs, "You never really wanted me here in the first place, so what difference does it make?"

"If it's death from a Darchadian hand that frightens you, then you should've stayed at home, your real home back in the mines!" Adrian insults.

Victor scoffs in annoyance and hears Damian sigh impatiently from behind. He then turns his attention towards him and dejectedly asks, "What?"

Dismayed, Damian lowers his Gauntlet and informs, "You split the team up, and your carelessness gave the Darchadians a chance to attack us!"

"I didn't leave on purpose!" Victor attempts to clarify, "I was trying to help the others!"

"What others?" Elena carefully asks with a concerned look.

Hoping to justify his case, Victor calmly explains, "When I saw him, there were slaves being held captive underground."

"Oh yeah, what kind of slaves?" Damian mocks.

Victor stares at Damian intensely, and answers, "Human, what else?" Elena places her hand over her chin, concerned by this news as Adrian chuckles, uncaring to Victor's sentiment. "Those people are dying, we should go back and help them!" He rationalizes.

"It doesn't matter anymore!" Damian expresses, "We should never have trusted you, and now they're gone."

"All of them!" Adrian chimes in with a serious tone.

"I'm sorry you lost people on this mission, but there are worse problems sitting right in front of us." Victor contests.

"You're right." Adrian argues, "The real problem here is that you place your own feelings above everything else. Duty, obligation, tradition, it all means nothing to you!"

With an intense glare, Victor faces Adrian and firmly states, "It means everything to me, my heart tells me my duty, and I follow it."

"In some ways, you're a brilliant warrior." Elena professes, "You're brave, loyal, but you don't trust your heart enough at times. I'm beginning to wonder if you even have one."

"This assignment has made it quite clear that we are very different people, all of us." Victor frustratingly denotes.

"Maybe too different." Adrian insultingly adds.

"There must be a lot of things that we still don't know about each other," Elena sadly states, "Even more so than I realized."

"Quite a few actually, but the feeling's mutual." Victor remarks. Unable to process her mixed feelings, Elena looks away in disappointment as Victor stares back at Damian and Adrian, both of whom look away in disgust.

"I see how it is, I can take a hint!" Victor says angrily, "If you won't help those people, then I will!" He then activates his wings as he prepares to take off for good.

"Wait!" Elena calls with her arm extended as she quickly approaches him, "Where are you going?"

"Talia's out there somewhere!" Victor bellows while motioning into the distance with his hand.

"I know she's out there, but there's nothing we can do about it right now!" Elena rationalizes, "You swore an oath to the Arch; if they saw you breaking it now, what would they say?"

Trying to maintain his composure, Victor faces Elena with a worried look and claims, "I don't know, but I have to find her before it's too late. I know it's risky, but a shot in the dark is better than nothing."

"But you're putting your career at risk for her!" Elena stresses.

"Elena, I would've expected you of all people to know that friendship must dare to risk or else it's not friendship." Victor harshly states.

"Don't be irrational, Victor." She explains, "We need to strategize our next move before we can move on together." Victor takes a deep breath, attempting to calm himself as she inquires, "What are you going to do?"

"I'm going to find her." Victor firmly replies.

"Why?" Damian questions, uncaring to his claim.

"Because, she'd find me." Victor professes with a calm tone as he looks into the dreary night sky, "It appears I'm not alone in this world like I originally thought."

"What do you mean?" Elena cautiously inquires.

Victor turns to face her once more, looking intense and queries, "How could you miss a group of slaves being held captive here? And why didn't you tell me there were others like me?"

Shocked by his intense approach, Elena looks away shamefully, and mutters, "I'm sorry, I didn't know."

Victor looks at her with a pained expression then drops the dark crystal shard to the ground and suddenly takes off into the sky, surrounded by energetic lightning. Everyone looks on in disappointment as Adrian swings his arm back in anger, and arrogantly exclaims, "Well good riddance to him!"

"We better head back to the outpost where it's safe for now." Yuri informs as he powers down his Gauntlet. "And if I know Kael, he should still be up there waiting for us." Marcus surely states while powering down as well. As everyone heads back towards the second Arch ship, Elena stands frozen, still looking into the sky for a moment in distress. "I'm so sorry, Victor." She whispers, "I thought you were different."

As Elena turns her attention back, she sees the dark crystal shard still lying on the ground where Victor dropped it and kneels to pick it up. After examining it closely, she places it in her garb for safekeeping and takes off with the others back to their ship to rendezvous at the Archadian outpost with Kael.

Sometime later, the distraught team arrives at the Archadian outpost above Pretoria to assess the damage. Marcus and Yuri depart the ship and head to the armory followed closely by Valorie and Vennessa. Distressed, Elena enters the main chamber and falls to her knees, feeling she failed to honor her crown as Damian and Adrian enter seconds afterward. Attempting to regain her Angelic composure, Elena closes her eyes and tries to meditate as Adrian takes off his Gauntlet and throws it against the wall in anger. Damian follows suit as he pounds a crystalline table and leans over it in anger of their defeat. Sensing their internal struggle, Elena quickly opens her eyes while turning her head and sighs disappointedly. Moments later, Kael enters the chamber as Damian and Adrian look upon him with concern.

"Oh great, that's all we need." Adrian scoffs impatiently.

"I had half expected this operation to run smoothly." Kael states, "What took you so long?"

"Let's just say they don't scare so easily," Adrian comments, "At least not in the way we thought they would. The Arch also forgot to mention one of their security precautions against such ferocity."

"You're back much later than the Arch expected." Kael denotes then quickly demands, "Damage report!"

Trying not to let Kael see his troubled composure, Damian straightens up and informs, "We ran into some trouble, but I'm sure you already knew that."

"Not in the way you might think." Kael utters, "What happened?"

Elena stands up and faces Kael, feeling the weight of the outcome entirely on her shoulders. "Needless to say, they got careless, therefore we had no choice but to diffuse the situation." She explains, "As we expected, the distress call was trap. We were all ambushed, and barely escaped with our lives."

"They attacked without provocation, though fortunately for us we were able to cope with them." Damian chimes in, trying to justify their defeat.

"And not by much from what I saw." Elena mentions to their annoyance. She then looks back at Kael and states; "We wanted to know if they had improved their tactics, guess we have our answer now."

Surprised by this news, Kael sternly surmises, "And the results I assume were quite drastic. But you've only just begun to witness their extreme savagery, for none of you have yet to even see half of what they can truly do."

"I think it's safe to say we've seen enough already, for we have met the enemy up close and it is quite fierce!" Adrian begrudgingly comments, "A war was started here today and we didn't even fire the first shot."

Elena nods in response, and clarifies, "They weren't trying to determine our intent, they simply wanted to see who would strike first."

"Definite proof of their savagery." Damian crossly remarks, "Their power is far more reaching than anyone we've ever encountered."

"Perhaps it is the notion of raw power that keeps their agenda hidden and somewhat immortal." Elena explains with concern evident in her voice, "For years there's been barely a whisper out of them."

Adrian holds his hand up before him, gripping his fist tightly then snarls, "And for no apparent reason, they seem to be back with a roar."

Alarmed, Kael looks upon the trio and asks, "How could this happen?"

"It appears we all became distracted." Elena reluctantly admits.

"Considering the amount of training you've all had together, I didn't think that was even possible for someone of your caliber." Kael states.

"Neither did I, but it's all about the Artifact." Elena informs, "That's what they wanted and that's what they have." She looks away and states, "Seems we greatly underestimated our enemy, which has cost us dearly."

"Yeah, no thanks to Zyas!" Adrian cynically scoffs.

Elena glances at Adrian with discontent as Kael looks around with concern and inquires, "If Victor's gone, where's Talia then?"

Sighing disappointedly, Elena reluctantly replies, "They took her, it's my fault. I shouldn't have left her behind the way I did."

"And Victor?" Kael hesitantly asks.

"Probably hiding like a coward!" Adrian frustratingly mocks.

Elena scowls upon him, and exclaims, "Adrian enough already!"

Angered, Damian steps between them with his arms extended and argues, "He fled when we needed him the most, Elena!"

"I don't believe that!" Kael firmly proclaims.

Annoyed by his claim, Adrian scoffs as he approaches Kael, saying, "Believe what you want, *old man*, but he wasn't there!"

"That doesn't sound like him at all." Kael justifies while shaking his head in disbelief, "Something must have drawn him away; something you all apparently missed."

"We didn't miss anything!" Damian firmly responds.

Feeling shameful, Elena looks upon Kael and calmly articulates, "We found him afterwards; harsh things were said, and he left." Kael sighs disappointedly and says, "I hate to say it, but I'm very disappointed in all of you!"

"For getting our asses kicked, or ridding ourselves of the weak link?" Adrian irately grunts. Taking this moment to teach them all a valuable lesson, Kael patiently explains, "Defeat is nothing more than education at this point, the first step to something better. And being a team isn't about reputation or status, it's about doing what's best for everyone, not just yourselves."

Damian and Adrian glance at each other then sigh impatiently.

"Being the warriors that you are, you think you can't make mistakes, but you're wrong about that." Kael sternly points out.

"Are we?" Damian selfishly inquires, thinking this is all Victor's fault.

"To lead a team, you must be calm and detached, but right now none of you have that anymore than him apparently." Kael states as he approaches them, "You must never confuse your feelings with your sacred duty." Elena glances at her colleagues, feeling shameful as they try not to speak out of line in his presence. "It's impossible for someone to be right all the time you know?" Kael stresses. Confused by his profound statement, Damian faces him and peevishly asks, "Are you saying that this is all just a simple misunderstanding? Over one's misguided conscience?"

"It wasn't simple, not for him anyway." Kael sternly informs, "The fine line between love and hate is actually quite small." Damian and Adrian glance at each other with concern as Elena listens closely. "It was probably all he had left to hang onto." He continues, "Deep down, I think his hatred has been the only thing that's kept him going all this time, till now that is."
Adrian scoffs, saying, "Sounds like nothing but superstitious garbage to me!"
Annoyed by his arrogance, Kael looks directly at him and says, "So you think, but if you let that kind of mentality get to you then you've already lost."

"Oh yeah?" Adrian scornfully retorts, "Lost to what exactly?"

"On the battlefield, a soldier never questions why they're fighting." Kael explains with a stern tone, then motions towards each of them and states, "The outcome of this battle was decided beforehand when you chose to let your petty differences get in the way."

"So what are we fighting for then?" Damian edgily inquires.
Facing the Eudenian Champion, Kael implies, "In time you'll see."
Expecting clarification, Adrian questions, "Answer me this, General, who exactly do you think we are?"

"We are warriors, hired by a noble cause." Kael enlightens as he approaches the entrance overlooking the sky with his arms crossed behind his back, "But a true warrior fights not because they hate the one in front of them, but because they love those left behind them." He then turns back and finishes, "We still have power and an enemy that threatens to destroy us, what more reason do we need at this point?" Damian and Adrian glance at Elena, unsure of how to strategize without Victor present. "Being challenged in life is inevitable, being defeated is optional." Kael harshly implies, "Though if you prefer, you can always return home and forget this whole thing altogether."

"That won't be necessary, General, for we are all capable of exercising self-discipline." Damian calmly defends, "I hate to admit it, but without Zyas, we are in a very serious and potentially dangerous situation."

"Which is why I implore you all do something about it." Kael adds, "We're a team which makes us family now so start acting like one."
Realizing them to be hesitant on the matter, Elena steps forward, "He's right you guys!" She stops beside Kael and finishes, "We have to make this right!"

"It is crucial for a team to function well, and it always starts with the leader." Kael proclaims whilst trying to get through to them.

"Or one with the most heart to set the overall tone, just like music in a sense." Elena chimes in encouragingly with a calm demeanor.

Kael turns to face her directly and states, "At the moment, it is you who is setting the tone." Elena grins in response to his inspiring remark, as Damian nods in agreement. "To fight the enemy, you must first understand the enemy." Kael further explains, "But you can't possibly expect to understand the enemy if at first you aren't willing to understand each other." The trio shares a glance with one another, realizing that he speaks the truth.

"When a team is strong, nothing can ever defeat it." He resumes, "Despite your differences, you must learn to work together, when you do, each individual will be a link in a chain that will be stronger than crystal itself." Damian looks away, contemplating his words carefully as Kael notifies; "You cannot possibly retaliate against the enemy if you let him go."

"I've already sent Valorie and Vennessa to help find him." Elena informs with slight hesitation.

"That's not good enough!" Kael replies as he shares a firm glance at each person present then finishes, "You all know what has to be done as well as I do, for we cannot allow egos to deter us from our ultimate goal." Elena glances at Damian and Adrian as they look back with determination. "The situation is grim, but right now it's preceded by a resting state." Kael implies. Adrian nods in agreement and says, "The calm before the storm."

"That's right, let's use this calm while it's still dormant." Kael says with a grin, "Setbacks are only temporary as long as you don't give up."

Now determined, Adrian walks over to pick up his Gauntlet off the floor and places it back over his arm, saying, "This encounter took almost everything we had. I don't know how we're going to handle the next one."

Everyone glances at each other as Damian unexpectedly prepares to take his leave, "Let's not wait around then." He declares, "I'll do it."

Surprised by his sudden change of heart, Elena looks upon Damian who prepares his Gauntlet by grabbing a few new crystal shards to power it up.

"Are you sure?" Kael respectfully asks.

Damian shakes his head and calmly replies, "No, but it feels right."

"Better you than me," Adrian says sarcastically, "Two hot heads don't mix very well considering the circumstances."

"Well in this case, let's hope that cooler heads prevail then." Damian responds, "We've been compromised by a force of unknown size and intent. We're still the first line of defense, so we must assume the worst." He claims.

Elena nods in agreement as Damian nods back in respect then leaves to find Victor aboard a small Archadian ship. Still disappointed in their attitude towards his lifelong protégé, Kael looks upon Adrian and Elena in a stern manner for a brief moment then takes his leave as well.

As Adrian prepares for combat, Elena looks into the night sky in sorrow, hoping to make amends with Victor for their thoughtless judgment upon him.

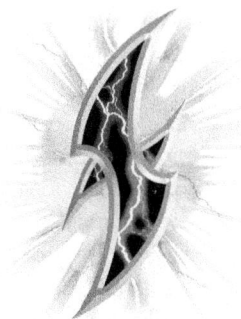

CH: 44
THE DARK AND THE DANGEROUS

Back at the Darchadian fortress beneath the surface of Pretoria, Raiven and Celeste arrive with Talia in their custody before Traganus in his throne room as he looks upon them in annoyance.

"Well, is this it?" He sternly inquires.

Raiven and Celeste nod sheepishly as Traganus looks upon Talia in curiosity of her presence. Annoyed, Traganus points firmly towards her, and questions, "You mean to tell me this is the only remnant of our enemy?" Sighing impatiently, Raiven and Celeste glance at each other for a moment then shove Talia to the ground as she looks upon him in fear. "I suppose one is better than none." Traganus murmurs as he stands from his crystalline throne and approaches them.

Out of anger, Talia suddenly jumps to her feet and attempts to strike, but is stopped by his energy aura as he waves his hand in front of her. Traganus looks upon her curiously as she looks back in shock of his Darchadian power.

"You know for an Archling, you're a little confident, aren't you?" Traganus mocks with a curious expression. Struggling to break free, Talia scowls back as he grins. Intrigued, he suddenly forces Talia back onto the ground then calmly kneels before her. "Seems you didn't come back as empty handed after all, sisters." Traganus commends.

Raiven grins, confident of Talia's capture as Celeste frowns upon her. Traganus waves his hand over Talia's face as she stares back, concerned for her life. "I sense much power in this one, she'll make a fine addition to our ever-growing clan." He proclaims, "You belong to me now!"

Talia scowls back, and exclaims, "My friends would not approve!"

Confident of his position over her, Traganus crudely informs, "Your friends have deserted you, they're not coming back."

"He'll come for me!" Talia boldly asserts, "I know he will!"

Amused by her strong-willed claim, Traganus chuckles softly then curiously inquires, "And who might that be I wonder?"

"My dearest friend, who else?" Talia proudly retorts.

"It appears you have no friends, but you soon will." Traganus cynically states as he stands and turns away towards his crystalline throne.

"I do have a friend and his name is Victor!" Talia exclaims as Raiven and Celeste attempt to hold her back. Her anger causes the entire chamber to darken which catches Traganus' full attention as he stops in his tracks, then turns and looks upon her with great surprise.

"How unfortunate." He says as he looks towards Raiven and Celeste in annoyance, then mutters, "Seems our Intel has been slightly misplaced."

Disgusted by his dark presence, Talia looks around for a moment and sees dozens of captured human slaves hanging in their cages including Tristan and Michael. Sensing Talia's intuitive observation, Traganus looks upon her and says, "You're probably wondering why I have so many."

Surprised by his remark, Talia glances back at him and replies, "Yes!"

"They were merely a gift from someone very important, a token of appreciation for my good deeds." Traganus proudly reveals.

Concerned for her friends, Talia disputes, "You must have great need to see all of us suffer like this!"

"Ha!" Traganus scoffs as he sits back down in his crystalline throne, "I need nothing of the sort!"

"Liar!" Talia cries furiously while trying to break loose from Raiven and Celeste's grip, "Let me go!"

Traganus shakes his head confidently and states, "Not yet."

"Whatever it is you're after, they won't give you what you want!" She shouts angrily on the Arch's behalf.

"Oh, and what is that?" Traganus humorously inquires.

"To break their spirit of course!" Talia snaps.

Chuckling once again, Traganus with a snide grin responds, "You think that's what I really want?" He uses his dark energy to make Talia float before him once again, pulling her from Raiven and Celeste's grip then explains, "If breaking their spirit will suffice, then that's what I'll have, as well as yours."

"Never!" Talia cries, her voice echoing throughout the chamber.

With his patience wearing thin, Traganus firmly retorts, "Perhaps you can join the rest of them until you learn some manners, *girl!*"

Traganus suddenly drops Talia to the ground and signals another Darchadian to take her away. Looking back in anger, Talia keeps her focus on him and shouts, "He'll come for me! He'll come and take me away, to paradise!"

As the Darchadian leaves the chamber with Talia held tightly in her grip, Traganus stands from his crystalline throne once again, looking upon his two female associates and asks, "Have you located the second Artifact?"

"Not yet, we traced its signal, but are unable to take possession of it at this time." Celeste replies, "Thanks to the Champions standing in our way."

"Really, is that all?" Traganus sternly inquires.

Sighing in response, Celeste reluctantly admits, "Unfortunately no; our opponents gave us more trouble than we thought we could handle."

With a curious face, Traganus probes, "What do you mean they gave you trouble, what kind of trouble?"

"We fought the Archadians, and while our numbers were greater, still they overpowered us." Raiven attempts to justify, "We thought it wise to return alive and gather a larger force in retaliation."

"So, they remain free?" Traganus contests with a disgruntled tone, "You're both aware of the penalty for failure."

"Give us one more chance, and we will succeed!" Raiven pleads.

"I am not in the giving vein, this day or any other." Traganus firmly warns, "You're Angels are weak, it's no surprise that your mission failed!"

"Forgive us, Lord Traganus." Raiven defends, "We had them on the defense, and still they attacked strong and fierce."

"They descended several of us in the process!" Celeste chimes in.

With a cold shoulder, Traganus walks past the deadly duo, and questions, "They defeated you, and yet you alone escaped?"

Raiven and Celeste sigh impatiently, annoyed by his unwillingness to understand their position on the matter. As Traganus steps towards a large window, he looks upon the fleet of Darchadians below in cryo-sleep, and says, "It is good that I have a loyal batch still asleep, awaiting their awakening to succeed you both should you falter again."

"With all do respect, Master!" Raiven finally snaps, "It appears neither side had correct operational knowledge."

"We did what we could and got out, simple as that!" Celeste defensively adds to support her claim.

"Seeing as how you were allowed to stage the assault yourselves, why didn't you finish them off then?" Traganus furiously inquires.

"It seems apparent, but we would've died trying!" Raiven attempts to clarify before regaining her composure, "Besides, someone else interfered."

Traganus turns his head from the window, and asks, "Really, is that so?"

"Listen to her!" Celeste exclaims as she approaches Traganus, "Our sister speaks the truth! We couldn't have anticipated the Princess of all people showing up at the temple when she did!"

"The Princess, huh?" Traganus queries, sounding intrigued.

Raiven nods in response and replies, "You heard right!"

"Given her current status with the world congress, her interference should be of no surprise to either of you." Traganus points out as he turns away from the window and approaches them intensely, "You've been trained for such contingencies, have you not?"

The troublemaking sisters glance at each other and sigh impatiently.

"Yes, but we've never seen nor encountered an enemy like this before." Celeste defines, "Their size, their strength, they're not typical warriors, they appear to be beyond that."

"That's unacceptable!" Traganus warns while violently raising his voice, which darkens the entire chamber slightly and immediately silences his two sassy officers. "I expect you to complete your mission, therefore I don't want to hear anymore excuses!"

Annoyed by his aggressive reaction to their pleas, Raiven and Celeste scowl while trying to keep their strong composure in his powerful presence.

"Despite what the people of Earth may think, I don't believe in fairy tales." Traganus enlightens after calming himself, "It's what society has reduced our people to; nothing more than a forgotten myth lost in shadow." He then turns away and adds, "The world we currently reside in has many laws, but all written by feeble gods and men. And because of that, power can change everything in the blink of an eye. Thus, the fallen shall rise again; during which time, I shall wreak terrible vengeance upon the entire planet."

Dropping to her knees with Celeste following suit beside her, Raiven respectfully requests, "Please, Master, we beg your forgiveness."

"As do all of us who wish to faithfully serve only you." Celeste adds.

"It would be a pity to waste our talents." Raiven rationalizes.

"Save your pity for yourself if you fail again." Traganus warns.

Feeling reassured by his sudden change in attitude, Raiven and Celeste cool down with a sigh of relief as Traganus turns his head and orders, "Take what troops and resources you need to resolve this matter personally."

"We were not suggesting that we go back out there so soon." Raiven cautiously defends.

"Then you should not have spoken!" Traganus snaps, "Capture these so-called Champions, however you can. Use innocent people as bait if you must." He then waves his hand forward and commands, "Leave immediately! When you find them, signal back and an attack force will join you shortly, or I will follow myself if need be."

Raiven and Celeste bow their heads in respect, both saying, "Yes, Master."

Traganus turns to face them once more with a stern look, and proudly declares, "Soon we will rule this planet, for no one will stop us in our quest to reclaim absolute victory from the Arch, as well as the Gods themselves."

Raiven and Celeste bow once again in respect then quickly take their leave as Traganus looks on with confidence of his peoples' future, assuming the pair can handle things on their own without his direct involvement.

CH: 45
THE STORM WITHIN

Somewhere near the outskirts of Pretoria, beyond the now destroyed Archadian Temple, a despondent Victor flees in search of his dearest friend, Talia. After making his rounds above the surface from above, he lands on the edge of a cliff and looks out onto the horizon in a crouched position. While observing his Gauntlet intensely, Victor sighs disappointedly from his failure to use it properly to prevent Talia's capture. Turning his attention behind him, he sees the same statue with broken wings and approaches it. Hesitant to touch it, Victor caresses his hand over the name, *VICTORIA* engraved on the statue's base, disheartened by the fact that he'll never meet his real mother. He then sits in front of it on the ground to gather his thoughts while looking into the thunderous night sky overhead. Moments later, Damian suddenly appears and finds Victor sitting near the Angelic statue, hoping to work things out with him personally.

"I know you're there so if you've got something to say just say it and be done with it." Victor grumbles.

"You're not going to find your answers out here, you know that." Damian respectfully informs.

Victor faces him, surprised by his presence, then turns back in annoyance. "Leave me alone, Damian!" He gripes, "I feel bad enough as it is!"

Damian slowly approaches him, calmly saying, "I know, I was hoping you'd come to your senses by now."

"Forget it, I'm not going back!" Victor impatiently retorts. He looks back at Damian and states, "If you're so eager to die, then go right ahead, but I've still got something to live for!"

"We all have something to live for, Victor." Damian infers.

Sulking from his previous humiliation, Victor professes, "I screwed up, I don't belong on the team anymore! I'm a freak, and don't belong anywhere!"

Surprised by his response, Damian reminds, "You may not be like us, but you swore an oath just like everyone else."

"It's your team, not mine." Victor grumbles.

"I can't believe I'm even saying this, but we need each other if we are to overcome this dark adversary." Damian reluctantly points out.

"I need no one!" Victor snaps.

"Don't push your luck any farther than you're capable!" Damian quickly counters, "When something bad happens you can let it define you, destroy you, or you can let it strengthen you."

While observing his Eudenian comrade as if to size him up, Victor firmly denotes, "You seem to have walked away just fine."

"You have a problem with that?" Damian scoffs in annoyance.

"Call me old fashioned, but I'm not too sure I can a trust anyone without a dark side no matter how good they seem to be on the outside." He spitefully implies.

"Let's just say you haven't seen it yet!" Damian argues edgily.

Trying to diffuse the argument, Victor angrily justifies, "Fear drives all men, and right now, I'm in the grip of forces you couldn't possibly understand."

"Cut the crap!" Damian argues, annoyed by his attitude, "We can't trust your senses anymore, your taste for darkness has screwed them up."

Now angered, Victor stands up as he looks upon Damian eye-to-eye, and exclaims, "My senses are fine!"

Damian extends his arm; signaling Victor to keep at bay and firmly cautions, "Back off! I didn't come here to fight!"

"Then what did you come here for?" Victor disputes as he steps past Damian towards the edge of the cliff.

Following his movement, Damian replies, "I simply came here to reason with you, but I see that's not possible at this point."

"And why is that I wonder?" Victor snaps as he turns his head back.

Annoyed by Victor's constant negative attitude, Damian approaches him from behind, and strictly contends, "Hey! Stop complaining! The Arch believes there's a great power sleeping inside you. So use it, rely on it, face your fears with dignity, as we all have to do."

"What are you getting at?" Victor questions irritably as he faces Damian from the cliff.

"You'll laugh at your fears when you find out who you really are." Damian states as he stands beside Victor overlooking the horizon from the cliff, "Don't quit what's right for you or others just because it isn't easy. It's time to grow up and handle things for yourself."

Victor scoffs in response, saying, "Unlike you, I've never had the leisure of handling things myself. I know all about the rules, and your world has lots of them. There hasn't been a time when someone hasn't told me what to do."

Damian sighs impatiently, realizing he's still unable to get through to him.

"I'm half human, remember?" Victor infers while stepping closer to him, "Is that why you still won't accept me for who I am? Well, is it?"

Disappointed, Damian looks directly at him, and clarifies, "With the way you've been acting, it's you we can't entirely trust. Your actions alone have been a source of contention in this team that have put others including yourself at risk."

"You're just like everyone else, you know that?" Victor sneers, "You think the whole world revolves around you, don't you?" Damian scowls in annoyance as Victor circles around him on the cliff, and mocks, "As if there aren't enough people without guidance through problems of their own!" Damian looks away, sighing impatiently once again as Victor continues to rationalize, "People everywhere are suffering, while you and everyone else are ordered to look the other way and pretend it doesn't exist!"

"Stay on point, Victor!" Damian maintains, "This isn't about them, it's about you. All you can think about right now is yourself!"

"Is that a crime on this planet?" Victor defends, "Nobody else ever thought about me, so as far as I'm concerned I don't' need anyone else!"

"As much as I hate to admit it, you need us, and we need you." Damian calmly points out, trying to diffuse his anger.

Victor stops in his tracks, coldly facing him and exclaims, "Yeah well guess what? I was doing just fine until I met you!"

"You think your actions qualify as just fine?" Damian argues as the tension rises, "Going a-wall whilst risking the safety of our team? I mean come on, who are you trying to kid here?"

"What do you want from me?" Victor questions furiously.

"You still don't get it, do you?" Damian sternly counters.

Victor offensively points towards him and angrily contends, "Don't push it, Damian! You can't expect me to come back and fall in line again like a mindless soldier!"

"You want to know the difference between a soldier and a warrior?" Damian contests, "A soldier is given orders and simply does what he is told, whereas a warrior already knows what to do and does only what is right."

"I am doing what's right!" Victor snaps as Damian scowls in response, feeling completely insulted at this point. "I have faith in something far greater than that, always have!" He continues harshly.

As a violent storm draws overhead with a rumble of thunder, the pair begins to circle around each other as Damian defensively retorts, "My faith as a leader is what guides me, and this soldier didn't have to come all the way out here to find you! Why do you challenge this?"

"I don't put my faith in anything that selfishly puts a man on his knees!" Victor exclaims, unwilling to back down.

"No man fears to kneel before that which he trusts." Damian disputes with a calmer tone as he motions towards the Angelic statue, "Without faith or belief in something, what are we?" Victor looks away in anger towards the statue whilst pondering the thought. "Besides, you seem to have no problem praying the Gods!" Damian mockingly continues as he points toward the Gods' symbol over Victor's chest.

Glancing at the symbol over his chest, Victor sighs in sorrow then turns his attention back towards Damian in anger, breathing heavily.

"Yeah, well whoever said I wanted to be lead in the first place?" He shouts, "I'm better off calling my own shots, so you better get used to it!"

"I'll get used to it when you start calling the right shots!" Damian begrudgingly informs.

"Give me a break!" Victor barks, extreme anger evident in his voice.

"I'll give you the facts!" Damian proudly argues, "You're far from ready!" Stepping between Victor and the statue, he finishes, "You're impatient and hot tempered, but lastly and more importantly, I'm better than you and you know it!"

Victor chuckles in response, saying, "You know something, Damian, you may be right about a lot of things, but I have to disagree with you on that one!"

Positioning himself in a battle stance, Victor stands ready to fight as Damian shakes his head and pleas, "Don't do it, Zyas, you're better than this."

Victor powers up in anger as energetic lightning begins to surround his body then declares, "I'm done taking orders from the world, *Trag*, especially you!"

Without warning, Victor suddenly strikes Damian in the chest, knocking him back into the statue, breaking it in two. Surprised by his intense rage, Damian realizes he'll have to knock some sense into him the hard way. With his wings activated, Victor turns his back towards Damian who quickly pulls himself up from the debris caused by the statue.

"Stay out of my way!" Victor viciously threatens, "I'm warning you!"

As Damian rises to his feet and swings his purple cape over his shoulder, he looks upon Victor and contests, "Are you threatening me?"

Catching Damian off guard, Victor turns back to face him with eyes glowing and furiously states, "You bet I am!"

Accepting his challenge, Damian powers up as he slowly steps away from the broken statue and approaches Victor. The rain falls heavy with lightning filling up the sky, followed by a loud rumble of thunder as Victor and Damian stand in battle stances for a moment then suddenly rush towards each other and the fight begins. The two warriors display tremendous strength with semi-equal fighting prowess as they try their best to subdue each other.

"You think toying with my anger is funny?" Victor yells as he attempts to strike several times, putting Damian on the defensive.

"There's nothing funny about anger," Damian calmly retorts, "But once it consumes you, then soon enough..." Victor strikes again, but misses as Damian quickly dodges behind him and sternly finishes, "You lose sight of everything, including yourself." Infuriated, Victor's eyes light up as he quickly turns to strike but misses again as Damian strikes him back instead.

Damian then grabs Victor's wings and tosses him to the side, causing him to yell in anger. Ready for more, Damian stands ready as Victor attempts to strike once again, this time locking hands with the Eudenian Champion in a true show of force, both trying to over power each other whilst causing an energy wake around them that causes the ground beneath their feet to crack. Damian looks on with a concerned expression as Victor's rage intensifies, which inevitably allows him to subdue him on the ground. Victor stares onto Damian in anger with glowing eyes then after a few seconds, he realizes that his rage almost got the best of him. As his eyes begin to dim, Victor backs off for a moment in shock. Damian takes this moment to pull himself off the ground, breathing heavily as he places his hand over his shoulder to wear off the soreness caused from the fight.

"It's over, Victor." Damian calmly relieves, "Let it go."

Feeling shameful over his actions towards his comrade, Victor observes his hands for a moment before him then closes his eyes in despair.

"May the Gods forgive me." He whispers, "I'm sorry."

Damian is surprised by his sudden change in attitude, as Victor opens his eyes and spreads his wings. Victor flees to get away from the pain within as Damian raises his hand to stop him, and calls, "Victor, wait!"

Victor flies into the stormy sky with tears in his eyes whilst breathing heavily. Damian looks away towards the broken Angel statue, feeling he failed to get through to him after all. A sudden high-pitched hiss grabs his attention as he quickly turns with his Gauntlet aimed.

"Why hello." Raiven sneers, "Out on night maneuvers, are we?"

"Not exactly!" Damian sternly retorts, keeping his guard up.

"The Eudenian Champion, all by himself?" Raiven taunts.

Realizing that he's surrounded by Raiven and several other Darchadians, Damian looks around then warns, "Don't think me defenseless!"

"Oh, but you are!" Raiven scornfully teases. Preparing for the worst, Damian readies his Gauntlet as the Darchadians hiss.

"Take him out, now!" She wrathfully demands.

Damian suddenly fires upon Raiven with an energy blast, knocking her back and defends himself against the other furious Darchadians. He fares well for a moment until Raiven suddenly strikes him in the chest with a negative energy attack. Raiven laughs as Damian drops to his knees from his Soul Gear suddenly malfunctioning, causing him to grunt in pain.

"What do you want with me?" He frustratingly inquires.

Raiven approaches him with a devious grin on her face and happily informs, "Our Master has a message for you and your people. One he would like to give personally." Damian tries to blast Raiven again but misses as the Darchadians finally subdue him. From a distance, Victor hears Damian yelling in agony then quickly turns back and calls, "Oh no, Damian!" Victor flies towards his location at full speed, hoping to help him before it's too late.

"Hang on brother!" He frantically yells.

Damian is taken aboard Raiven's ship along with the other Darchadians as Victor flies towards it. Angering Damian, Raiven waves his Gauntlet in front of him, saying, "Not so tough without your Gauntlet, are you?"

"Whatever you have planned for me, know that my people won't stand for this!" Damian angrily retorts.

"Just accept the fact the no one is coming after you." Raiven scorns.

Suddenly, a rumble is heard outside the ship as Raiven and Damian look around curiously. Realizing who it is, Damian grins with confidence and surely mutters, "Sounds like someone is."

Raiven looks upon Damian and scoffs then turns to address a couple of Darchadians, "Take care of it!" She orders.

The Darchadians nod in response then take their leave towards the ship's exterior. Raiven turns back and glances at Damian who grins. Outside, Victor grabs on to the ship's hull in an attempt to save his comrade as a few Darchadians rise to the surface and try to blast him away. The Darchadians lose site of him as he quickly maneuvers around the ship and takes them out one by one. The ship vibrates from the commotion outside as Raiven looks around in anger, then shouts, "He's still out there!"

"It's the hybrid, we're having trouble tracking him!" one of the Darchadians aboard the ship reluctantly informs.

Raiven sighs in annoyance then quickly takes her leave to the settle the matter personally. Damian looks upward toward the ship's hull, hoping Victor is successful in his rescue attempt. Outside of the ship, Victor makes his way towards the front as Raiven suddenly appears behind him.

"Hoping to save your friend?" She taunts with a devilish smirk.

Victor quickly turns and looks upon her in anger as he powers up.

"Such a noble creature, and pathetic!" Raiven mocks as she stands atop the ship, "I didn't know there were humans in service to the Arch."

"As far as I know, I'm the only one!" Victor says determinedly.

Victor attempts to strike Raiven but is pushed back by a sudden energy blast from her Gauntlet. Chuckling, Raiven approaches Victor whilst floating in the air with her wings, and says, "A half breed spawn of a human and an Angel?" Attempting to strategize his next move, Victor stands his ground as he balances himself atop the ship.

"I've heard tales of your kind, but have never seen one before." Raiven remarks as she readies her Gauntlet.

"Oh well, you're still going to die regardless." Raiven suddenly fires an energy blast as Victor quickly maneuvers out of the way and finally strikes her in the face. As she looks upon him in fury, Victor smirks and exclaims, "Take that you bitch!"

"How dare you!" Raiven furiously spits as she places her hand over her face then immediately strikes him back towards the ship's edge. Struggling to hold on, Victor attempts to fly as Raiven places her foot on his hand.

"Humans, not only useless in battle but completely helpless as well." She scorns venomously, "I know somewhere you can go!" Victor looks upon Raiven with determination as she fires an energy blast, forcing him downward away from the ship. "That'll teach him!" She confidently mutters while turning back towards the ship's hull. After crashing into the rocky mountain top below, Victor pulls himself up and sees the ship flying into the distance, realizing he can't catch up to it in time. Angered over Damian's capture, Victor pounds the ground furiously with his fists, and yells, "No!"
While looking upon the bright moon piercing through the stormy sky in despair, Victor falls to his knees, feeling he failed once again.

Back at the Archadian outpost above Pretoria, Elena stands beside a crystalline pillar on the balcony of the armory whilst staring into the stormy night sky, concerned for Victor and Talia's safety.

"I hope you find her, wherever you are." She whispers.
Reaching her hands out, she allows the rain to fall into her palms then calmly wipes the cold sweat off of her face whilst brushing her fingers through her hair. After taking in the cool purified air from the falling rain, Elena steps back into the armory from the balcony, whilst observing the pink Gods' symbol on her Gauntlet as she gently caresses it with her fingers.

Within the Darchadian fortress, Talia sits in one of the many cages hanging from the ceiling along with Tristan and Michael. Talia carves the Gods' symbol into the door panel with the Angel figure's wings whilst humming Victor's tune. She then places her hand on the carved symbol surrounded by Angelic wings and sighs in despair. Tristan coughs from the pain of starvation whilst lying down next to Michael as Talia picks up a jug of water sitting in the cage and rushes to their side with it.

"Here, drink this." She caringly urges, "Save your strength."
Tristan takes a small drink from the water jug and looks upon her for a moment in appreciation. He then pushes the water jug back and turns the other way as Michael shares a disappointed expression with her. Talia looks away in distress, feeling helpless as Tristan continues to cough violently.

"Hang in there, alright?" Talia says gently.

Tristan and Michael look away in sorrow of their capture as they try to sleep away their misery in the cage. Talia senses Victor's pain as she looks around and sees others held captive well. After studying her dark surroundings, she looks downward and sees a legion of Darchadians gathering in the center of the chamber. Unexpectedly, Lithia appears before her and chirps as she looks upon him in relief through the cage.

"Lithia!" She says quietly, "How did you find me?"
Lithia chirps once again as he attempts to break her free by biting the energy bars. Talia sighs disappointedly, knowing Lithia isn't strong enough to break the cage just yet. While panting, Lithia stands on one of the energy bars as Talia pets his head to comfort him.

"I appreciate your help, Lithia, but you must leave this place at once." She sadly advises. As Lithia continues to pant, he looks upon her with a concerned expression. "Find Victor, he'll know what to do!" She whispers. Determined, Lithia chirps then quickly takes off to find Victor as requested. Talia sighs in relief of his safety then turns her attention back towards the bottom of the chamber and looks on curiously. The Darchadian fleet bows in unison as Traganus enters the chamber. Raiven enters the chamber shortly after with Damian in her grasp and shoves him aggressively to the ground. Traganus looks upon Damian in delight as he looks back in annoyance.

"Well done, sister." Traganus compliments.
Raiven bows her head in respect, as Celeste stands by, annoyed by her sister's praise. Talia looks on from her cage in panic and whispers, "Oh no!"
Damian looks around the chamber, trying to assess the situation as Traganus approaches him, "Who is this hybrid?" He sternly inquires, "What's he doing with a team like this?" Damian looks upon him and scoffs, unwilling to answer. Angered by his lack of cooperation, Traganus suddenly grabs Damian by the throat and holds him up before everyone in the chamber to see.

"You will answer!" He furiously exclaims. Still refusing to answer, Damian grunts in pain. "Then hang with the rest of them until you break!" Traganus threatens before violently throwing Damian to the ground with great intensity, causing Raiven and Celeste to grin. Damian grunts again from the pain as Talia continues to watch, concerned for Victor's colleague. Traganus turns and looks upon the Darchadian fleet as well as the slaves hanging from their cages who look back in fear.

"Do not forget why you've all been chosen!" He firmly announces, "You are here because the outside world enslaves you! This is your family! Rise now, or fall forever!" Talia grips the bars of her cage as she listens carefully. "They have their army, we have ours!" Traganus adds as he motions towards his Darchadian fleet. "Let this be thy first decree; those who do not pledge themselves to me shall be destroyed as the new age begins." The Darchadians chant in response, signifying their dominant status as he explains, "What I offer you is simply the gift of freedom!"

"Freedom from tyrannical dreams, laws, and gods!" The slaves look on in fear whilst pondering his provocative statement, "It is not merely that we search for a purpose, but that our destiny is calling for us!" He continues as he holds his hands out before him, gripping his fists tightly, "I myself have paid the price for such vindication, in blood, tears, and broken dreams!"

Raiven and Celeste glance at one another as if to size each other up.

"Unlike the Arch, who demands that you kneel before them and the Gods, I require only that you stand!" Traganus proposes as Talia looks on curiously whilst pondering his words as well, "The least of us survive the uncaring world by earning the right to bear Darchadian wings, for we work in the dark to uphold the light!" Traganus firmly declares while gazing upon the slaves intensely who look back fearfully. After a long pause, Traganus' eyes light up brightly in red as he straightens up his torso and proudly concludes, "Forever be accepted, or forever be forgotten!"

Traganus takes his leave as the Darchadian fleet disperses within the fortress. Raiven stops to look at Celeste in disappointment as she stares back in annoyance, then spitefully teases, "Well sis, it looks like you failed to bag your prize once again." Celeste's face cringes with anger as Raiven persists with a devious grin, "I believe that's two for me, and none for you."

Raiven begins to chuckle and walks off to follow Traganus as Celeste yells in fury over her defeat. She then turns and sees Talia hanging in her cage from above and grins with an idea. Celeste flies up to the cage unexpectedly and as Talia turns her attention behind her, she looks back in fear as Celeste sneers and attempts to reach for her through the cage. Raiven follows Traganus into his throne room and denotes, "You seem troubled, Master."

"More so than I should be," Traganus professes as he approaches his crystalline throne, "Something about this hybrid vexes me."

"Like what?" Raiven carefully inquires.

Traganus comes to a halt, standing by his throne and firmly replies, "Something familiar, perhaps something from the past."

"If he truly is of Angel descent as you say, he'll likely show up soon enough I'm sure." Raiven assures, attempting to ease his mind.

"I'm expecting so." Traganus says confidently, "We shall make him in our image, and when we are done he will not need to be locked below in the darkness as a criminal like I was, but will join us up above in the light." He divulges, "Fully restored, and we shall embrace him as one of our own."

Concerned by his sentiment, Raiven inquires, "Why is this man so valuable that you continue to spare him?"

"It's possible that he holds the key to our salvation, a power that has been lost between our people for some time now." Traganus clarifies as he turns away, looking upwards with a hardened expression, "May the Gods help him if he cannot provide it for me." Curious to her master's consternation, Raiven looks on as he takes his leave to gather his thoughts in solitude.

As the storm settles above Pretoria near the Archadian outpost, Elena continues staring into the night sky from the balcony of the armory. She observes the full moon illuminating the outpost through the darkened clouds as Kael walks up from behind to address her.

"Do you think he'll come back?" Kael calmly inquires.

Surprised by his presence, Elena quickly turns to acknowledge him then turns back and answers, "I don't know."

"There's no need to worry, believe me, he'll come back when he's good and ready." Kael reassures.

Elena sighs, and mutters, "I truly hope so, but for now I need this time to think, as does he I'm sure."

"What exactly does he need to think about?" Kael carefully asks.

"His life, and why there's any reason for me to be a part of it." Elena reluctantly answers, "Though I hope it doesn't take too terribly long, for if I have to I'll go out there and find him myself."

"Leave it to Victor to find his own path towards those most precious to him." Kael assures, "He gave you his word, didn't he?" Elena nods in response, "As an Angel my dear, you can stake your life on that." He confidently states, "I have a feeling he'll return soon enough."

Turning back to face him once more, Elena calmly asks, "For what?"

"Answers." Kael quickly replies as he steps onto the balcony beside her and clarifies, "The Darchadians will surely be on the hunt for him. But a man like that has a will made of tempered crystal, he'll be extremely difficult to defeat no matter how many mistakes he makes along the way."

Looking distraught from the thought of Victor being harmed, Elena glances at him and softly murmurs, "I hope you're right about that."

"A warrior's path like his is a solitary one," Kael proudly states, "But he's resilient, I'm sure he'll find his way back eventually."

"I pray he does." Elena mutters softly, "His new status in life was never meant to be this difficult, nor mine."

"Perhaps not, but when one such as him builds a life from struggle, their courage never fails." Kael states as he looks upon Elena for a moment, sensing her internal struggle, he then respectfully denotes, "I see you've grown fond of him, that's good."

"Not sure if that's a good thing at this point." Elena says with a dreadful grin, "I've never wanted someone who only knows the light. Is it strange that I'm comforted by the darkness in someone like him?"

Facing her directly, Kael professes, "We all have a side that we try to hide, for it's easy to fall in love with someone who shows you their soul. Which is why I sense your concern for him runs deeper than you've let on, milady."

Elena grins and says, "A keen observation." She then faces him and amusingly retorts, "It's good that you watch over us so diligently, but I fear you watch us too closely sometimes."

"It takes nothing for someone as observant as I to notice such things, Princess." He says while stepping near the balcony's edge, "We don't always get choose the things we believe in, sometimes, they choose us instead."

"I'm sure he admires me as much as I do him." She reveals, "He's a force of nature, for he's determined, and truly unstoppable in some ways."

"Some would call that arrogant." Kael snidely comments.

"He's just strong, inside and out." Elena replies, feeling assured.

"Yeah, that he is." Kael mutters in agreement, "Sometimes if you truly love someone then you must let them go, and if they come back then you'll know it was truly meant to be. In some ways, you can't really explain what you see in a person, but you know deep down that it's there."

"I suppose sometimes it's just the way they take you to another place nobody else can." Elena professes, "No words can fully describe all the feelings I have for him, but to me, love is about being able to see the light inside of a person who sees nothing but darkness."

"Like him?" Kael respectfully probes.

Feeling comforted by his attitude, Elena calmly confesses, "The world is so guarded and fearful; I appreciate his rawness so much and when I'm around him, it feels so right that it scares me. You see, it's the first time in my life that anyone has ever treated me as a woman, and not as some Angelic warrior. In some way, I knew I would become more attracted to him the more we stayed together. I greatly feared it, but in a way, I needed that from him."

"He needed it from you as well." Kael respectfully adds, "Like Talia, I believe you are the light in his darkness, the calm to his storm."

Smiling in response, Elena clarifies, "Perhaps, but you see, he's the only person who doesn't care about my position, not even for personal gain. He simply respects me, not out of fear or lust, but compassion."

Kael nods in agreement then slowly turns and states, "Victor is truly devoted to those he cares about, he needs you."

Shaking her head, Elena looks upon Kael and replies, "No, what Victor needs is a woman, a real woman, not a Princess. He deserves a family, but I don't know if I could ever give him that. At least not in the way he might expect."

"Why not?" Kael carefully probes, "He finds you quite endearing."

Elena looks away and explains, "And I him, but you forget, it's forbidden for me to stray from my sacred duty for such a thing, at least at this point in my life." She then looks directly at him and continues, "But I'm not going to deny him those things, even if he wants me to. I simply won't do it; I couldn't live with myself knowing that he's become disappointed with his life."

With a slight pause between them, Kael nods, unsure of what to say to comfort her. "Some relationships just can't work, no matter much you want them to." She dishearteningly concludes, "Besides, why would the Gods allow such a union anyway?" Elena abruptly walks away in sorrow to gather her thoughts as Kael looks on and sighs, sensing her true feelings for Victor.

CH: 46
PARADISE LOST

Dejected, Victor runs to the edge of a cliff in Pretoria; ready to throw his Gauntlet into the distance as he yells, feeling angrier and alone than ever before. He reluctantly resists while looking upon the Gauntlet and clutches it tightly in his hands. Victor sighs in sorrow then places it back over his arm as an eerie and dreadful sound of air flows viciously around him.

"The Edge Of Beyond is calling you home, isn't it?" Traganus indicates as he suddenly appears behind Victor from the shadows.

In retaliation, Victor powers up and quickly turns with his Gauntlet aimed as Traganus moves in and out of the shadows. Trying not to waste any more energy, Victor questions, "What do you mean?"

Traganus appears out of the shadows, revealing himself and replies, "It calls to me as well, for we are both children of the damned." Not seeing him as a threat at the moment, Victor powers down his Gauntlet and looks away. "Is it becoming clear to you yet?" Traganus probes as he circles around him, "Look at yourself, standing there cradling the Gauntlet bestowed upon you. If it means nothing to you, why protect it?" Victor lowers his Gauntlet to his side and sighs in disappointment. "I know who you are, Victor." He crudely meddles, "I know your pain, for I am just like you."

Shaking his head in disagreement, Victor angrily retorts, "You don't know what you're talking about!"

"Yes I do, we are the orphan children of uncaring parents, in this case, the Gods." Traganus says in a hateful tone.

"My mother cared for me till the bitter end!" Victor firmly snaps.

"And your team?" Traganus inquires as he stops in front of him.

Victor looks downward in shame, realizing that he speaks the truth then says, "I'm close to very few, but those few people mean everything to me."

Traganus grins in response and mutters, "I'm sure they do." He then turns his back towards him whilst looking upon the starry sky above in a curious manner. "I thought this might happen." He states as Victor looks upward as well. As Traganus walks past him, he claims, "They never really accepted you. I was just trying to show you that, but I understand your position."

Enraged, Victor suddenly whips around and fires another burst of energy at Traganus but is quickly deflected by his dark power.

"You don't understand anything!" He furiously exclaims.

"No?" Traganus angrily retorts as Victor continues to attack, lashing out in anger. Traganus is put on the defensive as he attempts to block every attack with his Darchadian power giving him considerable strength, and yells, "I don't know what it's like to be the outcast?"

Striking back, Traganus puts Victor on the defense as he leaps into the air with his wings fully spread, and disputes, "To not be accepted, to be hated, to long for a family?"

Their show of force in the air escalates until they're shrouded in a blanket of dark shadows and blue lightning. Victor lands on the ground gracefully then looks around stern and alert as Traganus suddenly appears behind him, and warns, "You will regret your impulsiveness!" Victor quickly turns and blocks as Traganus attempts to neutralize his Arch aura with his bare hands.

"Painful? You don't know the meaning of the word." He cruelly taunts, "Tell me, do Angels fear death as much humans?"

Victor glances back at him intensely whilst struggling to break free of his grip. After a brief moment of trying to over power him, Traganus suddenly neutralizes Victor's Arch aura and forces him down into the ground face first.

"That's only the beginning of what I'm truly capable of." Traganus informs, "I should've known you couldn't handle this kind of power just yet, but you're too weak to think that you could ever survive it. Though in the end, it only makes you stronger, but you're too stupid and timid to utilize it properly." He explains as Victor grunts from the pain of trying to regain his strength, "It comes and goes at first, I probably should've told you that, unfortunately now you both have to die."

Victor raises his Gauntlet in anger, assuming that he's referring to Elena as he attempts to fire upon him.

"Stand down, you know it's useless to fight against me!" Traganus sternly warns as Victor raises his head and scowls upon his dark adversary.

Aiming his Gauntlet towards Victor, Traganus threatens, "I could destroy you, but that would defeat the purpose and wouldn't be as exciting." Victor continues to grunt in pain as Traganus paces around him, "Perhaps you should listen when your elders speak." He strongly advises, "You cannot win this fight, no matter how hard you try."

Attempting to stand up, Victor shrugs off the pain and determinedly retorts, "Perhaps I'm not trying hard enough then."

"Your aggression is highly misplaced." Traganus cautions.

"What would you know about it?" Victor questions as he tries to power up but fails miserably.

Traganus scoffs, amused by Victor's unwillingness to give up then professes, "You're not the only one whose people have been victimized in this world, for I myself have learned to live with something terrible, thus, we're not that different." There's a look of compassion on Victor's face as he listens closely.

"All those years in the darkness I thought, no one else knows what this feels like." Traganus explains, "But now I've seen first hand that I was wrong." Curious to his meaning, Victor follows him as Traganus resumes; "Everything that's happened was preparing the path to guide you here. Why else do you think your mother died, leaving you as the sole survivor?"

Pondering the thought, Victor replies, "I've wondered that my whole life, but I have found a new purpose in serving the Arch."

"There are many who have spoken out against the Arch." Traganus instigates, "You shouldn't allow them to anathematize you, for it kills our intuition as well as our natural instincts."

Taking a moment to regain his composure, Victor states, "I don't know about my intuition, but my instincts have always guided me forward."

"They will soon fail you if you aren't careful," Traganus forewarns, "If you do not seek retribution then you dishonor your own kind."

Traganus steps onto a higher platform on the rocky mountaintop as Victor follows closely behind and claims, "I do not cling to the past as you do, for I've dishonored no one."

"Perhaps not, but you will." Traganus implies as he comes to a stopping point, "I will honor the memory of my fallen. Who will you honor?"

"The Gods, for they will forsake you." Victor firmly retorts.

Traganus chuckles softly in response and contends, "A fate that has yet to work in their favor it seems." The two Angelic adversaries lock eyes, a brief moment of association. "Why discard yourself by becoming one of them?" Traganus probes, "You were chosen to survive, as I was, but you don't have to be alone, Victor."

Traganus attempts to make a real offer, reminding Victor of Elena speaking the same words earlier in Archadia as he steps towards another Angelic statue atop the rocky hill.

"I was like them at one point, that is until I reached the age of reason." Traganus enlightens, "The Arch destroys anything unique, every trace of individuality erased." He then turns to face him directly, "I accept you for who and what you are, and I know my legion of thunder will too."

Surprised, Victor's expression softens and he trustingly asks, "Me?"

"Yes, the clan embraces you." Traganus affirms, "Your power is a gift only to those with the confidence and courage to wield it." He then gestures towards the Angelic statue, "Why, just look at what we can do."

Out of curiosity, Victor looks upon his reflection in the statue's crystalline surface, trying to deduce his rival's exact intention.

"Ask yourself, what goes together better than light and dark?" Traganus insinuates as Victor approaches the statue apprehensively, "You have the light, but you must embrace the other side as well, become one with the darkness within." Keeping his gaze onto the reflection from the Angelic statue, Victor holds out his hands and observes them curiously.

"Our power is different for each of us, but one thing remains true for us all." Traganus influences, "We grow stronger the more we fully embrace our divine gifts."

Upon closer inspection, Victor looks upon the fractured reflections of themselves cast in the crystalline statue and is shocked to see his wings, one light and one dark.

"You see?" Traganus gladly points out, "Your spirit represents that of a forgotten age."

Victor shakes his head and retorts, "I'm not the spirit of any age. I'm at odds with everything, I always have been."

"Denying who and what we are only means that we are lost in the scramble for our own identity." Traganus informs.

"I know who and what I am!" Victor contests, becoming annoyed.

Traganus scoffs, and says, "So you think, but in order to see the light, you must first risk the dark." He then turns to face the statue as Victor continues to listen, "My fall from grace symbolized the fall of a century, but you are a true reflection of the world's broken heart. You are special, in more ways than you may ever know."

Victor continues looking upon his reflection in the statue and sighs disappointedly, struggling to cope with the storm within.

"That which you seek inside, a shadow heart you will find." Traganus states as he steps away from the statue, then finally offers, "Will you follow me into the very heart of darkness, so that light may shine through in the way it was always meant to?"

Victor closes his eyes, contemplating his decision to turn against the Arch, knowing there's a chance things could get much worse for him if he stays.

"I know exactly what you want, Victor, what you've always wanted." Traganus indicates, "You will be one of us, and you will no longer be alone. We can make them see, we'll give them a world where everything is…"

Opening his eyes, Victor turns to face him and utters, "Dark."

Realizing how this looks, Traganus attempts to clarify, "Life is dark, so dark, but it can also be free. Though in order to survive the dark, you've got to become dark yourself."

Victor shakes his head in discordance, trying to ignore the sudden urge to let his inner rage take over his emotions once again.

"No matter you much you try to hide it, everyone has a dark side, some even darker than others." Traganus enlightens.

"More reason to keep that part of me away from others." Victor pointedly argues, "Otherwise no one in this world would truly accept me for who, or what I am."

"Perhaps, though how can anyone accept you if you aren't willing to accept yourself?" Traganus probes as Victor looks away, caught off guard by the question while contemplating his next move. "They'll accept both of us, no matter who or what we are, for we take care of our own." He assures, "Think of all those people down below who would be free to choose their own destiny. Now, can we be allies?"

Seriously considering the offer for his peoples' sake, Victor stares upon Traganus intensely whilst thinking of the possibility of freeing them, then finally, he answers, "No, we cannot." Surprised by his reply, Traganus looks upon him with a concerned expression. "They'll fear both of us, and that's not what I want at all." Victor vindicates, "If you call that paradise, then I'll flee from Heaven, and take my chances in Hell."

Annoyed by his stubbornness, Traganus articulates, "Call it what you will, even still, every culture on this planet shares a common dream of a place from which creation and eternal bliss exists equally. For us though, that place will soon become reality, with or without you." Turned off by his pushy attitude, Victor turns to walk away as Traganus looks on and states, "Like me, you clearly see things that others do not."

"I believe they call that madness." Victor sarcastically mutters.

"Victor, be reasonable, for you truly are a living miracle." Traganus attempts to sway his hybrid prey.

Victor places his hand next to a crystalline pillar and leans against it, trying to make sense of everything then calmly responds, "Thanks for your concern, and your sanctimony, but no thanks. The price is a little too high for me, and I don't like what it would take to have."

As Victor attempts to walk away, Traganus steps forward and convincingly claims, "You contain the answers so many of us seek."

Sighing impatiently, Victor turns to respond, saying, "I seek only what is equitable, my own answers, always have and always will."

"Of course you do, there can be no argument on with that." Traganus eases, trying to diffuse his anger again, "Stay with us, help us unlock the Gods' work, so we can understand those answers and more, together."

Victor steps forward in annoyance and insultingly professes, "When I was young, my mother used to tell me stories about your defeat at the hands of the Holy Trinity. Being a prisoner for so long as a result should've taught you the value of mercy."

"Don't think me merciless!" Traganus says defensively, "Sometimes it's better to be feared than respected."

"Sometimes, but not always." Victor confidently mutters.

"I assume you dream?" Traganus inquires as Victor sighs impatiently and nods in response, "I've spread my dreams under your feet, so tread carefully." He cautions, "When you have found what people fear most, you will have discovered the key to their madness, and the means to control it."

"It's not enough that you take me under your wing, is it?" Victor contests, "Like the others, I have to give myself freely and completely to the darkness within, to you."

Amused by his profound assumption, Traganus mocks, "Don't flatter yourself! I've overseen the dissension of countless Angels, even before you were born, you are no different!"

Finally sensing his' true intention, Victor angrily retorts, "You're lying!" Traganus stops in his tracks as he quickly turns to face Victor, who continues, "You desire more than just another Darchadian drone, you want a being with a mind of their own. One who could bridge the gap between humanity and the Arch. You simply want a counterpart, but I resist the temptation." He then concludes as he approaches Traganus intensely, "I will fight it, and you!"

Traganus scoffs, and disputes, "There's no fight to be had, for it's only a matter of time before you give in to your true self."

"I already know my true self!" Victor proudly exclaims.

Knowing he is oblivious to his point, Traganus counters, "The Arch may have given you a second chance in life, but they could not restore your faith in the world. Could they?"

"No," Victor sadly replies, "But as you already know, they're not all to blame for that."

As Traganus steps closer to him, he firmly defends, "Don't forget, life made us this way, I'm not responsible for the man you've become."

"And I will not be damned like you!" Victor snaps, bringing an annoyed expression from Traganus. He then turns his back towards him and warns, "Now for the last time, leave me alone!"

Frustrated by his forceful non-compliance, Traganus states, "You can't even begin to imagine the life you are denying yourself. What I offer is clearly beyond your comprehension." Confused, Traganus looks on, not expecting Victor's response. Then his eyes flame with anger, feeling vulnerable from his rejection. The time for negotiation is over as Traganus quickly changes his attitude and says, "Very well. You want to be left alone? Done! But first, there's just one minor detail with which I ought to make you familiar."

Sensing that his adversary has some trick up his sleeve, Victor stops in his tracks as Traganus snaps his fingers, and Celeste unexpectedly appears with Talia in her grasp. Victor quickly turns and frantically calls, "Talia!"

He looks on in panic as Talia struggles to break free and yells back, "Victor!"

Enraged, Victor looks upon Traganus while gripping his fists tightly and to his surprise he mysteriously powers up his Gauntlet once again in retaliation.

"She said you'd be back, and here you are!" Celeste scornfully teases.

"Let her go you coward!" Victor yells in anger as his eyes flare up.

"Is that a dare?" Traganus scoffs, "If so, then we'll soon find out who's the better Angel."

"You dare to threaten her life!" Victor angrily retorts.

"I dare anything, for I am Traganus, the Prince of Darkness!" Traganus proudly declares as his dark aura causes a brief energy wake, "Stand down and pledge yourself to me, or you will join her in another dimension."

"It's not her you want, it's me!" Victor snaps, "It's only between us!" Traganus waves his hand and furiously shouts, "Silence!"

Victor and his young female companion glance at each other for a moment with concern over his words. There's terror in Talia's eyes as she screams from Celeste clenching her tightly with her hand.

"I'm warning you!" Victor threatens, "Let her go, or I'll destroy you!"

"If you're willing to risk her life for revenge, then you may not care about her safety after all." Traganus spitefully scorns.

"Don't you dare tell me I don't care about her!" Victor exclaims.

Becoming impatient, Traganus states, "I grow tired of this. I had planned to offer you help, but I've changed my mind due to unexpected circumstances." Traganus signals Celeste to kill Talia with her bare hands as Victor extends his arm out in panic and says, "Please, don't hurt her!" Talia continues to struggle as Celeste spitefully laughs at their expense. Victor regains his composure and frustratingly asks, "What do you want?"

"Maybe I want nothing!" Traganus mocks with a devious grin.

"If that were true, then you would've killed her already!" Victor angrily deduces, thinking he has the upper hand.

"I still might," Traganus torments, "Perhaps we can still reach an accommodation that benefits both of us."

"What sort of accommodation?" Victor cautiously inquires while keeping his focus on Talia, hoping to keep her calm.

Traganus holds his hand out and demands, "The Gauntlet, give it to me!"

Knowing he means business, Victor replies, "I might, but that depends."

"On what?" Traganus asks out of pure amusement.

"On what you want it for, I vowed to keep it out of the wrong hands, yours to be more precise." Victor sternly defends.

Expressing a confident grin towards his Angelic foe, Traganus proudly states, "Technically, it's already in the wrong hands."

Victor grips his arm bearing the Gauntlet in a protective manner, as Talia looks on, concerned for both of them.

"Your allegiance to her is much more important than some sacred oath." Traganus cynically deduces, "Am I right?"

Talia looks upon Victor in despair as he struggles to keep his composure for her sake. His furious energy settles as the darkness within finally subsides.

"Fear is a great motivator, now hand it over and I'll let her go peacefully." Traganus devilishly persists, "If it hasn't become clear to you by now, your kind have a bad habit of interfering with other peoples' business." Confused by his crude remark, Victor disputes, "What are you talking about? I have no kind!"

"Don't give it to him, Victor!" Talia cries frantically.

Celeste shakes Talia out of anger and shouts, "Silence you little brat!"

Talia struggles to get loose, but Celeste only tightens her firm grip around her neck. She can hardly breathe, struggling to get away from the Darchadian.

"Do it, Victor, give us what we're after or your friend becomes a tragic memory." Traganus teases, "Don't be tempted by flesh." Victor glances at Talia as he struggles to make a decision. "Give up the little bitch and embrace your true nature." Traganus viciously taunts.

Becoming angrier by the second, Victor furiously exclaims, "Apparently you don't know what my true nature is!"

"Once this dirty business is complete, and our way home reopened, her part in this dark fairy tale will seem ever so small." Traganus declares.

Feeling cornered, Victor steps forward and yells, "Damn you!"

Traganus smirks devilishly, expecting his reaction and replies, "Too late for that, though the feeling's mutual." As Traganus approaches Talia, Victor looks on, trying desperately to hold himself back from doing anything that my cause her harm. Talia squirms in Celeste's grip as Traganus caresses her youthful face. "Her welfare consumes you, like that of a wild flame." Traganus denotes, "Very admirable, but it's time to extinguish it for good."

Knowing he has no choice in regards to her safety, Victor powers down.

"I don't want you to worry about her having a father figure." Traganus assures, "After all, there's only room for one alpha male in this picture, and I think we should put the poor kid out of her misery, don't you?" Victor trembles from the inner rage building up again, as Traganus turns to Talia and says, "No hard feelings, kid, I'll make it as quick as possible."

"You're a monster!" Victor shouts angrily.

"Join the club." Traganus scoffs with a devious grin.

Hesitating to make a decision, Victor finally takes the Gauntlet off of his arm and reluctantly hands it over. Traganus takes the Gauntlet and holds it before him with pride as Victor looks on in despair. Talia's energy begins to rise exponentially from the pain as Celeste looks upon her curiously.

"I must say, I expected more resistance from you, but you've made the right decision." Traganus assertively remarks.

"I only did it for her!" Victor angrily informs, "I can't let her live like this, I have to think about what's best for her first."

"I know, and I bet you promised that you would give her a good life, didn't you?" Traganus mocks, "But you know what, Zyas, you're really not doing a very good job, are you? In fact, you're kind of a natural disaster."

There is a short silent pause as Traganus examines the Gauntlet closely.

"Alright, you got what you wanted, now let her go as you agreed!" Victor shouts as he backs away, hoping to keep Talia from further harm. Talia struggles to keep her composure as she looks upon Celeste in anger, with her eyes beginning to glow unexpectedly as the ground begins to shake.

"No!" Traganus insultingly deceives, "You say you want to be alone, so be alone!" Lithia suddenly appears and bites Celeste in the neck as Talia yells furiously, giving her a chance to strike the Darchadian back with her energy through a rock fixture. Celeste shrieks as she hits the ground and looks up wrathfully. Lithia growls with his spinal shards glowing as she raises her Gauntlet and fires an energy blast towards Talia, knocking her back into a crystalline crevasse. "No!" Victor shouts with extreme panic in his voice. Victor can't believe what he's seeing as Lithia spreads his wings and immediately flies down, attempting to save her from the dangerous fall.

"The Arch did not teach you well!" Traganus ridicules. Enraged, Victor looks on as his eyes begin to glow brightly in blue. "You're strong no doubt, but not strong enough it seems!" He teases. Out of instinct, Victor charges towards Traganus and attempts to strike but is forced back by his Angelic wings. Victor stands up, holding his arm in pain as Traganus lifts the Gauntlet in front of him. "You're nothing without your Gauntlet!" Traganus proclaims just as he breaks the Gauntlet over his knee, cracking it in two. Light explodes from the Gauntlet as terror comes into Victor's eyes, causing him to clutch his chest as if in pain from the sudden energy connection.

"A pity you could not have cooperated." Traganus scorns, "If you're the best the Arch has to offer, then you're just as stupid as they are." Victor breathes heavily; trying to regain his composure as Traganus slowly approaches him, saying, "Know that my quarrel is not with you, though your defiance is unforgivable. This turn of events is a real shame, for you would've made a fine Darchadian. Like myself, you showed a rare talent for it."

"You're mad!" Victor angrily retorts.

"In some way, we're all mad." Traganus taunts, "Most simply aren't mad enough to admit it." Extending his arm out, Victor reaches towards him furiously as he finishes, "Lucky for you, your death will be slow; the girl isn't so fortunate." Traganus suddenly fires a burst of energy from his Gauntlet, slamming Victor back into the crevasse behind him. The wall cracks as Victor comes loose and falls downward into the chasm below with Talia and Lithia. Traganus and Celeste approach the edge of the crevasse and chuckle at his demise. "Ha!" Celeste scoffs, "We won't be seeing him anytime soon!"

"When one Angel falls, another shall rise." Traganus wickedly states as he tosses the broken Gauntlet down into the crevasse below, "May your grave bring you solace during these final moments."

"*Puny human!*" Celeste coldly remarks.

Traganus and Celeste activate their wings and suddenly take off into the sky at full speed as the broken Gauntlet lands in front of Victor and Talia. It's cold and dark, Victor feels weaker than ever before. Battered from the fall, Victor slowly looks over and sees Talia lying unconsciously on the ground. Victor panics as he rushes to her side and says, "Talia, are you hurt?"

Talia wakes up and shakes her head in response but is emotionally hurt. Emotionally hurt himself, Victor tries his best to comfort her, and mutters, "Despite all my gifts, my whole life has been nothing but a cosmic joke. It's over for us, I'm afraid there's no help coming this time."

"You came." Talia comforts with a smile as he pulls her closer, cradling her in his arms as Lithia climbs out of the rubble and shakes his body to remove the debris as he chirps. "I'm so sorry guys, this is all my fault." Victor expresses with a shameful tone. Lithia walks towards them and places his head next to Talia's to comfort her as she pets him. "Apparently my best intentions have brought nothing but harm to us both." He mutters while holding Talia tightly as she closes her eyes for a moment in despair, "He was right, I cast a shadow on everything." He sadly professes, "Perhaps I am unworthy of someone like Elena after all."

Distraught, Victor sighs as Talia opens her eyes. She's never seen him like this before; it's heartbreaking as she struggles to finally accept that he and Elena have an unbreakable bond just as they do. "Victor…" She says softly. Upon hearing her voice, he looks at her as Lithia pants. "As long as I've known you, you've always come charging to my rescue." She happily acknowledges.

Feeling appreciated, Victor grins and softly replies, "Well, I do my best."

Talia smiles back as tears roll down her face then states, "Oh, Victor, after all that's happened, and everything you've been through to get this far, you must be so disappointed. I know I am."

"Yeah, but not as much as I could be." Victor mutters, "We're so used to being disappointed that it's become a second nature for us both."

"I'm so sorry." Talia says softly, hoping to comfort him.

"Don't be, I love you just the way you are." He comforts, which brings a smile to her face. "I suppose I should let you be who you want to be, regardless of what anyone else thinks."

"Well, as long as I've got you and Elena I don't need anyone else." She lovingly admits.

Leaning back, Victor sadly mutters, "If it wasn't for bad luck I wouldn't have any luck at all." Then with a sigh he says, "It seems when I fall, I fall hard."

"When life knocks you down you simply roll over and look at the stars." Talia proudly mentions as she looks upwards beyond the crevasse.

Following suit, Victor sadly remarks, "I thought you were dead once, so if I had died, I suppose it wouldn't have mattered anyway."

Talia's expression hardens with determination as she encouragingly tests, "What do you mean it wouldn't matter?" Victor looks upon Talia, surprised by her innocent fortitude as Lithia chirps. "If one of us is ever in trouble, the other can't quit!" She positively stresses while tugging on his shoulders.

Deeply discouraged, Victor looks upward towards the top of the crevasse and sadly mutters, "In this case, it's probably best that I do."

Talia places her hand on his cheek to knock some sense into him, and says, "You once told me that no one should ever give up, no matter what."

Feeling grateful for her strength, Victor looks upon her with glossy eyes and says, "Perhaps you're right. In many ways, I've come back from worse. I must find a way to defeat them, though it seems utterly impossible as this point."

Attempting to get his full attention, Talia places her hand on Victor's chin and softly encouragingly, "It's only impossible until it's not."

Victor smiles; impressed as always by Talia's profound intuition as he grips her hand firmly within his and says softly, "Talia?"

"Yeah?" She replies whilst looking into his eyes compassionately.

"Will you sing for me?" He calmly requests with a painful grunt.

With a soft nod, Talia smiles and begins to hum Sonya's tune. Lithia joins in as Victor closes his eyes in relief. As his two sidekicks hum the ancient melody together, Talia looks upon the broken Gauntlet still lying on the ground and suddenly gets a thought as her eyes widen. Talia's expression hardens with determination as she grabs the blue crystal shard lying next to it.

"Hey, what are you doing?" Victor asks as he quickly opens his eyes, distracted by her movement. Talia holds the shard before him as it pulses brightly with light. Lithia chirps as she motions towards the Gauntlet then looks back at Victor. She then grabs the broken Gauntlet and hands it to him as he hesitates to take it. To counter his despair, Talia convinces him with a cute gesture to unlock his inner power so they can escape. She places the crystal shard back into the broken Gauntlet then smiles upon Victor.

"It's going to be alright, you'll see." She heartens with a soft voice, "You just need a little faith." Determined to put his mind at ease, Talia continues to hum the same melody as Lithia joins in again. The crystal shard in Victor's broken Gauntlet reacts to her notes and begins to flash. He looks upon the Gauntlet in shock, realizing that musical notes with various pitch intervals can in fact cause different energy reactions from crystals. "You see?" She comforts with a promising smile, "Even when you're at your weakest, you're actually at your strongest, you just may not know it yet. As Elena once told me, you must always keep the faith because greatness is inside of you, and the blessings are just around the corner."

Inspired by this revelation, Victor is able to restore the Gauntlet's full power by humming the notes along with them. He then places the Gauntlet back over his arm and activates it as it repairs his Archadian Soul Gear.

Sighing in relief, Victor feels fully reenergized as Talia and Lithia look on with excitement. Rising to his feet, Victor proudly stands whilst observing his body curiously, and states, "So that's why the Gods chose me, I truly am an Angel." Relieved by his regained strength, Talia smiles then turns her attention upwards towards the moon still shining brightly above them.

"The thing I fear the most contains the very thing I need." He recalls in acceptance of utilizing his power in a positive manner despite what Traganus may have meant by it, "I suppose even the best fall down sometimes, but only the best get right back up and start over." Talia nods in response, pleased his willingness to believe in himself once again. She then attempts to climb the crevasse wall, seeming a simple task for her from growing up in the crystal mines with her old gear, but she suddenly falls and lands back in his arms as he quickly catches her. "Don't worry, Talia, I've got you." Victor caringly reassures.

Comforted by his presence, she whispers, "I know, and for that I'm glad."

"My life force has started to regenerate thanks to you." Victor remarks in appreciation, "It may not last, and if it doesn't, always know that I'll do everything I can to protect you."

Lithia flies onto his shoulder and chirps as Talia smiles back and gently says, "I know you will, my life always seems to fall into your hands."

"Once again I am in your debt." Victor admits with a crooked smile.

"You can pay me back later." Talia says with a soft smile.

Looking above them, Victor motions upward and says, "Sometimes when you hit rock bottom the only way out is up, right?" Talia smiles in appreciation to him remembering as he looks back at her and suggests, "What do you say we get out of here now?"

"Sounds good to me!" She happily retorts.

Victor smiles determinedly, as Talia presses the blue Gods' symbol over his chest, which causes his wings to activate. He then powers up, saying, "Hold on tight!" Seconds later, he flies out of the crevasse into the sky followed closely by Lithia. Holding onto him tightly, Talia closes her eyes and smiles in relief as they head back to find the others. Watching from a short distance away, Valorie and Vennessa see them pass by then share a concerned glance.

"I knew it, just as I thought!" Valorie says impatiently.

Turning to face Valorie, Vennessa responds, "Seems you were right, sister, your intuition in these matters never fails."

"We should probably head back and inform Elena." Valorie suggests as she activates her wings and steps towards the cliff's edge.

"We can possibly make it back before he does, assuming he's gone to find her." Vennessa implies as she activates her wings also.

"Right!" Valorie replies as they prepare to take off, "Let's go then!"

With her wings activated, Valorie flies off towards the Archadian outpost, followed by Vennessa, attempting to make it back in time before Victor does.

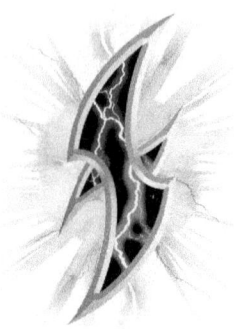

CH: 47
THIS IS WHO I AM

Sometime later in the Archadian outpost above Pretoria's surface, Elena reenters the armory then senses a familiar presence as she turns and sees Victor and Talia arriving with Lithia. She smiles in relief as Victor lands gracefully with Talia and smiles back. After gently placing Talia on the ground, Victor approaches Elena and embraces her tightly.

"Praise the Gods," she says softly with a heavy sigh relief, "I knew you'd come back eventually."
Smiling back, Victor replies, "Glad somebody still had faith in me."
Talia approaches Elena and embraces her in relief as well.
"I'm so glad you both are safe." Elena comforts.
Looking up at her two dearest friends, Talia joyfully retorts, "Me too."
Elena looks upon Victor and Talia in relief as Lithia flies onto her shoulder and chirps. Amused by his friendship, Elena chuckles as she pets his head and jokes, "I'm glad to see you made it back as well, Lithia."
Lithia purrs in appreciation then licks Elena's face, which causes her to laugh along with Victor and Talia. He then flies back onto Talia's shoulder, perched in his typical strutting manner.
"How did you find her?" Elena inquires.
Laughing softly in response, Victor calmly replies, "Let's just say there's a lot to be found in the dark when you shine a light."
Elena smiles appreciatively, knowing Victor has learned a valuable lesson from her as he smiles back with a new sense of confidence in him. Two Archadians quickly approach Elena from behind as Victor looks upon them with a concerned expression.
"Milady, our apologies for having to do this." One of them informs.
Apprehensive, Elena looks upon the two Archadians as Talia stands beside her with Lithia. The Archadians nod at one another then they suddenly attempt to take Victor into custody.

Acting Victor instinctively shoves them both back as Elena tries to intervene. Panicked, Talia watches as Marcus and Yuri arrive at the scene and stand between them to guard her. Unwilling to back down, the two Archadians grab Victor once again as he tries to safely subdue them.

"Sisters, what are you doing?" Elena questions in a troubled tone.

"Following orders, Princess!" The other Archadian states as she tries to effectively deactivate Victor's Gauntlet.

Becoming angry, Victor presses his chest piece and activates his wings; forcing them back in retaliation. Trying to keep the situation from escalating, Elena firmly stands in-between as she looks upon them intensely, saying, "Everything's been worked out! This has all been a grave misunderstanding!"

As the two Archadians pull themselves off the ground, one of them informs, "According to the Arch council, it isn't!"

"What are you talking about?" Elena inquires with a confused look.

The Archadian points towards Victor, who scowls back, then states, "He's the reason the Darchadians attacked in the first place!"

"They tracked him there!" The other chimes in aggressively, "Like us, they can sense one of their own!"

"That's absurd, sister!" Elena defensively disputes, "He's not one of them I assure you!"

"We don't like this anymore than you do, Princess, but we have our orders." The Archadian firmly proclaims.

"The council received word from two of our fellow sisters who supposedly saw this human fleeing the Darchadian lair earlier tonight." The second Archadian informs.

Elena looks upon them, confused by their outrageous claim, as Victor stays calm to avoid any further confrontation, "Who then?" She edgily inquires on his behalf, "Let them step forth and speak now!"

Valorie and Vennessa suddenly arrive in the armory as Elena turns and looks upon them in disappointment, knowing it's them who reported him.

"It's true, Princess." Valorie reluctantly informs, "We tracked him all the way back here from the surface. We're sorry."

Disheartened, Elena sighs then looks away and mutters, "I'm sorry too."

Feeling frustrated, Elena closes her eyes for a moment and asks, "Is this true, Victor?" She then turns to address him directly and carefully questions, "Did you know the Darchadians would attack us the way they did?"

"Of course not!" Victor defensively retorts, "How could I?"

"What were you even doing there in the first place?" She asks, hoping he has a definite answer whilst giving him the benefit of the doubt.

Talia steps forward to intervene as Elena looks upon her in relief, knowing deep down that Victor is telling the truth.

"He came for me!" Talia chimes in as she looks towards Victor.

Victor smiles back as Lithia chirps in his defense as well.

"He probably led the Darchadians to her!" Vennessa intolerantly accuses, "How else could they have possibly known where she was?"

Unable to answer, Elena glances at Victor, hoping he can explain everything. Valorie steps closer to Elena and warns, "Your team is broken, Princess."

"That doesn't make him a traitor!" Talia defensively proclaims, "He saved me!" Elena turns her attention towards Talia, hoping she is right.

Eager to diffuse the argument, Elena approaches Talia and kneels as she places her hand on her shoulder then calmly asks, "I know you have no reason to lie, but are you absolutely certain about that, Natalia?"

Talia nods confidently in response as Elena sighs, feeling reassured as she looks back towards Victor in relief.

"Stay out of our business, *child*, unless you want to join your friend!" Vennessa rudely states.

Elena stands whilst guarding Talia to keep her from agitating her fellow comrades. Realizing his actions appear to have no merit, Victor firmly states, "I know none of you have any reason to trust me at this point, so just listen." Everyone looks upon him as he prepares to address them all. "Their leader means to destroy you if something isn't done." He explains, "We must act before he can do anymore harm."

"We no longer require your help, *human*!" Vennessa snaps.

Victor scoffs in response, and sarcastically retorts, "That's too bad, because I know something you all don't."

"That's improbable, for you are no more aware of the current situation than we already are!" Valorie argues.

"Listen to me!" Victor edgily illuminates, "I've seen what he can do first hand, and it's going to take everything we've got to stop him!"

"We don't trust him, Princess." Valorie snaps, "He's a nothing more than a deserter to us and the Arch!"

"We don't know that for sure," Elena defends, "He's still an Angel."

Vennessa scoffs in annoyance as she turns towards Elena, and denounces, "He was an Angel when he ran, but as of now he's no more Angel than the wild beasts that dare to threaten us below. Your Majesty, please, destroy him and be done with it!"

Elena sighs, displeased by Valorie and Vennessa's attitude over the situation.

"The Arch nor the Senate will take kindly to this human's actions going unpunished," Valorie cautions, "He's done enough damage already."

Elena looks away with a saddened expression, knowing she can't help Victor until there is sufficient evidence to free him of this current charge.

"I understand, sisters." Elena reluctantly submits.

Vennessa turns to address the other Archadians, and orders, "Bind him!"

Without hesitation, the two Archadians nod then quickly approach Victor and take his Gauntlet away.

As he glances at Elena, she shakes her head as a warning not to fight back. Disappointed by their choice, Victor stands his ground with a prideful expression as they place energy shackles over his arms and legs. Rattled by the sight, Talia covers her mouth as tears run down her face. Victor remains calm on her and Elena's behalf as Valorie approaches him.

"Your level of cooperation is somewhat surprising," She curiously regards, "Surrendering is your only option at this point."

"I'm not surrendering to you," Victor proclaims as he calmly motions towards Elena, "I'm surrendering to her."
Elena looks on in shock of his valor as he turns his attention towards Talia. Valorie and Vennessa glance at Elena in curiosity as Talia begins to weep.

"Very noble, Zyas, but either way you're only making this easier for yourself, not her or your friend." Valorie crudely states as she motions towards Talia who looks back with an emotional scowl.

"There's nothing easy about it!" Victor says intensely.

"We cannot allow the Arch to be debased with his presence any longer, therefore he must be punished!" Vennessa insultingly proclaims as she signals the two Archadians to take Victor away, "Escort this vermin out of our sight, far from here!"

"No!" Talia cries out in despair as Elena tries to comfort her.
Victor passes by with the two Archadians and quickly kneels before Talia, who hugs him tightly. "Be strong, Talia." He softly encourages into her ear, "Pray for us both if you can." Talia nods determinedly as Victor reluctantly stands back up to leave, which causes Lithia to pant in a sorrowful tone.

"Prepare him for immediate deportation!" Vennessa sternly orders, "He's going back to Titania where the Senate will decide his fate."

"They will likely make an example of him." Valorie harshly chimes in.
Struggling to keep calm, Victor exclaims, "You're making a big mistake, you'll need my help!" Elena looks away in despair as she stares into nothing for a moment with great trepidation. "Angels like him are extremely powerful and almost invincible!" Victor warningly adds.

"Come on, enough of this!" The Archadians demand as they escort Victor to be imprisoned, but he quickly stops to address Elena.

"I'm sorry, Elena." He humbly apologizes, "I failed you all."
Fighting the sudden urge to free him herself, Elena sadly confesses, "No, Victor, we failed you. I'm so sorry for what has happened. You inspired us to follow our hearts, and we repay you by ruining your life."

"No," Victor calmly retorts, "You just opened my eyes to how broken it really was. And for that, I am indebted to you."
Elena closes her eyes for a brief moment, trying desperately to regain a strong composure in front of Valorie and Vennessa.

"My actions may seem dishonorable, but I am what I am, regardless of the blood in my veins." Victor discouragingly murmurs.

"I've never doubted that." Elena professes, "I know you're a man of honor, I've known that from the moment I met you, and Talia knows it too." Victor nods towards Talia with his arms tied behind his back as she nods back sorrowfully, acknowledging his attempt to keep his cool. "Looks like we won't be a team after all." Elena sadly mutters.

"Oh, Elena, I would give up a thousand wings if I could stop this." Victor expresses whilst trying to relieve her emotional pain.

"I doubt even the Gods could stop this now." Elena eases, "I'll do what I can to see that they go easy on you."
Shaking his head, Victor calmly retorts, "We both know they won't." He then looks directly into her eyes and says softly, "You have to believe me, for no one else will." Elena looks back into his eyes passionately, feeling helpless. "Let's face it, I don't fit in your world, and probably never will." Victor mutters as he locks eyes with her passionately, "Elena, I wish you could understand, but no matter what happens, please, never forget who I am."

"I won't." Elena replies with a confident nod as she tears up, fearing the worst for him, "But how can I possibly care for a man in prison?"

"I guess that depends on whether or not you can ever forgive me." Victor carefully implies.

"I already have." Elena softly replies.
As the two Archadians take Victor away, Talia approaches Elena with Lithia perched on her shoulder. Marcus and Yuri glance at each other, concerned for their Angelic comrade as Elena and Talia look on in sorrow. Valorie and Vennessa follow the two Archadians towards the exit then stop to address Elena as Talia scowls upon them once more.

"You've put an awful lot of faith in him, Princess." Valorie warns, "Perhaps too much."

"What do you see in him anyway?" Vennessa irately questions.
Hesitating to answer, Elena looks away and states, "A hero, though he may not know it yet, nor us for that matter." Valorie and Vennessa glance at each other, unmoved by her keen observation as Elena looks upon Talia, feeling hopeful. "It doesn't matter to me where he comes from, or what he's done." Elena firmly explains, "I have to believe in something, even for the greater good in someone other than myself, and my people."
Valorie shakes her head in disbelief as Vennessa scoffs, "And look where that's got you." Elena sighs disappointedly as Valorie and Vennessa take their leave with the others to supervise Victor's deportation to Titania personally.

"There's got to be something you can do." Talia woefully suggests as she tugs on Elena's arm to get her attention.
Elena looks upon her and sadly replies, "At this point, I wish there was."

"What are they going to do with him?" Talia frightfully inquires.

"I don't know, but it's out of our hands now." Elena explains as she looks upon her young protégé, "Let us pray the Gods are on his side."

"And if they're not?" Talia asks softly.

"Then pray they're on ours." Elena softly retorts.

Talia looks away with teary eyes as Lithia attempts to lick them off her face. Holding her young friend close, Elena suddenly remembers the dark crystal shard she placed in her garment earlier and pulls it out. She looks upon the shard intensely and grips it tightly in her hand, looking determined as she receives a Gauntlet transmission from her parents above.

"Word has it you turned over one of the sacred Artifacts to the Darchadians upon your defeat earlier." Rosalyn mentions.

"It's not like we didn't put up a fight on our end." Elena defends.

"They've tried and failed to get their hands on those Artifacts for years." Josephus scolds, "And it seems they've started to succeed."

"Not yet," Elena justifies, "They don't have all three."

"No, but it's still one less than us now." Josephus warns, "Do you have any idea what it means if they are to get control of the Artifacts?"

"They'd be invincible." Elena denotes with a worrisome tone.

"Then stop them," Rosalyn orders, "You're the only one who can."

"Not anymore," Elena remarks, "We still have Victor on our side."

As her parents share a look of disbelief, the transmission ends. Elena turns towards Marcus and Yuri, signaling them to meet her elsewhere as they bow their heads and take their leave. Elena glances at one of the smaller chambers within the armory and sees the captured Darchadian from earlier struggling to break free. Focusing her attention back onto the shard in her hand, she grips it tightly and says, "Perhaps this is the key to setting you free."

Concerned, Talia looks up with teary eyes and asks, "What does that mean?"

Determined to investigate the matter further, Elena places the shard back in her garb and firmly answers, "The will to act in defense of another."

Talia shares a curious glance with Lithia as Elena looks upwards then quickly takes her hand and says, "Let's go you two."

Now on a mission, Elena reluctantly releases the wounded Darchadian from his energy shackles as he drops to the floor and looks upon her savagely, saying, "What the hell are you doing, *Archadian*?"

"Something I should've done long before now!" Elena replies.

"What?" The Darchadian spitefully barks, "You're foolish, *Princess*!"

"Perhaps, but I'm also determined." She proudly informs to his surprise, "You're coming with us, there are questions that need answering and you're going to oblige me whether you like it or not."

Elena grabs him by the collar and forcefully drags him outside while Talia and Lithia look on, surprised by her intensity. While dragging him onto the landing platform, Elena leads Talia and Lithia towards an Arch ship and prepares to take off towards Archadia to confront her parents about the shard as well as Victor. Kael steps outside and watches the Arch ship take off to the skies, then shakes his head with a grin, knowing exactly what Elena is up to.

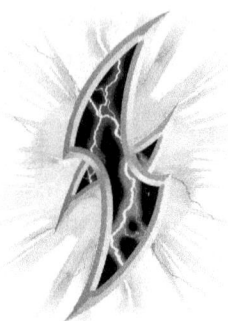

CH: 48
THEOLOGICAL REVELATIONS

Afterwards within the throne room of the Archadian Temple, the Arch council converses amongst themselves. Elena suddenly enters the chamber with a Darchadian in her grasp that was subdued previously after their first battle in Pretoria, as Marcus and Yuri stand by to listen.

"The world acts as if there is no such threat, but here's my proof!" She sternly announces. Rosalyn and Josephus look on with concern as Elena aggressively shoves the Darchadian to the ground several feet before them.

"What is the meaning of this, Elena?" Rosalyn questions irritably.

Elena steps forward with an intense look and confidently states, "I was hoping such questions might be answered myself while I'm here. Let's take a moment and discover them together, shall we?" Elena suddenly kicks the Darchadian with black trauma lines over his eyes towards the Arch council, causing him to grunt in pain, "I figured if we hear both sides regarding this investigation then we would all be enlightened, because hearing only one will keep us forever in the dark."

The Darchadian looks upon the Arch council heatedly for the first time as Rosalyn and Josephus stare back with stern expressions.

"You have our permission to speak, Darchadian, but choose your words carefully, and your time wisely." Josephus seriously informs.

Refusing to speak, the Darchadian stares back, chuckling in spite then Elena swiftly strikes him from behind and forcefully demands, "Talk damn you!"

Rosalyn raises her hand to calm Elena's intensity and calls, "Elena!"

Annoyed, Elena glares upon Rosalyn for a second then stands back to let him speak. "Seems you're arresting people everywhere these days, another form of terrorism no doubt." The Darchadian mocks, "Imprisonment under your wings is not something my people think highly of."

"I've seen what your people do to your prisoners!" Elena contests, "Like those who have enslaved humans, such people are not to be trusted."

"Traganus himself would not be pleased with this sort of treatment." The Darchadian scorns, "Surely you remember your old comrade in arms?"

"We remember a traitor!" Rosalyn scornfully replies.

"We are greatly superior in every way." The Darchadian arrogantly proclaims, "You will taste no victory in your pathetic attempts to stop us!"

"You will taste your own blood!" Elena furiously interjects as she strikes the Darchadian from behind once again. Josephus raises his hand to stop her as she stares back impatiently. "The Arch has always had a knack for violating people's rights." The Darchadian crudely comments.

"That's ludicrous!" Elena disputes, "We uphold the people's rights, we do not violate them as you do." The Darchadian turns towards her and scowls as she continues, "The Arch has a strict policy of no interference with other cultures, for it is our prime directive in case you've forgotten!"

"Your directive apparently doesn't include spying on and judging other cultures." The Darchadian cynically implies as he turns his attention back towards the Arch council, "The Arch, as well as society thinks of us as criminals, but not long ago it was also said that humans were once the same."

"Ridiculous to look upon someone un-righteously enslaved as a criminal, don't you think?" Elena scorns.

"My point exactly." The Darchadian crossly remarks, "Familiarity and repetition breeds such conformity, but in our case, contempt." Rosalyn and Josephus glance at each other, concerned for the sanctity of their kingdom in the presence of their dark enemy. "Oppression on the other hand, spawns obedience." The Darchadian adds with a condescending tone.

"What's your point?" Elena snaps.
The Darchadian slowly faces her with a devious grin and proudly clarifies, "We are many, and you are none."

"That's a contradiction if I've ever heard one." Elena scoffs, "Like us, you Darchadians have a collective consciousness, except one that is both dark and twisted. There is no such individuality that I'm aware of."

"Like the Arch?" The Darchadian mocks with a smirk. Elena scowls in annoyance as the Darchadian looks upon the Arch council intensely, and declares, "We're not going anywhere, and we aren't going to play by your rules anymore!" Concerned by his declaration, the Arch council glances at one another as he resumes, "There are many who would heed our call, most of which are already aware and fully support our Master's plan."

"It doesn't matter what your reasoning is, you've committed crimes against us, the people of Earth, and the Gods!" Elena argues, "Is this your sick way of justifying your recent actions?"
The Darchadian sighs impatiently and states, "Being the wise leader that he is, Traganus knows exactly what he's doing; therefore, our actions do not need justification from anyone, including yourselves."

"The Arch seems to think otherwise." Elena firmly contests.

Shaking his head defiantly, the Darchadian scoffs as she states, "You claim to be a civilized culture, yet you've committed acts of utter barbarity. You think you're all in control, but truthfully you are the ones being controlled." The Darchadian fiendishly illuminates, "Your Gods with their divine power have controlled you so completely that you've lost even the slightest desire to question it." He then turns to face Elena once more and smugly questions, "Ask yourself, what happens when that control goes away?"

"Stop it!" Elena furiously exclaims in response, "You destroy lives simply because we have something you'll never have!"
The Darchadian deviously chuckles at her expense and mockingly says, "Would you please enlighten me then?"

"Gladly!" Elena proudly explains, "Our people have hope, trust, faith, and great potential. You on the other hand do not. Case in point, we do not murder people in an attempt to save our own skins!"

"Maybe not now, but you will." The Darchadian devilishly implies, "Soon you'll have no choice but to answer for your worldwide mistakes."

"You sure about that?" Elena retorts, slightly amused.

"Absolutely!" The Darchadian confidently replies.
Elena straightens up in a relaxed manner to retain her composure and calmly informs, "Well you're wrong, our purpose is to rise."
Amused himself, the Darchadian shakes his head once again and proclaims, "No, your purpose is to fall, just as Traganus prophesied." With a lowered brow, he looks upon the Arch council to address them directly, and announces, "There are more of us than you fail to realize." He then queries, "Have any of you stopped to think that maybe you've become the minority?"
Elena glances at her parents with a deeply concerned look as he wickedly threatens, "Something is coming, both vast and dark."

"What's coming?" Elena questions, feeling irritated.

"You can't miss it." The Darchadian pompously infers, "Like a raging storm, it's going to light up the sky."
The Arch council looks on, angered by his threats as Elena instinctively powers up and aims her Gauntlet towards the Darchadian in anger.

"You must have a death wish, *Darchadian!*" She angrily threatens.
Knowing Elena is bound by her code, the Darchadian scoffs and calmly retorts, "There is nothing beyond death, only the next dimension."

"Maybe not for you!" Elena warns as she powers up her Gauntlet.
Surprised by her sudden intensity, the Darchadian glances back at her, realizing that she's willing to kill him at any second despite her sacred oath.

"That's enough!" Rosalyn shouts impatiently.
Elena looks towards the Arch council with an intense glare then retains her composure as she powers down and pulls her Gauntlet back by her side. Rosalyn signals a couple of Archadians to take the Darchadian away, as Elena looks on, deeply concerned over her unexpected reaction.

"You will all come to know the truth!" The Darchadian decrees as the two Archadians escort him out, "Angels of the night shall rule the world, and there will be no one powerful enough to stop us!" Elena looks directly at her parents who express extreme displeasure. "Archadia will fall eventually!" Rosalyn and Josephus shake their heads in annoyance as Elena pulls out the dark crystal shard form her garb and examines it carefully.

"Traganus has gone too far this time!" Rosalyn asserts, "He enjoys what he mistakenly believes to be his control over us."

"Why is that?" Elena inquires.

"In his mind, his time in Archadia was merely a chess match, and we are his pawns to move as he sees fit for his pleasure." Josephus explains.

"But like most children, he seems to forget that all games must end, for there can only be one victor." Rosalyn adds.

"I see." Elena murmurs as she suddenly throws the shard towards Josephus who instinctively catches it. "Now maybe we'll be able to get some things straightened out."

"We may indeed." Josephus mutters while he and Rosalyn observe the dark crystal shard intensely as it glows brightly, he then cautiously inquires, "Where did this come from?"

Elena steps forward to address the council directly and decisively expresses, "That's what I'm here to find out. We're being probed in a very methodical manner, and pattern. I'd like to know why."

Continuing her curious gaze upon the shard with Josephus, Rosalyn denotes, "It's a chaos crystal no doubt, and radiant with great negative energy."

"With my own eyes, I saw the enemy subdue our finest warriors." Elena reluctantly mentions, "It seems my fellow sisters, Baptiste and Voltaire have defected as well." Rosalyn and Josephus look upon her with surprised expressions as she continues, "There's more, we've tracked their trajectory."

"Archadia we presume?" Josephus infers.

"Never before has an enemy dared to attack us here!" Elena stresses, "As far as I know anyway." Concerned by their daughter's profound intuition, Rosalyn and Josephus glance at each other for a moment and frown unexpectedly. "Our kingdom is not as impregnable as the world may believe." Elena aversely points outs, "Please, you must tell me what you know."

The Arch council glances at Rosalyn and Josephus with grave concern and is signaled to exit the throne chamber. "Leave us!" Josephus demands.

Bowing their heads, the Arch council members take their leave as Elena looks upon them curiously, knowing her parents are hiding something from them as well. As the council members close the chamber doors behind them, Rosalyn begins, "Light has always been our sole weapon against the forces of darkness amongst the people of Earth. But that power seemed insufficient to some, thus, a great debate arose among us." She explains, "Should another source of power be exploited, one we had long sworn should never be used?"

"Which was?" Elena carefully inquires.

"Darkness." Josephus reluctantly reveals, "But the power was too unpredictable, and the chance of corruption far too great. So, in the best interest of the Arch and the entire planet, we ultimately decided against it. All of us that is, except for one."

Elena listens closely as her parents finally reveal a mystery of the past...

Many years earlier in in the depths of Archadia, a young male Darchadian with long black hair battles the darkness within him whilst standing within his private chambers, trying also to channel the light.

"Alone, this Angel conjured a power from which he could never escape." Rosalyn explains, "He wanted to prove that light and darkness could both be mastered equally, by constantly digging into the full potential of an Angel's power through the mind, body, and spirit. Though sadly to his dismay, it appeared he dug too deep." The Angel powers up, trying desperately to balance his energy inside and out to sustain both light and dark.

"His intentions were pure, but his hopes were hopeless and naïve." Josephus explains, "He perfected a means of bringing to the surface all that was evil and negative within, which in turn caused it to erupt and spread. In time, his Angelic aura seemed to have formed a second skin, dank and vile. Consumed by the darkness within him, the Angel inevitably fell, and became the very evil he swore to destroy."

After a brief moment of channeling his inner power, the Angel retains his composure as the dark energy surrounds him and his red Angelic wings.

"He became known as, Traganus, the first Darchadian, or as we prefer to call him, the Fallen." Rosalyn divulges, "A name that will never be forgotten, for he was the first of his kind to rise up against his true masters."

"Like all Darchadians, their beliefs are based on a natural order that's extremely predatory." Josephus adds, "Thus, for the planet's safety and our own, the Holy Trinity was sent to subdue him before his power could negatively influence others in Archadia as well."

High above the planet's surface on the edge of a crystalline cliff, Korina, Kitana, and Kiara of the legendary Holy Trinity battle Traganus in a fateful and deadly duel. He puts up a good fight against the divine trio but is eventually defeated as they finally subdue him. Angered by his defeat at their hands, Traganus looks upon the Holy Trinity and yells ferociously.

"For a brief moment, it seemed as if his unparalleled strength would overcome them, but seeing how they worked together as a unit..." Josephus recalls, "Fortunately his opponent's cunning was more than a match for him."

"He would've pushed the boundaries even further had we not stopped him in time." Rosalyn adds, "And after his defeat, one of us was charged with imprisoning him."

"And who amongst us at the time was charged with such a feat?" Elena inquires as they glance at each other, both hesitating to answer.

An Archadian wearing an Angelic cloak takes Traganus into custody, personally exiling him somewhere deep within Pretoria under the surface.

"Victoria Zyas." Rosalyn finally reveals as Victoria places Traganus in energy shackles within a small crystalline prison beneath the Earth's surface heavily guarded by Archadians, and says softly, "I'm sorry, Gabriel."
Disappointed by her actions, which aided in his capture, Traganus stares back intensely and asks, "Are you?" As Victoria turns to take her leave with two other Archadians, Traganus scowls back and threatens, "You think your family's safe?" Victoria slowly turns, surprised by his perceptive remark. "One day, I will reclaim what you have taken from us!" He viciously exclaims, attempting to get a rise out of her. Bothered by his threat, Victoria frowns upon him as she signals the two Archadians to leave the chamber.

"I know what your greatest secret is, Victoria." Traganus fiercely warns with a confident grin, "Neither the Arch, nor the Gods will stop me in my quest for vengeance!" A short pause leaves Victoria unnervingly silent as Traganus attempts to conjure the strength from within which causes the entire chamber to suddenly darken slightly. "I will find him eventually, and make him one of us!" Traganus declares as he attempts to reach for her, failing to break his energy shackles in the process as the chamber trembles from his dark energy. A tear rolls down Victoria's face as she takes her leave from the chamber with the others. Moments later, the prison doors close engulfing the whole chamber in shadow as Traganus looks down in despair.

Elena turns in disappointment of this revelation, realizing Victor's origin to be even more dark and mysterious than previously thought.

"Throughout his attempts to rise against us, he appeared to feel very little, but all people have their breaking points." Josephus states.

"At the time, we were bound by our oath as Angels to find a cure and make him and his followers whole again." Rosalyn explains, "Though times have greatly changed, which doesn't allow us the luxury of showing mercy in any form towards their kind."

"Upon his fall from grace, we had determined that the heretical teachings of him and his followers to be inconsistent with the harmonious life here in Archadia." Josephus explains.

"But he escaped," Elena curiously points out, "How?"
Rosalyn and Josephus glance at each other with concern, as Elena looks upon them, waiting impatiently for an answer.

"We aren't sure exactly, for it seems our patient efforts to silence revolutionary voices such as his have utterly failed." Josephus reluctantly admits with a disgruntled tone, "What we do know is that he's been feeding upon the fear in others, growing stronger and more powerful over the years."

"He's become a symbol of lethal purpose, completely unseen, that is until he strikes." Rosalyn chimes in, "And if history has taught us one thing since the Arch's inception, it's that evil begets evil."

"Well I've got news for you regarding him and the Darchadians, it's not ancient history anymore." Elena firmly comments.

"It's possible that he intends to eventually unleash the Darchadians on a full-scale assault." Rosalyn surmises, "Legions that have likely been awaiting his return since his fall from grace. And the saddest part is, he can't see the difference between saving the Arch, and destroying it altogether."

With her back turned against them, Elena stresses, "And in the process, he's planning to take his revenge on you, and destroy the Arch once and for all." She then turns back to address them directly, "If that's the case, then we have no choice but to intervene, for it is our sacred duty to wage war against any and all enemies that dare to threaten us, especially any Darchadian horde." Elena approaches Rosalyn and Josephus closely as they look back, listening closely. "To protect our kingdom, we must be able to defend ourselves, and retaliate without question if necessary." She determinedly states.

"We will act accordingly to the Senate's wishes." Josephus informs.

"Which is to remain neutral at this time." Rosalyn adds.

Shocked by their apathetic stance on the matter, Elena frowns upon her parents and says, "What?" Gripping her fists tightly, Elena struggles to keep her composure as Yuri turns to address Marcus in the back of the chamber.

"This just keeps getting worse." Yuri denotes.

"No doubt about that." Marcus sarcastically comments.

Elena regains her composure as she looks upon her parents once again intensely, saying, "Permission to speak freely, if I may?"

"I suppose we have little choice." Josephus amusingly retorts.

"Forgive me for not understanding the council's ruling, but this is absurd and you know it!" She disputes with an angry tone, "A menace of this magnitude could eventually wipe us out! Your inaction could cost the lives of many if they haven't already!"

Rosalyn sighs impatiently and justifies, "The Arch must be protected, Elena, even with or without apology sometimes. Without knowing their exact location, attacking them now would provide no strategic advantage, and could cause more damage in the long run for us, and the people of Earth. You have to appreciate the position of this council as well as the Arch in general."

Elena swings her arm back in anger of the situation, "I do, but you don't seem to get it, do you?" She argues, "Traganus isn't planning to defeat the Arch, he's planning its annihilation! For our own security, we must dare to have a preemptive attack. If we're not careful, his sins will mark us and our children for many generations to come."

"We aren't any less aware of the consequences than you are, Elena!" Josephus sternly informs.

"Maybe not, but are you prepared to have that kind of blood on your hands?" Elena irately questions.

"The blood, as you so well put it, will not be on our hands, but his and his alone!" Rosalyn defensively attests.

"Traganus simply wants to rule the Arch, and if Earth's forces win, he will abandon his claim to it forever." Josephus affirms.

Annoyed by their unwillingness to budge, Elena scoffs, "Don't count your blessings, forever may not be long enough."

Angered over their apathetic decision, Elena quickly turns to leave, as Talia looks on, fearful for Victor and the Archadians. As Elena rushes past her crew impatiently, she exclaims, "Let's go guys, we're done here!"

"Well, she's pissed!" Marcus jokes.

"Really, you think?" Yuri sarcastically retorts.

Elena signals Talia and says, "Come along, Natalia."

Talia glances at Lithia who chirps while perched on her shoulder then follows Elena with Marcus and Yuri in tow. Elena and her crew exit the chamber as Rosalyn and Josephus continue observing the dark crystal shard before them curiously. Josephus becomes enraged by its negative energy and slams the shard against the counter before him, unable to break it with his own power.

Sometime later, Adrian and the remaining team gear up for battle in the armory within the Archadian outpost. Concerned for their safety upon her return, Elena quickly approaches him, hoping to intervene and warns, "Adrian, you can't do this alone! The danger is too great!"

Adrian places a new crystal shard in his Gauntlet, then stops for a moment and says, "Well you can forget all that sympathetic crap now because danger is imminent at this point, Princess. I'm afraid we no longer have a choice in the matter for we've all been reassigned." He explains, "Like you and the Eudenians, we Enfurians are made from a hardy stock. Besides, the greatest honor one can ever achieve is to live with great courage and to die with their people in battle for the safeguard of their own home."

Elena nods in agreement, and kindly replies, "Spoken like a true warrior. I understand if you're a little anxious, I would be too."

"Only fools have no fear, but real courage is being scared to death and going into battle anyway." Adrian professes, "Understand, it is very difficulty for me to depend on anyone for anything, especially for my life."

"I know the feeling, but with a team you have to do that everyday, for everyone depends on everyone else to protect them in some way." Elena inspires, "So you must overcome it eventually just like the rest of us."

With a stern gaze, Adrian looks upon her and states, "In time perhaps, but it will always be my enemy regardless."

Elena nods in respect as Adrian signals the others to prepare their departure.

"Give me enough time to convince the council, I can call for help." She perceptively implores.

"The Senate has requested that we head out as soon as possible." Adrian responds while grabbing his new combat gear, "Your efforts will be ineffective by the time we reach Pretoria anyway."

"What about Damian?" Elena inquires as she follows him out.

Contemplating his Eudenian comrade's fate, Adrian stops in his tracks and denotes, "They won't kill him, he's too important."

"Not to them, but to us he is, just like everyone else on this team." Elena regards out of respect.

Turning his attention outside the armory onto the horizon, Adrian groans and states, "I know they're waiting for us to come back. They killed the others, and they could've killed us, but for whatever purpose, they didn't."

"Be glad for that." Elena eases with a comforting tone.

"Whatever it is, he's alive for a reason, and they know that we're not going anywhere as long as he still lives." He affirms.

Elena looks onto the horizon as well, and responds, "When you put it like that, it sounds like they were planning this all along."

"Indeed," Adrian retorts with a nod, "I bet they were."

With a curious expression, Elena questions, "You're saying their attack on us was not arbitrary, but part of some devious tactic?"

"Yeah, but the only way to find out for sure is to go back out there." Adrian replies while motioning towards the horizon outside the armory.

"I suppose you're right." Elena sighs disappointedly as she looks away, "It's truly unfortunate that Victor won't be there to help you this time."

"Zyas was right about one thing though…" Adrian reluctantly mentions as she looks upon him curiously, "As it turns out, the Darchadian fortress was in the same vicinity as our previous encounter."

Elena shakes her head, somewhat relieved to hear this and warily denotes, "No wonder he fell into enemy hands so easily. It probably didn't help the situation any considering I was too hard on him from the start."

"Yeah, though technically we all were, but keep in mind his absence still cost us dearly back there." Adrian civilly asserts.

"I'd worry more about how we fight them than who is to blame at this point." Elena firmly states.

"Last time we fought them, we didn't even make a dent." He implies, "Still, it's a shame he turned out to be less than we expected."

Bothered by Adrian's mindset towards Victor, Elena responds, "I'm sorry you feel that way, but your evidence regarding the Darchadians and their location will surely prove his innocence."

"Possibly, but until that time, he'll have to remain a prisoner and face the Gods like the rest of us." Adrian concludes as he turns to take his leave.

As Adrian and the other troops pack their gear to head out towards their ship, Elena looks on, fearful for their safety as well as Victor's.

CH: 49
DISORDER IN THE COURT

Back in Titania within the Senate Hall in Edge City, the Senate meets for another summit to discuss the current situation. Sitting amongst the crowd, Hammond and Griffin look on, knowing the Senate will not be merciful towards Victor. "It is decided!" The Chancellor announces from his seat, "LT. Braxel will lead the remaining troops back to Pretoria!" As Tannis glances at Elena with a devious grin, the Chancellor turns to address her directly and infers, "Seems your human has failed us, Princess."

With sadness evident in her eyes, Elena looks around the Senate Hall and rationalizes, "He didn't fail us, Chancellor, we failed him." The Senators begin to argue amongst themselves as she explains, "I warned you about the Darchadians beforehand, but you wouldn't listen! He's still a valuable asset and too important for you to turn your backs on him now!"

"Ignorance is not the same as innocence, thus we cannot allow naivety of the law to become a defense!" The Chancellor exclaims, "Many lives were lost in the process; therefore, we can ill afford such a tragedy here!" Bothered by his unbending stance, Elena sighs impatiently and contests, "Such prejudice never shows much reason, for there can be no real justice so long as laws are absolute. Even life itself is an exercise in exceptions."

"Yes, but his recent actions are far too suspicious for us to ignore." The Chancellor sternly remarks, "Which is why we only respect those who respect our laws without question."

"Good thing we live in a world where suspicion alone does not constitute a crime, and where people such as yourselves respect the rule of law in all forms." Elena cynically points out."

"This is the rule of law, Princess!" The Chancellor snaps, "For a crime unpunished is a crime in and of itself."

"Tell me this, Chancellor, when has justice ever been as simple as a rule book anyway?" Elena intriguingly argues.

"You make a valid point, but whether or not it was an accident we still retain dominion here, and he'll suffer the consequences for his actions!" The Chancellor resolutely announces, "As it stands, let the record show that this committee holds him solely responsible until proven otherwise."

"And what fate has the Senate decided for him?" Elena cautiously inquires, unsure if she's ready to hear the answer.

Tannis finally steps forward and happily announces, "Death of course!"

"No!" Elena exclaims in despair as she looks towards Tannis with disgust, "What about due process?"

"Actually, we prefer justice!" Patrayous arrogantly chimes in as the crowd hollers in response.

"You can't be serious!" Elena angrily disputes.

"We have no choice but to remand him at the Palace of Justice for processing." Patrayous contentedly informs.

"It would appear that this court has shown an extreme level of discrimination." Elena firmly disputes.

"This court has shown no bias in this case!" The Chancellor defends.

"But you have, a distinct prejudice against the accused, his case, and his counsel." Elena argues on Victor's behalf.

"This is a classic example of what happens when you argue with feelings instead of facts, for no one believes in the guilty no matter how innocent they may appear." Tannis selfishly adds with a devious smirk, "And since humans have no such legal rights in our society, it is forbidden to place one like him on trial."

"He's right, Princess." The Chancellor respectfully interjects, "The only course of action at this point is penalty of death."

Angered and hurt by the situation, Elena slams her hand on the crystalline podium, as Hammond and Griffin look on, concerned over her demeanor.

"This is unlawful and you know it!" She furiously exclaims.

"The law is the law; our peace has always been based upon that principle!" Tannis announces as he faces Elena to taunt her with a quiet chuckle, "Don't worry, Princess, it will be swift and just."

Elena looks upon him and Patrayous, trying desperately not to lose her cool.

"Heroes aren't always what they're cracked up to be anyway!" Patrayous cynically ridicules, "Our concern is for the public safety of our people, not your wounded pride, *Saltora!*" Elena scowls towards the overzealous General in annoyance as he continues, "And because of that, we're left with only one other option!" Zepherus growls in support of his master as Tannis glances at Elena with a grin, angering her even further.

"Princess Elena, please know that we take no real pleasure in prosecuting him, but a capital charge of this scale requires that we put aside our passions and sympathies towards his hybrid status by letting ourselves solely to the truth itself." The Chancellor respectfully explains.

"And what truth is that?" Elena carefully questions.

"The fact that he was positively and unimpeachably identified at the scene of the apparent crime." The Chancellor further clarifies, "For he had motive, opportunity, and he most certainly had animosity for his own team which was confirmed by his testimony alone."

"There was much reason for his animosity towards them." Elena points out, "Imagine how much anyone in his position would be despised at first for ever daring to take on the challenges that he has amongst his peers."

"Another valid point to be sure, thus if the team provides empirical evidence by the time they return, then you have our word, the word of this congress that no harm will befall him." The Chancellor humbly discloses.

Elena bows her head in respect and calmly replies, "Thank you, Chancellor."

The Chancellor stands up from his seat, regarding everyone in the hall, and announces, "In the mean time, let us hope they can handle the situation on their own and end this conflict once and for all!"

Malik raises his fists, cheering in response by shouting, "Here, here!"

The Senate applauds in response to the team's expected success as Hammond and Griffin look towards Elena with concerned expressions.

"Meeting adjourned!" The Chancellor calls as he pounds his gavel.

The Senate disperses as Elena looks away, disappointed by their cold decision. Hammond and Griffin nod at one another then quickly take their leave as Malik watches them curiously from above. As Elena rushes out of the Senate Hall impatiently, Tannis faces Patrayous and grins, feeling pleased by his selfish political victory over her. Moments later outside the Senate Hall, Kael arrives and sees Elena exiting then quickly approaches her through the political crowd. "I'm sorry, Princess, I got here as soon as I could." He quickly mentions before asking, "So, what's the verdict?"

Feeling hesitant, Elena faces him and replies, "He's been branded a traitor, and it appears they want to extradite him under the table." Then with a calm breath she says, "Isn't it amazing how quickly people can turn against you?"

"You must convince them to rethink their position on this matter." Kael sternly requests on Victor's behalf.

Distressed, Elena places her hand over her tiara and states, "Believe me, I tried, but they won't agree with my sentiment, no matter the cost."

Sighing disappointedly, Kael looks away and grumbles; "Once again the Senate sits in apathy whilst our enemy grows stronger. It seems pretty clear to me what they're trying to do, which is making an example out of him."

"It would certainly seem that way, or perhaps it's all just political propaganda to further their gain along with Tannis." Elena angrily denotes.

"When is it not?" Kael says with a disgruntled voice.

"I wish there was something I could do for him, but I can't go against the Arch." She says with a disheartened tone, "We both know it is forbidden, even for someone in my position."

"Like everything else it seems." Kael implies, "Our ways may be different from theirs, but deep down we both know what is right."

Elena nods in agreement, and calmly retorts, "That we do."

"It's conceivable that the true objective is not to engage them in battle just yet." He carefully denotes.

"Why do you say that?" Elena asks with a confused look.

"Right now, our main goal is to insure Damian's safe return, as well as Victor's freedom." Kael patiently explains, "Perhaps at the moment we can best accomplish that here."

Overwhelmed, Elena sighs and murmurs, "You know for an Angelic warrior like myself, I've never felt so helpless before in my life."

"Forgive my composure, but sometimes the best way to fight is not to be there at all." He encourages, "For thee who triumphs knows when to fight, and when not to."

Elena grins in response and says, "Sounds like you've been keeping up with our customs. Seems the Arch is still adamant through their teachings of Archadian strategies."

"I pray your people have the strength to do what is necessary, so that they don't repeat the same mistakes of our ancestors." Kael firmly states.

"This is all so unfair." Elena gripes, "I once thought people of the world were better than this, apparently I was wrong."

"I too wish the world was a place where fair was the bottom line, where the kind of idealism you show is rewarded not taken advantage of." Kael expresses, "Unfortunately, we don't live in that world."

"I've always believed the world is what we make of it." Elena jokes.

"So did I at one point." Kael humbly adds.

Highly determined, Elena looks onto the horizon through the city towers, and declares, "I can't just sand by and do nothing; I have to help him!"

"Then you already have the strength," Kael advises, "You just have to embrace it and take action."

Amused by his sentiment, Elena jokingly scoffs and retorts, "I'm surprised you aren't trying to convince me otherwise."

As the crowd clears out of the Senate Hall, Kael states, "In any other case I would, but sometimes we must go beyond what is expected of us, and push towards the edge of greatness."

"Seems my people have forgotten that lately." She remarks, "Like Victor, you don't say much but when you do, it's very thoughtful and wise."

"There are two types of people in this world that don't have much to say really." Kael mentions, "Those who are too busy planning something wrong to say much, and those who whole heartedly believe that actions speak louder than words and talk only when they truly have something worth saying in the presence of others."

"I have a feeling he's the second type, as a matter of fact, I'm sure of it." Elena favorably affirms then faces him, placing her hand on his shoulder in appreciation, "Thank you, General, your words will never be forgotten."

"I hope not." Kael says with a cunning expression.

With a heroic grin, Elena proclaims, "I know now what must be done."

Kael bows his head in respect as he prepares to take his leave then turns back to respond, saying, "Whatever you choose to do, Princess, know that your secret will always be safe with me."

Surprised by his remark, Elena looks upon him, knowing that he's referring to her bond with Victor. As Kael takes his leave, Elena looks back onto the city and smiles with determination, now fully knowing what she must do.

High above the city within Tannis' throne room, he and Patrayous watch the ships take off from the window as Adrian and the dejected team take off in an attempt to rescue Damian, and end the Darchadian threat alone. Raina and Lucian enter the chamber shortly after as Zepherus growls.

"Be calm, Zepherus." Patrayous says as he lays his hand on his head.

Raina and Lucian approach the window as Tannis turns to face them and infers, "Well my Lords, it looks like the human couldn't keep himself out of trouble after all. Though it's unfortunate to hear about Trag's recent capture."

"The rest of the team is on their way to resolve the issue against the Darchadians in Pretoria." Raina informs.

"Let us hope Braxel and the others are up to the challenge then." Tannis says with a confident grin.

Lucian steps forward and proudly states, "If anyone is going to end this conflict then it might as well be one of mine."

"Thanks to this *human's* interference, my Champion is still missing in action." Raina irately claims.

"I'm sure the rest of the team can handle it, and if they can't..." Tannis proclaims as he motions towards Patrayous, "I'll gladly send my General and his troops to take care of it themselves."

Patrayous steps forward, signifying his willingness to do battle, and declares, "Just give the command, and I will face these Darchadians myself."

Raina and Lucian share a glance, annoyed by Kraven's arrogant claim.

"There's absolutely nothing to worry about my King and Queen," Tannis reassures, "We'll act immediately if things get out of hand."

"Let's hope so for your sake, Emperor." Lucian warns while pointing towards Tannis intensely, "If I lose my Champion as well in this battle, we'll hold you responsible." Annoyed by their powerful stance, Tannis stares back with Patrayous and calmly mutters, "Understood, my Lords."

"Good day, *Marquis*." Raina edgily concludes as she and Lucian take their leave in a cold manner.

Zepherus raises his head and growls fiercely as Tannis and Patrayous glance at each other, knowing full well that there's a furious storm on the horizon.

Meanwhile outside the Senate Hall, Hammond and Griffin walk with their noble servants as Elena quickly approaches them.

"Senator Hammond!" She calls.

Hammond and Griffin quickly turn, surprised by her insistence.

"Everything alright, Princess?" Hammond carefully asks.

Elena stops before them and respectfully informs, "I need to speak with you at once if you don't mind."

"As you wish." Hammond calmly replies as he signals Griffin and his servants to leave, "Give us a moment if you don't mind, Julius."

"Of course, Nikolas." Griffin responds while bowing his head in respect. He then turns to Elena and says, "Farewell, Saltora."

Elena nods back in respect as Griffin takes his leave with the others.

"Now, what can I help you with, milady?" Hammond queries.

"Victor…" She quickly retorts, "Where is he?"

Amused, Hammond expresses a grin and warns, "Don't trouble yourself, you can't get anywhere near him at the moment."

"No, but I'm guessing you can." She implies with a confident smirk.

Hammond looks upon her with surprise as she discloses, "I need your help."

"It's been a long time since an Angel has asked a favor of me." Hammond jokes, "What exactly do you need?"

"Your help to free him." She clarifies, "As you already know, I can't directly go against the Arch to do so myself."

Holding his hands up in a worrying manner, Hammond affirms, "It's very tempting but at this point it's quite impossible. You see my hands are tied in this the same as yours I'm afraid. Is he really worth all this trouble?"

Elena looks away for a moment, contemplating her duty to Victor as well as the Arch then mentions, "He's shown greater courage than anyone I've ever known. The team needs him if they are to survive this debacle."

"What makes you so sure he can be of help to them at this point?" Hammond asks with a concerned expression.

"We both know they'll be overpowered without him." She construes.

Checking to make sure they aren't being watched, Hammond quietly asks, "Do you really think the Darchadians could come up with numbers greater than our own this quickly?"

"I know I'm asking a lot from someone of your political position, but he'll face execution if we don't act fast." Elena concedes.

"The Senate made a bad call; it's very divisive of them considering their duty as a working government is to protect people not run their lives." Hammond recognizes, "Regardless of his apparent innocence, they seem to hate him now; such is the irrefutable nature of politics in this world."

"Sadly yes." She gripes in a resentful tone, "More people from your realm would learn from their mistakes if they weren't so busy denying them."

Unbeknownst to them, Malik steps onto a balcony outside the Senate Hall, watching from above in suspicion.

"How much time do you need?" Hammond inquires.

"Just long enough to take him away from Titania for good." Elena clarifies with a respectful grin.

"The Emperor won't be pleased to know that he's escaped captivity again." He strongly cautions whilst looking around suspiciously.

Elena steps forward, looking upward at Tannis' tower and states, "At this point I don't really care what the Emperor thinks…" she turns back, then finishes, "And neither should you."

"They don't call this place the land of trade for nothing," he remarks, "You must have something to offer in return for such a risky request."

"If you help me, I swear to help you win the World Congress election as Chancellor in the next term of service." Elena persuades.

"A very enticing offer." Hammond muses as he brushes past her, "Should he be victorious, it would help me win by popular vote alone." He then turns back and asks, "But what guarantee do I have that he'll be able to find Trag and make it back alive with the others?"

Elena shakes her head as she grins in response and answers, "You don't."

Hammond suddenly waves his hand towards Griffin, signaling him to create a diversion with the Titanian guards. As Griffin heads towards the Palace of Justice, Hammond faces Elena and cautions, "You are treading on dangerous ground, milady. If your plan fails, then it will be both of our heads at risk."

"I know; that's why you're going to help me." She presumes.

Hammond chuckles softly and jokes, "You're a slave driver you know that?"

Amused by his ironic reference, Elena smirks as he says, "Tell your men to meet Griffin at the Palace of Justice near the slave chambers in ten minutes."

Bowing her head in appreciation towards him, she gratefully responds, "Thank you, Nikolas, you won't regret this."

"I hope not, for both our sake." He says sarcastically, "I'll get you your window." Elena nods once more then turns to take her leave as he warns, "Better hope he has some fight left in him cause if he doesn't then we'll both be joining him in the slave pit."

Turning her head, Elena mutters, "The world itself better hope he has some fight left." She then rushes off as Hammond shakes his head and grins.

After watching from above outside the Senate Hall on the balcony, Malik steps back inside still unnoticed by them. Minutes later, Elena rejoins Marcus and Yuri to confront them about her plan as Hammond takes his leave to avoid suspicion. "Well, what is it this time?" Yuri jokingly probes.

"I need your help guys." Elena states as she stops before them.

Wary of her intentions, the pair shares a glance. "Let me guess, it has something to do with Victor, doesn't it?" Marcus skeptically denotes.

Elena nods and retorts, "You know I can't allow the Senate to take his life."

"We can't just go knocking on the prison doors requesting his freedom you know?" Yuri says while sharing a concerned glance with Marcus.

"Not to worry, I've bought you guys some time." Elena assures as she turns her attention behind her.

"I'm not sure I want to know, but how exactly did you pull that off?" Marcus inquires apprehensively.

Grinning with determination, Elena turns back and states, "Let's just say I'm not the only one who sees Victor more valuable alive than dead."

"We get the idea." Yuri proclaims, "We'll take care of it."

"Are you sure?" Elena questions with her head slightly tilted.

"If you've got some help pulling strings in this corrupt place, then it shouldn't be a problem." Yuri confirms.

"Good call," Marcus deduces, "I'm sure the team could use his help right now as it is." Contemplating the worst-case scenario, Elena carefully responds, "Actually, I need you guys to take him someplace safe, far away from here. Eldria might be a good place to start."

Surprised by her request, Marcus and Yuri share another concerned glance.

"Let me get this straight, you want us to break him out and take him away from the fight?" Marcus questions, slightly annoyed.

"Yeah what gives?" Yuri curiously chimes in.

"I fear Tannis would still find a way to punish him even if he and the team were to succeed." She reluctantly clarifies, "He deserves more than what their kind has to offer."

"Understood." Yuri retorts as he and Marcus nod in esteem.

Relieved by their cooperation, Elena sighs heavily and says, "Thanks guys, you have no idea how much this means to me."

"More than you realize actually." Marcus chuckles in response.

"You know this won't go unnoticed by the Senate either." Yuri forewarns, "There will be consequences to pay for his release."

"I know, but it's my burden to bear." Elena calmly asserts.

Marcus willingly steps forward with Yuri and says, "Not anymore it seems."

"I have to do this." Elena states as she turns to take her leave.

Marcus smiles back and asks, "To uphold your sacred duty once again?"

Elena stops in her tracks and replies, "A promise." She then quickly turns and informs, "Whatever you do, do it quickly, we haven't much time."

With a grateful nod, Elena takes her leave to find Hammond as Yuri glances at Marcus and says, "Let's get going then!"

"I'm with you, bro!" Marcus determinedly retorts.

The pair head towards the holding cells to meet with Griffin as Yuri suddenly stops beside him and says, "Hold it! Are you thinking what I'm thinking?"

Marcus shakes his head and replies, "I hate to say it, but I'm afraid so."

"You know the three of us could be of assistance out there." Yuri suggests as he studies their surroundings in the city.

Marcus scoffs, surprised by his partner's sudden suggestion and queries, "Wait! You're telling me you want to join them on their suicidal mission?"

"If Victor chooses to fight then the team could possibly succeed," Yuri replies with a nod, "Wouldn't you agree?"

Amused, Marcus shakes his head and mutters, "I've been around you too long and it's starting to creep me out a bit." He then looks towards the Palace of Justice and states, "All right, let's do it! We owe it to Elena anyway."

"Exactly." Yuri confirms with a determined grin as he and Marcus continue walking through the city.

"Do you really think this is a wise course of action?" Marcus probes.

"We're about to find out." Yuri comments, "You've been craving some real action lately so you should be just as excited as me."

"I am, but what makes you think he'll even fight anyway?" Marcus inquires, concern apparent in his voice.

Yuri chuckles quietly and replies, "Just a hunch, but I'm betting he will." He then jokingly bets, "Ten to one odds?"

"Now you're talking!" Marcus says excitedly as he and Yuri once again pound their fists together in agreement.

The Empyrian duo head towards the Palace of Justice in an attempt to free Victor with what little time they have left.

Moments later, Elena finds Hammond who rushes towards her to converse.

"Everything is set, milady." Hammond gladly informs, "I suggest you get him out of here while you still can."

"My men are already on their way as we speak." Elena quickly reassures, "My apologies for getting you involved in all of this."

"Think nothing of it." Hammond humbly replies as he continues to look around for any spies then informs, "Griffin will distract the guards long enough to give them a chance to escape."

"Once again you've helped a very noble cause." Elena commends.

"I suppose this makes up for not warning you a while back when he fell into Tannis' grip." Hammond apologetically infers, "But first we shall see what he's truly made of. Do you think he'll even succeed?"

Without hesitation, Elena avows, "I believe in him."

Impressed with her diligent attitude, Hammond praises, "Your conviction shines now more than ever, Princess, for you truly are a model of virtue."

"If I'm truly a model of virtue, in this particular case, then Victor surely is one of valor himself." She remarks.

"Seems my people still have a lot to live up to in that regard after all these years." Hammond politely entails.

"Let's pray you're right about that." Elena conveys with a quiet chuckle as she looks upon Archadia floating in the sky overhead while Empyria hovers above Earth's atmosphere. Hammond follows suit as they take a moment to pray for their kingdoms' safety against the Darchadians.

Deep within the Darchadian fortress in Pretoria during mid-day, Damian is placed in energy shackles within a cell as Raiven and Celeste observe his Eudenian Gauntlet in curiosity.

"This will make a fine trophy, huh sis?" Celeste cynically infers.

"Yes, our Master will be very pleased with this." Raiven retorts.

Traganus suddenly enters the chamber as they look back in amusement.

"Indeed I will." Traganus confirms with a devious grin. Raiven and Celeste glance at each other and grin also as Traganus approaches them and conceitedly announces, "Let's see what our Champion has unlocked from his past battles, shall we?" Angered over his capture, Damian struggles to break free from the energy shackles but is unsuccessful.

"What of this Eudenian trash?" Celeste savagely queries as she motions towards Damian. Traganus looks back at him and sternly demands, "Get him to talk! I need to know where the pureblood is."

"Yes, Master." Celeste respectfully replies.

Raiven pulls Damian to his feet and callously orders, "This way, *slave!*"

Damian attempts to formulate an escape plan whilst being escorted by Raiven and Celeste. Making sure they don't notice, Damian pulls out a crystal shard from his garb and quickly tosses it to the side as they take him towards the holding cells for interrogation. Unbeknownst to them, the shard lights up brightly in purple, acting as a tracking device for Adrian and the team.

Traganus suddenly receives a holographic transmission from a mysterious figure, which appears before him and demands, "Report, Lord Traganus."

"I have retrieved the Artifact as requested and have successfully captured the Eudenian Champion." Traganus proudly states.

"Excellent, you've done well, Darchadian." The mysterious figure commends, "I trust you're presently unlocking the data from his Gauntlet?"

"That I am." Traganus replies with a firm nod, "It shouldn't take long to uncover its hidden power in conjunction with its internal mapping."

"I assume the team recently deployed by the Senate will be taken out without any further assistance then?" The mysterious figure inquires.

Traganus motions towards a large chamber behind him, and informs, "As you can see for yourself, I have a whole armada currently in status as we speak and will awaken them momentarily."

"See that you do." The mysterious figure reverently instructs, "I want them ready to launch as soon as possible."

Determined to exploit the opportunity given to him, Traganus grips his fist and assures, "As the prime leader of the Darchadian order, it will be done."

"Initiate your plan now then." The mysterious figure concludes, "This has been a long time coming for us both; I'll be expecting good news."

As the transmission ends abruptly, the holographic reading from Damian's Gauntlet catches Traganus' attention as he examines it closely, looking surprised by its mysterious genome results.

CH: 50
THE WORLD NEEDS YOU NOW

Right outside the Palace of Justice in Edge City, Marcus and Yuri approach Griffin who's standing outside the entrance as he waves them in.

"This way guys!" Griffin calls.

Marcus and Yuri nod in respect and rush inside as Griffin keeps an eye out for any trouble. Inside, Marcus and Yuri make their way towards the holding cells and find Victor sitting alone, looking distraught.

"You just can't catch a break, can you?" Marcus teases.

Surprised by their presence, Victor quickly turns and sees the two comedic Empyrians standing before him.

"I bet you're happy to see us, aren't you?" Yuri sarcastically implies.

Victor scoffs and mutters, "Let me guess, you came to restrain me?"

"No." Yuri calmly replies. Curious to their intentions, Victor looks upon them as he finishes, "We came to give you hope."

Annoyed by their positive stature, Victor looks away and grumbles, "Look, if you're here to gloat, spare me, there's nothing more I can do."

Marcus and Yuri glance at each other and grin.

"We thought you'd say that." Marcus states with a confident grin.

To Victor's surprise, Yuri suddenly breaks the locking mechanism on the holding cell with his energy sword extended from his Gauntlet.

"What are you doing?" Victor suspiciously queries.

"A dear friend of yours has risked her neck to save you." Marcus informs, trusting he will get the hint.

Concerned, Victor looks away; realizing who it is and murmurs, "Elena," he then turns back and inquires, "But why?"

"She's ordered us to get you out, assuming you want out." Yuri reveals as his energy sword retracts back into his Gauntlet.

"I see," Victor suspiciously retorts, "So you're just following orders then? As in you really don't care what happens to me?"

"Not quite," Marcus clarifies, "The team needs your help actually."

"My help, for what?" Victor questions with a surprised look.

Yuri crosses his arms in a stern manner and probes, "You've been to the Darchadian lair, yes?"

Victor nods and reluctantly says, "I have, but why should I be expected to fight for those that enslave me?"

"If you won't fight for us, then fight for yourself." Marcus inspires as he points directly towards Victor.

Victor hesitates to respond as he carefully ponders the thought for a moment.

"You can choose to flee, and we'll take you some place safe." Yuri explains, "Or you can fight for redemption. Either way, it's your choice."

Amused by their offer, Victor chuckles and sarcastically denotes, "I thought humans such as myself were pathetic and useless in combat?"

"You may be human, but you're still important to the team whether anyone else sees it or not, including you." Marcus states in a respectful tone.

"And if Trag is still alive you can help us rescue him." Yuri adds.

Victor looks around the holding cells, considering their proposal.

"Elena will be disappointed to know you won't help them," Marcus surmises, "We thought you were her friend?"

"So did I." Victor mutters disappointedly.

"What should we tell her then?" Yuri carefully asks.

Victor looks away whilst struggling to keep his composure then replies, "Lie if it makes you guys feel any better. All in all, it's probably best that she knows the truth about me anyway."

"And what truth is that?" Yuri probes with a curious grin.

Unable to answer, Victor sighs impatiently as Marcus and Yuri look upon him, disappointed by his negative attitude.

"What is it with you?" Marcus inquires, "We're supposed to be on the same side, and the Arch really needs your help right now."

"We really need your help right now." Yuri respectfully adds.

"I'm sorry, I just can't." Victor says in a cowardice voice.

As Marcus turns to leave with Yuri, he states, "She thought you were different, I guess she was wrong."

"I am different!" Victor defensively exclaims.

Marcus and Yuri glance at each other, smiling, then turn back to face him.

"Then show us." Yuri contests, "Here's your chance to redeem yourself and do what's right; I would take it."

"This is the time when it truly matters." Marcus adds encouragingly.

Searching within to find the strength he needs, Victor sighs and finally gives in, "I've lived helplessly under the lash of my enemies my entire life, but, I would be honored to fight and die beside you."

"That's the spirit!" Marcus says excitedly as he swings his fist in a cheerful manner.

Amused himself, Victor chuckles quietly in response to their excitement and states, "Even I can accept failure from time to time, but what I can't accept is not trying. Besides, if I can't do it, then who else will?"

"Spoken like a true Angel." Yuri compliments with a grin.

Shaking his head, Victor grins then looks upon his Angelic comrades and jokes, "I figured you guys would grow tired of me by now."

"So did we, but you're worth way more than you think, even in Elena's eyes." Yuri inspires.

"Don't disappoint her." Marcus firmly warns whilst pointing at him.

"I won't." Victor declares, looking determined, "Damian is still my comrade; I can't allow him to pay for my mistakes."

"Good choice, Victor." Marcus praises.

Yuri sees that the Titanian guards are returning to their posts and informs, "Now that that's settled, we must go, quickly."

Marcus and Yuri lead the way as Victor hesitates to step out of the holding cell. Noticing his hesitation, Yuri quickly turns and calls, "Come on!"

Overcoming his fear of imprisonment, Victor flees the holding cells and follows them out as they attempt to board a ship.

Making their way outside the Palace of Justice, Victor follows Marcus and Yuri as Griffin stands by and extends his hand out respectfully.

"Good luck, Zyas." Griffin encourages.

Victor shakes his hand and replies, "Thanks, I'll need it where I'm going."

Yuri points towards a docking station holding their ship and quickly directs, "Over there guys! Let's get the ship ready for take off as soon as we can!"

"Come on Victor, follow us!" Marcus guides.

Victor turns back to address Griffin one last time and says, "Thanks again."

"Don't mention it." Griffin replies with a humble nod.

After expressing his typical crooked smile, Victor boards the Arch ship with Marcus and Yuri in tow as they prepare to take off. As Yuri enters the cockpit, he fires up the ship and calls back, "You guys ready?"

"Yeah, let's do this!" Marcus jokingly shouts.

"Alright then, here we go!" Yuri announces as he turns back to focus on the control deck in the cockpit.

The Arch ship floats above the landing platform and quickly departs the docking station as Elena takes notice from her position near the Senate Hall.

"Farewell, Victor." She whispers in a sorrowful tone as she watches the Arch ship take off, hopeful for Victor's safety.

Meanwhile in the outskirts of Pretoria, Adrian and the team finally arrive and prepare for battle, knowing they may not survive an expected skirmish with the Darchadians. As the ship lands, Adrian stands to address everyone and firmly announces, "Prepare yourselves, and kill anything that moves faster than you, got it?"

"Got it!" The Eudenian and Enfurian troops respond with a hail.

"We've brought the fight to them!" He continues, "Let's show them who they're messing with and why!"

Everyone shouts in unison and power up their Gauntlets in anticipation.

"Alright everyone, move out!" Adrian orders as he motions towards the landing platform at the back of the ship.

Adrian and the remaining team depart the ship, ready to take on anything standing in their way as they cautiously scout the area for Darchadians.

"Don't power up your Gauntlets just yet," Adrian cautions quietly, "We don't want to give our position away." The Eudenian and Enfurian troops lower the energy levels of their Gauntlets to avoid signal spotting as Adrian turns to address the Enfurian Captain and orders, "Captain, tell the men to use their scouters."

The Enfurian nods and replies, "Yes Sir!" He then signals everyone to use their scouters, saying, "Power on your scouters, and check the perimeter!"

Everyone follows suit as they power on their scouters, which shift over the left side of their faces in search for any oncoming threats.

"Just because you don't read anything doesn't mean they're not out there!" The Eudenian Captain informs, keeping his eyes open for any perils.

Adrian looks around cautiously, sniffing a familiar scent just like before and grumbles, "They're out there alright."

As to not draw any attention to themselves, Adrian and the team continue cautiously through the rocky terrain in search for the Darchadian fleet.

Deep within the Darchadian fortress below the surface, Raiven and Celeste aggressively interrogate Damian whilst striking him in turns.

"Tell us where the pureblood is!" Celeste furiously demands.

Struggling to retain his composure, Damian scowls upon them and exclaims, "For the last time, I don't know what the hell you're talking about!"

Raiven and Celeste attempt to strike him once again in unison as Traganus suddenly grabs their arms from behind.

"At ease sisters, he's neutralized." He calmly informs.

The sassy duo glance at each other as Traganus frees their arms then swing them back in anger. A couple of other Darchadians enter the chamber to address Traganus as Raiven and Celeste look upon them in annoyance.

"What is it?" Traganus sternly inquires, sounding impatient.

"My Lord, an offensive force has landed near the outskirts of the base!" The first Darchadian informs.

"Their numbers are small compared to ours, but their power appears to be fairly strong!" The second one adds.

Amused by this news, Traganus scoffs, "How foolish! I didn't expect them to play right into our trap so easily."

"Guess they didn't learn from our last encounter." Raiven sneers.

"Apparently not." Traganus remarks whilst looking directly at the two Darchadians then asks, "Is the Enfurian Champion amongst them?"

"We can't confirm that yet, but he likely is." The Darchadian replies.

"Let us take a squad out and eliminate them once and for all!" Celeste ambitiously requests.

Traganus extends his arm towards his two anxious officers to calm them, saying, "Patience, sisters, you'll get your chance soon enough. Assuming they stay on their present course."

In light of this news, Damian looks upon Traganus in provocation and informs, "You're going to lose, all of you!"

Angered by his intrusive comment, Raiven suddenly strikes him in the face once more and screams, "Hold your tongue!"

"Enough!" Traganus furiously shouts as the chamber begins to suddenly darken from his intense power.

Raiven and Celeste sigh impatiently, as Traganus faces Damian directly and queries, "What makes you think your fallen team has a chance in Hell?"

"You may have the numbers, but your arrogance has blinded you!" Damian proclaims.

Traganus chuckles quietly and threatens, "The arrogance of your people is what brought you here. Your team will soon meet their end when I unleash terror in the skies above."

"It would be our pleasure to see the big brute fall to his knees!" Raiven maliciously comments.

"Even if you succeed, you'll have to answer to Raina and Lucian, and there's still the Angels to consider." Damian points out, "I know for a fact you wouldn't last long in that fight."

"Ha!" Traganus scoffs, "You think your mighty King and Queen are a threat to me?" Damian looks upon Traganus, surprised by his response as he continues, "Even together they've never been able to match my power. As for the Angels, they masquerade as mere saviors, but are worthless fairies."

"They can't be too worthless if you still see them as a threat." Damian mocks, attempting to argue.

With a confident grin, Traganus states, "They won't be a threat for long. The Arch as well as the Gods have yet to recognize our autonomy."

"Why should they?" Damian scorns, "You've threatened the entire planet, putting many lives at risk just to accomplish your own selfish goal."

"You may see my efforts only to be selfish, but in truth they are righteous and pure." Traganus justifies, "A necessary compromise."

"More like appeasement." Damian angrily counters.

"Is it appeasing to place people's lives at their beck and call, regardless of their hopes and dreams, like that of the Arch?" Traganus heatedly contests. Hesitating to respond, Damian ponders the thought, ignoring his valid point. "You'll soon understand; we've been moving slowly, cautiously for many years now." Traganus continues, "We've been extremely careful to cover our tracks as to not arouse suspicion. That is of course, until the time was right."

"And now it's too late, isn't it?" Damian sadly mutters.

"For you that is!" Raiven threateningly chimes in.

"Well put, sister." Traganus compliments with a turn of his head towards Raiven, then faces Damian once more, "The seeds of destruction have already been planted, setting the course of war in motion. Survive your people will today, but tomorrow brings darkness upon the Earth."

"What do you mean by that?" Damian cautiously inquires.

"Let's just say you won't always have the Arch to save you from oblivion." He cruelly explains, "The hierarchy of this age will soon crumble down before your own eyes. It is inevitable."

"We'll be ready when it does." Damian confidently retorts.

As Traganus straightens up, he states, "I doubt you'll have the pleasure, LT. There's no one else left to fight, no one to come to your aid."

"Someone surely will." Damian says determinedly.

"If you seriously think there's someone else who will take a stand against us, you're dead wrong!" Celeste viciously scorns.

Surprised, Damian sees the Angelic Artifact in Traganus' grasp and expresses a concerned look, unsure of what it is.

"With access to the Gods' realm, we will separate from the rest of the world and together, we will light up the entire planet." Traganus proudly enlightens, "Imagine the fear that will roll before us."

"The Arch will not comply with your demands!" Damian argues.

"In order to save themselves, they will give us what we want." He firmly states, "Only then can we reclaim our birth rite and finally be free. Soon they will know that our time has finally come, for I will bring our world crashing down upon theirs."

Damian attempts to strike Traganus but is held back by the energy shackles as Raiven and Celeste chuckle at his expense.

"Time to show this fallen Champion what it means to have your faith destroyed." Traganus proclaims as he turns to address Raiven and Celeste, waving his hand, "Awaken the others, it's time they spread their wings."

Raiven and Celeste glance at each other and deviously grin in anticipation.

"In order to demonstrate their abilities, we must let them leave the nest." Traganus informs, "Be sure to kill them this time, sisters."

"Our pleasure, but we don't need your advice on that." Raiven reassures as her and Celeste pound their fists together with determination.

"You may take a squad out, Celeste." Traganus allows with a firm wave of his hand.

Celeste bows her head in respect and grins towards Raiven as she takes her leave to do battle against the team.

"I will leave you to your thoughts, LT. As you can see, I have a war to wage." Traganus claims as he quickly turns away from Damian then orders, "See that he doesn't leave his cell, there may be others."

The two Darchadians nod as he takes his leave, followed closely by Raiven.

"Master!" Raiven inquires, "What about me?"

Traganus stops in his tracks then turns to face Raiven and calmly orders, "Take your squad away from the battle and await my command." He then informs, "We don't want to alert the Arch to our full presence just yet."

"What about him?" Raiven queries as she motions towards Damian.

Glancing back at him curiously with a confident grin, Traganus assures, "Don't worry, he'll soon overstay his welcome here."

Raiven bows her head then takes her leave as Damian looks on, hoping that someone will come for him eventually. As Raiven exits the chamber, she quickly looks behind her to see if anyone's looking then raises her arm to set up a transmission with her Gauntlet.

"What is your location, sister?" Raiven quietly asks.

"Come to join the action, huh sis?" Celeste counters with a laugh.

"You got it." Raiven confidently replies.

"I should've known you wouldn't let me have all the fun." Celeste jokes; pleased by her willingness to join her in battle.

Raiven chuckles quietly and devilishly retorts, "Of course not."

"I suppose I could share a little carnage with my own sibling," Celeste sarcastically states, "What are sisters for anyway?"

"Causing trouble and taking names." Raiven cynically replies with a devilish grin as she looks upon the coordinates displayed through the holographic image projecting from her Gauntlet.

"Don't keep me waiting, sis!" Celeste warns.

"Not to worry, sis, I won't." Raiven says quietly.

Just as the transmission ends, Raiven quickly takes off against Traganus' orders to do battle alongside Celeste against the team outside their underground fortress.

CH: 51
THE BATTLE FOR PARADISE BEGINS

In the outskirts of Pretoria, Adrian and the team continue scouting the perimeter as they unknowingly venture towards the Darchadian fortress. With his Gauntlet drawn securely, Adrian looks around cautiously and quickly turns, sniffing a familiar scent once again.

"They're here!" He warns.

The team is suddenly ambushed by a small fleet of Darchadians flying in from above in all directions like burning comets from the sky.

"Fall into attack positions!" The Eudenian Captain shouts.

The Darchadians hiss savagely as they charge towards the team without hesitation, attempting to take them out quickly and efficiently.

"Stand your ground and wait till they break formation!" Adrian orders as he steps into attack position, "Everybody stay tight on the enemy horde and don't let them catch you out in the open! Keep your Gauntlets at the ready, here they come!" A few Darchadians see Adrian and hiss ferociously as they eagerly fly towards him at high speed. "Bring it fairies!" He proudly exclaims while aggressively pounding his chest in a warrior like manner, ready to take them on singlehandedly.

As the Darchadians attempt to strike, Adrian catches them off guard as he backhands them several feet in the air. The battle ensues as the Eudenian and Enfurian troops stand together to keep the Darchadians at bay.

Aboard the Arch ship heading towards Pretoria, Victor prepares for battle with Marcus as Yuri puts the ship into autopilot. He then steps away from the cockpit to gear up as well and surprises him with his mother's Gauntlet still intact.

"Try and hang on to this if you can." Yuri encouragingly jokes.

Victor grins in appreciation then places the Gauntlet back over his arm and activates it, which powers up his Angelic Soul Gear once again.

"I've adjusted it to perfect efficiency," Yuri proudly informs as Victor examines his Gauntlet in appreciation, "Thanks to the shard you had within it, you should be able to draw more energy than before now."

"Thanks, Yuri." Victor replies with a nod, "I greatly appreciate it."

"I don't know exactly where you got the crystal contained within, but it's even more powerful than that of our own." Yuri jokingly states.

With a crooked smile, Victor retorts, "Call it a gift if you must."

Amused by Victor's renewed confidence, Marcus approaches him and gags, "I sure hope you know how to use that thing."

Victor powers up his Gauntlet to its full potential, looking determined then faces Marcus and sarcastically replies, "Better than you do!"

"Yeah right!" Marcus chuckles, "We probably should've warned you beforehand; this may turn out to be extremely dangerous."

"I'd be very disappointed if it wasn't." Victor says with a smirk.

A bit of laughter escapes Victor also as Marcus motions outside the Arch ship and denotes, "I bet the odds are against us, aren't they?"

"You could say that," Victor sarcastically utters, "At least I'll know where they're coming from and when this time."

There is a slight pause as Marcus nods then proclaims, "Sounds like fun!"

Yuri looks out from the ship's hull and sees the team battling it out against the Darchadians below. Suddenly, the Arch ship is struck by a couple of random energy blasts from the surface, causing the trio to hang on tightly. Marcus approaches the back of the ship and opens the landing platform as he observes the battle below in amusement.

"Would you look at that." He jokingly mutters, "Who started a party without me?" An energy blast zooms past the ship as Marcus grins and exclaims; "Now that's what I'm talking about!" Victor and Yuri look out towards the ship's hull as well and see the battle intensifying below. "Time for some payback, *bitches*!" Marcus announces determinedly as he powers up his Gauntlet and prepares to take off.

Concerned by his Empyrian comrade's sudden confident attitude, Yuri calls back, "Marcus, what are you doing?"

Marcus quickly turns to respond, saying, "You two find Trag! I'm going to help them before Braxel takes all the glory!"

"In the midst of that battle, are you crazy?" Yuri questions.

"Yeah sometimes; wish me luck!" Marcus says with a hand wave.

"I would but this isn't part of the plan!" Yuri cautions, "I don't see the odds in your favor and it's too dangerous for you to go down there now!"

Laughing in response, Marcus turns to face Yuri and informs, "But that's when all the action takes place!" He then looks directly at Victor and shouts, "Hey Victor!" Surprised, Victor curiously looks towards him as he inspires, "Make it back in one piece, alright!"

"I will!" Victor confidently shouts back over the noise with a grin.

Marcus smiles back then suddenly jumps off the ship's landing platform, falling head first towards the battlefield below.

Yuri shakes his head, amused by his spirit as he and Victor look down below from the landing platform.

"Damn fool!" Yuri teases, "That guy never ceases to amaze me!"

"It's up to us now!" Victor motivates, "Let's find Damian so we can help the others!"

"I'm with you!" Yuri quickly retorts as he closes the hatch and heads back towards the cockpit to pilot the ship manually.

As Yuri takes the ship back into manual control, Victor stands by the landing platform and looks out the window with a slight heavy breath, determined to redeem himself before the eyes of his team and the Gods.

Making his way downward towards the battlefield, Marcus presses the Gods' symbol over his chest, which activate his wings and slow him down. Moments later, Marcus gracefully lands on the ground with his fist hitting the dirt, scattering several Darchadians in the process.

"Oh yeah!" He proudly exclaims.

Angered by his sudden entry, several Darchadians rush towards him in the air, attempting to strike but Marcus holds his own, taking them on one at a time.

Outside the Darchadian fortress, Victor and Yuri land the Arch ship and attempt to infiltrate the base alone. As Yuri steps away from the cockpit, he approaches Victor and asks, "You ready?"

Fully energized, Victor raises his Gauntlet and proudly states, "Affirmative!"

"Good," Yuri replies, "Feel free to lead then."

Victor grips his Gauntlet determinedly as he steps onto the landing platform, and states, "It's about time I did."

As Victor departs the ship, Yuri follows closely behind in an attempt to look for Damian. Yuri presses a random button on his Gauntlet, which causes a holographic schematic to appear before him.

"So how do we expect to find him exactly?" Victor inquires.

"That's the easy part," Yuri explains, "I've calibrated our Gauntlets to pick up his energy signal. He apparently left a distress signal from one of his shards for us to follow so we better act quick."

Victor looks upon his Gauntlet curiously and also presses a button as the same holographic schematic appears before him as well.

"Great idea." Victor remarks, "This will make it much easier for us."

"Assuming he's still alive, we should be able to find him in no time." Yuri suggests whilst following vigilantly.

"Let's hope so anyway." Victor sarcastically mutters.

As Victor and Yuri approach the back entrance to the fortress, they look around cautiously with their Gauntlets drawn.

"It's awfully silent around here, don't you think?" Victor denotes as he attempts to find a visual trace of the Darchadians.

"Yeah, they probably all left to do battle." Yuri assumes.
Stepping cautiously forward through the mysterious fortress, Victor surmises, "I don't think so, they wouldn't leave this place unprotected for long."

"You're probably right about that." Yuri jokes.

"I don't believe they know that we're here, yet." Victor deduces.
Yuri suddenly stops as he looks upon Victor curiously and carefully asks, "How's that, because they haven't shown their ugly faces yet?"
Victor suddenly stops in his tracks as well then faces him and seriously informs, "No, because they haven't attacked us, and we're still breathing."
Concerned by his assumption, Yuri looks upon his Archadian comrade as he carefully follows him deep into the Darchadian fortress.

On the battlefield outside the Darchadian fortress in Pretoria, Marcus catches up with Adrian, as they take on the Darchadians side by side. The team holds up their defense against them, but know full well that there are plenty more Darchadians on the way.

"Nice party!" Marcus puns, "Mind if I crash?"

"You call this a party?" Adrian sarcastically retorts.

"What, you're not having any fun?" Marcus asks.

"I think it's fair to call this hostile territory!" Adrian professes as he strikes a Darchadian back several yards away with his elbow. "I must say, I'm kind of surprised to see you here!"

"Someone told me there was a battle going on!" Marcus informs.

"Oh, it's going alright, though how well I can't say!" Adrian retorts as he deflects an attack back towards a Darchadian, "We've got things under control for the moment anyway!"

"Come on!" Marcus insists, "I can't let you fight Darchadians all by yourself, now can I?"
A couple of Darchadians swoops in unexpectedly and attempts to strike as Marcus and Adrian retaliate by striking them back together.

"Phew, that was close!" Marcus jokes as they stand back to back once again, attempting to hold their ground against their deadly foes.

"The heat is on!" Adrian warns, "Better get out while you still can!"

"And let you have all the fun?" Marcus scoffs, "I don't think so!"
Adrian turns his head and grins, amused by Marcus' willingness to join him in battle against the Darchadians.

"Yuri and Victor went after Trag!" Marcus informs, "We just have to hold them off till they get back!" He then faces the Enfurian Champion directly and asks, "Are you up to it?"

"Of course!" Adrian sarcastically retorts, "Though I never thought I'd be fighting alongside an Empyrian!"

"Well, technically we're both Enfurian, but I get your point!" Marcus ironically infers with a smirk.

Another Darchadian swoops in as Adrian quickly ducks, allowing Marcus to take them out single-handedly.

"Don't tell me you're getting soft on me already?" Marcus teases.

Feeling challenged by his Empyrian comrade, Adrian grins and proudly declares, "Not at all, I'm just warming up!"

"Good, cause ready or not, here they come!" Marcus warns as he and Adrian see a few Darchadians flying towards them at full speed.

"Yeah, come and get if fairies!" Adrian exclaims as he pounds the ground with his fists, which causes various crystalline pillars to pop out from under the dirt whilst scattering the Darchadians in a more forceful technique.

"Amen to that!" Marcus jokingly harmonizes.

Marcus and Adrian continue fighting together, displaying tremendous power against the vicious Darchadians in an attempt to buy Victor and Yuri enough time to find their Eudenian comrade, Damian.

Deep within the Darchadian fortress, Victor and Yuri continue their search for Damian and unexpectedly come across a large cavernous area containing hundreds of cryogenic chambers.

"What is this place?" Victor questions, looking distraught.

"A stronghold of some sort," Yuri deduces, "Looks like Traganus has been preparing a Darchadian army right under our noses."

The pair looks around cautiously as they enter the chamber and see dozens of Darchadian hexagonal cocoons waiting to emerge.

"So, this is how Angels are made?" Victor sarcastically grumbles, "It's not exactly what I imagined growing up."

"This isn't how true Angels are made, this is something else entirely." Yuri comments, greatly concerned by what they're seeing.

As the powerful duo makes their way deeper into the chamber, Victor denotes, "They're like a hive mind."

"It would appear so," Yuri affirms. Victor places his hand on the side of his head, feeling strange atmospheric vibes in the chamber as Yuri looks upon him with concern and asks, "You good?"

"Yeah." Victor replies as he continues his focus on the wicked looking hexagonal cocoons, "It's strange, I feel linked to them somehow."

"Not too much I hope." Yuri sarcastically implies.

Victor and Yuri suddenly hear a hissing noise as they quickly draw their Gauntlets and stand back-to-back, ready to defend themselves.

"Did you hear that?" Yuri carefully asks.

"Unfortunately." Victor firmly replies whilst gripping his Gauntlet.

"What was it?" Yuri inquires whilst gripping his tightly as well.

While studying their dark and mysterious surroundings, Victor smirks then confidently retorts, "I'd say we have company."

"Great, that's all we need." Yuri grumbles.

As the Darchadians begin to move in their cryogenic cocoons, Victor notices his Gauntlet glowing brightly in blue and expresses a look of concern then turns to him and says, "Yuri?"

"Yeah?" He carefully replies.

"I think they heard you." Victor jokingly mutters.

Surprised by his comment, Yuri looks around with his Gauntlet drawn as the Darchadians begin to awaken from their hexagonal cocoons.

"Hide, now!" Victor quickly warns as they take cover behind a couple of crystalline pillars while the cryogenic chambers open. The Darchadians exit their cocoons, activate their Angelic wings and fly near the top of the fortress. Shocked by the sight, Victor and Yuri glance at each other as they watch a large amount of Darchadians heading towards their comrades outside.

"The Arch council isn't going to believe this!" Yuri states with a raised tone to counter the loud screeching noise made by the Darchadians.

"We have to find Damian before the team is overrun with these damn things!" Victor cautions.

"Right!" Yuri replies with a nod as he hurriedly raises his Gauntlet to set up a transmission, "Better inform Elena while we're at it. She needs to know what we just saw!"

Saddened by the sound of her name, Victor looks upward and sighs, yearning to see her again as Yuri attempts to contact Elena by sending a transmission through his Gauntlet's higher functions.

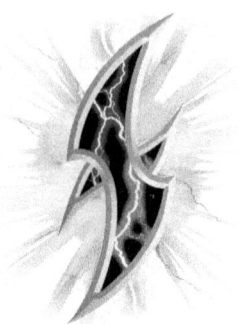

CH: 52
WORLD DISTORTION

Meanwhile, inside his throne chamber within the tallest and most extravagant looking tower of Edge City, Tannis meets with a small Titanian media crew to make an announcement to the world through a live broadcast.

"Ready when you are, Lord Tannis." A media crewmember informs.
As Tannis prepares to give his speech, people the world over watch the broadcast in anticipation through various forms of visual and audio media.

"Greetings, my fellow citizens of Earth..." Tannis begins.
Patrayous stands by with Zepherus as the Titanian media crew listens closely with their advanced video and audio equipment.

"It has come to my attention that our collective trust has been placed upon someone who has recently dishonored it." He reveals as citizens from around the world glance at each other curiously of this news.
Outside Tannis' tower in Edge City, Elena tends to Talia with Lithia at her side as Kael stands by with his arms crossed, listening to the broadcast overhead on a large holographic screen.

"A recent skirmish in Pretoria has put the safety of our people at risk; to retain worldwide security we must maintain a state of order." Tannis explains, "Thus, action will be taken swiftly against those who dare to threaten our way of life." Concerned by the Emperor's meaning, Kael glances at Elena who places her hands around Talia to comfort her as Lithia growls.

"The cost of sanity in today's society is a certain level of alienation..." Tannis continues as the city lights start to flicker unexpectedly, "For that which keep us secure, also keeps us free."
Elena and Kael look around, confused by the sudden power surge as the holographic screens showcasing the broadcast throughout the city begin to flash. Guarding Talia closely, Elena attempts to deduce the exact cause of the visual disruption as the broadcast screens suddenly go blank worldwide.

Back in the tower, Tannis looks around in annoyance as the Titanian Media Crew scrambles to solve the issue with their equipment.

"What's happening, did we just lose the feed?" He questions irritably. As the crewmembers frantically check their equipment, one of them looks back and replies, "We don't know, Sir!"

Patrayous looks out the window passed the crystalline throne, sensing a mysterious threat as Zepherus growls with his spinal shards glowing and retracting, sensing it as well.

"We've lost the transmission!" another crewmember states.

"What?" Tannis angrily inquires, as he steps away from the window, "How is that even possible in my kingdom?"

Concerned by this mysterious interruption, Patrayous looks towards Tannis as the media crew attempts to solve the issue as fast as they can.

"Something's over riding our signal!" A crewmember carefully states. Tannis glances at Patrayous, angered by this interference then turns back and furiously mutters, "Of course it is!"

To Patrayous' surprise, Tannis slams his fist onto the table in anger and approaches the window overlooking the city as the Titanian media crew struggles to locate the disrupting signal in time.

Outside the tower, Elena and Kael look around cautiously and see hundreds of Titanian citizens starting to panic due to the broadcast's interruption.

"What's going on?" She carefully inquires.

"I don't know," Kael replies while shaking his head in annoyance, "Whatever it is it can't be good."

A high-pitched noise suddenly roars throughout the city, causing fear and disruption amongst the citizens present as Traganus suddenly appears in shadow upon every holographic display around the world. Everyone looks on in shock as the mysterious Darchadian leader positions himself into full view.

"Inhabitants of Earth, heed our warning." Traganus begins.

Surprised by his sudden and unwanted presence, Elena looks back at Kael who scowls in annoyance of the startling broadcast.

"Your leaders have withheld the truth from you about my kind for far too long." Traganus illuminates, "Thus, the time for revelations has come to pass for all who would listen. For those that have fallen, I am their voice."

Tannis looks out from his throne chamber in the tower and scowls angrily over the prohibited broadcast.

"You are not alone in this world." Traganus reveals, "We have lived among you, hidden in secret for years, but no longer. The Arch thought they had rid themselves of me and my kind for good, but when darkness falls upon the planet, they're going to discover their grave mistake first hand."

Titanian citizens watch the broadcast in shock of Traganus' presence as he resumes, "In time, you will see that we can destroy your cities at will, unless of course you turn over the Princess of Archadia to us."

Kael shares a deeply concerned expression with Elena as she and Talia look upon the broadcast in shock.

"Until you do so, we will continue as planned to do what we had originally set out to do, which is to take control of every kingdom on this planet." Traganus viciously threatens to their surprise.

"He can't be serious!" Kael scoffs.

Talia looks into Elena's eyes, concerned for their lives as she looks back and smiles to comfort her as Lithia supports with a cheerful chirp.

"And if you resist, we will destroy the world as you know it, for our mission is not of peace, but freedom and retribution." Traganus menaces with a stern voice, "Your time is over; we're bringing the war to you."

Raina and Lucian watch the broadcast from aboard their ship sitting in Titania and glance at each other in anger of his self-proclaimed superiority.

"Make no mistake; this is the day when your world changes forever, for peace is no longer considered a justifiable deterrent." Traganus states, "If the Arch fails to comply with our demands, then war will break out like a plague across the entire planet." Citizens of all types from around the globe watch in horror as he continues with his life-threatening speech, "Your oceans will become caverns, your cities like graveyards, and your loved ones into ashes. Our enemies will soon be destroyed, and from those ashes a new kingdom shall arise. My people seek paradise, and they shall have it."

Lithia growls in anticipation with his spinal shards glowing as Talia attempts to calm him by petting his head.

"There is no escape." Traganus warns, "Succumb to our rule, or die. In order for you to understand the true nature of your choice, a small demonstration of our power from my legion of thunder."

Several Darchadian fleets fly downward from the sky like burning comets towards various parts of the planet in an attempt to showcase their growing dominance by taking the world hostage. Kael continues watching the broadcast and scoffs as waves of Darchadians are shown flooding various cities within continents, excluding Titania.

"You call that small?" Kael mutters in annoyance.

Elena looks upon him in admiration of his strength during this dark time then refocuses her attention on the broadcast.

Patrayous continues looking out the window from Tannis' throne room with Zepherus and sighs, angered of this worldwide treachery.

"And to my fellow Angels, I say this…" Traganus clarifies as Rosalyn and Josephus watch the broadcast from above in their throne chamber in Archadia, glancing at each other with grave concern over the matter. "Either stand with us, or stand against us." He firmly warns.

Rosalyn quickly signals an Archadian to get in contact with Valorie and Vennessa near the area as she and Josephus continue watching the dreadful broadcast impatiently.

"Enough blood will be shed once we've taken our rightful place back from those who have selfishly taken it from us." Traganus proclaims, "As we cleanse the surface, darkness will soon blanket the world in shadow."

Valorie and Vennessa receive orders from their Gauntlets and nod at one another before taking off from an Archadian outpost to find Elena in time.

"From nothing we have risen, and from nothing we shall soar." Traganus proclaims while gripping his fist, "The invasion of Earth has begun." With the tension building worldwide, he pauses briefly then resumes, "Understand that what we do, we do for the goodness of all mankind. This won't be understood now, but the destruction to come will vindicate our rewarding faith, for violence is the only truth that can cleanse the corrupt establishment of this world from its hypocrisy and systematic inequality."

Elena stands ready with her crystalline staff to protect Talia and says, "Kael?"

"I know!" Kael frustratingly retorts.

Guarding Talia with her life, Elena powers up her crystalline staff, as Talia looks on in fear, holding Lithia close as he chirps.

"The fallen has risen from the ashes of chaos, from the darkness, and into the light." Traganus concludes as he finally reveals himself up close, "Justice has revealed its true face, and thus, vengeance has come at last."

Everyone worldwide looks upon the holographic broadcast in shock as Traganus' helmet shifts back, finally revealing his face. The broadcast ends abruptly as Elena receives a sudden transmission from her Gauntlet.

"Princess Elena!" Yuri calls, "Are you there?" Elena quickly raises her Gauntlet to respond as Talia and Kael look on curiously. "You're not going to believe this!" Yuri states.

"At this point I'll believe anything." Elena jokingly scoffs.

"As it turns out, there's a whole chamber full of Darchadians that have just been awakened, which I assume are to do battle against the team." Yuri reluctantly informs.

Without hesitation, Elena quickly asks, "What is your location?"

"Pretoria, I'm in the Darchadian fortress as we speak." He reveals.

"Is that so?" She sarcastically retorts.

"Are you surprised?" Yuri jokes.

Elena glances at Talia and mutters, "No, not really."

"Then you won't be surprised to hear that Victor is with me as well." Yuri gladly reveals.

Shocked yet relieved by this news, Elena glances at Kael as he smiles back with a nod. Talia looks upon Elena in relief who looks back with a smile and says, "That's wonderful news, Yuri." She then covers her mouth in relief as a tear runs down her face, feeling slightly emotional over his well-being.

"I'd say so, considering the grim circumstances." Yuri replies.

Hoping to comfort Elena, Talia places her hand next to hers as Lithia perches himself on her shoulder.

Elena regains her composure as she places her hand on Talia's shoulder in appreciation, and denotes, "So that would-be tyrant, Traganus has been building an army after all, which means he's been planning to attack Archadia for some time now."

"It would appear so, yes." Yuri explains, "An army of this scale could definitely threaten the entire populous if we don't stop them."

Disappointed by this dark revelation, Elena firmly comments, "Our enemy has been recruiting right in front of us, for survival no doubt, and yet as always we were too blind to see it."

"Excluding ourselves, I can't disagree with you there." Yuri puns.

"Victor was right all along then." Elena sadly murmurs as she looks onto the horizon beyond the city.

"Yes," Yuri regards, "Seems there's more to him than what everyone else chooses to see. But you believe in him, and I'm starting to as well." He says, nodding towards Victor in approval as he smiles back. "Braxel and the team are already engaged in combat with the Darchadians, so we have to act fast." He informs.

"Watch his back, Yuri, and report back immediately when you find Damian." Elena orders.

"Understood, milady!" Yuri acknowledges, "We're tracking his signal now. With Victor's help, we should be able to find him quickly, but we're going to need a lot of back up if we are to survive this deadly skirmish."

"Not to worry, help is on the way." Elena reassures as she looks upwards and sees Valorie and Vennessa approaching them from above.

Talia smiles in relief of Elena's attitude as Lithia climbs onto her shoulder, ready for action as he growls. "Copy that!" Yuri concludes, "Yuri out!"

The transmission ends as Elena looks away disappointedly whilst placing her hand over her tiara on her forehead, realizing that the team is in far greater danger than previously thought. "I'm so sorry I ever doubted you, Victor." She whispers to herself. "How are we going to evacuate entire cities?"

"We can't; people are going to die." Kael sternly replies.

Talia looks upon Elena, concerned for her emotional wellbeing whilst sensing her true feelings towards Victor. Elena wipes away her teary eyes then looks upon Talia and smiles. "How much of the team remains?" Kael inquires.

"Last I checked, less than a third." Elena replies, "He's raising a vast army, how is that possible that a single man can cause so much devastation?"

"From what we know about him, it's in his nature." Kael informs.

As Kael looks away, Valorie and Vennessa land from above to address them.

"Your highness!" Valorie calls as Elena quickly turns and looks upon them, curious to their intentions. "We've been ordered to bring you back to Archadia." She informs. Becoming impatient, Elena asks, "Why?"

"The council has requested that we get you out of harms way before Traganus has an opportunity to capture you here." Vennessa explains.

Frustrated by her parents' callous decision, Elena steps forward and stresses, "I can't go back now; there are more important matters at stake!"

"We're just following orders, Princess." Valorie strongly advises, "It's probably best that you don't anger the council any further."

Elena glances at Kael and Talia in disappointment, contemplating her next move then turns impatiently towards the Arch ship as she prepares for battle.

"What are you doing?" Valorie inquires.

"Redefining what it means to be a Princess; if the Arch won't take a stand then someone has to!" Elena firmly rationalizes, "I'm not going to sit back and watch them die!" Valorie and Vennessa glance at each other, concerned over her ambitious attitude as she continues, "I have to help them in any way possible, regardless of what the council wishes at this time."

"Why may I ask?" Vennessa queries with a stern expression.

As Elena powers up her Angelic Soul Gear, she quickly turns and answers, "The Arch can't expect them to do this alone, and neither should we."

"It's too dangerous to go out there!" Valorie warns as she approaches the Arch ship to stop her.

"Incase you haven't noticed, sisters, it's going to be dangerous no matter where I go at this point." Elena mockingly retorts, "That alone is why I don't go by typical protocol, for I lead from the heart not the head."

"Nevertheless, you should come back with us and wait for the Arch to take action!" Valorie advises in an attempt to counter her defiance.

"By that point it will already be too late." Elena expresses as she prepares a couple of crystalline staffs for battle, "Traganus is a far greater threat than we anticipated. Therefore, as a Princess of Archadia, I must insure he does not reach the final stage of his plan, for it could be ruinous for us all." She proclaims whilst preparing a green Soul Gear pendant for Talia.

"There's a low survival probability out there," Vennessa insistently warns, "You know you can't do this alone."

Stopping her tracks, Elena quickly turns to face her female comrades and carefully indicates, "I'm not; you're going to help me."

Valorie and Vennessa glance at each other, amused by her bold request.

"Help you, how?" Vennessa scoffs, "If you go out there like this, you'll be turning your back on your own people."

"Can't you see I'm trying to help my people?" Elena contests, "Actual belief in one's duty is demonstrated by action, not profession."

Vennessa sighs impatiently as she resumes, "You must do everything possible to convince the Arch to intervene. If they stand by apathetically in this matter, then the Darchadians will come for us next."

"What makes you think they'll even listen to us?" Valorie inquires.

"You heard Yuri's transmission!" Elena explains, "That should be more than enough evidence to convince them."

Elena takes a brief moment to connect with her fellow sisters as she stands before them and places her hands on their shoulders to comfort them, saying, "I know it won't be easy, sisters, but you have to try." Valorie and Vennessa contemplate the idea as Elena quickly turns to address Talia and informs, "Talia, you're coming with me!"

"Yes, your Highness." Talia replies with a firm nod.

Lithia chirps excitedly, which causes Talia and Elena to grin in response.

"You can't fly out on the Arch like this!" Vennessa stresses.

"Why not?" Elena contests, "I do it all the time."

"Because you're a political envoy, more so now than ever." Vennessa adds, trying to convince to her otherwise.

"No, I'm a warrior Princess." Elena proudly declares.

"With responsibilities mind you." Vennessa confirms.

Elena sighs edgily and proclaims, "Such responsibilities are worthless without action, which is why my true responsibility at the moment is combat."

"You're going to risk your own life and this child's life as well?" Valorie firmly questions as she motions towards Talia. Elena turns back towards Valorie and Vennessa with a concerned look. "Are you so ready to die that you would risk the safety of our people?" She irritably questions.

With a serious gaze, Elena responds, "Archadia won't survive if we don't take action." She then points towards them with her crystalline staff and says, "If either of you have any concern for our people, then you will do what I ask."

As Valorie and Vennessa glance at each other once more, Elena turns back to address Talia and asks, "Ready, Talia?" Talia nods determinedly as Lithia flies onto the Arch ship and chirps. Elena smiles, appreciative of their courage as she motions towards the ship and says, "Get on board then." As Talia boards the Arch ship with Lithia, Elena looks on with a determined stance then turns back to address Valorie and Vennessa one last time. "Go back and put a face on what's happening out there, make the council see what they choose not to." Elena respectfully orders before turning back to board the ship.

Valorie steps onto the landing platform and carefully asks, "What if we fail?" Stopping in her tracks once more with her back turned, Elena firmly replies, "We'll all fail on this day if we don't try." She then turns back to face them and concludes, "I pray the Gods give you strength, sisters."

"And you, Princess." Vennessa responds with a respectful nod.

Elena nods in return then quickly turns back to board the Arch ship as Kael approaches the landing platform next to Valorie and Vennessa.

"Take care of yourselves." Kael encourages.

"We will." Elena affirms with a steady nod.

As the landing platform closes, Kael stands back with Valorie and Vennessa. The Arch ship hovers above the dock and suddenly takes off towards Pretoria, as Valorie and Vennessa look upon Kael, unsure of their next strategic move in regards to the Darchadian threat looming about.

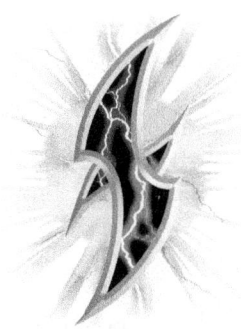

CH: 53
A HERO WITH WINGS

In the outskirts of Pretoria, Adrian and Marcus continue their battle against the Darchadians alongside the team. Observing the intense battle from above, Raiven and Celeste arrive on the battlefield whilst floating in the air with their wings fully spread. "An Enfurian and an Empyrian fighting together?" Raiven taunts. Adrian and Marcus apprehensively look up and see the pair floating above them as they grin. "Fascinating!" She teases.

"Though you have to admit, sis, they're not much to look at." Celeste ridicules with a devious grin.
Annoyed by their wicked presence, Adrian scoffs and sarcastically retorts, "We weren't meant to be pretty!"
The deadly pair chuckle manically, "Apparently not!" Celeste scorns.

"What are you doing out here, *Darchadians*?" Marcus questions.
The two Darchadians grin as Celeste replies, "Looking for playmates, and it appears we've found them."

"We didn't realize we were going to be this entertained whilst destroying your pitiful force." Raiven sneers.

"Yes, how exciting." Celeste snickers.

"Give it up, ladies!" Marcus seriously warns as he steps forward defensively, "You can't take us both on!"

"That's what you think!" Raiven says with a condescending laugh.

"Don't flatter yourself, *fool*, we're Darchadian elites!" Celeste proudly informs, "Top of the line!" Adrian chuckles in response as Marcus looks upon him, surprised by his confident attitude towards the situation.

"You may be Darchadians, but I hunt fairies like you for breakfast!"
Adrian declares as he aggressively pounds his fists together.
With a harsh chuckle, Raiven derides, "Fairies, such a juvenile term it hardly fits. Truth be told we're vindictive little bitches."

"Sounds like the big guy didn't get his fill this morning, and must be hungry!" Celeste cynically mocks.

"Indeed, sis." Raiven adds as she waves Adrian and Marcus over to them, "Catch us if you can, *big boys*!"

Annoyed by their arrogance, Adrian and Marcus power up then charge towards the deadly duo and the fight begins. With the battle ensuing, Raiven and Celeste prove too quick for them as Adrian and Marcus try their best to take them down through the intense battlefield full of deadly opposition.

High above the planet's surface in Pretoria, the Arch ship flies towards the battlefield as Lithia stands perched on Talia's shoulder then looks towards Elena and chirps, ready to take on anything. Elena approaches the cockpit to address the two Archadians flying the ship.

"Keep the ship steady, sisters." She advises, "We don't want to alert the Darchadians by coming in too hot."

"Yes, your Highness." The Archadians respond together with a nod.

Elena turns away from the cockpit and approaches Talia who's sitting in the back of the ship with a nervous look then kneels before her as she pulls out a small custom made Archadian Gauntlet. "Here, take this Gauntlet, Talia; you may need it." She instructs. Lithia nudges his head against Talia's as she takes the Gauntlet and observes it in appreciation. "The time to use it may be near at hand. This angelic tool is not a toy so bear it well and use it wisely." Elena informs as she places the green decorative piece on Talia's chest and presses the Gods' symbol, which activates her Soul Gear. Talia watches with wondrous eyes as the Soul Gear forms over her body for the first time.

"I think I could be brave enough." Talia proclaims.

"I'm sure you could, but battles are ugly affairs." Elena calmly warns.

"Are we going to help Victor then?" She inquires in a hopeful tone.

Elena places her hands on Talia's shoulders firmly for a moment and councils, "I need you to listen to me carefully, for this is really important."

Talia nods and replies, "Alright, if you say so."

"Good," Elena instructs, "I need you to stay on the ship when we land. I can't afford to lose you, you're too important. You understand?"

Nodding once again, Talia replies, "Yes." She then expresses a deeply concerned look and questions, "You're coming back, aren't you?"

Hesitant to answer, Elena looks away then faces her and replies, "I don't know honestly, but I have to keep you safe. It's what he would've wanted."

Concerned for his safety, Talia looks out the ship's window in a sorrowful manner and mutters, "I hope he's all right."

Amused as always by Talia's loyal affection for Victor, Elena smiles and respectfully denotes, "You really care for him, don't you?"

Talia pulls out the Angel figure from her garb and observes it intensely before her eyes and admits, "I always have, as he's always cared for me."

Lithia hums Sonya's melody as Victor and Yuri fight their way through the Darchadian fortress whilst searching for their comrade Damian.

"He never gives up, and always puts everyone before himself." Talia softly explains, cheering her hero on in her head. Damian sits alone in his cell, and sighs, hoping someone will come to his rescue soon as she continues, "When darkness falls, he shines a light to show you the way."
Victor takes out a couple of Darchadians single-handedly and signals Yuri to continue following him through the forsaken fortress.

"He fights with a bravery no one else could ever understand." Talia happily professes, eyes still gazing upon the Angel figure as Elena listens closely, "He inhabits the shadows and preys upon those who prey on the weak, waiting for the right moment to strike."
Hidden in shadow, Victor suddenly ambushes two more Darchadians and takes them out with ease. Surprised by his intensity, Yuri looks upon Victor who stares back with determination then nods in respect as they continue searching for their comrade Damian.

"You can always count on him to be there when you need him the most." Talia acknowledges, "No one could ask for a better friend than him."
Victor and Yuri make their way closer to Damian as he looks around, sensing the commotion near by. A tear drops from Talia's hazel eyes as she looks through the blue Angel figure and sees Elena who looks back and grins.

"You've been through a lot together, haven't you?" Elena denotes.
Talia nods in sorrow and replies, "We grew up together, both orphans trying to survive in the mines. We found a home in ourselves, looked out for each other." She explains, "His unique strength set him apart from everyone else. When the Pretorians sent him on all the most dangerous missions, he took me with him sometimes, right by his side, and with each venture our bond grew. He took me in when everyone else saw nothing but a wild animal with only my raw talents to guide me, and that's the absolute truth."

"Whatever the truth, the death of his loved ones hold him back, and only the Gods can help him if he listens." Elena remarks.

"I used to have nightmares when he wasn't around." Talia adds.

"He watched over you, protected you." Elena acknowledges as Talia nods in response, "Well that's my job now." Elena places her hand on the Angel figure and hums a musical notation, triggering an organic chain reaction, which causes it to fix itself by naturally patching up all the cracks.

"This is what we Angels like to call harmonic convergence, for compassion is the remedy that heals a broken spirit." She reveals, "And to accomplish great things with such power, we must not only act but also dream, not only plan but also believe. Even the Earth has music for those who are willing to listen."
Talia looks upon the pristine Angel figure with excitement then hugs Elena in appreciation and happily whispers, "Thank you so much."

Elena embraces Talia whilst taking in the moment of her comfort like a daughter. After a warm embrace, Talia places the now fixed Angel figure back in her garb as Lithia chirps excitedly. "I can tell you mean a great deal to each other, and that you both share a special connection." Elena implies.

"You share it as well, Elena, he loves you." Talia reveals.
Worrisome over the fact, Elena grins with a saddened expression and mutters, "That's what I'm afraid of."

"I think you're afraid because you love him too." Talia respectfully professes to her surprise. Touched by Talia's kind words, Elena closes her eyes for a moment in joy and despair. Talia is saddened by her reaction, knowing that she truly does care for Victor as much as she does if not more. With her eyes still closed, Elena murmurs, "Just like him, you also see things in a way that most do not, but as they truly are."

"How could one not see such beautiful things?" Talia encourages, "You're just as important to him as I am."
Elena opens her eyes in relief, feeling grateful for Talia's acceptance of her shared bond with Victor. Talia smiles as Elena looks upon her with determination and states, "Then let's not disappoint him." She then kneels before her once again and calmly apprises, "I cannot allow you to fight, but do us both a favor and pray for his safety, as well as the others."
Determined now more than ever, Talia firmly replies, "I will."
Elena smiles in response to her young companion then stands back up and proclaims, "We'll make it through this; don't you worry."

"So will he." Talia confidently supports.
Lithia chirps in agreement as Elena and Talia chuckle, having faith that Victor will prevail in honoring them both.

Through the depths of the Darchadian fortress, Victor and Yuri make their way to the holding cells and take out a few more Darchadians. Surprised by their unexpected entrance, Damian sees Yuri approaching and sighs in relief. "Yuri, how did you find me?"

"It wasn't easy, that's for damn sure." Yuri jokes.
Curious as to who else is with him, Damian inquires, "Where's Elena?"

"Knowing her, she's already on her way." Yuri postulates.

"Good, we'll need her help." Damian comments, sounding hopeful.

"We've come to free you." Yuri gladly informs as he breaks the locks on the holding cell with his energy sword protruding from his Gauntlet.
Confused, Damian looks upon Yuri and asks, "We?"
To Damian's surprise, Victor approaches the holding cell with a crooked smile on his face while saluting and says, "Hey there."
Damian shakes his head, amused by his presence as he looks upon him and remarks, "So, you honored your sacred oath by coming after all."

"We're comrades, remember?" Victor proudly states as Damian nods in respect, "Teamwork isn't about ego, it's about we go. Therefore, we must stick together in the good times and bad."

"Seems you have finally learned what I could not, I'm sorry I misjudged you, Victor." Damian professes, "Can you ever forgive me?"

Surprised by Damian's sentiment, Victor shakes his head with a smile and mutters, "Forget it." He then turns his attention away and states, "We have to get you out of here before more of those things show up."

Damian rises to his feet to address them face-to-face but falls back down and says, "There's not much I can do without my Gauntlet. He took it from me."

Concerned, Victor looks upon Damian and probes, "Traganus?"

With a nod, Damian grunts in pain and replies, "Yeah!"

Victor helps Damian to his feet as Yuri holds his Gauntlet securely in front of him to scan his vital signs.

"He's too weak to make it past the blockade." Yuri cautions.

Worried for his Eudenian comrade, Victor looks upon Yuri who motions towards the exit and says, "We have to take him back to the ship and get him to safety as soon as possible." Victor glances at Damian and notices others being held captive, realizing he's back where he first encountered Traganus.

"Yuri, I need you to do something for me." Victor mentions.

"What now?" Yuri says sarcastically.

Motioning towards the cages floating above them, Victor points out the slaves held captive as Damian and Yuri express a look of shock.

"Instead of helping us, I need you to lead these people to safety if you don't mind." He respectfully requests.

"What about you guys?" Yuri questions.

Damian nods towards Victor, willing to fight beside him once again.

"We'll meet back with you once we're done here." Victor confirms.

Yuri looks upon Victor with a concerned expression and carefully cautions, "You don't have to do this, Victor."

With a solemn glare, Victor looks upward towards the slaves and firmly states, "Yes I do. We all do what we have to do, you know that well I think."

Damian looks upon Victor in admiration of his determined attitude as Yuri nods in respect. Victor sets Damian down and kneels before him as he places his hands on his chest. "What are you doing?" Damian asks suspiciously.

"You'll see." Victor assures with an assertive grin as he begins to use his Gauntlet, attempting to heal Damian's wounds.

As Victor's energy passes through Damian's body, Yuri watches, surprised by his abilities. After a brief moment, Damian stands fully healed and looks upon him, amazed by his power and inquires, "How did you do that?"

Victor grins in response as Yuri glances at him whilst shaking his head in amazement and regards, "You truly are of Angel descent."

"I don't care what I am anymore, it's who I am that truly matters." Victor expresses. Surprised by his honesty, Damian nods in agreement.

"I may be human as well, but I don't quit and never have, no matter what they throw at me." Victor proudly states.

Looking around cautiously for any possible oncoming threats, Damian strongly advises, "Time's running out so we better move!"

Victor, along with Damian and Yuri free all the slaves held in captivity. Tristan and Michael look on from their cage and are relieved to see Victor as he quickly approaches them once again. "Tristan, Michael!" He calls.

"Victor, it's really you, isn't it?" Tristan cheerfully questions in relief while admiring his friend's Angelic Soul Gear. Victor nods back to comfort them as he uses his Gauntlet to break the energy locks on their cage.

"We knew you would come back for us someday!" Michael happily states which incites a comforting grin from Victor.

Hoping to get them all to safety, Victor informs, "We haven't much time, boys. I need your help, that is, if you're willing."

Determined to follow their champion, Tristan and Michael nod in agreement.

"Of course we are!" Tristan proudly declares.

"We'd do anything for our hero!" Michael adds excitedly.

"Good," Victor says as he motions towards the exit, "Follow Yuri back to the ship, he'll lead you guys out safely."

Damian approaches Victor from behind after freeing the last group of slaves in captivity, and informs, "We have to go!"

Victor quickly turns and firmly replies, "I know." He then turns back towards Tristan and Michael as they look upon him in curiously, "Hurry guys! Take care of the rest of them for me, will you?"

"No problem, you can always count on us!" Michael proclaims.

"Yeah, we believe in you, Victor!" Tristan joyously adds.

Appreciative of their friendly cooperation, Victor smiles and retorts, "Thanks guys, I believe in you as well." Tristan and Michael smile back in appreciation as Victor motions towards the exit and caringly instructs, "Now go!"

Determined to honor their friend, Tristan and Michael honorably salute.

"Yes sir!" Tristan happily decrees.

"Come on everyone, let's get out of here!" Michael announces as the other slaves gather around to escape the fortress with them for good.

As they take their leave with the other slaves, Yuri approaches Victor and Damian, cautioning, "I sure hope you know what you're doing."

"Don't fret, it'll come to me." Victor says with a smirk.

"I trust you have a plan then." Yuri jokingly implies.

With a determined grin, Victor replies, "I'm an Angel, aren't I? I'll improvise, by doing what I do best."

As Victor turns to take his leave with Damian, Yuri inquires, "Which is?"

Stopping in his tracks, Victor quickly turns to face him and jokingly retorts, "Attract trouble, but don't worry, I'll wing it if I have to."

Victor turns back to move on with Damian as Yuri shakes his head in amusement and states, "I'll take it from here then, you guys be careful and whatever you do, do it quickly."

"We'll be fine once I find my Gauntlet." Damian informs as he turns back to acknowledge Yuri's hard work, "Take care, Yuri."

"You too." Yuri replies with a nod, "Stay alive you guys."

Yuri quickly heads off with the human slaves to lead them safely out of the fortress as Victor and Damian begin their search for the Eudenian Gauntlet.

In the outskirts of Pretoria, the Arch ship sets down as Elena looks out from the landing platform, determined to find Victor and help the team in battle. Talia holds Lithia close to keep him calm as Elena faces the two Archadians in the cockpit and orders, "Keep the ship ready, sisters! Protect Talia at all costs, and take off if your position is compromised! Got it?"

"Yes, your Highness!" The Archadians reply with a nod.

Talia approaches the landing platform with Lithia as Elena faces her and instructs, "Stay close to them, there may be Darchadians lurking about."

Fearful for her safety as well, Talia tugs on Elena's hand and persistently pleads, "I want to go with you!"

Elena faces her impatiently and scolds, "We've been through this already. If it gets too dangerous my sisters will head back to Archadia."

"We can't just leave you here!" Talia caringly pressures.

Leaning against the ship's outer wall, Elena looks out onto the horizon and murmurs, "You may not have a choice when the time comes."

Feeling discouraged, Talia looks upon her with a concerned expression. Elena kneels before Talia to comfort her while gripping her hand and encouragingly says, "I'm counting on you, Natalia. I'll be back as soon as I can."

Talia sighs disappointedly and says, "Alright."

Elena grins then turns back towards the landing platform and presses the pink Gods' symbol over her chest, which activates her wings. Without hesitation, Elena takes off into the sky to help the team, as Talia looks onto the horizon, feeling hopeful for their safety and whispers, "Be safe."

Lithia chirps as Talia turns to acknowledge him then turns back and sighs once more, wishing she were old enough to aid her friends in combat.

CH: 54
WHEN WARRIORS CLASH

In the outskirts of Pretoria, the battle rages on as Adrian and Marcus continue fighting the deadly duo, Raiven and Celeste. Celeste suddenly grabs Marcus from behind, putting him a headlock as he struggles to break free.

"Come on, Empyrian!" She viciously teases as he grunts, "I know you can do better than this!"

"You're playing with us, aren't you?" Marcus queries, followed by a devious grin from Celeste.

"Well, play this!" Adrian shouts while coming up from behind, attempting to strike her down as she senses him charging towards her.

"Nice try, but it won't be long before we send you both to another dimension!" She spitefully claims.
Celeste quickly turns around and shoves Marcus towards Adrian as Raiven suddenly flies in overhead and strikes them both from behind, knocking them to the ground. The pair chuckle maniacally as they float back into formation.

"These heightened senses are quite a kick, huh?" Celeste teases.

"I hope that's not the best you've got, or we're going to be very disappointed!" Raiven cynically adds.

"Damn it!" Adrian roars as he pounds the ground with his fist, which unintentionally knocks back a few Darchadians in the process. As Marcus humorously looks back with surprise, Adrian grunts heavily and exclaims, "They're too fast! I think we're going to need some back up after all."
Adrian and Marcus attempt to catch their breath whilst assessing the situation as Raiven and Celeste circle around them in unison, still floating in the air.

"You take them from the front if you can," Marcus suggests as he discharges the crystal shard from his Gauntlet and places another back in, "I'll come in from behind."
Adrian follows suit as he nods and replies, "Got it!"

Raiven and Celeste hiss ferociously whilst preparing to charge towards Adrian and Marcus once more but immediately stop as everyone suddenly senses something powerful coming towards them at high speed from above.

"What is that?" Adrian inquires, unable to detect the exact presence. Marcus looks up with a confident grin and jokingly states, "You know that back up you inquired about earlier?"

"Yeah!" Adrian suspiciously answers.

"It's finally here!" Marcus proudly informs.

Raiven and Celeste look on in anger as Elena suddenly flies in from above, stopping instantly above the ground between them whilst causing an energy wake. Everyone is taken aback by Elena's sudden entrance, and is slightly blinded by her pink illuminated wings then turn to see who it is. As the dust finally settles, Elena opens her intense eyes and looks towards her former female comrades with serious intent.

"So, the Princess has finally arrived!" Celeste spitefully sneers, "An appearance she'll soon regret."

"You've come looking for a fight, and we're happy to oblige." Raiven cynically chimes in as her and Celeste float above the ground in battle stances, ready to take on their former Archadian colleague.

With her colorful pink wings fully spread, Elena walks past Adrian and Marcus without hesitation and sternly comments, "Looks like you're in need of a woman's touch out here, a woman in arms."

"Nice of you to drop by, Princess." Adrian says sarcastically with a surprised expression, "What's the occasion?"

As Elena approaches Raiven and Celeste, she replies, "Divine intervention!"

"Where have you been anyway?" Marcus questions.

With a quick turn of her head, she answers, "Watching you fail!" She then turns back and looks upon Raiven and Celeste intensely.

"Come to join the party, *sister*?" Celeste taunts.

"This party's over!" Elena firmly declares.

The two Darchadians chuckle in response to her intensity as Elena stares back, annoyed by their pompous attitude towards her.

"You don't really think we were kept in the dark about your true intentions, do you?" Raiven deviously questions.

"That's right, *Princess*, patience is one of our virtues." Celeste adds.

"We didn't go after you, instead we allowed you to come after us." Raiven happily informs, "More dramatic that way don't you think?"

"Yes, the one thing our people share is a love of theater, and you've put on a fine show." Elena sarcastically remarks.

"Indeed we have." Celeste mockingly jeers.

Elena scowls in anger then quickly turns to address Adrian and Marcus once more and orders, "These two are a handful, so you guys help the others!"

"What about you?" Marcus protectively inquires.

Looking determined, Elena faces her deadly adversaries with a firm posture and declares, "I'll be fine; this Princess fights her own battles when need be!" Angered by Elena's intrusion, Raiven and Celeste hiss ferociously.

"Better do what she says, Braxel." Marcus jokingly advises.
Adrian glances at Marcus and scoffs, "Guess you're right." He then faces her and respectfully informs, "They're all yours, Elena!"
Adrian and Marcus quickly take off to let Elena fight Raiven and Celeste alone in her own way.

"Well now, it looks like the Princess is willing to get her hands dirty after all!" Raiven mocks.

"Only when I have to!" Elena firmly retorts. Raiven and Celeste chuckle in response as she stares back and denotes, "I see Traganus has recruited you both to his cause. Since when are you on his side?"

"Ever since the Arch decided to herd us all like sheep." Celeste scornfully replies, "Traganus simply wants world peace."
Elena scoffs and sarcastically says, "More like pieces of the world."

"He only wants what's best for us, unlike the Arch!" Raiven snaps.
Unmoved by their claims, Elena frowns upon them with disdain.

"You see, we aren't their ornate play things anymore." Celeste proudly declares, "Our clan is owned by no one, including the Gods!"

"Your tastes have always been poor." Elena challenges, "It's unwise to idolize someone of his nature, for he's no God."

"Ha!" Raiven harshly ridicules, "Neither is your *human*. No good comes from that kind of hero worship, especially for those who are greatly unworthy of such titles."
Celeste raises her Gauntlet and suddenly fires a warning shot, trying to intimidate Elena as she moves her head just slightly enough to dodge the blast without flinching. The pair chuckle as Elena sighs in annoyance.

"You'll pay for what you've done," Elena calmly threatens, "Your actions won't go unpunished."

"You know, out of all our siblings, we despised you the most." Celeste joyfully scorns, "Traganus will be pleased to know his prize has fallen right into our deadly trap."
Unwilling to back down, Elena states, "I don't know what your so-called master is up to, but the Arch will never fall into is hands, nor will I."
Angered by her tenacity, Raiven and Celeste float in the air and circle around Elena in unison, trying to intimidate her.

"Your forces will stand down!" Elena sternly exclaims whilst holding her ground, "The Arch will not abet this madness!"

"You hold no sway here, *Princess*, for we are in command now!" Celeste sneers in response, disregarding her previous oath.
Following their movements without turning her head, Elena angrily mutters, "You stain Archadian honor with such treachery!"

422

"There is no such thing anymore!" Raiven mocks with a cruel laugh.

"Of course there is!" Elena disputes, "Angels like myself are divine, not damned, for we rise by lifting others. Thus, we are to temper the world's aggression, not enable it!"

Amused by Elena's noble efforts to sway their own point of view, Celeste snaps, "Traganus showed us the truth a long time ago, for the world's aggression cannot be tempered, only quelled!"

"You mean slaughter the innocent?" Elena spitefully scoffs in return, "I'm afraid your master has beguiled you both."

"Your people must be awfully weak willed if you are to be their future Queen." Raiven ridicules.

Standing her ground, Elena firmly states, "Where I come from we learn the ways to protect more than the ways to destroy. Thus, we are to give service, help the innocent, save the lives of friend and foe. That has always been our custom since the very beginning."

Raiven and Celeste instinctively hiss as Elena lowers her brow upon them.

"How dare you lecture us on the Arch code!" Celeste barks.

"I don't seek to lecture, I seek to depose." Elena calmly informs, "It doesn't have to be like this, sisters. There are more constructive ways for you to control your fear, inside and out."

"No thanks," Celeste wickedly informs, "We're having too much fun eliminating the competition."

"We must rebuild what Traganus threatens to destroy, together." Elena attempts to plea to her former comrades.

Moving in and out of formation with Celeste in the air, Raiven spitefully taunts, "Your path is folly, *Princess*. Deep down, you're a killer, just like us."

"No!" Elena disputes, "We are to unite the world's people, lessen man's aggression, and overcome it with love and compassion!"

"We no longer need the approval of your precious Arch!" Celeste belittles, "We ourselves are more powerful than you as it is."

Determined to prove them wrong, Elena looks upon them with a confident grin and contests, "Oh yeah? Prove it then!"

"Oh, we will!" Raiven proclaims while rudely pointing towards her, "Then soon Traganus will have your soul."

"Come and get it if you like, but I think I'll be keeping my soul intact!" Elena declares as she positions herself in a battle stance.

Ready and alert, Elena stands with feet firmly planted and her crystalline staff in hand as her Archadian tiara forms over her head into a helmet. Elena powers up then spins her staff in preparation as the two Darchadians hiss. Taking a deep breath, Elena conjures the power from within as Raiven and Celeste ferociously charge towards her and the fight begins.

Meanwhile in the Darchadian fortress, Victor and Damian walk into a chamber and find the Gauntlet floating above a small crystalline platform. Damian looks upon the Gauntlet in relief then quickly grabs it and places it over his arm as it powers up his Soul Gear once again.

"That's better!" Damian states, which brings a smile to Victor's face.

"If I had to guess, I would say you were more concerned about your Gauntlet this whole time." Victor teases.

"My Gauntlet I like, it's you I'm not so sure about." Damian jokes.

"Wait till you get to know me better." Victor says sarcastically.

"I'm trying to." Damian says he as he turns to face him then informs, "We should head back and help the others as quickly as possible."

"Assuming we still can." Victor sarcastically mutters.

"Why do you say that?" Damian inquires.

Victor looks around cautiously with his glowing Gauntlet drawn, sensing a powerful presence and replies, "Because we're being watched."

"How can you tell?" Damian questions out of suspicion.

"I feel a familiar yet unwanted presence." Victor reluctantly reveals. Taking no chances, Damian quickly draws his Gauntlet as well and cautiously stands back-to-back with him. Unexpectedly, Traganus ambushes them, knocking Victor to the ground with a kick and Damian through a wall. Traganus faces Victor and grins as he attempts to strike but is knocked back again. Victor is slightly wounded as Traganus chuckles at his expense.

"I see you've been revitalized." He callously mocks, "I didn't realize the Gods were in the habit of rewarding such failure."

"Funny, I could say the same about you." Victor says with a grin, "Though like you said before, what doesn't kill you only makes you stronger." Traganus waves Victor towards him and grunts aggressively. Anxious to take him down, Victor jumps to his feet and attempts to strike Traganus once again as he blocks, locking their hands together powerfully.

"So, you've come to avenge your people?" Traganus cynically teases, "*The Great Archelus!*"

"Unlike you, I fight for more than vengeance, Traganus!" Victor exclaims with a confident smirk. Traganus scoffs as Damian jumps to his feet and looks around the chamber within the fortress, trying to devise a plan that could help them. "I fight for what my mother once believed in, and what you've tried to corrupt!" Victor declares, his power growing as their auras cause an energy wake in the fortress, which causes the floor to crumble.

"You're a slave to their dogmatic view, but we could've helped you, had you accepted my gracious offer." Traganus insults with a stern tone.

"I don't need your help!" Victor angrily retorts whilst attempting to overpower his dark adversary, "Never have and never will!"

"Are you awake yet?" Traganus sneeringly teases, "You'll find it's not so easy to kill an Angel of my caliber."

"Keep him busy if you can!" Damian shouts back towards Victor to get his attention whilst still devising a plan.

Victor glances back at Damian and jokingly replies, "Sure thing, no problem!"

"Why attack your own kind?" Traganus teases, trying to overpower his half human foe once again, "We see something in each other neither one of us likes, or maybe we're just looking into a mirror."

Their energy auras push each other back, causing a brief standstill.

"You threaten the Arch, I'm here to protect it!" Victor proclaims.

"Even now you're too blind to see the nihilistic drawback to Archadian methodology." Traganus ridicules whilst shaking his head in disappointment, "The Arch itself is derided for its shrill sanctimony."

Confident of his position over him, Victor snaps, "You have no right to be so sanctimonious given your lurid past!"

Victor fires an energy blast from his Gauntlet, pushing Traganus back for a moment then quickly maneuvers around and strikes him from behind as he yells in anger. Leaping gracefully, Victor lands in a crouching position and grins as Traganus turns and angrily states, "That was a mistake."

"No mistake, I only kill when I have to." Victor assures, "You on the other hand kill for pleasure."

"If you're referring to the Angels who died during our first encounter, you should know that their deaths were bittersweet." Traganus taunts, "You should try it sometime, for it would appeal to you in some way."

"You know nothing about what appeals to me!' Victor barks.

"Don't I?" Traganus cynically teases, "How will the blood of your fellow Angels taste once they've reached their end?" Victor straightens up as Traganus continues, "You've wondered what it's like to take a life out of passion, haven't you? Curiosity clouds your senses, you can't help it, especially for the Princess." An expression of shock covers Victor's face in light of this conjecture. "You look at her and your blood pumps. Tell me you haven't confused that hunger for something else I hope." Traganus belittles.

"I'm not confused!" Victor claims as he leaps towards Traganus and forces him back several feet, "For I know exactly why I'm here."

Surprised by his tactic, Traganus remarks, "You're a little more resourceful than I thought, and more foolish." Victor stands in a battle stance as Traganus slowly approaches him, and states, "You reek of the Arch, but I knew it was only a matter of time before you returned. Now you will surrender to me, or die here where you were created."

"What do you mean, created?" Victor carefully inquires.

Traganus gestures towards the entire chamber, and exclaims, "Take a look around! You think your fellow Angels were born?" Victor studies his surroundings as Traganus clarifies, "They were created, to do what they were told for all eternity…" He then points towards him and says, "Just like you!"

Victor scowls upon him as Damian looks around and sees a row of energy generators linked up to the main chamber. Unexpectedly, a couple of Darchadians appear and attempt to take him down as Damian defends himself against their vicious attacks. "Like the Gods, I too have sought to unravel the mortal coils of life." Traganus reveals, "I've been trying to replicate your extreme level of power for quite some time now."

"I've seen your so-called creations, and I must say I'm not impressed whatsoever." Victor mocks.

"Once unleashed, they're truly invincible, the perfect killing system that answers only to me." Traganus proudly remarks.

"Perhaps too perfect." Victor scoffs in disbelief, "Damn fool, your own creation nearly destroyed you all those years ago."

"As well as the Arch, mind you." Traganus cynically adds.

"You will be stopped, one way or another!" Victor threatens.

"By who, you?" Traganus sneers with a confident grin. Victor stays in battle formation, waiting for him to strike at any moment. "You see, when the chips are down and the pressure is on, every being on the face of this Earth is interested in one thing and one thing only..." Traganus confidently states as he raises his Gauntlet and suddenly fires upon Victor who quickly deflects the energy blast by backhanding it elsewhere, "Its own survival!"

Annoyed by his cynical viewpoint, Victor grunts angrily as Damian attempts to take out the two Darchadians and suddenly fires upon each energy generator in the next chamber with his Gauntlet in the process.

"The irony is impeccable, for the Gods use the Arch as a shield to protect them against their own mistakes." Traganus enlightens as he floats above Victor with his Angelic wings, "By building their hierarchy, they challenged my power. Needless to say, you don't destroy one's work then let them live to finish or recreate it. I'm here to beat them at their own game."

"Yeah, we'll see about!" Victor snaps while following his movements, "You seem to think we're all created for a purpose; I definitely think so. My mother gave me this power as a blessing from the Gods; I believe she wanted me to slay you, safeguard the Arch." Determined to take him out for good, Victor attempts to power up as energetic lightning surrounds his entire body. Traganus looks down from above, amused by his daring persistence and scorns, "I would've thought you had learned from out last encounter."

"I'm a fast learner when it suits me." Victor confidently retorts.

"You're stronger than before no doubt, but my powers are beyond your mortal imagination." Traganus decrees. Victor activates his wings and flies towards him, attempting to strike as Traganus looks back in anger.

"You're a fool to face me alone!" Traganus roars as he comes to blows with Victor in the air.

"I've been alone my whole life, so what difference does it make?" Victor contests, becoming furiously irritated with each strike.

"So be it!" Traganus mutters as he quickly lands on the ground. Yelling in anger, Victor charges head first towards him from above and strikes as Damian defeats the two Darchadians and fires an energy blast, knocking Traganus back. Victor sees Damian re-enter the chamber with his Gauntlet aimed, relieved by his company. "Sorry about that." Damian jokingly greets. Shaking his head with a grin, Victor sarcastically retorts, "No you're not." Damian grins in response as Traganus bursts through the rubble intensely. Victor and Damian stand in formation as Traganus approaches them and wrathfully shouts, "Fools! How dare you assault me!"

"Just doing our jobs!" Damian firmly counters.

Victor grins as he and Damian hold their ground in preparation for another attack against the fierce Darchadian leader.

"You're capable of far worse than I!" Traganus scornfully states, "I stood for my fellow Angels, for reason and justice! But the Gods molded them into their image, the way they saw fit! The Arch is nothing more than a flawed creation, and I was to bow down to them?"

Sensing his energy dark energy rising, Victor and Damian prepare for the worst as Traganus powers up and declares, "No longer shall I remain a slave!"

"That makes two of us!" Victor boldly chimes in.

Without hesitation, Victor charges towards Traganus alone and locks fists with him once again. Traganus chuckles, sensing the darkness within Victor growing, and states, "You're afraid, good. I too know what it's like to live in fear, to see my people killed and my family taken away." He articulates as Victor attempts to overpower him, "But even as I was left with nothing, I vowed to rise above the fear of the Gods and liberate the oppressed people of this world, and the next."

"Then why an army of Angels?" Victor probes as Damian defends himself against pair of random Darchadians attempting to defend Traganus.

"Well, you need Angels to conquer other Angels." Traganus implies.

"Or maybe you need Angels to conquer people in general." Victor denotes with a scowl, "To control those who follow you, and to rid yourself of those who won't." Traganus stares back, surprised by his supposition as Victor calmly states, "If you truly believe in peace, then let's keep it. The Arch wants nothing more to than to harmonize with the world, and we have the answers you seek back in Archadia. Please, just let me show you."

"No, let me show you!" Traganus viciously threatens as he attempts to overpower Victor, "I'm going to use what the Arch itself taught me, by destroying what they built. And upon that floating rock of would-be Angels, I will build my own sanctuary."

"Not if I stop you first!" Victor bravely counters.

"Even you can't run from your own demons, especially when they control you." Traganus derides.

"I won't let you control me!" Victor angrily retorts.

"You don't need to be controlled, you need to be unleashed." Traganus proclaims, "The road to Hell is paved with good intentions, but is inevitably marked by our sins." He then questions, "Why bow in the light when you can stand in the dark?"

"I'm not like you!" Victor snaps as Damian forces the Darchadians back and notices the generators malfunctioning from his attack earlier.

"Give it time, such power will make you invincible if it doesn't kill you first." Traganus warns, "You're weak and selfish to think we can ever set ourselves apart, for I'll always be a part of your future." Victor struggles to force him back, eyes glowing brightly in anger as Traganus taunts, "What makes you any different than I?"

Damian looks on from his position, surprised as Victor's eyes suddenly dim from retaining control of his inner rage.

"Because I choose to be." Victor calmly declares as he quickly forces Traganus back aggressively. With the energy generators becoming unstable, Damian turns his attention behind them as Traganus' eyes glow brightly in red. Pushing for time, Damian places his hand on Victor's shoulder to get his attention and prudently informs, "We have to move, those generators are going to blow any second now!"

Victor regains his calm composure whilst staring Traganus down and with a determined voice says, "No point standing around here then."

"Don't deny your own destiny!" Traganus demeans, "Get off your knees, open your eyes, and let the dream take flight."

With a crooked smile, Victor retorts, "Your dreams of glory no longer fit the time. They belong buried in the past, along with you and your disciples."

"And to think, had you come to your senses and awakened from the dream, we could've been friends." Traganus wickedly taunts.

"Maybe once upon a time in another life, but your time is over, whereas mine is just starting." Victor strongly counters as he and Damian power up then suddenly blast Traganus back through a wall to buy themselves enough time to escape. As the two Champions share a glance for and nod, Traganus yells in anger, his voice echoing throughout the entire crystalline fortress. Taking this opportunity to flee, Victor activates his wings then wraps his arms around Damian from behind and shouts, "Hang on!"

Victor quickly takes off with Damian in his grasp as Traganus attempts to chase after them. As they reach the top, Traganus is caught in the rubble from the exploding energy generators. Reaching out towards them in anger, he fiercely exclaims, "You can't escape what you are!"

Trying to escape the blast, Victor flies upwards at full speed with Damian into the sky as Traganus attempts to use his energy aura to deflect the debris. Unable to break through, the Darchadian fortress comes crumbling down on him as he yells out violently in rage.

CH: 55
RAISE THY WINGS

Miles away from the battlefield in Pretoria, Talia sits aboard the Arch ship with Lithia by her side as the two Archadians look onto the horizon from the landing platform. Prepared to defend her with their lives, the pair stands ready with their crystalline staffs in hand. Sensing immediate danger, Lithia's spinal shards glow with a sudden screeching noise that catches Talia's attention as a few Darchadians suddenly approach the Arch ship from above.

"Get down!" one of them warns as she waves her hand back.
Taking no chances, Talia quickly hides with Lithia as the Archadians fire upon the Darchadians approaching. One of the Archadians takes out a Darchadian in the air but is suddenly struck by an energy blast. Two more Darchadians attempt to board the Arch ship and attack the last Archadian. The Archadian takes out one of the Darchadians by hand but is quickly taken out herself by an energy blast. Talia is knocked back from the blast towards the front of the control deck as the last Darchadian boards the ship with her Gauntlet aimed.

"You can't hide from me, Archadian!" The Darchadian taunts.
With a calm panting noise, Lithia motions towards a crystalline staff lying on the floor as Talia attempts to grab it. With the staff gripped tightly in her hands, Talia takes a deep breath and quickly stands to face her deadly foe with determination as the Darchadian hesitates to fire by the sight of her.

"Why, you're just a child." The Darchadian sneers with a devious grin, "You don't look so dangerous."
Talia scowls back as she successfully powers up the crystalline staff.

"No matter!" The Darchadian confidently mutters as she raises her Gauntlet and suddenly fires upon Talia.
Determined to fight back, Talia quickly dodges and uses the crystalline staff to fire an energy blast in retaliation, taking the Darchadian out with ease. Lithia chirps excitedly as Talia looks back and grins.

After taking a brief moment to settle her composure, Talia rushes towards the landing platform of the Arch ship and looks out for others as Lithia flies onto her shoulder and chirps.

"We have to help Elena!" Talia declares.

Lithia tilts his furry head with a confused expression then motions towards a certain direction and howls.

"Let's go, Lithia!" Talia commands as she takes off running.

Lithia chirps once again and follows close behind in the air as Talia heads towards the battlefield in an attempt to find her friends, Elena and Victor.

Through the intense battlefield in Pretoria, the battle rages on between the team and the Darchadians. In the midst of dodging and deflecting energy blasts, Adrian runs out of power from his Gauntlet as he looks towards Marcus and exclaims, "I'm out!"

Marcus quickly turns and tosses a crystal shard towards Adrian who instinctively catches it then replies, "Here, make it count!"

Adrian and Marcus discharge the crystal shards from their Gauntlets and place the new ones inside as they power back up. Moments later, Victor and Damian catch up with the team as they land gracefully before them.

"About time you guys showed up!" Marcus teasingly remarks while shaking his head, "I assume you were held up?"

"We had a little trouble along the way and ran into some old friends." Damian jokingly retorts, "Looks like you guys have been busy yourselves."

Marcus sighs in relief and says, "We've had our hands full out here."

Adrian looks directly towards Damian and teases, "Guess they couldn't keep you down for long, could they?"

"Actually, I had some help." Damian responds with a confident grin as he motions towards Victor.

"You're the last person I expected to see here." Adrian comments.

"I'm part of the team, aren't I?" Victor responds with a smirk.

"Looks to me like your place is with us after all." Adrian remarks, acknowledging his redemption. He then nods in respect and states, "Never thought I'd catch myself saying this, but it's good to see you, Victor."

"Did you miss me?" Victor jokes with a crooked smile.

Adrian scoffs and mutters, "Don't kid yourself."

Observing the intense battle before them, Damian quickly turns to Marcus and informs; "We'll take it from here if you don't mind."

"Sounds good to me." Marcus gratefully replies as he looks around for his partner in crime, "Where's my old pal, Yuri?"

Damian points towards the large cloud of smoke and debris caused by the Darchadian fortress caving in and notifies, "He's helping the slaves who were held captive there. We need you to help them to safety as well if you're not too busy at the moment."

"No problem," Marcus sarcastically ensures, "I think I've had enough action for one day as it is."

Concerned for Elena's whereabouts, Victor looks around the battlefield and inquires, "Where's Elena?"

Adrian motions towards the hill in the distance and informs, "She's over there fighting those two bitches that ambushed us before."

Victor turns and sees several energy waves clashing back and forth in the distance. Determined to give her a helping hand, Victor prepares to take off and proclaims, "We have to help her before it's too late!"

Marcus quickly extends his hand towards him and humorously reassures, "Don't worry, bro, she can handle herself. Trust me."

Victor sighs in relief, hoping Elena can hold her own against them. While swinging his purple cape back, Damian steps forward whilst gripping his Gauntlet tightly, and announces, "Alright guys, it's time for some teamwork so let's pull it together. Let's get to work!"

"Right, time for some crowd control!" Adrian sarcastically states as he prepares for more combat against the Darchadians, "Cover me, Victor!" Surprised, Victor looks upon his large Enfurian comrade who sarcastically adds, "I'll punch a whole, you follow me through. Think you can handle that?" Adrian suddenly takes off towards the others, aggressively knocking back each Darchadian that attempts to fly in and strike.

Amused by his determination, Victor grins, feeling one with the team again and shouts, "Right above you, big guy!" He takes off to join Adrian in battle, flying through waves of Darchadians above the team below.

"Good luck guys!" Marcus encourages, "You're going to need it."

"I think we've got our good luck charm back now." Damian jokingly retorts as he watches Victor fight several Darchadians single-handedly in the air then says, "We'll be fine."

Marcus nods in respect then quickly takes off to find Yuri. Gripping his fists tightly, Damian faces the Darcahdian horde, ready for action and proudly states, "Let's see how well these things handle all three of us."

Showcasing his revived power, Damian enters the fray with Adrian and Victor against the Darchadians, fighting together as a team for the first time.

Over the hill near the battlefield in Pretoria, Elena continues her intense duel with Raiven and Celeste as the rocky surface around them gets destroyed in the process. Faring well against the deadly duo, Elena strikes Celeste back and prepares her crystalline staff as Raiven moves in and fiercely states, "Not bad, for an *Archadian*."

"You're not too bad yourself, *Darchadian*." Elena confidently retorts.

"Your looks betray your loyalties, *Princess*." Raiven scorns, "You've only ever been a servant to the Arch, not the Gods."

"Actually, I serve both!" Elena proudly retorts as Celeste flies in from behind and attempts to strike.
Elena pushes Raiven back and quickly dodges the attack as Celeste sneers, "Victory will hasten our father's return, and all shall bow before him!"

"I wouldn't flutter on his return," Elena contests as she positions herself in a battle stance, ready for more, "That's a bet you'll never win."

"Our Master expects death upon defeat, and we shall give it to you." Celeste threatens, angering Elena further.

"And your friends will die with the rest of them!" Raiven chimes in.
Elena holds steady, locking her intense blue eyes upon Raiven and Celeste and quarrels, "Don't count on it!"
Raiven and Celeste suddenly turn their attention behind Elena and see Talia approaching them with Lithia beside her.

"What a surprise!" Celeste cynically teases.
As Talia comes closer, Elena looks behind her and panics. With a screech, Celeste suddenly flies towards Talia at full speed, attempting to catch her off guard. Elena forces Raiven back and swiftly cuts Celeste off as Talia attempts to power up her Gauntlet in defense. In retaliation, Elena knocks Celeste to the ground and sees Talia powering up.

"Talia, no!" She shouts frantically.
Raiven uses this opportunity to catch Elena off guard from behind, putting her in a lethal headlock as Celeste stands up and chuckles. Lithia growls ferociously with his spinal shards glowing as Talia begins to enrage from her fear within and successfully powers up the Gauntlet with ease.

"What now, *Princess*?" Raiven viciously teases, "No one to save you from your own demise, how tragic."
Talia aims her Gauntlet directly at Raiven and Celeste as she looks upon them and angrily shouts, "Let her go now!"
Amused by her fortitude, Raiven and Celeste turn their attention towards Talia and see her aiming her Gauntlet at them as they begin to chuckle.

"Or what?" Celeste mocks, feeling unthreatened by her, "Put that thing away girl or someone could get hurt!"
Determined to defend her friend, Talia powers up as Elena reaches out and orders, "Get out of here, Talia!"
Raiven aggressively pulls Elena's hair back and screams, "Silence, *Princess*!"

Feeling confident of their control over the situation, Celeste grins and slowly approaches Talia who stares back and panics. "What's it going to be little one? We won't wait forever."

"Come on while we're still young!" Raiven viciously chimes in.

With tears running down her delicate face, Talia is pushed to the edge as she closes her eyes and furiously screams, "Stop it!"

Talia's raging energy causes the ground to crumble and suddenly forces Raiven and Celeste back as they struggle to hold their ground.

Surprised by this feat, Celeste glances back at Raiven as Talia calmly opens her eyes. Struggling to break free of Raiven's grip, Elena grunts angrily as Celeste takes this calm moment and flies towards Talia at full speed then suddenly stops just inches in front of her. Talia is taken aback for a moment in shock as Celeste floats before her and chuckles, "You look out of place, *girl.*" She spitefully claims. With her Gauntlet aimed, Talia slowly backs up as Celeste ridicules, "Definitely not a warrior like us, not even in the slightest."

Talia's energy begins to rise exponentially as Elena expresses a look of shock, sensing her inner strength, knowing Celeste is unaware of her true power.

"Farewell then, *sister!*" Celeste cunningly declares as she powers up and aims her Gauntlet directly at Talia to finish her off.

Talia stands frozen, hesitating to fire back as Raiven looks over and shouts, "Sorry kid; you just don't have it in you!"

Angered by Raiven's mockery, Talia closes her eyes once again and suddenly yells in anger as the ground around them begins to shake. Everyone looks on with concern as Talia opens her glowing eyes and unexpectedly fires upon Celeste with her Gauntlet, knocking her back several yards onto the ground. Elena looks on in shock as Raiven scowls back at Talia and hisses ferociously.

"That's my sister!" She screams violently, "How dare you!"

Pushing her to the edge, Talia's energy rises even more for a split second as Elena strikes Raiven back and quickly takes cover.

"Do it Talia!" She encouragingly shouts.

Raiven grunts in pain as Talia suddenly fires and knocks her back as well. Realizing the odds to finally be in her favor, Elena pulls herself up and is surprised to see Raiven and Celeste out cold. Talia stands motionless from the excitement as Elena gracefully flies towards her. Lithia chirps excitedly as Elena places her hand on Talia's Gauntlet to calm her down.

"It's alright." She says calmly. Talia looks up, trembling from the sudden energy flow as Elena comforts, "You can let go now."

With a careful nod, Talia lowers her Gauntlet to her side and calmly mutters, "I never knew I had it in me."

Pleased to see Talia maintain control without proper training, Elena smiles, hoping to comfort her as Talia tries her best to calm down from the intense anger within after bravely facing the two Darchadians.

As the battle rages on, Victor continues fighting alongside Damian and Adrian against the Darchadians whilst displaying tremendous power as a unified team for the first time together.

"A little help, oh fearless one!" Adrian sarcastically shouts as he forcefully grabs a Darchadian flying towards him. Adrian snarls at the Darchadian who hisses then tosses them into the air as Victor swoops in from above and strikes them back through waves of foes.

The two Champions nod to one another in respect then continue fighting as Adrian sees Damian fighting and shakes his head in amusement.

"I've been meaning to ask, what's with the cape?" Adrian queries.

Damian forces a Darchadian back with an energy blast from his Gauntlet, as he turns to face Adrian and says, "What about it?"

"What purpose does it really serve in combat?" Adrian inquires.

"I'm glad you asked that, cause it's time you found out!" Damian jokingly replies as a Darchadian flies towards him from above.

The Darchadian attempts to strike but is caught off guard as Damian throws his royal purple cape towards them, catching them in midair then slams them into the ground and tosses them several yards away with ease. Damian turns towards his comrade once again and grins determinedly as Adrian chuckles.

"Never mind!" Adrian jokingly mutters whilst shaking his head.

The two Champions continue fighting the enemy horde as Victor takes on several at a time, flying gracefully through the air like a true Angelic warrior.

Some distance away, Talia calms herself down, taking steady breaths as Elena kneels before her and jokingly states, "You're either the bravest kid I've ever met, or the craziest."

Talia grins in appreciation and says, "Is that a good thing?"

Elena chuckles in response, "For the time being I suppose."

Apprehensive about her actions, Talia looks up directly at Elena and says softly, "I didn't wish to do that, I'm sorry."

With a comforting grin, Elena shakes her head in amusement and calmly retorts, "Don't be, it's always better to do what is right, not what is easy."

Talia smiles back in relief, as she adds, "I can tell you've been around Victor too long but let me give you some guidance. As an Angel, don't kill if you can wound, don't wound if you can subdue, don't subdue if you can pacify, and don't ever raise your hand until you've first extended it gracefully."

"That's definitely some advice worth remembering." Talia states.

As Lithia perches himself back onto Talia's shoulders, he chirps, bringing a warm smile to their faces whilst acknowledging the profound advice just given. A sudden screech catches their attention as they turn and see Raiven and Celeste attempting to pull themselves up.

"Get behind me, Talia!" Elena orders as she quickly positions herself in a battle stance once again, "I've got this one."

Talia stands behind her as Raiven and Celeste stand up, both looking ravaged.

"You'll pay for that you little brat!" Raiven furiously scorns.

Elena powers up her Gauntlet and exclaims, "Give it up you two, it's over!"

"No, *Princess*, not merely so!" Celeste angrily spits as she wipes the dirt from her face.

Without hesitation, Elena quickly presses the pink Gods' symbol over chest, activating her wings in preparation for an attack from her former comrades.

"We shall rip the flesh from your bones!" Celeste threatens as she and Raiven prepare to attack.

As Elena guards Talia intensely, Raiven points towards them and declares, "Witness, *girl*, the end of your meaningless life!"

"Do you even know who we are?" Celeste scornfully chimes in.

"You're murderers for all I care!" Talia quickly snaps, followed by a defensive growl from Lithia.

"Foolish bitch!" Raiven shrieks as she and Celeste power up.

Elena stands ready in front of Talia, waiting for the two Darchadians to make a move towards them and says, "Excuse me for a moment if you will."

"We'll kill you both!" Celeste screams as she and Raiven suddenly charge towards them in a blind rage.

Frightened, Talia covers her eyes as Elena continues her intense glare and grins. Raiven and Celeste fly towards them at full speed as Elena quickly leaps away from Talia and performs a spin attack with her Angelic wings in-between, forcing them to the ground and knocking them out simultaneously. Elena lands gracefully then turns as she looks upon Raiven and Celeste in an intense manner and firmly states, "Sorry sisters, but I don't think so!"

Talia looks upon Elena, surprised by her sudden intensity as Lithia lands before Raiven and Celeste and attempts to roar, signifying their defeat.

CH: 56
I AM ETERNAL

As the battle comes to a close, Victor finishes off the remaining Darchadians alongside Damian and Adrian. Damian clashes with the last one and strikes them from behind towards Adrian, who grabs them aggressively.

"Hey Victor, think fast!" Adrian calls while forcing the Darchadian back towards Damian who strikes them into the air with his cape as Victor leaps in from above and strikes them down with great intensity. Victor lands gracefully and faces Damian and Adrian as they nod back with determination. The three of them stand together in their respective battle stances once again in preparation for more as everything suddenly becomes quiet all around.

"Huh, is that all they got?" Adrian sarcastically remarks.

"Looks like it." Damian replies.

"Now what?" Adrian sarcastically inquires, "Don't tell me that's it." The ground beneath their feet begins to shake and crumble as the trio struggles to keep their balance. Amused by Adrian's competitive nature, Damian turns to him and mocks, "You had to jinx it for us, didn't you?" Adrian shrugs his shoulder in response as Victor floats a few feet above the ground to avoid the shaking. To their surprise, Traganus suddenly bursts out and shoots upwards into the sky above. The Champions look on in shock as Traganus floats high above them with his red wings fully spread in furious anger. "Now you die!" He warns.

"Is that who I think it is?" Adrian mocks.

"Yep, unfortunately." Damian jokingly replies. Victor lands back on the ground between Damian and Adrian as Traganus stares back for moment whilst raising his left arm with an open hand.

"I am eternal!" He firmly declares with a loud thunderous voice. As the trio prepares for the worst, Traganus suddenly flies downward like a raging comet and lands hard on the ground, causing a large energy wake as the team struggles to balance themselves once again.

Victor looks on through the debris determinedly as does Damian and Adrian. As the dust settles, Traganus raises his head intensely and opens his glowing red eyes. "Well if it isn't the world's finest, together at last." Traganus mocks as he rises to his feet, "You've interfered with our affairs for the last time."

"Stand ready guys!" Damian cautions as he powers up his Gauntlet, "We don't know how much power he truly has!"
Prideful of their chances against their deadly adversary, Adrian exclaims, "Give it up, Traganus, you can't take on all three of us!"

"What makes you think you're even a challenge to me?" Traganus confidently retorts with a devious grin.

"We're not afraid of you!" Damian sternly informs.
Traganus chuckles and sneeringly replies, "You should be!" Cautious of his intentions, Victor remains silent and looks on with a concerned expression.

"I'm giving you one last chance," Traganus sadistically warns, "End this without further bloodshed!"

"Too late for that!" Adrian scoffs.

"Surrender now, or parish!" Traganus firmly threatens as he raises his Gauntlet and powers up as a warning. He then turns his attention towards Victor directly and scorns, "Ha! I see you've continued to ally yourselves with this pathetic excuse for an Angel." Victor scowls back in anger as Traganus mutters, "He still has yet to learn his place in the world."

"He has chosen his place!" Adrian proudly announces as he nods towards Victor in approval of his place on the team. "Among us!"
Amused by their willfulness, Traganus grins and proclaims, "A battle between Heaven and Hell, fought here on Earth." He then motions towards the ground and sky, "We are both part of the same prodigious game, but sadly we have found ourselves on opposing sides of the board. Haven't we, Victor?"
Annoyed by his arrogance, Victor frowns as he resumes, "Have you stopped to think which side you're really on?"
Trying to refrain from letting his anger grow, Victor stares back and firmly retorts, "I have, and it looks like you're on the losing side, Traganus!"

"Ha!" He ridicules, "You rejected my family in favor of theirs?"

"You bet I have!" Victor replies with a crooked smile.
Lowering his gaze in a stern manner, Traganus mutters, "Very well then." As his Soul Gear fully armors his entire body, more so than the Champions have ever seen, Traganus stands ready to fight and shouts, "Prepare to die!"

"I found my family along time ago, I just didn't know it yet." Victor states as he motions towards Damian and Adrian, who grin in appreciation.

"Anyone can love you when the sun is shining, it's in the storms where you learn who truly cares for you." Traganus cryptically reveals, "The truth is you never had a family, you've always been the uniquely created Angel, for you are neither human nor Archadian but the evolution of both."

"That's a lie and you know it!" Victor aggressively disputes whilst gripping his fists tightly in anger.

With a soft chuckle, Traganus states, "It is not merely that we search for the darkness within, but that darkness has always called upon people like us."

Listening closely, Victor lowers his brow as Traganus continues, "Like me, your power is all that was ever needed to reach The Edge Of Beyond."

As Damian and Adrian look on with determination, Traganus points towards them and proclaims, "For us, there's no such thing as family and friends, for we are each our own kingdom with temporary allies and enemies. Those fools you've dragged along with you aren't necessary."

Victor grips his fists tightly, struggling to keep his composure as Damian and Adrian glance at their hybrid comrade with concern.

"It's true that I was alone for the longest time, I was always on my own for the most part." Victor professes as he takes a deep breath, "But if I had stayed that way, the only thing I could ever attain myself would be a world that is meaningless to me. That kind of life is nothing!"

Damian and Adrian stand next to Victor defensively, ready to take on the mighty Darchadian leader as a team.

"Very well then, fulfill your dying fate!" Traganus shouts as he swings his arm back intensely and waves them over, "Have at you!"

"Enough talk!" Victor exclaims.

"Yes, quite enough." Traganus calmly retorts.

Victor stands ready in a battle stance next to Damian and Adrian as Traganus charges towards them at full force, and the fateful battle begins.

Several yards away over the rocky hill, Elena looks upon Raiven and Celeste, both still unconscious then turns to address Talia as Lithia chirps.

"That was too close, Natalia." Elena carefully scolds, "I thought I told you to stay on the ship with the others?"

"I had no choice!" Talia calmly defends, "The ship was attacked and they killed the others. I'm sorry."

Elena sighs in annoyance then smiles towards her young companion and calmly states, "I'm just glad you're safe." Talia smiles back; relieved by her attitude as Elena looks around and mutters, "We need to find another ship, it's too dangerous for you here."

"But we've come all this way!" Talia adds, with a disgruntled tone, "We can't leave Victor, not now!"

Amused by Talia's caring persistence, Elena shakes her head and jokingly infers, "You're as stubborn as he is, aren't you?" Feeling slightly embarrassed, Talia blushes in response as Elena concludes, "Alright, stay close to me and try not to draw too much attention to yourself."

"Will do." Talia happily affirms.

Elena wraps her arms around Talia, activates her wings and quickly takes off into the sky with Lithia to catch up with Victor and the others.

After a brief and intense duel, the three Champions are overpowered by Traganus and take a breather to assess the grim situation.

"Giving up, and so quickly, how disappointing." Traganus teases.

The trio scowls upon their dark adversary in response to his imperious deride.

"The Arch fears me now, as do the Gods." Traganus proudly affirms as the team stares back towards their dark adversary, annoyed by his superior power while trying to regain their strength. "Their pathetic attempts to rule the world shackle me no more." Traganus firmly declares as he takes a step forward to intimidate them then points towards Victor and implies, "I know you can feel it, Zyas, the end of all things." Damian and Adrian glance at Victor, unsure of his meaning as Traganus extends his arms out to taunt them, "Surely you can feel the spiritual pull towards it; you're on the edge of control now, with death only inches away."

"What are you babbling about now?" Victor furiously questions.

"Does it burn inside you, the hunger for flesh and blood?" Traganus continues to taunt with a devious grin.

"It burns, but not for anything you yourself desire." Victor defends.

"So be it." Traganus sternly utters.

Damian glances at Victor and jokingly asks, "You done?"

"Yeah, for now anyway." Victor replies with a smirk.

"We've somehow lost control." Damian reluctantly professes with a deep breath, "I can't tell if we're winning or losing."

"Me neither." Adrian retorts, aggravated by their current standstill, "We need to think of something, and fast!"

Damian holds his Gauntlet out before him and points out, "Every move we make against him greatly affects our ability to defend."

"And here I thought that we were the good guys." Adrian jokes.

"So did I." Damian says with a cunning grin as he turns to address their hybrid colleague, "Well, Victor, any ideas?"

Victor looks back towards Traganus for a moment whilst trying to formulate a tactful plan of his own. "I see your so called advanced tactics provided by the Arch have proven… inadequate." Traganus sinisterly mocks.

Annoyed by his remark, Victor turns his attention back towards his comrades and proposes; "He thinks we're afraid; I say we use that against him."

The trio looks back at Traganus as he stares upon them intensely. To his surprise, he sees Elena arriving with Talia followed by Lithia and furiously exclaims, "It's the pureblood!" Confused, the trio looks back at Elena as she lands gracefully with Talia and Lithia. Traganus grips his fist tightly in front of his face; confident of his victory over them and the Arch then proudly declares, "At last, the Princess has fallen into my grasp."

Elena guards Talia protectively as she and Victor glance at each other and share a comforting smile. Traganus takes this opportunity and flies towards her at full speed but is blindsided by Victor as he leaps in and strikes his face.

Acting instinctively on his behalf, Elena swiftly flies in and strikes Traganus to the ground intensely with her fists. Angered, Traganus looks up and sees them floating in front of Talia defensively, signaling the right of challenge as an Angelic pair. Relieved to see her lifelong friend still holding up in the fight, Talia looks upon Victor and expresses, "Victor, you're alive!"

With a crooked smile, Victor turns his head and caringly retorts, "You bet I am, and so are you apparently."

Sighing in relief of his presence, Talia smiles back as Lithia chirps excitedly.

"How dare you stand in my way; the Princess is mine!" Traganus furiously exclaims as he fleetingly pulls himself off the ground.

Annoyed by his claim, Victor slowly turns back and firmly states, "If you want her, then you'll have to go through me first!"

Traganus is angered even further as Damian and Adrian move beside Victor and Elena in defense as well, unifying as one.

"How heroic, but your resistance is futile." Traganus taunts.

"Last chance, Traganus!" Adrian confidently warns as he pounds his fists together as a sign of victory over him.

As Traganus straightens up, he warns, "Have it your way!" He then begins to power up and threatens, "I'll take care of you three, then I will claim my prize." He points towards Talia and finishes, "I'll take the small one as well."

"I'll die before I let you touch her!" Victor protectively alerts as he begins to power up himself, surrounded by energetic lightning.

Following suit, Elena supportively defends, "As will I!"

Everyone is taken aback as Elena begins to power up as well, causing the ground to shake around violently them. Adrian quickly turns to address Damian and inspires, "No more hiding our true power, it's now or never!"

"Alright guys, do your thing!" Damian proudly announces as a leader next to Talia and Lithia, "Power up, and give him everything you've got!"

"Attack as one!" Adrian adds as he positions himself before Talia.

"Give it up, Zyas!" Traganus fiercely taunts, "You may have powers similar to mine, but you have zero imagination on how to use them. Don't you realize you're that you're both up against the perfect weapon? Face it, you and your crew aren't good enough to beat me!"

With a cunning grin, Victor strongly counters, "Yeah, maybe I'm not…

"But we most definitely are!" Elena finishes standing next to him.

Surprised by their willingness to fight him singlehandedly, Traganus looks upon the Angelic pair intensely and states, "Let's end this, shall we?"

Determined to end this universal threat, Elena glances at Victor who nods back, then expresses a confident posture and retorts, "With pleasure."

Acting fast, Victor and Elena power up as Traganus is slightly taken aback by their energy showcased together as the most powerful Angels on the planet.

With energetic lightning surrounding them, Victor and Elena swing their arms back, then furiously charge towards their mighty foe with a war cry.

Damian and Adrian stand back next to Lithia to guard Talia and the epic fight against the fallen Angel resumes.

Several yards away, Raiven awakens while rubbing her hand over her head and notices the huge clash of energy waves beyond the rocky horizon.

"Master!" She mutters to herself, feeling helpless. Deciding between fight or flight, Raiven turns and sees Celeste still unconscious on the ground then decides to flee without her, "Sorry to leave you hanging, sis, but I have my orders the same as you."

Raiven activates her wings and quickly flies away from the battlefield whilst screeching loudly, leaving her partner in crime behind to fend for herself.

As the second round commences, Traganus forces Victor back as Elena comes in to strike but is forced back as well.

"Pathetic!" Traganus proclaims as he taunts the two Angelic heroes.

"Come on you demon!" Elena shouts as she and Victor swiftly fly in with their wings and take on Traganus single-handedly in the air.

"Judging by your energy readings, it would seem that the two of you aren't so pure!" Traganus savagely taunts, "Tell me, *heroes*, whose world do you really belong to? There's, or mine?"

"Here and now!" Victor strongly retorts.

"It's just you and us; we will see you pay for your sins!" Elena scorns. While defending himself against each of their attacks, Traganus teases, "Do you dare? Who's truly fighting me under those wings, you or the Angel?"

"You better hope it's just us!" Elena exclaims.

"Otherwise you're in a world of hurt!" Victor finishes.

"That's the real difference between us, isn't it?" Traganus sinisterly mocks, "You wear a weapon, whereas I am a weapon!"

Talia and the others watch in awe as their Archadian comrades fight the mighty Darchadian leader blow for blow high in the sky while Victor and Elena strike wildly, taking the fight upward for a moment. As the two Angelic warriors rise several yards above the surface with their movements in perfect harmony, Traganus floats overhead then lowers his arms and fires a couple of energy blasts from his hands towards Victor and Elena who instinctively raise theirs and fire back. Both combatants brace for impact as the powerful energy waves collide, lighting up the sky with blue and pink energetic lightning. Yelling aggressively, Traganus attempts to push them down, but Victor and Elena utilize their impressive strength and are able to push back, causing the intense energy waves to eventually explode in the sky between them.

Near the battlefield, Celeste finally awakens and looks around as she notices that Raiven has left her behind. Angered by her absence, Celeste yells in anger and mutters, "Thanks for the help, sis!"

Celeste looks onward and sees the energy clash beyond the horizon darkening the sky then quickly activates her wings and takes off towards it in an attempt to help her master, Traganus.

CH: 57
RISE OF THE FALLEN

Taking the fight down to the surface after their intense bout in the sky, Victor and Elena spread their wings and lead Traganus back towards Damian and Adrian in an attempt to take him out together. As Talia and Lithia stand by safely and watch, the Angelic pair suddenly stops midair and dodge as Traganus attempts to strike them down. With a fierce war cry, Adrian charges forward and rams his head into Traganus' chest cavity, causing him to yell but is knocked back. Damian attempts to strike as well; landing one good hit to his side and is also forced back. Enraged, Victor takes on Traganus single-handedly once again whilst leaping into the air and strikes, slightly injuring him as Elena gracefully leaps forward in return and strikes with a fist, breaking his crystalline helmet in half. Before they can land another hit, Traganus instinctively strikes them down towards Damian and Adrian. Slightly dazed, Traganus feels around his head and notices that his helmet is severely damaged, revealing half of his trembling face.

"Anyone recognize that smell?" Damian mockingly implies.

"Sure do, and it's not pleasant!" Adrian sarcastically replies with a grunt as Talia chuckles softly, followed by a snort from Lithia.

Amused, Victor glances at Elena and says, "I believe that's called fear."

"And a true sign of defeat." Elena confidently claims.

Traganus places his hand over his chest in pain from Victor's fierce attack as the group takes another breather, realizing that despite their valiant efforts they are still too weak to defeat him alone.

"Enough, your lesson is over!" He furiously exclaims as he extends his hand out and uses his dark energy aura to keep them all at bay.

Victor and Elena float before Talia and Lithia while using their wings to block them from any damage caused by the energy aura as Damian and Adrian stand by in their defense and take cover. After regaining his composure, Traganus fires a powerful energy blast, forcing them back even more.

"Well, Saltora, I must say that the two of you fight well, but it's not enough!" He firmly decrees as Victor and Elena glance at each other, "Even with your so called Champions at your side, you cannot match my strength!" Realizing what's at stake for them against the Darchadian leader, Victor turns to face Elena directly and nods his head, signaling her to flee the battlefield. Elena nods back in response then quickly turns to address Talia as she wraps her arms around her once again to take flight with Lithia.

"Talia, we must go now, we're distracting them!" She carefully warns. Talia reaches out towards Victor as Elena takes off with her in her arms, followed closely by Lithia who chirps. As Victor watches them leave, he grins for a moment then approaches Damian and Adrian who they stand in their respective battle stances to begin the third round against Traganus. While holding their positions next to Victor, the Champions look on, exhausted and distraught as they try to regain their strength to fight once again.

"It's going to take more than mere skill to overcome this guy, even with all of our tricks combined." Adrian reluctantly informs to their dismay.

"In case you were wondering, this is far from over!" Traganus warns of his powerful position over them. The trio looks around in gloom as more Darchadians unexpectedly arrive to aid their master. As they fiercely hiss in unison, Traganus chuckles softly and taunts, "What now, *Champions?*" Discouraged, the trio shakes their heads as he raises his arms, signifying his sheer dominance while motioning towards the Darchadians and states, "Seems my family is much greater than yours; behold my legion of thunder!" The Darchadians steadily approach the team and hiss, as Victor stands back-to-back with them warily. "Well guys, looks like this is it!" Damian warns.

"I knew you were going to say that!" Adrian sarcastically retorts.

"It's not over yet!" Victor adds determinedly.

Damian chuckles in response and says, "Don't know if you've noticed, but it doesn't look like we're getting out of this one."

"Maybe not, but at least we'll die trying!" Adrian proudly states as he grips his Gauntlet tightly.

"Too bad Elena didn't stick around, we could've used her help after all." Damian jokes with a disappointed frown.

"Have a little faith, guys." Victor encourages with a crooked smile. Unsure of what to do at the moment, Victor closes his eyes with a calming sigh and tilts his head back as if to pray.

Some distance away from the battlefield, Elena lands near the slightly damaged Arch ship with Talia as Lithia turns with his spinal shards glowing and chirps. Elena and Talia turn and see the sky becoming darker beyond the horizon from the powerful explosion. Talia quickly faces Elena in panic and says, "Look like Victor's in trouble!" Talia suddenly takes off with Lithia by her side as Elena reaches out to stop her and calls, "Talia, come back!"

Sensing that Victor and the others may need her help after all, Elena shakes her head impatiently and chases after Talia. As Talia rushes back as quickly as she can, Elena flies in from above and gracefully picks her up from the air as they head back towards the team with Lithia flying close behind. Talia looks up at Elena and teases, "I knew you couldn't resist."

"Looks like you guys are starting to rub off on me too." Elena jokes. Looking determined, the pair shares a comforting smile then continue flying back towards the battlefield to aid Victor and the team as Lithia kicks into high gear with his wings fully spread and chirps.

While continuing to pray for a positive outcome in the surrounding battlefield, Victor sighs calmly once again with his eyes closed as Damian and Adrian stand by apprehensively.

"The girl will make a fine addition to the clan, don't you think?" Traganus savagely teases. Angered by his remark, Victor quickly straightens up his posture and opens his blue eyes in anger towards him as he viciously taunts, "Her innocence will be ravaged!" Victor steps away from Damian and Adrian towards the Darchadian leader and furiously yells, "You'll die!" Traganus looks back with a devious grin, feeling confident over his ability to get under Victor's skin and mocks, "Will I?" Concerned more than ever for their lives, Damian and Adrian look up and see the sky becoming darker as Victor powers up intensely out of rage, surrounded by energetic lightning once again.

"Victor, don't!" Damian frantically warns with a pained expression, "This is exactly what he wants!"

"I don't care what he wants anymore!" Victor angrily retorts whilst shaking his head and gripping his fists tightly.

"You've come for answers, time to see what the truth brings you." Traganus taunts, "Come, child of the dark, sample the taste of vengeance with me. Achieve what no one else in this world can offer you." Knowing that he's finally pushed him to the edge, Traganus grins as Victor suddenly flies towards him at full speed, yelling furiously. Victor attempts to strike with a deathblow as Traganus quickly blocks then dodges and strikes him in the gut, which knocks him to the ground aggressively.

"Well that's just great!" Adrian grumbles whilst shaking his head, frustrated by the situation, "Now what are we supposed to do?" Damian shakes his head also and sighs, unsure of how to get a grip on the grim situation. Reveling over his apparent victory over the team, Traganus grabs Victor by the neck then holds him up and informs, "Fear has overcome you; embrace it." Breathing heavily from the attack, Victor grunts in pain as he struggles to break free of his grip. "In the absence of light, darkness prevails." Traganus profoundly states as he turns to face Damian and Adrian while holding his coveted prize before them, "Stand down, or he dies!"

Victor desperately struggles to overcome his fear and anger from within as the Darchadians stand by, awaiting the signal from their master to attack the now defenseless team. Damian and Adrian look upon Traganus and sigh disappointedly as the sky darkens even more overhead.

"My darkness spreads, for it is the end of all things pure." Traganus declares. Too afraid to act, Damian and Adrian glance at each other, unsure of how to help Victor, much less themselves.

"Many will be wasted in their foolish resistance against it," Traganus proclaims, "Now is the dawn of my rule!"

Panic flashes in Victor's blue eyes as he struggles to break free. Realizing there's no way out of this, he calms himself and closes his eyes as if to pray. Amused by his sudden change in composure, Traganus looks upon him and viciously mocks; "Yes that's it, pray to the Gods as your way of life ends."

Victor keeps his eyes closed and squints as he struggles to retain a peaceful composure in the presence of his powerful enemy.

"Come on, Braxel, it appears that we don't have a choice!" Damian strongly advises as he powers up his Gauntlet in an attempt to help Victor.

Adrian follows suit and jokingly mutters, "I wish you were wrong about that."

"So do I." Damian sternly replies.

Traganus chuckles in response to Damian and Adrian's attempt and ridicules, "Disgraceful! You and the Princess might have over powered me without this fool's interference!"

"Leave them out of this!" Victor quickly retorts as he opens his eyes.

Keeping his gaze upon Damian and Adrian, Traganus viciously scoffs and warns; "Don't worry about your friend here, for you'll be joining him soon in the next dimension!" Damian and Adrian stand together, preparing for the worst, as Traganus looks upon Victor, confident of his defeat and informs, "Say your goodbyes to this world and behold my new order. Even at the end, the forces of darkness will thwart the Gods."

"You're nothing but a god of destruction!" Victor exclaims.

"Yes, and sadly their fate, will now be yours!" Traganus declares as he raises his Gauntlet to kill Victor once and for all.

Panic suddenly strikes Damian and Adrian, who yell, "No!"

Victor looks upon his dark adversary in a calm manner and begins to laugh unexpectedly. Traganus pauses; concerned by his attitude then laughs as well.

"I see you've finally come to your senses." Traganus denotes, "You are facing death with extreme composure, as well as fate with an unexpected sense of tolerance and acceptance."

The Darchadians approach Damian and Adrian from all directions, trying to intimidate them as they hiss. "Have you accepted the fact that you're alone?" Traganus pompously inquires as he pulls Victor closer to him.

"Who says I'm alone?" Victor replies with a crooked smile.

"You've got no way out of this!" Traganus threatens.

"Really? Victor counters, "Like you, I see things a bit differently, which is why every day and night I dream with my eyes open."

"Then you can see the darkness rising to embrace you." Traganus retorts as the sky darkens even more.

"The dark may embrace the light, but can never eclipse it." Victor contests with a sense of true belief, "I've learned that being an Angel is not about the act of fighting, it's about being so prepared to face a challenge and believing so strongly in the cause you are fighting for that you refuse to quit." Traganus notices the Gods' symbol on Victor's Gauntlet glowing brightly in blue then looks upon him in anger as beams of light suddenly shine through the darkened sky. "Cause or not, your Gods choose to remain silent, while mine live within me, now and forever!" He confidently states.

"I do not fear you, *demon*!" Victor bravely scorns, "In fact I pity you, for you've already lost."

Turning his attention to the sky, Traganus looks on in shock as Kael unexpectedly arrives aboard an Arch ship with Valorie and Vennessa, leading a small fleet of Archadians in a powerful call to arms. "It can't be!" He angrily exclaims, "No, this world is my right!" Kael begins firing upon the Darchadian horde with his Gauntlet as Traganus yells, angered at the sight of the Archadian fleet attacking his own people. Elena arrives shortly after with Talia and Lithia in tow then quickly approaches Damian and Adrian to help.

"You summoned them, through prayer?" Traganus angrily denotes.

"You've got your family, I've got mine." Victor confidently replies. Traganus looks back at the two Champions as Elena stands next to them and stares off against him intensely. "Once again the Arch meddles in my affairs!" He furiously mutters, "No matter, for my power is far beyond theirs."

"Maybe so, but it's not beyond mine." Victor counters with a grin.

"Tell me, what blood mingles within yours?" Traganus queries, "Who took your mother under their wing? They couldn't have possibly been human! Who gave you the strength to overcome my legion of thunder?"

"Someone stronger than you apparently." Victor says sarcastically.

"That's doubtful." Traganus snarls, "You may have minimized the destruction, but the final strike will still turn this monumental occasion along with your legacy into your own tomb." Angered by the situation, Traganus pulls Victor close and proclaims, "Enough of this! I will finish you off, then I shall reclaim my rightful place into the kingdom of paradise, for all eternity!" Traganus suddenly takes off into the sky with Victor still in his grasp as Elena and Talia look on in panic and frantically call, "Victor!"

Talia covers her mouth in fear as Lithia growls with his spinal shards glowing and quickly flies towards Traganus, attempting to save Victor himself.

"You've done well, Princess, but it's too late!" Traganus announces as he flies upward with Victor held tightly in his grip.

Damian and Adrian continue their intense battle against the relentless Darchadians as Kael suddenly joins in, "Alright boys, let's get to it!" He confidently advises, "Try and keep up if you can!"

To their surprise, Kael showcases his seasoned yet impressive power against the Darchadians single-handedly with his Gauntlet, taking them on several at a time by utilizing his Empyrian fighting skills.

"Well damn, he's pretty fast for an old guy." Adrian humbly jokes.

"Old, but still strong and not obsolete." Damian respectfully admits.

"Not yet anyway." Adrian sarcastically affirms.

In an attempt to finish the battle quickly, Valorie and Vennessa signal the rest of the Archadians to attack with full force then join in on the battle themselves. Lithia flies upward in the sky and approaches Traganus, who fires several energy blasts towards him. Victor looks downward, appreciative of Lithia's efforts as he dodges each blast by rolling and zigzagging through the air with his wings. With a confident grin, Traganus fires one last shot and finally blasts Lithia back, causing him to lose momentum as he howls in a sorrowful tone and retreats back towards Talia below. As Lithia flies downward with an injured wing, Talia rushes underneath to catch him.

"Lithia!" She frantically calls, "Are you alright?"

Resting in her arms, Lithia looks up at Talia and licks her face as she sighs in relief. Overwhelmed by the intense battle between both sides, Elena continues her intense gaze towards Traganus as she prepares to take off.

"This war is not yet over!" Traganus exclaims as he stops high above the planet's surface with Victor still in his grasp, "Behold your ruin, and witness my ascension into the kingdom of paradise!"

With the wave of his hand, Traganus creates a dark energy field that shields him and his hybrid captive high above the planet's surface. Victor looks around in shock, overwhelmed by this turn of events as Traganus informs, "You've been imprisoned within this energy field, which only I can dissolve."

More determined than ever, Elena attempts to fly to Victor's aid but is distracted whilst trying to fend off several Darchadians in the process.

"Damn you, Traganus!" She shouts angrily from below.

Damian and Adrian continue fighting then look up and see Traganus floating high above them with Victor but are distracted by several Darchadians as they quickly defend themselves. Kael breaks away from the fight and hastily approaches Talia to get her to safety as she carries Lithia in her arms. Elena crosses her arms in a kata pose and quickly extends them, causing a powerful energy wake with her Arch aura, which separates several Darchadians.

Realizing this to be her only shot; Elena looks on determinedly and quickly flies through the Darchadian horde in an attempt to save Victor herself.

Knowing his army will eventually be defeated without him; Traganus holds his position in the sky and looks directly upon Victor with a scowl.

"This is the end my friend." He informs, "Earth has lost, now so shall you!" Traganus mocks as Victor grunts in pain, struggling to break free, "Unlike you, I was meant to be beautiful." He enlightens, "The world would've looked up to the sky and seen hope, instead, they will look up in horror, as its greatest Champion comes crashing down before them." Victor yells furiously, trying desperately to overcome his rage in the clutches of the Arch's most dangerous foe. "You are nothing, you were never meant to be. You're just as much a failure as I was, and just as afraid." Traganus proclaims, trying to break his spirit, "Well, I used to fight my fears, but now that I've tasted its true power, I'll never go back."

"I'm not a failure!" Victor angrily retorts as he scowls back.

"The Arch asked for a savior, a hero of sorts, instead, they settled for a slave." Traganus taunts with a devilish smirk.

"In that case, I suppose we're both disappointments at this point in time." Victor says sarcastically.

"Yes, I suppose we are." Traganus concurs, "You wear the Gauntlet of the Angel who imprisoned me, and thus shall suffer the same fate." He reveals to Victor's surprise, "Knowing her, she sacrificed herself to save you, what a tragic waste." Victor looks upon his Gauntlet for a moment, distressed over his mother's fate then suddenly gets an idea. "Once I have conquered your world, I will have all the strength I need to defeat the Arch and destroy the Gods once and for all!" Traganus firmly declares as he powers up in an attempt to crush Victor onto the surface below.

"Hang on, Victor, I'm coming!" Elena calls from below as she flies towards the energy field, attempting to break her way through.
Hearing Elena's voice in the distance, Victor expresses a look of compassion as he turns his attention downward and whispers, "Elena."

"The Princess, I sense your compassion for her has grown strong." Traganus denotes with a devilish grin, "But your feelings betray you, which is why I'm not envious."
Continuing his gaze towards Elena, Victor calmly retorts, "You should be."
Elena tries desperately to break through the shield barrier as she attempts flying towards it at full speed, fully determined to save Victor from the clutches of their most dangerous adversary.

"Damn fool!" Traganus mocks, "Such a thing is not meant to last."

"I guess that depends on the ones willing to try." Victor disputes.

"You can't go anywhere, or do anything freely cause it's forbidden, by them." Traganus informs as he points upward with his finger, signifying the Gods' rule from above in complete safety within their kingdom Empyria.
Victor looks up and sees Empyria orbiting above Earth's atmosphere, wondering if he'll ever one day be worthy of their divine presence.
After regaining his strong composure, Victor scowls upon Traganus and spitefully scorns, "I sense no soul in your blackened heart."

"Which is why I have no fear." Traganus sternly retorts, "No one will remember you, or what you've done."

"I don't need to be remembered!" Victor snaps, "All that matters is that I'm here, now, in this moment." He suddenly closes his eyes once again determinately as the energy from his Arch aura begins to rise exponentially beyond that of Traganus'.

To his surprise, Elena forces her hands through the shield barrier, nearly breaking through in her attempt to save her one and only true love.

"Impossible!" Traganus exclaims as he looks down towards Elena then turns his attention back towards Victor with surprise, sensing his energy aura rising rapidly before his eyes. Victor's eyes suddenly open with a glow as he stares directly onto Traganus intensely. "What is this power?" He questions furiously, "I must know!"

More confident than ever, Victor calmly stares back with a crooked smile, eyes still glowing, then says, "Surprised? Well so am I."

"This energy you possess, Victor, we can use it, together!" Traganus proposes, trying to sway him at the last minute. Victor tilts his head back and scoffs in response as Traganus pleads, "You and I friend, just think of what we could achieve! We could accomplish so much together with it!"

As Victor's eyes begin to dim, he looks upon Traganus with a soft expression and calmly informs, "I'd rather not."

"Together we can rule the planet!" Traganus persuades once more.

"It's not going to happen, cause it's not ours to rule, not now, not ever." Victor firmly retorts.

Enraged by his unwillingness to cooperate, Traganus' eyes begin to glow brightly in red as he places his free hand on Victor's chest and furiously threatens, "I'll take it all then, every last ounce of your strength!"

Victor is taken aback as Traganus attempts to absorb his Angelic power, then assertively states. "You can try, but my power is far beyond yours."

Traganus pulls Victor close once again, staring into his eyes intensely as he declares, "If I can't harness your energy, then I will destroy it! For I and I alone, am eternal!"

"If you truly want my power, then take it." Victor offers as he quickly discharges the blue crystal shard from his Gauntlet given to him by Talia.

"You still have a choice you know." Traganus scornfully teases.

"Forgive me," Victor says calmly to his foe's surprise as he grips the blue crystal shard tightly in his hand, "For I've already chosen." He then reluctantly stabs it into Traganus' backside.

Shocked by this daring tactic, Traganus roars out in pain and is weakened from the positive energy contained within whilst struggling to pull it out.

A look of solemn compassion covers Victor's face as he looks back in disappointment, feeling disheartened in having to cross the line between life and death with someone who could've meant so much to him.

"What have you done?" Traganus shouts frantically.

"I chose, for I've finally found a sense of family I've been yearning for ever since I was a child." Victor illuminates as the shield barrier weakens, giving Elena a chance to finally break through. Traganus attempts to grip Victor's neck even tighter but struggles against the pain.

"Consider it something you can't take back," Victor proudly informs, "A parting gift, to another dimension."

Traganus struggles to retain physical control as he scowls upon him and furiously spits, "I will not be descended by you!"

"Are you afraid?" Victor calmly inquires with a crooked smile. A confused expression crosses Traganus' face as Victor mocks, "A man who fancies himself a god suddenly feels a very human chill crawl up his spine."

Shocked by his power, Traganus' eyes widen as Victor enlightens, "If there's one thing I've learned, it's that the true test of an Angel is not without, for it comes from within. That is where we meet the challenge, for it is the weakness inside us that an Angel must overcome, above all else."

Elena powers up while flying to Victor's aid at full speed as beams of light begin to emit from Traganus' body in reaction to the crystal shard in his back.

"We have to accept responsibility for our failures, mistakes, as well as our glories." Victor finishes, "Only then can we truly be worthy of other people's belief in us."

Traganus yells in pain from the crystal shard; it's destroying his body by attacking the negative energy contained within him. As he stares into Victor's eyes intensely, Traganus exclaims, "The Arch will not take away my victory!"

"No, but I will!" Victor proudly retorts.

"You would die for them?" Traganus painfully questions.

Taking in the moment of his powerful foe's defeat, Victor solemnly enlightens, "Some ideals are worth dying for. I've risked my life for a lot of stupid reasons, this is the first one that makes sense to me."

"And only you!" Traganus angrily retorts.

"All my life I wanted to become an Angel so that I could serve others in need." Victor professes, "And because of that, I've lost everything, but I've also gained everything in return."

"I hope for your sake; the price is worth it." Traganus contests.

"A heavy cost to be sure, but I pay it gladly." Victor proudly states.

With Traganus quickly losing power inside and out, the shield barrier below them finally weakens, allowing Elena to burst through, breaking it into pieces as she flies towards Victor in an attempt to save his life.

"Bear in mind, your struggle to resist our nature can't last forever." Traganus forewarns, "One day, the urge for vengeance will be even stronger, and you won't be able to fight it any longer."

"We'll see about that." Victor counters with a confident grin.

"Seems you will never fulfill your destiny," Traganus taunts, "For you will never understand the true power hidden inside you."

"Guess I'll just have to find a way to live with it then." Victor retorts.

"Savor your petty victory, for no matter how fast you fly you can't possibly save everyone, not even the ones that truly matter to you." Traganus exclaims as he attempts to tighten his grip on Victor. "Should you prevail, I shall see you on the other side, at The Edge Of Beyond!"

"Don't wait up on me then." Victor decrees as he grabs him by the neck as well, "When one Angel falls, another shall rise. Farewell, *Dark Prince!*"

"Just so you know, there are some things far more frightening than death." Traganus whispers, "You cannot withstand the coming storm."

"I am the storm!" Victor confidently retorts as he suddenly strikes Traganus back several yards in the air and begins to fall downward from his Gauntlet being powerless without the crystal shard. Using all the power she has, Elena swiftly flies towards Victor, trying to save him before it's too late.

"I'm coming, Victor!" She calls with determination I her voice.
Traganus grips his fists tightly in anger at his side, losing complete control over his body as he leans back in the air and yells, "I am eternal!"
Beams of light shoot through Traganus' entire body as he continues to yell furiously. Suddenly, an explosion is caused from the energy reaction within him in conjunction with the shield barrier in the sky, blindsiding Elena for a moment as she attempts to track Victor through all the debris.

"Victor!" She frantically calls once again.
Talia and Kael look onto the sky and see Victor falling from the explosion as Lithia leans his head upward with his spinal shards glowing and chirps.

"Somebody help him!" Talia says while attempting to help Victor.
Kael quickly stops her by placing his hand on her shoulder and shakes his head. Disappointed, Talia turns her attention back towards the sky and sees Elena flying towards Victor at high speed as she covers her mouth with grave concern. Victor continues to fall towards the Earth's surface below, still unable to fly as he passes out for a brief moment and unexpectedly hears a familiar voice from beyond the grave, that being Sonya's.

"Never forget where you come from." Her voice whispers to him, which causes Victor to smile.
As the debris from the explosion fills the sky, Elena suddenly appears through the fiery clouds with her wings fully spread. Coming in from above at full speed, she reaches for Victor whilst gripping his hand and gracefully catches him in midair. "I've got you this time." She whispers passionately.
Victor slowly opens his eyes in relief of seeing Elena as she smiles back.
Down below, Damian nods towards Adrian in relief as Victor and Elena finally come to a stopping point, landing softly on the ground. Valorie and Vennessa, along with the other Archadians, force the enemy horde back as they eventually corner them.

The remaining Darchadians are outnumbered and quickly flee to fight another day as they screech loudly in anger of their defeat. The dust settles from the intense battle as Elena helps Victor walk through the debris.

Over the horizon, Celeste pulls herself upon the rocky hill, observing the battlefield from a distance and angrily grumbles, "No!"
Realizing that Traganus has finally been defeated, Celeste tries to stay out of sight then suddenly receives a transmission from her Gauntlet.

"We must flee, sister." Raiven irritably informs, "Revenge will soon be ours for the taking." As Elena stops for a moment with Victor, she turns and sees Celeste standing upon the hill as they stare each other down for a moment. "This isn't over, *Princess*!" Celeste furiously shouts.
Riled at the sight of her defeated clan, Celeste activates her wings and flees to fight another day as she screeches loudly. Elena sees her fleeing, but chooses not to stop her as she sighs in relief of the battle finally coming to an end.

Darchadians from around the world sense Traganus' sudden defeat and flee each respective kingdom, screeching loudly as Earth's citizens look on in relief. Tannis approaches the window of this throne room from above in Edge City, surprised by this turn of events as the Titanian Media announces the news broadcast worldwide. "If Traganus and the Darchadians have truly been defeated, then perhaps there's more to worry about than we originally thought." Patrayous remarks as Zepherus growls in response.
Amused by his General's comment, Tannis turns and mutters, "We shall see."
Raina and Lucian stand high above their people from their own citadels, raising their fists as a sign of sovereignty over the rising Darchadians. The Eudenian and Enfurian crowds begin to cheer as Raina and Lucian delight in their superior reign over the planet once more.

Back in Pretoria, the Archadians attempt to assess the damage from the strenuous battle against the Darchadians. Victor can barely walk as Talia rushes to help him board an Arch ship. Elena and Talia carefully place Victor on the landing platform so he can catch his breath as they look upon him and sigh in relief. Feeling out of place, Talia backs away to give them a moment as Lithia flies up to her shoulder and chirps.

"You came back for them, your faith brought you to the battlefield to save lives." Elena happily commends, "In turn you honored your angelic halo and risked your own life to save everyone here."

"Guess I'm not the only one." Victor regards with a crooked smile, "You were right, a woman's touch was needed, and I know of none better."

"I should hope not." She teasingly retorts.

"You fought well today yourself." He compliments.

"Slaying Angelic beasts?" Elena jokes, "What a cruel courage."

"I suppose whatever presents itself to honor your people as well as the Arch, you'll gladly do it." Victor teases.

"I'm just a hard worker like you really." Elena says sarcastically.

Victor nods in agreement and respectfully says, "That will surely come in handy when you're Queen someday."

"I'm hoping so." Elena humorously comments.

"Your duty was to stay home, but your heart told you to break the rules." Victor remarks, "How did you decide between them?"

"Well, it wasn't easy, but by following my instincts I wound up doing the right thing." Elena professes, "I guess I've finally learned that my duty has and always will be to my heart."

"Makes perfect sense to me." Victor says sarcastically.

Elena smiles in response as Victor gently takes her hand and grips it tightly within his. A joyful tear runs down her face as she looks upon him and states, "Light has overcome darkness, and our kingdom remains safe thanks to you."

"And you." Victor compliments, slowly rising to his feet as Elena helps him up. "Let's face it, you're beautiful, in more ways than one."

"And you're combative at times, but I think we can work on that." Elena counters with a soft chuckle.

"I have been known to be stubborn amongst others so it might take a while to adapt." Victor jokes with a comforting grin.

"You know, sometimes you talk too much." Elena teases.

"Good thing I'm the strong silent type then." Victor puns.

Sensing his internal struggle, Elena looks upon him curiously as he focuses his attention upon the sky now filled with sparkling ash and mournfully sighs.

"What's wrong?" She calmly inquires, "You look awfully blue for someone who just saved the world."

Facing her, Victor grins and replies, "I guess you're right, I've even got the marks to prove it." Elena smiles as he looks back towards the sky once more and says, "I've always embraced life. How difficult after all these years to be forced to destroy it, one of my own, but sadly, there was no alternative."

Hoping to ease his busy mind, Elena places her hand on Victor's shoulder and encouragingly says, "The courage you showed doesn't mean you aren't susceptible to being afraid, it just means you don't let fear stop you. You did what you had to do, by honoring your sacred duty, and your people."

"I didn't want to do it," Victor says with disappointment in his voice, "But I suppose the gift of these powers will be my burden till the day I die."

"I know, but we all do what we have to even in times of desperation." She calmly heartens.

"I wonder if they'll ever truly understand though." He queries.

"Don't forget, you still have Talia and I." She assures with a smile.

"I'm glad for that." Victor remarks as he looks towards Talia, relieved by her safety as well as Elena's. Elena smiles towards Talia also as he continues, "Traganus has finally been defeated, but I fear his death will only give rise to a more treacherous foe." He reluctantly expresses, "But if another shall rise, I hope that I'm strong enough to overcome them as well."

"You and me both." Elena comforts as she places her hand on Victor's face and holds her hand close to his cheek. Talia smiles in approval of their affection as Elena extends her hand out towards her and says softly, "Natalia." Talia glances at Elena curiously whilst hesitating to approach her.

Victor smiles upon Talia as Elena places her hand on her shoulder as well, saying, "The Gods have chosen well, sister."

Surprised, Talia looks upon her and questions, "Sister?"

With a heart-warming smile, Elena nods in approval towards her and proudly decrees, "You have proven yourself worthy of Archadian wings, and as a divine result, I proudly welcome your sisterhood into our kingdom."

"That's my girl!" Victor jokes to lighten the mood, "About damn time if you ask me!"

Feeling appreciative, Talia smiles upon her two friends as tears of joy roll down her cheeks. Victor places his hand on Talia's shoulder to comfort her as Lithia licks her tears away once again.

"I don't know what to say." Talia humbly utters, shaking her head.

"Don't say anything, just go with it and see where the dream takes you." Victor encourages with a comforting smile.

Talia laughs in response as Victor and Elena join in.

"Victor!" Damian suddenly calls from a short distance as Victor turns and sees him approaching them. "You know, for someone who doesn't take orders, you did fairly well." Damian professes, bringing a smile to his face, "You fought with honor; I owe you my deepest gratitude."

Esteemed, Victor nods back in respect as Damian follows suit.

"As do we!" Adrian announces from a short distance as everyone looks behind them and sees him approaching with Marcus and Yuri in tow.

"Not bad, for a human." Marcus jokes.

Victor grins in response as Yuri walks up as well and respectfully commends, "You're the toughest one I've ever met for sure."

"I'll heal." Victor jokingly retorts as he grunts slightly from the pain.

"At least your personality is still intact." Adrian teases with a chuckle.

Laughing in response, Victor replies, "Yeah, we'll see how long that lasts."

"Looks like you won the bet today, Victor." Yuri informs.

"Oh really?" Victor asks with an amused expression, "How's that?"

"Because you proved everyone wrong today." Yuri answers, "And with great finesse I might add."

Marcus brushes past Victor and jokingly implies, "Though it seems you had a little help along the way."

Grinning in appreciation, Victor expresses, "Thanks guys, I couldn't have done it without you. And I'm sorry you all had to endure this horrific battle."

Damian and Adrian glance at each other, knowing they owe Victor their true honesty. "No, we're the one's who are sorry." Adrian reluctantly admits, "We were too close minded to see you for who you really are."

"A good leader is open to new ideas amongst new friends, so please forgive us." Damian professes in respect towards their comrade.

"There's nothing to forgive," Victor happily retorts, "You all helped me, even when you didn't have to."

"No, the truth of the matter is, you helped yourself." Yuri replies. Remembering the slaves held captive in the Darchadian fortress, Victor looks around frantically, saying, "I almost forgot! Did you get the people to safety?" Marcus and Yuri chuckle in response to Victor's concern over them.

"They're safe, don't worry about it." Yuri reassures. Victor sighs in relief then turns and sees Tristan and Michael in the distance with the others and raises his hand to acknowledge them. Tristan and Michael smile excitedly and wave back as they board the Arch ship with the other slaves while being carefully escorted by a group of Archadians.

"We'll see to it that they stay out of harms way for good this time." Marcus ensures as Victor nods in respect. Feeling relieved over their safety, Victor looks back towards Elena and asks, "So, what happens now?"

"I believe that's for you to decide, though we should probably stick together this time around." Elena suggests.

"For survival?" Victor implies.

"No, for each other." Elena confidently replies. Damian extends his arm out towards him and says, "Come, Victor, it's time."

"For what?" Victor queries as he shares a curious glance with Talia.

"To take your place among the people of Earth." Adrian adds.

"And me." Elena softly chimes in. Surprised by Elena's faith in him, Victor looks upon her as they smile at one another. Talia holds onto Victor's left arm whilst petting Lithia's head with her other hand as Damian and Adrian extends their arms out in approval. With a crooked smile, Victor nods then grips each of their hands in respect.

"Does this mean we can finally go home?" Talia carefully inquires as she looks up at Victor, feeling hopeful.

"Yes, Talia, we're finally free." Victor happily replies with a smirk. Talia grins with excitement, followed by an excited chirp from Lithia. As everyone boards their ships to head back home, Victor follows Elena and Talia onto the Arch ship while Valorie and Vennessa calmly welcome them aboard by graciously extending their arms out. Marcus and Yuri board the ship shortly after as Victor suddenly stops and slowly turns towards Kael, who's standing several yards away on the landing platform of another ship. Elena stops for a moment as well, realizing that something has caught his attention then approaches him. Grateful to have him be such a big a part of his life, Victor waves his hand in appreciation as Kael respectfully nods back with his usual stern expression.

Relieved by his mentor's survival as well as his own, Victor lowers his arm then smiles as Elena gently places her arms around his shoulders to get his attention and says, "Come on, Victor, it's time to go."

Victor looks back at Elena and grins as he follows her aboard the ship next to Talia and Lithia. Amused by his powerful protégé, Kael sighs with a grin as he briefly looks onto the horizon then turns back to board the Arch ship.

Aboard their own Arch ship, Victor looks upon Elena in relief of their safety as Talia quickly approaches them and says excitedly, "You did it!"

"No, we did it." Victor remarks, proudly acknowledging them both, "It's more apparent to me now than ever that we're in each other's lives for a reason." He happily expresses, "Thanks for showing up."

Touched by their shared bond, Talia comes in close to hug them with tears in her eyes and whispers, "I love you guys."

Victor and Elena embrace Talia like a family unit for the first time, accepting each other as one. While taking in the heartfelt moment, Victor and Elena glance at each other in relief of Talia's safety and their own as Lithia howls with his spinal shards glowing once more. Amused, Victor pets his head, which causes him to purr loudly and chirp.

"Everyone ready?" Yuri calls back from the ship's cockpit.

"All my life!" Victor jokes, inciting a chuckle from Elena and Talia.

"Alright then, here we go!" Marcus announces as they fire up the ship and prepare to take off. The light from the sunset shines through the windows as the ship takes off towards Archadia. Comforted by their unified presence, Talia gently grabs Victor and Elena's hands and places them jointly as they lock together once again, showcasing their true bond as she places hers on top. Victor and Elena look into each other's eyes passionately; hands still locked as Talia rests between them with Lithia in her arms and closes her eyes with a sigh of relief. After a brief moment of true connection, Victor and Elena grip each other's hands tightly as they lean towards one another and gently rest their heads together whilst sharing a compassionate smile.

"And so it was; when one epic tale ends another begins." Kael profoundly narrates, "First comes the day, then comes the night. When lightning split the sky, thunder shook the Earth, then all was clear, peaceful, and serene. As legend tells: some are born great, some achieve greatness, and some have greatness struck upon them. Thus, many are lost in the storm; some are born in it, while others simply triumph by the spark of destiny. A divine spark, which ignites a furious bolt of lightning; it's there to remind us even in the worst of times through the darkness that there's always a flash of light, perhaps even a flash of hope."

As the Arch ship takes to the skies, Victor and Elena look out the window with their heads still rested together, enjoying the beautiful sunset with the promise of a new day, full of hope and wonder.

CH: 58
THE GIFT OF FREEDOM

Days later in Archadia on a bright sunny day, a ceremony is held as waves of Angels fly through the kingdom, leaving vapor trails full of fireworks in celebration of the Arch's victory over Traganus. Many have gathered to witness the Arch's full recognition of the Champions of Earth as Damian and Adrian walk up the castle stairs and bow before Elena to receive their honor before the crowd. Talia, who has a crystalline green and purple Lotus flower in her hair once again, stands next to Elena whilst holding a crystalline box. Elena turns towards her as she opens the crystalline box and gracefully pulls out a couple of crystal shard necklaces. Honoring her sacred duty as the Princess of Archadia, Elena hands the necklaces over to Kael who nods and gently places them around Damian and Adrian's necks.

"According to the customs of greater Earth, I would like to present these as gifts of peace, from one kingdom to another." Elena announces, "Nothing can buy the honor which you have so passionately fought for." Kael shares a respectful nod with Damian and Adrian as she resumes, "You have forever earned the respect of me, and my people. Your bravery and gallantry will never be forgotten."

Damian and Adrian glance at their crystal necklaces in appreciation then look upon each other and nod in respect as they grin. In closing to this part of the ceremony, Elena holds her arms up before Damian and Adrian, and proudly decrees, "Rise, Champions of Earth!"

Never having this much recognition for their efforts, Damian and Adrian take deep breaths as they stand up before the crowd, who cheers and applauds. The two Champions respectfully shake hands then step out of the way as Victor slightly stumbles, bringing a smile to Elena's face. Victor finally makes his way up the castle stairs to receive his honor as Talia looks on with excitement while Lithia stands perched on her shoulder as usual and chirps.

"The Darchadians enabled one man to inflict his rage upon the entire planet. In turn, he used all his powers against us but in the end goodness and strength prevailed." Elena firmly announces, "Let him, his disciples, and his memory be consumed by his darkest passions, rather than extricate them from despair." Kael steps back as Elena gracefully grabs the third and final crystal necklace from Talia, both of whom smile.

"Harmony enables even the smallest things to flourish while the lack of it destroys what greatness we all have inside us." Elena proudly adds, "Out of suffering have emerged the strongest souls, for even the most massive characters in history are seared with scars." As Victor reaches the top of the stairs, he kneels before Elena who gracefully places the crystal necklace around his neck with excitement and smiles. Rosalyn and Josephus step up to address the crowd as Victor smiles towards Kael who nods back and grins.

"While some may find his methods to be less than appealing," Rosalyn announces while the crowd listens closely, "His appearance and demeanor may not even reflect what is believed necessary to carry out one's sacred duty. He's even challenged what we adhere as a time-honored tradition that for years have been the very backbone of our divine society."
Everyone in the crowd looks on with anticipation as Rosalyn continues to speak, "Though, nothing wrong can be found in his attempts to improve the quality of life for us and those around him." She proudly announces, "There is no fault in one's ambition to pursue and further their knowledge based on our celestial practices and theories."
Rosalyn and Josephus look upon Victor with pride as he smiles back.

"In fact, we applaud such passion and willfulness." Josephus proudly acknowledges, "Your power is amongst the highest class of us Angels, and therefore we are grateful to claim you as one of our own."
A tear rolls down Victor's face as he slowly closes his eyes for a moment in appreciation of finally being accepted.

"Along with your crass, and your somewhat disdainful behavior, we recognize that you carry with you an inspirational bolt of lightning." Josephus continues, "One which we could only hope will spread through the kingdoms of Earth as well as our own like a wild storm."
Victor bows his head in respect as Rosalyn and Josephus step aside, allowing Elena to step forward once again to address the gathered crowd.

"Though his time as an Archadian has been brief, his defeat of Traganus will be remembered as long as the Arch exists." She announces, "In symbol, and in legend. He and his team have exhibited great courage, leadership, and the willingness to protect those they hardly knew. His actions alone are a reminder of why the Gods chose each of us, for only those who dare, drive the world forward."
Shifting his intense focus elsewhere for a brief moment, Victor glances at Talia who happily smiles back with excitement.

"To maintain peace and prosperity, by upholding balance, to overcome fear, and destroy evil wherever it may hide." Elena continues, "As Angels, we must all fight as one, no matter how small we may seem. And though our wills haven't always been united, I believe it's time they were."
Victor looks up at Elena as they briefly smile at one another.

"Know that the genuine wealth of this world isn't in the ground or up in the sky, for it's all around us in the minds and hearts of those who uphold its true value." Elena proclaims, "My people, the Gods who guide us in all we do today, sanctifies a union that will be a blessing for all of Earth." She then firmly declares, "The Arch embraces you, and by the Gods' grace I decree, slave no more." Feeling relieved, Victor closes his eyes once again, eternally grateful to finally be rid of his previous slave status for good.

"Rise, Victor Zyas." Elena proudly instructs. Victor opens his eyes while gazing upon her in appreciation as she smiles back and happily concludes, "You are free." After taking a deep breath, Victor stands before her as she places her arms around his shoulders and gently kisses him on the forehead. "Make your mothers proud, both of them." She whispers.
Surprised by her kind gesture, Victor smiles, "If only they could see me now." As Elena turns away from him to face the crowd, everyone cheers and applauds as Victor stands tall and proud for the first time in his life. Tristan and Michael stand by Hammond and Griffin as they cheer in approval of their hero finally becoming one with the people of Earth. Unsure of how to act, Victor nods towards the crowd in appreciation then raises his Gauntlet fist up high, signifying his Angelic status before the people of Earth. After a moment of taking in the crowds' reaction, Victor turns his head towards Elena and smiles as Talia quickly rushes over with Lithia to hug him.

"We made it, just like you said we would!" She says excitedly.

"Yes we did." Victor happily retorts, "Guess those stories had some truth to them after all." Talia smiles and embraces him tightly as Victor looks upon Lithia while humorously petting his head and instructs, "Take good care of her, Lithia." Talia looks upon her furry companion standing on her shoulder and smiles in appreciation of his company, "She's truly an Angel now." He compliments.
Lithia chirps in response then licks Victor's face as Talia laughs in relief of their victory. After sharing a moment with Talia, Victor turns and sees Rosalyn and Josephus approaching and bows his head in respect.

"We'd like to express our profound gratitude." Rosalyn professes, "I'm sure your mother rests well knowing you have truly avenged her."

"One can only hope, right?" Victor says sarcastically.

"Protecting oneself is considered self-defense, but protecting others is highly angelic." Rosalyn compliments, "You were willing to give your life to rescue them, even when the odds were stacked against you. And to our humble surprise you never folded."

Slightly embarrassed, Victor humbly replies, "How could I? Sometimes you must be willing to work in the dark to serve the light. I did what I had to just like everyone else, even if it was against my oath." He then places his hand on Talia's shoulder, signifying her importance as she grips it and smiles back.

"If we knew nothing else about you, that would truly be enough." Josephus states, "But you also fight when you should withdraw, and that is Angelic too. To our surprise, you've even influenced our daughter, though hopefully for the better." Elena stands by and jokingly frowns in response as Victor laughs. "Let us hope your passion is contagious amongst others as well." Josephus respectfully finishes. With a crooked smile, Victor sighs as Elena places her hand on his shoulder. "Perhaps there is a divine spark in you after all," Rosalyn adds, "Maybe even a hero as well."

"I'm no hero." Victor chuckles, "Thank my comrades, they're the real heroes. I'm just a nobody with a great idea about certain things."
Elena smiles at Talia to acknowledge her presence as she pets Lithia's head, which causes him to raise his hind leg and scratch himself like a dog.

"In time, I suppose we'll see what you're really made of, but as of now you serve as a strong and righteous example for all of our kind." Josephus compliments while motioning towards the surrounding kingdom.

"And know that heroic deeds do not go unnoticed by the Gods." Rosalyn respectfully adds as she motions towards the new crystal shard around his neck, "You've been awarded for conspicuous valor."

"The citation engraved on the crystal reads honor and faithfulness." Josephus adds, "May we be the first to offer our congratulations to you. Your family's good name has finally been restored."
Victor looks upwards towards the sky and sees Empyria still orbiting above Earth's atmosphere and smiles, hoping he has truly honored them.

"When a person is motivated by a true sense of justice and genuine sincerity in their actions, then they conform to what we call the Celestial Way." Rosalyn graciously finishes, "Seems you've finally found your higher purpose after all, and for that we are glad." Turning his attention back, Victor looks upon Elena and Talia and places his hands on their shoulders, signifying their importance to him as he replies, "Yes, it seems I definitely have."

"Within you lies the light of the world," Rosalyn explains, "Your Earthly companions will one day be shadows in the next dimension when you are a name living forever in history as the most glorious shining light of youth next to that of our daughter." Elena slightly blushes as Rosalyn continues, "Forever young, forever inspiring, never will there be an Angel like you."

"And just so you know, we'll be watching you." Josephus warns.

"Who isn't at this point?" Victor says with a smirk.

"We all have shadows, and sometimes if we're not careful, they tend to overwhelm the light inside us." Rosalyn concludes as she and Josephus bow their heads in respect then take their leave.

Victor bows his head in return then looks upon Elena for a moment as they laugh together in amusement. Elena glances back at Talia and smiles in approval as she walks through the crowd with Victor. Amongst the large crowd are Hammond and Griffin, who stand by and bow their heads in respect. "Our sincere compliments and congratulations, Victor." Hammond commends as he shakes his hand in approval, "You're truly one of a kind." Victor nods in response as he turns to shake Griffin's hand as well.

"You've turned calamity into victory." Griffin praises, "The world is grateful and forever in your debt."

"Thank you, Senators, that means a lot coming from you." Victor acknowledges as he nods once again in respect. Hammond and Griffin bow their heads then take their leave as Damian and Adrian approach him to pay their respects while Kael stands by with pride.

"You're impertinent, Victor Zyas." Damian denotes. Victor glances at Kael, smiling in response as Damian continues, "You're rash, volatile, and extremely opinionated." Damian looks towards Kael with a grin then jokes, "Seems Kael found another just like him, may the Gods help us all." Kael nods in amusement towards Damian then places his hand on Victor's shoulder, which causes him to laugh. "Though despite your insufferable arrogance towards protocol…" Damian continues.

"Just spit it out, Damian!" Kael jokingly interrupts to their surprise. Damian looks upon Kael in a serious manner then starts to grin and clarifies, "We've come to admire your valor, and unique fighting abilities." Prideful of his lifelong protégé, Kael glances at Victor and encouragingly states, "He'll make a mighty ally for sure."

"I have no doubt of that." Damian kindly remarks. Victor shakes Damian's hand in appreciation, and says, "Thanks, Damian."

"No, thank you." Damian respectfully retorts. Surprised by his remark, Victor looks upon Damian who finishes, "I'd say you've finally earned your place among the people of Earth." Victor smiles as Adrian steps forward from behind, saying, "And among us, brother." Everyone quickly turns as Victor nods towards him in appreciation. "I may be considered a young warrior the same as you, but I'm not too stubborn to admit when I'm wrong. I'm sorry I misjudged you, there it is."

"That's good enough for me." Victor says sarcastically.

"We're truly honored to fight beside you." Adrian salutes. Feeling grateful for their long-awaited respect, Victor looks upon them and says, "Thanks guys." Adrian suddenly smacks his hand on Victor's shoulder in approval and jokes, "Welcome to the pack, brother!" Kael chuckles as Victor tries to balance himself correctly, laughing as well.

"We need to consider solidifying this team." Damian mentions.

"Agreed, someone should be watching." Victor concedes, "The way I see it, no one is before the other, from now on it's about teamwork."

"Sure you won't be too busy upholding the balance with Elena?" Damian inquires, "I've seen the pressures of her crown."

"Not at all." Victor assures whilst sharing a final nod with them. He then sees Marcus and Yuri standing beside Valorie and Vennessa in the distance and nods towards them, acknowledging their presence as they all nod back. "I knew he could do it!" Marcus jokes as he jabs Yuri's side.

"Guess we both won that bet." Yuri jokingly retorts.

"What are the odds of that ever happening again?" Marcus puns.

"Guess we'll find out soon enough." Yuri implies as he and Marcus begin to laugh. Slightly amused by their Empyrian counterparts, Valorie and Vennessa shake their heads and grin. As Victor approaches them, Marcus shouts, "Hey, Victor!" Victor looks directly at Marcus and Yuri as he stops before them. "How did it feel taking on the world's biggest threat, and flying through the depths of Hell?" Marcus jokingly inquires.

With a slight chuckle, Victor replies, "Well, I suppose it's the closest I'll ever be to Heaven." As Elena approaches him, Victor looks upon her passionately with a crooked smile and mutters, "Hopefully not though."

Marcus and Yuri share a chuckle then take their leave with Valorie and Vennessa in tow. Shaking his head with a sigh of amusement, Victor turns as Elena embraces him, "You fought for me." She whispers with excitement.

Victor holds Elena close for a moment in relief, resting his head against hers and softly retorts, "What can I say, you're worth fighting for."

Excited to finally share her world with him, Elena and Victor stare into each other's eyes passionately. "One day they'll tell a story, and some below will say it was just a fairy tale, about a fearless human who flew in from the sky above and changed our world." Elena tributes as she motions towards the kingdom surrounding them, "But I'll know, and so will they. Archadia thirsts for a new perspective, someone who understands the surface world, someone who will lead us into the next century. The Arch needs a beacon, and maybe it's you."

"Protecting the ones I love will suffice, though I can't say I've ever felt this way before." Victor blissfully mutters.

"What do you mean?" Elena questions with a curious grin.

"For the first time in my life, I'm exactly where I want to be." Victor happily concedes as he embraces Elena and looks over her shoulder towards Talia, who's standing next to the Tree of Life with Lithia still perched on her shoulder. "Everything's going to be just fine." He whispers with a wink.

"I pray so, fighting for your dreams isn't easy, but it's worth it." Elena softly adds, acknowledging the three of them, "In a way we're all part of a grand fable waiting to be told, so in the end, let's make it a good one."

Talia has the biggest smile on her face, illuminated by the bright morning sun as she laughs joyfully. Lithia proudly raises his head and attempts to roar successfully for the first time as Talia continues her wondrous gaze upon Victor and Elena, hoping the absolute best for them.

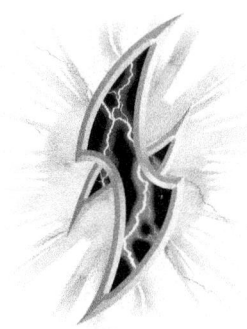

CH: 59
MYSTERIOUS FIGURES

Deep within the heart of Edge City in Titania during the night hours, Celeste enters a secret chamber and is greeted by Malik, who stands by the doorway with a stern glare.

"I must speak with him at once." Celeste firmly requests.

Malik looks around cautiously, making sure she isn't being followed and asks, "You're alone I presume?" Celeste nods in response as Malik extends his arm towards the entrance at the end of the corridor and respectfully informs, "Very well, this way then."

Malik leads Celeste down the corridor and into a dark chamber. Two beams of red and blue light illuminate two sections of the floor as Malik points towards the red spot. Celeste nods as Malik quietly takes his leave, she then steps into the red light and kneels. As Malik closes the chamber doors behind him, Celeste looks around for a moment in curiosity then suddenly hears a mysterious voice.

"What is it?" The mysterious entity questions.

"I've come to tell you in person, Lord Traganus has been defeated." Celeste regretfully informs.

The unknown entity scoffs and retorts, "It seems Traganus was blinded by rage, how easily he was convinced the Arch would ignore his rise to power."

Celeste looks away in anger of Traganus' defeat as the mysterious entity continues; "Yet this hybrid still lives. You have failed me, Darchadian!"

Annoyed by his implication, Celeste looks up intensely and justifies, "We were overpowered! As you well know, the Arch aided them in their victory."

"Your incompetence is becoming most taxing!" He sternly scorns.

Celeste sighs impatiently with a disgruntled tone, and defensively argues, "Our enemy was underestimated, even by you."

"Perhaps." The mysterious entity slightly chuckles to himself then asks, "What of the pureblood?"

Hesitant to respond, Celeste looks away once again in anger and grumbles, "She has allied herself with the Champions of Earth, and the human."

"It appears he and the Princess are more powerful than we originally thought." The mysterious entity denotes, "No matter, for neither Earth nor Archadia can withstand the coming onslaught. It is time, for Atom will soon be free, and the planet will be ours for the taking."

Celeste slowly raises her head, looking frustrated and carefully inquires, "What would you have me do?"

Unexpectedly, Raiven enters the chamber and kneels into the blue light as she and Celeste glance at one another with slight disdain.

"Welcome, Raiven." The mysterious entity calls.

Raiven and Celeste scowl towards each other then turn their focus back on the shadowy figure once more.

"Perhaps I should ask you what went wrong?" The entity probes.

"Something you didn't count on." Raiven reluctantly reveals.

"Oh really, and what was that?" The mysterious entity persists.

Raiven shares a glance with Celeste and replies, "Archelus."

With a soft chuckle, the mysterious entity comments, "I thought that was just a silly superstition at this point."

"He's real enough, but he simply won't die." Raiven remarks.

"Not now anyway. The two of you were Traganus' left and right hand Generals." The mysterious entity informs, "Prepare yourselves, his war is over, now mine begins." The shadowy figure finally leans into the light to reveal himself up-close, and to their surprise, it is Tannis Marquis.

"As with any keen ruler like myself, the true key to success is playing the hand you were dealt like it was the hand you always wanted." Tannis confidently implies, "For I have other means of remedying his failure, as well as my own." With a cunning smirk he concludes, "The devil is in the details and unlike most people on this planet, I have long-term vision."

Acknowledging his master plan, Raiven and Celeste deviously grin in response as Tannis chuckles maniacally while holding the Angelic Artifact tightly in his hand that was previously in Traganus' possession.

END OF ACT: 03

EPILOGUE: 01
BEYOND THE DARK

Atop the waterfall in Archadia, Talia stands by with Lithia as Victor stands before Elena, both gripping their hands together. In her honor, Victor wears the new Soul Gear presented to him earlier in her quarters. Like his previous suit, this one bears the Gods' symbol in blue below the neck as well as a new V design on the torso, signifying his name.

"Archadia sure is a wonderful place." Victor remarks, "The art, the music, and especially the people."

"You sure took to our customs fast enough." Elena playfully denotes.

"Thanks for showing them to me, I'll never forget what I've learned." Victor happily acknowledges, "I truly wish I didn't have to go."

"So do I." Elena sadly professes.

"Take care of her for me." Victor requests in regards to Talia.

With a determined nod, Elena assures, "I sure will, you have my word."

"There are dangerous forces at work that will likely come back stronger the more we try to vanquish them." Victor warns with his attention behind him, gazing upon the sunset sky with determination. "War is on the horizon…" He says before turning back to face her, "I'll be back soon."

Elena looks upon Victor passionately, knowing she won't see him for a long while and retorts, "I know, and we'll be here waiting for you."

Relieved by her sentiment, Victor holds her hands close to his chest plate and says, "The storm within has finally been calmed, but when it comes calling, know that I will one day return."

"What about your sacred duty?" Elena inquires with a curious grin.

"I now have a duty to honor what is in my heart." Victor professes, "Somehow I'll make it all work, though I should probably keep a foothold in both worlds. Besides, it will help repair relations if I'm seen helping out."

"Well said; like myself you are a gifted warrior and a natural leader." Elena acknowledges, "I'll be praying to the Gods for your safety."

"And I you." Victor replies with a crooked smile then kisses her hands as she smiles in response, "I've learned many things from your world in a short amount of time, and most of all I think I now know my parents better, whoever or whatever they were."

"You've taken a mighty leap into the future." Elena compliments.

"I'll be sure to tell others about this place, how one woman with hope and courage found the strength to endure." Victor praises, "One who's inner light is bright enough to rid the world of darkness forever."

Touched by his kind words, Elena embraces Victor then kisses him as she looks upon his new Soul Gear and caresses the custom V design.

"How do you like it?" She eagerly asks.

Victor extends his arms out to showcase his comfort with the new armor and happily replies, "It's perfect, the advancements will prove useful in the field."

"Really?" Elena retorts excitedly, "I'm glad it suits you. Your scars tell a tragic story; wear it like armor, and it can never be used to hurt you."

"I'll be sure to wear it with pride." He proudly states, "Thank you."

"You're welcome." Elena says with a smile. Talia looks on from behind with Lithia as the two lovebirds share smiles. "I wish I could convince you to stay, but I know you have a duty to uphold, as do I." She inspires.

"I'll serve you better out there anyway." Victor assures, "But, if you should ever need me, I trust you'll know where to find me."

Elena nods in response as she kisses Victor one last time and says softly, "Even the brightest light is worth nothing if hidden in darkness."

"I don't want the legacy of this place or my people to be the destruction of its civilization." Victor caringly professes.

Motivated by his words, Elena holds her arm up in a warrior-like manner and declares, "Then let us join together and share our light with the entire world."

Victor takes her arm in his, signifying their warrior like bond and also declares, "Don't worry, Princess, I promise you, in time I will see you again."

"That which you have promised, you must now perform." Elena replies with a confident smirk.

"This is my dream, ours, everyday, a new adventure, new people to discover." He proudly informs, "Therefore I shall start a new course, and you'll be at my side naturally."

"All my life, I've felt weighed down by this crown." Elena confesses, "Full of restraint and responsibility." Victor shares a comforting smile as she resumes, "Then there comes this guy, who's not like anyone I've ever met before; he doesn't want to fight if he can help it. Not because he's afraid, but simply because he already knows he can win, even more so now than ever."

Appreciative of her words, Victor bows his head in respect, acknowledging her sacred duty as an Archadian Princess. "I feared nothing could ever be good again in this world, that is until you arrived." She finishes.

"I'm just a man fighting for his home." Victor humbly remarks.

"How others view us is of little consequence." Elena explains, "How we perceive ourselves is much more important, and your name like it or not…" She states as she places her fingers over the V design on the new Soul Gear, "Will be a rallying cry." Victor turns his attention behind him once more, weary of what lies ahead. Curious of his intentions, she kindly asks, "Your heart is free, but do you have the courage to follow it?"

"You know I do." Victor confidently replies.
Elena nods in agreement and inquires, "Where will you go?"

"I don't know where I'm going exactly or what I'll find when I get there." He replies with a sigh, "If I stay with you, the darkness will seek me out, and how would I protect you then?"

"I'll show you if you let me." Elena says encouragingly.

"It's not safe to be with me." Victor cautions.

"Well, it's clear to me that by your side is the safest place there is, for both of us." Elena jokingly inspires.

"I can't make you any guarantees." Victor jokingly warns.

"I know, but I'm willing to take that chance." She says passionately, "I'm not a woman who likes to be kept waiting, but in this case, I'll gladly make an exception for you."

"Well then, I'll do everything in my power to make sure that your patience is rewarded, as well as mine…" He assures with a daring smirk, "For it seems a different pair of Angels now maintain the home front."

"And what a daring pair we make." Elena cunningly denotes. Surprised by her sentiment, Victor's eyes widen passionately as she gently grabs his hand by placing it over her chest near her heart cavity and concludes, "Keep this with you, and Archadia will always be near."
Feeling light as a feather from her deep affection, Victor replies, "You were right, it was you who brought me here from the very beginning."

"And it will be I who brings you back, as well as her." Elena proclaims as she motions towards Talia, acknowledging her presence.
Victor grins for a moment then steps away as he kneels before Talia who still has a crystalline Lotus flower in her hair. Talia is extremely saddened by his departure as she weeps in despair and professes, "I don't want you to go!"

"I know you don't, but I have to." Victor says with a hard swallow.
Disheartened by not having a choice in the matter, Talia looks away impatiently, and mutters, "It's not fair!"

"Why do you say that?" Victor asks with a comforting grin.
Talia quickly turns back to face her lifelong friend and sadly expresses, "Because, you belong here, with us."

"I know I do, but no matter where I am…" Victor reassures while raising Talia's chin with his hand as she looks into his eyes for comfort, "I'll always be with you, Talia." Deeply touched by his words, Talia tears up even more as Victor kisses her forehead, which causes a glint of light to appear.

As Victor keeps a comforting gaze upon his young friend, Talia struggles to keep her composure then suddenly hugs him tightly, feeling she'll never see him again. Victor holds her close with tears in his eyes and looks upon Elena with sadness as she glances back, sensing their extreme pain from being apart.

"You've shown me that the world is full of miracles, even ordinary ones that happen everyday." Victor calmly inspires as Talia stares deeply into his blue eyes, hoping he's right, "Don't' be sad, the sun hasn't set on us yet," Victor encourages as he gently pulls her away from him, "Storms come and go but they don't last forever, not even darkness lingers eternally."

"But Victor, what if I fall?" Talia asks in disbelief as her emotions quickly overcome her.

"Oh, but Talia, what if you fly?" Victor hearteningly whispers as he places his hand on Talia's face to comfort her. Feeling encouraged once again, Talia smiles as he inspires, "For once we know where we belong. It's time we make our own life, our own destiny. We've finally found our place in the world, and in a way, it's right back where we started, but the difference is, from now on, we finally get to choose." Attempting to be strong for him, Talia smiles whilst trying not to cry. "I trust the keys to the kingdom will be safe while you're here." Victor carefully implies.

Talia nods as Victor holds out the letter she wrote him earlier back in the mines. Taken aback, she is surprised to see that Victor still has the letter as he smiles and places it back in his garb.

"Your words bring hope, even in the darkest of times." Victor heartens, "This will keep me company while I'm away." Talia tears up with joy, feeling grateful for Victor's strong compassion towards her. To his surprise, Talia pulls out the Angel figure from her garb, bringing a warm smile to his face. "If there's one thing I've learned since we first met, it's that one of the best feelings in the world is knowing your presence and absence both mean something to someone." Victor happily reveals, "Which is why we must always respect the past when forming the future." The Angel figure illuminates under the morning light in her hands as Victor smiles in appreciation of how much she clearly values it. "Always be who you are, not what the world wants you to be." He encourages, "You've got something special inside you, I just hope I'm there to see it when you let it all out."

"Me too." Talia replies with a sad smile, "I'll miss you, so much."

"And I'll miss you, milady." Victor whispers with a crooked smile, "We have a bond stronger than crystal, we're friends and we'll always come back to each other, no matter what." Saddened herself, Elena tears up, knowing this is equally hard for them as they lock hands together for a moment, once again showcasing their unbreakable bond. "Love has given me wings, and so I must fly." Victor says determinedly. Inspired by his words, Talia gently presses her hand against the Gods' symbol over Victor's chest, which activates his wings as they emerge from his spinal armor fully spread.

"You are truly one of a kind, always remember that." She happily compliments with a joyful smile whilst caressing them with her fingers, hoping to one day have a set of her own.

"You have a purpose just as we do, one mightier than yourself." Victor encourages, "Find it, learn how to use it, and fully embrace it."

"I promise I won't let you down." Talia proudly assures.

"The best teachers are those who show you where to look but don't tell you what to see, so learn from her example, for she is very wise and you are the future." Victor encouragingly points out while motioning towards Elena, "Whatever you face in life, meet it knowing that you will eventually figure it out. Keep a positive attitude and always remember your own strength." Talia nods in response as he motions towards Elena once more, saying, "I'll come back for her someday; I trust you'll make her great."

"You know I will." Elena happily assures, "In the meantime, please take care of yourself; all our hopes and dreams now soar with you."
Lithia chirps as Victor pets him on the head, causing him to purr loudly. After a brief moment of giving Lithia some attention, Victor looks directly into their eyes compassionately and concludes, "Well…" He stands up then slowly turns to take his leave as Talia looks on, reaching out to him and says softly, "Forever yours…" With his usual crooked smile, Victor slowly turns back and happily answers, "Beyond the dark." Talia smiles in relief as Victor suddenly jumps off the edge of the waterfall. Elena looks on with a sad expression as Talia runs along the top of the waterfall with Lithia following closely behind, trying desperately to catch up with Victor then quickly stops on the edge, unable to fly. She gazes upon the beautiful sunset sky with Lithia perched on her shoulder as Elena approaches them from behind and smiles.

"Goodbye my friend; I hope to see you again soon." Talia whispers with teary eyes as she watches her dearest companion fly off into the sunset.
Victor flies gracefully in the air whilst spreading his Archadian wings proudly. Hoping to comfort her, Elena holds Talia close from behind as she weeps in despair. Lithia begins to hum Victor's melody as Talia holds the Angel figure tightly against her chest. With a constant gaze beyond the kingdom, Elena looks onto the horizon with Talia, hopeful of Victor's inevitable return.

"At first their humanity was seen as a weakness, and yet it proved to be their greatest strength." Elena narrates compassionately, "Perhaps we're not so different after all, and as our enemy grows stronger, so will we. This fight has been won, but the war rages on. The battle for paradise has just begun, though darkness surely awaits us all. Ties will be severed, and bonds will be made as we struggle to unify our people. Tolerance is willing and acceptant, for the least among us are the most important." She concludes.
With a confident smile, Victor flies towards the horizon at full speed with his wings fully spread, surrounded by energetic lightning and disappears into the sunset high above Earth's surface.

EPILOGUE: 02
SUPREME MEDIATION

High above Earth's atmosphere, the large space station known as Empyria orbits the evolved planet. The five ruling Gods observe the Earth from above through a large crystalline window in curiosity of recent events below the surface.

"Earth remains safe on our watch." The first God assuredly states.
The fifth God approaches the window and denotes, "Yes, the Angels have proven themselves victorious in our grace once again."

"Their forces have gained in strength thanks to Earth's Champions, and this unknown hero." The third God curiously points out with his hand rested over his chin.

"Seems humans can make a difference as well." The fourth God remarks as she turns to face the others, "Who'd of thought?"

"He is but one man, a mere human, nothing more." The third God cynically comments with her arms crossed.

"That may be, but what if others were to follow in his example?" The second God questions as he kneels before the window facing them, "It would seem that with his ever-growing power he's also become an ideological ally, and quickly I might add."
Annoyed by the notion, the fifth God firmly grips a crystal shard in his hand and sternly chimes in, "The Edge Of Beyond is no place for his kind, nor does it need their protection with us still in reign over this ethereal realm."

"Perhaps now it doesn't, but what of the near future?" The second God carefully implies as she gracefully extends her arm out and motions towards Earth floating before them in space.
The five Gods glance at each other for a moment with concern then continue gazing upon the planet below their kingdom in curiosity.

EPILOGUE: 03
PROMISING YOUTH

Beneath the kingdom of Archadia, Talia and Lithia follow Elena underground to officially begin her training as an Archling. Elena approaches a large crystalline doorway and comes to a stop as she hums an ancient tune, which causes the doors to suddenly open before them.

"We'll meet again here, should you succeed with your training that is." Elena wisely informs, "Only one who is able to overcome the trials that await here will be acknowledged by the Gods to be a true Angel."

As Lithia sniffs around curiously, Talia looks through the dark entrance apprehensively and asks, "How will I know if I'm worthy?"

Elena turns to face her and carefully instructs, "Trust your instincts, follow your heart and no matter what, don't ever give up."

Determined, Talia looks upon Elena directly with a clenched fist and states, "I'm not sure if I have what it takes to be an Angel, but I'll do my best."

"I expect nothing less from you." Elena calmly stresses, "But if you fail to purge the darkness within, you will surely fall to your death." Talia looks onward with slight hesitation as Elena strongly articulates, "Like many who have come before you, your mind, body, and soul will be tested, pushing you beyond your limits. You must rise above the trial of the Gods."

With a concerned expression, Talia carefully steps forward then turns to face Elena and inquires, "What exactly am I supposed to do?"

"Survive." Elena firmly instructs, having faith that she'll prevail.

Talia nods in response then turns back to enter the darkness as she holds her Gauntlet tightly. Lithia chirps as the crystalline doorway behind Talia closes with a loud boom. Now alone, Talia looks around curiously as the shadows subside then ventures into the dark catacombs, determined to make Victor and Elena proud by successfully completing her training as an Archling.

THE END

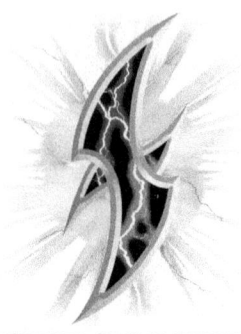

SOURCE MATERIAL: CHARACTER INFO

1.) <u>Victor Zyas:</u> Archelus, Archadian Warrior, Male, White
Age: 27, Height: 6', Eyes: Navy Blue, Hair: Silvery White, Sign: Scorpio
2.) <u>Talia Andreas:</u> Archling Apprentice, Female, White
Age: 14, Height: 4'10, Eyes: Hazel, Hair: Blonde, Sign: Aquarius
3.) <u>Elena Saltora:</u> Princess of Archadia, Female, White
Age: 27, Height: 5'10, Eyes: Sky Blue, Hair: Blondish Brown, Sign: Libra
4.) <u>Alexandre Kael:</u> Empyrian General, Male, White
Age: 52, Height: 6'2, Eyes: Brown, Hair: Grayish Black, Sign: Sagittarius
5.) <u>Lithia:</u> Seraphine Guardian, Male, Animal
Age: Unknown, Height: 1', Eyes: Green, Hair: Purplish Blue
6.) <u>Damian Trag:</u> Eudenian Champion, Male, White
Age: 26, Height: 6'1, Eyes: Brown, Hair: Black, Sign: Capricorn
7.) <u>Adrian Braxel:</u> Enfurian Champion, Male, Samoan
Ager: 26, Height: 6'5, Eyes: Green, Hair: Reddish White, Sign: Aries
8.) <u>Marcus Durrante:</u> Empyrian Warrior, Male, Black
Age: 29, Height: 6'3, Eyes: Brown, Hair: Black, Sign: Leo
9.) <u>Yuri Kuran:</u> Empyrian Warrior, Male, Oriental
Age: 29, Height: 5'10, Eyes: Blue, Hair: Black, Sign: Virgo
10.) <u>Valorie Vonstrutton:</u> Archadian Warrior, Female, Hispanic
Age: 26, Height: 5'9, Eyes, Brown, Hair: Black, Sign: Virgo
11.) <u>Vennessa Fantine:</u> Archadian Warrior, Female, Black
Age: 26, Height: 5'11, Eyes: Brown, Hair: Black, Sign: Aries
12.) <u>Tannis Marquis:</u> Emperor of Titania, Male, White
Age: 45, Height: 5'11, Eyes: Blue, Hair: Blonde, Sign: Taurus
13.) <u>Kraven Patrayous:</u> Titanian General, Male, White
Age: 52, Height: 6'2, Eyes: Hazel, Hair: Grayish Black, Sign: Leo

14.) <u>Raina Demuera:</u> Queen of Eudenia, Female, White

Age: 46, Height: 5'10, Eyes: Blue, Hair: Black, Sign: Capricorn
15.) <u>Lucian Drakhan:</u> King of Enfuria, Male, Egyptian
Age: 47, Height: 6'4, Eyes: Green, Hair: None, Sign: Aries
16.) <u>Terrence Malik:</u> Titanian Senator, Male, White
Age: 54, Height: 5'10, Eyes: Brown, Hair: Grayish Brown, Sign: Pisces
17.) <u>Julius Griffin:</u> Titanian Senator, Male, Black
Age: 48, Height: 5'11, Eyes: Hazel, Hair: Grayish: Brown, Sign: Taurus
18.) <u>Nikolas Hammond:</u> Titanian Senator, Male, White
Age: 56, Height: 5'10, Eyes: Brown, Hair: White, Sign: Cancer
19.) <u>Raiven Baptiste:</u> Darchadian Warrior, Female, White
Age: 27, Height: 5'10, Eyes: Blue, Hair: Black, Sign: Pisces
20.) <u>Celeste Voltaire:</u> Darchadian Warrior, Female, White
Age: 26, Height: 5'9, Eyes: Green, Hair: Red, Sign: Gemini
21.) <u>Traganus:</u> Darchadian Leader, Male, White
Age: 47, Height: 6'2, Eyes: Green, Hair: Black, Sign: Scorpio
22.) <u>Tristan Mohr:</u> Human Slave, Male, White
Age: 14, Height: 5'1, Eyes: Blue, Hair: Blondish Brown, Sign: Sagittarius
23.) <u>Michael Richter:</u> Human Slave, Male, White
Age: 14, Height: 5'0, Eyes: Brown. Hair: Brown, Sign: Capricorn
24.) <u>Sonya Grace:</u> Human Slave, Female, White
Age: 50, Height: 5'8, Eyes: Brown, Hair: Brown, Sign: Aquarius
25.) <u>Rosalyn Saltora:</u> Queen of Archadia, Female, White
Age: 62, Height: 5'11, Eyes: Blue, Hair, Grayish Blonde, Sign: Sagittarius
26.) <u>Josephus Saltora:</u> King of Archadia, Male, White
Age: 64, Height: 6'2, Eyes: Green, Hair: White, Sign: Cancer
27.) <u>Victoria Zyas:</u> Archadian Warrior, Female, White
Age: 32, Height: 5'11, Eyes: Blue, Hair: Blondish Brown, Sign: Capricorn
28.) <u>Zepherus:</u> Seraphine Guardian, Male, Animal
Age: Unknown, Height: 5', Eyes: Red, Hair, Yellowish Black
29.) <u>Korina:</u> Archadian Holy Trinity Warrior, White
Age: Unknown, Height: 5'10, Eyes: Blue, Hair: Brownish Blonde
30.) <u>Kitana:</u> Archadian Holy Trinity Warrior, Oriental
Age: Unknown, Height: 5'8, Eyes: Brown, Hair Black
31.) <u>Kiara:</u> Archadian Holy Trinity Warrior, Indian
Age: Unknown, Height: 6'0, Eyes Green, Hair: Red
32.) <u>The Gods:</u> Supreme Rulers of Earth, Various

THE WRITER/DIRECTOR/PRODUCER

Razael Alucard Wickham is an American Writer/Director/Producer who has been developing a Spiritual/Sci-Fi/Fantasy franchise entitled, The Edge Of Beyond for nearly twenty years. Born October 24th 1983 in Ft. Leonard Wood, MO and growing up in a military family in places such as Frankfurt, Germany and Tacoma, WA, Raz began his artistic journey as early as 1991 with various world building concepts, but it wasn't until 1997 when T.E.O.B. as a name came to fruition as well as the main story concepts supporting it. Unable to pursue a career in film after finishing high school in 2002 due to his status and location, he finalized what creative elements he could for T.E.O.B. before swaying towards a dormant side of his artistic self.

By default, in 2003, Raz inevitably changed his artistic course in pursuit of the same ultimate goal and became a full-time musician being the Writer/Singer/Guitarist for the Thrash/Metal/Symphonic band of the same name. That same year, he founded R.A.W. Productions LLC as an official-business entity to carry out his future plans for T.E.O.B. as a multimedia franchise. Spending several years writing, recording, and performing, he would come to find a natural groove behind his musical axe on stage, a blue Jackson King V-4 guitar along with two others whilst pioneering an original presence and sound that paid homage to the likes of Megadeth and Metallica.

After moving to Nashville, TN in October of 2007, he attended Audio Engineering courses at S.A.E. Institute and continued pursuing a music career for five years there. To his chagrin, he would end up being forced to walk away from the stage entirely in 2011 and back into the literary realm, reluctantly right back where he started. Sidetracked by the performance side of things for nearly 10 years, Raz took a long break from the world of music to refocus his career path and specifically hone the literary side of T.E.O.B. with a graphic novel series in the works. With the graphic novel falling through as a T.E.O.B. related project, Raz re-emerged with R.A.W. Productions in early 2012 to bring his epic story into a more tangible format.

In the fall of 2012, Raz started writing the official trilogy in screenplay form, which ended up taking nearly two years to complete. As Writer/Director/Producer, Raz is currently building up T.E.O.B. as an iconic brand through R.A.W. Productions, with all intents and purposes of using his flagship franchise to build a multimedia production company, which is aimed at helping to produce other creator owned projects in need of professional services. Sticking to what he knows best, Raz has continued developing his life's work in full, with T.E.O.B. remaining his overall legacy.

With three scripts already in his arsenal and several more on the way, Raz is now in the final stages of reverse engineering by releasing each of his screenplays into novelization with the first book, Rise Of The Fallen, now released in 2015, the second, Wings Of Destruction, to be released in 2016, and the third, Twilight Of The Gods, to be released in 2017, and the official source/art book, Angelic Artifacts to be released in 2018. To add more credibility to his already profound design, Raz has been working with a local scientist named Weston Warren, Chief Research Scientist and co-inventor behind the world's current PCO technology, who for the past year has been acting as Scientific Advisor, which in turn has brought more real-world plausibility to the innovative concepts already supporting the story and overall vision behind T.E.O.B.

T.E.O.B. is currently being launched as a full-length Spiritual/Sci-Fi/Fantasy franchise supported by various forms of visual related material. While building a fan base with the novel series through various convention circuits, Raz intends to crossover his epic saga into other forms of artistic media such as graphic novels, videogames, television, and more importantly film. With every interactive event Raz and his team does in regards to T.E.O.B. specifically, all footage is currently being captured for future use in the upcoming documentary, The Edge Of Beyond: Rise Of An Icon.

THE PRODUCTION ARTIST/ASSISTANT

Jaclyn Barrows is the official Production Assistant for the Spiritual/Sci-Fi/Fantasy multimedia franchise, The Edge Of Beyond. She joined R.A.W. Productions LLC in the summer of 2015 after first meeting local author, Raz Wickham on a local film set. Since then, Jackie has been working on different visual aspects for the project, including but not limited to putting together all the cover art for entire novel series. She has also helped Raz to make a full-length teaser video for T.E.O.B. regarding the first book to be used through social media outlets as well as in theater promotions.

Jackie graduated from Stephens College in Columbia, MO in December of 2013 with her Bachelors of Fine Arts in Digital Filmmaking. She is currently working directly with Raz to put the cover art together for the second book as well as compiling all the footage to be used in the upcoming documentary, The Edge Of Beyond: Rise Of An Icon. She also works on many of her own creative ideas for short films, animated television series, and full-length features in her spare time. Her ultimate dream is to one-day make her own artistic ideas come to life on the big and small screens alike.

THE SCIENCE ADVISOR

Weston Warren is the CEO and Chief Research Scientist for Weston Scientific. Weston is responsible for strategic development and intellectual property of advance technologies such as PCO that helps to reduce bacteria, virus, and volatile organic compounds that exist in the air and on surfaces. These safe and effective technologies are vital to the safety of food, health care, and commercial building industries. Weston Scientific has also developed photon water through advance water physics by restructuring the water molecule to maximize the health and immune systems of organic plants and animals. His development of photon water revitalizes both H2O and soil structure to increase mineral uptake and optimum cell health. He is also the holder of many U.S. patents and is an accomplished public speaker of three decades, as well as having top honor degrees in biochemistry, and environmental science Summa Cum Laude.

THE GRAPHICS DESIGNER

Damion Cronin, curious explorer of the digital and musical realms. After meeting Raz for the first time back in 2010 during a metal band audition in Nashville TN, Damion then worked side by side with Wickham and his original concept drawings in early 2011 to help remodel the original 2003 TEOB logos into what is currently used by R.A.W. Productions. Damion is a skilled image manipulator by trade and desire, as well as a self-taught designer and manifestor of creative thought and experience. According to the creative mind that is Damion Cronin, while dabbling in various forms of music, food, software, and architecture, he occasionally sleeps.

'Seize the day' and 'memento mori'.

GO BEYOND AND MAKE IT EPIC!

R·A·W·

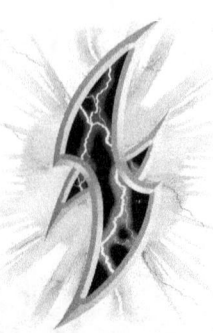

R.A.W. PRODUCTIONS PRESENTS
THE EDGE OF BEYOND TRILOGY:
RISE OF THE FALLEN
WINGS OF DESTRUCTION
TWILIGHT OF THE GODS
THE OFFICIAL NOVELIZATIONS

THE SAGA COMES TO AN END...BUT THE LEGEND FOREVER LIVES ON.